What was the mysterious relationship between Leonardo da Vinci and his Milanese assistant Count Francesco Melzi and why did this young man inherit all of Leonardo's drawings and notebooks? In this historical novel entitled *Leonardo da Vinci: The Melzi Chronicles* the author J. K. Kulski reveals the basis and evolution of their intriguing friendship and their interactions with the noble Italian and French families who helped to nurture and realise their ambitions during the tumultuous times of the Renaissance. Francesco Melzi, a trusted member of a brilliant group of acolytes and royalty in Leonardo's power, reveals how, despite the political uncertainty, they excelled with a breadth of diverse techniques and ingenuity (beauty, science, and reason) to combat the evils of necromancy, deceit, and ignorance that prevailed in their time.

And surely if this Necromancy did exist, as is believed by small wits, there is nothing on the earth that would be of so much importance alike for the detriment and service of men, if it were true that there were in such an art a power to disturb the calm serenity of the air, converting it into darkness and making coruscations or winds, with terrific thunder and lightnings rushing through the darkness, and with violent storms overthrowing high buildings and rooting up forests; and thus to oppose armies, crushing and annihilating them; and, besides these frightful storms may deprive the peasants of the reward of their labours. -- Now what kind of warfare is there to hurt the enemy so much as to deprive him of the harvest? What naval warfare could be compared with this? I say, the man who has power to command the winds and to make ruinous gales by which any fleet may be submerged, -- surely a man who could command such violent forces would be lord of the nations, and no human ingenuity could resist his crushing force.

— Leonardo da Vinci

By the same author

China Heist (a crime novel)

Next Generation Sequencing: Advances, Applications, and Challenges (edited volume)

DEDICATION

To Mark and Danker, two modernistic Leonardeschi who led me onto the rocky and winding path towards undertaking this challenging and never-ending project. To my dear wife Tina for her support and for putting up with me when I was much too often embedded at my computer screen and lost in the clattering word processing software instead of attending to the right stuff. A hearty 'woof - woof' to my two cavaliers Charlie and Sascha for lifting flagging spirits when needed. And a very big 'thank you' and much love to Naoko, Ruslan, and Jan, and *domo arigatou* to Lila and Yura for their loyalty, love, and cheerfulness. In the memory of my mother Valerie and my father Wladyslaw.

LEONARDO DA VINCI: THE MELZI CHRONICLES

Count Francesco Melzi of Vaprio, painter, art historian, and Leonardo da Vinci's secretary and heir, chronicles the life and times of his mentor Leonardo, and recounts the principles that they lived by and the volatile political events that shaped their ambitions.

J. K. Kulski

Historical novel with illustrations and bibliographical references.

Leonardo da Vinci: The Melzi Chronicles

ISBN: 978-0-6480653-1-9: softcover
ISBN: 978-0-6480653-2-6: e-book

A CiP catalogue record is available for this title from the National Library of Australia.

First Edition: 2017v1

Published by Jerzy K. Kulski

www.jerzykulski.com

Cover design by Jerzy K. Kulski

Cover image is *Portrait of a Youth*, 1514 Oil, by Raphael. With permission from the collection of the National Museum in Krakow, Poland, and the collection of the Princes Czartoryski. Wartime loss. Web Gallery of Art.

Table of Contents

Part 1: The Melzi, Medici, and Sforza Connections

Chapter 1. The End and the Beginning at Chateau du Cloux.. 1

Chapter 2. Leonardo and the Melzi of Milan and Insubria 14

Chapter 3. Sforza's Milan, 1447 to 1480.. 35

Chapter 4. A Simmering Florentine Kitchen, 1476 to 1480.. 56

Chapter 5. First Diplomatic Mission to Milan, 1480 to 1481.. 68

Chapter 6. Back in Florence, 1481... 80

Chapter 7. Leonardo's Milanese Kitchen, 1482 to 1485.

War Against the Republic of Venice and Fear of the Black Death.. 89

Chapter 8. Peace, Travels, Portraits, and Courtside Intrigues, 1485 to 1488 110

Chapter 9. Love, Marriages, Births, and Festivities, 1488 to 1493 128

Chapter 10. Auguries. The Death of the Magnificent Florentine in 1492 and

the Passing of Leonardo's Mother, 1494.. 161

Chapter 11. Ludovico Sforza's French Alliance, and the Suspicious Death of Gian

Galeazzo Sforza, the Sixth Duke of Milan, 1494 166

Chapter 12. The Investiture of Ludovico Sforza, the Seventh Duke of Milan,

Betrayer and Usurper, and the Tragic Death of His Wife Beatrice.. 180

Chapter 13. Leonardo's *Last Supper*, Coded Messages, and Allegories of the

Dark Beast of Milan.. 198

Chapter 14. Colours and Symbols of the Sforza Books of Prayer.

A Prelude to the End of Milan's Ruling Dynasty... 211

Chapter 15. Leonardo's Liaison with Mona Lisa, the Princess Isabella

Aragon Sforza, at the Corte Vecchio in Milan 217

Chapter 16. Ludovico Sforza's Demise by a French Takeover, 1498 to 1500 233

Part 2: Continued … Italian-French Connections 245

Chapter 17. Farewell to the Mona Lisa and Self Exile in the New Millennium.

The Wandering Years 247

Chapter 18. Romagna Campaign with Cesare Borgia, the Illegitimate Son

of Pope Alexander VI, and Other Fortification Commissions 261

Chapter 19. Back Home in Florence, World Maps, and the Battle of Anghiari 270

Chapter 20. Leonardo's Family and Florentine Disputes,

and His French Recall to Milan 283

Chapter 21. Milan's French Kitchen, 1508 to 1513 297

Chapter 22. Leonardo's Apocalyptic Novel of the Deluge: *The Prophet of Mt. Taurus* 311

Chapter 23. A Roman Sojourn 319

Chapter 24. Leonardo's Final Farewell to Milan and Vaprio d' Adda 346

Chapter 25. A French-Italian Welcome in Amboise, 1516 351

Chapter 26. Fair and Gallant Ladies 375

Chapter 27. Fireside Royal Chats. Politics, War, Health, and Envy 394

Chapter 28. Leonardo's Philosophies and His Studies of the Brain and the Soul,

Mechanics, and the Pyramidal Law of Nature 414

Chapter 29. Post Mortem and Adieu 432

Acknowledgements 458

Source of Quotes in the Text: 459

FIGURE CREDITS 463

ABOUT THE AUTHOR 467

PART 1

THE MELZI, MEDICI, AND SFORZA CONNECTIONS

All communities obey and are led by their magnates, and these magnates ally themselves with the lords and subjugate them in two ways: either by consanguinity, or by fortune; by consanguinity, when their children are, as it were, hostages, and a security and pledge of their suspected fidelity; by property, when you make each of these build a house or two inside your city which may yield some revenue and he shall have...; 10 towns, five thousand houses with thirty thousand inhabitants, and you will disperse this great congregation of people which stand like goats one behind the other, filling every place with fetid smells and sowing seeds of pestilence and death; and the city will gain beauty worthy of its name and to you it will be useful by its revenues, and the eternal fame of its aggrandisement.

— Leonardo da Vinci

Young Francesco Melzi by Boltraffio

CHAPTER 1

The End and the Beginning at Chateau du Cloux

While I thought that I was learning to live; I was only learning how to die.

— Leonardo da Vinci [S1]

A Sad Farewell and Renewal (*Triste Vale et Renovare*)

Leonardo Ser Perio da Vinci died peacefully in his bed while in the tender arms of the young French King, His Most Christian Majesty, Francois Premier at Cloux in Amboise at 10:20 pm on Friday, May 2nd, 1519.

I, Francesco Melzi of Vaprio, know this because I was there. I saw and heard Leonardo gasp, 'I see the light' as he died in the arms of the French king.

Twenty-five years later, Giorgio Vasari, the Florentine art historian, visited me at the Villa Melzi in Vaprio d'Adda to ask me about Leonardo's history as a painter, sculptor, and architect. This is what Vasari wrote in 1550 about Leonardo's death in his book *The Lives of the Most Eminent Painters, Sculptors, and Architects*:

> When Leonardo finally became old, he lay ill for many months, and, feeling himself near to death, he wished to be carefully informed about the Catholic faith, and about the path of goodness and the holy Christian religion; and then, with much lamenting, having confessed and repented; and although he could not raise himself well on his feet, supporting himself on the arms of his friends and servants, he devoutly took part of the most Holy Sacrament. The King, who often and lovingly visited him, then came into the room; wherefore Leonardo, out of reverence, sat up in the bed, giving the King an account of his sickness and the circumstances of it, showed withal how much he had offended God and mankind by not having worked at his art as he should have done. Thereupon he was seized by a paroxysm, the messenger of death; for which reason the King arose and took hold of Leonardo's head, in order to assist him and show him favour, so as to alleviate his pain, and Leonardo, knowing that he could receive no greater honour, expired in the arms of that king at the age of seventy-five years.

Leonardo was only 67 when he died and not 75 years of age as reported by Vasari who did write some confusions about Leonardo's life in his books, most of which I have corrected in my account here wherever or whenever I have remembered to do so. But, Vasari and I have told the solemn truth that Leonardo met with death whilst in the arms of the French king. This cannot be disputed. Yet, many who were not in attendance at the moment of Leonardo's death somehow know better than I do, and they dispute this event and say that the King was in Paris signing government documents or that he was in attendance at his second son's birth at Château de Saint-Germain-en-Laye.

When the king gives permission to his ministers to sign government documents, his ministers sign them in proxy in his absence. This occurs commonly enough - the young king at 24 years of age liked to delegate responsibility to his ministers. I know. I was there when he delegated, so you cannot dispute what I saw. After Leonardo's death, I was the King's falconer and Secretary of his Bedroom Chamber and his constant companion for a few years before I returned to Milan and Vaprio d'Adda in April 1522.

And yes, one month earlier, the king, His Most Christian Majesty Francois Premier, House of Valois-Angoulême, attended his son's birth at Château de Saint-Germain-en-Laye. His second son Henri II was born on March 31 to Claude of France at the Château de Saint-Germain-en-Laye in the department of Yvelines about 19 km west of Paris and 233 km or a six-day horse ride from Amboise. Four weeks later, on the 23rd of April, the king returned to Amboise with his wife and two sons, so that he could spend time in the company of his new mistress Francoise de Foix, Comtesse de Châteaubriant. She and her husband Jean de Châteaubriant had been summoned to the Amboise court to assist with the ceremony and baptism of the king's new son Henri. Françoise de Foix was *La mye du Roi* (The Sweetheart of the King), the king's first official mistress. The king made his affections obvious to the Court, which displeased his wife Queen Claude, the Duchess of Brittany, and also upset his mother Louise of Savoy who greatly disliked the de Foix family. However, the king's sister Marguerite of Navarre was fond of the king's mistress, possibly to spite her sister-in-law Queen Claude because they were in courtly competition, and possibly because she had once passionately loved Francoise's dead relative, the handsome Gaston de Foix, Duc de Nemours, nephew of the dead King Louis XII.

The Dauphin's baptism was scheduled for the 29th April, and Leonardo and I had been invited to attend. While I accepted at the insistence of Leonardo, he was too ill to attend. 'Go and see the king and his new son and tell me all about the goings on,' he said. And so I went. The king's wife Queen Claude, the king's mother, his sister, his daughter, and his mistress and other ladies-in-waiting were all there, and I had much intrigue and good humour to report back to Leonardo.

At 8 pm on May 2nd, Leonardo's health suddenly turned for the worst, and the priests began the last rites. Leonardo struggled for breath and was close to death. A messenger was sent immediately to the king to inform him that Leonardo was entering death's door. At 9.30 pm, the King appeared from out of the underground passage that connected the Castle Amboise with the Cloux, and he entered the kitchen and immediately rushed up into Leonardo's bedroom. The king was relieved to see that Leonardo was at peace and still alive. Leonardo welcomed his King with a kiss, and he expressed joy to see His Majesty once more before his imminent death. The Maestro described his symptoms to his king and admitted his regrets that life is much too transient and short-lived. Sadly, he had left much undone and unfinished. He was happy to now meet with his maker and express his sins and regrets. He hoped that his godsons, Salai and I, would complete his affairs as he had instructed us to do to his material and spiritual satisfaction. The king looked at him and nodded, saying, 'we will see that they both have opportunity to complete their responsibilities to you, Maestro. Rest easy and happily in peace. Your works will not be forgotten and will be your legacy and scions well into posterity.'

'You've come in time my King for us to see each other and to talk together for one last time,' said Leonardo. 'I already have one leg stretched out through death's door. My time with you, your Majesty, is my last great adventure in this, my mortal coil. I have greatly offended you and God and mankind by not having worked better at my art as I should have done.'

'Don't despair, Mon Pere, you will be loved and remembered by God and mankind long after we have gone. We'll sit in admiration and awe at your feet in Paradise, Mon Pere.'

With those heartfelt and generous words from the king, Leonardo cried out in a spasm, sighed, and died in the king's arms. The young king honoured Leonardo with his presence, and he expressed his personal admiration and appreciation to Leonardo for having provided him with the blessed opportunity to spend his early, formative years with the likes of whom he would never see again; and so he wept with immense sadness that he had lost a great companion and mentor.

Apart from me, Francesco Melzi of the family Melzi da Vaprio d'Adda, and the French king, the others who were present in Leonardo's room to bear witness to his soul's departure from our material world and into Paradise were Leonardo's maid, Maturina (Mathurine in French); his servant Battista, and the two Franciscan friars Francesco de Corion and Francesco da Milano. They can bear testimony to the truth that Leonardo had died in the arms of the French king.

I fell to my knees beside Maturina and Battista and the friars, and we began to pray in unison with tears in our eyes and with a flickering flame of sadness in our hearts. When we stopped for a moment, the king rose from Leonardo's bed and addressed us without releasing any further tears.

'We will have Leonardo da Vinci's body in his casket tomorrow and moved to the chapel here for four days. Members of my court and family will visit you and Leonardo at the chapel on Sunday. We will inform the priors and rectors of St. Florentin, St. Denis, and St. Gregoire to begin their first masses for Leonardo tomorrow evening. On Tuesday, we will transfer Leonardo's casket to St. Florentin with a fitting procession according to his will and testament. He will lie in view until Wednesday night, and then he will be transferred underground to a temporary crypt until we decide upon the proper arrangements for his permanent burial. Tomorrow, Francesco, you will remind us and show us what Leonardo has written in his will, and we shall try to fulfil his wishes the best that we can. We will also discuss what death notices our secretaries should begin to deliver. Our secretaries will inform Milan, Rome, Florence, Chambery, Venice, and Naples. But, we ask you to write to his brothers, to Salai, and to the Duchess of Bari. We will correspond separately with the Duchess at a later time. You can mention this in your letter to her Illustrious Highness, the Duchess of Bari. You can use our couriers or your own if you prefer. We will leave you now to your sorrow and your own private moments with your beloved Papa. God bless Leonardo da Vinci and all of you.'

The king turned away from us, returned to Leonardo's bed, knelt before the body, said a silent prayer, stood up and then quickly departed back into the underground passage and to his castle on the high parapet. It was now 11:30 pm at night.

The friar Francesco de Corion said that he would allow Leonardo's body to rest in his bed for the night, and that he and the other priests and their assistants would come to transfer his body to a casket before daybreak and leave him at the chapel of the Chateau Cloux before arranging the funeral march and his transfer on Tuesday to the St. Florentin Church located in the grounds of the fortress castle of Amboise on the bank of the Loire River.

Maturina and Battista said that they would stay with Leonardo throughout the night until the priests arrived to transfer his body to the casket. I kissed the face of Leonardo and hugged Maturina and then Battista and retired to my room to pray and meditate.

Later that night, unable to sleep, I sat down with a collection of burning candles and wrote my first draft letters to Leonardo's brothers and sisters, to the Duchess of Bari, and to Salai. One month later, I rewrote these letters and sent them off via a Gondi on the first of June.

A draft letter to Leonardo's brothers:

> To Ser Giuliano and his honourable brothers and sisters.
>
> I am sad and distressed to inform you of the death of your brother Maestro Leonardo da Vinci, who passed into the starry night in Amboise while in the loving arms of His Royal Majesty, King Francois I.
>
> He left this present life, on the second day of May, with all the sacraments of the Holy Mother the Church, and well prepared for his journey into the next life. May Almighty God give him eternal rest.
>
> It is impossible for me to express the anguish his death has caused me, for he was to me the best of fathers, and while my body holds together I shall feel perpetual sorrow, and not without justice, since he showed me every day a deeply felt and most ardent love,

as the giver of life himself. It is for each one of us to lament the death of such a man that nature has not the power to re-create again.

Leonardo da Vinci has appointed and willed me to be the lawful executor of his last will and testament and I shall execute it in full honesty and expediency according to that which he has narrated to me and his constituted Testator empowered by the Most Christian King. You and your brothers have been willed to be heirs of a sum of money held in the hands of the treasurer of Santa Maria Nuova in the city of Florence. The aforesaid Maestro Leonardo has deposited in Santa Maria Nuova in the hands of the Camarlingo 400 gold scudi in marked and number notes, bearing interest at 5 per cent, which on the 16th October will have been there for 6 years, and also there is a property at Fiesole which he desires to be distributed among you. The transference of the property and willed sum from the treasurer to you will be arranged by me, the Testator, and the treasurer of Santa Maria Nuova over the next year. After one year's grace I as his lawful executor will contact you with the appropriate letters and documents for you to procure and receive your rightful entitlements from the treasurer of Santa Maria Nuova as deemed in your brother's last will and testament.

The will does not contain anything more that concerns you, *nec plus ultra*, except that I offer you all my powers most speedily and most readily to do your will and I continue to recommend myself to you.

May he, my father and your loving brother, Leonardo da Vinci rest in Paradise with the full grace of our Maker for we will never see the like of him again.

Francesco Melzi, Count Palatine, Executor and tenant of His Royal Majesty, King Francois I.

Your faithful servant and executor of Leonardo da Vinci's last will and testament. [S2]

I also wrote to Leonardo's sister Piera di Leonardo from his mother's side to inform her and her three remaining sisters and brother of Leonardo's passing. My next letter was to my mother and father at Vaprio d'Adda in Lombardy, who both love Leonardo as much as I do. Little did I know that as I wrote this letter to my parents that my father was unwell, and that he would die in Vaprio d'Adda one year later, almost two years before I would return home to have him honour me with the inheritance of his Villa and the full title of Count Palatine with legal endorsement from Charles V and the Holy Roman Empire.

Then, I wrote to my 'brother-in-arms' Salai, Leonardo's adopted son and personal assistant, describing the last hours before our Maestro's death, what kindnesses Leonardo had said about him, what the king had told me about Leonardo, and I relayed some of my fondest remembrances of our time together. I allayed Salai's anxieties about his inheritance by pointing out what our beloved father Leonardo had bequeathed to him in his will. He already had many of Leonardo's paintings and inventions in his possession in Milan and a substantial sum of money accumulated to him with the help of Leonardo. It was a long and sad letter that I wrote.

Still awake and unable to sleep I wrote my fifth letter. It was to Princess Isabella Sforza of Aragon, the Duchess of Bari. Leonardo and she had loved each other very much, and at an auspicious time they would have married if only protocol would have allowed it. But, it was not to be. The Duchess was issued from a much too royal line, and although Leonardo was a gentleman and a genius, his bloodline was far too removed from her superior lineage. The courts and church would never have allowed her to keep her Royal titles had she and Leonardo married. And so they had to part ways and follow their own separate journeys along the roads and with the experiences that they were fated with by Lady Fortune, although not necessarily the one and only God (and the other Gods) of privilege that they may have encountered along the way. While Leonardo's corpse lay with me in Amboise, the Duchess was alive and well at her Royal Court in Bari, a thousand miles and lifetimes away from us.

I knew the Duchess would be much distressed by the news of losing her past lover and loyal confidant. Maybe, she would find solace and sympathy in the arms of another - I thought this to myself graciously as I began to compose the letter. She had many pursuers after she was widowed from the young duke Gian Galeazzo Sforza who died under suspicious circumstances at the age of twenty-five years. But, she remained in mourning dress in the memory of her young Duke and that of the much older Leonardo for the remainder of her life, the blessed and beautiful Duchess of Bari.

Most Illustrious Highness and Duchess of Bari

It distresses me to inform you of the loss of our beloved, Leonardo ser Perio da Vinci. He died last night in the arms of the King of France at 10:20 pm in his bed in Cloux. It was a starry, starry night and we watched his soul rise reluctantly at first, but then burst and soar into the heavens at a speed greater than an exploding comet.

He called out your name saying how much he loved you and the young Duke Gian, and how you were both an inspiration to him and especially how he admired your beauty, grace, intelligence, integrity, bravery and your joy of life in his presence. His one regret was that you were absent from his presence in the later years of his life. His message to your Illustrious Highness that he passed on to me as the lawful executor of his last will and testament was to please tell the Duchess that he hopes that you will continue to support him and be his patron of the Arts and to remember him as your faithful servant and once betrothed and to burn your favourite candles for him each month for a year at the face of the gracious and forgiving Madonna that you both love so much and that he painted for you in remembrances of the past when you spent your time together in full love and joy.

I am in great pain, Duchess, for having just lost my Godfather and Teacher. He was more than a father to me and I know when we look up at the stars at night he will look back down at us, his shining light twinkling with love and encouragement reminding us to face our demons with bravery and with a forgiving humour.

I am unsure of my future right now, but I do hope very much to visit you and your court in Bari some day that is convenient and propitious to us both.

The French King, His Illustrious Majesty Francois I, has asked me to pass on to you his royal respects and his own sadness at the loss of Leonardo. He will also write to you directly regarding Leonardo's time in his court, and he thus forthwith apologises beforehand, should my letter reach you before his own message of condolence does. We both pass on our best wishes to your gracious daughter, Bona Sforza, the Duchess of Bari in extensia and with the greatest of respect, we ask your grace to inform your daughter and other admirers of Leonardo about our sad news of his passing; Leonardo da Vinci, master painter, and the best and gentlest friend that we could ever have.

Leonardo's most favourite portrait of you, that we call the Bella Lisa, is now in my possession. However, the French king is desirous to own it and we are in a protracted negotiation about its worth and subsequent entitlements. He proposes to house it at his residence in Amboise while he is alive and then have it transferred to the Royal Gallery of Paris after his passing. I would very much like to receive word of your thoughts about your picture passing into the hands of the French king, who loved Leonardo greatly and was a generous and gracious host to us both.

Your loyal servant and admirer

Count Francesco Melzi da Vaprio d'Adda, Executor and tenant of His Royal Majesty, King Francois I.

Having finished my draft of the five letters, I collapsed at my desk, fast asleep.

Battista woke me before sunrise. 'The priests are here to transfer Leonardo from his bed to his casket. They have washed him with embalming fluid to ensure the preservation of his body during the funeral and at least for the duration of a month or longer.'

Leonardo was in the open casket on a bier, clothed, and ready to be transferred to the chapel to allow people to view him. An hour before the arrival of the priests, Battista, Maturina, and three nuns from the nearby convent had washed and dressed him in his favourite kaftan. Maturina had trimmed, washed, and combed his beard. He looked peaceful, serene, happily dreaming in his casket. I sketched in my mind the image of how he lay there, like Jesus on the Shroud, his hands crossed over at his hips. I smiled at his wonderful serene face and my eyes filled with tears until all was distorted before me. I wiped my watery eyes and stood back for the nuns and priests to add their prayers and blessings over his body.

The king had sent soldiers to guard the entrances and placed them at strategic positions on the grounds of the chateau. They were already in the house, inside and outside the chapel, solemnly at attention long before the friars were allowing mourners to enter and visit the chapel and view Leonardo. Word spread quickly through the local and Italian community in Amboise that Leonardo da Vinci was dead. Throughout the day, large numbers of people gathered to view and pray for him. Many members of the large Italian community in Amboise filed past his casket, stopping to make the sign of the cross with the prayer of 'in the name of the Father (forehead) and the Holy (chest) Spirit (right shoulder)' or to express a private silent prayer wishing him well into the afterlife. There were Italian monks and friars, masons, stone-dressers, sculptors, master glaziers, wrought-iron craftsmen, carpenters, joiners and cabinet-makers, painters, goldsmiths and silversmiths, and landscape gardeners. They were in Amboise to beautify the Royal Castle. The Neapolitan tailors had brought fabrics and embroideries to dress the French nobles and make the magnificent shimmering clothes and costumes for court revelries. They all knew Leonardo and had met him at one time or another during his short, three-year stay in Amboise.

After an hour with Leonardo in the chapel, I returned to my room to sleep. Maturina woke me to say that a small offering would be ready in an hour, and that I should join her and Battista in the kitchen, for we had to eat and regain some strength for the days ahead. I asked her to stay with me for a little while to allow me to read out Leonardo's last will and testament to her before she went back to the kitchen. She sat down in the chair on the other side of the desk from me. Leonardo was lying quietly in his coffin on the bier in the chapel, and I could hear the visitors and mourners filing around outside. I withdrew a copy of the will from the drawer of my desk and read it out to her in full, occasionally looking across to watch her reaction. She remained calm until I had finished reading the entire will.

Leonardo's Last Will and Testament

Be it known to all persons, present and to come that at the court of our Lord the King at Amboise before ourselves in person, Messer Leonardo da Vinci painter to the King, at present staying at the place known as Cloux near Amboise, duly considering the certainty of death and the uncertainty of its time, has acknowledged and declared in the said court and before us that he has made, according to the tenor of these presents, his testament and the declaration of his last will, as follows.

And first he commends his soul to our Lord, Almighty God, and to the Glorious Virgin Mary, and to our lord Saint Michael, to all the blessed Angels and Saints male and female in Paradise.

Item. The said Testator desires to be buried within the church of Saint Florentin at Amboise, and that his body shall be borne thither by the chaplains of the church.

Item. That his body may be followed from the said place to the said church of Saint Florentin by the collegium of the said church, that is to say by the rector and the prior, or by their vicars and chaplains of the church of Saint Denis of Amboise, also the lesser friars of the place, and before his body shall be carried to the said church this Testator desires, that in the said church of Saint Florentin three grand masses shall be celebrated by the deacon and sub-deacon and that on the day when these three high masses are celebrated, thirty low masses shall also be performed at Saint Gregoire.

Item. That in the said church of Saint Denis similar services shall be performed, as above.

Item. That the same shall be done in the church of the said friars and lesser brethren.

Item. The aforesaid Testator gives and bequeaths to Messer Francesco Melzi, nobleman, of Milan, in remuneration for services and favours done to him in the past, each and all of the books the Testator is at present possessed of, and the instruments and portraits appertaining to his art and calling as a painter.

Item. The same Testator gives and bequeaths henceforth for ever to Battista de Vilanis his servant one half, that is the moity, of his garden which is outside the walls of Milan, and the other half of the same garden to Salai his servant; in which garden aforesaid Salai has built and constructed a house which shall be and remain henceforth in all perpetuity the property of the said Salai, his heirs and successors; and this is in remuneration for the good and kind services which the said de Vilanis and Salai, his servants have done him in past times until now.

Item. The said Testator gives to Maturina his maid a cloak of good black cloth lined with fur, and a bolt of cloth and two ducats paid once only; and this likewise is in remuneration for the good and gracious service rendered to him in past times until now by the said Maturina.

Item. He desires that at his funeral sixty tapers shall be carried which shall be borne by sixty poor men, to whom shall be given money for carrying them; at the discretion of the said Melzi, and these tapers shall be distributed among the four above mentioned churches.

Item. The said Testator gives to each of the said churches ten lbs. of wax in thick tapers, which shall be placed in the said churches to be used on the day when those said services are celebrated.

Item. That alms shall be given to the poor of the Hotel-Dieu, to the poor of Saint Lazare d'Amboise and, to that end, there shall be given and paid to the treasurers of that same fraternity the sum and amount of seventy soldi of Tours.

Item. The said Testator gives and bequeaths to the said Messer Francesco Melzi, being present and agreeing, the remainder of his pension and the sums of money which are owing to him from the past time till the day of his death by the receiver or treasurer-general M. Johan Sapin, and each and every sum of money that he has already received from the aforesaid Sapin of his said pension, and in case he should die before the said Melzi and not otherwise; which moneys are at present in the possession of the said Testator in the said place called Cloux, as he says. And he likewise gives and bequeaths to the said Melzi all and each of his clothes which he at present possesses at the said place of Cloux, and all in remuneration for the good and kind services done by him in past times till now, as well as in payment for the trouble and annoyance he may incur with regard to the execution of this present testament, which however, shall all be at the expense of the said Testator. And he orders and desires that the sum of four hundred scudi del Sole, which he has deposited in the hands of the treasurer of Santa Maria Nuova in the city of Florence, may be given to his brothers now living in Florence with all the interest and usufruct that may have accrued up to the present time, and be due from the aforesaid treasurer to the aforesaid Testator on account of the said four hundred crowns, since they were given and consigned by the Testator to the said treasurers.

Item. He desires and orders that the said Messer Francesco Melzi shall be and remain the sole and only executor of the said will of the said Testator; and that the said testament shall be executed in its full and complete meaning and according to that which is here narrated and said, to have, hold, keep and observe, the said Messer Leonardo da Vinci, constituted Testator, has obliged and obliges by these presents the said his heirs and successors with all his goods moveable and immoveable present and to come, and has renounced and expressly renounces by these presents all and each of the things which to that are contrary. Given at the said place of Cloux in the presence of Magister Spirito Fieri vicar, of the church of Saint Denis at Amboise, of M. Guglielmo Croysant priest and chaplain, of Magister Cipriane Fulchin, Brother Francesco de Corion, and of Francesco da Milano, a brother of the Convent of the Minorites at Amboise, witnesses summoned and required to that end by the indictment of the said court in the presence of the aforesaid M. Francesco Melzi who accepting and agreeing to the same has promised by his faith and his oath which he has administered to us personally and has sworn to us never to do nor say nor act in any way to the contrary. And it is sealed by his request with the royal seal apposed to legal contracts at Amboise, and in token of good faith.

Given on the XXIIIrd day of April MDXVIII, before Easter. And on the XXIIIrd day of this month of April MDXVIII, in the presence of M. Guglielmo Borian, Royal notary in the court of the bailiwick of Amboise, the aforesaid M. Leonardo de Vinci gave and bequeathed, by his last will and testament, as aforesaid, to the said M. Battista de Vilanis, being present and agreeing, the right of water which the King Louis XII, of pious memory lately deceased gave to this same de Vinci, the stream of the canal of Santo Cristoforo in the duchy of Milan, to belong to the said Vilanis for ever in such wise and manner that the said gentleman made him this gift in the presence of M. Francesco Melzi, gentleman, of Milan and in mine.

And on the aforesaid day in the said month of April in the said year MDXVIII the same M. Leonardo de Vinci by his last will and testament gave to the aforesaid M. Battista de Vilanis, being present and agreeing, each and all of the articles of furniture and utensils of his house at present at the said place of Cloux, in the event of the said de Vilanis surviving the aforesaid M. Leonardo de Vinci, in the presence of the said M. Francesco Melzi and of me, Notary &c. Borean. [S1]

'Maturina, will you wear his cloak to his funeral?'

'I don't know, Francesco. I'm still too stunned by sadness to think about my costume.'

'I'm sorry, Maturina. I didn't mean to be insensitive to your feelings. You know that he left the cloak in his will to you because he didn't want the unscrupulous accusing you of stealing it from his wardrobe. This way it clearly belongs to you in law. Also, you have his documents and a share in the Salamander Tavern. Apart from the king's share, it all belongs to you.'

Maturina began to sob, and I felt sorry that I had read the Last Will and Testament out to her. It was cruel and insensitive and boorish. She looked tired and distressed.

'I will write a copy out for the king to read tomorrow and give you this copy after the funeral.'

'I have to tell you a secret, Francesco. It may not be a secret for too long.'

I nodded and waited for her to continue.

'I'm pregnant with Leonardo's child.'

'What?' I was stunned. Had I heard correctly? 'What did you say, Maturina?'

'I'm pregnant with child. I haven't bled for three months.'

'Is Leonardo the father?'

'Yes, it cannot be anybody else's child. I have only slept with Leonardo.'

'Maturina – if only this is true – it would be a miracle – God's gift to us all.'

I stumbled from my chair, moved around the table to where she was seated and knelt down beside her and rested my head on her stomach and began to cry. She stroked my head and neck and said, 'do not cry for me, Francesco. Leonardo has left me a far greater treasure than his cloak, and he didn't even have to declare it in his lawyer's last will and testament.'

After I regained some of my senses, I looked up into her face and asked, 'will you tell the king that you are carrying Leonardo's child?'

She smiled back at me and said, 'no. I'll wait to see if he notices any physical change in me over the next few months and whether he can guess correctly?'

Suddenly, I understood why Leonardo had instructed me a few weeks previously to give Maturina one of our copies of the Madonna with imaginary child that I had helped him to finish painting only recently. For Maturina was not only Leonardo's model for the painting, but she in fact was his Madonna with his unseen baby.

***

After lunch, I went outside away from the gathering crowds to a little grove of beautiful trees beside the river L'Amasse Ou la Masse that trickled through the grounds of the Chateau. I sat on a bench and stared up through the canopy of leaves that created a speckle of shadows on the ground. This was Leonardo's favourite spot to sit and meditate or converse quietly with his King or with his retinue of friends. I glanced around me and saw nobody about in my line of sight. It was lovely and peaceful – it seemed to be a fitting place for the great Leonardo da Vinci to have come to live out the last years of his life and to die peacefully if not contentedly, his enormous spirit somewhere high in the sky, finally flying as he always dreamed to do one day.

Why had we come here to Amboise? Why did Leonardo, the Maestro in his old age leave Milan in Italy and bring us, Battista, his valet and servant; Salai his adopted son and assistant, and me, his personal secretary and painting assistant, here to Amboise in the Loire valley to live in the chateau of His Majesty the French king Francois I, the first king from the House of Valois? The answer is simple. It was because of our French connections or as Leonardo liked to called it, the French kitchen. We came here to Amboise because we had no choice. The king summoned us here to cook for him, and so we obeyed him or else the French rulers in Milan might ostracise us and our families. By disobeying the king's invitation, we and our loved-ones could easily suffer the consequences, lose our properties, and lose our freedoms. Were we forced against our own will to leave Italy and move here to France as the King's prisoners or insects? No. We were pressured, but, in the end, it was our own choice. It was a way to best protect us and our families and our interests from the foreign occupation of the French and yet expand our own horizons. It was Leonardo at his diplomatic best, knowing that he might die a foreigner in a foreign land, yet willing to sacrifice himself for his family, the Melzi family, who he loved dearly and who loved him in return. The French king and France ruled over us in Milan, so it was better to be with him in France than with the duplicitous Pope Leo X in Rome, who was prepared to ruin us all if we continued to stay there. Florence was in political turmoil in 1516, and Leonardo had no desire to return there and face his grasping stepbrothers and stepsisters and the generational divide. The young King Francois, his wife, his mother, and his sister were most welcoming, and they received us with open arms and accommodated us at their private property in Amboise with great warmth and generosity.

As I write this in the year of 1560, Milan and much of the Italian peninsular is now officially under the rule of the Spanish because of the Treaty of Cateau-Cambresis that was signed last year between Henri II of France and Phillip II of Spain. France and Spain were constantly at war with each other over the ownership of the Duchy of Milan at least since 1525 when Charles V's Spanish forces were dominant in Italy. So it is difficult for my children and

9

grandchildren to understand that Milan was once the relatively peaceful domain of the French when Leonardo and I were living and working there with my family, the Melzi of Vaprio, on the Adda River, and with the ruling family of Milan, the Sforza. Before Leonardo had died there were three different invasions of Milan and Pavia in Lombardy by the French kings, Charles VIII, Louis XII, and Francois I. Two of them lay claim to Lombardy and Savoy through their bloodlines with the Visconti and the Savoy. They also lay claim to Leonardo as a representative of Milan, Florence, and the Italian kingdom of Rome.

The French kings Louis XII and Francois I had seen Leonardo's *Last Supper of Jesus* in the refectory of the Convent of Santa Maria delle Grazie, Milan, and they were spellbound. Nobody had every seen such a life-like, magnificent piece of artwork. Leonardo's mastery of perspective into infinity and his visual story telling had overwhelmed them. It was as if you were actually before Jesus and the disciples when you stood or knelt in the refectory and looked up at the painting. Jesus and the disciples were alive, they were there in three dimensions projecting out of the refectory wall, and they stunned you with their emotional intensity and agitation. Jesus had just told them that one of them was going to betray him to the Jews and the Romans. Or was Leonardo also telling us another story, one that was more relevant to his times in Milan? When King Louis XII saw it, he immediately wanted to take it back with him to Paris. 'How do we take this wall back with us across the Alps,' he asked his engineers? And, thus began the many invitations to Leonardo, first from Louis XII and then Francois I, to live and work in the French court.

For many years, Leonardo had resisted a move to live and work in France despite the offers from the French king Louis XII and other high nobles. He had no intention to live in France because he loved far too much the sun and mild weather of Lombardy, Tuscany, and the other vibrant places of the Italian northern peninsula. The south of Italy was far too hot for him and in this case, if given a choice, he might have preferred to live in the milder climate of the beautiful Loire valley. However, he avoided the first French occupation in Lombardy by moving to work in Ferrara, Florence, and elsewhere mainly in the services of Cesare Borgia, Niccolo Machiavelli, and the Signoria of Florence, respectively. But, the French were persistent, and they forever offered him commissions for the things he loved to do with fortifications, construction, hydraulics, architecture, and city planning.

During the French occupation, Leonardo eventually called Italy his French-Italian connection, his French kitchen, a place of foreign intrigue where he would need to cook up his most inventive recipes and his best, nutritious, vegetable soups to survive or to sustain himself. My family also had strong diplomatic ties and a history with the French kings. My great grandfather had visited Amboise for the proxy wedding between Bona of Savoy and the Duke Galeazzo Maria Sforza, the then ruler of Milan.

When King Francois invaded Lombardy in 1515, Leonardo on the insistence of the King and the wishes of the Pope Leo X met with him in Bologna and presented him with a gift, a mechanical lion that opened up and displayed the king's heraldic flowers, the livre. In a private audience, the king immediately invited Leonardo to return with him to Amboise and his royal court. The king's mistress Marie Gaudin suggested that Leonardo should join her king on his return back to France once matters were stabilised on the Italian peninsula. Leonardo thanked the King and his mistress for their gracious invitation, and he reminded the king that he was still under contract to Giuliano de' Medici, Duke of Nemours, the brother of Pope Leo X, and that he now resided in the Vatican apartments with commissions for the de' Medici family. The young French King understood and said that he wasn't offended by Leonardo's non-acceptance, but observed that Rome was an unstable place, and if things were to change for the worse for Leonardo while he was there, then his, the King's, invitation was still open to him. At first Leonardo seemed to be more than content in the Eternal City. We had rooms in the Beldevere, and Leonardo had two studios and workshops and various pupils and assistants working with him. We had many of Europe's greatest artists, scientists, classicists, nobles, celebrities, and others of great note in our near vicinity. I also had access to a small Melzi family apartment in a notable area of Rome. The French king was prescient, however; he had foreseen Leonardo's misery in Rome. Leonardo was in dispute and in trouble with German glassmakers working for the Vatican. There were unpleasant rumours about the loss of his abilities and his procrastination, and suddenly he was out of favour in Rome. His options were dwindling rapidly. Milan was as unstable as Florence and uninviting as Rome. Amboise, all at once, seemed to be the best option for Leonardo and me and our remaining small family of the faithful.

***

On the third day of the vigil at Leonardo's casket, the king's equerry, Count Galeazzo Sanseverino, the best horseman in Europe, arrived in a sudden flamboyant rush. He grabbed me by my shoulders and hugged me vigourously. 'Little one, I came as soon as I received word from the king's pigeon. I was in Fontainebleau. I will tell you more later on. But now, little one, take me to your Master, I have to see him in repose.'

Sanseverino was six years younger than Leonardo and his long time friend since their days together in Milan. Leonardo had resided in Sanseverino's palace in Milan at various times in the 1480s and 1490s and used his collection of horses to model the planned equestrian monument of Francesco Sforza. They shared many adventures and philosophical debates before Sanseverino moved to France after 1504 when he was appointed firstly as a councillor of the state, then as king Louis XII's chamberlain, and lastly as the Grand Ecuyer de France. Sanseverino was an Italian condottiere, a general in Ludovico Sforza's army before the latter's capture, imprisonment, and death in France. Sanseverino had survived in the hands of Louis XII, because in 1494, he had been awarded a knighthood of the Order of Saint Michael by the king of France Charles VIII. So, Galeazzo Sanseverino had become a chivalrous servant of the French kings, and he was one of a number of advisors who favoured Leonardo's appointment to the French court as King Francois's chief architect, painter, and philosopher.

I led Sanseverino to Leonardo's open casket, and he dropped to his knees and wept for the death of his friend. After a while, he stood up and leant over the casket and kissed Leonardo on his cold, stiff lips. Then, he took my hand and said, 'my condolescences, little one. We will talk later. You will have to help me with organising the banners, effigies, and carriages for the funeral procession.' He let go of my hand and rushed out, crossing himself while he exited.

Day four after Leonardo's death was Tuesday, the day of the funeral procession. Sanseverino had arrived at sunrise to organise the horses, the carriages and carts, the cavalier escorts, all appropriately dressed in black silk. A large crowd of mourners had gathered at the Cloux a few hours after the sun had risen in the east. The small Italian community of Amboise was gathered outside the grounds of Cloux ready to accompany Leonardo's body to the churches along the way. Amboise was steeped in the Italian art of living and entertaining. Italian was spoken in both the town and court of Amboise. The mourners were sombre and quiet, many in tears, waiting patiently for the cortege to begin its procession. Amboise was full of people in the streets. People had been travelling from the nearby towns and villages of the Loire valley including Tours and Blois.

After prayers and with the monks singing Latin dirges, the procession, attended by the collegium of Saint Denis and Saint Florentin, left the grounds of the Cloux and proceeded first down the main streets of Amboise to the church of St. Denis and then along the narrow street between the merchant houses and the castle and on towards the entrance of the castle rampart and upward to St. Florentin Church located inside the castle walls on the left bank of the Loire River. As the cortege left the Chateau du Cloux, the column of cavaliers rode ahead of

Leonardo's two mules Pedro and Paola. They led the procession of horses pulling carts bearing effigies and banners of Leonardo's portrait in profile and his paintings of *St. Anne* and *St. John, the Baptist*. Then, it was Count Galeazzo Sanseverino in black silk and chest armour riding tall on his magnificent white stallion ahead of a small column of cavaliers in support and ahead of Leonardo's hearse bearing his casket with an effigy of a lion lying on its lid. The first carriage after Leonardo's hearse carried an effigy of the Virgin Mary with a solemn, but serene face, standing with her arms outstretched towards Leonardo's casket. Behind this carriage strode the church rectors, priors, vicars, chaplains, deacons, sub deacons, friars, and lesser friars in full church regalia. Behind them were the carriages of the old clerics and nuns who were unable to walk, and the carts of the household staff (Maturina and Battista were there among them), and the other workers from the Chateau du Cloux. They were followed by a long procession of mourners on foot holding candles or images of Leonardo made available to them at different points in Amboise. I walked alongside Leonardo's hearse together with eight other dignitaries from the King's castle. We meandered about the streets of Amboise enclosed by houses and shops covered in black cloth. Throngs of people lined the route of the procession. We passed the Salamander Tavern that was co-owned by the King and Leonardo. Black drapes hung from its balconies with images of salamanders and lions side by side and banners with words proclaiming *Long Live the King* and *Rest in Peace, Maestro Leonardo*. Mourners stood on the balconies, holding lit candles.

As we moved forward in orderly fashion, I heard the gathering crowd of workers, farmers, and merchants crying out, *goodbye, Maestro, goodbye, Leonardo. We will miss you Maestro. We will miss your wine and festivals. Rest in peace gentle Lord Leonardo. Rest in peace.* The sun was shining bright over the horizon behind the castle as the procession proceeded slowly along the designated streets. In accordance with his last wishes, sixty paupers carrying torches accompanied his body in broad daylight. The early morning farmers and merchants left their usual duties behind them and they joined the cortege that transported the body of the Maestro to the ramparts where the castle guards were at standby ready to prevent the uninvited masses from following the official retinue through the castle gates. The king's castle loomed above us and cast a large black shadow. The Royal Castle of Amboise and its fortification was built on a rocky spur known as the Promontoire des Chatelliers, an ideal observation post at the confluence of the Loire and one of its affluents, the Amasse. Since the Iron Age, this site was a place of craftwork and commercial exchanges, and now it was to be the site of Leonardo da Vinci's funeral and burial place.

My eyes filled with tears as we slowly trudged up the rampart onto the parade grounds of the castle, winding our way to the Chapel. The church was filled to capacity with black ravens. Once inside, Leonardo's casket was placed on a bier and the bishops, abbots, and priests began their chants while the rector and prior of St. Florentin looked down solemnly on the gathered mourners. The Dominican nuns attending from the priory adjoining the Cloux now filled the Chapel with their gentle singing. An attendant led me to a corner pew, and I sat down, my head was spinning with tiredness. I looked about me and saw that the young King, his wife, sister, and mother were all in attendance sitting together away from the nobles and other members of their court. The King was dressed in a red, white, and blue cape over his shoulders; the priests were in reds and whites, many in black. Some altar boys were in blue. Here and there, I could see the Italian contingent, the Italian artists, humanists, and engineers who had come to work in the Amboise court, the craftsmen, masons, painters, goldsmiths, cabinet-makers, tailors, and musicians. I was soon hallucinating with the memories of Leonardo. I felt faint and thought that I would soon follow Leonardo and die from inhaling the incense forever growing stronger about me. In an hour or two, they would transfer Leonardo to another bier for further prayers and a viewing of his coffin. Could I last until then without the need to leave for a breath of fresh air and some welcomed sunlight?

And then, before I could catch my second breath, the King of France stood at the pulpit of St. Florentin, and he told us and his entire country that, *'there had never been another man born in the world who knew as much as Maestro Leonardo da Vinci, not so much about painting, sculpture, mathematics, and architecture, and he was a very great philosopher. He was divine, and for each one of us the death of this man is a great loss because it is not possible that life will ever produce his like again. On the second of May 1519, at the age of 67, Leonardo da Vinci, one of the greatest visionaries in Christendom finally joined God, the one that he called, "the operator of so many marvellous things." After all, was it not Leonardo who also said, "not to value life, all life, is not to deserve it?" And now, with his passing from this, our material world, into the Kingdom of God, Leonardo will discover why and how we are all put together on this Earth to live and to die, and why our Lord, the Saviour, wants us all to live in peace and with love in our being, and to die with grace and honour.'* And with these simple words King Francois pronounced the end to one of the most beautiful of funeral orations I had ever heard; and he and I and the congregation wept tears of sadness. The young king and his family had welcomed Leonardo with open arms – but time rushed by – it was all too short – and now Leonardo was dead, unable to be heard or to respond to the King's eulogy. I heard a threnody, a hymn in Praise of God.

While I sat weeping after the king's funeral oration, my head filled with thoughts and images of Leonardo. I thought of his beautiful paintings, and the da Vinci-coded messages of the corrupt rule of the Duchy of Milan in his painting of the *Last Supper*; the symbolism and the identity of the beautiful and mysterious ladies in his Madonna paintings, his love for the *Mona Lisa*, the *Lady and the Ermine*, and *La Belle Ferronniere*; the solution to his coded messages in his paintings of Gian Galeazzo Sforza the young Duke of Milan and of the brilliant mathematician Luca Pacioli. I thought of his marvellous inventions, the festivities, his troubles and travails, his loves and his foes. He created performances, entertainments, magic, and fun like nobody else with whom I shared my life and ideas. I thought of the man with the dangerous and beautiful mind, the man who almost lost his own liberty and life to unsubstantiated accusations from the envious and jaundiced, and the unreasonable investigations into his life from the dark forces of the Florentine Officers of the Night. He dedicated his own life to inquiry, observation, and the rules of science and natural philosophy that challenged the teachings and mendacity of the church. He confronted the authority of the tyrants and yet generously provided them with his service and genius in order to survive. I thought about his life and times with the Florentines, and the Lombardians, and the disruptive wars with France, the political betrayals, the continuous changes in culture and authority, his loves and disappointments, the enormous challenges, disadvantages and prejudices that he needed to overcome, the masterpieces he created, the interruptions to his creativity, and his duels with Fate and Fortune. I sat thinking about the life and times of Leonardo da Vinci, the wars, and the intrigues … here was a marvellous story to tell.

The incense burnt my eyes and nostrils intolerably. I felt nauseous and faint. I tried to cry out to the Saviour for freedom from my own internal primal scream from somewhere deep inside my own sealed coffin. Without a sound, I collapsed into a numbing, malodorous, glutinous darkness of seeming contradictions and then nothingness …

CHAPTER 2

Leonardo and the Melzi of Milan and Insubria

Good day to you Messer Francesco. Why, in God's name, of all the letters I have written to you, have you never answered one? Now wait till I come, by God, and I shall make you write so much that perhaps you will become sick of it.

— Leonardo da Vinci

Who Was Leonardo?

I wish to tell you the true story of Leonardo da Vinci, about his life and times and how he confronted the stresses and challenges in his life. Leonardo represents many different things to many people. I can only tell you what he was to me, Francesco Melzi. He was my godfather, mentor, teacher, friend, companion, and the inspiration to be a good person, a loving and generous family man, and a bold painter. His fable of the eagle best illustrates his own life of renewal and his dream to always strive for the truth like Icarus's high-flying ambition to leave the bondage of mediocrity and ascend to the stratosphere.

A majestic old eagle lived alone on top of a very high mountain. One day he sensed that the hour of his death was not far off. With a mighty cry he summoned his sons who lived lower down the mountain. When they were all gathered together, he looked at them one by one, and said:

'I have provided for you, and bought you up so that you might look directly at the sun. Those of your brother's who could not tolerate the sun's face I have allowed to die of hunger. For this reason, you deserve to fly higher than all the other birds. Any who want to preserve their lives will not attack your nest. All the animals will fear you and you shall never harm those who respect you. You shall allow them to eat up the scraps of your prey. Now I am about to leave you. But I shall not die here in my nest. I shall fly very high, as far as my wings will carry me. I shall stretch out towards the sun to take my leave of it. The sun's fiery rays will burn my old feathers. I shall fall towards earth and finally into the water. But miraculously I shall rise again from the water, rejuvenated and ready to begin a new existence. Such is the lot of eagles, our destiny.'

With these words the eagle took to the air. Majestic and solemn he flew round the mountain where his sons stood. Then, suddenly, he turned upwards towards the sun, which would burn up his tired old wings. [S3]

I will continue with my testament of Leonardo da Vinci and reveal his thoughts and feelings about various matters later on in my chronicle. He was envied, misunderstood, and vilified by some, and I will set the record straight in his defence. But first, I will tell you about my family the Melzi, patricians of Milan, and how we are intertwined with the life and times of Leonardo da Vinci.

Francesco Melzi, Count Palatine of Vaprio, and Insubria (1491 to Present)

My name is Giovanni Francesco Melzi, Count Palatine of Vaprio d'Adda in Insubria (Lombardy), the Duchy of Milan. I am a councillor, painter, art historian and the curator of Leonardo da Vinci's notebooks and drawings and the author of his *Treatise on Painting* that I published after his death. My mother, father, grandparents, uncles and aunts, brothers and sisters, all call me Giovanni or *Cesco,* but I am better known as Francesco amongst my friends, colleagues, and acquaintances. Leonardo called me *Messer Francesco,* and the historian and painter Giorgio Vasari referred to me as Francesco Melzi in his book *The Lives of the Most Eminent Painters, Sculptors, and Architects.* And so, I will refer to myself as Francesco Melzi in this book of my reminiscences of Leonardo da Vinci, my thoughts and memories of his and my life in Milan, Italy, France, and elsewhere.

My eight children know me well. But let me to introduce myself to you in some greater detail to allow you to better appreciate my story about the Maestro. My ancestors are the Melzi, the della Torre, the Tanti, the Visconti – and other nobles of the Lombardy and Milanese history. We are a well-connected and wealthy group of families with properties inside the city and lavish estates and palaces outside the city in Lombardy and other states. Even today, we are still addressed as patricians of the city of Milan and its dominions, an ancient and noble family of the Duchy of Milan who nurtured and encouraged Leonardo da Vinci to become one of us.

Fig. 1. Francesco Melzi. Self-portrait.

Here, I have added my self-portrait that I drew and painted with some assistance from the Maestro one year after I became his student and secretary in Milan in 1508. I also have added my self-portrait which I finished in 1525 when I was 34 years of age more than six years after I had served Leonardo da Vinci for 11 years and another three years serving the French King Francois I.

The House of Melzi

I have many Melzi, della Torre, Tanti, and Visconti relatives scattered throughout the Duchy of Milan and other places. I can trace my Milanese nobility to at least Antoniolo Melzi who was Counsellor of the first Duke of Milan and General Counsellor of Milan. My mother's ancestors, the della Torre (or Torriani), also were intimately involved in the rule of the Milanese Duchy in the 13th and 14th centuries. The members of the House of della Torre were overthrown as the rulers of Milan and Insubria in 1277, and they battled unsuccessfully for thirty years with the rival Visconti family for power until 1311. Thereafter, the della Torre either moved out of the Duchy of Milan to other territories or stayed on and faithfully served the Milanese ruling families, first the Visconti and then the Sforza family.

My father's family, the Melzi of Insubria, were always loyal to the incumbent Milanese ruling families from the della Torre to the Visconti, from the House of Sforza, and to the two French kings Louis XII and Francois I who were the first kings representing the House of Valois-Orleans and the House of Valois-Angouleme. Now, after the overthrow of the French in 1529, Imperial Spain and the House of Habsburg use their proxy Governors to rule us. Many of the Melzi served as Treasurers, Ducal Counsellors, Senators, and General Counsellors of Milan and its territories. Today, I myself am a General Counsellor of Milan and Prevost of Pontirolo and landlord of an estate near the village of Sant'Antonio in Brolio that is located between Florence and Siena in chianti country. Some of my past Melzi relatives, such as Antonio Melzi, were ducal engineers in Milan especially in building and maintaining the waterways from the times of the della Torre and the Visconti rulers. Other Melzi relatives are well established within the locality of Santa Maria Assunta, a commune (now know as Magenta) of orchards, streams, and irrigation canals on the Ticino River, 20 km west of the city of Milan, near the Lombardy and Savoy (Piedmont) border.

Fig. 2. Francesco Melzi of Vaprio d' Adda, Count Palatine 1525, self-portrait.

In addition, the Melzi of Insubria represented the Holy Roman Emperor as grand counts appointed to represent him in his electorate of Insubria. My great, great granduncle Bartolomeo II was Imperial Valet of the Emperor Friedrich III who then bestowed on him the title of Count Palatine of Insubria because of his bravery while fighting in the Hungarian and Bohemian wars. The coveted title of Count Palatine, granted by the Emperor to Bartolomeo II, was on behalf of all his descendants, the privileged male members of the family Melzi of Insubria.

Since the life of Bartolomeo II, my great grandfather Giovanni, my grandfather Giovanni Bartolomeo III, and my father Gerolamo and his brothers, and I inherited the title of Count Palatine with Imperial diplomas granted to us while serving the ruling Holy Roman Emperor Fredrick III from 1452 to 1493, Maximilian I from 1493 to 1519, Charles V from 1521 to 1558, and now Ferdinand I from 1558 to 1564. Accordingly, as the Count Palatine of Insubria, I am responsible for the proper administration of the Holy Roman Emperor's properties in an area stretching approximately between the Adda river in the east, and the Sesia river in the west, and between the San Gottardo Pass in the north, and the Po river in the south, that is to say, the entire Milanese region and the countryside about it.

The Insubres founded the city of Milan 600 years before the birth of Christ. They were of Ligurian origin from northwestern Italy who spread and settled in different surrounding regions of Milan, but especially along the Adda and Sesia rivers and up North in the area of the pre-Alpine lakes (Como, Lugano, and Maggiore) around the towns of Como and Varese. The name Insubres is visible in the middle portion of the *Tabula Peutingeriana*, the Roman map of the roads dating from the fifth century after Christ. The Melzi symbol and flag is based on the symbol of Insubria in the quartered Milanese Ducal flag and the Imperial eagle, but without the child-swallowing serpent of the Visconti.

The Illustrious Giovanni Melzi, Count Palatine of Milan and Insubria (1410 – 1483) and His Good Christian Wife Brigida de Tanzi

My great grandfather Giovanni Melzi was the archetypal patrician of Milan, wise, generous, and well respected by all. He died eight-years before I was born, but I learnt a lot about him from my father and Leonardo da Vinci. He never became the signore or the ruler of the Duchy of Milan, but nevertheless, he was an important and influential nobleman and official of the state. He was *Difensore della Liberte*, Senator of Milan, Ducal Counsellor, and Count Palatine with an Imperial diploma from the Emperor of the Holy Roman Empire. He served five rulers of Milan; Filippo Maria Visconti, the Ambrosian Republic, Francesco Sforza, Galeazzo Maria Sforza, and Gian Galeazzo Sforza under the guardianship of Bona of Savoy and later, under Ludovico Sforza, Duke of Bari, and he was the Ducal Consul to four of them. He was highly religious and followed a number of edicts of St. Ambrose, patron saint of Milan. He travelled to France regularly on the highest diplomatic missions for the welfare and the service of his Dukes. He was a friend of two French kings (Charles VII and Louis XI), and he counselled them wisely, which helped to maintain a lasting peace between France and Milan during his lifetime of service. His achievements are numerous and outstanding. Although my great grandfather Giovanni Melzi is beyond the realms of this tale about Leonardo, he does warrant a remembrance in his own right, and I encourage one or more of my grown up children to research and undertake this project and provide us with his history with pride and deserved love. In Milan, he lived mostly in his private rooms beside the Sforza castle and on the estate of his father-in-law Pietro Tanzi in Casoretto, a small commune outside the city walls and not far from the Martesana canal, which runs between the northeastern city gates and the Adda River. It was at Casoretto that he had one of the best and largest private libraries in Milan having collected many codices, manuscripts, and ancient texts that he shared with his family and friends. Years later, after his death, some of his books were bought by the newly established central library of Milan.

His life is impossible to summarise in a page or two, but it is worth pointing out a few facts as a reminder to my readers of our strong family connection to the French and Milanese courts that would prove useful to me and to Leonardo in later years. First, my great grandfather had aggrieved the Sforza from 1450 until his death in 1483. He was a Doctor of Law who wrote on ethics and Christian morality and who distinguished himself at the time of the Ambrosian

Republic as ambassador to the Republic of Venice (1447-1450), and then later he was the ducal Counsellor of Francesco Sforza and his son Galeazzo Maria Sforza. He had many dealings with the French as a representative of the Duke and Duchy of Milan, but also as a representative of the Holy Roman Emperor from 1469 until his death in 1483. The title of Count Palatine from the Emperor was a powerful position to have for the Duchy of Milan was still a vassal of the empire and the towns were ultimately in their possession. The Palatine counts were judges, governors, and administrators; special representatives of the Holy Roman Emperor entrusted with much more extended power than any of the ordinary counts of the empire. They were also the Emperor's spies to check on the support and the independent tendencies of the great tribal dukes, like the Sforza. The office of the palatine counts is hereditary, so I was in line to be Count Palatine after the death of my uncles and father. Amongst our various duties as a palatine count of the Milanese Duchy, we had to show loyalty to the Emperor and the Holy Roman Empire, but also to suppress rebelling counts or dukes, and to settle frontier disputes between Milan and the French kingdom, and between Milan and the Republican states like Venice and Genoa. As palatine counts for the Holy Roman Empire, we had to support the pro-imperialist Ghibellines in their fight against the anti-imperialist Guelph who supported the Pope and the papacy. Coincidently, my mother's side of the family, the della Torre, were once enthusiastic Guelph supporters, whereas the Melzi were always on the side of the Ghibellines and the Holy Roman Empire. Although this sounds simplistic, it was a big reason for my role in Leonardo's French kitchen where I was required to advise and support King Francois I in his bid to be elected the Holy Roman Emperor in 1519.

My great grandfather was buried at the Church of Santa Maria Bianca (Saint Mary White of Mercy) in Casoretto. His father-in-law Pietro Tanzi owned the church, and in 1404, he elected the congregation of the Lateran canons of Santa Maria della Frigionaia Lucca, which belongs to the Order of Canons Regular, to run the church. My great grandfather's wealth helped the Augustinians to finance the building of the Abbey of Casoretto. The Canons Regular (priests living in community under the Rule of St. Augustine) took on the vows of common property and stability in the form of chastity, poverty, and obedience. They are not cloistered, and they engage in public ministry of liturgy and sacraments for those who visit their churches. In 1406, Don Pietro Ordo from Padua was appointed the first prior of the Church of Santa Maria Bianca in Casoretto. Because the church was small, the Augustinian canons first lived in Pietro Tanzi's villa. Later, the church and monastery of Casoretto became an important seat of the Congregation of the Canons Regular of the Lateran who stand out as wonderful examples of virtue, poverty, and holiness. Consequently, the church needed to expand with a new cloister (an open space surrounded by covered walks) adjoining the church. The Solari family of architects who also worked on the Santa Maria delle Grazie in Milan and San Pietro in Gessate rebuilt the church with its three naves and side chapels from 1470 to 1480. One of the side chapels of the church has a beautiful fresco by Pisanello of the White St. Mary as Our Lady of Mercy. The Virgin Mary is portrayed in the act of worship with baby Jesus, lying on a background of black grass. The Madonna is depicted beautifully dressed in a white robe edged with gold, a simple design of the Child Jesus, and a scroll with the written phrase, *Ecce Maria genuit nobis Salvatorem (Mary generated our Saviour)*.

The families Melzi and Tanzi held the funeral of my great grandfather at the Church of Santa Maria Bianca. Many of the luminaries of Milan attended including Leonardo da Vinci, members of the Sforza families, and other high officials and friends from the Milan Duchy. The church was full to overfilling, and the Duomo (Cathedral) in Milan held two further memorial masses, two months apart, for other family, friends, citizens, diplomats, and church dignitaries of Italy and Europe to attend. My father was overwhelmed by the support and the love that was shown to the House of Melzi with the passing away of his grandfather. He thought at the time that he could never fulfil his grandfather's achievements for they were living in different times, and they were generations apart in polite courtly manners and conduct. He feared that the Melzi power would soon begin to wane after the deaths of his grandfather and father; it was now up to him and his elder brothers Bartolomeo IV, Beltrame, Michele, Andriotto, and Lancillotto to divine and successfully manage Fortuna's blessings on the House of Melzi.

***

A few months after the death of my great grandfather, his good and most Christian wife Donna Brigida de' Tanzi invited Leonardo da Vinci to visit her in her villa in Casoretto to ask for his advice about a painter who her dearly departed husband had commissioned to prepare a triptych for them to hang above the church altar and over their grave site in the nave of the church.

'He is Giovanni Ambrogio Bevilacqua. Do you have knowledge of him, Maestro Leonardo?'

'Of course I do,' said Leonardo. 'He was a pupil of Vincenzo Foppo, and he is a master painter of mixed media panels. Yes, an excellent choice, yes, indeed, Countess. May I ask what it is that he has done for you?'

'Well this is it, Maestro Leonardo. I do not know. He has not been in contact with me, nor with my husband for some time. I have not seen his drawings, nor his designs, and I am getting on in years, and I will soon be joining my beloved Giovanni in our church together. I would like to see the triptych before I die. This is why I need your help. If you know Master Bevilacqua would you see him as soon as you are able on my behalf and implore him to hurry up and come here to show me his masterpiece that I am waiting for.'

Leonardo said that he would immediately intercede on her behalf, but he was worried because he had aligned himself with the de' Predis brothers' studio, and they were now in the process of bidding to paint a Madonna for a church confraternity in Milan. He wondered how Bevilacqua would interpret his intervention on behalf of Countess Tanzi and whether he had also put in a bid for the Madonna.

Luckily, Bevilacqua was most hospitable and pleased to see Leonardo and very enthusiastic to show him around his studio. He wanted Leonardo to tell him all the latest gossip about the Florentine painters, sculptors, goldsmiths, and metal workers; and so they were soon firm friends drinking Bevilacqua's favourite Milanese red wine.

'Apologise to Countess Tanzi for me for I have been extremely busy for the Sforza family. You and I will bring her some drawings and designs that I have already made. She will be very excited. I can finish everything in two or three months. She will not die so soon. She is much younger than her husband who unfortunately died only this year before I could show him my finished triptych. I will finish the triptych for the countess. No problems. Here, Leonardo, have some more wine.'

And so it was that Bevilacqua recruited Leonardo to help him finish the triptych to the Contessa's satisfaction. When Leonardo and Bevilacqua hung it in the chapel for the Contessa to see with her own eyes, she almost fainted right there and then in ecstasy to see such a beautiful image with God above her and her husband and Jesus and the Saints, St. John the Baptist, and St. John the Evangelist. She fell back into Leonardo's arms while Bevilacqua rushed off to find her a chair to sit on and some refreshing wine for her to sip. When she recovered, she couldn't stop gushing about its sanctity, beauty, and glory. Later, she provided Bevilacqua with a little extra above his written fee and a small bonus for Leonardo for his help to assist and encourage Bevilacqua to finish the work in time before she died. In fact, the triptych hung in the church for twelve years before she died and was buried beside her beloved husband Giovanni.

I first saw Bevilacqua's triptych in 1496 when I was a 5-year-old. It was when my mother and Leonardo took me to the church in Casoretto for a holy mass in memory of my grandfather and great grandfather and great grandmother. Since then, I have copied it many times as a painting exercise to distribute among my Melzi and Tanzi relatives.

The triptych painting, oil on wood panels, hangs over the altar of the church. It depicts the Resurrection of Christ at the centre and in the two side planks, to the left Count Giovanni Melzi is presented by St. John the Baptist, to the right his wife Brigida de' Tanzi is accompanied by St. John the Evangelist. Giovanni Melzi is white haired and elderly, he is kneeling in pray with his body covered in a precious cloak of damask red as if he were a rich cardinal. His wife, with wrinkled face, also kneels in prayer, dressed in a modern black and brown outfit of the time, and she has her head covered with a smooth white cap adorned with veils. In the lunette above the images of my great grandparents and above the saints and Christ, is the figure of God the Father blessing those below him. Christ the Risen is the central subject of the triptych. He stands above the marble sarcophagus in which he was entombed and now from which he has arisen after his death. It is a heroic and forgiving pose, rangy, and vigorous. Christ, the Son of God, stands covered with a white cloak, his right hand raised to heaven for this is the Resurrection, the Transfiguration, and the Ascension presented as a single image. In his left hand, Christ carries the Cross of Ambrose, the Red Cross on a white background, the flag that is the symbol of the Ambrose Republic of Milan at a time when Count Giovanni Melzi was their honoured ambassador to Venice. The Red Cross is also the flag of the Crusades and the symbol of victory over death, a victory that Count Giovanni and his wife had hoped to share with Christ.

St. John the Baptist who presents an elderly Count Giovanni Melzi to Christ holds a lamb in one hand (*Behold the Lamb of God who takes away the sin of the World*) and has the other hand resting reassuringly on the shoulder of the Count. The colour of the background behind God the Father, Christ the Risen Our Saviour, and the two saints is a shiny dark royal blue representing heaven. The picture testifies that the spouses Giovanni and Brigida have reached the end of their earthly life, but that they still have faith in their future resurrection with the intercession of St. John the Baptist and St. John the Evangelist. The triptych still hangs in the church, and I often visit to look at it and think of my great grandparents, my parents, Leonardo, and Bevilacqua.

Because my great grandmother loved the triptych of herself and her husband in their old age so much, she commissioned Bevilacqua to paint a votive portrait of her husband as a young man receiving the blessing of Jesus.

'Aren't women funny', Bevilacqua would say to Leonardo with a wink and big smile, and Leonardo would have to agree with him for there was no point in arguing about the weird pleasantries of life.

Brigida de' Tanzi and her daughter Michele commissioned a few additional works from Ambrogio Bavilacqua who was now known to them as 'il Liberali'. They wanted him to paint a younger Giovanni Melzi with an enthroned Madonna and Child and accompanied by Saint John the Baptist and Saint Bernard of Clairveaux. This is an exquisite tempera and gold on wood panel about 24.5 cm wide and 34.3 cm high. I have made many copies of this work in miniature. The Virgin Mary with a blue mantle symbolising heaven is seated, enthroned, on a marble throne, looking in contemplation down towards the viewer, her head higher than the standing saints on either side of her, with her left hand placed on an open book resting on her left leg. Perhaps this book is the Old Testament or simply a symbol of wisdom or a book from Giovanni's library. The Christ Child with an amulet around his neck stands in his mother's lap, or right leg, facing Giovanni Melzi and blessing him with his right hand. Saint John the Baptist as the patron saint introduces Giovanni Melzi to the Christ Child. While Melzi has white hair in the triptych of the *Resurrection of Christ*, here with the Madonna and the Christ Child, Melzi is portrayed as a younger man with black hair at the peak of his powers at an age of thirty or forty years. Saint John with a cross on his bare chest beneath his vest of animal skin also holds a cross with a spiralling scroll inscribing *'ECCE AGNUS DEI'* (*Behold the Lamb of God*). To the left of the Madonna, St Bernard of Clairveaux, the French founder of the Cistercian Order, wears his white habit and holds his pastoral staff. Above them all, the face of God, the Eternal Father, looks down from his lunette atop of the throne in the tympanum bordered by Renaissance scrolls.

The background that Bavilacqua provides in this picture for his conservative donor is the architectural detail of classical columns with delicate niches and a dominant, blinding gold background; features that Leonardo and his school of painters purposefully left out from their paintings when they modernised the painting movement. My great grandmother kept this painting of her beloved Giovanni with the *Madonna and Child* in her bedroom until her death; after which it was donated to the Cistercian abbey of Chiaravalle four miles south east of Milan where Giovanni had spent time in his youth to learn canon law and the art of contemplation and to study the books of *St. Bernard*, including the *Rule of the Knights Templar*, and the *Five Books on Consideration*, and the book on *Two-fold Knowledge*. Giovanni Melzi preached the teachings of St. Bernard to my father and even to Leonardo da Vinci who committed them to his memory for he often liked to oppose them in their debates. While Giovanni was a supporter of the Knights Templar as an order of monks devoted to military combat in the crusades, and he saw them as noble, fearless, holy, and following a higher calling, Leonardo thought of them as no different to any of the contemporary knights or the ordinary ones of the past for their vanity, greed, fantasies, wanton violence, and pointless existence. But, like St. Bernard and Giovanni Melzi, Leonardo was a Marian, and he had great love and honour for the Madonna and her children, and her heartfelt consideration for healing the afflicted and the poor. And it was this purity of vision in an age of transition that made his painted Madonnas such extraordinary figures of natural beauty.

While Bevilacqua's commissions ran smoothly in the 1480s, Leonardo and the de Pedris brothers' commission for the altar painting *Virgin of the Rocks* fell into difficulties. Leonardo was now coming to realise the grim reality of Milanese politics and social feuds.

Giovanni Bartolomeo III Melzi, the Poet and Diplomat of Milan, and Citizen of Lodi (1432-1478)

The illustrious Hungarian poet Janus Pannonius (1434 to 1472) in his well-read oeuvre dedicated the following poetic epigram to my grandfather Giovanni Bartolomeo III Melzi, praising his eulogy that he had written in praise of the Sforza rulers and presented to the incumbent Duke of Milan, Galeazzo Maria Sforza. The poem by Janus Pannonius is written in Latin in distichs or couplets. It is swarming with mythological allusions paying Giovanni Bartolomeo III the highest praise, an exuberant laudation to a person younger than himself. I unapologetically have translated it as follows:

> Giovanni Bartolomeo Melzi of Milan.
> I am pleased to inform the Apollonian students
> That you have spent time with the Muses.
> Bartolomeo, I congratulate you on your talent.
> The news of your celebrated songs reached our ears
> As you walked towards us singing so many beautiful songs,
> A heavenly voice, a notable triumph,
> Especially your praise of the Sfortiadam,
> You lead the way to the stars
> Imperishable songs worthy of heaven,
> Clarions worth shouting out to the stars.
> I am surprised by their intelligence,
> I am surprised by the troops of words that you have chosen,
> And the charm to distort and mix them with gravity.
> Your place is at the breast of the poet Smyrneus,
> Although your own is more extensive,
> Apollo himself gave you his faith.
> Now, wearing his laurels, you are right to say that after his death
> Hippocrene's lips drunk from the sacred waters
> Of the nymph Castalia
> And he clearly saw
> Her sisters in the Muses' valley,
> Which together with old Ascreus
> They had seen before. [S4]

The Milanese poem that Janus Pannonius refers to is to the laudation that my grandfather Giovanni Bartolomeo Melzi composed and entitled in Latin as *Bartholomei Melcii in laudem Galeaz Mariae versus* (*Bartolomeo Melzi's praise of Galeazzo Maria*). They are hexameters devoted to Galeazzo Maria's father Francesco Sforza and the events related to his official instalment as the 4th Duke of Milan on March 25, 1450 when he replaced the deceased Duke of Milan, Duke Visconti, who left no male heirs to replace him. In his poem, my grandfather writes about the empty triumphal carriage with the canopy over the seat, referring to the events at Francesco's official instalment. His mother and father as leading citizens of Milan meet with the Sforzas when they are approaching the city from the direction of the Ticinese gate, and they invite their new duke to enter the city in their highly decorated triumphal carriage. Francesco Sforza refuses to do so, saying that such dignities only befit kings. Thus, my grandfather Bartolomeo

III pays homage to the humility of Francesco Sforza and, perhaps, he provides a pointed hint to the new one, Galeazzo Maria Sforza, the 5th Duke of Milan, to also rule with humility.

My grandfather also stresses the loyal role of his father Giovanni Melzi as *Difensore della Liberte* and Ducal Counsellor, '*tantum quaeso te digneris parentem meum virum tibi animo certe ac tota mente deditissimum et me in tuorum fidelissimorum grege dinumerare,*' which I have translated as, '*I only ask you to deign to my father who devoted his whole mind to your highness to count him and me into your most faithful flock.*'

The Melzi family and the poet Janus were all good friends with their Lord Galeazzo Maria Sforza. The poet Janus knew the duke from their student days in Ferrara, and he knew that the Sforza family had enormous respect for the Melzi. Both Galeazzo and Janus were students of the scholar Guarino in Ferrara. Janus was studying with Guarino, when in 1452, the eight-year-old prince Galeazzo Sforza delivered one of the Latin orations in honour of the visiting Holy Roman Emperor Fredrick III.

Baldo, the Duke's Preceptor (teacher), wrote a short biography of the Melzi family, some of which I quote as follows: '*The Melzi were more than respected patricians and patrons of the arts, and they held key positions at the courts of Milan and were also representatives of the Holy Emperor of the Holy Roman Church. Thus, they were highly steeped in canon law and finance and administration, educated in Latin, Greek, Italian, French, German, and Spanish.*'

The teacher Baldo stresses Bartolomeo III father's prominence as being the Count Palatine of the Insubrians in the office of the Imperial Palace of the Holy Roman Empire, a prudent son of the esoteric Council, Baron, adviser, and the Treasurer of the Duke of Milan, and emphasises that my grandfather Bartolomeo III inherited his father's office as Quaestor, a public official who supervises the financial affairs of the state and conducts audits. In 1466, when Bartolomeo III was 34 years of age, his good friend, the newly inaugurated Duke of Milan Galeazzo Maria Sforza bestowed upon him the title of Citizen of Lodi and all the rewards that it entailed. In 1478, two years after the murder of Galeazzo Maria Sforza at the church of St. Stafanos in Milan, the poet Bonus Accursius Pisanus dedicated his verse, *Dicta Plautina, the Comedy*, to Bartolomeo (III) Melzi who had died that year at the age of 46 years from a festering wound while he was on his way back from a visit to see Leonardo da Vinci in Florence.

My Father Gerolamo (Jerome) Melzi (1460 to 1520): Leonardo's St. Jerome and the Vitruvian Man

My grandfather Bartolomeo III made regular visits to Florence, and on one such occasion in 1478, he requested an allegorical painting from Leonardo of St. Jerome in the wilderness, a dedication to his son's patron saint. He requested that Leonardo should paint St. Jerome in the likeness of his own father Giovanni and to add his 18-year-old son Gerolamo as a tortoise in search of goodness and stability, and Leonardo himself, as the lion with a burr in his foot. He wanted the Italian Alps in the background and his castle to stand out beside lake Como. He also requested that Leonardo place some riddles about anatomy into the painting for they both enjoyed riddles and entertained each other by the telling of them. Leonardo started the painting in 1478, but the commission was far from complete when Bartolomeo III suddenly died that same year. He gave the unfinished painting to my father in Vaprio in 1499, and he said that he had not finished it because it was disrespectful to his father's memory to do so. In later years, when Leonardo and I looked at this unfinished painting together, he drew my attention to some of the riddles.

'Look at the tail of the Lion. Yes, it is me, Leo the Lion, curling my tail, the paintbrush, around your father, the tortoise. But is it really a tortoise or is it something else perhaps, a skull or even an image of half of your father's brain, the hemicranium? Who is protecting whom in our friendship here? And look at the head of St. Jerome. It looks like the old head of your great grandfather Giovanni, but it is your father, depicted as the aging Jerome. His head will soon be bald, and it could be the image of the brain's lobes and the *falx cerebri* in all its grandness, could it not? If your grandfather Bartolomeo was alive and had seen the painting as it looks now, he would have enjoyed the joke. Unfortunately, your father doesn't see its humour in the same vein as I do or the way your grandfather would have. Keep this tragic painting for your children, Francesco, and let them know that St. Jerome and I are protecting you and them in this image of your great grandfather, father, and me, the lion in repose. It's the holy trinity you know, without the real image of Bartolomeo, although he is there somewhere in the image of the Alps and the lake or in the villa that you and your father now live in. He could be in the cave with the Ark of the Covenant, could he not?'

The painting (1 metre by 80 cm) is on wood panels, walnut, oil over tempera. It shows the maestro's love and mastery of anatomy, and the saint's emotion through the figure's gesture and expression. Leonardo was depressed by the news of my grandfather's death. Somewhere in one of his notebooks, Leonardo writes: *'why do we suffer so? The greater one is, the greater grows capacity for suffering. I thought I was learning to live: I was only learning to die.'*

We see the saint's suffering and penitence through his pose and expression. St. Jerome left Rome to live in solitude in a cave and perform his life's work to translate the Bible into the Latin vulgate. Where is he and the lion from whose paw he removed a thorn? Are they in the desert of Syria or in Sinai with Mt. Sinai and the Red Sea in the distance or is he somewhere else? Is the stone in the saint's right hand for beating himself in self-chastisement or is it for something else? And the cardinal's chair below the opening of the cave, is it a comment about the status of the Church? If Leo the lion's tail curls around a tortoise then maybe, this animal, the tortoise, is a conventional representation of reticence and of chastity, a homebody carrying its own home on its back, solid, and firm. But in reality, Leonardo has not drawn a tortoise. It is a section of the skull, a midline section of the brain showing the intracranial dura and venous system with sinuses and major deep veins. And what of the opening of the cave to the saint's left? Is it really a cave?

This is an extraordinary painting, unfinished, and yet finished with pulsating foreboding images never before seen in a painting. It raises so many questions that are not easy to answer. On occasions when I stare at it, I find riddles and outlines within the shadows that Leonardo may have added much later and that should not be there. The images of Bella Isabella (*Mona Lisa*) and my mother and her mother appear before me, and yet, they come and go as ripples in a pool, just like Leonardo's continual reworking of the shadows in *St. Jerome* for over twenty years. Those ghost's are there and yet they are not there. It is a mystical work, finished, yet unfinished; for me it is a continuing paradox. My children cannot understand its profoundness, that it is a study of the brain, its *dura mater*, its *falx cerebri*, and its illusions. They can only see it as an unfinished, depressing picture, a drawing of a person's suffering. They believe it requires the immediate addition of bright, glistening, complementary colours in order to finish it. And to a degree my children are right and so am I, for we are inside Leonardo's mind, inside his brain, inside his skull. He is the lion, and they are inside a cave with St. Jerome. It is Leonardo's cave. It represents Leonardo's skull, his artist's mind looking out through the open spaces, his eye sockets, one to the left and the other to the right. St. Jerome is his nasal cavity, and the lion is his distorted, broken mouth. In this sense, it is a wild abstraction, filled with meaning.

My grandfather Bartolomeo III commissioned Leonardo to paint *St. Jerome* as a dedication to his son, my father Gerolamo (Jerome) Melzi. But, the painting he would have received from Leonardo if he was still alive would have surprised him. It is a painting by Leonardo about Leonardo, and it is also an image of my father and what my father saw that was of importance to him, the Alps and the lake of Como through the left eye, and the church and villa in Vaprio through his right eye. And my father (St. Jerome) is depicted as having inherited wisdom in an

old head (my great grandfather or grandfather) on his own strong and young body (my father).
Also, look in a straight line from the rock in Jerome's hand, up and across and along his arm
and shoulders, and from his right eye out to a cross, just barely visible through the opening of
Leonardo's skull. It looks like St. Jerome (my father) is about to throw a stone with enormous
strength and force at a crucifix and building outside the right eye socket of Leonardo's skull.
Meanwhile, Leonardo, the lion, looks at Jerome in shock and awe and with a mouth wide open
while his tail curls about a rock-like image of a brain in surprised contemplation.

Fig. 4. Leonardo's St. Jerome *on the left-side and* Vitruvian Man *on the right-side.*

When I look at the painting, I see the contradictory nature between the saint and the man
who was my father. Unlike St. Jerome, my father was not prone to self-chastisement and
flagellation. Although St. Jerome obviously was a man of God and a servant of the church with
a love for his bible, my father was a military man and an engineer of war weapons and canals
and irrigation and devoted to Insubria (the Duchy of Milan). He was powerfully built, not bald,
and he was clean-shaven in face like Leonardo's *Vitruvian Man*. At 30 years of age, he was
Leonardo's unidentified *Vitruvian Man*, proud and serious, argumentative with his father and
grandfather, but gentle and loving with my mother and me. Leonardo has captured the tension
between his military and spiritual nature. On the one hand, he is St. Jerome, the holy man in
the wilderness taking care of an injured lion. On the other hand, he is a warrior, a human
catapult hurling rocks at the crucifix, the church, and other objects outside his domain.

I asked Leonardo, why is St. Jerome preparing to throw a rock at an unclear depiction of
the church and crucifix? He told me it was to remind him of his time in Florence when Pope
Sixtus IV tried to assassinate Lorenzo de' Medici, the most illustrious Lord of Florence, in the
Pazzi Conspiracy, and then, as retribution for his failed murder attempt, he excommunicated
Lorenzo and Florence from the Church of Rome, and further, declared war against Florence
by sending his papal mercenaries and the troops of the King of Naples to fight against
Florence. Leonardo told me that, 'the crimson chair beside St. Jerome represents the absence
of true moral authority in the Church of Rome at the time of the Sixtus Papacy, but do not tell
your father that I told you so, for he is a man of the church and far more religious than you
and I are, Francesco.'

Leonardo explained to my father and me that the painting was an allegorical depiction of his own crumbling skull with an image of him, the artist as a lion in front of his painting of my father, St. Jerome. It is the creative abstract moment when Leonardo has conceptualised the painting and so, while he looks at and examines Jerome with an intensity to devour him, his lion's tail, which is his paintbrush, encircles his own brain as a metaphor of his creative inner or third eye. Leonardo used the interior of his rock-like skull as a backdrop in some of his other paintings such as his *Virgin of the Rocks*. The man was a courageous and creative genius, and this is why I love him so much and feel forever grateful to have served such a wise and ferocious warrior, a lion in name and a lion in nature. This is also why I have his painting of *St. Jerome* as a shrine in my study, ironically to remind me of my father and Leonardo arguing together in their happier days.

Recently, I saw Titian's finished painting of *St. Jerome* (the 1552 version). He has paid homage to Leonardo's painting by depicting St. Jerome with stone in hand ready to hurl it towards Jesus hanging from a crucifix before him. The symbol of the rocks, the conifers, the skull, and the slumbering lion are all there in the picture. Titian chose the colours that he imagined Leonardo would have used to finish his own painting of *St. Jerome*. Some years later, he began to paint another slightly different version of St. Jerome in a cave among the rocks, but this I have not seen as yet.

Leonardo sketched my father the *Vitruvian Man* into a squared circle and provided him with a man's ideal proportions. Possibly in jest, he even sketched in an inguinal hernia on the left side of his groin, although my father always claimed that he never had such a problem. Despite Leonardo's crude depiction of my father's physique and face, he and my father remained the best of friends all their lives, like the best of loving brothers. My father lasted to the age of 59 years and died in 1520 at Vaprio one year after the death of Leonardo.

My Mother Tommasina della Torre (1469 to 1550)

My mother Tommasina della Torre met my father Gerolamo in Bergamo in 1483 when she was 14 years of age and he was twenty-three. He and Leonardo were laying siege against the city for the young duke of Milan Gian Galeazzo Sforza and his uncle the Governor Ludovico IL Moro Sforza. My mother comes from the ancient and prestigious della Torre (Torriani) House of Milan. Her grandfather was a former Ambassador to France. Her father was a Ducal engineer. Her mother Caterina served Bona of Savoy as a Lady-in-Waiting, and she helped to raise the young duke Gian Galeazzo Sforza and his two sisters, Bianca Maria Sforza (5th April 1472 – 31st December 1510) who married the Holy Roman Emperor Maximilian I, and Anna Sforza (21st July 1476 - 2nd December 1497, Ferrara) who became Hereditary Princess of Ferrara when she married Alfonso I d'Este. One of my mother's brothers was a city engineer and the other was a medical doctor and a distinguished army surgeon. Tommasina was strongly attached to the other della Torre clans who had left Milan because of harassment from the Visconti regimes and settled in Bergamo and in Verona. Leonardo met and worked with the della Torre families from Bergamo and Verona for the patriarchs of both families were distinguished doctors in their own cities and assisted Leonardo in his medical and anatomical projects.

Her distant cousin Professor *Doctori* Marcantonio della Torre became a great friend of Leonardo da Vinci, and they worked together during 1510 and 1511 at the University of Pavia where they refined their techniques of anatomical investigation. It was the time when Leonardo produced the most exquisite and precise anatomical drawings of his career as artist of anatomy and the human spirit. I mentioned this to the painter and historian Giorgio Vasari and showed him the anatomical drawings, and he wrote about this in his book on Leonardo:

Leonardo attended, but with greater care, to the anatomy of men; helped, and helping one another in this, by Mister Marcantonio della Torre, a profound philosopher, who then taught at Pavia and wrote upon the subject. It has been said that he was one of the first who began to illustrate the science of medicine, by the learning of Galen, and to throw true light upon anatomy, at a time of thick darkness of ignorance. In this he was marvellously served by the genius, work and hands of Leonardo, who made a book about it.

Leonardo worked alongside Professor Marcantonio who allowed him direct access to his human material with the excellent results that are evident in the drawings. Professor Marcantonio performed the dissections and named the anatomical parts while Leonardo sketched them and focussed on drawing the bones, ligaments, and muscles in red chalk and ink. As Leonardo's personal assistant at that time, I provided them with the hand-written notes that they had dictated to me while they performed their anatomical work. Of particularly profound analysis was their embryological studies and philosophical discussion concerning the foetal soul and the link between body and soul.

Unfortunately, the fruitful anatomical collaboration between them suddenly ended in 1511 when Marcantonio died unexpectedly at the age of 30 years when he was struck down by the plague on his visit to Riva del Garda. Thus, the *Treatise on Anatomy*, which these two highly distinguished scholars had intended to publish, never saw the light of day.

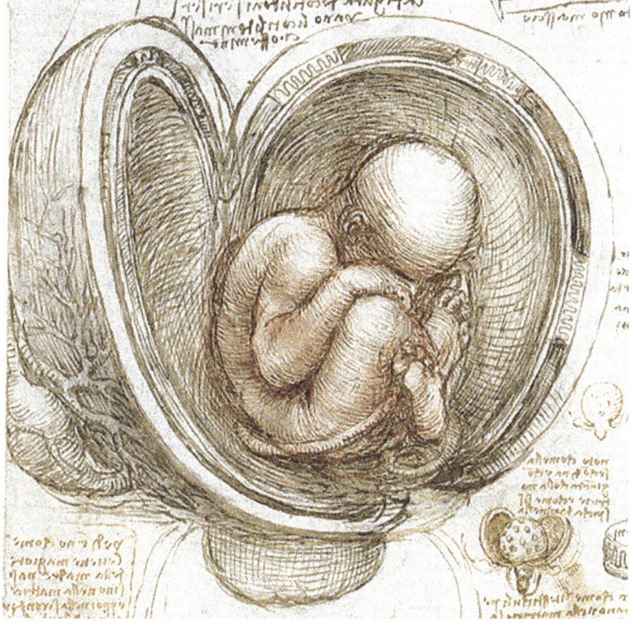

Fig. 5. Leonardo's drawing of a foetus in the womb.

Marcantonio's father Geromamo who was Professor of Medicine at the University of Padua and his brother Giulio who also graduated in Medicine in Padua University, together with the financial assistance of my father and mother, commissioned the sculptor Andrea Riccio of Padua in 1501 to build a tomb with eight bronze reliefs for Marcantonio to be placed at their family villa in Verona. Riccio of Padua consulted with Leonardo da Vinci about a possible narrative for the tomb's reliefs. Leonardo provided some sketches that were eventually adopted by Riccio for this tomb. Unfortunately, Riccio did not realise this funerary monument until 1521, and so my father and Leonardo never saw its completed splendour. The tomb contains a bronze relief of Marcantonio based on his death mask. The five main bronze reliefs show the illness of della Torre, the first is where he is visibly ill and close to death; the second is a sacrifice for his cure offered to Esulapius, the god of medicine; the third is the death of the scholar; the fourth is the funeral and dedication of the scholar's tomb; and the fifth is Marcantonio the scholar teaching anatomy to his students dressed *all'antica* at the university. The tomb is an extraordinary masterpiece. The scenes represent various moments of the life and death of Geromamo and Marcantonio della Torre, father and son, both distinguished Professors of philosophy and medicine, one from the University of Padua and the other from the University of Pavia.

Leonardo's friend Marcantonio della Torre died too soon and tragically of plague and his father followed him fourteen years later.

Tommasina had two other influential uncles, Luca della Torre who served Francesco Sforza in the Milanese Council and Giacomo Antonio della Torre who was bishop of Cremona from 1476 to 1486. She had many brothers and sisters. Giacomo Antonio was a prothonotary apostolic and an advisor to Ludovico IL Moro Sforza.

The Melzi Connection with Leonardo da Vinci

Leonardo was born on the 15th of April 1452 in a farmhouse outside the town of Vinci in Tuscany of the Republic of Florence. His father who never married his mother lived and worked in the city of Florence as a successful notary. Leonardo first lived with his mother and stepfather and then with his grandfather and uncle in Vinci, until, at the age of fourteen, he joined the workshop of Andrea del Verrocchio as his apprentice in the city of Florence. He moved from Florence to Milan when he was thirty, and it was in Milan where he eventually served the ruling Sforza family officially as a master court painter, architect, entertainer, master of ceremonies, and fort and canal builder for thirteen years from 1487 to 1500. The House of Melzi sponsored Leonardo for forty-eight years starting in Florence from 1471 until his death in France in 1519. During this time, he served my grandfather Bartolomeo (died 1478), my great grandfather Giovanni (died 1482), my uncle Bartolomeo (died 1488), and my father Gerolamo (died 1520). I knew Leonardo all my life, from the day I was born in 1491 until he died in my presence in 1519. He was my godfather, and he was present at my baptism at the Church of Santa Maria Bianca. He was a close friend of the entire Melzi family, and he often stayed with us at our villa and estate in Vaprio d' Adda in the Duchy of Milan. He taught me how to draw and to paint, and he provided me with my first rudimentary lessons in anatomy. My maternal grandmother Caterina was a lady-in-waiting and a favourite of Leonardo's in the Sforza court. Leonardo oversaw my father and mother's romance and wedding, and it was one of the many happy events that he attended to in the Sforza court of Milan between 1488 and 1493, before things began to turn sour for him and the Sforza duchy after 1496.

The Melzi clan first met Leonardo da Vinci in Florence in 1471 when as a noble family of Milan they accompanied the Sforza Duke Galeazzo and his wife the Duchess Bona with great pomp and ceremony on their first state visit to Florence at the invitation of the signore Lorenzo de' Medici. While in Florence, the Sforza and the Melzi men visited the workshop of Andrea del Verrocchio to inspect and commission some of his art works. It was here where they were introduced to the 19-year-old Leonardo da Vinci and learnt about some of his prodigious talent and scholarship. Verrocchio showed his illustrious guests the painting of the *Baptism of Christ With Two Angels* where the amazing vibrant angel was painted by Leonardo, and the statue of *David Beheading Goliath* that was Maestro Verrocchio's representation of Leonardo in his youth. The Milanese duke was highly impressed with the Verrocchio sculpture and approached him with a possible commission for an equestrian sculpture to honour his father, the Duke Francesco Sforza. Verrocchio declined, but recommended his budding pupil Leonardo da Vinci as a potential future candidate for the commission if the Duke of Milan was willing to wait long enough for Leonardo to graduate as a master from the Guild of St. Luke and gain maturity with a few more works and years behind him. They then came to some sort of agreement for such a possible future undertaking.

The Melzis had never met anybody before like Leonardo da Vinci. He was handsome, intelligent, well mannered, and diplomatic, yet vibrant and highly original and imaginative. He lacked formal education in Latin, law, and foreign languages, yet he made up for these deficiencies with a profound knowledge in the art and science of painting, engineering, architecture, mathematics, alchemy, and anatomy. He told the Melzis that the subjects that he needed to master in future were those that would provide him with a better understanding of the true nature of man and the world, and that would improve his ability to draw, paint, and sculpture the human form with a dynamic interplay between the truth and mystery of God, and not just mirror man with realistic proportions and dimensions and without a soul. Although he thought Latin was useful for accessing the classical books and writings, he was less sure about the value of law and foreign languages for the enhancement of his chosen endeavours. Moreover, Leonardo surprised my great grandfather and grandfather with his skills and knowledge about forts, fortifications, and the modern weapons of war. They arranged to meet with him a few days later and have him take them on a tour of the public fortifications in and around Florence and along the Arno River. They were even more surprised when he provided them with cartology and aerial maps of the regions that they intended to visit. They particularly admired Leonardo's maps and his drawings and thoughts about the Arno River running through Florence and Tuscany and his expertise in canals, rivers, fortifications, and weapons design, for the Melzi men were river engineers and canal and fortification builders in their own right, especially with respect to the Adda, Po, Lambro, and Ticino rivers. They soon became firm friends and my great grandfather offered Leonardo accommodation and sponsorship for him to visit Milan in the coming years. Leonardo declined, until, he eventually visited Milan first in 1480 and then in 1483. In the meantime, during the next nine years the Melzi followed Leonardo's progress with interest, and they travelled often to Florence to meet with him and discuss his many projects and varied interests, even arranging to sponsor him in some of his preliminary studies on weapons and armoury. Consequently, Leonardo set up a secret laboratory within the convent rooms of the building next to a Military Armoury in Florence where he began to build and test some of his amazing and often quite outlandish ideas about the art of war.

In 1472, with modest fanfare, Leonardo at 20 years of age qualified as a Master in the Guild of St Luke, the guild of artists, and doctors of medicine. As a graduation present, his father, a wealthy Florentine notary, helped him establish his own small studio. However, Leonardo still preferred to collaborate and work at Verrocchio's large and established workshop rather than consolidate his father's help. In 1476, while still collaborating with Verrocchio, he was suddenly involved in a most unsavoury scandal that darkened Florence for him forever. He was anonymously accused of sodomy. Although he had been falsely accused and all the charges were dismissed, the stain of the accusation remained over his name, and he began to feel increasingly persecuted and unhappy in the City of Bankers. He was constantly under strict surveillance by the Soldiers of the Night who wanted to catch him committing some crime of moral turpitude. He was growing more paranoid and frustrated in Florence, and each year he was developing a greater desire to visit Milan. However, with the attempted assassination of Lorenzo de' Medici in April of 1478, Leonardo felt obliged to stay on in Florence and support Lorenzo de' Medici and his followers, until Lorenzo eventually succumbed to the continuous requests from the Melzi clan, and he sent Leonardo on his first diplomatic mission to Milan in April of 1480.

The Villa Melzi at Vaprio d'Adda

> Niccolo Machiavelli,
> *Men could forget the loss of their fathers more rapidly than that of their property.*

The Villa (or Palazzo) Melzi in Vaprio d'Adda is my family residence that sits on top of a rock face on the west bank overlooking the river Adda and the neighbouring navigable canal, Naviglio della Martesana (also known as Naviglio Piccolo). The commune of Vaprio d'Adda is in the province of Milan located 35 km east of Milan city. It is easily accessible along the navigable Martesana canal that starts south of Trezzo sull' Adda just a few kilometres north of us at Vaprio (also known as Vavero). It is a strategic and convenient location because it is approximately half way along the Adda River between Lecco where my grandfather Bartolomeo and my uncle Beltrame and aunt Maria Antonia lived at the southern point of Lake Como in the north (38 km) and Lodi in the south (36 km). There is a similar distance (49 km) along the Adda River between Lodi and Cremona to the southeast as there is between Vaprio and Lodi. The Adda River flows from Lake Como in the north and joins the Po River in the southeast at Cremona. Hence, the Adda River is an important navigable river with considerable merchant, farming, industrial, and military activity on its waters and along its shores. We also have the Martesana canal below our house at Vaprio that runs all the way to the north-eastern docks of Milan City finishing a short distance from outside the main gate of Porta Nuova at the Spanish Wall and the minor gate of Porta Tosa where the statue of the Donna Impudica entertains the little boys and the perverted old men who gather there to look at the impudent display of her genitalia. The canal is part of Milan's trade waterways connecting with the other transportation and navigation and irrigation networks. Our earnings come from the Canal's Custom and Tax House below our residence and the ferry services at the Vaprio ferry landing that we provide across the Adda River between the communes of Vaprio in the Duchy of Milan and Canonica d'Adda in the Republic of Venice. I also own and manage the up-river Imbersago ferry landing that connects Imbersago and Villa d'Adda on the way to Bergamo about 12 km to the east. Imbersago is about 15 km north of Vaprio.

Fig. 6. Sketch by Leonardo da Vinci of the Villa Melzi at Vaprio d'Adda.

Leonardo da Vinci spent a considerable amount of his time along the Adda River and at Imbersago sketching and designing locks, mills, pumps, irrigation outlets, and ferry services in this region. One of his sketches that I show you is of the Melzi Villa of Vaprio where he often lived with us.

He also added the Vaprio castles, parts of the Adda River and its valleys and bridges, and the Lombardy Alps in a number of his paintings, including *St. Jerome in the Wilderness, Mona Lisa, Virgin of the Rocks,* the *Virgin and Child with St. Anne, Madonna of the Yarnwinder, St. John the Baptist,* and *Leda and the Swan.* I also added these scenes in my own paintings *Vertumnus and Pomona* and the *Madonna with Flowers,* scenes that I will show you later on.

If you travel along the 40 km of the Martesana canal and the barge tow paths between Milan and Vaprio, you will see communes, aristocratic villas and their gardens, parks, farms and rural settlements, factories, mills, washhouses, hydraulic wheels, wooded bluffs, water features, churches, castles, palaces, and tree lines marking out the road ways radiating away from the canal corridor. You will pass the communes and municipalities of Inzago, Gorgonzola, Bellinzago Lombardo, Melzo, and Truccazzano and see the lavish villas between Cernusco and Cassano d'Adda that are rich in architecture. Leonardo sketched into his notebooks the buildings and their structures and the architectural features such as the porticos, loggias, portals, balconies, and front yard decorations. The Raverti Villa where Ambrose Raverti, the husband of Lucia Marliani, the Duchess of Melzo, and his family resided in Inzago is of special interest to many who visit Martesana.

The Adda river valley in Lombardy is an irrigation plateau with marshlands, farmhouses and farmlands, orchids, mulberry trees, silkworm rearing, silk spinning factories, industrial sites, small village communes, and aristocratic villas and their gardens. The landscape is divided by a dense network of *rogge* (small irrigation ditches) partially derived from the springs and local rivers and partially from the Naviglio itself that irrigate the fields. The irrigation network is regulated by a profuse series of little hydraulic features (gullies, manhole covers, and water sharing systems), and dams. Isolated, monumental trees border the country roads and canals, and wooded banks form boundaries between the properties, farmlands, and the canals outside the city of Milan.

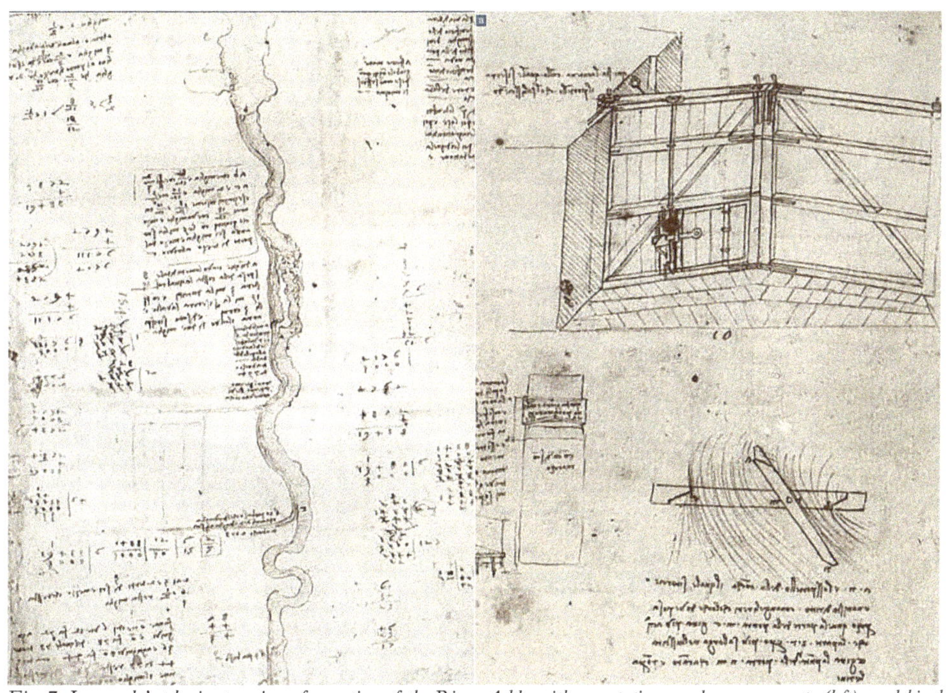

Fig. 7. Leonardo's planimetry view of a section of the River Adda with annotations and measurements (left), and his design for a hatch with moveable wings in a lock in the Martesana Canal.

East of Vaprio and across the Adda River, we have the Lombardy plains situated between the Adda River in the west and the Serio River in the east, and Cremona to the south, and the Bergamo ditch (Fosso Bergamo) in the north, which is part of the Gera d'Adda with the town centres of Treviglio and Caravaggio. This region is of political and historical interest because of its numerous fortifications and clashes and wars between the Duchy of Milan and the Republic of Venice and the rulers who aspired to dominate the area. Today the municipalities of the area belong to the diocese of Milan and Cremona, but not to the Diocese of Bergamo. One reason that the Melzi family purchased the Vaprio Palazzio is that it is in close vicinity to our Melzi farming properties in the Fara Gera d'Adda (Massari Melzi), Badalasco, and Pontirolo, and it has allowed us more flexibility to manage the local affairs and administer justice for the 350 residents in these areas.

Originally, the site of the Palazzo Melzi Vaprio was a fort that belonged to the della Torre family before it was transferred to the Visconti house and then later on to Francesco Sforza I, the 4th Duke of Milan. His son Galeazzo Maria Sforza, the 5th Duke of Milan, inherited the property and passed it on to his mistress Lucia Marliani in 1474 for whom he had also given the title of Duchess of Melzo. Later, with the exile of the Duchess Bona of Savoy from the Duchy of Milan, Ludovico took over the Villa Vaprio d'Adda and other properties from the Duchess of Melzo on behalf of his nephew Gian and himself. Ludovico then sold the house and property at the site of Villa Vaprio d'Adda to his compatriot Giovanni Melzi, Count

Palatine, for defensive and strategic reasons. The site on the edge of the Adda River is perfectly located on the border between the Duchy of Milan and the Republic of Venice with a ferry crossing that allows the transfer of goods and passengers across the river. Because the Duchy of Milan and the Republic of Venice often have territorial disputes along the Adda River, the Sforza family set up defensive military factories both on and outside the grounds of the villa with strong fortifications. In 1480, the count Palatine Giovanni Melzi bought the land together with an extensive irrigation system surrounding the estate from his Lord Ludovico, and with the architectural help of Leonardo, we built a mansion with three terraces overlooking the river Adda, the Martesana Canal, and the ferry crossing. This quickly became a lucrative administrative centre for taxing the canal traffic and ferry crossings with a transportation tax. Thus, the site of the Villa Vaprio d'Adda was of economic and politico-strategic importance endorsed by Ludovico Sforza who received a substantial commission from the Melzi. Moreover, the duke of Milan endorsed my father when he was appointed captain of Martesana and the Adda River to guard the line of the Adda and to collect toll fees in the name of the city for the use of the rivers and canals and for excavations such as ditch digging to access the canal and river waters. My father also enjoyed an extended jurisdiction and a greater authority in some cases to judge the life of his subjects with the death penalty.

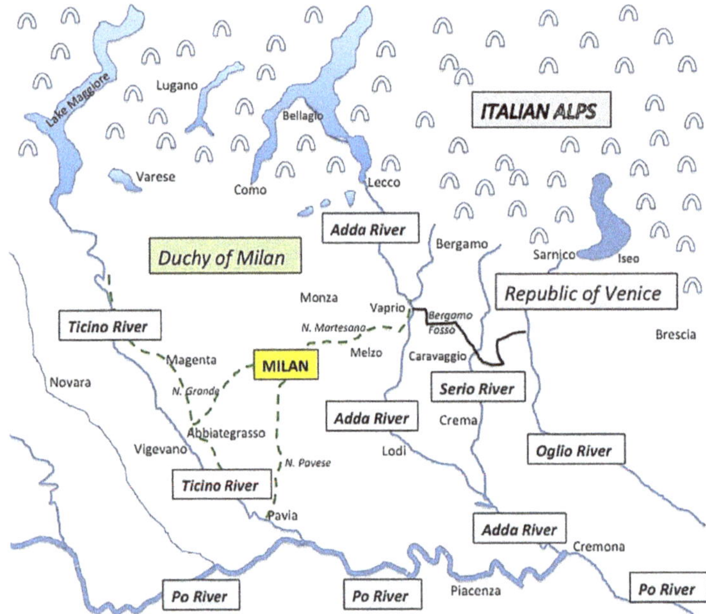

Fig. 8. Map of the main rivers (solid blue lines) and canals (green dashes) of the Duchy of Milan and western region of the Republic of Venice.

Leonardo was given his private rooms for perpetuity in the Villa Melzi to use as his living chambers, library, and studio. He also had his own workshops in the military factories on and outside the grounds of the villa. North of the villa was the Castelbarco, church of San Colombano, and the monastery and the fields of the Cistercian friars.

Soon after the death of Giovanni Melzi, my father Gerolamo (Jerome) and his five brothers inherited the villa, and then later, it became my possession and my families' home. My father was a Count Palatine, and he was a Milanese captain of the militia, superintendent of the construction of the fortification walls with which Gian Galeazzo and Ludovico Sforza wanted to have maintained near to the city of Milan. When Leonardo was appointed advisor on fortification to the Sforza court, he provided my father with his engineering expertise and assistance. My father also served as captain of the militia of Milan under the French king Louis XII and a military engineer under Maximilian Sforza. He retained all the privileges granted to him by the previous government under the French king Francois I of Valois who confirmed them to him in writing in 1516 a few days before Leonardo and I left Milan to live and work at the King's court in Amboise.

Leonardo often stayed at the Villa with my parents and me during my childhood, and he was my tutor on various subjects, especially music, mathematics, drawing, and painting. I also had many other tutors teaching me Latin, Greek and the classics, Spanish, German and French,

Christianity, and other subjects of little interest to me, but which I was forced to learn. Leonardo was my favourite tutor, and I loved his lessons on the art of observation, diplomacy, and warfare. In 1498, when I was 7 years of age, Leonardo's friend Fra Luca Pacioli taught me mathematics, card games, chess, and his system of double entry accountancy and book keeping. He said this would help me if I grew up to be a notary with a solid background on how to solve problems ethically and to evaluate the true value of properties and mortgages. Of course, this did help me to act as an accountant for Leonardo and my own family businesses later in life. Leonardo and his assistant Giovanni Boltraffio sketched and painted my portrait a number of times before they left Milan for Florence in 1500. Leonardo didn't return to Milan again until 1507. The Villa Melzi d'Vaprio was again home for him on and off between 1508 and 1513 and in 1516 during the new French occupation. He spent much time here redesigning the canals and preparing drawings and maps. His plan was to completely restore our building to look and function more like a French chateau, but with aspects of mature classicism, and hints of Roman architecture. He added decorative facades between the ashlar angles, corbels, and eaves for contrasting light and shade. He wanted to renovate the tower for his own comfort and to use a large room on the top floor to draw, paint, and meditate on his inventions. Many of his machines and inventions were already stored at our adjoining factories and workshops, and they were the things that he didn't want to leave unguarded at his workshops in the city of Milan.

Soon after Leonardo's and my father's death, I returned to Lombardy from France in 1522 to manage the Melzi properties at Vaprio d'Adda and in the area of the Giarra d'Adda, and various properties in the city of Milan and in the towns of Valsassina, Bellagio, and Valmadrera that are a few kilometres west of Lecco in the Lake Como region, Magenta west of Milan city, and in the towns of Lodi and Pavia. My portfolio of ownership was large and often taxing and out of hand, even with the loyal assistance from other members of my family and relatives.

The History of the Purchase of the Villa Melzi from Ludovico Sforza

My grandfather with the encouragement and support of his father wanted to purchase the Sforza fort because the Melzi already owned extensive farmland in the region on either side of the Adda River at Vaprio. Moreover, the fort sat above a canal with a custom and tax house that could be used to charge boats that trafficked goods between Vaprio and Milan along the Martesana canal. The ownership of the fort and surrounding property was in dispute because Galeazzo Sforza had presented it as a gift to his mistress Lucia Marliani rather than to his wife Bona of Savoy and their son Gian Galeazzo, the 6th duke of Milan. Bona of Savoy nevertheless claimed ownership of the fort and estate for her son, and then, in order to spite her husband's mistress, she agreed to sell it to Bartolomeo Melzi. But, Bartolomeo died before the deeds could be properly prepared and signed. Nevertheless, the Melzi persevered. Two years after the death of Bartolomeo, Bona was exiled from Milan by her brother-in-law, the new governor Ludovico IL Moro Sforza, and as the new regent of Milan he took over running her and her son's affairs. My great grandfather convinced Ludovico Sforza to sell him his brother's fort and estate on the grounds that in return he would provide Ludovico with lifelong support, loyalty, and service that he seeked from the House of Melzi.

As soon as Giovanni Melzi received the deeds of purchase of the Vaprio fort and estate from Ludovico Sforza, he and his grandsons arranged with Leonardo to travel together to visit Vaprio and to inspect their newly acquired property. On the way, they gathered at Giovanni's home in Casoretto where the villa and estate, now as then, are both large and are managed and supported by a substantial household and estate staff who provided welcomed visitors with the maximum of comforts. Leonardo stayed there with the Melzi for a few nights, and they talked about the new purchase that was located only 16 km directly east from where they were in

Casoretto. They told Leonardo about the history of modern Milan and the Sforza family and how the current signore Ludovico Sforza had taken the city's power away from the Duchess Bona of Savoy and her son Gian, the young Duke of Milan, who was the hereditary ruler of Milan. They attended a mass at the Santa Maria Bianca, located within a short walking distance of the Villa. Later, Giovanni told Leonardo that they would travel along the Martesana canal to reach the River Adda, and that he wanted to have Leonardo's opinion about the adequacy of the fortifications along the canal and those of the fort at their destination in Vaprio on the River Adda. The fortifications have to be impenetrable so that they can protect the Melzi for many centuries ahead of them.

Fosso Bergamo

> A very old ditch, which divides the territory of Bergamo from Giarra d'Adda and from Cremonese, State of Milan, which rises from the river Oglio and discharges itself at the Adda, with no precise memory of its construction…

Fosso Bergamo is an artificial ditch or channel about 35 km long and five metres wide (three Venetian steps) that crosses the plains of Bergamo starting at the river Adda where it meets with the Brembo river near Vaprio and runs north of Fara Gera d'Adda and Pontirolo where it ends and then starts again at the Serio river to run east past Cortenouva to the Oglio river near Calcio. Documents suggest that the ditch was dug between the late thirteenth and early fourteenth century following an ancient Roman channel formerly known as *Circa Cortenuova.* The start date for the major work on the Fosso Bergamo was March 9, 1267 when a truce was signed between the towns of Cremona and Bergamo following the war that had involved the Lombard cities allied with my mother's family, the Guelph of della Torre (or Torriani), and with those who had sided with the Ghibellines and were led by Buoso of Dover, the Lord of Cremona Soncino. The importance of this ditch is that it was used as a central border of disputes and battles between the various rulers of past times and those of today. The channel in the historic document is named *Fossatum Bergamaschum* (Fosso Bergamo), and the Republic of Venice used it from 1427 to define the western limits of their State and the land that borders the territories of the Duchy of Milan. It is comparable to the moats that surround the fortifications of villages and differs greatly from the yellowtail irrigations that dot the entire lowlands of Bergamo. This artificial channel defines the northern borders of our properties of the Fara Gera d'Adda, Badalasco, and Pontirolo. The Palazzo Melzi at Vaprio d'Adda is therefore the main centre for the administration of our farming and industrial properties across the Adda River to the east, below the line of the Fosso Bergamo, and in the Duchy of Milan.

CHAPTER 3

Sforza's Milan, 1447 to 1480

There are three classes of people: Those who see. Those who see when they are shown. Those who do not see.

— Leonardo da Vinci

The Birth and Battles for the Ambrosian Spirit, and the Topography of Lombardic Milan

For the many of you who do not know much about Lombardy and her origins, let me inform you of the evolution of the Duchy of Milan to which I will refer frequently in my remembrances of my home and my friends and their interconnected histories; the intertwining invisible and visible threads of the Duchy that resonate strongly within me even now. The Duchy of Milan is a dukedom, a fiefdom, worthy of control and defence for it guarantees great wealth and influence and the possibility of eternal remembrance. It is a constituent state of the Holy Roman Empire in northern Italy with more than thirty towns and a large, fertile, rural area, and numerous rivers and lakes in its territory.

The Duchy of Milan is known commonly as Lombardy, and we the residents are the Lombards. At one time the entire territory of Italy was referred to as Lombardy (*Longobardia Major and Minor*). The Lombardic Kingdom of Italy (*Regnum Italicum*) was established in northern and central Italy and some parts of the south by Germanic tribes known as the Lombards who were constantly seeking new lands to conquer south of the Germanic territories. The kingdom of Lombardy was at its zenith in 751 AD under king Aistulf, and it stretched from the Northern Alps down to the southern end of the Italian Peninsula. The Byzantines still controlled small pockets of Italy, mainly Rome, Sardinia, Calabria, and Sicily. Fearing the loss of Rome to the Lombards, Pope Stephen II recruited the assistance of the new king of the Franks, Pepin the Short, to regain his territories in a campaign against Aistulf. The Lombards quickly lost a substantial amount of their territory to the King of the Franks when he crossed the Alps and invaded Italy and defeated Aistulf in the year of 753. The lands that Pepin conquered from Aistulf were returned to the papal state in a decree known as the Donation of Pepin. When Pepin's son Charlemagne (Charles I) visited Rome in the year of 756 as King of the Franks and Patrician of Rome, he reconfirmed his father's donation of Aistulf's territories to the Pope in Rome. Now, it is only the northwestern part of Italy that is referred to as Lombardy or the Duchy of Milan.

For much of its existence, the Duchy of Milan was wedged between the Duchy of Savoy and Montferrat to the west, the Republic of Venice and Duchy of Mantua to the east, the Swiss Confederacy to the north, and separated from the Mediterranean by Genoa and the Duchy of Modena to the south. Only the Duchy of Savoy separates the Duchy of Milan from France. Our current owner Phillip III, the King of Spain, rules us from across the Mediterranean Sea, and he is even further away from us than the French kings ever were. Today, we are known as the Dominion of Milan, and we are Europe's most prosperous commercial gateway into Italy.

The city of Milan is situated on the Lambro River, and bordered by two canals, the Naviglio Grande connecting to the Ticino River in the west, and the Naviglio Martesana connecting to the Adda River in the east. An abundance of waterways provides us with a sustainable lifeline for transport, trade, irrigation, and industry. The city is bordered by five accessible rivers that run from the north to the south, and to the east and to the west of the city. Apart from the Adda to the east and Ticino to the west, there are the Seveso and the Lambro on the eastside and the Olona on the westside that run through the outer reaches of the city and mostly underground. Fifty km to the south of the City, the River Po runs 189 km from the French border in the Cottian Alps in the west all of the way to the east into the Adriatic Sea near Venice. It runs through Turin and Pavia and connects to Milan through a network of channels called *navigli* that Leonardo da Vinci helped to design.

Fig. 9. The Italian States at the time of Leonardo's life in Milan.

There are distinct social classes in Milan like those in other city-states, the clergy, the nobles, the military, the merchants, the artisans, the tradesmen, and the unskilled workers. The city has many precincts or trade halls and parish churches with large and small convents and monasteries. There are a number of hospitals and houses for the poor that are dependent on the church and the charity of the people. Overall, it is a city for nobles, gentlemen, traders, and the merchant class. The nobles live on large estates outside the city walls. They own most of the city's land and control the rule of the city. They serve as military officers, church leaders, court advisers, and as politicians, and they are patrons of the church, arts, and sciences. I am an example of the noble class with inherited titles and ownerships, albeit, I say this with modesty and humility and with Fortuna looking over my shoulder for I know that my privileges were not attained by divine right. Milan is the moral city of Italy and its patron saint is St. Ambrose.

A Venetian ambassador visiting Milan in 1520 while I was at the time still living in Amboise in France made the following observation about the city:

> The city of Milan is large and has the highest population in all of Italy. There are many poor and they eat cornmeal. There is also a great quantity of gentlemen who have incomes ranging from eight ducats to 10,000 ducats. They spend greatly on their households: on horses, clothing, and food and also on charity … there is a great number of artisans, more than any other Christian city, who make every type of work and goods, which are exported

throughout the world, such as armour, bridles, and saddles, etc. And thus this city always hopes for war, so that it can sell its wares. [S5]

Milan, with a population of 300,000 people compared to 50,000 in Florence and 180,000 in Venice, is a leading city of the Italian peninsular. It is a walled-fortress city, circular shaped and bordered by inner and outer moats. The outer walls are called the Spanish Walls built between 1546 and 1560 at the will of the Spanish Governor Ferrante Gonzaga, and there are nine main bastions, and seven minor bastions that fortify them. These bastions projecting outward from the Spanish Walls are based on the original designs of Leonardo da Vinci that were not built until long after his life-time in Milan. He sketched many aerial maps of Milan. These were bird's eye views of the canalisation, city gates, and major roads that he had planned in 1508 as part of his intended canal projects for Charles d'Amboise, the French governor of Milan. Here, I provide you with one of Leonardo's sketches of an aerial view of Milan, a constructed 3-point perspective within an ellipse that shows the layout of the city and its confining ring-shaped canals. In this plan, he has inverted the names of the city gates to orientate himself to the familiar monuments as if he were walking around the outer circle of the city. He is like a bird surveying the area from a distance, considering it from high-up. Which part of the city should he investigate in more detail?

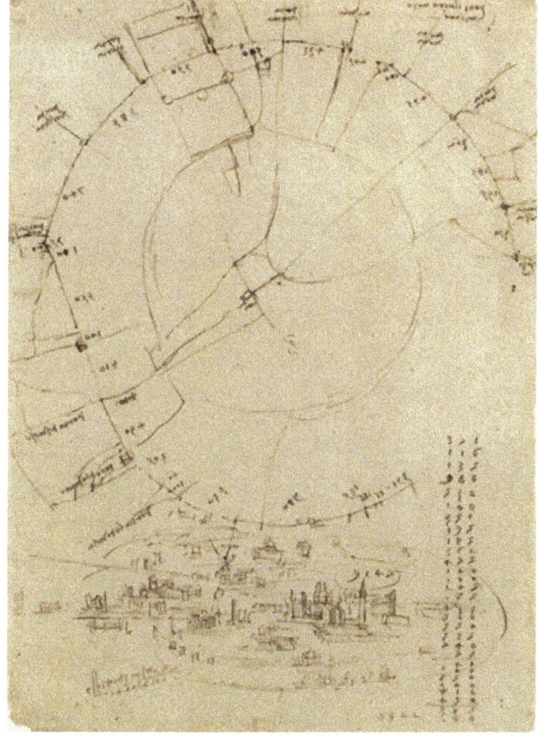

Fig. 10. Leonardo da Vinci's 3-point perspective map of Milan city 1508.

The inner and outer walls of the defensive moat, the *Cerchia dei Navigli,* were built to encapsulate and protect its citizens, although not always successfully. Fredrick Barbarossa easily breached the inner walls and moat and razed the city to the ground in 1158. Also, the inner walls and moat didn't protect its occupants against a French invasion and their entrance into the city on at least two occasions, once in 1499 and then later in 1515. At the times of the French invasions, the citizens were as much captured within the walls as they were protected. At least the walls protect us against wandering wolves, wild pigs, and marauding bandits. Mostly, the walls provide for a better sense of community and the collection of taxes and are a barrier to keep out the large majority of the unwashed, unclean, and unwanted. While the moat has not helped much as a defensive work, it has helped to form the nucleus of our system of canals that has brought us great wealth from transportation and trade.

The eight main gates to enter and exit through the Spanish Wall, running counter clockwise to the Sforza castle, are Porta Vercellina (now called Porta Magenta), Porta Ticinese, Porta Ludovica (formerly Porta di Sant Eufemia, Porta Tenaglia or Porta Sempione), Porta Romana, Porta Tossa (or Porta Vittoria [Victory]), Porta Orientale (Porta Renza, Eastern Gate, Porta Argenzia, Porta Vigentina or Porta Venezia), Porta Nouva, and Porta Comana (or Porta Comasina). There are six main gates and ten posterns (secondary gates) to enter into and exit from the inner city circle. The six old gates or districts are Porta Vercellina, Ticinese, Romana, Orientale, Nouva, and Comana. The Porta Ticinese leads towards Pavia and its inner gate contains a marble relief of Madonna and Child with St. Ambrose proffering the model of the City. The old Porta Nuova that leads towards the town of Monza also has a marble relief of Madonna and Child and Saints. The secondary gate of the Pusterla di San' Ambrogio is a fortress in its own right and in the vicinity of the Basilica of San' Ambrogio. There you can see the three saints Ambrogio, Gervasio, and Protasio. The gate Sempione (Simpion) or Porta Giovia (Jupiter's Gate) is now part of the Sforza Castle.

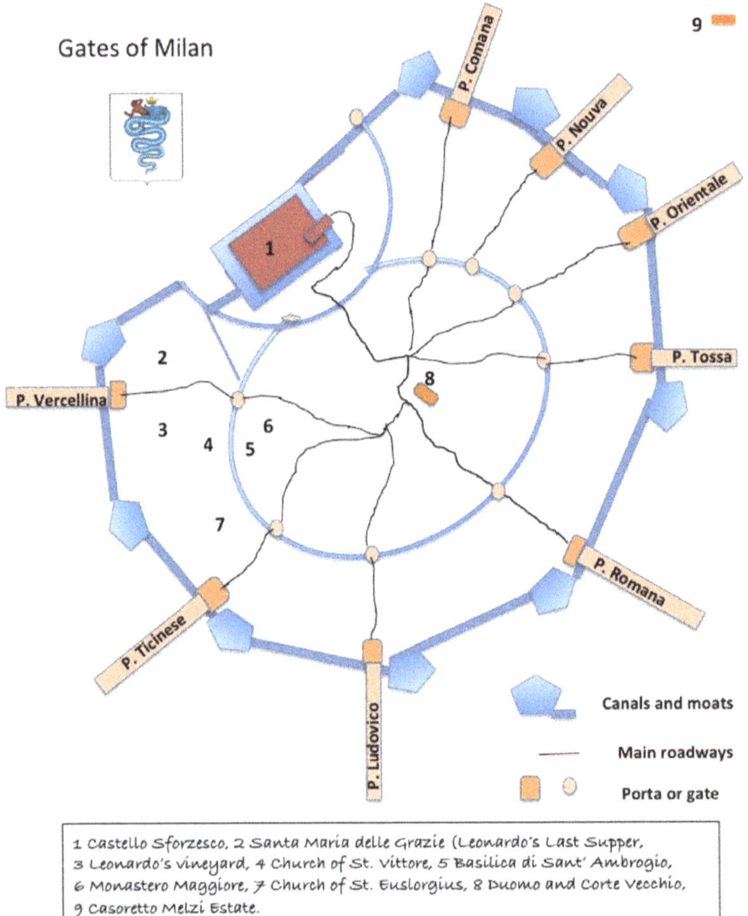

Fig. 11. Map showing the eight main gates of the walled city of Milan. The internal and external canals are not shown.

My own sketch of an aerial map of Milan shows you the location of the eight gates at the outer wall and the approximate positions of the Sforza Castle, the Monastery of Santa Maria delle Grazie where Leonardo's painting of the *Last Supper* is located, his vineyard, the Duomo, the Corte Vecchio where Leonardo worked and resided in Milan, and the location of the Melzi estate in Casoretto.

Milan's main gates are found at all four cardinal points of the compass, and inside the city there are a great abundance of churches (priories and parishes) and hospitals. We have the royal and government residences at Palazzo del Broletto Vecchio, a cathedral (duomo), a senate building, and the castle fort that we refer to as the Sforza castle (Castello Sforzesco), which sits on the periphery of the city at the northwest end extending outside of the city walls. We have well defined areas where people can congregate to play and to celebrate. Also, there are areas for the visiting dignitaries and ambassadors, factories, workshops, horse corrals, monasteries and convents, schools, and banks, and of course the markets and the shops of the merchants. While I could elaborate on our government organisations, administration offices, and municipal structures in much more detail than is necessary, it is sufficient to know, dear reader, that overall Milan has been well run historically despite some moments of failure, destruction, and invasion, and I would say that it still is run reasonably well today. Of course, the Melzi and the della Torre families have had no small part to play in the foundations and running of the city for they have long held important positions in the city's protection and prosperity as militia leaders, politicians, ducal advisors, senators, councillors, and city administrators, as well as ducal engineers, magistrates, and lawyers.

Milan arose as a settlement in antiquity well before the emergence of the Roman Empire and the birth of Christ and Christianity. The settlement was guaranteed freedom of religion for Christians by Emperor Constantine in 313 after the birth of Christ with the Edict of Milan. Milan's moral and spiritual compass arises from St. Ambrose. He was bishop of Milan from the years 374 to his death on 4th of April 397 AD. He is the patron saint of Milan, the French Commissariat, candle makers, domestic animals, education, and students and bees and beekeepers. His Saint's title is Confessor and Doctor of the Church. He was educated in Rome where he studied law, literature, and rhetoric. One Ambrosian mantra that the Melzi admire and agree with was his stand on poverty and the poor. According to Ambrose and the Melzi, *'the poor are solidary people united in our humanity and not a group of outsiders to be ignored. Giving to the poor is not to be considered an act of generosity, it is a repayment of resources that God had originally bestowed on everyone equally and that the rich had usurped.'*

Leonardo da Vinci was most impressed artistically and spiritually by Ambrose's powerful Mariology, his belief in the virginity of Mary and her role as Mother of God.

> The virgin birth is worthy of God. Which human birth would have been more worthy of God, than the one, in which the Immaculate Son of God maintained the purity of his immaculate origin while becoming human? [S6]

Leonardo, like Ambrose, believed that virginity is superior to marriage, and that Mary, the Madonna –Mother of God, is the ultimate model of virginity. *'We reject the natural order of things when we confess that Christ was born from a virgin and that he was conceived from the Holy Spirit and not from a man of sin.'*

It is in this context that Leonardo wrote his often to be quoted jibe about the absence of purity in the act of sexual intercourse:

> The act of procreation and anything that has any relation to it is so disgusting that human beings would soon die out if there were no pretty faces and sensuous dispositions.

Some say Leonardo was Platonic, whereas I believe he was Mariologic, a devotee of Marianist art and symbolism, an ideology which he tried to represent in his own ideals.

Three hundred and seventy-seven years after the death of Ambrose, Charlemagne conquered Milan, and he became the 'King of the Lombards'. His conquest saw Milan subsequently become part of the Holy Roman Empire. After Charlemagne, Milan became the seat of the nobles and counts whose authority was overshadowed by the prestige of the archbishops. Various wars followed, particularly with the Germans and the Swiss from the north. Despite its wars with German emperors and internal wars of dispute and differences between the Guelph and the Ghibelline cities, Milan grew steadily to prosper as an important centre of European trade because of the rich plains of the Po, the surrounding rivers and tributaries, and its strategic position along the routes into Italy from across the Alps from France, Switzerland, Germany, and the other states and countries to its north and west. Eventually, the nobles and burghers entered into compacts and guilds, and the power of the merchants grew at the expense of the archbishops and clergy. Long periods of peace favoured agriculture, the wool and silk industries employing more than one hundred thousand men. Interestingly, my mother's ancestor Pagano della Torre was elected Lord *Capitano del Popolo* by the executive branch of the city government in 1240; and later his nephew Martino della Torre ruled by dictatorial powers in 1259. Together, they paved the streets, dug canals, and taxed the countryside. Their rule ultimately angered the population, and the nobles began instead to favour the della Torre's traditional enemies, the Visconti. Eventually, of the two families from my mother's side, the Visconti successfully overthrew the della Torre and became the ruling family of Milan and its territories. Many of the della Torre families of today were exiled from Milan as a potential danger to the rival Visconti families.

Visconti and the Birth of the Duchy of Milan, 1395

For the price of 100,000 gold florins, the King of Germany and Bohemia, Wenceslaus IV bestowed Gian Galeazzo Visconti with the title of the 1st Duke of Milan in 1395, and he raised Milan and the other Visconti territories in Lombardy to the status of a duchy. The duke Gian Galeazzo Visconti considered his cities collectively as the Duchy of Milan, and he appointed his son Giovanni Maria heir to different areas —the duchy of Milan and the duchy of the cities of Brescia, Cremona, Bergamo, Como, Lodi, Piacenza, Parma, Reggio, and Bobbio. However, the duchy of Milan was constantly changing shape under different rulers including the Visconti and the Sforza families and the French kings. Many of the cities listed in the investiture of 1396 were lost from the duchy: Vicenza was taken by the Republic of Venice in 1404, followed by Verona and Reggio in 1405; and Brescia and Bergamo were lost to Venetian forces in 1426 and 1428, respectively. The definition of the duchy of Milan wavered according to the ever changing statutes ranging from the whole area ruled by the duke to clearly naming the city, suburbs or surrounding territory of the duchy of Milan and excluding other cities owned by the duke such as Parma and Piacenza so as to not offend them as subordinates to the city of Milan and its suzerainty (position or authority of a powerful state, the suzerain). Thus, by 1450, the 4th duke of Milan Francesco Sforza also was addressed as count of Pavia and Angera and signore of Parma, Piacenza, Novara, Lodi, and Como. The cities had little option but to accept the new Sforza edicts even though they had a one-to-one relationship with the duke as their elected signore and not with the entire Chancery of Milan.

Maximilian I, the Holy Roman Emperor and King of the Germans, officially bestowed '*the duchy of Milan and the countships of Pavia and Angera with their remaining cities and lands*' on Ludovico Il Moro Sforza during the start of his rule as the 7th Duke of Milan in 1496, a diploma which was more restricted than those previously covered by Gian Galeazzo Visconti's three diplomas. However, the duchy of Milan at least covered all the duke's territories (outside of Pavia and Angera) under a single title. Maximilian's diploma provided Ludovico with a new definition of the Duchy of Milan because the Holy Roman Emperor had just married Ludovico's niece Bianca Maria Sforza shortly before bestowing him with his investiture. The precedent established in 1495 was followed by the investiture granted to Louis XII in 1505. That diploma gave him '*the duchy of Milan and the countships of Pavia and Angera, which Louis king of France himself at present holds and possesses, and with which the dukes of Milan, the predecessors from whom he descends, were invested.*' Since 1499, the lands of Milan have changed five times under different rulers. The French king Louis XII had taken the area in 1499 and again in 1500; Maximilian (Massimiliano) Sforza won it back in 1512 with the help of the Swiss; the French King Francois I became ruler in 1515 following his victory at Marignano; Francesco Sforza II assumed control during the period of conflict from 1521 to 1525 with the help of Emperor Charles V who inherited the title when it devolved to him with the death of Maximilian Sforza, and that he subsumed into his own dominion. Milan has kept its duchy lands from 1395, albeit with changing borders, right up to the present with the new law code issued in 1541 by Charles V, the Emperor of Rome and King of Spain, who assumed control of the Sforza possessions and saved the term 'duchy' for the capital and surrounding jurisdiction.

Official documents still refer to the district surrounding Milan as its duchy. However, today, as I come closer to the end of my life, the Milanese Constitution no longer wants to call Milan and its regions a duchy in the sense that it is a mere collection of towns and cities under a common ruler. Rather, it now wants to be known as Milan and its dominions, a clear geographical entity with a capital city, a territorial unit that has acquired a common identity over its history of more than one hundred and sixty years, at least since Gian Galeazzo Visconti's investiture in 1395 as the 1ˢᵗ Duke of Milan, including the ownership of his conquered cities and towns that have still remained as part of the duchy. However, in my tale about Leonardo da Vinci's time in Milan and its *contoda* (the region surrounding or belonging to a city in a city state), I will refer to the Milanese territories mostly as the Duchy of Milan (the duke's territories and possessions) and occasionally as Lombardy, Insubria or Liguria (when including Genoa in the territory).

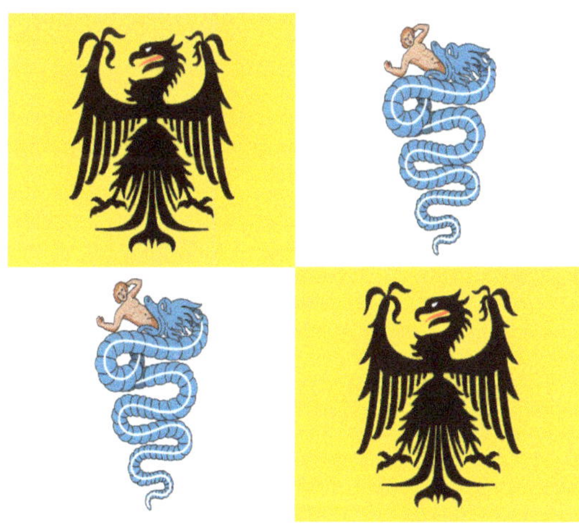

Fig. 12. Heraldry of House of Visconti and the House of Sforza.

Nevertheless, the Duchy of Milan is best known to my family and friends as Insubria or Lombardy, an area inhabited by the Insubres stretching out from the Adda River in the east and the Sesia river in the west, and between the San Gottardo Pass in the north and the Po river in the south. Later, it was stretched out further south to Genoa and Modena. Our motto in Insubria is '*Insubres sumus, non latini*' ('*We are Insubrians, not Latins*') for we Insubrians believe that we were once of Celtic Gaul origin, and that our sacred symbol was always the *El Dragh Bloeu* (*The Blue Dragon*), and that it was part of the Visconti coat-of-arms that was transferred to the Sforza coat-of-arms. The Visconti symbol and coat-of-arms of the biscione (a blue dragon or serpent) swallowing a Saracen still is a sacred symbol of Milan and Lombardy today.

Francesco Sforza and the Visconti Legacy: the Haunting of Milan by Valentina Visconti's Ghost and Her Royal French Descendants

From the start of his rule soon after 1447, Duke Francesco Sforza, Seigniory (feudal lord) of the Duchy of Milan, believed that he and his dynasty had only one critical foe and rival from the west to seriously contend with for the rule of the city and the duchy of Milan. He worried mostly about the French descendants of Valentina Visconti who he believed would challenge the Sforza's right to rule and possibly even initiate a French Italian war campaign over their perceived claim of an ancient filial right and written contract to their rightful rule of the Duchy of Milan. But how did this dangerous feud with a French arm of the Visconti house arise?

The noble Visconti dynasty rose to complete dictatorial power in Milan when they ruled from 1277 to 1447. The founder of the Visconti Milanese dynasty was Ottone who wrested control of the city from my mother's other ancestors, the della Torre family. The branch of the Visconti family that came to rule Milan originated from a village above Lake Maggiore when they were entrusted with the lordship of Massino, which they controlled from the twelfth century. Decades before that, before 1070, they had gained the title of Visconti (Viscount), which was inherited down the male line. The Visconti ruled Milan first as Lords, then, from 1395, with the mighty Gian Galeazzo Visconti who endeavoured to unify Northern Italy and Tuscany, they ruled as Dukes of Milan until 1447 with the death of his descendant in charge Filippo Maria Visconti who left no male heirs. With the extinction of the Visconti House, a short-lived Ambrosian Republic was established that elected my great grandfather Giovanni

Melzi to represent them as their ambassador to Venice. A few years later Filippo Visconti's son-in-law Francesco I Sforza (1401 to 1466), who had married Bianca Maria Visconti in 1441, was elected the 4th Duke of Milan, and he established the reign of the House of Sforza, which maintained power on and off for about 90 years. My great grandfather Giovanni Melzi was now an advisor to the new Duke of Milan Francesco I Sforza.

Surprisingly, the most feared rival of Francesco Sforza and his descendants during their rule was the ghost of Valentina Visconti who had lived in Milan and France when the Visconti family was at the height of their power. She was born in Milan in 1371 as the second of the four children of Gian Galeazzo Visconti, the first Duke of Milan, and his first wife Isabelle, a daughter of King John the Good of France. After her mother's death in childbirth in 1373, Valentina and her siblings were raised by their paternal grandmother Bianca of Savoy and aunt Violante Visconti. Valentina was betrothed to various suitors before her father finally negotiated her marriage to his nephew-by-marriage Louis, Count of Valois and Duke of Touraine, the second son of King Charles V of France and brother of the reigning king Charles VI. Because of the close relationship between bride and groom, a Papal dispensation was granted for them on 25th November 1386. For security reasons, Valentina remained in Milan until after the end of June, before she was escorted to France by her paternal cousin Amadeus VII, Count of Savoy, and a retinue of 300 knights and finally delivered into the protection of Louis's envoys who had waited anxiously for her safe arrival. The formal marriage took place in the city of Melun on 17th August 1389.

The marriage contract had already been signed on 27th January 1387 in Paris, and Valentina received a dowry of the County of Vertus, the city of Asti, 450,000 florins in cash, and 75,000 florins in jewellery. **Most importantly, it was stipulated in the marriage contract that if the continuation of the Visconti male heirs should end then Valentina's heirs would inherit the Visconti dominions including the Duchy of Milan**. It was this particular Valentina Visconti contract that would always haunt the Sforza family, and because of it, her grandson Louis XII of France would later claim the Duchy of Milan for himself and embark on his Italian Wars, just as Francesco Sforza, the first Sforza duke of Milan, had always feared.

Valentina's union with Louis produced eight children. Two of them Charles Duke of Orléans (born 1394 and died in his Château d'Amboise, Indre-et-Loire, 1465) was the father of King Louis XII of France, and John Count of Angoulême (born 1399 and died 1467) was the grandfather of King Francois I of France. Both of these French kings lay claim to their rightful ownership and rule of Milan and its regions. The title of Duke of Orléans was first created during the 14th century, and it was reserved for the French royalty, and given, when available, to the oldest brother of the king. Thus, the Dukes of Orleans formed a collateral line of the French royal family with an eventual right to succeed to the throne should any of the more senior princes of the blood line die out. The Orléans branch of the House of Valois first came to the throne with Louis XII (1498-1515), and their branch have continued to rule right into my old age with the reign of King Francois's eldest son Henri II (1547-1559) whom I had known when he was a 4-year-old boy in Amboise, and his two successors, Francois II and Charles IX. The latter was recently crowned in 1561. Remember, I served King Francois while I was in Amboise from 1516 to 1522.

The role of the Melzi family as noble and loyal servants of the Sforza rule was to keep a close eye on the Dukes of Orleans and the Counts of Angouleme and to monitor their ambitions and manoeuvrings for the control of Milan. Thus, most in the Melzi clan were well versed in French as well as in Latin, Spanish, German, and Italian. As I mentioned earlier, Count Giovanni Melzi was a friend to two French kings (Charles VII and Louis XI), and he counselled them wisely, which helped to maintain a strong and lasting peace between France and Milan during his lifetime of service and at least until 1499. Giovanni Melzi counselled his Duke that he should consider marrying a Visconti because the mingling of the Sforza and

Visconti bloodlines might dilute out the controversial claims for the Milan dukedom by Valentina Visconti's French descendants. Therefore, by marrying a Visconti, Francesco Sforza believed that his children now had complete legitimacy to rule Milan in their own right for they all now carried the Visconti bloodline. After all, Valentina Visconti was born in Milan in 1371, and she died in Paris in 1408 as the wife of Louis de Valois, Duke of Orléans (the younger brother of King Charles VI of France) and as Sovereign Countess of Vertus (a commune north-east of Paris) and Duchess consort of Orléans, but she never inherited the title of Duchess of Milan. It seemed unlikely that any of her descendants would possibly want to claim the coveted Duchy of Milan thirty-eight or more years after her death in France. So, with the wise counsel and diplomacy of Giovanni Melzi, the duke of Milan stayed calm, but vigilant.

Galeazzo Maria Sforza, Fifth Duke of Milan, 1466 to 1476: Ascension, Marriage, and a Murder Most Foul

Under the moderate and skilful rule of Francesco Sforza from 26th February 1450 to 8th March 1466, the city and duchy of Milan was modernised and quickly become one of the richest city-states in Europe. He created an efficient system of taxation that generated enormous revenues for the government. His court became a centre of learning and culture, and the people of Milan grew to love him. He founded the Ospedale Maggiore, restored the Palazzo dell'Arengo, and added the Naviglio d'Adda, a channel connecting the eastern outskirts of Milan with the Adda River, and built an effective administration with the help of the Melzi and the remaining loyal della Torre and Visconti families.

To stave off French opposition and rivalry, the Duke decided that his eldest son Galeazzo Maria should marry a French royal or a Savoy. An alliance between the Sforza and the royal house of France was rumoured from as early as 1460, and in June 1464, Bona of Savoy was officially offered to Galeazzo as his betrothed by letters from the King of France and the Duke of Savoy. But, Francesco Sforza changed his mind because he now wanted to restore the once traditional alliance with the Gonzaga family of Mantua. Previously, the Gonzaga family had abandoned their long-held alliance with Milan and instead had formed an alliance with Venice, a long time enemy and rival of Milan. So, seeing an opportunity for a new alliance with Mantua, Francesco Sforza changed his mind, and in 1466, he married his son Galeazzo to Dorotea Gonzaga in order to form the Sforza's much-needed alliance with the Gonzaga noble family that had ruled Mantua from 1328.

When Francesco Sforza died unexpectedly on the 8th March 1466, his son Galeazzo was at the head of a military expedition in France with Giovanni and Cristoforo Melzi in attendance to help King Louis XI in his fight against Charles I of Burgundy and the 'League for the Public Good'. Called back home by his mother, Galeazzo returned to Italy anonymously in order to pass through the territories of the Duke of Savoy, the family enemy who had earlier made an unsuccessful attempt on his life for having jilted the saddened Bona of Savoy. However, Galeazzo re-entered the city of Milan safely on 20th of March, and there, he was proclaimed by the populace as the rightful heir to rule the Duchy of Milan.

And then, about one year after Francesco Sforza's death, Galeazzo Sforza's wife Dorotea Gonzaga died mysteriously on 20th April 1467, and surprisingly, Galeazzo married Bona of Savoy a year later, on 9th May 1468. Why this sudden change of heart and the need to marry a Savoy? I remind you, dear reader, that the Duchy of Savoy is the western neighbour of the Duchy of Milan, and that it provides Milan with a strategic buffer against an invasion from France. The House of Savoy is an ancient, prosperous, and influential royal family stemming from the Alpine region between the regions of France and Italy where they resided and controlled the strategic mountain passes through the Alps. The House of Savoy descended from Hubert I, Count of Sabaudia, in 1003. They resided mostly in Chambery and on occasions in Turin, Pinerolo, and Piedmont. However, when Charles VIII of France invaded Savoy, Piedmont, and Italy in 1494, and conquered Naples in the same year, the House of Savoy moved from the alpine region of Chambery and established their main residence in the lower lands of Turin. In 1553, with most of Savoy in French hands, the Duke of Savoy Emmanuel Philibert served the House of Habsburg and the Netherlands to slowly regain his territory from both the French and the Spanish, including the city of Turin to where he had moved the capital of the Savoy duchy from Chambéry.

In the 1460s, the females of the House of Savoy were well represented in the court of the French king Louis XI, monarch of the House of Valois. This included his second wife Charlotte of Savoy who he had married in 1451 when she was a mere 9-year-old and he was 27 years old after the death of his first wife Margaret of Scotland who had died of a fever in 1445 at 20 years of age. Louis XI, either for the love of his new wife or to accrue political advantages, welcomed his three sisters-in-law including Bona of Savoy whom he hoped to marry off to a wealthy or influential suitor. Although the King's offer of Bona of Savoy as a wife was at first spurned by Galeazzo and the Sforza house, now with the death of Francesco Sforza and Dorotea Gonzaga, Galeazzo suddenly saw Bona as great prize for the Sforza rule in Milan. She was a great beauty, a Princess of the ancient House of Savoy, and she was blessed by the patronage of the King of France. To win Bona of Savoy's hand with the blessing of the French king would be seen by all as a sign of legitimacy that Galeazzo Maria Sforza was acknowledged to be the 5th Duke of Milan and the rightful ruler of its domain. Appearances do matter.

The French King Louis XI felt obliged to Galeazzo Sforza for assisting him in his fight against the Duke of Burgundy and the League for the Public Good and believed that he deserved a special reward in return. Galeazzo Sforza, the great grandson of the peasant from Cotignola, was looking for a connection with the king's own royal house, and so, the king offered him the hand of Bona of Savoy, the 'Heir Apparent' to the Duchy of Milan. This time Galeazzo Sforza accepted her with an unbridled glee. However, this alliance was most unpalatable to the bride's family in the Duchy of Savoy, and it met with a great deal of opposition, particularly from Bona's four brothers, Amadeus IX, Philip II, Louis, and Jacques. But, King Louis XI was resolute, and he ordered Amadeus IX and his brothers to accept his decree for the marriage. So, the betrothal of the affianced pair took place in 1468 at the Castle of Amboise, when Tristan Sforza, the Duke's half-brother, arrived there as the proxy for the bridegroom.

My great grandfather Giovanni Melzi who was Difensore della Liberte, Senator of Milan, and Ducal Counsellor, and Count Palatine with an Imperial diploma from the Emperor of the Holy Roman Empire, accompanied Tristan Sforza to Amboise to witness the ceremony of the proxy marriage, and he then accompanied Bona of Savoy and Tristan back to Milan. After the ceremony, Giovanni Melzi and Tristan Sforza wrote a long dispatch to their Duke in Milan describing the whole event, the long procession of lords and ladies, the princes, the Queen and her maids, and how the King holding the exquisitely beautiful bride by the right hand led her into the church before placing the nuptial ring on her finger. The bride was dressed in a white cloth of gold with the royal crown on her head and her hair spread over her shoulders, revealing her renowned purity and grace. After the solemn mass and the wedding service, their Majesties, the bride and the proxy bridegroom Tristan retired to the King's own rooms where he presented Bona with the jewels sent to her by her husband, the Duke of Milan. These gifts were received with great joy and satisfaction and much applause. All the marriage celebrants then went upstairs to a reception hall where feasting and dancing occupied the rest of the day.

Although King Louis XI showered Tristan and his party with extreme cordiality and hospitality, Tristan Sforza remained suspicious and highly guarded against any treachery towards the Milanese Court. A few days after the wedding, Tristan and Giovanni Melzi escorted the bride to her new home and her waiting husband Galeazzo, taking great care to avoid the Savoy territory in case that somebody from the House of Savoy, in an endeavour to dishonour the Duchy of Milan, might attempt to kidnap the bride and prevent the marriage from being consummated. The bridal party travelled by way of Marseilles and Genoa; and the marriage between Galeazzo and Bona was successfully celebrated and consummated at Pavia on the 6th of July 1468.

In the first two years after his father's death, Galeazzo and his mother Bianca Maria Visconti ruled jointly. But, before he married Bona of Savoy, he had successfully ousted his third brother Ludovico and their mother from Milan to the town of Cremona that was her dowry gift from her now deceased husband Francesco Sforza. Galeazzo also had a large number of brothers and sisters to take care off either for their betterment or to contend with their worse intentions. He had six legitimate brothers and three legitimate sisters and a large scattering of illegitimate half brothers and sisters. His living legitimate brothers were Filippo Maria (born [b,] 12th December 1449) - Count of Corsica from 1464, Sforza Maria (b, 18th August 1451) – Duke of Bari from 1464, Ludovico Maria (b, 3rd August 1452), Ascanio Maria (b, 3rd March 1455) – Abbot of Chiaraville from 1465 and Bishop of Pavia from 1479, and Ottaviano (b, 30th April 1458) – Count of Lugano from 1467. His sisters were Ippolita Maria (b, 18th April 1446) who in 1465 married Alfonso II of Naples (King of Naples 1494 to 1495) and was the mother of Isabella of Aragon (b, 1470), and Elisabetta Maria (b, 10th June 1456) who in 1469 married Guglielmo VIII Paleologo, the Margrave of Montferrat.

Of all his brothers, Galeazzo had the most trouble with Ludovico, and he imagined that he might have to go to war against him one day because their mother Bianca had groomed Ludovico to be a future Duke of Milan, and he never hid his burning desire from Galeazzo or his other brothers. This ambition may have soured and festered when his mother died suddenly and suspiciously on the 28th of October in 1468. She left her residence in Cremona to travel and take part in the continued ceremonies and celebrations of her son's marriage to Bona of Savoy in Milan. She was in good health when she left Cremona, but unexpectedly died in transit at Melegnano. It was immediately rumoured that her ungrateful son Galeazzo poisoned her. His court poisoners were reportedly seen in Melegnano at the time that she had fallen ill. After the untimely death of his mother, Ludovico Sforza stayed on in Cremona and away from Milan and his brother, the Duke, and he waited patiently in the wings for his opportunity to revenge his mother, the Dowager Duchess Bianca Maria Visconti. That day would come to him much sooner than he expected.

In July of 1469, Lorenzo de' Medici, the Magnificent, arrived in Milan from Florence to share in the celebrations and baptism of the Duke and Duchess's first son Gian Galeazzo. Lorenzo was the signeur and ruler of the Florentine Republic, and he belonged to a rich and influential banking family, the Medici. As godfather of the boy Gian Galeazzo Sforza, Lorenzo brought beautiful gifts of diamonds and pearls for his godson's mother Bona, the Duchess of Milan. One diamond was so large and brilliant that it inspired Galeazzo to exclaim, *'you must be the godfather to all my children!'*

In 1471, when Leonardo da Vinci was 19 years of age, the Duke and Duchess of Milan reciprocated Lorenzo's visit and travelled to Florence with great pomp and ceremony. The Melzi House as nobles of Milan travelled with the Duke within his group of chief vassals and councillors to visit and to honour the Magnificent One, Lord Lorenzo de' Medici, and the Republic of Florence. The visit was a triumphant success for the Sforza rule and standing in Italy. Thereafter, the Duke and Duchess ran the Milan Duchy together in unison, the Duke often on campaigns and skirmishes with his neighbours, while the Duchess applied her skills and diplomacy to soundly administer Milan and its regions. With advice from the Melzi elders and other councillors, the Duke was actively encouraged to improve agriculture by constructing canals for irrigation and transport, introduce the cultivation of rice and the manufacture and commerce of silk and wool. He was also a major patron of musicians, artists, poets, and scholars and founded a number of academies of the sciences and the arts. He was particularly proud of his assembly of Franco-Flemish composers, musicians, and singers and his musical ensembles that he had gathered together from Europe for his Sforza chapel. The Duke also continued the reconstruction of the Castello di Porta Giova (Sforza Castle) that was started by his father Francesco Sforza, and with the assistance of the architect Benedetto Ferrini, he commenced the construction of the tower named after Bona of Savoy. The Sforza plan was to reconstruct the Visconti fortification into a princely residence and citadel for the ruling Sforza dynasty.

Although always busy, the Duke and Duchess also managed to find time to issue forth four children, Gian Galeazzo in 1469, Hermes Maria in 1470, Bianca Maria in 1472, and Anna Sforza in 1476. The Duke had four illegitimate children with his mistress Lucrezia Landriani and many more with various other women. Among the illegitimate was the remarkable Caterina Sforza born in 1463 who became the Countess of Forli and the Lady of Imola and will always be remembered for her distinguished beauty, her bold, impetuous, and militant character, her passion for hunting, her friendship and experiments in alchemy with Leonardo, her military occupation of the fort Castel Sant' Angelo in Rome in order to influence the election of a new Pope, her internment as a prisoner in Castel Sant' Angelo by Cesare Borgia and his father the Pope Alexander VI, and her slaughter of the many families that she thought were involved in an uprising against her and her husband in her fiefdom of Romagna. She was the mother of eight children, and she died relatively young in Florence at the age of 46 years of a fever on 28th May 1509, forever to be remembered as the Tigeress of Forli.

Over the years, although Galeazzo had done many good things for Milan, his rule had become cruel and intolerant, and he began to annoy a large group of the Milanese nobles who saw him as a tyrant. His cruelties, vices, and evil passions excited the rage, disgust, and hatred of many of his subjects and some of his courtiers. He was a notorious womaniser who shared his conquests with his courtiers, and he was known to have raped the wives and daughters of many of his nobles. His mania for hunting made him act at times in a manner so brutal as to be deemed by some to be entirely insane. When the most trivial of violations angered him, he forced some of his staff to eat uncooked animals until they died from bloat and blockage. Where was the reasonableness and compassion required of a just and sane duke? His behaviours bordered on the insane, and consequently, they led to conspiracies against him.

His counsellors, including Count Giovanni Melzi, advised him diplomatically to temper his rule and to rein in the unfair tax collections and his veracious sexual appetites whereby he was seen to be abusing the wives and daughters of his own nobles. They wanted him to follow the example of his father who was a wise and moderate ruler who followed the counsel of his advisers. Then, what his Counsellors, including Count Giovanni Melzi, had all feared actually happened. He was brutally assassinated attending his church, the Santo Stefano, the day after Christmas. Even Galeazzo himself knew from the many unusual presentiments on this day that all was not well. Before leaving home to go to the church, he met with and took leave of each of his children and with Bona of Savoy as though he knew that he would never see them again.

On St. Stephen's Day (26th December) in 1476, the three principal assassins, supported by about thirty friends, waited in the church for the duke to arrive for mass. When Galeazzo Sforza arrived, Giovanni Andrea Lampugnani knelt before him, exchanged some mumbled greetings, rose briskly, and then stabbed Sforza in the groin and chest. Gerolamo Olgiati and Carlo Visconti followed with further stabbings to the head and body, as did Lampugnani's servant.

Sforza was dead within a matter of seconds. All three assassins quickly made their escape from the church, although Lampugnani was quickly caught and killed by an incensed guard. His corpse was dragged through the streets by a mob that finally hanged the remains upside-down outside his house and beheaded him. Visconti, Olgiati, and the servant were soon apprehended, interrogated under torture, and after confessing, they were executed and their corpses displayed in a public ceremony as a warning to others.

The three principal assassins were high-ranking officials with grievances at the Milanese court. Lampugnani's grievance was a land dispute where his family had lost considerable wealth and property and Galeazzo Sforza had failed to intervene on their behalf. Visconti had accused Galeazzo Sforza of raping his sister and stealing her virginity, whereas Olgiati was a Republican idealist wanting to return to the good old days of the Ambrosian Republic. The assassins' teacher, the humanist Cola Montano, was blamed for instigating and encouraging the assassination because Galeazzo Sforza previously had him publicly flogged and imprisoned for the crime of sodomy. Montano disappeared from Milan immediately after the assassination, but he was eventually found, arrested, tortured, tried, and hanged for teaching, supporting, and inspiring the three assassins to kill Galeazzo Sforza on the grounds that he considered the duke to be a classical tyrant in the image of a Julius Caesar. Because of his Republican beliefs, Montano encouraged his students to re-enact the deed of Brutus and kill the tyrant Galeazzo Sforza as they should with all tyrants. There were rumours that the French king Louis XI had encouraged the assassination. Yet, nobody from Milan was game to charge, arrest, and interrogate the French king despite the strong rumours and accusations against him.

The assassins had hoped that with the tyrant's death all the citizens would rise against the Sforza dynasty and assert their freedom and independence. But, they were bitterly disappointed because this didn't happen. Instead, the citizens and councillors later consented to the succession of the Duke's little son Gian Galeazzo Sforza who was only 7 years of age.

The day after Galeazzo's assassination, the Duchess Bona of Savoy displayed the Duke's corpse in the chapter of the church where he was killed. She placed three rings and a seal of great worth in the coffin with her husband who was only 33 years old at the time of his death. She dressed him in a suit of white cloth in which he expressed a wish to be buried. She allowed the choir to wail for a few hours, a mass to be heard for half a day, and then she removed his body from the church for it never to be seen again.

'The peace of Italy is dead!' exclaimed Pope Sixtus IV when he read the news of Galeazzo's murder in a letter from his widow. In spite of her husband's crimes and follies, she begged the Holy Father to issue an edict absolving her dead husband from his many and grievous sins. She promised to atone for any of his perceived crimes by providing reparation to those whom he had wronged, and offered to build churches and monasteries, endow hospitals, and perform other works of mercy. The Pope never issued the requested absolution, and instead, he took advantage of Bona's distress and sadness to hurry the marriage of Caterina Sforza, the dead Duke's illegitimate daughter, to his own nephew Girolamo Riario, a marriage which had previously been arranged by Galeazzo Sforza in 1473. The wedding took place in Milan in April of 1477 with great pomp and ceremony when Caterina was only 14 years of age. One year later, she was in Rome to have her first child, a daughter named Bianca after both Girolamo's mother Bianca della Rovere and Caterina's paternal grandmother Bianca Visconti.

The New Regime: Bona of Savoy, Cicco Simonetta, and the Boy Duke Gian Galeazzo Sforza

The conspirators' hopes that the whole town would rise and throw off the Sforza ducal yoke after Galeazzo Maria Sforza's murder were not fulfilled. The Duke's 7-year-old son Gian Galeazzo Sforza succeeded him, and his mother Bona of Savoy was appointed Regent and guardian during his minority. Francesco (Cicco) Simonetta who had served the deceased Duke as his secretary was named as the Duchess's Chief Councillor and Director. Bartolomeo (III) Melzi also had been nominated for the position of Chief Councillor, but he did concede that

Cicco had the better experience and the credentials for the position. Cicco was small and tough minded. He was born in Caccuri in Calabria in 1410 and moved to Naples in his youth where he obtained diplomas in civil and canonical law. He served as Francesco Sforza's secretary and was rewarded for his service with the Governorship of Lodi. He was a member of the ducal chancellery and the Secret Council and wrote up the constitution and ordinances for the chancellery. He expanded his influence in 1452 by marrying Elisabetta Visconti, the daughter of Gaspare Visconti. In 1477, the Duchess appointed Cicco as ducal secretary, and he had the powers of a Prime Minister to maintain stability and to contend with the many endemic conflicts, interstate alliances, and the continued wars between the Guelphs and Ghibellines. However, these appointments annoyed many in the ducal chancellery including some in the House of Melzi who were now siding more strongly with the Sforza brothers' complaints. Ludovico, the deceased Duke's younger brother, resented that the Chancellery and the Council had appointed Bona of Savoy as Regent and not his eldest living brother Filippo Maria, the Count of Corsica, for he felt that it was he or one of the Duke's brothers that should have been appointed as the guardian of Gian Galeazzo. In fact, it was Ludovico who was actually plotting to seize the duchy.

Ludovico Sforza and two of his brothers were returning from a holiday in France over Christmas when they heard about the murder of their eldest brother Galeazzo. They had been in France to visit the court of Louis XI at Tours, Paris, and Angers. On hearing of their brother's death, they rushed back to Milan and blew the clarion call to summon their supporters. Ludovico disputed the Council's decisions and demanded to participate in the regency putting himself on a collision course with his sister-in-law Bona and with her minister Cicco Simonetta. He claimed the right of his eldest brother to be the regent and guardian of his nephew Gian, the Duke of Milan, and questioned the legitimacy of Simonetta's appointment. Ludovico protestations were heard and supported by the Condottiere Roberto Sanseverino and his Ghibelline followers who had a passionate and violent hatred of Cicco Simonetta and were ready at a moment's notice to raise troops to overthrow the new regime of Bona and Simonetta.

When Ludovico asked for support from the Melzi family, Gerolamo and Beltrame were quick to give it to him while Giovanni was temperate and reserved in his opinion. Bartolomeo III, on the other hand, accepted the decision of the Chancellery and the Council to support the legitimate regency, and he thought that Cicco had the experience and intelligence to be a good Chief Councillor. In an attempt to resolve the disputations, the Chancellery and the Council on advice of the Melzi invited the Marquis from the neighbouring state of Mantua to mediate and rule independently on the matter of the legitimacy and reasonableness of their appointments and decisions. And so, in February of 1477, Simonetta and the governing council invited Ludovico III Gonzaga, the Marquis and ruler of Mantua, to visit Milan and to mediate and end the dispute between Bona of Savoy and the Sforza brothers. Gonzaga convinced everybody involved that the best solution to end the dispute was for the three Sforza brothers to leave the Duchy of Milan as exiles each with a compensation of an annual pension of twelve thousand and five hundred gold florins, a residency in the city, and some castles in the duchy, which they could visit or return to whenever they were allowed to by the Ruling Council and ratified by the young duke Gian, his mother the Duchess Bona, and the Prime Minister Cicco Simonetta. The Sforza brothers accepted the verdict and the compensation. A calm returned to Milan for a short period while Bona of Savoy and Cicco Simonetta established their own rule over the city and the duchy.

Despite the continued protestations from the Sforza brothers, Cicco Simonetta, secretary of state, proclaimed that the young Duke Gian was the Prince regent and that his mother the Duchess Bona was to be the Regent during the minority of her son. He proclaimed two other decisions. One was that the State Rule was to be located in the castle and the other was that

Justice was to reside in the Ducal Palace, the Corte Vecchio, located across from the Duomo, the central Cathedral of Milan. He also publicly deplored the murder of Galeazzo Maria Sforza, the 5th Duke of Milan. To keep the peace with the citizenship and to better reconcile the new government with the population, he abolished the most troublesome taxes, and he reduced the price of grain. Thus, he bought some temporary peace to the city and some breathing time for himself, the Duchess Bona, and the people of Milan. The regency took advantage of the peace to celebrate the marriage of Caterina Sforza to Girolamo Riario in April of 1477. While Bona allowed Simonetta to run the Duchy, she administered to the needs of her children, especially the young duke, keeping him aware of all their State decisions.

With Simonetta and Bona now ruling Milan in the absence of Galeazzo Sforza, there was growing concern and fear amongst the Court Councillors and Senators that their rule might favour Louis XI and the French Court in future decisions of state. But Louis XI no longer seemed overly obsessed with wanting to possess or rule over Milan, possibly because he was still recovering from his wars and troubles with the Duke of Burgundy in France. Moreover, Bona showed no intention of favouring the French in any way, and to the great annoyance of Galeazzo's brother Ludovico Sforza, she simply followed the advice of her Chief Counsellor Cicco who had gained the upper hand in the Court and ruled Milan for the Milanese and not for the French as Ludovico had hoped he would.

To celebrate their new authority, Cicco Simonetta struck a gold double ducat of 2.4 cm diameter and 7 grams and a silver coin (the single testone or big head) of 2.8 cm diameter and 10 grams with the portrait of the Bona of Savoy as the Regent of the Duchy of Milan on behalf of her son Gian Galeazzo Sforza who inherited the symbolic ducal imagery of his deceased father Galeazzo Maria Sforza.

Fig. 13. Gold and silver coins of Gian Galeazzo Sforza, the 6th duke of Milan, featuring the portrait of his mother Bona of Savoy, the Regent of the Duchy of Milan, and her symbol of the phoenix rising from the fire.

It was Bona of Savoy's husband Galeazzo Maria Sforza who in 1474 issued the first testone coin of the Duchy of Milan with a portrait of his own head in profile engraved by Cristoforo Foppo. The coin had a value equal to one pound or a quarter of a scudo (subdivided into 6 lire or 20 soldo (copper coin worth one twentieth of a lira). While the scudo bore the coat of arms of authority, the testone bore the portrait of authority, a recognisable head in profile. The gold ducat and the silver testone of the Bona of Savoy, Regent and Duchess of Milan, were designed with her profile on the observe side of the coin bordered with the Latin script, *BONA . 7 . IO . GZ . M . DVCES . MELI . VI* (*Bona et Ioannes Galeazzo Maria Duces Mediolani Sextus*) that translates as *Bona and the seven-year-old Gian Galeazzo Maria, Sixth Duke of Milan*. This was the first time that the head of a woman was on an Italian coin since the time of the Roman Empire. On the reverse side of the gold and silver coins, the engraved image was either the head of her son Gian or a phoenix rising above the flames bordered by the Latin words *Sola facta, solum Deum sequor* that translates to *alone, I follow only God*.

The Shameful Infatuation of the Duchess Bona, Regent of the Duchy of Milan

New anxiety, shame, and discontent returned to the court of Milan when Bona of Savoy suddenly lost her dignity and perspective and became infatuated with a new favourite in her court, a lowly and opportunistic servant and meat carver by the name of Antonio Tassino. Rumour and innuendo were spreading about her incapacity to properly rule as Regent because her head was clouded by an indiscrete love affair. This sudden and calamitous change in perception by a growing band of her critics was that she was *'under the influence of unsavoury forces and becoming a woman of low tastes and habits and behaving in a manner that was immoral and undignified.'* This view fanned and spread by the Sforza brothers and reflected by some members of her court was to have a disastrous effect on her life. The French Ambassador wrote to his king that she had become *'une dame de petit sens', a lady with little sense!* She had fallen in love with one of her servants, Antonio Tassino, a handsome man, five years younger than herself, and he was selfishly and inappropriately influencing her governmental decisions to the detriment of all the good gentlemen of Milan. Tassino was of low birth, and he had been her husband's servant, an appointed carver at the royal table, serving the duke slices of his favourite meats. Now, with the death of her husband, this servant and carver of meats had become the favourite of the Duchess Bona, even ahead of her son, the very young Duke of Milan. She quickly promoted this meat carver above his station from servant to her personal advisor against all reasonable advice from her elected councillors. She arranged to have his room moved next to her own, and she was often seen horse riding alone with him in the woods instead of spending valuable and productive time with her children, friends, and council advisors at the royal court. The Duchess had fallen head over heels in love with the handsome rogue and was using him as her advisor at the expense and humiliation of Simonetta and the other court advisors. The Duchess was now 30 years of age, portly, and plain of face with an overabundance of unruly long hair. Yet, in the presence of Antonio Tassino, she was flirtatious, youthful and joyful, light upon her feet and with infatuated eyes, hands-a-twirling, and a merry laugh only for him. The roguish Antonio flattered her as a great beauty, and she, vain and snobbish about her royalty and stately bearing, easily believed his flattery. She showered him with gifts and unrequited love. My grandfather Bartolomeo Melzi advised her to be more cautious and discreet for the sake of her son and the Regency, but she dismissed his good intentions and accused him of jealousy. Others would not abide by her dismissals of jealousy, and they soon turned and plotted against her and Simonetta. Indeed, the enemies of Simonetta and Bona quickly realised that Antonio Tassino was the chink in her armour, and so they began to pressure and pester the Duchess against her own Chief Counsellor. Ludovico saw that his opportunity had arrived, and while in exile, he energised his plotting to further destabilise the current regime. He began his campaign by writing simpering letters to Bona begging for her and the young Duke's forgiveness, hoping that she would forgive him sooner than later. With unrequited love in her head and heart, Bona believed Ludovico's lies and expressions of servitude.

Il Moro. The Dark Beast Rises from the Ashes and Swallows Milan

The four Sforza brothers, Ludovico il Moro, Ascanio (the Abbot of Chiaraville), Sforza Maria (the Duke of Bari), and Ottaviano Maria (Count of Lugano), recruited Roberto Sanseverino to assist them in their opposition to Bona and Cicco Simonetta. The eldest Sforza brother Filippo (Count of Corsica) decided to stay neutral and told his brothers, *'good luck, my most esteemed brothers, but I won't be actively undermining Bona and her son Gian Galeazzo or the memory of his father, the late Duke Galeazzo, for their son is the rightful heir to the Duchy'*. The remaining Ludovico band of brothers and Roberto Sanseverino debated whether or not to invade Milan and overthrow Bona and Simonetta immediately or to summons greater support before they did so.

Instead, the shrewd Simonetta easily manipulated them to first subdue an insurrection in Genoa, the port town on the west coast of the Italian Peninsula, and to restore the authority of the Duke of Genoa, a strong ally of Milan. The Sforza and Roberto Sanseverino easily won the battle at Genoa in a few days, and so with the confidence of a victory, they then returned to Milan to attempt to overthrow Simonetta. However, Simonetta enjoyed the sympathy of the people, and he had by now effectively organised his citizen militia, and nobody dared to assist the conspirators. Next day, a strong band of Simonetta's militia drove the conspirators out from the city. The condottiero Roberto Sanseverino with drawn sword still in his hand rode out of the city through the Porta Vercellina and in great haste crossed the Ticino River and did not rest until he was in the safety of his cousin's French domain of Asti to the east of Turin and under the protection of the Duke of Orleans. On the other hand, the young Ottaviano Sforza, in his great haste to escape the Milanese militia, drowned while trying to cross the rapidly flowing Adda River, not far from the location where my father and his brothers would later build their villa in Vaprio. Ottaviano's other brothers, Ludovico, Sforza and Ascanio, escaped with their lives, but they were immediately exiled from the Milanese regency. Ludovico went to Pisa, Sforza to Bari, and Ascanio to Perugia. Ascanio later became Bishop of Pavia and eventually a cardinal in Rome before he died in 1505 at the age of sixty years. Filippo Sforza (Count of Corsica), the eldest of the living brothers, who was described as weak in intellect and with no ambitions of any consequence, was allowed to live contentedly and peacefully in Milan until his death in 1492.

With Galeazzo Maria's rebellious brothers out of the city and in exile, the year of 1478 and the first half of 1479 were periods of peace for the Duchy in which the regency took advantage on 24th April 1478 to celebrate the coronation of Gian Galeazzo Sforza as the young Duke of the city and Duchy of Milan. He was the 6th Duke of Milan at the age of almost nine years.

A few months after Gian Galeazzo's coronation, my grandfather Bartolomeo Melzi died in Lodi from a festering wound to his leg and a raging fever. He was buried at his church in Lodi, but had a memorial service at the Milan cathedral attended by the young duke, Bona, and the Prime Minister. My father Gerolamo was 18 years of age when his father died, and he was highly upset and agitated because he believed that the court doctor and the medical treatment had failed his father. Bartolomeo's personal doctor was away at the time giving a lecture at Padua University.

Despite this peaceful time in Milan, Ludovico, although technically in exile in Pisa, was still plotting to take over the Duchy. He complained to Lorenzo de' Medici in Florence that he was just wasting the best years of his life away from Milan. His friend Lorenzo could only counsel patience, for although he sympathised with the banished prince, he was the godfather of Gian Galeazzo the young Duke of Milan and still closely allied with the rulers of Milan. Ludovico was disappointed with Lorenzo de' Medici's response, and he believed that his only hope of seeing his native land again was to seek the support of Ferdinand I (Ferrante I), the King of Naples, the sworn foe of the Medici. This monarch looked on Simonetta as a traitorous villain who had taken advantage of Bona's weakness to usurp the supreme power in Milan. He wrote to King Louis XI begging him to come to his kinswoman's help and assist in restoring the Duke of Bari and his brothers with their legitimate rights. But, the French king had no wish to be drawn into the quarrel. When Ferdinand I failed to obtain the restoration of his exiled kinsmen, Ludovico Sforza resolved to try the fortunes of war once more. Roberto Sanseverino again placed his sword at Ludovico's disposal, and together they knew that they had the secret support of their Sforza and Visconti kinsmen in Milan.

Then, sometime in July 1479, Ludovico's luck changed for the better when his brother Sforza Maria, Duke of Bari, passed away due either to poison or natural causes for the duke was known to be excessively stout and unhealthy. This was good fortune for Ludovico for it meant that he might inherit the title of Duke of Bari if he played his cards properly. He knew that the title would give him extra gravitas to try and re-enter the Milanese circle of influence. His brother Sforza Maria had been granted the duchy of Bari by Ferdinand I, the King of Naples, as a reward for his betrothal to his daughter Eleonora d'Aragona. Also, Sforza Maria's sister Ippolita Maria Sforza had married the King's son in 1465, and she was a great ally of her brother. So, Ludovico immediately hurried to Naples to seek support from his sister and her royal father-in-law. They were suitably appalled with the tales of Ludovico's portrayals of Bona's scandalous behaviour with her servant boy Antonio Tassino. The disgusted King Ferdinand I of Naples immediately granted Ludovico the vacant Bari dukedom and promised him troops to overthrow Bona and Simonetta in Milan. As a consequence of the Pazzi conspiracy to kill the Medici in Florence, the King in support of the papacy was now at war with Florence and Venice, and he was looking for any ally in Milan, somebody like Ludovico. So, Ludovico gratefully accepted his title of Duke of Bari, and then as if he was already the regent of Milan, he quickly reconfirmed the betrothal between the two first cousins, the young duke of Milan Gian Galeazzo Sforza and Ippolita Maria's daughter Isabella of Aragon. This confirmation by Ludovico was an unnecessary ingratiating ploy for they had been already betrothed to each other when they were only 3 years of age during Galeazzo Maria Sforza's rule of Milan in 1472, and it was never contested or overturned by his widowed wife Bona of Savoy.

Ludovico returned to Pisa from Naples and abandoned his intended plan to invade Milan with Roberto Sanseverino. Instead, he once again inundated Bona with letters of apology, swearing allegiance to her and her son, and requesting their forgiveness and permission to return to Milan. In addition, he recruited Tristan Sforza's widow Beatrice, Caterina Sforza, and other Sforza supporters to write to Bona to say that they deplored the growing arrogance of Simonetta, and that they lamented the success of his intrigues against Ludovico who was his sister-in-law's nearest relative and rightful protector. These letters helped to widen the breach between Bona and her Prime Minister. Ludovico also bribed Antonio Tassino to continue encouraging the Duchess to reconcile with him as her most loving and trustworthy brother-in-law. Acting on these suggestions, the Duchess eventually relented and sent a messenger to invite Ludovico to return to Milan in his nephew's name Gian Galeazzo Sforza, the 6th Duke of Milan. When Cicco Simonetta learned of the decision from Bona, he told her '*I will lose my head, but you will lose the state.*'

And so it happened - on the night of September 7, 1479 - Ludovico Sforza secretly entered Milan with only a few friends as an escort, and he immediately took the oath of allegiance to the young Duke Gian Galeazzo Sforza and the Duchess regent Bona of Savoy. Cicco Simonetta congratulated Ludovico on his return and received him in the most courteous manner. When the news of these events reached the rival camps outside Milan, a truce was proclaimed, and the leaders on either side disbanded their armies. A few months later, without the support of the Duchess of Savoy or the young Duke Gian Galeazzo Sforza, Ludovico arrested their Prime Minister Cicco Simonetta, along with his son Antonio, his brother Giovanni the historian, and all their friends of influence.

After the arrest of the Calabrian Prime Minister, the reins of government quickly passed into the hands of Ludovico il Moro, and he ignored the proclamations of the young duke's mother and instead entrusted the supervision of Milan to a few of his most trusted friends. He surrounded himself with loyal supporters and then skilfully attracted towards himself most of those who had previously enjoyed the favour of his sister-in-law Bona of Savoy. My great grandfather Giovanni retained his previous positions, and Roberto Sanseverino was elected as the new head of the militia forces commanding more than two thousand men organised into small companies of fifty to eighty men.

Congratulations poured in from all the Sforza kin. The illegitimate daughter of Duke Galeazzo, Caterina Sforza, who had been brought up by Bona with her own children wrote from Rome to her uncle rejoicing over the fall of the hated minister; '*quelo nefandissimo Cecco the murderer of our family and our flesh and blood.*' Then, she added, '*I will be able to visit Milan and see my beloved mother once more in peace and safety.*' And her husband's uncle Pope Sixtus IV wrote to congratulate both the duke and duchess on the arrest of Simonetta and the restoration of peace and tranquillity. Ludovico was now the Duchess Bona's chief adviser in the regency, and he recalled and advanced his brother Ascanio to the office of Archbishop of Pavia. He established a peace treaty with Florence, and then with the full approval of King Ferdinand I of Naples, the Duke of Ferrara officially announced that Ludovico Sforza was betrothed to his daughter Beatrice d' Este, and that they would marry when she was ready and had reached the right and proper age.

Pandolfini the Florentine ambassador who with Leonardo da Vinci had watched the public events unfold in Milan with profound interest in 1480 sent a report to Ludovico's friend Lorenzo Medici, the Magnificent.

> Signor Ludovico is very popular here, both with the people and with Madonna Bona. Madonna trusts much in Messer Ludovico's good nature. The whole government of the kingdom is placed in Ludovico's hands. With what ability and skill he has effected this sudden change! I tell him, if he uses his opportunities well, he will become the arbiter of the whole of Italy. [S7]

Now that the government of Milan was fully established in the hands of Ludovico, he began to remove all those who he considered to be a thorn in his side. On October 7, 1480, Antonio Tassino and his father Gabriele who had been appointed as the commander of Porta Giovia were suddenly stripped of their Milanese possessions and driven out of Milan into exile to Venice to live with their memories, gifts, treasures, and jewels from Bona of Savoy. The arrested Prime Minister Cicco Simonetta was ordered to redeem himself by paying forty thousand florins that he held on deposit in certain banks of Florence. He refused to hand over any property and payment, and so as punishment, he languished for a year in the prisons of the castle of Pavia where he was tortured in an attempt to extract from him his secret deposits. When that failed, he was beheaded on October 30, 1480. His poor, loving wife, a Visconti, went mad and died in terrible despair soon after her husband's execution. The executed husband's brother Giovanni Simonetta, however, was pardoned and released from prison. He was an able and learned scholar and lived to write the Sforziada, a history of Duke Francesco's great deeds, which he dedicated to the Duke's son Ludovico. He had survived, and he was forever grateful to Ludovico and his supporters.

In the last months of 1480, the Duchess Consort Bona was outraged and distraught, and for a written promise that her son Gian Galeazzo now 11 years of age would remain the rightful Duke of Milan, she signed over her son's protection to Ludovico Il Moro Sforza, the new ruling Governor of Milan. Totally humiliated, she was obliged to leave Milan with rivers of tears gushing from her eyes while Ludovico was left smiling, fully satisfied with his safe and unchallenged position as the new Regent and Governor of Milan. On November the 2nd, 1480, Bona of Savoy left Milan for Vercelli, and she was soon exiled under guard to Abbiategrasso. My father told me that she eventually left the fort of Abbiategrasso, visited the court of Louis XI, and settled for a short time in Savoy in the lands of her nephew Philibert II of Savoy without ever receiving those promised payments from Ludovico and the Milanese Duchy. For some reason, Ludovico had rescinded on his promise. And yet, she would return to Milan nine years later to see the marriages of three of her children, Gian Galeazzo Sforza to Isabella of Aragon, Princess of Naples, on 15th February 1489; Anna Maria Sforza to Alfonso I d'Este, future Duke of Ferrara, on 16th January 1491; and Bianca Maria Sforza to the Holy Roman Emperor Maximilian I on 30th November 1493.

By Christmas 1480, His Lordship Ludovico IL Moro Sforza is back in his castle at the Castello of the Porta Giovia as its rightful owner. He is just 28 years of age, in his prime physically and intellectually. He looks in the mirror and sees himself as the splendid figure that he is. *Il Splendido*. He is perfectly groomed, tall, good-looking, sultry brown eyes, dark skinned, long, beautiful curly black hair, solid jawed, wide mouthed with a big smile. He is Il Moro, the regent of Milan and its territories. His father the first Sforza duke of Milan is dead, his brother the second Sforza duke of Milan is dead, and he, Ludovico Il Moro, is now the official guardian of the third Sforza duke over whom he has full control. His mother the wonderful Bianca Maria Visconti is dead, his half-sister Elisabetta Maria is dead, and three of his other brothers Sforza Maria, Francesco Galeazzo Maria, and Ottaviano Maria are dead. His worthless elder brother Filippo Maria is content to be his minion, and his youngest living brother Ascanio Maria is content to be the Bishop of Pavia. His sister Ippolita Maria and his beautiful niece Caterina Sforza are married with excellent husbands of influence, and he knows that he can continue to manipulate them all to his greater benefit.

Ludovico forced his brother's widow Bona of Savoy out of Milan, and so, he must be careful, wary about reprisals from her and her brother-in-law king Louis XI of France and her nephew the Duke of Savoy. Still, he already has proven himself to be a canny and successful diplomat. He has stopped the attack of Naples and the papacy against his good friend and ally Lorenzo de' Medici, the Magnificent of Florence. In return, Lorenzo has promised to reward him with Leonardo da Vinci and Atalanti Migliorotti, two of the Florentine's very best artists, engineers, and architects from Florence, to beautify the Sforza castle and the churches of Milan. Yes, he's already done well in the diplomacy stakes. Soon, he will have Naples, the papacy, and Florence in the palm of his hand to manipulate them against each other. He is Il Moro, the Prince, the Regent of Milan, and the Duke of Bari. He is the poet, the architect, and builder of a new world in Milan. He is Il Moro, yes, Ludovico Maria (misspelt as Moro on his birth diploma) Sforza, the blackest and the best ruler of Milan, ever. He can hear the chants in the streets outside the walls of his castle. 'IL Moro, IL Moro. Merry Christmas, IL Moro.'

Yes, Ludovico Moro, that hero of patience and cunning, at last, has attained his lifelong objective. He is the sole Regent of Milan. *'Merito e tempore (Merit in Patience)'* is his motto. It is illuminated on the vellum pages of his favourite books and placed in golden letters on his shield. He was of the firm belief that all good things come to the man like himself who can learn to bide his time. Now, his head appears together with that of his young nephew on all the new coins and medals of Milan with the inscribed words, '*Ludovico patrue gubernante (Ludovico uncle and governor)*'. His silver testone will quickly replace that of the Bona of Savoy, and with patience and clever management his head one day might even replace that of his nephew.

Fig. 15. Testone of Gian Galeazzo Sforza, the 6ᵗʰ duke of Milan (left) with his uncle, Ludovico Sforza, governor of Milan (right).

CHAPTER 4

A Simmering Florentine Kitchen, 1476 to 1480

Salt may be made from human excrement burnt and calcined and made into lees, and dried by a slow fire, and all dung in like manner yields salt, and these salts when distilled are very pungent.

— Leonardo da Vinci

1476: Vile Accusations, Anger, Love, Death, and Distress

When Leonardo da Vinci was 19 years of age, he witnessed the first visit of the Duke of Milan Galeazzo Maria Sforza and his wife Bona of Savoy to Florence. This visit in 1471 was highly successful and popular, and it cemented a strong relationship between Milan and Florence for the next five years. So, it was an enormous shock to the Medici and many of the Florentine nobles, merchants, and bankers when Duke Galeazzo was suddenly assassinated in December of 1476. Florentine diplomatic representation was quickly sent to Milan to gauge the political climate and to provide a strong show of moral and political support to the Duchess Regent and her young son Gian Galeazzo Sforza who had inherited the dukedom and became the 6th Duke of Milan. There was also a strong concern that the insurrection in Milan might encourage similar provocations in Florence for it was known that some nobles were discontent with the Medici dynasty, and that they were accusing them of acting as tyrants. This was making Lorenzo de' Medici very nervous.

The year 1476 was particularly distressful for Leonardo da Vinci. He was 24 years of age and wondering where his next commissions were going to come from in order to pay the rent and the wages of his three apprentices. Lorenzo de' Medici's commissions were all bypassing him and going to others, and he was worried that he had lost favour in the Medici court. Some money was coming in for his drawings and inventions from Bartolomeo Melzi whenever the count visited Florence from Milan or Lodi, but this was not as much as he had hoped for. He had reached a hiatus, and the portents weren't good. And then, a series of disasters seemed to descend upon him in quick succession. Only eight months before Galeazzo's murder in Milan, Leonardo da Vinci faced his own personal horror in Florence. On April the 9th 1476, six days before his 24th birthday, he was accused, arrested, and charged for the crime of sodomy. The accusation was anonymous and unfounded, yet it had to be investigated by the Magistrate at Bargello, the Palace of the People. The Magistrate read out the text of the anonymous and damaging accusation found by the prelates (those who exercise the public power of the church) in the people's drum outside the Palazzo Vecchio on the 8th of April.

I hereby notify the Officers of the Signoria with a certain fact, namely, that Jacopo Saltarelli, brother of Giovanni Saltarelli, lives with the latter opposite the goldsmith's shop in Vacchereccia. He dresses in black and is about seventeen years. This Jacopo has been an accomplice in many vile deeds and consents to please those who ask for such wickedness. And in this way, he has had many deals, that is, he has served several dozen people about whom I know many things, and here I will name a few of them: Bartholomeo di Pasquino, the goldsmith who lives in Vacchereccia; Leonardo di Ser Piero da Vinci, who lives with Andrea de Verrocchio; Baccino, the tailor, who lives in Orto San Michele and recently opened a tailor's shop on the street where there are two large tundish shops leading to the loggia dei Cierchi; and Leonardo Tornabuoni, known as Teri, dresses in black. [S8]

This was a serious and slanderous accusation, and Leonardo had much to worry about. If he was found guilty of the offence of sodomy, his punishment could be death either by hanging or being burnt at the stake. The best defence for him and the four others who were accused and tarnished by the same pen was that it was an anonymous and scurrilous accusation dropped into the *bocca di leone (mouth of the lion)* at the Palazzo Vecchio (Townhall). It was not unusual for anonymous informers to drop similar letters of false accusation into the receptacle with the Lion's head located at the town hall. Such invidious *delatores (denouncers)* were rampant in those times of conspiracies against the Medici house, which allowed the infamous *tamburos (letterbox)*, the denunciation boxes, to be used as a perfidious trick to protect their house from perceived enemies. But, this meant that many a good citizen like Leonardo da Vinci and Leonardo Tornabuoni were accused falsely. It is likely that the prelates, the Dark Companions, the Ufficiali di Notte (the Officers of the Night), the Night Watch or the Dark Watch as Leonardo called them, were themselves, the actual accusers in order to keep their businesses viable. More than half of the male population of Florence had already been accused of sodomy using the denunciation boxes, and consequently, Florence had gained the reputation throughout Italy and other European states as being the City of Sodomy. Although the accusation boxes were controversial and annoying to the male population of Florence, Lorenzo de' Medici used them as a necessary evil to keep him informed of possible plots and assassination attempts. However, his logic seemed flawed because if anybody was planning to assassinate him, it was most unlikely that they would announce it via his accusation box.

After a worrying afternoon in the prison cells of the Bargello Palace, Leonardo and his co-accused were released on the same day of their arrest on a bail paid to the magistrate's office by a Medici official. The co-accused Leonardo Tornabuoni was closely related and allied to the ruling Medici family. His uncle was the Medici banker Giovanni Tornabuoni. His aunt was Lucrezia Tornabuoni, the wife of Piero di Cosimo de' Medici, son of Cosimo de' Medici, and she was the mother of Lorenzo 'il Magnifico', the current Lord of Florence. Leonardo Tornabuoni thought that this accusation against them was an attack on the Tornabuoni and Medici families and their allies. Jacopo Saltarelli was already a known sodomist, previously accused and charged, and because he was an easy target, the other accused were meant to be guilty by association. According to Tornabuoni, it was the Pazzi, the stinking Pazzi family, a rival Florentine banking family who were besmirching the Tornabuoni and de' Medici name. They were allied to the papacy, Pope Sixtus IV and his nephew, or as some say, his illegitimate son Girolamo Riario, who was married to Caterina Sforza. Leonardo Tornabuoni predicted that this wasn't the end of the matter and that more trouble would follow, especially for the Medici.

Six days later, on April 15th 1476, Leonardo turned 24. He was three months older than Ludovico Moro Sforza who was in Cremona at the time already plotting against Bona of Savoy and Cicco Simonetta in Milan, and he was three years younger than Lorenzo de' Medici, the perceived tyrant of Florence. Leonardo was still in Andrea del Verrocchio's employ, but as a collaborator rather than an assistant. On the day of his birthday, he was at Verrocchio's workshop where a table was laid out with food and drink for him to celebrate amongst his friends and supporters. Also, on this day, he had received a final payment for his extraordinary portrait of the beautiful Ginevra de' Benci from her patron who she was soon to marry. It was a welcome sum that was brought to the party by her brother Giovanni de' Benci who was a close friend and strong supporter of Leonardo. The mood was boisterous, loud, and forgiving, and Leonardo was feeling happily relieved eating and drinking with his favourite colleagues, friends, and apprentices from the Florentine arts and intellectual community rather than locked in a dirty, smelly prison cell at the Palace of the People. The painters, Andrea del Verrocchio, Sandro Botticelli, Pietro Perugino, Lorenzo di Credi, Domenico Ghirlandaio, Francesco Botticini, Baccio della Porta, and Filippino Lippi; the sculptors Mino da Fiesole, Antonio

Pollaiuolo, and Benedetto da Maiano; and the poets, writers, and musicians, Bernardo Bellincioni, Pico della Mirandola, Bernardo Rucellai, Atalante Migliorotti, and Luigi Pulci were all there to enjoy Leonardo's birthday celebration. Others who visited to lend their support included the Vespucci brothers, Petro, Marco, and Amerigo, and there were Giuliano de' Medici and his companions, the mathematician Fra Luca Pacioli, and Leonardo's co-accused Leonardo Tornabuoni.

Leonardo partied in the city for the next few days, and then he rested with Simonetta Vespucci at her villa to recover with welcomed relief. She was weak and unwell, but happy for him to visit and to provide her with his loving and charming company while her husband was away from Florence on business. Leonardo was overjoyed to again be in her presence, and he sang her songs, played his fiddle for her and told her the latest Florentine gossip including about the false and malicious accusations against him. She comforted him and allowed him to exert his manhood in his sweet, gentle, loving way. He worried about her health and brought over a physician of his acquaintance in whom he trusted to examine and provide her with a healing panacea and relief. The doctor told him that she was dying of consumption and nothing could be done for her, only rest, time, and a miracle cure. A few days after Leonardo last saw Simonetta Vespucci in her villa, her condition deteriorated quickly, and she died of consumption on the night of the 26th April 1476.

Leonardo and the entire city of Florence were in sorrow. They mourned her death greatly. Thousands followed her coffin to its burial. She was only 22 years of age. Here death was a shock to all. She was celebrated for her beauty and popularity at a jousting tournament, the La Giostra, just the previous year. It was held at the Piazza Santa Croce in her presence where she was popularly and gloriously nominated the 'Queen of Beauty', the most beautiful woman of the Renaissance. She was also known as the 'unparalleled one', and she was Leonardo and Botticelli's favourite model. Leonardo drew many portraits of her, and she featured posthumously in a number of his later paintings, *Virgin of the Rocks, Adoration of the Magi, Madonna with Child,* and other paintings. Simonetta Vespucci also featured in Botticelli's paintings as one of the three graces in *Primavera* and as Venus in the *Birth of Venus*, although Leonardo disputes this and says Venus is Caterina Sforza when Botticelli met and painted her in Rome. Nevertheless, Sandro Botticelli, like Leonardo, had fallen in love with the beautiful Simonetta, but unlike Leonardo, Botticelli told all who would listen to him after her death that he wished to be buried at her feet in the Church of Ognissanti, the parish church of the Vespucci. When Sandro died in 1510, his wish was indeed granted, and he was buried at the foot of Simonetta's grave.

About four years after Simonetta's death, Piero di Cosimo painted a sensational portrait depicting her as Cleopatra ready to commit suicide with an asp wrapped around her neck. Leonardo da Vinci hated this portrait, which he called 'despicable' when he saw it, for he considered that it created an evil dispersion against her good name and saintly, generous character. She had no intention of killing herself. She loved life far too much and tragically died young of an unintended illness. Leonardo was not a fan of Piero's style or technique of painting, and he thought that his life style bordered on the bizarre. Simonetta's husband Marco Vespucci had found life difficult in her shadow, and her death was a relief for him. He soon remarried and happily raised a large family with his new wife who never received the same adoring attention and fuss that his previous wife Simonetta had received from various artists, poets, and the many other gentlemen of Florence.

Then on June 7, 1476, while Leonardo was still recovering from the loss of his beloved Ginevra de' Benci to an arranged marriage with an elderly banker, and with the death of his mistress Simonetta Vespucci due to consumption, the stain of besmirchment struck him again. He was again accused anonymously and charged with sodomy. However, these new charges against him and one of his pupils were dismissed immediately for lack of evidence. In fact, the

Magistrate dropped all the charges against him including the previous April the 9th charges. There were no witnesses to testify against him, and there was no evidence to support the anonymous accusations. He even received a gold-edged letter pardoning him, '*absolute cum conditione ne retamburentur (absolutely on the condition of the tuamburini accusation),*' where the term '*tuamburini*' was the name given to the anonymous warrant cases of the Night Police.

Fig. 16. Simonetta Vespucci by Leonardo da Vinci (top left and right), by Piero di Cosimo (bottom left) and by Leonardo da Vinci (bottom right).

Sailing the Wild Seas, 1476 to 1477

During the remainder of 1476 and most of 1477, Leonardo turned his attentions away from Florence, and he travelled to distant towns and lands. He first travelled to Lodi where he met with Bartolomeo Melzi to discuss his problems and future plans. Later in Pisa, he joined Piotro Vespucci's fleet of traders, financiers, bankers, cartographers, and landscape artists, and he sailed with them across the Mediterranean to Marseille in France. While in France before Christmas, he visited the court of Louis XI in Angers and met up with Ludovico and his brothers where they spent a few days together to visit Tours. In 1477, he sailed with Piotro Vespucci and the Medici traders and bank representatives to Sicily and Constantinople and through the Bosphorus into the Black Sea in the company of Transylvanian and Hungarian delegates of King Matthias Corvinus. He spent his time on board listening to the tales of the Florentine poet and trade delegate Luigi Pulci, playing the violin for the sailors and passengers, and learning about sailing, piracy, and the art of naval war. In Constantinople, he participated with the traders to open up new opportunities for trade between the Ottoman Empire and Florence. He also took the opportunity to visit the Ottoman seats of learning and to obtain translations of the great Ottoman and Persian scholars, scientists, and mathematicians like Ibn al-Shatir, Nasir al-Din Tusi, and Ali Qushji. He visited Cyprus and the beautiful port town of Antalya where his Armenian mother Caterina had been abducted and sold as a slave to Venetian traders who brought her across to Venice and sold her off to the Florentine banker Vanni di Niccolo di Ser Vann who used her as a young house-maid and servant at his house. She was freed from Vanni di Niccolo's household and the stigma of slavery when the Florentine banker died and Leonardo's father inherited her and the banker's house and other collateral for an unpaid debt.

By the end of 1477, Leonardo was back in Pisa to stay at the monastery where Ludovico was living in exile. They spent a few days together, and he was a willing ear to Ludovico's plans for ruling Milan if he would ever become governor and protector of his nephew the young duke Gian Galeazzo. While in Pisa, Leonardo took the opportunity to examine the fortifications and the restrictions of the Arno River's flow through the city and into the harbour and the sea. Leonardo was back in Florence for Christmas with his father and his third stepmother Margherita di Jacopo and to meet with his new brothers and sisters. He was now looking forward to the beginning of a new future with an increased stability in his life.

The Virtuous Ginevra de' Benci, the Divine Enchantress

To celebrate his return to Florence, Leonardo spent the first day of the New Year as a house-guest with his good friend Giovanni de' Benci for he wanted to hear the news about Giovanni's sister Ginevra de' Benci. She was Leonardo's first beloved in Florence when he was 20 years old and she was sixteen, just a few years before her father married her off to an elderly Florentine banker who had commissioned Leonardo to paint her portrait a year or two before he had left Florence to escape from his unhappiness there. She was highly intelligent, well educated, and with a phenomenal memory. She could recite and interpret any verse from Dante's *Divine Comedy*. At the age of thirteen years, she had already published her own book of religious verse. Leonardo was very much in love and had hoped to marry her, but her father reminded him that he was a bastard and that she was of noble birth who required a husband with great wealth and the right blood-line and worthy credentials.

Leonardo had used Ginevra's face as the young Virgin Mary in his *Annunciation* painting. The angel Gabriel (modelled on Leonardo with the Vinci knot tied around his bicep) is in a Florentine palace garden on one knee with his wings raised vertically above his head and with his right hand raised in a gentle greeting. The 16-year-old Ginevra sits on a chair in three-quarter pose and raises her left hand in response to Leonardo's greeting. It is a tentative, almost guilty warning, '*please do not come any closer.*' Her belly is wrapped in a golden glow.

> If the poet says that he can inflame men with love… the painter has the power to do the same… in that he can place in front of the lover the true likeness of one who is beloved, often making him kiss and speak to it.

Fig. 17. Annunciation *by Leonardo.*

Fig. 18. Ginevra de' Benci *by Leonardo da Vinci.*

In Leonardo's *Annunciation,* it is obvious that she is from a rich and noble family, and not the Virgin Mary of Nazareth who was betrothed to Joseph the poor carpenter and who later in Bethlehem gave birth to Jesus in a manger in the presence of livestock (sheep, donkey, ox, and chickens). In the background of the painting, the Juniper trees stand erect and proud and envelope Leonardo's head and wings with Ginevra's virtue and honour.

While Ginevra and Leonardo's relationship was strong and pure even after she married Luigi Niccolini in 1476, he painted her second portrait with a degree of meanness and unhappiness in his heart, and it shows. Although she was pretty and radiant, he has painted a rather creamy, austere, and miserable Ginevra, moonfaced, porcelain white, and unhappy to lose her young true love Leonardo da Vinci to a rich and elderly banker. In this case, he uses the backdrop of the juniper trees ironically, both as a symbol befitting her name *'ginepro'* and in the sense that she had been unfaithful to him by spurning him as her lover in favour of another (juniper as 'virtue and honour'). The painting is a truly magnificent portrait in many different ways, but mainly because it is the first three-quarter frontal view of a woman looking out directly at or slightly beyond the viewer. This was revolutionary at the time. However, I find it a somewhat cruel depiction of his first great love. Neither she nor her husband liked it, and her brother Giovanni eventually sold it to the Venetian Ambassador to Florence Bernardo Bembo who had become Ginevra's platonic admirer and close friend. Leonardo eventually felt bad about this portrait, and he set about to do others of her in a more positive, flattering, and enchanting light such as the *Madonna and Child with Flowers* where the child is a representation of his own undying love for her.

On his return to Florence, he wanted to hear all the news from her brother about her marriage and her state of mind. He wondered if she still loved him as he did her. Her brother told him that after a few years of marriage, she had grown fond of her husband who was very kind and attentive. But, she had no children and appeared unlikely to ever have them. Instead, she gave birth to copious poems, and the poets of the Medici circle wrote poems to her in return, dedicating them to her great intellect and renowned beauty.

Happy to be back in the presence of his very good friend Giovanni de' Benci who also wanted to be an adventurer and traveller, Leonardo told him about his travels and the wonders of the world. In addition, he presented Giovanni with a gift, a map of the world, not as a globe, but one of unusual design that nobody in Florence had ever seen before.

Madonnas with Flowers

Leonardo was presented with the first commission of his professional career in Florence on January 10, 1478 for an altarpiece of the *Virgin and Child with Saints* for the Chapel of San Bernardo in the Palazzo della Signoria of Florence. On March 16, he received a payment of twenty-five florins for completing the first stage of the altarpiece. His first Madonna was Ginevra de' Benci in the *Annunciation* painted between 1472 and 1475. By the end of 1478, he left Verrocchio's studio and began two paintings of the *Madonna and Child* at his own studio that was funded by his father. One was the *Madonna and Child with Carnation* and the other was the *Madonna and Child with Flowers* (now known as the *Benois Madonna*). They both feature his lost love Ginevra de' Benci as the beautiful Virgin. In each painting, he is the lost child looking for love and grace. Both Ginevra de' Benci and Simonetta Vespucci had turned him into a devoted Marian artist.

In the interim between being presented with his first commission in January for an altarpiece of *Virgin and Child* and his departure from Verrocchio's studio in November of 1478, there was an attempted assassination on the life of Lorenzo de' Medici that was enormously disruptive on the lives of all Florentines including Leonardo, and he momentarily forgot about his Madonnas.

Fig. 19. Madonna and Child with Flowers *(left), and* Madonna and Child with Carnation *and the Alps in the background (right)*.

Lorenzo de' Medici Survives a Murder Attempt, the Threat of War with the Papacy, and Shuttle Diplomacy with Naples, 1478 to 1481

After the assassination of the Duke of Milan Galeazzo Sforza in 1476, the Medici rulers in Florence gradually lost support from the new Milanese administration of the Duchess Regent Bona of Savoy and the Governor Francesco Simonetta who were caught up in their own internal struggles. But, an even bigger shock and disappointment was to follow for the Medici in the Florentine cathedral during Easter mass on April 26, 1478 when members of the Pazzi banking family attempted to assassinate Lorenzo de' Medici in the presence of many thousands of people in prayer. While the court poet Angelo Poliziano (better known as Politian) saved the wounded Lorenzo from certain death, his younger brother Giuliano was less fortunate when Bernardo di Bandino killed him instantly by inflicting multiple stab wounds. The assassin managed to escape from the cathedral and leave the country. The conspiracy was brutally terminated by the de' Medici supporters when they lynched the Archbishop of Pisa and killed members of the Pazzi family who were directly involved in the murder of Giuliano de' Medici. This murderous insurrection quickly became known as the Pazzi Conspiracy.

The Galeazzo Sforza assassination sixteen months earlier in Milan appears to have inspired the Pazzi Conspiracy in Florence. In reality however, the Medici killing and assassination attempt was more complicated than just eliminating a perceived tyrant by a disgruntled group of Republicans. In this case, it was a personal power struggle between families. The Pazzi were not the sole conspirators, they had the support of the Salviati and the Pope of Rome. The murderous trio, Girolamo Riario, Francesco Salviati, and Francesco de' Pazzi, put together the plan to assassinate Lorenzo and Giuliano de' Medici, whereas Riario's uncle Pope Sixtus IV provided them with moral support. The Pazzi and the Salviati were the Pope's Florentine bankers. The war against the Medici was for control of the Florentine economy and its revenues and for the ownership of Pisa, Imola, and the rich alum mines at Tolfa. The Pope had made it clear that it would be of great benefit to him and the papacy to have the Medici removed from their position of power in Florence, and that he would deal kindly with anyone who did this. In addition, the Duke of Urbino Federico da Montefeltro was recruited to provide 600 troops outside Florence ready to ride into the city and to take it over by force the moment that he received word that the Medici murders were successful.

While Lorenzo was recovering from his wounds in his palace after the unsuccessful attempt on his life, the Florentine gangs and soldiers who supported him rounded up all the suspected conspirators and imprisoned them, killed them or drove them from the city and confiscated their properties. The Gonfalonier (Chief magistrate) Petrucci in his anger at the murder of Giuliano de' Medici had Archbishop Salviati and his brother and cousin and Jacopo Bracciolini hanged by the neck from the palace windows. The raging mobs cut to pieces all who were described as enemies of the Medici or friends of the conspirators. Their bodies were dragged through the streets and their heads and limbs were carried on pikes. Even the holy remains of a bishopric priest were pissed and defecated upon by angry Florentine citizens. Piotro Vespucci, commander of the Florentine galleys built in Pisa and father-in-law to the deceased Simonetta Vespucci, was thrown into a prison for the perceived crime of having assisted with the escape of a falsely accused conspirator. These were unruly times bordering on anarchy, and they disturbed Leonardo and many of his fellow Florentine artists.

Because of the failure of the Pazzi conspiracy that the Pope had supported and the Florentine orgy of revenge against the Pazzi and Pope Sixtus IV's supporters, the Vatican acted quickly against the Medici and Florence and condemned them of anarchy and rebellion against the Church. The Papacy seized all the Medici assets that they could find, excommunicated Lorenzo and the entire government of Florence, and in early 1479, put the entire Florentine city-state under an interdict to deny it all of its churchly administrative rights. Unsatisfied with the progress of his edicts and sanctions, the Pope then threatened war against them. In November 1479, His Holiness the Pope formed a military alliance with King Ferdinand I of Naples, whose son Alfonso, Duke of Calabria, gathered together an invasion force against the Florentine Republic. Lorenzo rallied the citizens and again tried to win the support from his allies in Milan, but with no success because of the on-going power struggles among the Sforza family. In desperation for a solution, Lorenzo thought of his old motto 'divide and rule' and decided to personally confront the King of Naples against all the good advice not to go and place himself unconditionally into his enemy's hands. He immediately called a meeting of a committee of forty of the chief citizens at the Palace of the Ten, not to take their advice, but to communicate his intention to them in his valedictory address.

> Florence needs peace, for the allies are not doing their duty. Since they feign to make war on me alone, it is for me to go in search of peace. When my enemies will have me in their power in Naples, we shall see if it is I alone they aim at. [S9]

That same evening, in early December 1479, knowing that the safety of his city and his dynasty were at stake, Lorenzo left Florence for Pisa and then to Naples by sea, placing his life in the hands of their king. This was a brave move for it was known that the king of Naples had a fierce reputation for killing and pickling the bodies of some of his visitors with whom he had disagreements. In February of 1480, King Ferdinand was totally won over by Lorenzo's charm and his persuasive argument that it would not benefit him and Italy to be divided by the Pope nor for Florence to be destroyed in a war. Thus, the king of Naples and the Medici came to an agreement. In return, Florence was required to pay an indemnity, rectify territories, and release the remaining imprisoned Pazzi. On the 6th March 1480, the king of Naples withdrew his troops from Tuscany, and Lorenzo returned to Florence on 15th March with the gift of peace, and his citizens received him with great joy as their heroic figure and leader.

A Lesson in Florentine Diplomacy

At the time of the Pazzi Conspiracy, Leonardo da Vinci had his own workshop, but was also looking for the patronage of Lorenzo de' Medici who had opened a school of philosophy, poetry, and art in his garden at San Marco. A month after the Pazzi Conspiracy, the Florentine Governing Council had called for tenders for a fresco in the church to commemorate the murder of Giuliano de' Medici and the murder attempt on Lorenzo. Leonardo and four other painters put forward their proposals. On the 21st July 1478, the Council of Eight came to the following resolution, which Leonardo noted: '*item servatis etc. deliberaverunt et santiaverunt Sandro Botticelli pro ejus labore in pingendo proditores florin quadraginta largos. (For his services rendered etc. Sandro Botticelli received forty large florin for his painting and for his consultation work on the santiaverunt traitors).*' Leonardo missed out, and Botticelli was awarded the tender and a payment for his painting of the '*proditores* (traitors)' whereby the members of the conspiracy that had been condemned to death were to be depicted in a fresco on the facade of the palace. (NB: This fresco was destroyed in 1494 after the death of Lorenzo de' Medici on instruction from the new ruling regime). No fewer than eighty conspirators were condemned to death including the assassin Bernardo Bandini who had escaped initially, but was arrested a year and a half later in Constantinople on 23rd December 1479. Bernardo Bandini was hanged by the neck from a window in the Palazzo del Capitano on the Via dei Gondi in Florence five days later. At this time, Lorenzo de' Medici was sailing away from Florence to Naples on his important and dangerous diplomatic mission, so, Leonardo drew for him his eyewitness sketch of the hanged corpse of Bernardo di Bandino Baroncelli and inscribed the sheet in his sketchbook with notes about the colours of the murderer's clothing:

> A tan-coloured small cap, a doublet of black serge, a black jerkin lined, a blue coat lined, with fur of foxes' breasts, and the collar of the jerkin covered with black and white stippled velvet Bernardo di Bandino Baroncelli; black hose.

Leonardo da Vinci captured the hanging of Bernardino di Bandino Baroncelli in pen and ink as a record for Lorenzo de' Medici's satisfaction for the criminal was none other than the murderer of Giuliano de' Medici in the conspiracy of the Pazzi. He was a descendant of an ancient family and the son of the man who, under King Ferdinand I, was President of the High Court of Justice in Naples. His ruined fortunes, it would seem, induced him to join the Pazzi conspiracy. He and Francesco Pazzi were entrusted with the task of murdering Giuliano de' Medici on the chosen day of the attack. On receiving the sign from Francesco Pazzi, Bernardo repeatedly stabbed the unsuspecting Giuliano de' Medici in the chest, twenty-times or more with a short sword until he fell backwards, dead. When Lorenzo saw the drawing, he told Leonardo that he should add it to Sandro Botticelli's fresco, but this never happened.

In the first three months of 1480, Leonardo was living at the Medici Palace and working on a sculpture in the Garden of the Piazza San Marco where Lorenzo de' Medici had established a Neo-Platonic academy of artists, poets, and philosophers. Soon after his arrival back to Florence, Lorenzo de' Medici summoned Leonardo da Vinci to a personal meeting and asked him to lead a diplomatic mission on his behalf to deliver gifts and deeds to the Duke of Bari Ludovico Moro Sforza in Milan and thank him for his valuable support and for sending kind words about him to the King of Naples. Apparently, Ludovico Sforza had smoothed the path for Lorenzo with King Ferdinand who believed that Ludovico was now a trustworthy ally who was worth listening to. Ludovico had pointed out in diplomatic dispatches to the King before Lorenzo's arrival in Naples that Italy needed Lorenzo at the head of the Republic of Florence in order to maintain stability and peace between the different states. Also, he was a wealthy banker who could finance some of the King's own ambitions. The intervention by Sforza had eased the tension between Naples and Florence, and so, the King of Naples was able to receive Lorenzo in a mood of reconciliation. If necessary, Lorenzo de' Medici still had one other negotiating chip to present to the King of Naples. He had secret information of an imminent invasion of the Kingdom of Naples by the Turks. However, Lorenzo held back this playing chip because of the effective influence of Ludovico Sforza in the negotiations. The king had admitted to Lorenzo that Ludovico had influenced him in his favour. In return, Lorenzo now felt a debt to Ludovico, and so, he requested Leonardo da Vinci to be his ambassador to express his and Florence's gratitude and support. Lorenzo knew that Ludovico and Leonardo had met before in France and Pisa in 1476 and 1477, and that they had taken a liking to each other.

As part of this diplomatic mission, Leonardo was instructed by Lorenzo also to visit and sound out the former Ducal Councillor and Senator of Milan, my great grandfather Count Giovanni Melzi. My great grandfather was the former Ambassador to Venice for the Milanese Republic in 1448 and 1449, and he had an important role in negotiating the peace settlement with Venice and Florence in the Treaty of Lodi in 1452. He still had some important influence in Venice as well as with the Medici. Furthermore, the Melzi family had been negotiating previously for two or three years on behalf of the deceased Duke Galeazzo Maria Sforza with the Medici and other Florentine officials to allow Leonardo da Vinci to visit Milan on a goodwill sabbatical tour. Now, was as good a time as any for Leonardo to visit Milan and for him to find out what the possibilities were to successfully recruit Milanese support against Pope Sixtus IV. And so, in April 1480, Lorenzo de' Medici dispatched Leonardo to Milan together with the engineer and poet Atalante Migliorotti, and a group of merchants and banking officials, and a small escort of soldiers with gifts for Ludovico Sforza, the duke of Bari and the new Governor of Milan, and for Lorenzo's godson the young duke of Milan - Gian Galeazzo Sforza and for his mother Bona of Savoy. Lorenzo reminded Leonardo and the other envoys that he was the godfather of Gian Galeazzo Sforza, and that he expected them to treat the young duke with the greatest of respect and courtesy. Word went out ahead by rapid messenger to inform Count Giovanni Melzi that Leonardo da Vinci was on his way to visit him and the Duke of Bari with important requests from Lorenzo de' Medici.

Lorenzo de' Medici Encourages the Turkish Invasion of Italy

In the summer of 1480, when Leonardo was already in Milan and Lorenzo was safely back in Florence and again running his banking, commerce, art, and state businesses, a force of nearly 20,000 Ottoman Turks under the command of Gedik Ahmed Pasha attacked and captured Otranto in southern Italy.

In order to force King Ferdinand I to withdraw his troops from Tuscany during their potential war with Naples, Lorenzo and his Florentine agents secretly pressed the Turks to invade Naples in 1479. The Venetians also, being jealous of the Neapolitan king's power and having obtained intelligence that he was directing his interests towards annexing the kingdom of Cyprus, encouraged the infidels with whom they had then concluded a peace treaty to defend their dominions against a likely invasion from Naples. Sultan Mehmed II was easily persuaded by the Florentine and Venetian Republics about Naple's hostile intentions, and he soon fitted out a formidable fleet at Valona on the coast of Epire ready to embark with an army to land in Calabria. This city in the south of Italy only had a small garrison and was unprepared for the coming siege. The Turks at length assaulted the city and massacred the clergy, the old, and the women with child, and they captured the youth for slavery and ravaged the matrons and nuns upon the altars, or at least that is what our unbiased historians have told us.

The news of the invasion astonished and alarmed all of Italy. In response, Pope Sixtus IV issued his second call for a Crusade, but receiving no support, he grudgingly bowed to necessity and made peace with Florence and Lorenzo in August of 1480. The king of Naples threatened the Pope that if he would not assist him against the Turks then he would conclude a peace with them and invade Rome instead. Sixtus immediately ordered twenty-four galleys to sail to Naples in support of the king. On the 16th of September, the Pope concluded an alliance against the Turks with Ferdinand I of Naples, the king of Hungary, the dukes of Milan and Ferrara, and the Republics of Genoa and Florence. King Ferdinand I having recalled his troops from Tuscany after making his peace with Lorenzo now sent Duke Alfonso into Calabria to oppose the infidels and requested the princes of Europe for assistance. In May of 1481, when Leonardo was back in Florence after his first visit to Milan, Sultan Mehmed II died in Constantinople, and the resulting succession crisis prevented the Turks from sending reinforcements to Italy. Duke Alfonso won back Otranto from the Turks on 10th of August 1481.

Thus, Lorenzo, having survived an assassination attempt and a war instigated by the Pope, had the last laugh on him and the papacy when Pope Sixtus IV died 12th August 1484. Lorenzo de' Medici felt further revenged when Pope Sixtus IV's nephew Girolamo Riario was stabbed to death on 14th April 1488 and his naked body was flung out from the castle walls and dragged throughout the streets of Forli by the angry populace. When Lorenzo de' Medici and the people of Florence heard of Riario's demise, they were much satisfied and praised God for a justice done. Moreover, Lorenzo maintained good relations with the Turks as the Florentine maritime trade with the Ottomans was a major source of wealth for the Medici and Florence. Thereafter, Lorenzo, like his grandfather Cosimo de' Medici, pursued a policy of maintaining peace and a balance of power between the northern Italian states and of keeping the other major European kingdoms like France, Spain, and the Habsburg rulers out of Italy. I know that Leonardo admired Lorenzo largely for his bravery and diplomacy, and he favoured and encouraged Lorenzo's policy of a balance of power.

CHAPTER 5

First Diplomatic Mission to Milan, 1480 to 1481

Every action needs to be prompted by a motive. To know and to will are two operations of the human mind. Discerning, judging, deliberating are acts of the human mind.

— Leonardo da Vinci

Leonardo in Milan, April 1480 to March 1481

The Florentine poet and historian Benedetto Dei wrote down his remembrance of the Florentine visitors in Milan on 15th June 1480 in his book *The Chronicle of the Years 1400 to 1500* as follows:

> And Luigi Pulci, Gian Perini, Manno Tenperani, Andrea Billieslomi, Dino Bettini, Iachopo di Tanai de' Nerlli, Franc Ciapellone, Franc Ghaddi, Lucha del maestro Lucha, and so on…. until… Leonardo da Vinci painter, Ridolfo Paghanegli di Pisa, Atalanta with viola, and Franc Cicho… and so on ….

Benedetto Dei was in Milan drumming up trade for the Florentine mercantile houses at the same time that Leonardo was there, and they quickly became friends. Leonardo enjoyed hearing about Benedetto Dei's business trips for he had travelled extensively to various places including Germany, France, England, the Middle East (Beirut, Jerusalem), and Africa. However, Leonardo da Vinci, Atalante Migliorotti, and Luigi Pulci already had been in Milan for a month before Benedetto Dei had dated their visit as the 15th June 1480. By then, they even had their first audience with the Duke of Bari and the young Duke of Milan and presented them with the *lira da braccio* (violin or fiddle) and the other gifts and messages from their Lord Lorenzo de' Medici.

When Leonardo and his servant Tommaso Masini and the poet musician Atalante Migliorotti first arrived in Milan, they stayed at the Medici house beside the Medici bank and the Florentine ambassador's quarters in an area where many of the Florentine diplomats and merchants lived. It was here that they met up again with my father and his grandfather who then escorted them to a scheduled meeting with Lord Ludovico Sforza and his nephew, the young duke Gian Galeazzo Sforza. The meeting at the Sforza castle was informal and highly entertaining.

The reception room in the Castle Sforza is light and airy and natural light streams from the outside over the northern wall and parapets and brightens the interior through the large, barred windows. The room was filled to near capacity with the presence of about eighty people. The young Duke, aged eleven years, and his uncle sat with their secretaries and attendants behind a long table, stretched out horizontally at one end of the room. A rectangular stage and wooden barrier separated them from the congregation of visitors who were standing in groups or seated on the benches set along either side of the room, but on the opposite side of the barriers, away from the Sforzas. The table in front of the Sforza was laden with the gifts from the young duke's godfather, his Illustrious Lord Lorenzo de' Medici. The young duke was smiling and holding the silver *lira da braccio* (fiddle) that was shaped like a horse's head and that Leonardo had personally presented to him. Leonardo, who was dressed in his magnificent Florentine black and red velvet coat, was soon invited to demonstrate his playing skills, which he did with much aplomb and showmanship while accompanying the poet Atalante Migliorotti who recited an ode in praise of the magnificent friendship between the Republic of Florence and the Duchy of Milan, and especially between the Medici and the Sforza families.

Leonardo performed a few frottole, and he sang his and Lorenzo de' Medici's composition in praise of the young Duke and the Sforza family. He also told some amusing riddles and presented Lord Ludovico and the young duke and his mother the Duchess of Savoy with further gifts of jewellery and other valuable art objects. Leonardo had an additional gift for Ludovico Moro Sforza from Lorenzo de' Medici. It was a set of 78 Tarot cards beautifully hand-painted by Botticelli. These cards were an updated and modernised version of a set that Lorenzo's grandfather Cosimo had gifted to Francesco Sforza, the 4th Duke of Milan, in 1461. Lorenzo told Leonardo that Ludovico made many of his decisions based on cartomancy, and that he wanted the Duke of Bari to have this special hand-painted 78 card set imbued with ancient platonic and hermetic wisdom introduced by Marsalio Ficino, the translator of *Corpus Hermeticum* and the founder of hermetic thought in Florence. Ludovico Sforza accepted the gift with much enthusiasm, but he was less interested in the hermetic wisdom of the ancients and more in the magical power of the Tarot that he wanted his astrologer and physician Ambrogio Varesi to use as a cartomantic and divinatory tool.

'Tell me, Maestro Varesi, what can you divine for our guests from this set of cards from our Illustrious Lord Lorenzo de' Medici?'

'Your Grace. If you allow me a few moments to familiarise myself with this pack, I will see what fortunes they have brought for us,' replied the wizard.

Leonardo looked on unimpressed at the card reading for he had a great contempt for cartomancy and necromancy, and he took an immediate dislike to the charlatan Maestro Varesi posing as Lord Ludovico's astrologer and physician.

After the fortune telling, Atalante Migliorotti recited some more poetry in praise of Lord Ludovico and the Sforzas, and he offered Lorenzo's heart-felt expression of thanks for the Duke of Bari's support and for his very fine references that he had given in praise of Lorenzo and Florence to the King of Naples. In return, Ludovico thanked Leonardo and Antonio for their visit and their very fine gifts from Lorenzo and the Republic of Florence, and he asked them what they proposed to do in Milan. They said they wanted to talk with the resident artists, architects, merchants, and bankers. Count Giovanni Melzi who was seated at the high table beside the young duke told Lord Ludovico that Leonardo would like to visit their properties in Milan, and that they would take him to see the canals and tributaries along the Adda River. Lord Ludovico said that he wanted to talk to Count Melzi about a number of important matters, and that he would schedule a meeting with him for discussions about these and other matters at another time depending on how his new set of cards fell and how Maestro Varesi interpreted the reading.

Both my father and his grandfather were at the attendance of Leonardo's meeting with the two dukes the Duke of Milan and the Duke of Bari, and they were highly impressed by the improvised recitations of the lyrical and narrative poetry of Migliorotti and Pulci while Leonardo accompanied them on the fiddle. The young duke Gian was entranced by Leonardo's skill with the violin and called him the doyen among performers upon the *lira*. He invited Leonardo to return a few days later to meet his mother the Duchess Bona of Savoy and to play his *lira de braccio* for her and her visiting French musician and composer Josquin des Prez. Leonardo obliged and quickly charmed the French visitor and the Duchess Regent, and he soon had his first court appointment as the young duke's musical tutor and teacher.

A few months after Leonardo's arrival in Milan, my great grandfather and father attended a meeting with the young duke Gian Galeazzo Sforza and his uncle Ludovico Sforza at their castle. The meeting was arranged for the Melzi to present their offer for the purchase of the disused Sforza fort at the commune of Vaprio on the edge of the Adda River. This meeting with the two Sforza princes was highly successful for my great grandfather convinced the young duke and his uncle to sell their fort and estate to him and his family in return for their loyal support and service to the court. As soon as Giovanni Melzi received the deeds of purchase, he and his grandsons asked Leonardo to travel with them to Vaprio to inspect their new acquisition. Ludovico IL Moro Sforza had no objections to the proposal, and he told them that he would accompany them in their inspection of the Vaprio fort to satisfy himself that he had not made a mistake in helping the Melzi to the disadvantage of the Sforza family. Giovanni Melzi thanked his Lord Sforza and spoke thus, *'no man should be afraid of improving his possessions lest they be taken away from him, or be deterred by high taxes from starting a new business. The prince should be ready to reward men who want to do these things and those who endeavour in anyway to increase the prosperity of his city and his state.'*

Ludovico laughed at the impudence of this quote from somewhere or other that he had heard before, and he replied, 'you have the deeds of possession. They are safely in your hands. Our young lord the Duke rewards you for your loyal service. He and I wish to see how your new property will increase the prosperity of our city and state and what security and fortifications you will help us with along the borders of the Adda River. Also, your first duty to us as part of your purchase of the fort and lands at Vaprio will be to take an account and survey for us of all of the properties currently claimed by the Countess of Melzo in the Melzo and Martesana region. This ledger contains all her claims. You know full well that every villa, farmhouse, barn, and mill on the Contessa's lands could be fortified and defended easily by the enemy. Maybe our friend, the Maestro Leonardo da Vinci, could provide us with maps and drawings and an architectural assessment of her villas and lands for our records?'

Leonardo stayed a few nights at the Melzi villa in Casoretto to talk with them about their new purchase at Vaprio located only 16 km further east. He heard about the history of the Sforza family and how the current signore Ludovico Sforza might plan to take away the city's power from Bona of Savoy and her son Gian, the 6th Duke of Milan. Later, they travelled along the Martesana canal to the River Adda, and Leonardo provided them with his opinion about the adequacy of the fortifications along the canal and in Vaprio on the River Adda. At Vaprio, they met with the Sforzas and discussed the issues of Countess Melzo's properties and domiciles in Milan and her remaining Marliani communes. Here, Leonardo heard the full history of Lucia Marliani, Countess of Melzo, and how she gained her titles, wealth, and prestige from Galeazzo Maria Sforza, the now deceased 5th Duke of Milan.

Lucia Marliani-Visconti, the Duchess of Melzo, and the Mother of Duke Galeazzo Sforza's Two New Sons Galeazzo and Octavian Visconti-Sforza

Lucia Marliani-Visconti was more than just a mistress or a consort of Galeazzo Maria Sforza, the 5th Duke of Milan. She was his special-new-primary wife, an object of beauty that he wanted to possess respectfully at any price. He had written out a Ducal contract to possess her as a chattel, ignoring his and her marriage contract before God that he had already written and made with Bona of Savoy, and that she, Lucia, had made with her husband Ambrose Raverti. The Duke had no intention of removing Bona from his life for she was an excellent and tolerant wife who helped him immensely in diplomacy and in running the governing of Milan. Yes, Lucia Marliani was special, she was an addition to the Galeazzo Maria's family, replacing his previous mistress Lucrezia Landriani with whom he already had eight children including the amazing Caterina Sforza, Lady of Imola. Caterina had become part of Bona's household and was previously raised by her paternal grandmother Bianca Maria Visconti, and she would soon be betrothed to Pope Sixtus IV's nephew Girolamo Riarlio. Caterina's natural mother Lucrezia Landriani was back with her husband's children, and she no longer was of much interest to

Galeazzo's venial cuckolding. Galeazzo was now spending all his time and passions on the young and beautiful Lucia Marliani.

My Melzi ancestors loved Francesco Sforza and his son Galeazzo very much, and this is the story that they told Leonardo about the Galeazzo's love affair with Lucia Marliani, for they knew her and her husband's family very well. Like the Melzi family, the Raverti family were from the District of Martesana, the region directly east of Milan, 25 km from Milan to the Adda River along the Martesana canal, including the municipalities of Inzago, Cassano, Gorgonzola, Bellinzago Lombardo, Melzo, and Truccazzano on the way to Vaprio. The Melzi and Raverti both had residences in the East Gate. Ambrose Raverti was a minor official in the ducal court when the Duke Galeazzo first set eyes on his 19-year-old wife Lucia in 1474. The Duke immediately fell in love and installed her in his newly purchased house, the Torelli mansion, next to his castle in Porta Vercellina. Moreover, he made a legal pact or covenant with her husband, 'that he, the Duke, has bought Lucia the wife of Ambrose Raverti who remains legally the wife of the afore mentioned Ambrose Raverti, but the Lord of Milan prohibits the husband to have *concubitus* or *carnalem cupulam* (sexual intercourse) with his wife nor she with him nor with any other man except the person of the Duke of Milan.'

The Duke had bought Lucia Marliani from her husband for the sole purpose of sexual intercourse, to have babies with her, and to be in her company for whenever he wished. For this special license, Ambrose Raverti, the lawful husband of Lucia, was made the mayor of Como, and he was named as one of the captains of Justice with responsibility to manage the District of Martesana. From that day until his death, the main concern of the Duke was to impregnate Lucia with his children and to shower her with gifts always more expensive and larger than before. The Registers of the Duchy of Milan from December 1474 to August 1476 show that she received enormous payments – 1,000 ducats as Christmas gifts and 1,000 ducats a year on revenue of Martesana, necklaces, rings, brooches with pearls, diamonds, and rubies from Genoese and Venetian merchants, but also the villages and the parishes of Melzo and Gorgonzola; with the castle and commune of Melzo with the attached rights and appurtenances; the place, the parish, and the land of Gorgonzola with all its present and future inhabitants. Within two months of her relationship with the Duke, she became the richest woman in Milan. In the following weeks, other lands including several possessions in the territory of Vigevano, the fiefs of Desio and Marliano, and the land that is dependent on the Castello di Vigevano, were added to her already vast properties. Never a day went by without the Duke spending large or small on Lucia Marliani; fabrics, clothing, jewellery, artwork, always of great quality and value, very often of immense value. In two years, she accumulated more than 110 properties and fiefs and was regarded as the 'richest woman in England and Italy.' But, this was not all. Apart from receiving the title of Countess of Melzo from the Duke, he granted her and their future children the right to bear the royal surname of Visconti. The Duke not only rewarded Lucia with a royal Milanese surname, but he also officially recognised that her father's family, the Marliani, was an old and trusted noble family of the District of Martesana and the Duchy of Milan.

Lucia was born in 1455, the daughter of Peter Marliani from Melzo and Catherine from Angera, a small village that borders Lake Como. The Marliani ancestors stemmed from Brianza in 1033 and later migrated to Milan. They were long lived at the East Gate nearby the Melzi family before some of them were appointed by Milanese officials as consuls of merchants and justices for the Visconti and Sforza families. They were once assigned as captains and defenders of the fief of Melzo. Five years before her birth, her grandfather was the Mayor of Melzo, and six years after his death, she married Ambrose Raverti who was from another well known merchant family from the Martesana district. The Duke was rewarding her with the wealth that he felt that the Marliani family deserved for their long and faithful service to Milan and the Melzo region. She was also rewarded with the implantation of the Duke's seed and the birth of their two boys, the elder - Galeazzo Visconti-Sforza, Count of Melzo, born on 17th April 1476, and the younger - Octavian Visconti-Sforza, born after the Duke's murder, and who later in life would be appointed as the Bishop of Lodi by Pope Julius II. As an investiture of their new family, the Duke drew up a new emblem stating that *'it be represented as a golden hill or yellow circle with the words Lucia Visconti, Countess of Melzo and Gorgonzola, and a shield in a circle divided into two parts, one the snake of the Visconti symbol and the other two small doves in the blue sky as a symbol of their love and tenderness for each other.'* His two sons by Lucia were also granted the Sforza surname. Lucia knew from day one that her husband Ambrose had sold her to the Duke, and she accepted it gracefully and without complaint. The Duke always called her 'Contessa' and never failed to prove his great love by showering her with gifts, even though she knew that he continued to have affairs with other women, and she knew nothing could be done to stop him.

And then, it ended suddenly and brutally. Galeazzo Maria Sforza was murdered in Milan in the church of Santo Stefano on the evening of December 26, 1476. Fourteen wounds were counted on his corpse. He was quickly transported from the church to the Cathedral where a funeral and mass were held for him on the same night. Before the sun rose and the cocks crowed the next day, he was taken away and buried somewhere unmarked. We now know that Lucia Marliani, Countess of Melzo, took the body of the Duke with the permission of the consort Duchess Bona of Savoy and without the knowledge of Galeazzo's brothers, and buried him secretly at the Church of St. Andrew in Melzo.

And now that the Galeazzo's brother Ludovico was the elected Governor of Milan, he wanted to strip the Countess of Melzo of all of her entitlements. And so, the committee of redistribution was formed to retake and redistribute her properties. My great grandfather was part of the commission to investigate her current wealth and standing with the communities and the militia representatives in her newly acquired fiefdoms.

The Duke Galeazzo was so much in love with Lucia that he wanted her to rule over her fiefdoms of Melzo and Gorgonzola independently of the Duchy of Milan. So, he decreed the *'priviegium feudal'* and had it written into the laws of his Duchy, *'these places they belong in one body with pure and mixed powers both in civil and criminal cases, separate and free from any obligation of obedience to the city and the Duchy of Milan,'* giving Lucia a state within a state with a power and a degree of autonomy not seen before in the Duchy of Milan. This was totally intolerable – even sacrilegious – to Ludovico, so this was the first extraordinary change that he insisted on as the new Governor of Milan.

It was the Melzi's responsibility to investigate the flaws in the Countess Melzo's documents and draw up the legal and strategic arguments for Governor Ludovico to confiscate the independent fiefdom's of Melzo and Gorgonzola from the Countess Lucia Marliani–Visconti, mother of the Duke Galeazzo's sons Galeazzo and Octavian Visconti-Sforza, and the Countess of the independent fiefs of Melzo and Gorgonzola.

When my father accompanied his grandfather, and he first met with the Countess of Melzo to discuss these matters of ownership and fiefs, he, like many before him, was immediately struck by her good looks, bearing, wisdom, and charm. She had already anticipated trouble from Ludovico Sforza about her wealth and properties and calmly organised copies of her rightful entitlements that she presented to my great grandfather. She sat naturally with her husband, secretary, and various visitors with a dignified poise as if she was the Duchess of Milan herself. She talked about her two sons who she had issued with the assassinated Duke and about her new children who she produced with her husband Ambrose Raverti because after the death of the Duke, he again was allowed to procreate with her, his wife. My father studied her noble bearing, her long fair hair, and flawless face, and he thought that she would make a lovely model for one of Leonardo's madonnas or saints. He knew that she had hoped that she wouldn't lose too many of her properties, but according to him it was better for the running of the Duchy if Ludovico succeeded and had all her properties confiscated and redistributed. She guessed that this would happen to her because even before my great grandfather had mentioned his intention to purchase the Duke's old disused castle beside the river Adda in Vaprio, she asked, 'I suppose you have big plans for the River Adda and our canal systems, Count Melzi?'

'Yes, Countessa. We have plans for the improvement of fortifications and better transportation along the Adda River and for expanding our canals between the Adda River and Milan.'

'My husband and I would surely like to help you in your plans for we know that new developments are needed to better our Duchy and the young Duke Gian,' she replied demurely.

My father and great grandfather both knew that her interest in the canals would be seen as trouble by Ludovico and that he would never allow her to side with Bona of Savoy nor influence the young Duke Gian in any decision making in the matters of state commerce or fortifications. There was a naivety in her that Ludovico would soon exploit, and consequently, take away many of her privileges.

Lucia held the fiefs of Melzo and Gorgonzola for four years by the time Ludovico IL Moro had made the countess sign them over to him and to the young Duke Gian Galeazzo on the 1st of February 1481. He also insisted that he be made guardian of her two Visconti-Sforza boys Galeazzo and Octavian to which she relented. However, she legally retained the right to call herself and her children born with the Duke Galeazzo's seed as Visconti-Sforza. In addition, Ludovico assigned to her a large dowry and the castle of Cusago in a commune 11 km west of Milan. Years later, on the 21st of January 1487, by the will of the young Duke Gian Galeazzo Sforza, now 18 years of age, his uncle and guardian Ludovico returned the estates of Melzo Marliano to her two Visconti-Sforza sons Galeazzo and Octavian who held on to the fiefdoms until 1500 when the Duchy fell into French hands and Ludovico was forced out of Milan.

The Countess Melzo had a long and remarkable life, and she died as Lucia de Reverti, aged 70 years, in her home in New Port, the parish of St. Bartholomew in Milan on December 15, 1522, of dropsy on the judgment of her physician Francesco Tatti. Although she wished to be buried at the Santa Chiara nunnery beside the Naviglio Martesana, she was buried instead at S. Pietro in Gessate in the chapel of San Michele owned by the family of her husband. Some say her daughters later moved her to the Santa Chiara and buried her in the nun's habit.

After the assassination of the Duke Galeazzo Maria Sforza, Lucia renounced many of her vast possessions and endless privileges, and she returned to her husband Ambrosio Raverta. She bore him four children, became a competent administrator of his goods, and she accepted Ludovico Sforza's new rules without questioning them, without complaining, without rebelling or demanding compensation for her lost privileges. For, as my father often said, 'she was fair and very wise and virtuous and would have made a wonderful Duchess of Milan if fortune or fate had allowed her such a possibility.'

Although the Duke Galeazzo Maria Sforza possessed many women, more than two or three hundred by some counts, Lucia de Raverti was his greatest love. She was his lover and Countess of Melzo and Gorgonzola for two years, and she outlived him by 46 years. The writer Bernardino Corio wrote this of the Duke: *'This prince was very dedicated to Venus and filthy lust, for which reason he greatly harassed his subjects, he kept a lot of women and, even worse, when he was satisfied with his appetites, he abandoned the unfortunate to his courtiers to dispose of them as they wished.'* Yet, she survived his lusts with great dignity and honour.

His wife the Duchess of Savoy wrote this of her Duke to her confessor, *'in vice of carnality, simony and notorious scandalous and various other innumerable sins for which he must pay is there a possibility that his soul has found at least a place in Purgatory instead of Hell.'* And the Duke said of himself: *'I have only the sin of luxuria, throughout perfection that I have used in all those ways and forms that can be done.'* Yet, he loved Lucia with a passion and tenderness fit for a romantic, poetic novel that is still waiting to be written by some great Milanese poet, somebody like my own deceased uncle Bartolomeo, Provost of Pontirolo, who died in 1489, a great admirer of their love affair.

Lucia and her husband lived on and off for a number of years in the Castle Cusago that was gifted to her by Ludovico Sforza. Later on, she and her husband and their children lived in a few different houses that they rented in the residential blocks southeast of the Sforza castle and immediately north of the Cathedral. Various luminaries and their friends resided in these areas including Beatrice d' Este, the widow of Tristan Sforza who my great grandfather had accompanied to France for his half-brother's proxy marriage to Bona of Savoy. Others living there were Filippo Maria Visconti, Maria Ghilini, Alosio Cagnola Lampugnani, and Prospero. Despite her scandalous affair with Duke Galeazzo and her humiliation of the Duchess of Savoy, Lucia Marliani was accepted and well established within the Milanese noble society, the Ghibelline faith, and the church of St. Ambrosio. Her uncle Michael was bishop of Tortona, her son Octavian had become Bishop of Lodi with the help of Ludovico Sforza, her nephew Fabrizio Marliani was bishop of Piacenza, and two of her daughters had become nuns, and she, herself, was very religious.

Leonardo da Vinci became a friend of Lucia de Reverti years later when she settled in her new house at Porta Nuova just northeast and within walking distance of the Sforza Castle. She had developed an eye for fine art and often invited Leonardo and his painting assistants to give her lessons about the history and value of art. Although they often offered to paint or sketch her portrait, she declined politely saying that she preferred not to see herself in her later years as a reminder of her lost youth. Yet, she did sit for some portraits and sketches, including on some occasions for Leonardo. But, I know of only two public displays of her image, one in the votive fresco at the Church Santa Maria delle Grazie (the church of the Gracious St. Mary) and the other, a medallion, in the courtyard of the Reverti villa in Inzago.

The votive fresco of Lucia and her Reverti family is in Lord Galeazzo Sforza's ducal chapel. It shows the intervention and dedication to St. Mary full of Grace who is dressed in black and white attire, in the favourite colours of the Duke Galeazzo Sforza. St. Mary stands in front of a background blazing with golden leaf foil that symbolically shows off Lucia's connection to Duke Galeazzo. St. Mary prays with devotion and blesses her infant boy Jesus lying on a blanket of gold leaf. One scurrilous interpretation I have heard is that the infant is not Jesus, but it is Lucia's baby given to her through the miraculous intervention of Saint Ambrose. The Reverti family is painted in profile, kneeling in the foreground, below and on either side of St. Mary. To the right of St. Mary, Lucia's husband Ambrosio Reverti and his two sons are dressed in black and kneel in prayer. Saint Ambrose in his red robes stands behind Ambrosio Reverti and introduces him to his wife and daughter. To the left of St. Mary, Lucia is kneeling in prayer and looking directly at her husband and not up towards St. Mary. She wears the rich crimson of the ducal court ladies. Her daughter in a fine red dress kneels in prayer in front of her mother looking towards her father and brothers. Standing behind Lucia is St. Lucia dressed in red and covered with a dark blue cloak. Lucia Marliani de Reverti is housewifely and devoted. She is on her knees facing towards the Christ-child and her two sons and her husband. Contrary to expectations, she is not painted as the beautiful, graceful blond who the Duke had fallen in love with. Instead, we see her in the votive fresco as a big blond woman with a typical Lombardi frown. This is probably the image that Lucia wanted to leave of herself in 1493, namely, that of a devout mother during a less dangerous time with her legal husband Ambrosio Reverti; but still remembered as the former very special lover of the Duke who had ruled the Duchy of Milan during the more splendid and yet dangerous times for her and her family.

Lucia Marliani has portrayed herself with her husband and legitimate children and with Madonna silhouetted against a golden background studded by a radiant ducal glow, such as she so often saw at the Castello Sforzesco where her duke Galeazzo Maria had worn the same black and white colours as the Madonna in the image. The memory and dedication is clear, and it is accepted by the Sforza court, the ducal secretariats, and the *observanti* residential Dominicans of the Church Santa Maria delle Grazie where Leonardo's painting of the *Last Supper* also resides. Lucia would not tell us who designed and painted the fresco, but Leonardo recognised the hand of Vincenzo Foppa among others, suggesting an input from only a few insiders.

Fig. 20. Madonna with Child, St. Ambrogio, St. Lucia, Ambrogio Raverti, Lucia Marliani, and Family *at Santa Maria delle Grazie.*

When the French ruled Milan after 1500, Lucia became a secret agent for the French king Louis XII the duke of Amboise in the purchase of Italian paintings, jewellery, and art objects. Unknown to Ludovico, she had kept many of the riches that the Duke Galeazzo had gifted her and that had not been officially registered in the Milanese fiscal records. My mother Tommasina della Torre also became good friends with Lucia, and she and I often visited her to socialise and catch-up on the latest gossip. She was always gracious and kind, and I became good friends with her children. Although her Visconti-Sforza boys were at least 14 years older than me, they were always polite and hospitable towards me, and I admired her son Octavian who became the Bishop of Lodi.

In 1522, a few years after Lucia de Reverti's death, I gave a few sketches and paintings of Lucia Marliani to one of Leonardo's previous students to construct a medallion of her in the courtyard of the Reverti family villa in Inzago. Those who knew her well have told me that it is a very good likeness, showing off her famous long blond hair with its beautiful copper hues.

The Sforza Court and de' Predis Brother Artists: Art and Patronage

Although Leonardo considered himself to be a successful Florentine diplomat, he was also a mercenary for the arts and engineering. He asked his sponsor the Melzi family to explain to him how patronage worked in Milan for he knew that each city and state in Italy had their own particular mores and quirks in regard to sponsorship. He needed reliable contacts and sponsors, and so he enquired politely about the required rituals to obtain commissions especially from the Sforza court. The Melzi pointed out to Leonardo that although the Sforza commissions brought prestige, the artists in Milan would not prosper until they were integrated into the wider economic and social networks. Painters and sculptors could not afford to rely on a single patron like the Sforza because the dukes and duchesses rarely paid their artists. Moreover, the Sforzas were notorious for their cost cutting and not employing their artists and engineers on a permanent basis. And even if the duke promised patronage, it was a hierarchy of courtiers and bureaucrats who dispersed payments and privileges. For patronage from the Sforza court, you needed the support of the signoria and the administrative council for success. In addition, the day-to-day control over the Sforza commissions lay in the hands of supervisors of ducal works. In 1478, with the death of Bartolomeo Gadio, the supervisor's position passed on to his assistant Ambrogio Ferrari who had multiple responsibilities, ranging from the maintenance of fortifications and weaponry to choosing a painter for a chapel's icons and polyptychs.

Of course, the Melzi were willing to help Leonardo to find the appropriate patrons and networks that would allow him to prosper in Milan if he wished to stay on. They told him that it would be best if he began by joining a guild or a well established and respected artist's workshop. A few names like the Florentine architect and engineer Bramante, and painters like the Zavattari brothers and Giacomo Vismara were bandied about until they chose the de' Predis brothers for first introductions because they already had firm connections with the ducal household and with the Milanese mercantile community.

The de' Predis seemed a good choice for Leonardo for they knew of his painting and architectural skills, and they were enthusiastic for him to join their workshop. The six de' Predis brothers had a good oeuvre of artwork behind them and a strong reputation as excellent portraitists, miniaturists, and manuscript illuminators. They belonged to a number of powerful guilds, they had good connections with the Sforza family, and they had conveniently located workshops for Leonardo to access, as he wanted. Moreover, Giovanni and Gerolamo Melzi recommended the Predis clan as reputable, peaceful, honest, and hardworking artists and businessmen. Giovanni Melzi was a committee member of the Confraternity of the Immaculate Conception at the Church of San Francesco Grande, and he knew that a commission was in the offing from them for a chapel altarpiece for the San Francesco Church in Vercellina. Leonardo met with the de' Predis brothers and he liked them, and it was established that he would collaborate with them once he was more settled in Milan. But first, he had to return to Florence for a year or two to fulfil a proposed contract that he had with the Augustinian monks of San Donato a Scopeto to prepare an altarpiece of the *Madonna and Child* for their chapel.

New Coins and Coat-of-Arms for the Sixth Duke of Milan, Gian Galeazzo Sforza

Early in the first month of the new year of 1481, the young duke Gian Galeazzo Sforza invited Leonardo da Vinci and the engraver Cristoforo Foppo to his reception room at the Sforza castle for suggestions and discussion about the design and the minting of a new gold coin and a silver testone that would feature only his head and coat of arms as the 6th Duke of Milan and not incorporate that of Ludovico Sforza as the Regent and governor of Milan. At first, Ludovico protested strenuously against this suggestion by the boy, but finally relented on good advice from his councillors. They told him that if he refused the young duke's request or protested too strongly he might be seen as attempting to usurp his nephew's inherited title, which would quickly destabilise his own rule as governor of Milan. Ludovico was already viewed with suspicion for having exiled the young duke's mother against her and her son's best interests. They told him that the coins would still have the engraved words *LV • PATRVO • GVBNANTE* (*Ludovicus Patruo Gubnante*; '*Ludovico, governing uncle*'). Ludovico had no choice, but to accede to the young duke's request.

Gian Galeazzo Sforza asked Leonardo to help him design his coat-of-arms using the symbols that he had inherited from his father the 5th duke of Milan, Galeazzo Maria Sforza. The inherited symbols were the coat of arms of the House of Visconti (an azure serpent in the act of swallowing a red Saracen child), the coat of arms of the House of Sforza (a crowned eagle in the first and fourth quarters and a Biscione in the second and third of an escutcheon), the ducal chain of interlocking golden rings tethered to a helmet, burning branches with two buckets hanging from them, a fertile conifer tree full of acorns, a white dog chained to the trunk of the conifer, a rider's crop, Borromean rings (three interlocking rings), and a cheesecloth filter bag. While the symbolic colour of the chest armour of Francesco Sforza and Ludovico Sforza was blue, Leonardo suggested that Gian Galeazzo should adopt the colours of red, green, and gold with green chest armour highlighted against a complementary red background. He also suggested that the white dog should be a symbol of freedom and liberty, and therefore, the dog should be unclasped from the collar still tied to the tree. This was an old idea probably first introduced in Lombardy for the Lord Bernabo Visconti during his reign of 1354 to 1385. His motto was 'do not tease the sleeping dog', in other words, 'no impunity for an attack on peace.'

Gian Galeazzo Maria Sforza welcomed these suggestions enthusiastically, and wanted most of them incorporated immediately into his Sphaera and allegory of the Sforza family's coat of arms. He especially loved his hunting dogs, and so the idea of the unclasped collar at the feet of a greyhound was his favourite.

Fig. 21. Allegory of Gian Galeazzo Sforza's coat of arms.

Most of Gian Galeazzo Sforza's coins from 1480 to 1494 were issued with his portrait and inscription on one side and that of Ludovico Maria Sforza as his governing uncle on the other side. The only coins issued in Gian Galeazzo Sforza's name alone were the gold double ducat and a small trillina engraved by Cristoforo Foppo and Leonardo and minted in 1481 when Leonardo was back in Florence. The gold double ducat is a beautifully engraved and a rare issue. On one side of the coin, the young duke wears a berretto with his long hair resting on his armoured shoulders. The inscription bordering his portrait is *IO • GZ • M • SF • VICECOS • DVX • MLI • SXT*. This translates to *Gian (IO) Galeazzo (GZ) Maria (M) Sforza (SF), Sixth (VI) Duke*

(DVX) of Milan (MLI). The reverse shows his coat of arms surmounted by crowned and crested helmets, a dragon-like Biscione on the left and a dragon with a bearded, human head on the right facing each other. The inscription is + *PP • ANGLE • Q3 • COS • 7C* that translates to *Count of Pavia (PP) and Angera south of Lake Maggiore (ANGLE).*

Fig. 22. Gold Double Ducat of Gian Galeazzo Sforza, the 6th duke of Milan, issued in 1481.

Departing Instructions and Lasting Impressions

Leonardo was well looked after by the Melzi family, especially by my father Gerolamo who was eight years younger, but had become his close friend. They had much to do in their time together as canal and fortification engineers in Milan city and the outlying regions. By mid summer, Leonardo had made no headway with convincing the Governor Ludovico Sforza to assist Florence and Lorenzo in their struggles against the Pope. He conveyed his forlorn message to Lorenzo in Florence who responded with a message for Leonardo to keep on trying.

A few days before leaving Milan to return to Florence, Ludovico summonsed Leonardo to provide him with his letters for Lorenzo outlining his views of the current political situation in Italy and what his political relationship was with Lorenzo and the Republic of Florence. Basically, he told Leonardo that he was a friend and ally of Lorenzo, and that he would provide him with the best support that he could, but that Lord Lorenzo should realise that the situation in Milan was not fully stable, and that he could not spare many troops or horses at this stage of his governorship. However, he would continue to diplomatically support Florence in its stance against any invasion by the Papal States, the Republic of Venice, the Kingdom of Naples or any other forces. He also provided Leonardo with gifts to pass on to his Lord Lorenzo de' Medici. Ludovico told Leonardo that he was welcome in Milan at any time that he wished to return, and that he, as the Governor of Milan, would assist him to find sponsorships in painting and engineering projects. And so, in March 1481, Leonardo bid farewell to Milan, and he and his servant Tommaso Masini returned to Florence.

What were Leonardo's overall impressions of Ludovico Moro Sforza when he left Milan for Florence? In 1481, Leonardo and Ludovico were both 29 years of age with Leonardo only a few months older. They saw eye to eye on many things aesthetically as dictated by the fashion expectations of the day. They both cared about their appearance and their own and other people's courtly manners. Ludovico was named *Lodovicus Maurus* (Moro), but had become better know by his nickname *Il Moro* because of his dark-eyes, long black hair, bushy eyebrows, and large swarthy face. He liked and encouraged the use of his nickname for he realised his name and appearance were unique and stood him out from the many. It was his badge of honour and his connection with the people. The black mulberry-tree and the Moor's head were his emblems, and he humorously encouraged his poets, painters, and courtiers to invent puns and devise artistic themes on the subject of Moors and Moorish proclivities. And, he was very pleasant in manner and gracious in speech, always gentle and courteous to others, ready to listen and never losing his temper in arguments. He displayed a fondness and respect for his nephew the young duke of Milan, Gian Galeazzo Sforza. And like Leonardo, he was of keen intellect with a discerning eye and fine taste and an appreciation for all forms of beauty.

Ludovico was taller and broader than Leonardo and strangely physically handsome in his own rugged way. In comparison, Leonardo had longer, wavy, lank hair, a handsome regular shaped face, a straight Greek nose, and a dimpled chin covered with a sparse beard. His beautiful, wide set eyes were hazel in colour, and they changed sometimes from an emerald green to dark brown in varying light. I don't know how Leonardo could change his eye colour at will, but I know that he could do so depending with whom he spent his time. He had a strong, lean, masculine build, not too thin and not too fat, and moved with great elegance. He was always extremely careful with his diet throughout his life and never became obese. He had impressed Ludovico enormously, and Ludovico wanted him back in Milan. Leonardo saw opportunities of sponsorship from the Sforza, and so at this time, he had no bad words or thoughts about Ludovico, despite his misgivings about the new Governor's treatment of Cicco Simonetta and Bona of Savoy.

In summary, I note the following dates and events during Leonardo's first visit to the Duchy of Milan:

April 1480. Leonardo da Vinci visited Milan on a diplomatic mission for Lorenzo de' Medici and the Republic of Florence.

May 1480. Leonardo presented Lord Lorenzo de' Medici's gift of a *lira da braccio* (violin) to his godson Gian Galeazzo Sforza, the Duke of Milan.

June 1480. The Melzi purchased the Sforza fort in Vaprio d'Adda, and Leonardo visited the site to plan renovations and improvements.

July 1480. Leonardo inspected the properties of the Countess of Melzo in Melzo and Gorgonzola for the Melzi clan and Ludovico Sforza.

July 1480. Leonardo taught the young Duke Gian Galeazzo the art of playing the violin.

August 1480. Leonardo joined the workshop of the de' Predis brothers.

October 7, 1480. Bona of Savoy's favourite Antonio Tassino and his father Gabriele were exiled from Milan.

October 30, 1480. Cicco Simonetta the previous Governor of the Duchy of Milan was beheaded.

November 2, 1480. Bona of Savoy was exiled to Abbiategrasso.

December 1480. Ludovico Moro Sforza was voted full Regent and guardian of Gian Galeazzo Sforza.

January 1481. Leonardo helped to design a new gold coin and testone for Gian Galeazzo Sforza, the 6th duke of Milan, with his portrait and his coat of arms.

February 1, 1481. Lucia Marliani-Visconti returned to Ludovico Sforza the fiefs of Melzo and Gorgonzola that had been bestowed to her by his brother, the 5th Duke of Milan.

❋

CHAPTER 6

Back in Florence, 1481

Every evil leaves behind a grief in our memory, except the supreme evil, that is death, which destroys this memory together with life.

— Leonardo da Vinci

March 1481. A Time to Paint and Reassess

When Leonardo returned to Florence in March of 1481, he immediately met with Lorenzo de' Medici to express the support sent to him by Ludovico Sforza and by the young duke of Milan Gian Galeazzo Sforza to assure his safety against Sixtus IV and the powers of the Holy See. Leonardo reminded Lorenzo that Ludovico was still building up his support and power base in Milan after he had exiled Bona of Savoy and hanged Cicco Simonetti for withholding his fortune in a Florentine bank. Ludovico also held his nephew the young duke of Milan in his strong grip of guardianship allowing him no leeway or privileges to rule. All of the young duke's decisions had to be discussed with and ratified by Ludovico and his councillors.

Lorenzo de' Medici confided in Leonardo about his past troubles, and he vowed to use his power and wealth better than before. He would do so through alliances, allegiances, and the art of diplomacy. He would do this with the help of Rome and the Papacy, Milan and the duchy, and France and its kingdoms. He lectured Leonardo on the strictures of diplomacy and warned him to heed his lessons well on homage, fealty, obedience, and loyalty. Leonardo enjoyed Lorenzo's lessons about the French and diplomacy, but the rest about homage, fealty, loyalty, and faithfulness, he had already learnt much of this from the church and its ministry, and he accepted it as a political reality for himself and his own survival.

The two years of war between Rome and Florence following the Pazzi Conspiracy, coupled with the decline of the Medici bank in 1479 and 1480, meant that Lorenzo's dealings with the Papacy and Rome had to change course. Throughout the war, the branch of the Medici bank in Rome was closed. Worse still, in 1478, the branches of the Medici bank in Apulia, Milan, Flanders, and London had closed down with huge losses due to the mismanagement of Tommaso Portinari who did more harm to Lorenzo than even Pope Sixtus IV. Consequently, to rebuild the Medici fortunes, Lorenzo decided to use more judicious political manoeuvring such as marriage alliances with the papal families, first with Sixtus IV and then Innocent VIII who reigned from 1484 to 1492. To patch up the relationship between Florence and Rome, Lorenzo de' Medici agreed to fulfil his promise to Sixtus IV and send a group of Florentine painters to Rome to decorate the walls of the Sistine Chapel. Four months after Leonardo's arrival back to Florence, Lorenzo sent Sandro Botticelli, Domenico Ghirlandaio, and Cosimo Rosselli to join Perugino in Rome to paint frescoes and restore diplomatic links between the two states. He told Leonardo that he was not suited to the destructive politics of Rome, and it was better for him to stay in Florence, finish his art commission with the Augustinian monks, and then return to Milan where he would better serve Florence and the House of Medici by orchestrating the patronage of Ludovico Sforza and the young duke of Milan Gian Galeazzo Sforza. This diplomatic mission back to Milan would be as important as any papal marriage alliance or diplomatic activity to decorate the Sistine Chapel in Rome. It was, *'to aid the City of Florence and the House of Medici'* and *'you must serve the vital link.'* In the meantime, Leonardo was invited to stay at the Medici residence in Florence and to assist a group of artists with some commissions on decorating Lorenzo's country residence in Cafaggiolo. Leonardo thanked his Lord Lorenzo for the opportunity to stay in his residence, and he explained that he first needed to complete his commissioned altarpiece for the Augustinian monks of San Donato a Scopeto at their abbey located below the hill of Bellosguardo outside the Porta Roma and the walls of the city. While in the meditative rooms of the monastery, Leonardo wanted to carefully assess his standing and future in Florence.

Leonardo's Unfinished Masterpiece: The *Adoration of the Magi*

The contract that Leonardo da Vinci signed with the Augustinian friars of San Donato a Scopeto was to finish an altarpiece of the *Adoration of the Magi* in twenty-four months or at most thirty months. He already had his vision for the painting. He would paint the *Adoration of the Magi* like nobody had ever seen before. The friars initially asked Sandro Botticelli to provide them with the painting, but because he was scheduled to visit Rome and decorate the Sistine chapel, Leonardo da Vinci was recommended in his place. Leonardo had seen Sandro Botticelli's *Adoration of the Magi* painted for a banker connected to the House of Medici, and he wanted to outdo him. He would extend Sandro Botticelli's themes in the painting and even shock him with his design and subtle changes in theme. The banker Gaspare di Zanobi del Lama commissioned Botticelli's painting for his chapel in the church of Santa Maria Novella, and it featured him and several members of the Medici Family as worshippers within the gathering. Madonna and Child are elevated within the centre of the painting. The Madonna is no other than Simonetta Vespucci. Below them are the three kings, Cosimo de' Medici (the Magus kneeling in front of the Virgin, his sons Piero (the second Magus kneeling in the centre with the red mantle) and Giovanni (the third Magus), and his grandsons Giuliano and Lorenzo. The picture was painted by Botticelli in 1476 at a time when Lorenzo already ruled Florence and when the other three Medici who are portrayed as Magi were no longer alive. The banker del Lama who commissioned the painting is portrayed as the old man on the right with white hair and a light blue robe looking and pointing out at us, the observers. Two versions of Botticelli himself at age 31 years are visible in the painting, once as the blond man with the golden/yellow mantle on the far right and the other as the dark haired man in the violet mantle on the far left. Both are looking out at the viewer. He also painted a handsome 24-year-old Leonardo da Vinci in profile in a brown cap and a red and dark blue wrap leaning forward behind the imperious painter Domenico Ghirlandaio in his silver/blue wrap with gold trimmings, and the Magus Cosimo de' Medici kneeling before the Virgin. Leonardo and Sandro were very good friends during the period of this painting and apart from sharing a love of painting, they enjoyed to prepare and serve food and drink, and consequently, they managed a tavern/restaurant called the Tavern of the Three Snails that was located by the Ponte Vecchio beside the thriving butcher shops. Botticelli honoured Leonardo as his business partner by including him in his painting.

Giorgio Vasari in his *Lives* describes Botticelli's *Adoration* in the following way:

> The beauty of the heads in this scene is indescribable, their attitudes all different, some full-face, some in profile, some three-quarters, some bent down, and in various other ways, while the expressions of the attendants, both young and old, are greatly varied, displaying the artist's perfect mastery of his profession. Sandro further clearly shows the distinction between the suites of each of the kings. It is a marvellous work in colour, design, and composition.

Apart from the three kneeling Magi in Botticelli's painting, there are 12 attendants to the left and 15 to the right of the Virgin, all standing, but well below her elevated position. In addition, there are two horses to the far left, one white and one brown. The painting is tempera on panel (111 cm x 134 cm) and it shows great attention to detail, such as the rendering of the garments. Also, Botticelli at this point of his career was heavily influenced by the paintings of Rogier van der Weyden from the Flemish school. This painting greatly influenced Leonardo for he thought it to be a masterpiece.

Fig. 23. Sandro Botticello's Adoration.

Admiring Botticelli's painting, Leonardo would take some elements from it, but he would do it in a different and radical way. He placed the Madonna's head into the centre of his design and he introduced his new painting technique of *sfumato* to create a monochromatic effect, He decided that the Holy Family would be portrayed in the central lower half of the picture, yet totally surrounded by a similar number of characters on either side of them and behind them. The two horses would be included, but this time with riders. The Virgin Mary and Child would be depicted in the foreground and form a triangular shape with the Medici Magi kneeling in adoration before them. The Magi would represent the three different ages of man: youth, maturity, and old age.

So, what else did Leonardo add to his *Adoration*? Perhaps, place a palm tree in the centre and to the right of the Virgin and Child and let it stretch up to heaven for the Virgin Mary is as 'stately as a palm tree.' Moreover, a palm tree symbolises victory today as it did for ancient Rome, or Christian martyrdom, triumph over death or triumph in general. Paint in a few carob trees to suggest Christ is the King of Kings and the Virgin Mary is the future Queen of Heaven. Add a few more horses in the background, at least four with riders in amazingly ferocious battle scenes. Remind the world that while we worship the Virgin and her Infant, the church and papacy wage a pagan-like war against Lorenzo de' Medici and the Florentine people. In the background on the left, paint in the ruin of a Florentine or Roman building where workmen, soldiers, and horsemen fight in a battle scene. Place yourself at the far right as a young shepherd boy looking away from the Virgin and Child and Pope Sixtus IV. Place the artists Sandro Botticelli, Domenico Ghirlandaio, and Cosimo Rosselli to the left and right looking glumly at the bareheaded Sixtus IV grovelling with the golden chalice in his hand; he who has demanded their presence in Rome to decorate his apartments and the Sistine Chapel. Model the Madonna on his and Botticelli's great love Simonetta Vespucci who had died only a few years before.

Leonardo's painting would be twice as large as Sandro Botticelli's. It would measure 246 cm by 243 cm on ten slabs of timber glued together. He painted the wood with a white lead primer and began to sketch out the underdrawings using black ink. He never started to paint on the white lead because when the Augustinian friars saw his drawings on the wood they were horrified by the unconventional images. To see the horsemen fighting and with the surrounding crowd looking like vultures around baby Jesus was far too much for the tolerant faithful monks of Jesus. Somebody recognised the depiction of the authoritarian Pope Sixtus IV in the foreground and told Leonardo that they could not have something so irreverent in their chapel because they would all be charged with sacrilege and heresy.

'*You are irreverent, Leonardo. Do not cross the border of decency and orthodoxy,*' they warned him. Indeed, many of Leonardo's unfinished works were irreverent against various systems of orthodoxy.

The Augustinian friars paid Leonardo for five months work and then withdrew his commission. They told him it was unsuitable for the San Donato a Scopeto. He started his painting in March, and he received payment each month until his last in September 1481. Whatever changes he suggested to appease them, it was now far too late, and the friars rejected them outright because of the sensational scenario that they had already seen. Fully expecting a traditional interpretation including the three wise men with haloes, oxen, donkey, stable, and St. Joseph, they were instead given a maelstrom of unrelated, half-emaciated figures surrounding the Christ-Child without his halo, as well as a full blown battle scene in the rear of the picture. It was an outrage to their highly tempered mendicant sensibilities. They chose instead to pay off Leonardo and let him sell his abomination elsewhere. They then commissioned Filippino Lippi, a previous student and apprentice of Sandro Botticelli, to paint a more acceptable version of the *Adoration of the Magi* that he completed for them in 1496. Domenico Ghirlandaio, expanding upon Leonardo's theme, completed a separate painting in 1488. Leonardo saw both and thought they were interesting and well executed, but not to the same level of excellence that he expected of his own painting if it had been completed.

Fig. 25. Adoration *by Domenico Ghirlandaio, 1488 (left) and Filippino Lippi, 1496 (right).*

Leonardo left his unfinished painting with his friend Giovanni de' Benci who sold it to the Medici family a few years later. Giovanni paid Leonardo a few ducats and a barrel of red wine and that was the last that Leonardo saw of it. Did he regret not finishing it? Yes, he did. Would he have changed the sensational scenes? No, because for the viewer that was what added to its psychological impact and historical interest.

A few years ago, I visited the Medici family in Florence to look at Leonardo's unfinished painting of the *Adoration of the Magi* with an aim of purchasing it and possibly attempting to finish it because Leonardo had told me what colour pigments he would have liked to use. To my horror somebody already had painted over it in an attempt to make it more 'valuable'. This new paint over was done in dull yellow and browns, and the dubious redrawing resulted in alterations of inferior quality to Leonardo's original design and use of the wooden panels. They had covered over his stable and animals including a donkey, oxen, and a baby elephant intended to further animate the scene with novelty, and some faces were blurred beyond recognition. I decided not to buy it nor restore it. Instead, I left it with the family's curators to let them contemplate about its true value and what damage they had already done to it for they had other agents expressing an interest in this unfinished painting at least as a historic artefact of Leonardo da Vinci, the Florentine master painter.

Leonardo was now at a loose end again. He had expected to be working on his painting at least for a full year and into the middle of 1483. Instead, it was September 1481 and his commission was terminated after only six months of work. This was not good for his reputation as a painter. It would be difficult to receive further commissions in Florence if this kind of bad luck continued.

Farewell to the da Vinci Clan and Remembrances Past

By the end of 1481, Leonardo closed down his studio. Lorenzo di Credi now ran Verrocchio's studio in Florence because Verrocchio had moved to Venice to start a new workshop and work on a commission to build an equestrian statue of Bartolomeo Colleoni. Leonardo had assisted Verrocchio to design and build the initial award winning clay models that were now in Venice. After Verrocchio left Florence for Venice, Leonardo moved into the Medici palace and joined a group of academicians, poets, and writers known as the Neo-Platonic Academy of Medici. He was now a Master of Art and Medicine, and he belonged to the guild of Doctors and Apothecaries and the confraternity of St. Luke, the patron saint of artists. He continued to visit the mortuaries of Florence and the Hospital of Santa Maria Nuova to practice his art of anatomy and dissection. Although Leonardo was receiving some commissions from a few members of the seniority and the church, he was feeling more resentful that the Medici were ignoring his talents and interests in art, science, and engineering. His lordship Lorenzo de' Medici had sent him on the diplomatic mission to Milan, and while he enjoyed being a diplomatic agent to the Prince of Florence, it was commissions in painting and engineering that he now wanted.

In comparison to the struggles of Milan with the Sforzas in 1480 and 1481, Florence and the Medici family had found a tepid peace amongst themselves after the Pazzi Conspiracy. Yet, Leonardo was unsatisfied, and he was considering his options outside of Florence. And then more shock – the Black Watch were back again. One of his students in his studio was exiled from Florence after being accused by the Black Watch of committing the crime of moral turpitude. Leonardo was worried. He sensed the Black Watch was still after him. Somebody was still out to humiliate him or worse still, they wanted him imprisoned and out of the way for a substantial length of time. Should he return to Milan before his good name was to be sullied even further if he stayed on in Florence? He was much impressed by Milan's opportunities and their different outlook with art and religion and the possibilities that could be gained there. It now was more about what does the future hold for a modernista like him rather than about supporting and practicing the classicism and the orthodoxy that was becoming highly rooted in Florence. He was feeling stifled in Florence with its high conservatism and obsession with moral turpitude.

Now was a propitious time for Leonardo to leave Florence and to find his fame and fortune elsewhere even though Lord Lorenzo Medici was still a good friend and that his father Messer Piero Fruosino di Antonio da Vinci was doing well financially in Florence as a civil law notary and living with his third wife Margherita di Jacopo whom he had married in 1474. The Melzi were writing to him, enquiring about his return to Milan for they had work for him as an engineer and a painter, and the young Duke was missing his musical lessons on the violin. Also, they wanted him to help them set up an academy in Milan and Vaprio. After further contemplation, he weighed up his options and decided to say goodbye to his mother, uncle, and his father and his new family, and return to Milan.

He was obliged to farewell a large extended family in Florence and the village of Vinci, and he knew that it would be hard to make a permanent break from them for he enjoyed to visit one or other of them regularly. In Vinci, his birthplace, he had five godfathers, five godmothers, an uncle, a birthmother, and a stepfather and their five children to visit. He loved and respected them all. Most of all, he loved to spend time with uncle Francesco on his farm in Vinci. He often spent Christmas with them in Vinci and for another few days with his father's family in Florence before returning to live and work at Verrocchio's workshop.

Leonardo was born out of wedlock to Caterina, a well-educated Armenian girl who had been abducted from her parents in Antalya and sold as a slave to Venetian traders before she ended up working for his father at a farmhouse outside Vinci. The birth was at a farmhouse 3 km north of Vinci in the locality of Anchiano (an estate of Masetti of Farrale) at 10 o'clock at night. His grandfather Ser Antonio da Vinci recorded the event.

> A grandson was born to me, the son of my son Ser Perio, on the day of April 15, a Saturday, at the third hour of the night. He was named Leonardo. He was baptised by the Priest Piero di Bartolomeo da Vinci in the presence of Papino di Nanni Banti, Meo di Tonino, Piero di Malvolto, Nanni di Venzo, Arigho di Giovanni Tedescho, Monna Lisa di Domenicho di Brettone, Monna Antonia di Giuliono, Monna Niccholosa del Barna, Monna Maria, the daughter of Nanni di Venzo, Monna Pippa di Previchone. [S10]

His grandfather was a notary, and he took special care in preparing Leonardo's birth and baptism certificate. He wrote down all that he wanted officially known about the birth of his grandson. His purpose was to affirm Leonardo with a legitimacy of the baptism and the ten godparents of high standing in Vinci and the neighbouring regions. It was to assure that Leonardo was fully accepted into his family and into the community, and that he was legitimately and respectfully entitled to all the same benefits conferred on to him as onto any other member of the Antonio da Vinci family. He was to be known as Leonardo di Ser Piero da Vinci where Ser was his father's Magister's title, a special prefix attached to the names of notaries, and Piero was his father's Christian name.

Leonardo's mother's name is missing from his birth certificate as if she never existed. According to Leonardo's grandfather, her name was suppressed purposefully to protect her identity from a vindictive family in Florence. He did not want her real name to be recorded and spread about the community and in Florence from where she had run away. He said that Caterina was a runaway from a noble family, and that she had found shelter working in the Anchiano farmhouse of Leonardo's father. Soon after giving birth to Leonardo, she married Antonio (Achattabriga) di Piero Buti del Vacca, and they eventually had five children in a happy long lasting marriage. His stepfather was known as Achattabriga the fighter, and he was a kiln maker and potter at the furnace of the Monastery of San Pier Martire where he also ran a bakery that was managed by Leonardo's uncle Francesco. Achattabriga worked as a farmer on Francesco's farm that adjoined Leonardo's grandfather's estate and large house. Achattabriga and Caterina lived in the small farmhouse in Anchiano outside Vinci and within short walking distance of the Monastery of San Pier Martire. Leonardo lived with them until he was 5 years old before he moved in with his grandparents and uncle in their much grander house in Vinci.

His father Ser Piero di Antonio da Vinci lived in Florence, and he had married Albiera di Giovanni Amadori, a 16 year-old heiress from a wealthy Florentine family, the same year that Leonardo was born. Albiera was Leonardo's loving stepmother until her untimely death when he was only 12 years of age. She died in childbirth in 1464 to the great sorrow of Leonardo and his father for they both loved her greatly. The same year, his paternal grandfather Antonio di Ser Piero died in Vinci. A few years later, his father married Francesca di Ser Giuliano Lanfredini, and she died childless in 1473. His father took on his third wife Margherita di Jacopo in 1474 with whom he had six healthy children. Leonardo visited his father and his family as often as he could and occasionally sketched the babies and children. He was much loved by all of his stepmothers whom he called mother, even those who were much younger than he was.

Leonardo and his uncle Francesco loved each other dearly. Francesco and his wife Allexandra had no children, and they treated Leonardo as their own son, and as a boy, he spent a lot of time on their farm helping them to plant and tend to their mulberry trees, medicinal herbs, olive groves, and vines. Leonardo ran about the farm and explored the plants and animals at his leisure, always encouraged by his uncle and aunt. But now, he had come to say goodbye to them. He was leaving for Milan, and he did not know how long he would be away. It was a bittersweet farewell, but they would remain in close contact by correspondence, and he hoped to visit them again, someday soon.

Leonardo da Vinci Farewells Lorenzo de' Medici and Florence

Before embarking back to Milan with his servant Tommaso Masini, Leonardo met with Lorenzo de' Medici to receive new diplomatic instructions for his return visit to Ludovico Sforza and the young duke of Milan who was Lorenzo's godson. Lorenzo outlined some of his political concerns that Leonardo needed to pass on to Ludovico and the Duke of Milan, and he handed him the gifts that he want Leonardo to present to them. It was March 1482, Rome and Florence were at peace with each other. In fact they were allies again, this time against the Turks who had invaded the kingdom of Naples at Otranto. However, what worried Lorenzo the most was that the Republic of Venice was not part of their alliance against the Turks, and that they had declared war against Ferrara who were near neighbours of Florence. Lorenzo worried about the true intentions of the Venetians, and he predicted that they would expand their wars from Ferrara to Florence and Milan if they were not prevented to do so. As an expert in fortifications, sieges, and military weapons, Leonardo might be able to advise the young duke of Milan in the art of war. Ludovico had little to learn, but he might not be sharing his knowledge with his nephew the duke of Milan. Lorenzo presented the appropriate references for Leonardo to pass on to the young duke and his lordship Ludovico Sforza, for, although they had previously met with Leonardo da Vinci, it was an established courtesy to be reintroduced in a courtly and diplomatic manner.

This is what Lorenzo wanted Leonardo to confide to Ludovico Sforza. The Lord of Imola Girolamo Riario, who was the nephew of Pope Sixtus IV and Ludovico's nephew by marriage to his niece Caterina Sforza, had formed an alliance with the Republic of Venice in May 1480, and then, following the death of Pino Ordelaffi, probably by poisoning, he became Count of Forli receiving the investiture from his uncle the Pope. Still unsatisfied with the new possessions that he had gained, Girolamo Riario now wanted to possess the entirety of Ferrara. With this in mind and with the full support of the Pope, he tried to persuade the Republic of Venice to wage war against Este, the duke of Ferrara. For these and various other reasons, including access to the lucrative salt mines at Comacchio and elsewhere in the region, Lorenzo predicted that the Republic of Venice would soon find a pretext to declare war against Duke Ercole and Ferrara. Moreover, he predicted that the Republic of Venice would ally with the Holy See in Rome, Girolamo Riario lord of Imola and Forli, Pier Maria de Rossi, the Genoese, the Marquis of Monferrato, and Earl S. Second in Parma. If he was right, then he, Lorenzo de' Medici of Florence, as well as the young duke Gian Galeazzo Sforza and his uncle Ludovico Sforza regent of Milan, the Marquis Gonzaga of Mantua, Giovanni II Bentivoglio of Bologna, and the Colonna family of Rome, who were in dispute with the Pope, had better watch out and be fully prepared for war.

On the Road to Milan to Seek Fame and Fortune

On his ride back to Milan with Tommaso Masini in March of 1482, Leonardo thought about Florence and Milan and the two ruling Houses at their core. To be the prince of a city was a dangerous business anywhere. It was wise not to stand out too much drawing on and draining the City's wealth or ruling cruelly and blindly like a tyrant. Leonardo knew this, and the tyrants knew it, and yet, he and they were drawn together to the seat of unstable power like moths to a flame.

On reflection, the Galeazzo Maria Sforza assassination in Milan in 1476 appears to have been the inspiration for the Pazzi conspiracy in Florence in their attempt to murder the ruler Lorenzo de' Medici while he attended High Mass at the Duomo before a crowd of many thousands of people in Florence on Sunday 26th April 1478. The killings in Milan and Florence were the manifestations of unstable and self-serving power. In Milan, it was payback for loss of honour and perceived injustice by a group of Republicans, disenchanted students, and their humanist mentor. In Florence, the Medici provoked resentment from the Pazzi and others who wanted to replace them as the papal bankers, and they received support from the sworn enemy of the Medici; Pope Sixtus IV, Jacopo Salvati - the Archbishop of Pisa, and Girolamo Riario – the nephew of Sixtus IV and husband of Caterina Sforza who was the niece of Ludovico Sforza. Lorenzo de' Medici was wounded while his brother Giuliano de' Medici was killed. Leonardo had hoped to provide Lorenzo with a painting of his version and interpretation of the Pazzi conspiracy and its immediate outcome, but it never happened. He contemplated his role as a Florentine agent and diplomat to Milan, and he fully realised that Lorenzo de' Medici was using him and the other Florentine artists as diplomatic currency to advance his family's interest.

So, who was Leonardo politically? How did he see himself? What was his political standing? Was he a spy or a diplomat or something else? Where did his loyalties lie? Were they to himself, to his father and mother, to his uncle, to the Medici, to Florence, to Milan, to the Sforza, to the Melzi, to the de' Predis brothers, to Italy, to France, to the church, to whom? Maybe, he was simply a servant of Nature and God and here on earth to explore and reveal the mysterious ways and secrets of the material world? He often sighed to himself, knowing that time would reveal that his loyalties lay mainly to himself and his God of Reason, but that the magnets and distractions and the Fates would pull him one way and the other along an enchanted pathway to the very end of his natural journey and life. But, for now, it was to Milan and the possibility of war with the Venetians.

In the portrait of Leonardo da Vinci that I show below (Fig. 26), in the shadows of the bookcase directly below the red book, there are at least three cryptic words that are written in small black letters that I can hardly discern. At best or worse, they appear from top to bottom to be VICO, LEO, and DHEVS. The meaning of these words is a mystery, but the LEO suggests that it might be about Leonardo da Vinci. Alternatively, the cryptic messages might refer to the titles, subjects or authors of the books on display.

Fig. 26. Leonardo da Vinci and dog, 1482. Looking to seek fame and fortune in Milan.

✳

CHAPTER 7

Leonardo's Milanese Kitchen, 1482 to 1485. War Against the Republic of Venice and Fear of the Black Death

I have already been to see a great variety of atmospheric effects. And lately over Milan towards Lago Maggiore I saw a cloud in the form of an immense mountain full of rifts of glowing light, because the rays of the sun, which was already close to the horizon and red, tinged the cloud with its own hue. And this cloud attracted to it all the little clouds that were near while the large one did not move from its place; thus it retained on its summit the reflection of the sunlight till an hour and a half after sunset, so immensely large was it; and about two hours after sunset such a violent wind arose, that it was really tremendous and unheard of.

— Leonardo da Vinci

Leonardo Befriends the Young Duke of Milan and Applies for the Position of War Engineer in the Sforza Court

On his return to Milan in April 1482, Leonardo visited my father at his apartments in Nuovo. Together, they went to stay for a few days with my great grandparents in Casoretto to catch up on the latest news and social and political gossip about the Sforza court and the city. Then, he called in on the de' Predis brothers to inquire about the commission for the altarpiece at the San Francesco Church in Vercellina. They told him that the Confraternity had not yet drawn up the contract for them; they had been waiting for his return to Milan and hadn't expected him back until about this time next year. It was a few more days before Leonardo paid a courtesy call to the Sforza court to announce that he was back looking for sponsorship in the arts and architecture. He wanted to settle and work in their city as a painter, engineer, architect, and entertainer, he said. He passed on all of Lorenzo de' Medici's civility, respectfulness, gifts, and messages to the Governor Ludovico Sforza and his nephew Gian Galeazzo Sforza who was now 13 years of age and a proper little duke of Milan.

Leonardo also had his own personal gift for the young duke hidden in a wooden box the size of a large olive oil barrel. He removed a longish handle from the side of the box, slotted it through a small opening, and cranked it furiously for ten to fifteen seconds. When the front cover of the box opened, an animal the size of a large mastiff sprung out and slowly trotted towards the young duke who stepped back in surprise and wonderment. The animal was covered in tanned horse skin with a lion's head covered in masses of long woollen brown hair. While the young duke stood frozen with amazement, two of his guards leapt across to protect him from a possible attack and mauling. Before the duke, governor, guards, and other attendants realised it was a wooden mechanical toy, the lion suddenly stopped and bowed down in deference to the guards and the young duke. There were a few seconds of grinding, grating growls from some mechanism deep inside the lion and then a stunned silence. Cheerful applause broke out when the young duke and Ludovico Sforza and all the others who were present realised that there was a trickster in their presence who had just momentarily fooled them with his expertise in the art of illusion and entertainment. The duke congratulated Leonardo on the construction of such a marvellous toy and told him that he would love to take it for a ride if it was only larger and faster.

Leonardo never tired of magical entertainments to shock and surprise. Giorgio Vasari wrote the following account about Leonardo in his *Lives of the Most Eminent Painters, Sculptors, and Architects*:

> Leonardo went to Rome with Duke Giuliano de' Medici, and knowing the Pope to be fond of philosophy, especially alchemy, he used to make little animals of a wax paste, which as he walked along he would fill with wind by blowing into them, and so make them fly in the air, until the wind being exhausted, they dropped to the ground. The vinedresser of the Belvedere having found a very strange lizard, Leonardo made some wings of the scales of other lizards and fastened them on its back with a mixture of quicksilver, so that they trembled when it walked; and having made for it eyes, horns, and a beard, he tamed it and kept it in a box, but all his friends to whom he showed it used to run away from fear.

After a modicum of calm had returned to proceedings at the Sforza court, Leonardo found himself fiddling on his violin again for the young duke who had made considerable inroads on drawing out a pleasant sound from the beautiful fiddle that was gifted to him by Leonardo during his previous visit. The young duke Gian Galeazzo Sforza had practiced punctiliously on the lessons given to him by Leonardo, and he now happily showed off the small smattering of skills that he had developed in the maestro's absence with the help of the visiting French musician Josquin des Prez. Leonardo was impressed and complimented the young duke for his progress, and he showed him some new improvements, arrangements, and additional scales and chords to practice with. When Leonardo was asked to play for the young duke and his small entourage, he bowed the strings of his instrument with great passion and vigour for he sensed the Sforza court was much unsettled with the expectations of war. Milan as yet had not officially declared their hand against Venice. However, their old ally and supporter General Roberto Sanseverino who once had been a loyal friend of Milan and Ludovico Sforza was now a sworn enemy for he had transferred his allegiance and mercenaries away from Milan and across to the Venetians.

A few days after Leonardo's concert, the talk at the court was mainly about the preparations for war. On one occasion while Leonardo was sketching war weapons for the amusement of the young duke, the duke's bodyguard and horse-riding instructor Galeazzo Sanseverino told them that Ludovico Sforza was looking to hiring engineers for his war efforts. Captain Galeazzo Sanseverino was Roberto Sanseverino's fourth youngest son, and he and his three brothers had stayed in Milan and sworn allegiance to Ludovico IL Moro Sforza. Gian Francesco Sanseverino was Galeazzo's oldest brother, the Count of Colomo and Caiazzo, and a loyal army general in the service of the Duke of Milan. My father Gerolamo Melzi was appointed a captain of the Militia Guard and Fortification Engineer of the Canals and Adda River, and he was also present at the gathering. He told them that Leonardo was a fully trained engineer and an expert in fortifications who was advising and assisting him with strengthening the fortifications and armaments at Vaprio and along the Adda River. The young duke laughed and said that if that was so then Leonardo should immediately give up playing his violin and apply for the position of armaments engineer, and that they all would help him draft his letter of application. So, it was there and then in the young duke's rooms at the Sforza court that my father with the help of Leonardo, the young duke, and Galeazzo Sanseverino wrote out in his own strong hand the application that Leonardo would present to Ludovico via the young duke for the position of fortification engineer for the Governor of the duchy of Milan. I still have a copy of this application in our family archives. It reads as follows:

> My most Illustrious Lord, having now sufficiently considered the specimens of all those who proclaim themselves skilled contrivers and masters of instruments of war, and that the invention and operation of the said instruments are nothing different from those in

common use: I shall endeavour, without prejudicing or discrediting anyone else, to bring myself to the attention of Your Excellency, for the purpose of showing Your Lordship my secrets, and then offering them to you for your complete consideration at your convenience and pleasure, and when the time is right to bring into effective operation all those things which are in part briefly listed below:

1. I have an assortment of extremely light and strong bridges, adapted to be most easily carried, and with them you may pursue, and at any time flee from the enemy; and others, secure and indestructible by fire and battle, easy and convenient to lift and place. I can also burn and destroy those of the enemy.

2. I know how, when a place is besieged, to take the water out of the trenches, and make endless variety of bridges, and covered ways and ladders, and other machines pertaining to such expeditions.

3. If, by reason of the height of the banks, or the strength of the place and its position, it is impossible, when besieging a place, to avail oneself of the plan of bombardment, I have methods for destroying every rock or other fortress, even if it were founded on a rock or so forth.

4. Again, I have different kinds of mortars and cannon; most convenient and easy to carry; and with these I can fling small stones like hail; and with the smoke cause great terror to the enemy, to his great detriment and confusion.

5. And if the fight should be at sea, I have many kinds of machines most efficient for offence and defence; and vessels which will resist the attack of the largest guns and powder and fumes.

6. I have means of arriving at a designated spot through underground mines and secret winding passages, constructed completely without noise, even if it was necessary to pass under a trench or a river.

7. I will make armoured chariots, safe and unassailable, which, on entering among the enemy with their artillery; there is no body of men so great that they would break them. And behind these, infantry could follow quite unhurt and without any hindrance.

8. In case of need, I will make big guns, mortars, and light ordnance of fine and useful forms, out of the common type.

9. Where the operation of bombardment might fail, I would contrive catapults, mangonels, trabocchi (movable platforms or bridges extended from land over water with extended antennae supporting nets or traps or scoops), and other machines of marvellous efficacy and not in common use. And in short, according to the variety of cases, I can contrive various and endless means of offence and defence.

10. In times of peace, I believe I can give perfect satisfaction and to the equal of any other in architecture and the composition of buildings public and private; and in guiding water from one place to another.

11. I can carry out sculpture in marble, bronze, or clay, and also I can do in painting whatever may be done, as well as any other, be he who he may.

The young duke reminded the writing party that Ludovico Sforza was still looking for a sculptor to prepare a bronze equestrian monument in remembrance of his deceased father Francesco Sforza, the first Sforza and the fourth overall to become Duke of Milan, and that Leonardo should offer to take on the honourable task. So, they concluded Leonardo's application with the following paragraph.

Again, the bronze horse may be taken in hand, which is to be to the immortal glory and eternal honour of the prince your father of happy memory, and of the illustrious house of Sforza. And if any of the above-named things seem to anyone to be impossible or not feasible, I am most ready to make the experiment in your park, or in whatever place may please your Excellency – to whom I commend myself with the utmost humility.

Your most loyal servant, Leonardo da Vinci.

They all applauded the brilliance of the letter, and once the application was concluded to everybody's satisfaction, my father wrote out three copies using the young duke's finest paper, a sealed copy was given to the young duke to pass on to the Governor Ludovico Sforza, a copy was given to Leonardo, and my father kept the third copy for his own archives.

Clapping with great enthusiasm and happiness, the young duke called out, 'Maestro, we must add some of your drawings of war machines to the application for Lord Ludovico to see them with his very own eyes.'

They sorted through the twelve drawings that the applicant had with him and decided on only including six of them. On sorting through some of Leonardo's drawings of war machines, the young duke voted the giant crossbow as the most impractical. 'How are you going to transport this monstrosity to the battle field?' he asked. 'You'll need at least ten African elephants to drag this out onto the field. And does it have wheels for easier transport or will we have to gouge out some sort of transporters for you to carry it over the land? And while we are in Africa to capture the elephants, we should capture six rhinoceros for them to pull back the bow with their horns to fire the giant arrow. Oh, this is such an enormously wonderful invention, Maestro. This would be considered money really well spent by Our Duchy,' and he started to laugh setting off his long golden locks to shake with accompanied mirth.

'Your most royal Excellency, I can always miniaturise the design for your own and any other's convenience, and of course, to save on cost in order not to bankrupt the duchy. Here (he shows the duke his picture of the giant crossbow), I was thinking big for your amusement. I think your idea for the elephants and rhinoceros is excellent. I will add them to the drawing.' With that, Leonardo started drawing African animals including monkeys, elephants, and rhinoceros for the young duke's amusement.

'I like your springald moveable cannon and the multi-barrelled, multi-shot gun the best of all. Of course, I will show my uncle and his chief of staff your other drawings including your giant crossbow after they have read and digested your application,' said the young duke.

On the same day, Galeazzo Sanseverino invited Leonardo and my father to visit his family palace and to see the large collection of stables and the beautiful and expensive horseflesh that they were breeding. 'If you wish to place the late Francesco Sforza on a beautifully sculptured war horse, you'd better come and see some real horse flesh to mould your sculptures from.'

Leonardo was greatly impressed by the Sanseverino stables and the beautiful collection of horses, and so it was that he and Galeazzo soon became firm friends for they had much to share, and they recognised an intelligence, humour, and courtly bearing in each other's character. After eating, drinking, and talking late into the night, Galeazzo Sanseverino offered his patronage to Leonardo's endeavours. This was a welcomed addition to the patronage that my father and great grandfather already had offered him with the intended renovations of the Vaprio villa and adjoining factories and farmlands.

Preparing Milan for a War Against the Republic of Venice

A few weeks after the young Duke of Milan submitted Leonardo's application to his uncle, the Governor and Regent of Milan Ludovico Sforza summoned Leonardo, Captain Galeazzo Sanseverino, and my father to join him in his reception room in order to hear his decision. At the appointed time, Ludovico's secretary ushered them into the reception room where Ludovico and his nephew and three other gentlemen, the military general Gian Francesco Sanseverino, the secretary Jacopo Antiquaio, and the director of military engineering Ambrosio Ferrere were waiting for them. After a cordial exchange of salutations and courtly good manners, His Excellency IL Moro invited them to be seated on the chairs provided, and he immediately addressed Leonardo about his application. Essentially, Leonardo was thanked for his enlightening and enthusiastic application, which would be given proper consideration in good time. But for now no decision could be made about the matter because of the general flux of finances and positions already filled in preparation for an approaching conflict with the Venetians, Genoese, and the warlord Girolamo Riario of Imola and Forli regarding the Ferrara matter and the Salt Wars. The Duke of Milan Gian Galeazzo had shown Leonardo's drawings and plans for new weapons of war to the Governor of Milan, and he was very impressed, but unfortunately, his current revenues were low and general expenditures needed to be reduced. Ludovico thanked Leonardo for his offer to construct an equestrian monument in the memory and honour of the Illustrious Duke Francisco Sforza, Ludovico's father and the young Duke's grandfather. This also would be taken into consideration at the appropriate time, but for now, he, the Governor and Regent of Milan, and the young Duke would like to see Leonardo's preparatory drawings and plans for the monument for which he would be paid a generous fee for his time and efforts. However, at this stage of the Duchy's preparations for war in what he saw as an inevitable conflict ahead of him with the Republic of Venice, he could not risk any new ventures and inventions in engineering other than those supporting the true and tested mechanisms that he, the Governor and Protector of Milan, had already approved. So, regrettably, at this time, he could not employ Maestro Leonardo da Vinci as a fortification engineer or sculptor that would be paid by the State finances. However, if Ser Leonardo was willing to give up his time and energies to support the cause of the Duchy of Milan in its conflict with Venice and the Papacy, then a number of the Milanese patrons and patricians, including those who were gathered at the present meeting, would be willing to support him financially for his advice, suggestions, and inventions. In this regard, all matters relating to those discussed on this day or any other day about his appointment and the operational or the diplomatic matters concerning this imminent conflict with the Republic of Venice had to be held in secret. Thus, Leonardo had to swear before all those in attendance that he would maintain the code of silence and not discuss any of these matters with anybody other than the seven who were with him at this gathering. Leonardo was handed a copy of the oath of allegiance, and he was instructed to read it out loudly to Ludovico Moro and all the others who were there with him on this day. And so, Leonardo was now fully absorbed into the politics and intrigues of Milan, much more than he expected.

After the oath, His Excellency Ludovico Moro gave everybody who was present an update of the situation about the salt wars between Ferrara and the Republic of Venice. It was now June 1482. The presentation by his Excellency Lord Ludovico Sforza, Duke of Bari, Governor and Regent of Milan, was the following:

'As you know this conflict before us is about territorial expansion. Last year, Venice declared war against Ferrara and Duke Ercole I d'Este on the pretext that the vicar and the bishop of Ferrara excommunicated their *Visdominio* (force master) and expelled him from Ferrara and the Venetian community in the lands of the Duke d'Este. The excommunication of the *Visdominio* was of little issue. In reality, Venice wanted the salt marshes and the tin mines of Comacchio for their own economy. The League of States and the Duchy of Milan attempted to prevent the Venetians from escalating on their dissatisfaction with Ferrara. But, they ignored us. They wish to become the Lords of Ferrara. Last month, the Venetian troops led by our newly founded enemy, the condottiero Roberto Sanseverino, attacked Ferrarese territory from the northeast, brutally sacked Adria and quickly overran Comacchio. They attacked Argenta at the edge of the saltmarshes and besieged Ficarolo and Rovigo causing those people much misery. They now stand ready to cross the river Po, and together with their navy, they are preparing to attack the walls of Ferrara and lay siege to that city. They are fully supported with contingents from the Republic of Genoa and the Marquis of Montferrat, and from Lord Girolamo Riario of Imola and Forli who, I am ashamed to say, is wed to my dear niece Caterina Sforza. We instead will support the Duke of Ferrara and his allies Frederico da Montefeltro, duke of Urbino, King Ferdinand of Naples, Frederico I Gonzaga of Mantua, and

Giovanni II Bentivoglio of Bologna. Ser Leonardo da Vinci tells us that Lord Lorenzo de' Medici and the city of Florence will stand with us, although they have yet to officially announce their position. Our military representatives in the League are Frederico da Montefeltro, lord of Urbino, and our Milanese general Gian Giacomo Trivulzio, and I have provided them with five hundred foot soldiers and two hundred horses for their cavalry. The bulk of our forces remain in the duchy until we are ready to deploy them when necessary. Our plan, on the best advice that we have received from our generals, will be to launch a diversion elsewhere rather than directly attack the Venetians at Ferrara. Further, we will not launch our attack until the Venetians are at the walls of Ferrara draining their own resources. Until then, we will gather and train our troops and muster our horses until we are fully ready to strike.'

Leonardo thought about presenting Ludovico and the others with his ideas about the tactics that could be used to defend against the siege of Ferrara. He was familiar with Ferrara because he had visited there in the recent past to study and record on their local fortifications, mills, locks, and dams. However, he realised that it would be highly presumptuous of him to do so in front of the Governor of the duchy of Milan who was more familiar with Ferrara than he had ever been. All of them at the meeting, including the Governor, had previously visited Ferrara numerous times, and they probably knew more about the lay out of the city than he did. In fact, only a few days earlier, my father had reminded Leonardo that the Ferrarese house of Este and the Milanese house of Sforza were on the most friendly terms because Ludovico Sforza was engaged to be married to Beatrice, the younger daughter of Ercole d' Este who was the duke and ruler of Ferrara. Ludovico had originally requested a betrothal to Isabella, Beatrice's older sister, but because she was already promised to Francesco Gonzaga of Mantua, Ercole offered him Beatrice instead, and he gratefully accepted her as his betrothed. What my father couldn't understand is why Ludovico Sforza had not as yet called on his troops to defend his betrothed and Ferrara against the Venetians, for this was the most chivalrous thing to do if you were engaged to a Ferrarese princess.

Patronage from the Milanese Knight Galeazzo Sanseverino

The relationship between Leonardo da Vinci and Galeazzo Sanseverino had grown into the very best of friendships. Galeazzo was not only Leonardo's official patron, but he was also his landlord, providing him with rooms for his accommodation and studios for his painting and science, and allowing him full access to all the other parts of the Sanseverino palace inside and outside the western gates of the city. This included the valuable books and historical documents in their extensive private libraries. On most nights Galeazzo and Leonardo would drink red wine and talk, for Galeazzo, like Leonardo, was interested in many things, especially mathematics, philosophy, the sciences, and the arts. Galeazzo was also an expert on warfare and the arts of combat, a subject that Leonardo wanted to learn more about, for although he was handy with a knife and a short sword, he knew full well that he was no master in a fight to the death, and up to now he had never killed anybody. Galeazzo, on the other hand, by the age of 24 years, had already killed more than twenty men in hand to hand combat when accompanying either his father Roberto the former condottiero of Milan or his brother Gian Francesco, the current General of the Milanese forces, in various battles.

Galeazzo's tutor was Pietro Monte, an Italian knight who was regarded by many to be the best sword man in Italy and beyond. At that time, Monte was travelling in Spain, but Leonardo would meet him soon enough, and he would be taught by Monte the game of darts and how to best fight with a sword or a lance while sitting on horseback. These lessons were valuable for Leonardo in his later years for preparing jousts for court festivities. Monte and Sanseverino advised him on selecting mounts and saddles for war and for the joust, gave details on preparing jousting armour and equipment, and provided directions on how to handle the lance (including targeting the opponent's horse) and on the correct posture to gain advantage in reaching over the opponent. Both Galeazzo Sanseverino and Pietro Monte also taught Leonardo the art of constructing battle armour for foot soldiers, and horsemen and horses, and for festivals.

Galeazzo enjoyed to talk for he had much to say, and Leonardo never discouraged him for he was a very good listener, especially while sketching in his notebook. He liked to listen and make little drawings and notes of the subjects spoken about. It helped him to relax and better remember various interesting aspects of their conversations. Sometimes, Galeazzo would ask Leonardo to show him what he was sketching, although generally it never bothered him because Leonardo could easily engage in conversation, heated or calm, while drawing or writing. Nobody seemed bothered by Leonardo's habit of constantly sketching in the company of others because they all knew or soon found out that he was an artist and a philosopher with a need to always have a pen and paper in hand, for these were the tools of his trade as well as the natural extensions of his hands and fingers. For Leonardo, drawing was the same as breathing while living and playing from day to day. The notebook was tied to his side or it sat in a side pouch entrapped by a belt, and he never had any shortage of pens or crayons.

This is what Leonardo learnt about the Sanseverino family over the first few nights of their conversations. Galeazzo and his seven brothers and five sisters were related to the Sforza, for his great grandmother was Elisa Sforza, the sister of Francesco Sforza, a previous Duke of Milan. Yes, the same dead duke that Leonardo had offered to immortalise by constructing an equestrian monument for Ludovico Sforza and the young duke Gian Galeazzo was Galeazzo Sanseverino's great granduncle. Galeazzo's mother was Giovanna da Correggio, and she gave birth to him in the Po valley in 1460, the 4th son of Roberto. Galeazzo Sanseverino's father was a highly successful condottiero who had loyally served the first two Sforza dukes Francesco and Galeazzo Maria, but had fallen out with Ludovico il Moro Sforza when he wasn't granted the rewards that he was promised for his past loyalty and service. Roberto was born in Milan, and he proudly saw himself as a condottiero who served various masters including three Dukes of Milan (1440 to 1481), the King of Naples (1460 to 1463), the Republic of Florence (1467), the Duchy of Savoy (1476), the Republic of Genoa (1478), and the Republic of Venice (1482 to 1487). When Roberto served the King of Naples Ferdinand of Aragon from 1459 to 1462, he received from the King the titled surname of Aragona. Roberto named two of his eight sons, Gian Francesco and Galeazzo, after the previous two Sforza dukes whom he had served. One of his sons, Frederico, Galeazzo's half brother, eventually joined the church and had ambitions to become a cardinal of Rome.

In 1476, Roberto resettled in Milan and later helped Ludovico IL Moro Sforza to overthrow Bona of Savoy and her grasping Counsellor of Milan, the hated Cicco Simonetta. After the execution of Cicco Simonetta and the exile of Bona of Savoy, Roberto expected that Ludovico as the new Regent of Milan would appoint him as the supreme military leader and grant him the properties of his hated enemy Cicco Simonetta. However, Ludovico didn't trust his cousin Roberto with the sole responsibility of the entire Milanese military and instead subdivided the various military divisions into the hands of various leaders under his own command. Roberto was given minor leadership of one of the military subdivisions. This greatly offended Roberto, and he and Ludovico had a massive falling out. Roberto accused Ludovico of treachery and failing to support him with the promises that he had made when he had supported Ludovico in his attempts to wrest power out of the hands of Bona of Savoy and Cicco Simonetta. Indeed, Ludovico previously had promised to give Roberto the estates of Cicco Simonetta after they were confiscated, but instead he retained most of them for himself and left some of them to Simonetta's brothers who had repented and sworn allegiance to him. Moreover, Ludovico's payments to Roberto for his services as a condottiero had fallen in arrears, and the debt was accumulating. Roberto felt totally betrayed and dishonoured by

Ludovico, and so, he left Milan in October 1481 to his castle in Castelnuovo along the Scrivia River near Tortona and Alessandria in the Duchy of Savoy to plot a suitable revenge. In response, Ludovico gave him an ultimatum to return to Milan in two days or be exiled forever from the duchy of Milan. In early February 1482, Roberto escaped arrest and chose exile in Venice where the Republic was after an experienced and fearless condottiero. To get back at Ludovico, he joined the service of Venice as their military leader to take on Duke Ercole I d'Este at Ferrara.

In the meantime, Roberto's two sons Gian Francesco and Galeazzo Sanseverino remained in Milan and swore to serve the young Duke of Milan and his uncle Ludovico. Leonardo sensed that the young duke Gian Galeazzo and his guardian the Governor Ludovico had great admiration and love for both Gian Francesco and Galeazzo Sanseverino. As luck would have it, Leonardo had taken the opportunity to propose a full-time position for himself in the Sforza court that would involve preparing the monumental horse statue, royal portraits, festival designs, and engineering commissions that Galeazzo Sanseverino and his brothers were willing to sponsor. However, Leonardo knew from previous advice that Ludovico Sforza kept employment in his court to a minimum by outsourcing individual projects as much as possible, and that it was unlikely that he would be granted a tenured position. Therefore, he was greatly honoured and relieved to have gained the patronage of the Sanseverino brothers.

Galeazzo Sanseverino was very much interested in Leonardo's life, and so Leonardo reciprocated by revealing his own history and tales about the Medici court and Florentine rule and governorship. Leonardo also talked about the golden ratio in architecture and perspective and showed him his drawings and the proportions of the *Vitruvian Man* based on the geometry of Vitruvius in Book III of his treatise *De Architectura*. They talked mathematics and about Euclidian geometry, and in this way their bond grew even stronger.

One time, Galeazzo Sanseverino told Leonardo that he was preparing to sponsor the publication of a new book on warfare to be written by Pietro Monte (the *Colecteanea*), and that he would like him to illustrate it. The book would be a classic replacement to the previous two great books *Art of the Sword* by Anonimo Bolognese and *De Re Militari (Concerning Military Matters)* by Vegetius Renatus who was a Roman scholar before the time of Christ. Leonardo told Galeazzo that he was already developing a treatise to replace Roberto Valturio's book entitled *De Re Militari*. He hoped that this would help him to gain the attention of Ludovico Sforza who as Governor needed to develop the military and the territories of the duchy of Milan. Maybe, they could combine their resources and produce a joint publication. Galeazzo said he couldn't draw or paint, and that he wasn't the best at producing scholarly texts. Instead, he offered to demonstrate to Leonardo some of the classical Pietro Monte sword fighting strokes, the forward thrusts and parries.

'The thrust. Hold your sword out straight, Leonardo. Point it at my chest towards the middle, just below my heart. Now turn sideways, as I do, but with your head held still and looking at me. You are left-handed, whereas I am right-handed. You can no longer attack my heart when I stand side on. Yet, when you stand side on, I can attack your heart under your armpit. Look out for the thrust towards your armpit. You can step forward or backwards to avoid such a thrust. Forward is better, and then, spin rapidly to your right to face your right-handed opponent and thrust your sword instantly into his belly. Then, while he is recovering from the shock, you can at your leisure thrust your sword right through your opponent's chest into his still beating heart. That's lesson number one.'

Leonardo prayed to God that he would never find himself in such an awkward thrusting position in actual combat.

'And now, Leonardo, for the thrusts, parries, and feints. A cunning and effective fighter refrains from impetuous attacks. Instead, he moves with speed and measure, anticipates and counters the opponents' movements, and quickly perceives their weaknesses. For cuts, thrusts, and feints, agility, lightness, and mobility are the assets of the best fighters. Ascending cuts are preferred over descending cuts. Use them in swift combinations of two or three strokes. Cuts and thrusts from left or right or high or low must follow one after the other without pause, always with speed, aggression, and deception. Keep everything simple and economical. So, here, watch this. I throw two ascending cuts at you, the first with left foot forward, the second with right foot forward, and then, follow with the instantaneous finishing thrust. You didn't even have time to blink, did you? The first stroke was a feint to provoke you, the second to wound you, and the third was to finish you off. Easy, isn't it. There's more, of course. But, let's rest and have a drink for this is thirsty work. Oh, by the way, next time, you must learn how to fall correctly in combat to avoid injury or from looking ridiculous, like you do now sitting back there on your arse.'

With that last comment, Galeazzo helpfully raised Leonardo up from the floor and back again onto his shaky feet.

Weapons of War and Lessons on How to Fly

Some days, while still waiting for the clarion call, Leonardo would join Galeazzo and the young duke on their rides to the park outside the castle walls looking to hunt for deer and other animals. On other days, they would ride to the castles and parks in Vigevano and stay over night to feast on the game that they caught at one or other of the hunting parks. Galeazzo was teaching the 13-year-old duke Gian Galeazzo the skills of hunting, chivalry, heraldry, and the way noble men should use their leisure time while waiting to be involved in a war. Apart from the occasional hunt, Leonardo busied himself in the workshops of Sanseverino and the Sforza preparing drawings and models of war as well as various siege instruments. The heavily fortified city of Milan had gained its name, fame, and prosperity from the manufacture of arms as far back as the 13th century. Following in this tradition, Leonardo tested various weapons in the military park of several acres inside the front section of the Sforza castle. He designed and tested offensive and defensive military machines and naval weapons and spectacular armour hoping that they would be helpful in the defence of Ferrara's delta along the river Po and allow them quick escapes, assaults, and manoeuvrability around the waterways. He offered the young duke and Galeazzo Sanseverino detailed advice on war galleys, diving gear, flying machines, and defence strategies hoping that his insights would be passed on and approved by Il Moro. Leonardo's early mechanical solutions for many of these weapons, machines, and strategies were often impractical, and Ludovico Moro chose to ignore them.

At times, Leonardo supposedly encountered embarrassing mishaps while testing his newly invented weapons in public. There were two popular tales told by many in Milan and elsewhere that embarrassed Leonardo whenever he heard them. One tale was that he invented a horse drawn machine that he called his Giant Barley Cutter. It was to be pulled along by horses through a group of marching enemy troops, mowing them down like barley in the field. When he demonstrated the cutter in a field outside the castle gates, it ran amok and killed six of the handlers who had been attempting to manage the horses. Ludovico Sforza deemed the contraception more dangerous to him and his allies than to the enemy. On another occasion, Leonardo demonstrated his Giant Cow Grinder for pulverizing dead horses in the battlefield to provide horseflesh to the hungry troops. Again, life was needlessly lost when the attendants climbed into the interior of the grinder to remove jammed horses or cows. Of course, none of these events or demonstrations actually happened. They were simply popular stories made up by the wandering minstrels and storytellers and competitive engineers hoping to harm Leonardo's reputation.

When bored with war appliances, Leonardo studied the anatomy of bats and birds, examined their strengths and proportions, compared strong and light-weight materials and the dynamics of air-flow and air currents, weighed the static capabilities of different pulley arrangements, designed models of jointed wings, and engineered specialised traction and torsion mechanisms. He developed an innovative design for human flight, a birdman or *ornitotero* (also known as an *ornaithopter*), a human operated machine that flies like a bird by flapping its wings. In drawing such wings to generate lift and thrust, he wrote in his notebook, 'method for how the wing becomes perforated when it rises upward and become all unified when it lowers.'

Leonardo instructed the young duke to watch carefully how birds fly when he was out riding and hunting, 'Instead of firing your crossbow at the first bird that you see, sit in a bush in a hollow or sit on top of a rise and watch how the birds fly and hover. It is a marvellous thing. Watch how their wings go down and the feathers fully overlap to block the air passing through them. Then, on the upstroke, the feathers spread apart to allow the air to flow between them. It's like our overarm swimming stroke in water, the same principle.'

'But, we don't have feathers, Maestro.'

'Our fingers on the ends of our hand are like bird feathers. They are our paddles in water. When swimming, we close our fingers to push back the water in order to push ourselves forward. For the next swimming stroke, we spread our fingers to reduce air-resistance when we lift our hand from the water and move it forward through the air to a position in front of us. For birds, their flying strokes are like swimming through air, it's marvellous to watch. Their flapping generates lift and thrust, just like your flapping does when you are sword fighting against our good lord Galeazzo Sanseverino. The bird's flapping creates a vortex behind their wings that we cannot emulate with our bony featherless arms.'

'But, maestro, your birdman wings are made of a thin stretched material that has no feathers. How can it fly without feathers?'

'Your Excellency, what other creatures do you know about that can fly without feathers?'

'Insects?'

'Correct, flies, bees, butterflies, dragonflies, and mosquitoes. They flap their paper-thin wings very fast, so fast that they create a vibration that we can sometimes hear them flying and hovering.'

'You mean the buzz of a mosquito?'

'Yes, the mosquito flaps its wings faster than any other insect, even the fly. It is the king of all insect flappers.'

'So your birdman wings are insect wings, not bird wings?'

'Not quite, your Excellency. What other creatures fly that are not insects or birds?'

'Bats?'

'Correct, your Excellency. My design is based on bat wings, not bird wings.'

'So, Maestro, you should call your contraption batman, not birdman.'

'I will, your Excellency, a marvellous suggestion, indeed. Yet, I have added something to my flying contraption that bats do not possess. Can you see what it is?'

'Tail feathers?'

'Excellent observation. I will make a scientist of you yet. The V shaped tail is important in bird flight. It is like the rudder of a boat. It controls the direction of forward movement.'

'I understand, Maestro. The wings of a bird or a bat work like the oars of a boat that propel it forward with every stroke. The V shaped tail feathers act as the rudder to give the boat its direction. Excellent design, Maestro.'

'Would you care to try out the bat wings?'

'It is best for all, including you, Maestro, that we keep our feet planted firmly on the ground or in the stirrups of a good saddle. We don't want to lose our lives just yet, do we? Instead, let us see how our falcons will take-off from our outstretched hands and destroy those little twittering birds of yours down by the creek? Shall we?'

War Reconnaissance and the Death of Giovanni Melzi, Patrician of Milan

In September of 1482, the Sforza court received word that Ludovico's condottiero the Lord of Urbino in the League of States had become ill with malaria in Ferrara and then died a few weeks later in Bologna at the age of sixty years. This was a sad loss for the Sforza's in Milan for Frederico da Montefeltro had fought many times for past Milanese causes, and he had been married to Battista Sforza, the daughter of Alessandro Sforza Lord of Pesaro, until her untimely death in 1472. Now, Frederico and Battista's only son and heir, Guidobaldo da Montefeltro was the Duke of Urbino. More importantly, Frederico da Montefeltro, while alive, had kept the Duke of Calabria and Ludovico from squabbling with each other. Now their differences were beginning to rise again without the wise intervention from another, and the squabbling would soon become uncontrolled jealousies. As a consequence, Ludovico attempted to set up a peace settlement between Ferrara and Venice, which the Venetians and Neapolitans ignored. Instead, Ludovico received word in November that Roberto and the Venetians had successfully surrounded Ferrara and held the city under siege. The Sforza courts already knew that the towns of Ficarolo and Rovigo along the River Po were in the possession of the Venetians. The Milanese military generals, like Gian Giacomo Trivulzio, were getting impatient, but Ludovico held them back telling them that 'our time is not ready yet.' He was worried about betrayal from his allies including those from Florence, Naples, and Mantua, and so, he kept his forces well watered and fed and at the ready close to the outskirts of his city.

In December of 1482, Leonardo accompanied the troops of Gian Giacomo Trivulzio for reconnaissance down the Po River eastward from Piacenza to as far as the captured fort at Ficarolo west of Ferrara. When they returned to Milan for Christmas, they reported that all was quiet for winter with few or no clashes or fighting along the Po. The encampments of both the allies and enemy appeared to be sheltered permanently against the elements with little or no troop activity.

In February of 1483, Leonardo joined Gerolamo Melzi and his brothers Bartolomeo and Beltrame at the Villa Melzi in Vaprio to plan the construction of bridges in preparation to cross the Adda River with an army into Venetian territory. They were there also to train gunners, twenty at a time. The trainees received 5 ducats a month once they had become masters of their weapons. Then, in March, my great grandfather the Patrician Giovanni Melzi caught a fever, and after a short illness, he died at his home outside the city in Casoretto at the age of 73 years. The funeral was held at the Church of Santa Maria Bianca, and the patricians of Milan, including the young Duke and his uncle Ludovico Sforza, attended. Leonardo was there, as well as the Sanseverino brothers, and other military leaders, and various diplomats representing the League of States.

A Contract for the *Virgin of the Rocks* 1483

On 25th April 1483, Leonardo joined the brothers Evangelista and Giovan Ambrogio de' Predis to sign a long and detailed contract for the construction of the large altarpiece that was to include his painting of the *Virgin of the Rocks* as the main panel to be displayed in the chapel of the Church of San Francesco Grande. The patrons were the members of the Confraternity of the Immaculate Conception (*Confraternita della Concezione*), and they already had contracted Giacomo del Maino to carve an elaborate wood frame for the altarpiece for which he had received his final payment. They had a long list of instructions for the Predis brothers and Leonardo on how they wanted them to paint the images of the religious figures and the angels. Among these instructions was the choice of the perfect colours for God (gold and ultramarine), the Madonna (gold and ultramarine) and her son (gold), the angels (variously in red, gold and green) with an emphasis on the liberal use of gold, and gold especially for the

Christ-child who had to be painted entirely in gold in order to be depicted as the Golden Baby. They wanted the Madonna and angels (playing instruments) dressed in the Greek style and the mountains and stones painted in colours different to the figures. The Predis brothers would provide the paintings of an angel on two large wood panels that would flank Leonardo's central painting.

Leonardo had his concept for the *Virgin of the Rocks* fully formed in his mind, and he was ready to start the preliminary drawings. It had developed from when he had previously visited Ferrara where he was impressed by the passionate intensity and directness of the paintings by Cosme Tura. However, he intended to depict a different mood and have a backdrop that would be similar to the one that he had painted in his image of *St. Jerome*, a symbolic scene of a fixed image within the interior of a skull, the cathedral of the mind. Yes, the rocks would be located within the artist's skull.

Little did Leonardo realise that when he signed his contract to paint the *Virgin of the Rocks* that he would have a long running dispute with the Confraternity for 25 years before they would give him his final payment for his finished painting. Furthermore, with the help of his assistants, he would paint two versions of the *Virgin of the Rocks*, just like there would be two versions of the young duke of Milan as the musical angels that bordered Leonardo's painting. For now, not knowing the future, he was elated with the commission, and he optimistically looked forward to paint another apocryphal fantasy masterpiece about the Virgin Mary for a church altarpiece, this time for a church just a short distance away from the Sanseverino Palace.

The Clarion Call to Invade Bergamo and Brescia

It was now more than two years since the Venetian Republic declared war against Ferrara. Although Roberto Sanseverino and the Venetians had surrounded Ferrara in November of 1482, Ludovico still had kept the bulk of his forces from engaging with the Venetians outside of the duchy of Milan. Then, in May of 1483, Pope Sixtus IV changed sides under the pressure of losing his Papal territories to the League of States. He suddenly abandoned the Venetian cause and joined the League of States; Ferrara, Milan, Mantua, Florence, and Naples, and launched an interdict on Venice in order to halt their possible advances. Ludovico Sforza still feared that his once good friend and now a mortal enemy, the condottiero Robert Sanseverino who was employed by the Republic of Venice, had his eyes and thoughts on the conquest of the Duchy of Milan after Ferrara. But, Ludovico also feared his ally Alfonso the Duke of Calabria even more than Roberto, for the Pope had given Alfonso permission to enter the territories north of the Po River and attack Brescia and then Verona. In addition, one of Ludovico's leading generals, the condottiero Gian Giacomo Trivulzio due to disagreements about his pay suddenly left Milan to work in the services of the French King Louis XI. So, soon after the interdict by the Pope, Ludovico called on his remaining generals to muster together all the available troops and horses for an offensive. The time now was propitious for the troops of the duchy of Milan to make their moves. Ludovico's strategy was simple. They would approach Ferrara from the north by first invading the Venetian town of Bergamo at a time yet to be announced.

Ludovico Sforza had given command of one division to the young Gerolamo Melzi who asked Leonardo to join him in his attack on Bergamo. Gian Francesco Sanseverino was to be the main General in Charge of a few thousand troops on behalf of Ludovico Sforza and the young Duke of Milan. Captain Galeazzo Sanseverino was ordered to remain in Milan with a brigade to protect the city and the young Duke of Milan who was not allowed to accompany his uncle on their march to Bergamo. Both Galeazzo and the young duke protested loudly, and consequently, they were allowed to follow the troops to Bergamo for no longer than a week or two. Then, they had to accept their responsibilities on the further command from Ludovico Sforza and General Gian Francesco Sanseverino to return to Milan and protect their city from outside forces and any allies that might turn and become treacherous against them.

Ludovico outlined his strategy in the war room at the Vaprio villa where the generals had gathered for their briefings in readiness to cross the Adda River and to march on to Bergamo. Essentially, they would invade and conquer all the Venetian towns and territories between Bergamo and Verona. They had the troop numbers and generals to accomplish the task without a large loss of life, but the financial cost would be enormous. The Milanese troops congregated along the Adda River from Lodi to the fort of Olginate in Como, which is along the border between the Duchy of Milan and the Republic of Venice. And so, Leonardo went out on his first military campaign for the Duchy of Milan in the company of the Governor Ludovico Sforza, my father, the young duke, and Captain Galeazzo Sanseverino.

As Niccolo Machiavelli has written in his History of Florence, Ludovico Sforza made a decisive tactical manoeuvre in 1483.

> Leaving the marquis of Ferrara to the defence of his own territories, he, with four thousand horse and two thousand foot – and joined by the duke of Calabria (Pope Sixtus' Legate to the League of States) with twelve thousand horses and five thousand foot – entered the territory of Bergamo, then Brescia, next that of Verona, and in defiance of the Venetians, plundered the whole country; for it was with the greatest difficulty that Roberto and his forces could save the cities themselves. In the meantime, the marquis of Ferrara had recovered a great part of his territories; for the duke of Lorraine, by whom he was attacked, having only at his command two thousand horse and one thousand foot, could not withstand him. Hence, during the whole of 1483, the affairs of the League were prosperous.

Overall, it is only 25 km between the cities of Milan and Bergamo and less than half that distance between Como and Bergamo. It is half a day's march from the borders of the Adda River to Bergamo. Troops can easily march such distances in less than five hours and set up a defensive position in an hour to camp overnight. The Sforza troops had strategic camps set around Bergamo one night after leaving their camps along the Adda River. They met with little or no resistance crossing the river tributaries, canals, fields, and marshes along the way. They successfully used Leonardo's portable bridges with few or no injuries and breakages to man, horse or equipment. Leonardo was pleased with the outcome and rested easily in the Melzi tent outside the city walls. Next day, the Bergamo governor and mayor negotiated with the Milanese generals and decided that there was no point resisting them for Venice had no spare troops available to defend them.

After a few further days of discussion, the gates of Bergamo were opened wide to the Milanese troops and generals. It was here that my father again met with the father and mother of my future mother Tommasina della Torre. My father's grandfather Giovanni Melzi when he was the Ambassador to the Republic of Venice was the best of friends with my mother's father Giovanni Francesco della Torre. They remained good friends and often visited each other across the border since it was only a one-day ride between their respective abodes. Now that Gerolamo Melzi was in Bergamo, he visited della Torre to report on his grandfather's death.

Giovanni Francesco della Torre received my father and Leonardo with great deference and goodwill and soon most of the Sforza hierarchy were also welcomed guests at the della Torre home. It was here that Gerolamo Melzi told Leonardo that he would woo the beautiful raven-haired daughter of Caterina Visconti to be his wife. She was 14 years old and Gerolamo wanted her to be his very own. Her mother the Donna Visconti also was very beautiful, and by any comparative measure it could be easily seen how the daughter would take after her mother in courtly manners and physical beauty. The Sforza, Melzi, and Leonardo da Vinci had quickly made themselves at home with the gracious hospitality of the della Torre family. Ludovico Sforza was so charmed by the Donna Visconti that he offered her a position back in the Sforza court as a Lady-in-Waiting to look after his niece Anna Maria Sforza who was the younger sister of his nephew the young Duke Gian Galeazzo Sforza. Anna, aged 7, was a difficult child, and Ludovico was tending to neglect his responsibilities as her official guardian. He needed somebody like Donna Visconti to take the child into a firm, but loving hand and lead her down the path of righteousness, good courtly manners, and proper grooming. Before leaving Bergamo, Gerolamo Melzi, aged 23 years, was officially betrothed to Tommasina della Torre with the blessing of her mother and father and the Sforza clan. He hoped that he would survive the war to savour and enjoy his wedding and honeymoon scheduled for the summer of 1488.

The Venetians until recently had not worried Ludovico Sforza about invading the Duchy of Milan. They had through their longstanding treaty with King Louis XI of France tried to convince the French king to provide them with troops to attack the League of States in Italy. Lorenzo de' Medici had so far succeeded in dissuading Louis XI from taking to the field in aid of Venice. But, Venice now pleaded with the French king to attack Milan and provide them with a diversion and protection against Ludovico in Bergamo and Brescia. The French king seeing an advantage agreed to conquer Milan with Venetian support, but before he could muster an invasion, he suddenly died on the 30th of August 1483. The planned invasion by the French was abandoned immediately when his 12-year-old son Charles VIII inherited the throne. His elder sister Anne of France acted as the regent jointly with her husband Peter II Duke of Bourbon to rule France until 1491, the year when the young king would be 21 years of age and ready to rule. Queen Anne who was known as 'Madame la Grande' withdrew the few French troops from any further participation in the Ferrara War in Italy, and this, of course, was a great relief to Ludovico because it opened up the way for his next venture.

After staying in Bergamo for a few months with no attack from either Venice or France, Ludovico plotted his next move. He would take Brescia. Here, he expected to meet with a much stronger opposition because Brescia was better fortified to defend against an invasion from him and his allies. Brescia previously had been under Milanese rule, and the Venetians believed that Ludovico wanted it back under his rule. And so, it was at the end of July that a large contingent of Ludovico and Alfonso's troops marched across the fields to Brescia. At their head was the Milanese general Francesco Piccinino, son of Jacopo Piccinino and grandson of Niccolo Piccinino, a past condottiero who had previously led military campaigns against Brescia in 1426 and 1438. Francesco Piccinino had a personal interest in winning back Brescia for the Milanese, and so, Ludovico let him lead the way.

They met with strong resistance just as they had expected. A high rampart of earth surrounded the city. The weak points were strengthened with walls of stone, bricks, and mortar. Outhouses served as fortifications, and garrisons and stockades were manned with soldiers, farmers, and citizens who were willing to fight to the death. Initial attacks from the Ludovico and Alfonso forces failed. They were forced to retreat after being greeted with cannon fire, arrows, spears, and buckshot. Grapeshot, stones, boiling water, and blinding hot lime showered on top of their heads when they attacked the city walls. The soldiers and the citizens of Brescia had gathered on the ramparts to resist desperately against the siege and the destruction of their city's subsistence. Meanwhile, Ludovico and Alfonso's troops surrounded the city, and they set up camps to settle down for a lengthy siege and a tedious existence of relative inactivity, prolonged sobriety, short marches with no fighting, boiled porridge, and never-ending surveillance for all of the day and all of the night. Occasionally, Alfonso and his troops busied themselves by devastating the surrounding country, burning the neighbouring villages, and destroying the unthreshed grain.

There was now a need for Leonardo's long cannons firing 100-lb iron balls and innovative field artillery to weaken the fortifications; and accurate long-range siege engines transported by light mobile carriages to provide tactical benefits for these weapons. General Piccinino, together with Alfonso the Duke of Calabria who was in charge of the troops of King Ferdinand of Naples, besieged Brescia for two to three months until finally starvation, disease, malaria, and pestilence forced open the gates of the city to allow the enemy to enter with medical relief and food. Leonardo looked forward to inspect Brescia for it had a great arsenal and a huge furnace big enough to cast large cannons and bombards. The commander of the arsenal Giovanni Donato, an explosives expert, was killed the year before in 1482 at the siege of Figarolo, and he hadn't been replaced. Leonardo found within this arsenal newly made metal cannon balls filled with poisonous gas, and others with shrapnel that hadn't been used against Ludovico or Alfonso, which was a great relief to all those on their side. But, Leonardo was interested most of all in the giant furnace as a potential site to cast his bronze statue of the Sforza horse.

I tried to imagine Leonardo out in the battle and siege fields in his Milanese armour that was beautifully constructed by the great armourer Antonio Missaglia and paid for by the young duke of Milan. I reread Leonardo's letter of application to Ludovico about his *instruments of admirable efficiency not in general use*. I looked at his drawings of the war machines that he showed Ludovico and his nephew the duke of Milan, and his subsequent preparatory drawings for his proposed book about the machines and fortifications of war. In my later years, I have observed war battles from a distance, but I personally have not participated in a battle or killed anybody, and now in my old age, I have no intention of ever doing so. In my mind's eye, I watched Leonardo in battle at Brescia, Verona, Ficarolo, and Ferrara with his machines and inventions overseeing his siege engineers and gunners. I wondered how he put all his bizarre machinery to any good use. The military enthusiasts tell me that there is a strategic use for all his weapons, such as his steam blowers, hydraulic saws, sledges for use on mud, devices for dredging ditches, movable siege ladders mounted on carriages for assaulting fortresses, scythed carriages for mowing down troops, chariots with incendiary barrels, the *architronitos* or steam cannons, catapults and trebuchets standing 15 metres tall for hurling heavy stones and incendiary barrels to breach the walls of fortresses, and much, much, more. I looked at Paolo Santini's 166-leaf vellum codex *De machinis* on the weapons of war, and I could more clearly understand why nobody could survive a siege from Leonardo's designed machinery. In the codex, Paolo Santini has a sumptuous painting of soldiers and cavalry in a siege camp at the edge of a flowing river with not a single boat in sight. There is a mix of coloured (red, green, blue, and brown) tents that are round, domelike, triangular, and cabin shaped with side poles held in place by external guys. They have notched-shaped doorways with doors hung from the top in the manner of a curtain. It is a wonderful picture, which I have copied many times for it reminds me of another time when the French and English kings and I gathered together at the campground of the Field of the Cloth of Gold near Calais in France for a meeting and lavish games only one year after Leonardo da Vinci's death at Amboise in 1519.

And among these war machines and the battles and sieges, Leonardo engaged in his other great intellectual interest - the anatomy and wounds of the injured and dying. He observed and sketched the dying and the dead on the fields and in the hospitals. He examined the open cankerous shrapnel wounds of the skull with the leaking brain matter, the chest wounds revealing exposed pink lung and shattered ribs, the gut wounds with twisted yellow and white intestine spilling from the cavities, and the amputated legs and arms thrown onto piles of bloody human organs. He examined eyeballs, protruding tongues, and the bizarre colour and texture of mosaic dead skin. The brains made visible by shattered skulls drew his particular attention for he already had dissected and studied a number of intact skulls during his time in the hospital mortuaries of Florence. Now, it was with a strange curiosity that he examined how the architecture of the head and the brain was irretrievably damaged in battle.

While Ludovico and his generals spared the lives of most of his captives, his ally Alfonso Duke of Calabria and the future king of Naples committed some of the worse atrocities of the war against the Venetians and their towns, villages, and farming houses during his attacks on Brescia and Verona. Along the way, while in charge of the troops of King Ferdinand of Naples, the Duke was met with little resistance, and yet he stole the farmers' pigs, cattle, and horses, and even their useless household goods and burnt down their hovels allowing them nothing to return to. Occasionally, on the road and fields, he and his troops encountered men with weapons in their hands, but the majority fled and sought concealment in the hope of not being seen and murdered. All knew resistance was useless against an organised raging and warlike throng of killers. And whether resistance was met or not, all were put to the sword, the children killed, the women's breasts cut open, the men's legs removed from their bodies, the villagers burned in their hovels and barns, and their animals collected and driven to the back of the columns to feed the invading troops. According to Ludovico Sforza, there was no mercy from a leader like Alfonso whose brain burnt with mad delight and intoxication to decapitate, eviscerate, incinerate, rape, and plunder as his basic strategy of war.

With the fall of Brescia and Verona, Leonardo turned his attentions to the city's architectural wonders and museums and galleries to find painters and paintings of interest. In Brescia, he met with Boninus de Boninis, a publisher of illustrated books. Boninis was originally from the Dubrovnik Republic, and they talked about Leonardo's interest to publish an illustrated book of his drawings of war machines and fortresses. He offered Leonardo encouragement and gave him a complimentary copy of *De Re Miltari* by Valturius that he had printed in Verona only half a year earlier. Leonardo was amazed by the fidelity of the illustrations of military devices, weapons, and castles in the book, for Boninis had visually separated the illustrations from the text providing them with a thin frame and given them captions in distinct black and white print. Boninis explained to Leonardo that he illustrated using woodcut plates prepared by the best woodcutters and illustrators that he could find. This allowed him not only to provide beautifully printed illustrations, but it also allowed him to decrease the size of the drawings to fit into the page margins and improve the overall design and layout of the book. Leonardo suggested engraved copper plates instead of woodblocks for printing illustrations. Surprisingly, Leonardo and Boninis never followed up on their discussions, and they soon lost touch with each other.

Leonardo also spent time with the great Brescian painter Vincenzo Foppa who, although back in Brescia at this moment, was a regular visitor to Milan and was well patronised by the Sforza court including Ludovico IL Moro. Foppa decorated the Medici bank in Milan and painted portraits of Francesco Sforza and Bianca Maria Visconti. He also painted the portrait of Ludovico's courtier Giovan Francesco Brivio who was the nephew of Ludovico's mistress Cecillia Gallerani whose portrait Leonardo later painted in 1489.

The End to the Salt War

The Venetian's war offensive was highly disrupted by the inroads and territorial possessions that Sforza and his allies had gained in the Venetian territory north of the Po River. Surprisingly, Sforza called for peace talks instead of advancing further towards Ferrara. He knew that he had the upper hand and wanted to consolidate before the war could spread to the Duchy of Milan. In order to retaliate against Sforza, the Venetians ordered Roberto Sanseverino to attack the Duchy of Milan under the pretext of supporting the rights of the Visconti heir Louis of Orleans who eventually would succeed his cousin Charles VIII and become king Louis XII of France in 1498. But this attempted diversion failed when Roberto

Sanseverino had to counter Alfonso Duke of Calabria who was sacking Verona to the north of Ferrara as part of his own diversion. The Venetians lost momentum in the spring of 1484 when their navy was attacked and damaged on the River Po. By August, Ludovico Sforza had made the Venetians agree to a treaty that ended the war.

Niccolo Machiavelli wrote the following conclusion in his *History of Florence*,

> The position of Ludovico being known to the Venetians, they thought they could make it available for their own interests; and hoped, as they had often before done, to recover in peace all they had lost by the war; and having secretly entered into a treaty with Ludovico, the terms were concluded in August, 1484.

With the treaty known as the Peace of Bagnolo, Venice retained almost all its conquered lands. Ercole I d' Este the second Duke of Ferrara regained Ariano, Corby, Adria, Melara, Ficarolo, and Castelguglielmo, but lost to the Venetians all of his other territories north of the Po, including the Polesine of Rovigo. The Peace of Bagnolo checked Venetian expansion in the *terra firma*, although ceding to it the town of Rovigo and a broad swath of the fertile delta of the Po. This acquisition agreed upon at Bagnolo marked the highpoint of the broad expanse of Venetian territory; never again would they control so large a territory nor have so much influence as they did in the last half of the 15th century.

Nevertheless, Pope Sixtus IV was not pleased with the terms that were reached without consulting him:

> The news of it literally killed Sixtus. When the ambassadors declared to him the terms of the treaty he was thrown into a violent rage, and declared the peace to be at once shameful and humiliating. The gout from which he suffered reached his heart, and on the following day— 12th August 1484— he died.

Pope Sixtus IV born as Francesco della Rovere was Pope for 13 years. In his time, he was an erratic Pontiff. His greatest accomplishments were his edicts against slavery and to build the Sistine Chapel and to have it decorated with frescoes by the likes of Sandro Botticelli, Domenico Ghirlandaio, Pietro Perugino, Cosimo Roselli, and Pinturicchio. He snubbed Leonardo da Vinci, labelling him as irreverent. He also sullied his rule by his nepotism, support for the Spanish Inquisition, his crusade against the Ottoman Turks, and his involvement in the murder attempt of Lorenzo de' Medici, and the murder of Lorenzo's brother Giuliano. He also meddled too much in the politics of different states and countries for his own and his nephews benefits encouraging the war between Venice and Ferrara, disputed with King Louis XI of France, placed edicts against Florence and Venice, and unsettled the Barons of Naples. He was replaced by Pope Innocent VIII who occupied the Papal throne for eight years until July 1492. Pope Innocent continued Sixtus's legacy and indulged himself in witchcraft, nepotism, the slave trade, and crusades against the infidels.

The Ferrara war was expensive for the Sforza and the citizens of Milan, costing the Sforza family nearly three quarters of their total budget. One of the likely reasons that Ludovico Sforza had fought the Venetians northwest of Ferrara was to keep the battlefront away from Milan and the Duke of Calabria away from invading his territories. When his secret dealings with the Venetians became known to the rest of the allies, they were greatly dissatisfied with him, for as Niccolo Machiavelli wrote in his *History of Florence*,

> … principally because they found that the places won from the Venetians were to be restored; that they were allowed to keep Rovigo and the Polesine, which they had taken from the marquis of Ferrara, and besides this retain all the pre-eminence and authority over Ferrara itself which they had formerly possessed. Thus it was evident to everyone,

they had been engaged in a war which had cost vast sums of money, during the progress of which they had acquired honour, and which was concluded with disgrace; for the places wrested from the enemy were restored without themselves recovering those they had lost. They were, however, compelled to ratify the treaty, on account of the unsatisfactory state of their finances, and because the faults and ambition of others had rendered them unwilling to put their fortunes to further proof.

The poet Francesco Filefo best describes the feeling and meaning of the Lombardy Wars from 1423 to 1453 in the following verse that I have extracted from one of his Odes. I believe it also captures the meaningless of the Lombardy war with Venice from 1482 to 1484 in which Leonardo and my father partook to support Ludovico IL Moro Sforza's campaign.

Thus commenced the wars between men in arms all across the land. The mobilisation of troops begins on the Adriatic coast. Leaping across the Po where the Adda borders the sunny fields of the Milanese, Mars now sows turmoil everywhere throughout the countryside. One catastrophe oppresses gods and men alike, for here the dread lion, like a whirlwind, lays waste the fields. And there the viper, whose body sleep had long possessed, now rages with anger, venom spewing from his mouth. And not only does the savage snake dare to fight the fierce winged lion and stand his ground despite his roaring and his might, but after he has grown more and more hot with rage, he pours out his regiments on the land amid weapons and slaughter. He levels everything; all things are thrown into disorder, and lie in ruins. Peace, long gone, now dies. While Mars rules, the world burns. The Pierian Muses withdraw from this place. They flee, turning their backs to the insanity. No virtues are born of such service. [S11]

It was a successful war, however, for Leonardo da Vinci's reputation, becoming renown as a master architect of fortifications and strategies of war. On the basis of reports on the outcome of the Salt War, he would be hired again for his expertise in fortifications in future campaigns: Ludovico Sforza hired him for fortification and town planning in Milan, Genoa, Como, and along the Adda River (1487 to 1499); Cesare Borgia (captain general of the papal armies) employed him for military architecture, field defence, and cartography for his campaigns in Tuscany, Urbino, Cesena, Porto Cesenatico, Pesaro, Rimi, Val di Chiana, Umbria, the Marches, and Romagna (1502/1503); Niccolo Machiavelli hired him for the Republic of Florence to design fortifications and canalise and straighten the River Arno for Florence and around Pisa (1503/1504); Isabella Duchess of Bari employed him for her castle fortification in Bari; and King Francois I employed him to construct and design fortifications and castles in France (1516/1519).

A Note About Genoa

The Republic of Genoa had supported the Venetians in their fight against Ferrara. Some people find that surprising because they believed that Genoa was always a part of Lombardy and under the rule of the Milanese dukes. In fact, Genoa has been a republic and an independent state in Liguria since 1005, incorporating Corsica in 1347. And that had been the case for some time. So why would Genoa support Venice instead of Milan? First, you must know that the Republic of Genoa borders the southern region of the Duchy of Milan and stretches across the Ligurian north west coast of the Ligurian Sea on a narrow strip of land bordered by the sea, the Alps, and the Apennine Mountains. To the west is France, to the east is Emilia-Romagna and Tuscany, and to the south is the Ligurian Sea. It is a harbour town, possibly first settled long ago by the Ligurians stemming from French and Iberian ancient tribes. Along with Venice, Pisa, and Amalfi, it is a maritime republic involved in shipbuilding, trade, and banking. It had enormous economic success in the past through its trade in spices from the Orient and silk from Constantinople. The French and the Milanese have long attempted to dominate Genoa with varying degrees of success. Generally, it remained a republic administered by a doge and a few influential families. The Milanese held control of Genoa under Galeazzo Maria Sforza from 1464, but with his death, Bona Sforza lost control of Genoa around August 1478 to Pope Sixtus IV who still held Genoa when Venice declared war on Ferrara in 1482.

With the death of Pope Sixtus in 1484, Ludovico turned his attention to regain Genoa after his peace treaty with Venice. Milanese troops were practically welcomed back to Genoa in 1487 when the Genoese cardinal was prepared to return the city to the young duke of Milan Gian Galeazzo Sforza and his guardian Ludovico Sforza who forced the Florentine troops to retreat from their intended quarry. The historian Machiavelli has a more detailed chapter than I can give on the history of Genoa in his book the *History of Florence*. Ludovico believed that he could help Genoa with the construction of ships that would help them deal with the pirates of the Ligurian Sea. Hence, he used Leonardo's ship and military engineering designs to support Genoa from 1487 until the French took over in 1499. Leonardo's only visit to Genoa was in 1498 to inspect the harbour that was badly damaged by the French in 1496. Ludovico had long wanted control of the city harbour of Genoa for it was the hub, the entry and exit point for trade in weapons, agriculture, exotic spices, and silk. Leonardo advised Ludovico and the Counsellors of Milan that they should take up trade with the Ottomans, and that Genoa was where they should develop their shipbuilding and merchant warehouses for such trade. He proposed and designed a series of canals and waterways to join the harbour of Genoa to the river Po near Valenza, which would then join the Milanese waterways and canals at Pavia and the Ticino River junction. This all changed after 1499 when the French won back control of Genoa and all the important Ligurian territories. Now, in my old age, Genoa is just another territory of the Spanish.

Plague of Milan, 1484 to 1485

A few months before the peace settlement with Venice, Leonardo da Vinci was back in Milan at the Predis' workshop working on his painting of the *Virgin of the Rocks*. Ironically, instead of the Venetian troops, a different pestilence entered Milan in August of 1484, and by the end of 1485, it had killed 50,000 of its inhabitants. There had been a previous mass attack by the great plague in 1449, but nobody could remember the exact number of deaths, perhaps 5,000 people. Once again, health officials and plague doctors were appointed to count the dead and to try to cleanse the city of its impurities. My father and Leonardo kept to themselves much of the time with Leonardo visiting my father at the Vaprio d' Adda to help with the renovations or occasionally staying with the young duke at his castles in Abbiategrasso or Vigevano. It was at this time that Leonardo was inspired to prepare a treatise on science and nature, and he began his extensive readings of books from the Antiquity and the Early-Ages that he borrowed from the Melzi, Sanseverino, and Sforza libraries or from any other person or family that possessed books about his interests. Luckily for my father and Leonardo, in 1485, the Milanese governor Ludovico Sforza sent them on a diplomatic mission out of Milan to meet with the kings of Hungary and Poland. By the time they returned back home, the death and disease due to the plague had greatly subsided in Milan.

Milan and Pavia were so badly affected by the plague that the Sforza's sought haven at their country estates in Vigevano. However, the pestilence had spread throughout the countryside and every town and village was affected. The plague had invaded Pavia previously in 1479, and the town officials of that time appointed Giovanni de Ventura as their plague doctor who drew up financial deeds, a cash advance, a house, and severance pay with them in order to perform his dangerous tasks and cures. Everyday, Giovanni de Ventura threw the dice and met with the sick, and working alone at night, he wondered whether he would survive to the next day without contracting the disease. He wanted a good reward for meeting with the damned and avoiding being infected on the basis of his faith, dangerous concoctions, and a strong dose of good luck. By many accounts, he survived throughout the earlier epidemic to work his miracles and bring relief and cures to many of his patients before fading away from view in the times of better health and fortune.

It was in 1486 that the young duke Gian Galeazzo Sforza asked Leonardo to draw up some architectural plans to improve and reconstruct the city's layout and infrastructure for a hygienic ideal city to avert such outbreaks in the future. Leonardo presented his plans to the young duke of Milan and his uncle Ludovico on how to develop the city into an urban environment with clean air and water and by taking appropriate measures on how best to avoid or manage contagions like the plague. Although he took measurements and provided architectural drawings, nobody acted on them, and they were soon forgotten.

The Great Plague or Black Death has raged in Europe for about two hundred years and still no cure is in sight, even to the present day as I write. Milan had another devastating outbreak of the pestilence in 1523 soon after I returned from France and resettled at Vaprio d' Adda. Luckily, my family and I were unharmed and for a time we lived in Bergamo and Como with my mother's relatives. By all accounts, and from what I saw, the symptoms are nasty and horribly painful and best avoided by moving away from the affected areas. I believe that the pestilence first spread from India, Tartary, Mesopotamia, Syria, Armenia, Palestine, and Cairo. The Venetian and Genoese traders and their galleys brought it with them to Sicily, Pisa, Genoa, and Venice from Kaffa in the Crimea and Constantinople and other ports on the Black Sea in about the mid 1340s. By 1350, it had spread throughout all of Europe causing great devastation and killing off half the continent's population. The astrologers and physicians of Europe blamed the great pestilence in the air on the conjunction of Jupiter and Mercury. The clergy and church blamed it on the wild irresponsible life of its citizens and *'everyone who tended to enjoy eating, drinking, hunting, hawking, and gaming.'* According to them, pestilence arrived as a warning of the coming Apocalypse. Soon the plague would be followed by War, Famine, Death and the Last Judgment as described in the Book of Revelation and told by Jesus Christ to John the Apostle. Yet, we all could see that the clergy, the pure and the innocent young children were victims as often as the fornicators and the sinners. Why should our young innocent children die of the horrible plague if Our Lord God is merciful and caring? Is this the reward for our atonement?

The great Florentine writer Giovanni Boccaccio provided us with a description of the plague in Florence in 1348 in one of his stories in the *Decameron*:

> Towards the beginning of the spring of the said year (1348) the doleful effects of the pestilence began to be horribly apparent by the symptoms that showed as if miraculous. Not such were these symptoms as in the East, where as issue of blood from the nose was a manifest sign of inevitable death; but in men and women alike it first betrayed itself by the emergence of certain tumours in the groin or armpits, some of which grew as large as a common apple, others as an egg, some more, some less, which the common folk called gavoccioli. From the two said parts of the body this deadly gavocciolo soon began to propagate and spread itself in all directions indifferently; after which the form of the malady began to change, black spots or livid making their appearance in many cases on the arm or the thigh or elsewhere, now few and large, now minute and numerous. As the gavocciolo had been and still was an infallible token of approaching death, such also were these spots on whomsoever they showed themselves. Which maladies seemed to set entirely at naught both the art of the physician and the virtues of physic; indeed whether it was that the disorder was of a nature to defy such treatment, or that the physicians were at fault and, being ignorant of its source, failed to apply the proper remedies; in either case,

not merely were those that recovered few, but almost all died within three days of the appearance of the said symptoms, sooner or later, and in most cases without any fever or other attendant malady. [S12]

While the people of Milan were still recovering from the pestilence by the end of 1485, Ludovico Sforza suddenly fell seriously ill with symptoms similar to those with the pestilence and most in his court thought that he was doomed to die. However, his physician and astrologer Ambrogio Varesi used the art of cartomancy and necromancy to miraculously cure him within a few weeks. As a justified reward, Ludovico asked the young duke of Milan to grant his physician the properties and the title of count of Rosate for having saved his life. In October of 1483, the young duke himself was plagued by a fever that Varasi cured within a period of a few weeks by evoking talismans, blood letting, and purgatives. (However, there are some like Giorgio Valla and Gian Giacomo Trivulzio who believed that Ludovico's physician had actually poisoned the young duke rather than cured him). So, Gian Galeazzo Sforza Duke of Milan felt obliged and grateful to Varesi for having saved him and his uncle, and he dutifully awarded the physician and astrologer with the said properties of Rosate and other rewards bestowed upon him by Ludovico.

◉

CHAPTER 8

Peace, Travels, Portraits, and Courtside Intrigues, 1485 to 1488

Principles for the Development of a Complete Mind: Study the science of art. Study the art of science. Develop your senses, especially learn how to see. Realise that everything connects to everything else.

— Leonardo da Vinci

Goodwill Visits to the King of Hungary in Buda on the River Danube and Then to Cracow in Poland, 1485

On March 16 in 1485, Leonardo witnessed a total eclipse of the sun and thought it was an omen for peace, at least for a little while. On April 23, Ludovico Sforza sent a letter to Maffeo da Treviglio ambassador to the court of Matthias Corvinus king of Hungary in which he stated that he has commissioned a Madonna from Leonardo on the king's behalf: 'a figure of Our Lady as beautiful, as superb, and as devout as he knows how to make without sparing any effort.'

After the conclusion of the Salt War, Ludovico rewarded Leonardo and my father for their good service during the war with a diplomatic mission to visit the King of Hungary in Buda on the river Danube to discuss the future marriage of his niece Bianca Maria Sforza to the King's only son Janus Corvinus. Bianca Maria was the 13-year-old daughter of the widowed Bona of Savoy and the brother of the young duke of Milan Gian Galeazzo Sforza, and she was engaged to Janus Corvinus on 31ˢᵗ July 1485. With this intended marriage, the Hungarian ruler wanted to secure his son's future inheritance of Hungary and Bohemia and to entitle him as the Duke of Austria.

The Hungarian King and the Sforza of Milan were long time allies and my Melzi ancestors also knew him well. My grandfather Bartolomeo Melzi was a good friend of the king's favourite poet Janus Pannonius who had praised my grandfather's excellence as a poet and a cultured and knowledgeable person. Both poets died relatively young, just two years apart, Janus in 1476 and Bartolomeo in 1478. As an upcoming ten-year anniversary for the remembrance of Janus Pannonius in Hungary, the King was keen to meet with Bartolomeo's grandsons and obtain some hand printed volumes of his poetry, which he wanted for his Royal Library, the *Bibliotheca Corviniana*.

King Matthias Corvinus had taken Beatrice of Naples as his third wife, and she strengthened his interest in contemporaneous Italian art and scholarship with a result that the earliest appearance of Renaissance style buildings and works outside Italy were seen in Hungary. As a consequence, he was keen to consult with an artist and architect like Leonardo da Vinci in order to embellish his new building projects, the Buda Castle and Visegrad in the Renaissance style. He also cultivated Hungarian and Italian epic poems and lyrical songs that were often performed at his court, and he had heard that Leonardo was a wonderful musician and lyricist who had entertained and mentored the young duke of Milan. The Hungarian queen Beatrice of Naples was the sister of Ludovico Sforza's ally Alfonso Duke of Calabria who had told the Hungarian king and queen much about Leonardo and his marvellous war architecture and engineering. Alfonso recommended Leonardo to the king as an expert who could assess and advise on the value and efficacy of rebuilding his forts along his southern frontier.

Consequently, the Hungarian King requested Ludovico to send Leonardo da Vinci to him as part of the goodwill visit. Because the king knew the Melzi from their previous Milanese and Palatine diplomatic missions, Ludovico had no hesitation in sending my father and Leonardo as part of his sixty-man team.

The Hungarian king was a devotee of the Virgin Mary and the Marinian cult, and so, Ludovico persuaded Leonardo to present the king with a painting of *Madonna and Child*. Ludovico who commissioned the painting wanted Leonardo to gift the king with the Madonna who was modelled on Simonetta Vespucci, but Leonardo was loath to part with it. Instead, Leonardo agreed to paint a likeness to present to the king for he wanted to visit and see the books and art works in the king's renowned library. A few months before leaving with the expedition, Leonardo worked harder and quicker than usual to paint a new version of his *Madonna and Child* for the king of Hungary. He modified the face of the new virgin so that she looked less like Simonetta Vespucci and more like Ginevra de' Benci. So, while the original continued to hang in a room at the Melzi Villa in Vaprio, Leonardo and my father packed the newly painted *Madonna and Child* among the other gifts for the king, including a suit of heraldry armour designed and constructed by Antonio Missaglia of Milan. Leonardo and my father were given strict and elaborate instructions on how to assemble the suit correctly.

While in Hungary, Leonardo and my father successfully arranged a marriage contract between Janus Corvinus and Bianca Maria Sforza to be wed by proxy on 25th November 1487. According to the terms, Bianca would receive several Hungarian counties as her dowry. However, due to the opposition and intrigues of Queen Beatrice, the formal marriage never took place. Instead, a marriage between Bianca and King James IV of Scotland was considered in March 1492, but soon abandoned. Two years later, on 16th March 1494, in Hall, Tyrol, Bianca Maria Sforza married the King of the Holy Roman Empire Maximilian I who had been a widower since the death of his much-loved first wife Mary of Burgundy. Ludovico arranged this marriage with the expectation that the Emperor would grant him the official title of Duke of Milan in exchange for a very large dowry and Bianca as his wife.

My father and Leonardo had a memorable time in Hungary and later in Cracow in Poland where Leonardo met with Filippo Buonacorsi, an Italian humanist, poet, and writer who now belonged to the Cracowski court of the Polish King Kazimierz IV Jagiellon. Leonardo was intrigued that Filippo had exiled himself to Poland and the court of Cracow because of accusations of sodomy against him in Rome. According to Filippo, he had written Platonic love poems that were misinterpreted as poems of sodomy and male sexual love. His enemies then spread falsehoods about his sexual proclivities. Filippo said that he was happily married to a Polish noble girl, and that they had a happy and active sexual relationship, which was blessed in the eyes of God and the church in Poland. A few years later, Filippo Buonacorsi was appointed (along with his wife) the Polish ambassador to Venice.

It was on this trip to Hungary and Poland that Leonardo realised that he needed to devote more time and effort to improving his Latin, the international language for the educated from different countries and nations to communicate with each other about all the different spheres of life in art, science, and diplomacy. I appreciated what my father and Leonardo told me about Hungary and Poland because after their deaths I visited both of those countries and remembered their favourable impressions and lessons bestowed upon me. I visited Poland to meet with King Sigismund I, and Queen Bona Sforza, who I had grown up with as children in Milan before she left at the age of six to Naples and later on to Bari. Her mother Isabella Aragon Sforza Duchess of Milan was a close friend of Leonardo da Vinci, and she was the proud wife of the young Duke of Milan Gian Galeazzo Sforza until his tragic death in 1494 at the age of twenty-five years.

When I visited Buda in Hungary to meet with King Louis in 1526, much of the surrounding land was in the hands of the Ottoman Turks. But, that is a story for another time.

A Visit to the Duchy of Savoy, 1486

On their return to Milan, after an audience with his Lordship Ludovico Sforza, they went about their separate businesses until Ludovico called them back together again for another diplomatic mission. This time, he wanted them to visit the Duke of Savoy Charles I and the Duchess of Savoy Blanche of Montferrat in Chambery to present them with letters about financial compensation for Bona of Savoy, the mother of the young duke Gian Sforza and her other children Bianca Maria, Hermes Maria, and Anna Maria. Leonardo leapt at the mission for he knew that this was his opportunity to examine and measure the Shroud of Chambery and its mysterious figure purported to be Jesus Christ himself. Leonardo said he would take the mission provided Ludovico could obtain permission for him to visit the Sainte Chapelle at Chambéry and to see and examine the shroud. This was all arranged for them before they left with a diplomatic team of thirty. This was going to be Leonardo's most difficult mission so far because the Duke of Savoy was still very annoyed with the unconscionable treatment of Bona of Savoy from Ludovico and his cronies. The diplomatic pouch carried an apology and an explanation as to why Bona was exiled. If this was unacceptable to the Duke of Savoy then there was a danger that Leonardo da Vinci's diplomatic team could be detained in gaol and ransomed.

Bona of Savoy was the daughter of the second Duke of Savoy Louis I who reigned from 1440 until his death in 1465. The territory of the Duchy then included Moriana, the Valle d'Aosta, and Piedmont. The Duchy of Savoy was still a relatively young fiefdom at this time having been formed in 1416 after Sigismund the Holy Roman Emperor awarded the new title of Duke of Savoy to Count Amadeus VIII. The Duke of Savoy during my father and Leonardo's visit in 1486 was Charles I the fifth duke. He was 18 years of age and also the titular king of Cyprus, Jerusalem, and Armenia. He ruled from 1482 to 1490. His older brother Philbert I at 7 years of age had preceded him as Duke of Savoy when their father Amadeus IX died in 1472 after having ruled for seven years. Philbert I married his cousin Bianca Maria Sforza in 1476 when she was only 21-months old and her mother Bona of Savoy was still the Duchess of Milan. When Philbert I died in 1482 at the age of 17 years of age, his widow Bianca Maria Sforza at only 10 years of age returned to Milan and was placed under the tutelage of her uncle Ludovico Il Moro who allowed her to indulge her own interests until at the age of 13 years she was engaged to Janus Corvinus, the son of King Matthias of Hungary.

When Charles I died in 1490, his 18-year-old wife Bianca di Montferrato (also known as Bianche of Montferrat) became the regent of the Duchy of Savoy from 1490 to 1496 until the accidental fall and death of her 7-year-old son Charles II in his bedroom in Moncalieri. It was under Bianca di Montferrato's regency that she with the support of Ludovico Sforza allowed king Charles VIII of France free passage through her duchy to invade Italy and conquer Naples. After all, Bianca di Montferrato had Sforza blood. She was the eldest daughter of William VIII Marquess of Montferrat and Elisabetta Sforza who was the daughter of Duke of Milan Francesco I Sforza and Duchess Bianca Maria Visconti, after whom she was named.

A Meeting with Bona of Savoy

On meeting with the Duke and Duchess of Savoy, Ludovico's diplomatic team discussed the situation of Bona of Savoy's exile from Milan and the impending marriage of her son the young duke of Milan to Isabella of Aragon the princess of Naples. The wedding was scheduled for February of 1489 in Milan, still two and a half years away. Yet, the Duke and Duchess of Savoy already wanted to know what role was proposed for Bona of Savoy, and they wanted to have assurances that she would be invited, and that she would be treated with the respect that she deserved as the mother of the young duke. Ludovico had instructed his diplomatic party to provide all assurances that Bona would be invited to attend the marriage, and that she would be given due respect, although she would not be allowed to remain in Milan after the wedding, and that she would be required to return to the Duchy of Savoy or to France if she preferred.

The Duke and Duchy of Savoy spoke on behalf of Bona for she had declined to meet with the Milanese diplomatic mission. However, she did request to have an audience with Leonardo, and he was happy to oblige her, for he liked Bona, as he did all women, even if they were flawed, and Bona was considered unjustly to be terribly self-centred, scatter brained, and bone headed. Leonardo and Bona spent a day together, and he gave her his account of her children and how her son missed her immensely, but was coping and developing well under the tutelage of his uncle Ludovico IL Moro. The young duke's aunt was Ippolita Maria Sforza, the first wife of King Alfonso II of Naples, and he was engaged to marry her daughter Isabella. Leonardo had not yet met with Isabella, and he had nothing to say about her. Instead, he spoke of her son's love for hunting, horses, music, and his gift for mathematics. He spoke nothing of her son's precocious growing sexual desires for sleeping with beautiful young girls. He was fearful this would spark memories in her of her husband's infidelities and enormously perverted sexual appetite.

Bona was desperate for news about her other children. Leonardo talked about his trip to Hungary to celebrate and discuss the engagement of her daughter Bianca Maria Sforza to Janus Corvinus the son of the Hungarian King. However, he warned Bona that this engagement might come to naught because he detected a resistance from the queen of Hungary Beatrice of Naples. Bona's youngest son Hermes Maria was now 16 years old, and he was the Marquis of Tortona, but still living in Milan under the tutelage of Ludovico. Anna Maria Sforza was only ten and rather neglected by Ludovico, but Leonardo tried to paint a rosy picture of her development and education. She was a pretty girl and was engaged from birth to Alfonso I d' Este who was in line to become the next Duke of Ferrara. Bona cried copiously at the memory of her children. How could Ludovico still refuse her to see or communicate with them? Leonardo had no answer for her, but he tried to comfort her and assure her that they still loved her dearly, and that when they reached the age of independence, they would surely visit her with the love and attachment that they always had for her as their loving and caring mother. He thought of his own mother and how he had not visited her since he left Florence four years ago.

Before parting, Leonardo heard a seditious secret from the lips of a distressed and bitter Bona. 'Leonardo, I have written letters to my children. Would you please deliver them without His Lordship Ludovico intercepting them? Do you know that this very Christmas will be ten years since my husband, His Lord, Galeazzo Maria, the 5th Duke of Milan, was murdered? I have asked my children to honour their father's memory and soul with a special mass and prayers, and if they are afraid to do so in public then they should do so in private. Please ensure that my son Gian the duke of Milan fulfils his mother's wishes and prayers and that he helps his brother and sisters to pray for and celebrate their loving father's memory. My husband, may his spirit rest in peace, is buried secretly in the apse of St. Andrew in Melzo. He is buried there because his mistress Lucia Marliani convinced me that it was the safest place to have his body buried secretly and avoid having his grave desecrated by the violent mobs that had called him a tyrant and by those who supported the murderers. Leonardo, I have asked my children to decorate the apse at St. Andrew where he is buried in memory of my murdered husband. I requested that you be the artist to help them decorate the chapel. You don't know, Leonardo, but I tell you that it was Ludovico who killed his brother Galeazzo. He arranged through his secret agents that Cola Montano and his students murder my husband on that fateful day after Christmas day. It was only I and my children and Ludovico's agents who knew that he would be there alone at the church of Santo Stefano Maggiore. I now worry so much for my son Gian Galeazzo who I fear will soon become Ludovico's next victim, for Ludovico will never release his grasp and power over my son. Instead, he will murder my son and make it look like an accident or natural causes. My son will be pushed from his horse and fatally injured or slowly poisoned by Ludovico's doctors. Ludovico is sly and evil, and he will never allow my son to take the ruling powers away from him, for he sees these powers as rightfully his. Mark my words Leonardo, please try to save my son from the awful fate that awaits him. I rather see my son alive in exile than dead like my husband, killed by that deceitful, canker spreading murderer Ludovico Il Moro Sforza.'

On Seeing the Shroud of Jesus

A few days after his meeting with Bona, Leonardo was given permission to view the Shroud of Jesus. The Duke and the clergy allowed him to sketch and measure what he saw and examined.

The chaplain Jean Renguis solemnly carried the Shroud in its silver-gilt case to a long table, unfolded the bundle of black cloth, removed the folded yellowish linen cloth from its red silk coverlet, and stretched it out on a long table. The attending clergy chanted prayers in its presence as testimony to its authenticity. Everybody knelt down to venerate it, and while still on their knees, they examined every part of it, kissing it with tender devotion. They told Leonardo that 'the Shroud's authenticity has been confirmed by it having been tried by fire, boiled in oil, laundered many times, but it was not possible to efface or remove the imprint and image.' The chaplain repacked the Shroud and carried it to the Chapel's high altar where they unpacked and unfolded the cloth again and hung it vertically from a specially constructed stand on a balustrade above them for the purposes of proper viewing. What my father and Leonardo saw amazed them. It was a linen sheet with an image of a fully-grown man, a corpse in repose, with his bloodied body clearly visible on each side of the hanging cloth. The images of the wounds were of a distinct colour, different from that of the rest of the body. This colour was brown, and it outlined the corpse as if the blood and serum and fluids from the wounds had clotted and dyed the cloth to reveal the image of the body. The blood itself was purple red in colour and situated more or less according to the position of the wounds. Leonardo stood on a scaffold especially constructed for him for the investigation, and he took his measurements of the cloth and the figure while the attendants told him the history of how the shroud came into their hands.

The Shroud was first seen in Jerusalem and Edessa 500 years after the crucifixion of Christ. It was not seen again for another 500 years until King Louis VII of France reportedly venerated it in Constantinople in 1147. The Shroud of Jesus became the possession of the French knight Geoffrey de Charny when he was in Constantinople in 1349. He wrote to Pope Clement VI to report that he had the Shroud, and that he would house it in a church for St. Mary in Lirey in France to honour the Holy Trinity for helping him escape from the English when he was their prisoner at a time during the Hundred Years' War. Expositions of the Shroud held in Lirey in 1355 attracted large crowds of pilgrims. The Bishop Henri did not believe that the Shroud was genuine so he ordered the expositions to be halted. This forced Geoffrey I de Charny to hide the Shroud at the Treasury. The English eventually killed him at the Battle of Poitiers on the 19th September 1356, and his son Geoffrey II inherited the Shroud. In 1390, Pope Clement VII and the Bishop d'Arcis ordered him to keep silent on the Shroud under threat of excommunication.

Geoffrey II died on 22nd of May 1398, and his daughter Margaret de Charny inherited the Shroud. She married twice, and it is recorded in the chronicles that she exhibited the Shroud in a meadow on the banks of the river Doubs on 6th July 1418, at Mons in 1448 and 1449, at Liege in 1449, and at the Germnolles Castle in 1452. In 1457, Margaret de Charny was excommunicated for not returning the Shroud to the Lirey canons. She died in 1464 leaving her Lirey lands to her cousin and godson Antoine-Guerry des Essars, but she transferred the Shroud to the ownership of Duke Louis I of Savoy. The Duke informed the church that he had acquired the Shroud, and he agreed to pay the Lirey canons an annual rent to be drawn from the revenues of the castle of Gaillard near Geneva as compensation for their loss of the Shroud. After the death of Louis I, his son Duke Amaedeus IX of Savoy inherited the Shroud, and he instituted the cult of the Shroud in the Sainte Chapelle at Chambéry. In the period between 1465 and 1486, the Shroud belonged to the House of Savoy, and it travelled with them on their various Court journeys from castle to castle including Vercelli, Turin, Ivrea, Moncalieri, Susa, Avigliano, Rivoli, and Pinerolo. Now, here on Leonardo's first visit to Savoy, it was in the presence of the chaplain Jean Renguis and the sacristan George Carrelet at the Sainte Chapelle in Chambéry, an inventory described as *'enveloped in a red silk drape, and kept in a case covered with crimson velours, decorated with silver-gilt nails, and locked with a golden key.'*

It took Leonardo three days before he was satisfied that he had examined the Shroud as completely as he was allowed. He remained sceptical, but he could not see how any artist could have achieved such an amazing likeness of an actual body. It could have been faked using some trickery of light. Alternatively, he surmised that somebody has actually been wrapped up into the shroud and by unusual or mystical odds had left an imprint on the cloth. But, why the negative image and not the positive one that he expected to see from an actual body imprint? This was the big question. They all looked at Leonardo waiting for the answer. He gave them nothing in return. They all remained silent until a priest began to pray, and then, all their prayers filled the room. After these prayers, Leonardo gave his audience a summary of the results of his measurements and impressions of the Shroud.

I cannot definitely say that this is the true burial cloth of Jesus of Nazareth nor can I say it is a fake. If it is a fake by an artist unknown to me, then it is the most beautifully constructed chiaroscuro painting that I have ever seen. The blood appears to be real, although it may be a little too much on the bright side of colour, for if it is real then it should have faded or darkened with time depending on the conditions and history of its storage and washings. But let me list to you my assessment of this extraordinary image as seen by the eyes of a painter and architect, one who at this time does not know how to best recreate this image with the techniques he has available to himself, not even by the camera obscura. First, the cloth is expensive and ancient, and still in an excellent condition. It is not from this time or place. It is beautifully woven with a thin thread, many hundreds of fibres fill the cloth. It is 6.4 braccia (4.4 m) long and 2 braccia (1.4 m) wide of straw-yellow colour containing the impression of a fully-grown adult man of about 32 years of age. He is naked, well proportioned, and muscular. His face is bearded, with a moustache. He wears a chinstrap to flatten out his beard underneath his chin. He has long hair. He is covered with pockets of blood visible both on the front and the back of his image on the cloth. The front of the cloth is the anterior view of a man being crucified. The back of the cloth is the dorsal view of the same man corresponding in a correct shape and size to the image on the front of the cloth. The body image is faint, and there is no saturation of the brown pigments. The bloodstains are much stronger in colour than the body image, which does not have well defined contours. The body measures 2.6 braccia (176 cm), the height of a normal man who is a head and neck shorter than me. His thumbs are not visible, possibly compressed onto his palms. As you say, this would happen if a nail was driven through the nerves of his wrist. His nose shows a distinct swelling as if it was broken. A body image on the back surface of the cloth is in the same exact position and with the same anatomic details as the body image on the front. Image details corresponding to grooves of his eye sockets and the sides of his face are fainter than the raised regions of the face. The ridges above his eyes, the nose tip, the moustache, his bottom lip, and his chin area are more clearly represented than the rest of his face. There appear to be coins placed over his eyes, but this I would need to study more closely. His anatomical details are in agreement with my normal human-body measurements, although his hands, calves, and torso appear to vary a little from the norm. The fingers in the image appear to be longer than average. The body image shows no evidence of putrefaction or tissue breakdown. The wounds on his back, hand, and legs are bloody and show that his was scourged with dumbbell shapes before his crucifixion. However, he was not maimed or disfigured as is often accompanied with a crucifixion. It appears to me that the bloodstains are exactly like those that are exudated or leaked from clotting wounds and transferred to a cloth in contact with a wounded human body. The wounds from the crown of thorns are clearly visible from the man's head. Yet, there is no body image formation at the sides of the body on both the frontal and dorsal sides of the cloth, as I would have expected if a real bloodied man had been wrapped in the shroud.

There is no evidence that I can see that this image was painted by human hands. I see no brush strokes, I see no clear pigments that I could scrape from the image and then dissolve into water or oil and use as a paint to retransfer onto paper or onto a canvas. If the image is trickery, it is trickery beyond my humble talents to detect them. The image is negative in density and opposite to that which an artist would paint. As an example, I show you a copy that I have made of the image's head. It is almost identical to what you can see on the cloth. The eyes have negative density on the cloth. Now, I show you the positive image that I have painted. See how I have filled the eyes with a positive density. These two paintings that I show you for comparison are examples of a positive and negative image, but the image on the cloth is negative as if it was made by some gaseous energy, light or force that has moved out of the body and painted the image directly onto both sides of the cloth. I could do that as an artist, to burn on a man's image using a mirror or camera obscura, but possibly with not such exact precision. The face and head are extraordinary. The face is sad, but majestically serene, as if it was Jesus himself suffering for all of mankind. I can give you no further insight than what I have told you and what you already know. It is an image and a cloth that should be displayed and venerated for its profound mystery and beauty. [S13]

The *Shroud Man* of Chambéry affected Leonardo enormously. He thought about it solemnly all the way on his return to Milan. His thoughts would lead to his reassessment of the eternal measurements of his *Vitruvian Man*, the design of his crucifixion painting at the apse of St. Andrew in Melzo in memory of the assassination of Galeazzo Maria Sforza, and how he would later paint his *Salvator Mundi*, the Face of Jesus (the *Shroud Man*), with the crystal ball in his hand. It took Leonardo almost twenty years to complete a version of *Salvator Mundi* for King Louis XII of France, and yet, many painters had already copied his earlier versions to sell to their clients. He visited Turin with me in tow in 1509 to see and compare the painted face of his *Salvator Mundi* to that of the *Shroud Man*.

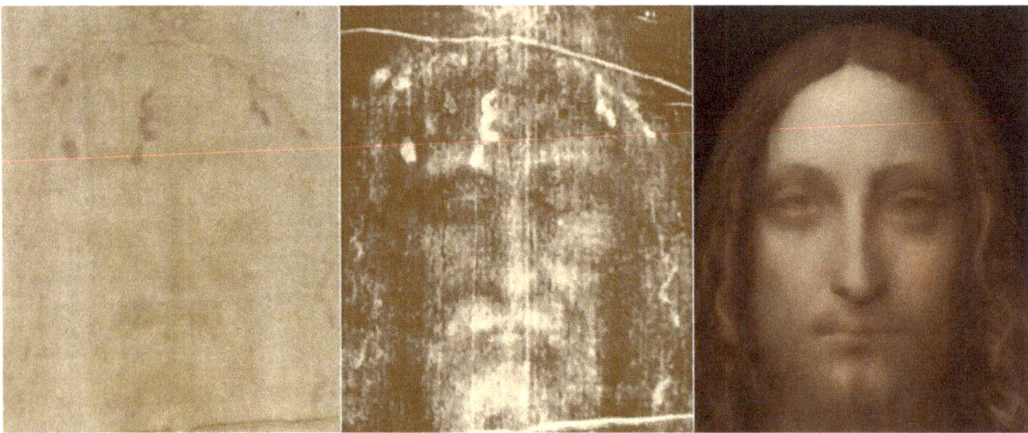

Fig. 27. A comparison between the head of the Shroud Man*'s negative (left) and reverse (middle) image and Leonardo's painting of the head of* Salvator Mundi *(right).*

All went well for Leonardo in the Duchy of Savoy. He accomplished his mission, and he charmed the Duke and Duchess to such a degree that they offered him a permanent position in their court as royal architect, painter, and musician. Leonardo only declined the offer a day or two before they set out to return to Milan after having accomplished most of their tasks for themselves and for Ludovico Sforza.

Mountaineering in the Savoy Alps

On their way back to Milan, my father and Leonardo decided to accompany a group of nine other adventurers to traverse the valleys and visit the base of Mont Blanc and then, to go on and scale Monte Rosa near the Savoy-Italian border. To reach the heights of Monte Rosa was a strenuous and technically difficult five- to eight-hour climb up steep grades and uncomfortable slippery walks along icy paths and glaciers at an altitude of up to 14,000 feet. They stayed the night below the summit without incident and huddled together all night for added warmth. Although they never succeeded to reach the top of the summit, this experience greatly impressed Leonardo, and he later wrote about it in his notebook.

> The river Arve, a quarter of a mile from Geneva in Savoy, where the fair is held on Midsummer Day in the village of Saint Gervais. And this may be seen, as I saw it, by any one going up Monte Rosa a peak of the Alps, which divide France from Italy. The base of this mountain gives birth to the four rivers, which flow in four different directions through the whole of Europe. And no mountain has its base at so great a height as this, which lifts itself above almost all the clouds; and snow seldom falls there, but only hail in the summer, when the clouds are highest. And this hail lies unmelted there, so that if it were not for the absorption of the rising and falling clouds, which does not happen more than twice in an age, an enormous mass of ice would be piled up there by the layers of hail, and in the middle of July I found it very considerable; and I saw the sky above me quite dark, and the sun as it fell on the mountain was far brighter here than in the plains below, because a smaller extent of atmosphere lay between the summit of the mountain and the sun.

Courtship Between Gerolamo Melzi and Tommasina della Torre

On their return to Milan, my father and Leonardo were pleasantly surprised to find that Donna Visconti and her daughter Tommasina della Torre were now in the employment of the Sforza court and residing at the Corte Vecchio (Palazza Reale). One year previously, Donna Visconti's husband Giovanni Francesco della Torre had taken ill and died. Ludovico Sforza had heard about the death and offered her and her daughter a position in Milan as ladies in-waiting. To overcome her grief for the loss of her husband and Tommasina's father, she accepted Lord Sforza's offer, for it was a generous one. Her sons, both older than Tommasina, had remained in Bergamo to look after the estates there and elsewhere, including those in Como. Ludovico wanted Donna Visconti to be present in his court because he had many festivities, ceremonies, visits, and entertainments planned, and he recognised that she had the education, a charm and naturalness that would please his many visitors and their wives. Now, that they were all together in Milan, Tommasina who was 17 years old and Gerolamo who was 26 years old began courting each other with unbridled passion.

Decorating the Church of St. Andrew (Sant' Andrea) in Melzo, 1486/1487 [S14]

In August 1486, Lucia Marliani Countess of Melzo on great insistence from Bona of Savoy commissioned Leonardo to prepare a private chapel at the apse of the Church of St. Andrew in Melzo in readiness for a Sforza family remembrance of the ten-year anniversary of the assassination of Galeazzo Maria Sforza the 5th Duke of Milan. The countess of Melzo would pay Leonardo his commission as well as those of other artists to decorate the chapel where the duke was secretly buried. Ludovico Sforza would provide token support for the undertaking, which had to remain a secret because Lucia and the Sforza family did not want the population of Milan to know where the duke was laid to permanent rest. Lucia Marliani, although married to Ambrose Raverti, had been the duke's special bride, his *Concubitus* by legal decree for a period of two years before his assassination, and she still retained most of her properties in Melzo that had been gifted to her by Duke Galeazzo Sforza before he was murdered. Lucia offered Leonardo da Vinci her residence in Melzo while he prepared the chapel of St. Andrew. The private church of St. Andrew retains its grace at the centre of the small town, which is neatly condensed with low residential houses and warehouses for the fishermen and farmers of the region. Leonardo accepted the commission graciously, and he stayed both in Melzo and at Vaprio with my father on the Adda River while he set about his work at St. Andrew.

Leonardo gathered about him the fresco painters and builders who were necessary to restructure the floor, walls, roof, and bell tower of the church of St. Andrew. For the next six months, he set about to prepare the chapel with his own frescoes and those of others. He painted the following fresco and designs:

1.   St. Andrew crucified on the diagonal cross, shaped like an X. The divine proportion of the martyr St. Andrew. Having seen the *Shroud Man* and his nail wounds to hands and feet, Leonardo decided to leave out the nails and instead paint the hands and feet tied to the cross in a less gruesome depiction of a crucifixion. As with his *Vitruvian Man*, Leonardo placed the diagonal cross and St. Andrew in a circle within a square. He decided on using similar colours that he saw with the *Shroud Man*, but he saturated his yellows and browns to allow them to stand out much more clearly. He painted on dry fresco plaster, a technique that was totally different to those of others who used the wet plaster method.

2.   The diagonal cross of St. Andrew. A simple design, two serpents coiled artistically about two swords, much like Caterina Sforza's logo of the X and the symbolic coiling of the Sforza/Visconti serpent. Yet, the two serpents coiled about an X has another much more personal meaning for Leonardo than the viewer might realise. His design of the serpents is similar to but much simpler than the one that he once had painted on a shield for a Florentine merchant client that had greatly impressed his father. Giorgio Vasari described the serpent shield in his book on Leonardo as one that *'he formed a great ugly creature, most horrible and terrifying, which emitted a poisonous breath and turned the air to flame; and he made it coming out of a dark and jagged rock, belching forth venom from its open throat, fire from its eyes, and smoke from its nostrils, in so strange a fashion that it appeared altogether a monstrous and horrible thing; and so long did he labour over making it, that the stench of the dead animals in that room was past bearing, but Leonardo did not notice it, so great was the love that he bore towards art.'*

3.   Quadrifoglio - the four-leaf clover - the X - the logo of the squared circle. While painting the fresco of St. Andrew on the diagonal cross, Leonardo finally squared the circle, a task he was working on since his time in Florence when he studied the architectural drawings of Vitruvius. He wrote in one of his notebooks, *'the morning* (crossed through and replaced by night) *of St. Andrews, after the candles and the paper I was writing on were consumed, I finally squared the circle.'* and later, ***'could you give me a place to be kept secret, like the church of S. Andrea in Melzo.'*** In celebration, he painted the squared circle logo, the four-leaved clover on the wall of the apse.

4.   Seven portraits of the *Warriors of Milan*. These *Warriors of Milan* resemble his drawings of the kings and warriors in his *Adoration of the Magi* in Florence, but here his seven portraits are the Sforza men, with Ludovico standing out as the il Moro, with his black face looking very sinister. A young Bona with her baby in her arms looks away in horror at the murder of her husband.

5.   The *Madonna and Child* painted under the shell is more classical than his usual depictions, and here he has modelled the Madonna on Bona herself. His assistants completed most of this painting.

6.   The child holding on to the hand of his mother looks like a slightly older version of the Madonna and Child in his *Adoration of the Magi* in Florence.

Later on, before the end of 1486, Catherine Sforza-Riario and her husband Girolamo assisted with the commission of the Apse of the Church of Saint Andrew. Her uncle Il Moro had invited Catherine Sforza-Riario to join him in 1487 to visit Melzo and commemorate the 10th anniversary of the murder of his brother and her father. She was the illegitimate, but the favourite daughter of Galeazzo Maria Sforza the 5th duke of Milan. She and Leonardo developed an immediate liking for each other, and they took active part together in the ceremonies practicing the allusions, metaphors, symbols, and alchemy of the arts that attracted them to each other. Her husband Girolamo who was Governor of the Papal States and the nephew of Pope Sixtus IV provided a substantial sum of money to renovate the apse, and he was rewarded with his portrayal as St. Jerome in the fresco together with his wife Catherine Sforza-Riario, the daughter of the assassinated duke. Another votive fresco is dedicated to Santa Maria from the Fountain of Caravazo with Francesco Sforza and Bianca Maria Visconti, the parents of Galeazzo Maria and Ludovico. Two majolica ceramic dishes depicting Caterina Sforza and Girolamo Riario are pasted into the wall of the Apse.

Apart from Leonardo's fresco and his designs, there are those of other painters and portraits of the commissioners, those who had commissioned the frescoes and symbols designed to seek pardon for the assassination of Galeazzo Maria Sforza the 5th duke of Milan. Bernardino Zenale under the instruction of Leonardo painted the Saints Catherine of Alexandria and Gerolamo supplicating the intercession of the Virgin and Child, with St. John the Baptist as the father for 'forgiveness'.

When I first saw these frescoes, a number of things struck me about them that I had not thought about at the time. There were contradictions and strange symbols in them that indicted to me and to others that Ludovico IL Moro was responsible for the murder of his brother the 5th Duke of Milan. The crucifixion scene of St. Andrew, the martyr, itself is contradictory with an extraordinary double meaning. Suddenly, the history of Galeazzo's murder was fully revealed to me in that one crucifixion scene because his assassin was Giovan Andrea (Andrew) Lumpugnani. Is it Andrew Lumpugnani the killer of the duke who in fact is being crucified in Leonardo's depiction? I don't know for sure. However, I do know that Leonardo believed that Ludovico was responsible for the murder of his brother Galeazzo Maria Sforza the 5th Duke of Milan and the murder of his nephew Gian Galeazzo Sforza the 6th Duke of Milan. Moreover, the two beams that form the cross of St. Andrew in the fresco are an allusion to the murderer's name. This is not any regular X; it is the X of death, the two knives of Ludovico IL Moro Sforza, a sign of his betrayal of the two dukes' of Milan. Yet, Caterina Sforza-Riario boxed the X, put it into an alchemical square, and used it as her personal emblem.

The *Lady with the Ermine*, Caterina Sforza-Riario

About a year after the commemoration of Galeazzo Maria Sforza at the Church of St. Andrew, the Forlesian Orsi family assassinated Girolamo Riario in Forli in April of 1488. Nine assassins slashed him to death and flung his body from the walls of the castle onto a nearby piazza where angry supporters further mutilated his body. Lorenzo de' Medici who regarded Girolamo Riario as one of the main instigators of the Pazzi conspiracy to kill his brother Giuliano and who had wounded him in the cathedral of Florence on 26th April 1478, celebrated his murder.

As for the widowed Caterina Sforza-Riario, she would go on to marry another two lords and give birth to eight children. She and Leonardo remained friends, and they would cross paths a number of times, the final time in Florence a year before her death on the 28th of May 1509, aged 46 years.

While Caterina Sforza-Riario was in Milan from January to April of 1487, she sat for a portrait by Leonardo. She was 24 years old with five children, but still beautiful and youthful looking. In this portrait, Leonardo drew and painted her as the royal lady with an ermine snuggled against her left arm. She is in three-quarter pose, her royal profile looking out at something or somebody to her left. She was an esteemed huntress and a warrior, and she loved her pet stoat because it would rather face death than soil its white coat. Befriending a stoat as a friend or neighbour before setting out on a journey was considered a good luck gesture against the poisons inflicted and encountered by its venom. Moreover, the ermine is a symbol of Caterina Sforza's late father Galeazzo Maria Sforza (and her uncle Ludovico Sforza) whose pure white paw points to the red blood that he lost during his assassination. The ermine also symbolises her husband Girolamo Riario who himself was murdered one year after Leonardo began the portrait of his wife. We know this is Caterina Sforza in the picture because Leonardo has included her emblem, the ribboned **X** within a square, her personal heraldry as designed by Leonardo. It is displayed on the golden brown vertical strip of her dress from the top of her right shoulder all the way down to the top of her right wrist. Somehow, Leonardo foresaw and captured the travails of destiny awaiting her by turning her towards her left and giving her and her ermine the dreamy gaze of confident expectation by having them both look out in the same direction where the elongated fingers of her right hand elegantly point towards her father's or her own Fortune. Leonardo wrote the following note about the painting in one of his manuscripts, '*the ermine with the mud. Galeazzo in tranquil times and a figure of Fortune.*'

Fig. 28. *Caterina Sforza-Riario as the* Lady with the Ermine *(usually mistaken to be Cecilia Gallerani) by Leonardo da Vinci.*

Fig. 29. *Caterina Sforza-Riario's symbol of the X in a square box displayed on her hair wrap.*

Caterina Sforza-Riario, her husband, her children, and her entourage returned to Forli in April before the completion of her portrait a few days before Leonardo's thirty-fifth birthday. She and Leonardo stayed firm friends throughout the remainder of their lives, and she also was a friend and model of the Florentine painters Sandro Botticelli and Lorenzo di Credi.

The Meaning of the White Ermine

The white ermine in Leonardo's picture is confusing for many who see it. The viewer can interpret the symbolism in many different ways. The educated citizens know that the white ermine is closely attached to the history of Milan, and that it also symbolises the Sforza court and the Sforza dukes. The patron saint of Milan is Saint Ambrose who was bishop of Milan in the year 347 AD. He is often depicted in illustrations while he is reading or writing and in the presence of one or more white ermine as a symbol of his ascetic, pure, and generous life style. The ermine is known to protect its immaculately white fur from soiling, even at the risk of death. The popes and bishops often wore red velvet garments or hats trimmed with white ermine. Leonardo wrote that the ermine would rather let himself be captured than flee into the soiled burrow, so as not to stain its white fur. Better dead than dishonoured is the ermine's motto. The white ermine is also the personal symbol of Ludovico Sforza. In 1486, he was inducted into the Order of the Ermine established by King Ferdinand I in Naples in 1465. The court of Sforza employed the white ermine as their symbol of honour and virtuousness, and the court poet Bernardo Bellincioni referred to Ludovico Sforza as a 'white ermine' and the protector of such values. This was ironic because Ludovico was also called 'Il Moro', the Moor or Dark One, and he loved to use the symbols of the 'black moor' as well as the dark or the deep blue mulberries from the mulberry tree.

Fig. 30. This picture copied from Bona Sforza's (the Queen of Poland) Book of Prayers *depicts St. Ambrose of Milan with the two Sforza ermine in the foreground, the brothers Galeazzo and Ludovico Sforza.*

Some people who have seen the picture of Caterina Sforza-Riario have informed me that it shows Ludovico's mistress holding him with unstained love, ermine-like, an adornment to Ludovico while he, the ermine himself, is her hunter and protector. No … big mistake. Leonardo did not use the white ermine as a symbol to show that Ludovico is in the arms of his mistress as some have told me, mistaking Catherine Sforza for Ludovico's mistress Cecilia Gallerani. No – the ermine sends a different message. If the ermine is Ludovico, the brother of Galeazzo Sforza, then he is the hunter and killer of the Sforza dukes as many in Milan believed.

The *Beautiful Jewel*, Cecilia Gallerani

Impressed by the beauty of the *Lady with the Ermine*, Ludovico IL Moro Sforza commissioned Leonardo to paint a portrait for him of his court companion Cecilia Gallerani who was 17 years old and beautiful as a jewel. Leonardo painted Cecilia as a mirror image of the *Lady with the Ermine* in three-quarter pose, but looking out of the picture frame a little apprehensively to her left side, towards the viewer. She has a small blemish of teenage youth to the left of her lower lip. Some people still make the error of thinking that the *Lady with the Ermine* is Cecilia Gallerani. They are wrong. Instead of an ermine, Leonardo placed a railing, a barrier, in front of her, alluding to the fact that she was the mistress of Ludovico and barred from attending the official proceedings at the Sforza court where his wife Beatrice d'Este resided. Cecilia Gallerani bore Ludovico a child, but she was not allowed into the legitimate court of the Sforza household because he was engaged to Beatrice d'Este, daughter of Ercole d'Este and Eleonora d'Aragona, and he married her in 1491. We know that this portrait is of Cecilia Gallerani by Leonardo because of the distinct Vinci bow ties on her shoulders and the Gallerani black and brown decoration on the embroidered top of her dress.

Fig. 31. Cecilia Gallerani as the Beautiful Jewel *or* La Belle Ferronnière *by Leonardo da Vinci.*

The court poet Bernardo Bellincioni had described Leonardo's portrait of Cecilia Gallerani as one that *'makes her seem to listen and not to speak'*, and he made no mention of an ermine on her arm because he, Bernardo Bellincioni, easily distinguished between the portraits of Caterina Sforza with the ermine and Cecilia Gallerani with the barrier. If Cecilia had an ermine in her arms, he would have said so. This painting of the *Beautiful Jewel* as Leonardo called her became known in French circles as *La Belle Ferronnière* because Cecilia Gallerani was the daughter of a successful ironmonger (ferronnier), an extremely rich merchant who Ludovico needed for the construction of his war machines and fortress defences.

On Leonardo's Portrait of Madonna Cecilia by Bernardo Bellincioni:
Nature, why are you angry? Who do you envy?
Vinci, who has painted one of your stars;
Cecilia, so beautiful is she
Whose lovely eyes make the sun seem a dark shadow.
The honour is yours, even if in his painting
He makes her seem to listen and not to speak.
Think, the more beautiful and vivacious she seems
The more glory will be yours in all the future ages.
Therefore, you may now thank Ludovico
And the genius and the hand of Leonardo,
Who wish to leave something of yours to posterity.

Whoever sees her like this, although it may be too late
To see her alive, will say: it is enough for us
To know now what are Nature and Art. [S15]

Portraits of the Young Duke of Milan, Gian Galeazzo Sforza

Fig. 32. The young duke Gian Galeazzo Sforza in his customary heraldic red and green and Leonardo's knotted bows and the interlocking ducal chains hanging over his chest.

By 1486, with the help of the young duke Gian Galeazzo Sforza who wanted more paintings from him, Leonardo rented his own studio at the Corte Vecchio (Corte dell' Arengo, Palazzo Reale or 'old court') where he attracted a number of young assistants. Two of his assistants Giovanni Antonio Boltraffio and Marco d'Oggiono were from good Milanese families and became life-long disciples of Leonardo. In 1487, Leonardo spent time between the homes and company of the Sanseverino, the Melzi, the Predis, and the Sforza, and he especially assisted the young duke to indulge in his musical interests. He experimented with various automated musical instruments; drum machines, flutes, and horns to present to the young duke, telling him, *'we will have some of these playing at your wedding celebrations.'* He, de Pedris, and Boltraffio spend much of their time painting portraits of the young duke wearing his distinctive green and red ducal colours and interlocking ducal chains in angelic poses with an arrow as a symbol of Saint Sebastian (his favourite saint), with musical instruments, and with angel wings, for he indeed was angelic looking.

Then, between July and September of 1487, Leonardo received payments to prepare drawings and a design for a domed-crossing tower for the Milan Cathedral. He hired the carpenter's assistant Bernardino de' Madis to build a wood model of the proposed *tiburio* because he would be competing against the best architects inside and outside Milan, the likes of Donato Bramante, Francesco di Giorgio, Giovanni Battagio, Luca Fancelli, Giovanni Antonio Amadeo, and Giacomo Dolcebuono. This was a competitive war worth winning for Leonardo, not for acquisition of land or wealth, but for the honour to produce the winning architectural design against the best of his peers.

❧❧❧❧❧

Fig. 33. *Duke Gian Galeazzo Sforza as* St. Sebastian *with an arrow.*

Fig. 34. *The young duke Gian Galeazzo Sforza by Leonardo da Vinci and de' Predis brothers' as the* Green Angel *and* Red Angel *that flank Leonardo's* Virgin of the Rocks *at the church of San Francesco Maggiore.*

Leonardo's Birthday Present and His Court Appointment, 15th April 1488

On Leonardo's 36th birthday on the 15th April 1488, the young Duke and his uncle Ludovico threw a party for him at the Corte Vecchio. With more than one hundred guests in attendance, the young duke officially welcomed Leonardo into the Sforza family. As a long awaited present, Ludovico finally appointed him as his chief Advisor on Fortifications and Master of Entertainments and Festivities and gave him the keys to his residential apartments at the old Royal Palace, the Corte Vecchio. Leonardo would reside only a few doors away from the room of my grandmother and mother, so he had devoted friends nearby to spoil him whenever he needed their attention. Another neighbour who Leonardo had befriended was Franchinus Gaffurius, the *maestro di cappella* at the cathedral across the piazza from the Corte Vecchio. For Leonardo, as Master of Entertainments and Festivities, a friendship with Franchinus Gaffurius was essential because this musician and composer wrote and conducted masses and motets for ceremonial occasions for his ducal employer. Gaffurius was a widely read humanist with a thorough understanding of contemporary musical practice, and Leonardo painted his portrait as the *Musician* (Fig. 35) to honour him and their strong friendship.

Leonardo was joyous on the day and night of his birthday, and he tried hard to stay sober for as long as he possibly could so as not to make a fool of himself and not spoil the immense occasion for himself or his guests. He was witty, courtly, and humble. It was hard work, but he had finally got there with recognition and reward, and there was much for him to do in the future as long as he behaved himself diplomatically and Fortune smiled upon him. The young Duke played the violin and sang on the night of the revelry with an expertise and a sensitivity that Leonardo had taught him well. The guests all recognised the young Duke as a talented musician, but also as a spoilt and sensitive gadabout. The young ladies of the court flocked about him like chickens to a cocky young rooster for at 18 years of age he had already developed a large reputation as being a great cock-smith among the virgins and the whores. He was young, pretty, and flamboyant, modelling himself on his artistic mentor Leonardo da Vinci.

One day after Leonardo's birthday, even before all the wine was consumed and the festivities were finished, the shocking news arrived at the Sforza court that Girolamo Riario husband of Caterina Sforza-Riario had been assassinated in Forli only two days before. His palace was sacked and his wife and children were held hostages. Ludovico immediately arranged for more than five hundred Milanese troops to be sent to Forli in an attempt to release Caterina and her children. Before Ludovico's troops had even reached Forli, Caterina had escaped from the Orsis assassins leaving behind her children as hostages. When the Orsis attempted to recapture her with the threat to kill her children, she stood on top of the walls of the Ravaldino fortress, exposed her genitals for all to admire, and shouted out at them, *'do it, if you want to. Hang all of them in front of me. I have the mould to make more!'* The Orsis were so shocked by her response that they freed her children, looted as much of the palace and commune of Forli as they could, and left before the arrival of the Sforza troops. Caterina with her great impudence had defeated her enemies and then regained possession of her fiefs with the help of her uncle Ludovico IL Moro. When Leonardo heard about her self-exposure, he composed a song about the legend of Caterina's impudence and shared it with his fellow painters. The question among them was who would immortalise her legendary impudence on wood or canvas? It was left to the Florentine Sandro Botticelli to do so.

At the end of June, Leonardo found out that his teacher and mentor, the great sculptor and architect Andrea del Verrocchio had died in Venice. With the assistance of my father and Galeazzo Sanseverino, Leonardo arranged a memorial service for Verrocchio at the Milan cathedral and a three-day wake at Sanseverino's palace and the horse stables to celebrate Verrocchio's past life with his fellow Florentine and Milanese artists, architects, sculptors, poets, goldsmiths, miniaturists, and artisans of all types. Verrocchio was still working on the completion of an equestrian statue in memory of the Condottiero Bartolomeo Colleoni, former Captain General of the Republic of Venice. He had finished the clay model, but died before it was cast in bronze. He willed that his pupil Lorenzo di Credi in Florence be allowed to finish the work, but it was finally cast many years later by the Venetian sculptor Leopardi. At the end of the wake, Leonardo announced to all those still present that the spirit of Verrocchio had entered him, and that he was now fully committed to the construction of the 'Sforza Horse' that would be bigger and more magnificent than anybody had ever seen before. Piero Alamanni the Florentine ambassador to the Sforza court in Milan wrote to Leonardo's friend Lorenzo de' Medici in Florence stating that Ludovico Sforza intended to commemorate his father, *'with an enormous horse in bronze, on which rides Duke Francesco in armour,'* and that he wished for, *'a few extra masters capable of finishing the work.'*

The Polyphonic Music of Maestro Franchinus Gaffurius

Like good food, music was a natural ingredient of all the entertainments and ceremonial occasions (birthdays, dinners, banquets, weddings, celebrations, funerals, and masses) at the Sforza court. For many of the cultured gentlemen and courtiers at the time, the ability to sing and play a musical instrument was as important as good horsemanship and understanding the finer points of falconry. The young duke and his uncle Ludovico were both great lovers and sponsors of musical performance in the tradition of the young duke's father Galeazzo Maria Sforza. The Sforza had their own choir at the Sforza chapel of the Santa Maria in Solario in San Fedele, whereas Franchinus Gaffurius the *maestro di cappella* of the Duomo assembled the most distinguished musical performers in Europe who crossed naturally between his large choir at the cathedral and the smaller polyphonic group at the nearby Sforza chapel. Franchinus Gaffurius wrote and conducted masses, motets, and hymns, and he also wrote three major treatises on the theory and practice of music. Leonardo often attended the polyphonic rehearsals conducted by Gaffurius at the Duomo, and he helped him to design new musical instruments for the cathedral and to maintain the old ones in good working order. Leonardo held music in high regard, but placed it second to the science of painting.

> Music may be called the sister of painting, for she is dependent upon hearing, the sense which comes second, and her harmony is composed of the union of its proportional parts sounded simultaneously, rising and falling in one or more harmonic rhythms. These rhythms may be said to surround the proportionality of the members composing the harmony just as the contour bounds the members from which human beauty is born. But painting excels and ranks higher than music, because it does not fade away as soon as it is born, as is the fate of unhappy music. On the contrary, it endures and has all the appearance of being alive, though in fact it is confined to one surface. Oh wonderful science which can preserve the transient beauty of mortals and endow it with a permanence greater than the works of nature; for these are subject to the continual changes of time which leads them towards inevitable old age!

Leonardo made numerous comparisons between painting and music, and one such comparison was in regard to measures:

> I give the degrees of the objects seen by the eye as the musician does the notes heard by the ear. Although the objects seen by the eye do, in fact, touch each other as they recede, I will nevertheless found my rule on spaces of 20 braccia each; as a musician does with notes, which, though they can be carried on one into the next, he divides into degrees from note to note calling them 1st, 2nd, 3rd, 4th, 5th; and has affixed a name to each degree in raising or lowering the voice.

Franchinus Gaffurius was born in 1451, and he lived and worked in Milan from 1484 and died there in 1522 at the age of 71 years, outliving Leonardo by three years.

Fig. 35. Leonardo's portrait of the musician and Milanese choir master Franchinus Gaffurius.

◉

CHAPTER 9

Love, Marriages, Births, and Festivities, 1488 to 1493

Love, Fear, and Esteem. Write these on three stones and serve.

— Leonardo da Vinci

Leonardo's Wedding Architecture and Festivals for the Sforza Family and the Duchy of Milan

The next few years for Leonardo were among his happiest at the Sforza court attending to his many different projects at his various studios including the one that he shared with Giovanni Ambrogio de' Predis. He attracted a number of talented assistants and pupils to work and paint for him. Among them were Marco d'Oggiono and Giovanni Antonio Boltraffio, and over the years he added other Leonardeschi among his pupils and followers including Bernardino Luini, Cesare da Sesto, Andrea Solario, Andrea Salaino, Raphael, Salai and, of course, I include myself among them. But now, Leonardo was an important and meaningful presence in the Sforza court with a generous budget to prepare for spectacular pageants, festivals, ceremonies, and joyous processions. He had responsibilities for the arrangement of at least three important royal marriages and the ensuing births of their royal children. But first, he attended to my parents' wedding celebrations.

The Marriage of Gerolamo Melzi and Tommasina della Torre, May 1488

The marriage between my mother and father was a momentous occasion for them as well as for me, although I was not yet on this earth to see it happen. It began with a full mass in the Cathedral, and the wedding celebration continued for many successive days over different locations. The first wedding banquet was held in the gardens of the old Royal Palace. More than four hundred guests attended the festivities at different times of the day and night. The young Duke and his sisters and his uncle attended as honoured guests. Leonardo's friends and acquaintances were in attendance, including the Sanseverino and de' Predis brothers, various other artists and artisans, and even a Florentine contingent who represented the Medici family. The bride and groom did not know where to look, whether at each other, their Lords, the Sforza, the elaborate decorations, the spectacular events or Leonardo bouncing about from one corner to another directing the processions and movement of the performers who were creating illusions and magic using his vast knowledge of alchemy. The grounds of the Palace were fully decorated with splendid tents, ornate columns, triumphal arches, Chinese lanterns, and beautiful images of Milanese saints and celebrities including images of the young duke and his uncle. Leonardo prepared giant sugar (marzipan) sculptures of his designs for the Melzi Villa in Vaprio, mythical gods and goddesses in various elegant poses, rearing horses, lumbering elephants, playful dogs, tender deer, and duelling knights, all lit up with coloured lights or draped with floral displays. Weird sculptures and strange designs were distributed throughout the gardens including some of his mechanical war weapons and robots that moved up and down the pathways, driven by their own locomotive powers. Buzzing machines pumped sparkling coloured waters through elongated glass pipes that hung high in the air creating the illusion of comets streaking across the heavens. Poets recited their tributes to the married couple and their families. Actors in elaborate costumes performed comical and dramatic mimes and theatre of the weird and wonderful. Wedding guests danced and drunk during the day and night, and they ate and nibbled from many courses of exotic foods that were prepared for either eating or just for beholding the wonder of it all. Mechanical flying objects, called helibirds or whirlybirds, fluttered or hovered in the air, occasionally dropping down dangerously into people's laps or on top of their heads. Towards the midnight hour, many more guests lurched about incoherently and collapsed from drunken stupor into the dark gardens. A flaming wheel of fireworks accidently collapsed and ignited some of the revellers. Occasional fights broke out among the overly enthusiastic knights displaying and testing their athletic prowess. Naked nymphets ran through the garden shadows and bathed exotically and erotically in the fountains. Four different orchestras switched from one to the other to play different sounds and styles to entertain the remaining guests between the dancing and the mock jousting. The celebrations and light shows were lavish, tantalising, and spectacular. Everybody present had a marvellous time and agreed that any future wedding would find it difficult to surpass this particular spectacular celebration of the marriage between Count Gerolamo Melzi and the Countess Tommasina della Torre.

In the morning, with little or no sleep, the bride and groom were transported by carriage in a wedding procession to their Casoretto estate. Here, they attended a celebratory mass in the Church of Santa Maria Bianca and were honoured by three days of festivities organised by the estate staff, friends, monks, and the people of the Church parish. The bride and groom and friends then travelled in a floating procession of ten colourfully decorated barges to continue feasting and drinking and dancing along the Martesana canal, all the way to Vaprio, where they disembarked for another two days of celebrations. The wedding party then travelled to Bergamo where they stayed for a week to celebrate with the della Torre and Visconti relatives and friends. They finally returned to Milan via their villas and estates in Lecco and Como. It had been close to a one-month wedding celebration, and they were utterly exhausted already by their short time of married life. They gradually returned to their previous routines with Gerolamo resuming his duties as councillor, engineer, and militia captain while Tommasina rejoined the ladies-in-waiting to care for Bianca Maria and Anna Sforza. Gerolamo and Tommasina were now husband and wife, but temporarily living apart to recover from their over-exuberant celebrations together.

Leonardo had travelled with the wedding party and performed his diplomatic duties for Ludovico Sforza in Bergamo, Brescia, and Como. He also escorted Caterina Visconti to some of the celebrations, raising questions and scurrilous gossip about whether they might become a permanent couple. Leonardo and Caterina encouraged the gossip with good humour, but to tell the truth, Caterina was too busy ensuring that her daughter looked and behaved at her very best during their exhausting proceedings and processions to give any serious attention to her own frivolous thoughts of love.

Tommasina was 19 years old and Gerolamo was 28 years old, and they had courted for at least two years. She shared rooms with her mother at the Palazzo del Broletto Vecchio while Gerolamo resided at Casoretto looking after his aged great grandmother who had her wish come true to see the two of them engaged and happily married. My great grandmother lived just long enough to see the birth of my sister (1489) and me (1491).

The marriage between Tommasina and Gerolamo allowed Leonardo to experiment with his preparations for the forthcoming weddings and festivities between:

1.   The young duke Gian Galeazzo Sforza and Isabella of Aragon (15th February 1489).
2.   Lord Ludovico Sforza and Beatrice d' Este (16th January 1491).

3.   Bianca Maria Sforza (Galeazzo's daughter) and Emperor Maximilian I (30th November 1493).

4.   Bianca Sforza (Ludovico's illegitimate daughter) and Galeazzo Sanseverino (20th June 1496).

A Meeting with Isabella of Aragon, Future Duchess of Milan

In August of 1488, Ludovico sent Leonardo on his fourth diplomatic Milanese mission. It was to Naples to meet with Gian Galeazzo's fiancé Isabella of Aragon and her father Alfonso II the Duke of Calabria to discuss the wedding arrangements and the associated festivities to be prepared for the winter of 1489.

Isabella's mother Ippolita Maria Sforza died in 1484, much too young at 38 years of age when Isabella was only 14 years of age. Ippolita was a beautiful and highly cultured and intelligent woman who corresponded with many of the Italian rulers, composed poetry, and produced manuscripts of her philosophies. She provided her daughter Isabella with the best possible education in the arts and humanities and Latin. Ippolita's grandfather was the fourth duke of Milan Francesco I Sforza, and she was the sister of the fifth duke of Milan Galeazzo Maria Sforza and the aunt of the sixth duke of Milan Gian Galeazzo Sforza who her daughter Isabella was engaged to marry. Thus, Isabella was the first cousin of his Excellency the young duke Gian and her uncles were Ludovico and his brothers, and Isabella's mother Ippolita Maria Sforza was Gian's aunt in this highly complicated marriage ancestry. Such close relationships are always far too complicated for me to calculate and sort out correctly, so I asked my children and a mathematician to explain to me all the connections and ramifications and to draw for me the lines linking together who is related to whom. What I hold clearly in my mind, however, is that Isabella's grandparents on her mother's side were the fourth duke of Milan Francesco Sforza and his wife the Duchess of Milan Bianca Maria Visconti, and that they were also Gian's grandparents from his father's side.

Things were different and slightly less complicated on Princess Isabella's father's side. Her father was Alfonso II of Naples and Duke of Calabria. He became the King of Naples briefly for one year in 1494 until 22nd February 1495. As Duke of Calabria, he was Ludovico Sforza's ally in their war against Venice during the War of Ferrara (1482 to 1484). He was a member of the House of Aragon that branched from the House of Trastamara, the counts of Barcelona, and the reigning House of Castile. They started the bloodline of the House of Trastamara in Naples in 1442 with Alfonso I, before becoming the House of Aragon. Their rule of Naples ended briefly with French rule from 1501 to 1504, before being restored again for 12 years from 1504 to 1516 with the rule of Ferdinand III and Joanna III. Isabella's brother Ferdinand (Ferrante) II became king of Naples briefly from January 1495 until the 7th September 1496 when he died at 27 years of age after a short illness while staying in Somma Vesuviana.

Isabella had a beautiful half-sister Sancha d'Aragona who was Princess of Napoli and Squillace from her father's side. Sancha's mother was Trogia Gazzela. Like Isabella, Sancha was very beautiful and a favourite of the artists and the poets in her time. Born in 1478, Sancha died young at 26 years of age in 1504. While in Naples, Leonardo sketched a few portraits of Sancha partly to tease Isabella, but also, because their comparable beauty impressed him.

Isabella's father, Alfonso, the Duke of Calabria, discussed with Leonardo the details of the wedding plans and his political expectations over the next few years. He believed that the wedding was essential to bring the two great states closer together because the Duchy of Milan and the Kingdom of Naples had drifted too far apart after the Ferrara war against Venice and Ludovico Sforza's self serving treaty, the Peace of Bagnolo. Alfonso was the next in line to the Neapolitan crown, and he saw the marriage between his daughter and the Duke of Milan as a way of protecting his throne of Naples from the claims of the French dukes of Anjou.

Leonardo was now a member of the Sforza court with monthly payments from their financier and a budget for his position as the Engineer and Architect of Entertainment and Festivities. He was delighted to meet with Princess Isabella for she at the age of 18 years was refined, pretty, and highly educated in the arts and humanities. As an Aragon princess, she was spoilt and beautiful, and Leonardo often thought of her as his ideal model for the pretty and demure Virgin Mary. She confided to him that she dreaded the thought of leaving Naples to marry and live in Milan. However, he provided her with confidence to look forward with excitement and optimism to her wedding in Milan. He quickly charmed the princess with his stories about her fiancé, her fiancé's uncle, the exciting city of Milan, the fields, hills, forests, rivers, canals, and mountains of Lombardy, and his equal love for Florence and its charms, and the painters, architects, musicians, and poets that he knew so well. He delighted in drawing sketches of her and her fiancé for her scrapbook. Leonardo was excited with the prospect of seeing her in Milan in the Sforza court, for he had fallen a little in love with her. He sang sweet songs for her about the birds and their twittering of love as if he was her actual suitor.

The Death of Count Palatine, Bartolomeo IV Melzi, 1488

On his return to Milan from Naples, Leonardo learnt of the death of my uncle Bartolomeo IV Melzi who was Count Palatine and Provost of Pontirolo and a well-regarded poet and classical scholar. He was the head of the Villa Melzi at Vaprio d' Adda, and he died suddenly at the Villa after a short illness and severe fever at the age of thirty. He was my eldest uncle who I never met because I was not born until after his death. Leonardo was greatly saddened by the death of Bartolomeo because he held him as his friend as much as he did my father. Bartolomeo was an intellectual and the curator of the extensive and valuable library of great books, codices, and classical manuscripts at the Villa that he had inherited from his grandfather, the patriarch Giovanni Melzi. Now all this and all the other properties were in the hands of his younger brothers, Beltrame, Michele, Andriotto, Lancillotto, and my father.

Fig. 37. Leonardo da Vinci's Virgin of the Rocks *commissioned by the Confraternity of the Church of San Francesco Grande.*

Leonardo and Predis's first version of the *Virgin of the Rocks* was finished and installed in the chapel of the Church of San Francesco Grande on December 8, 1488, the Feast Day of the Immaculate Conception. A few years later, Leonardo and Ambrogio de' Predis complained to Ludovico Sforza 'Il Moro' that the Confraternity had grossly underpaid them for the panel of the *Virgin of the Rocks* and the two flanking paintings of angels. The Confraternity had a host of complaints and dissatisfactions with the painting including that the holy mother and child didn't have haloes over their heads to depict their holiness, and there was an absence of gold paint on the Christ-child (the Golden Baby), and no golden brocade and distinctive wings for the angel Gabriel that had been requested by them in the written agreement. Moreover, the painting looked far too dark and mysterious for the Confraternity's liking.

Leonardo would ultimately have to withdraw his first version of the *Virgin of the Rocks* from the chapel and provide the Confraternity with a version closer to their wishes and requirements by adding the golden haloes for Jesus and Mary, a halo and cross for John the Baptist, and more distinctive wings for the Angel. Instead of placing the Christ-child in the middle of the painting and colouring him with gold paint, Leonardo covered the Madonna's belly in golden material to represent her pregnancy with the as yet unborn Golden Baby. He had painted the same 'golden belly' for the pregnant Madonna in his painting of the *Annunciation* (Fig. 17). In the original *Virgin of the Rocks*, Leonardo dressed the Angel Gabriel in the young duke's distinctive heraldic green and red colours, and made the Virgin look too much like the young duke's betrothed, Isabella of Aragon. The Confraternity accepted the grotto and the distinctive backdrop of the Lombardian rocks and the Alps in the distance and the illusion of the confluence of the Adda River running out from Lake Como. The illusionary backdrop is similar to the one he had painted previously in his image of *St. Jerome*; a symbolic scene within the interior of the painter's skull, the cathedral of the mind. Both versions are masterpieces in their own right, but the original surpasses the later copy by far in its delicacy, touch, and naturalism. The handling of the *chiaroscuro* (the contrast between light and shade) to create the illusion of three-dimensional forms is faultless. The hazy mountain tops in the distance adds to the perspective and depth of the painting to further evoke the mystery of the Immaculate Conception with the emergence of the holy figures from the dark shadows of their primordial cave. His peers immediately recognised the original painting as a masterpiece with its perfect perspective, the delicate smiles, movement, and grace of the figures, and subtle melting of the colours and shades of light. His reputation as an innovative and sensitive genius was assured.

The Most Celebrated Marriage Between Gian Galeazzo Sforza, Sixth Duke of Milan, and Isabella of Aragon, Princess of Naples, 15th February 1489

Of the many weddings on Leonardo's calendar for him to attend to for the next four or five years, the one between the Duke of Milan Gian Galeazzo Sforza and his cousin Isabella of Aragon, Princess of Naples, was the most challenging, demanding, and spectacular for him to achieve successfully for the couple and their family and the nobles of Milan. Preparations by Leonardo for this marriage began as early as 1487. The young duke had Leonardo's ear about his worries about his marriage to his beautiful and strong-willed cousin, and whether he could fulfil all his marital expectations. The Tarot cards read out to him by Ludovico and his chief advisor Ambrogio Varesi had warned the young duke against the marriage for if he married his cousin then he would die young. Others told him, however, that he would sire three or four children, have a happy and fulfilled marriage, and therefore, he should not worry about the prospects of his own death. Another prophecy was that he would inherit his full dukedom and rule Milan at the age of twenty-four years without any further interference from his uncle Ludovico. Some of these prophecies were right and some were wrong.

The young duke wanted a splendid wedding spectacle to impress all in his dukedom as well as all those in the other states of Italy, particularly the Kingdom of Naples and the Papal city of Rome. He persuaded his uncle Ludovico to provide Leonardo with a proper endowment to begin his wedding spectacle, neither to scrimp nor spare on the merest of trifles that were all fitting for the image and future fortunes of the Duke and Duchess of Milan. Indeed, the Duke of Bari provided Leonardo with an additional workshop and staff of workmen at the Corte Vecchio and instructed the treasury to begin to pay Leonardo his stipends in a timely manner. Leonardo had been appointed on the assistance of the young duke to the position of the Engineer and Architect of Entertainment and Festivities, and he was expected to produce a memorable event.

The marriage was planned to take place in Duomo at the main altar, across from the central piazza, and close to the location of Leonardo's main workshop. The wedding procession would leave from the Ducal court of the main castle and make way down the Via Dante to the Duomo where they would gather and meet with other dignitaries and clergy outside the main Cathedral entrance before entering into the bowels of the Cathedral.

The young duke's brother Hermes Maria Sforza was the Marquis of Tortona, and he had arranged for his uncle the governor Ludovico Sforza to prepare the official welcoming ceremony for his older brother's fiancé Isabella of Aragon at Tortona on the right bank of the Scrivia river and on the roadway between Genoa and Pavia. At Tortona, the poet Bernardo Bellincione paid homage to the *Eccellentissima* (Most excellent) Duchessa Isabella and recited a sonnet in praise of her beauty in the presence of her bridegroom Gian Galeazzo Maria Sforza and his uncle Lord Ludovico.

> For autumn, winter or spring
> Or when the sun is the lion of summer,
> Isabella always comes forth in style,
> More beautiful than the four seasons.
> Angelic welcome in her face,
> Serious, compassionate, with fine words;
> It is in her nature to mesmerise us all
> Her mother, Ipolita, so hopeful in the sky. [S16].

A spectacular banquet and an allegorical masque were held in their honour where the gods and goddesses of classical mythology served them at their triumphant table. Atalanta and Diana presented calf, wild boar, and stag, Iris served up peacock, Thetis and her sea-nymphs served fish, Pomona provided grapes, apples, and other fruits while Hebe filled gold and silver goblets with rare and delicious wines. The poet Bellincione, dressed in laurel as Apollo the god of poetry, music, art, and archery with a lyre and a bow and a sling of arrows, recited his own and others' classical verses, whereas shepherds and imps crowned with ivy sang songs in praise of Isabella of Aragon the new Duchess of Milan. The poet apologised to the Duchess for the absence of Leonardo from the entertainments for although he had designed the scenes and the costumes he was busy in Milan preparing the architecture, spectaculars, and entertainments for her forthcoming wedding.

On arrival in Milan, the betrothed and the accompanying dukes, nobles, trumpeters, and martial musicians were greeted with salvos of artillery. Hundreds of stradiots, mamelukes, and archers on horseback assembled before the Porte Romana outside the city walls to accompany the Duke and the Princess and their party into the city. The procession included the Princess's brother Ferdinand I who escorted the Duchess and Duke of Milan, both on horseback with a protective *baldacchino* held high over their heads to honour and shade them from the elements during their slow ride from the city gates, through the decorated city streets, and past the Duomo, all the way to the Castello Sforza on the opposite side of the city. The large crowds applauded and shouted their greetings enthusiastically and joyously all the way along the route where the houses beside the roadway were decorated with brocades, tapestries, ivy, and laurel hanging from the balconies and the walls. At the gate of the great Castello, the Duchess was greeted by her mother-in-law Bona of Savoy and the young Duke's sisters, the Princesses Bianca Maria and Anna, who escorted her to her rooms at the Camera delle Torre to rest in preparation for the wedding next day. The duke's mother Bona of Savoy had been allowed back into Milan to attend her son's wedding and to assist his betrothed in the preparation of her wedding day.

At dawn, on the day of the wedding, the Duchess Isabella was woken from her restless sleep, fed a light calming breakfast, and slowly and meticulously dressed by her maids and ladies-in-waiting into her exquisite wedding garments that she had previously worn in the Naples processions and celebrations only a month before. As in Naples, the day was sunny, bright and cloudless, and the Duchess sparkled in her long white robe of silver and golden brocade, sewn with pearls and diamonds while she rode seated in her covered chariot. Her escorts followed her in front of a long procession of knights and nobles all the way from the court of the Castello along the colourfully decorated Via di Dante to the centrally located Duomo where her bridegroom Gian and his uncle Ludovico waited for her in the *tiburio* (lantern tower) that was erected and decorated by Leonardo da Vinci and his team of architects, builders, artists, and carpenters.

The bridal procession and dignitaries, more than 2,000 strong, accompanied by musicians playing trumpets, flutes, and drums, moved slowly from the Castello to the Duomo along the street packed with cheering citizens and visitors. Garlands of ivy and juniper, portraits, tapestries, heraldic symbols, flags, and sparkling decorations hung from the roofs, balconies, and walls of private residences and the shops and studios of moneylenders, goldsmiths, artisans, and armourers. The Duchess smiled demurely until the crowd disappeared from her view. She had reached the Triumphal Arch that stood waiting for her passage through its main gate and along a floral guard of honour to meet with her bridegroom waiting for her within the giant *tiburio* that towered above the main door of the cathedral.

Together, the bride and groom passed through the central opening of the Triumphal Arch, whereas the accompanying dignitaries diverged through other adjoining openings. The bride moved gracefully and royally through the arcade to be met by her cheerful bridesmaids and the other noble Milanese women and pious clergy who had gathered to meet her at the entrance to the Duomo in a manner that alluded to her purity and virginal qualities. There, she kissed the cross that was presented to her by the bishop, and she and her noble women entered into the Duomo where others waited to witness the mass and formal wedding ceremony in the eyes of Jesus and God, the Father of us all.

It was Leonardo's duty as the Court Engineer and Architect of Entertainment and Festivities to organise the architecture, flora, ceremonies, friezes, decorations, symbols, honouriums, and all the other matters required for the splendid success and magnificent look of the wedding. He started his preparations for the wedding long before his appointment to the Court as its Architect of Entertainment and Festivities. In August 1487, he was commissioned by the cathedral as *Leonardus Florentinus* to partake in a competition to design and construct a wooden model in their workshop for a crossing tower, the *tiburio*. He enlisted Donato Bramante who was his friend from Florence and had migrated to Milan in the 1470s to become its city architect to help him resolve the stylistic and structural problems of the *tiburio*. He also hired the carpenter's assistant Bernardino de' Madis to build a wooden model that he eventually incorporated into the Ducal wedding decorations. Leonardo received regular payments throughout 1487 and 1488 to complete the wooden model that stood 50 braccia (braccia is 27 inches or 68 cm, the length of an outstretched arm) or 10 stories high and 30 braccia wide. In February 1489, the same *tiburio*, now carefully decorated, stood magnificently at the entrance to the nave and main altar of the cathedral as a reception area for the wedding party and families to gather beneath it and meet with the clergy and other important dignitaries before entering the interior of the cathedral. While the *antiporta*, a covered vestibule erected for the bridal couple and their guests to foregather before entering the Duomo, was common for the rich and the noble families, Leonardo's *tiburio* would outdo all the other *vestibuli portae* that were ever seen before or since. Not even the wedding of Ludovico IL Moro or that of Maximilian the Emperor of the Romans held at the Duomo a few years later could surpass the magnificence, size or grandeur of Leonardo's *tiburio*. This alone cemented his name in the annals of the greatest wedding architects, far surpassing anybody before him.

As a postscript, Leonardo's last payment from the cathedral for the wooden model of the *tiburio* was in May 1490. On June 27th of 1490, he was told that he had lost the design competition for the *tiburio*, which was awarded to the local Lombard architects and sculptors Giovanni Amadeo and Giovanni Dolcebuono. As a foreigner, *Leonardus Florentinus* couldn't circumvent Milan's guild system that was controlled by the local building trades to construct the *tiburio* for the top of the cathedral. Thus, his magnificent wooden structure that I played under when I was a child remained in the parklands of the Castello Sforza until it was finally used for firewood by the French occupying force in 1499.

Nevertheless, Leonardo's design and wooden model of the *tiburio* were legendary in Milan. Thus, the poet Giovanni Alberto Bossi, as an eyewitness of the decorations and splendour of the Castello Sforza, the triumphal arch and *tiburio*, and the processional way inside the Duomo, wrote the following odes in tribute to the wedding and its architectural structures.

The Castello Sforzesco
The citadel was crowded: the largest groups standing outside;
Purificatory chandelier illuminated with intense brightness.
Corymbiferis covered the royal palace, decked out with garlands,
All the Duke's insignias and symbols mingled with the light.
Most of the work, once adorned, added extra strength;
Laurus was born and thrived in our field,
He ran across a solid wooden porch with his bow,
Golden hair interwoven with juniper.

The Triumphal Arch and Tiburio
The triumphal arch narrates a lively tale about
Francisco (Sforza) as a previous strong leader.
High above the amphitheatre there is the rising star of Olympus,
A beautiful sacred vestibule stands in front of the house of God.
This is where I want to write my verse within,
For one and all to celebrate the glory of the past?
For whom does the entrance of the arch play and grant access to,
To cross through the cavernous dome, built by the hands of Pallas?
A long distance above lays the golden top of the tower
That powerfully binds together and encompasses the entire work.
Closed windows show off the narrated beauty and interior decor
Via circulating aisles shaped into a duplex.
I marvel that the pine trees and the machines
Used in the dome's construction cannot be seen,
Nor what contributed to its strength.
Inside are pleasing pictures, pictures laughing out at the viewer,
So varied that unskilled hands could not have placed them there.
I see a great painting and wonder if it is painted by Parrhasius
Or at least the grapes or the beguiling birds
Suggests a man of honours

Who knows how many waves make up the Libyan sea.
How the flowers emit their own colour,
Discerned by their fruit-hanging branches.
The grass snakes twist in and out of the marble everywhere
And a mixture of birds and small animals live together.
Many of the prince's insignias flow across the walls,
In between, the faces of the old leaders look out.
What terrestrial, sea, and mysterious animals abound in the deep and on land,
The statues arranged in a marvellous way.
In addition to the service of the empty arc above
It contains an enormous collection of polished wheels.
In addition, angelic beauties stand together in a group,
In heaven, but not in any way that it is usually presented.
They are not without their noble lady, nor at war with powerful Greece,
That Clio later foretold to be our own.
Finally, all the beauty of the paintings, showed Minerva's
Techniques skilfully learned and presented with the best of her knowledge provided.
For that reason I therefore hold my tongue and refuse any further contrivance;
Curio, I am now silent, glued between the two theatres.

The Processional Way Inside the Duomo
At the entrance: stands the shrine of the Virgin
For horse-riders and the noisy-footed to approach and honour.
I stand astonished like a stranger, and wonder
Who constructed this beautiful marble statue of the Virgin rising up from her abode.
I see another marvel: a straight line opens the way between spacious columns
Towards the chamber door of the Diety, which rushes me forward to the altar
Of Topia, that is constructed totally as a work of art.
For sure these delightful columns are bound and intertwined with shapely hangings.
These are green leaves and recurring golden fruit
Fastened with tawny metal tags.
Branches of ivy are weaved in tight circles,
Devoured by ferocious red vipers.
Moorish omens, signs, and Jovian winged-monsters represent the Duke of Bari,
Colour standards of the French Bona Sforza.
In addition to these declarations marble works
Rest on columns like a crown on Paris.
Wings soar above to assault the heavens,
Stories curve to ascend the opus.
But the rainbow arcs between them bend to
Highlight each town's emblems;
A signpost in the middle, the middle where a great singular
Body composed of one or two centaurians hover. [S17]

Giovanni Bossi was one of many poets and observers who wrote about the wedding architecture and spectacular decorations, but strangely he refrained to acknowledge that *Leonardus Florencescus* was the artist and architect responsible for the entire spectacle from the Castello Sforzesco, along the boulevard Dante to the Piazza Duomo, including the triumphal arch and *tiburio* and the passages and walkways through the nave to the high altar of the Duomo. Yet, all or most of the Milanese nobles, merchants, and artists knew of Leonardo's contribution for they saw his eccentric figure constantly rushing by them like a pulsating metronome along the boulevard Dante between his Duomo and Castello workshops during the months of preparation for this occasion.

I once asked Leonardo what he thought of Giovanni Bossi's description of the wedding decorations for Gian Galeazzo Sforza and Isabella d'Aragona. He was neither impressed nor stirred by any of the poets' descriptions or exultations. I made my own notes based on Leonardo's descriptions to King Francois of France and his drawings and notes of the courtyard of the Castello Sforzesco, the triumphal arch and arcade on the Piazza del Duomo, the *tiburio*, and the processional way inside the Duomo. I also have based my description of the spectacle on those of Stefano Dulcino and others.

Dulcino's account runs as follows:

> The Corte Ducale at the Castle was richly prepared with an elaborately decorated portico where the cortege assembled. The thick walls of the rectangular courtyard are amazingly high; the middle of the walls is covered all round by a dark blue frieze (a broad horizontal band of sculpted or painted decoration in low relief, especially on a wall near the ceiling) two cubits deep between the cornices (decorative ledge or framework at the junction of the wall and ceiling). Centaurs (man-headed horses, deer-centaurs, dog-centaurs) and woodland gods (Bacchus, Diana, Faunus, Feronia, Flora, Fulfluns, Nemestrinus, Pilumnus, Pomona, Terra, Antheia, Chloris, Cybele, Dryads, Nymphs and Satyrs) playing various games fill up the frieze. Above and below, wreaths of juniper, garlands of ivy and braids of laurel, like ropes, all intertwined with each other, girdle the whole enclosure in a leafy ring: from these hung the glittering insignia of the Duke's authority and of the subject states in spirals of ivy. In fact at the end of the large courtyard above the lobby of the corner, two eagles and the same number of hissing snakes with round crowns were let down in circular garlands. The fourth side was a temporary arcade towering over everything else, which continued each end of the limiting wall in the same direction. Columns, just like marble ones, made of juniper, supported leafy vaults with capitals covered with berries; so skilfully vaulted and smooth with tinkling gold that no spikiness, no inelegance of the leaves bound together could threaten the achievements of art; you would think that these things had just grown like that or had been produced by the brush of artists; the members of the Duke's procession mounted their horses under this portico, as though it were some pergola, and arrived undercover at the gate of the castle. [S18]

The full length of the main street, a little more than a kilometre from the castle gate to the Piazza Duomo, was fully decorated with the peoples' displays of their love and admiration. At the entrance of the cathedral square Leonardo built the majestic Triumphal arch composed of three entrance vaults, the middle one broader and taller than the other two, all showing off the spoils and trophies of Francesco Sforza's victories against the Samnites and the Milanese and over the cities of Caravaggio, Piacenza, Cremona, and Genoa. The top of the arch was decorated with the imperial standards, and beyond it, a promenade enclosed by columns covered with ivy and myrtle provided a delightfully beautiful walk to the entrance of the *tiburio*, the dome standing tall at the front of the church. This was a grand spectacle, a colonnade of eight columns supporting a soaring vault as high as the spire of the church. The columns housed in four niches per column 32 realistic statues of famous women including the Nine Muses (Clio, Thalia, Erato, Euterpe, Polyhymnia, Calliope, Terpsichore, Urania, and Melpomene) in female garb and formed with attributes and inscriptions. The Nine Muses were the daughters of Zeus and Mnemosyne, and they personified knowledge and the arts, literature, dance, history, and music. Some of the other 23 women presented by Leonardo were Melete, Mneme, Aoide, Portia, Lucretia, Penelope, Diana the huntress, Juno the daughter of Jupiter, and Vesta the virgin goddess of hearth, home, and family. There were two walking galleries to observe the wonders above, below, and around them that circumvented the Duomo and provided a view onto the piazza. Another walkway ascended to the roof crowned with triple rows of columns that narrowed into a conical shape. The entire building was covered in juniper, and water sprayed out through lead pipes and pumps hidden from view. This *tiburio* was a giant antechamber to the entrance of the Church where inside an enormous arcade of 17 equidistant pairs of columns of the same height and breadth as the doorway crossed the length of the church from the main door to a covered grandstand beside the main altar. The columns appeared to be marble, some decorated with the four-fronted head of Janus, others with circles of ducal and regal insignia, interconnected by circular nets of foliage and separated by intervals of foliate hangings carrying larger crests with representations of nymphs and centaurs. The gaps in the net permitted views of the roof and sides of the church for the guests who either stood or were seated at the sides of the arcade between the entrance and the high altar. This was a temporary architecture designed to create a phantasmagoria of performance art for the wedding party and their spectators.

Leonardo, as most other wedding artists, used the traditional and classical plant symbols of marriage, fertility, faithfulness, sacredness, triumph, and chastity so that tapestries of ivy, juniper, laurel, myrtle, and certain fruits covered the walls, columns, porticos, arcades, and the roof of the *tiburio*. Myrtle was sacred to the goddess Venus (Myrtea), and laurel was sacred to Apollo. Hesperides produced lemons, apples, and oranges for the sacred wedding of Zeus and Hera. Juniper is Juno's plant, and she is the guardian of women's chastity, marriage, and childbirth. Leonardo used Ivy, a favourite of his art as a symbol of longevity, triumph, and fidelity, as an aspiration that the marriage between Gian and Isabella and the alliance between Milan and Naples would be forever evergreen. Many of his ideas and designs originated from those described by Vitruvius and Alberti in their published books *De re aedificatoria* and *L'Architettura*. Whereas they provided some concepts and ideas, Leonardo da Vinci masterfully provided the actuality and the substance.

And what of the wedding party? After the morning wedding ceremony at the Duomo, the wedding celebrations were held within the banquet hall (203 feet long and 33 feet wide) and courtyards of the Castello where more than 500 guests ate, drank, sung, and celebrated well into the night before the wedding couple was allowed to retire to their bedroom for rest and appraisal. Leonardo and his one hundred assistants organised much of the feasting, festivities, and entertainments. He and his pantomimic dancers choreographed pastoral dances performed by shepherds and shepherdesses, torch dances by satyrs and nymphs, and the graceful dance steps of previous periods as well as those of the current times by knights and damsels. The young duke's love of music was heard clearly and abundantly throughout the courts and halls long into the night.

Watching the Wedding Bed and Waiting for the Royal Consummation

At a certain moment during the night well before midnight, the newly weds were escorted to their marital bedroom. The Duchess of Milan was prepared for bed in anticipation of her royal consummation with many words of praise and much encouragement from her sister-in-laws Bianca and Anna, her ladies-in-waiting, and her mother-in-law the Bona of Savoy.

Twenty minutes or so after the Duchess was in bed, Lord Ludovico, his brother the Archbishop, and a handful of the young duke's friends and retainers carried Gian Galeazzo to his marital chambers, dressed him in his nightshirt, and sang him lewd songs as he entered behind the diaphanous curtain hanging beside the bed where his wife Isabella nervously awaited him. Some ladies-in-waiting joined the men to provide incantations and words of encouragement to help the newly weds in readiness for their conjugation. After a short while, Ludovico Sforza mustered everybody out of the bedchamber, then he and his wizard Ambrogio Varesi returned to provide the newly weds further incantations and words of encouragement. Lord Ludovico and Ambrogio Varesi emerged an hour later from the bedchamber and announced to all within earshot that all they heard on the marriage bed was soft conversation between the two, and that they were sure that no jousting had taken place.

And thus, the young duke's uncle and Governor of Milan had sown the seeds of the rumour that the young duke was impotent and would not be able to father any children. The young duchess of Milan would forever resent Ludovico's demeaning of his nephew Gian and his unwelcomed and indiscreet lingering in her bedchamber well after everybody else had left.

Fig. 38. The Annunciation. *Gian Galeazzo Maria Sforza and Isabella of Aragon, the Duke and Duchess of Milan depicted as the Archangel Gabriel and the Virgin. In Bona Sforza's (Queen of Poland) Prayer Book illustrated by Stanislaw Samostrzelnik.*

A few weeks after the wedding ceremony, Gian and Isabella transferred from the Castello in Milan to the Castello in Pavia. The new Duchess of Milan and Princess of Naples Isabella of Aragon felt relieved to be away from her creepy uncle Ludovico and his intrigues and manipulations of her husband. Gian was happy to be back to his routine of hunting in the fields of Pavia. Now, he was accompanied by his wife Isabella who, he had to admit, was an accomplished horse rider and feisty huntress. Yes, now, he had his own Diana the Huntress by his side. While Isabella enjoyed the occasional hunt, her main interest was to improve the living conditions of the Castello in Pavia and to convince her husband to develop a greater interest in taking over the reins of government from their uncle Ludovico. She could see many areas of reform that could benefit the citizens of Milan, and as their Duchess, it was her duty to provide them with the most beneficial rule to improve their lives with a good education and profitable work. Also, she wanted to provide her husband with an heir, and so she set about to encourage him to perform his marriage duties, which he endeavoured to embrace secretly despite the rumours about his disability.

Galeazzo Sanseverino and Bianca Sforza's Betrothal in Vigevano on the 14th of December 1489

Ten months after Gian and Isabella's wedding celebrations, the Duke of Bari announced on behalf of himself and the Duke of Milan that the Jouster (Giostratore) Captain Galeazzo Sanseverino was to be betrothed to his illegitimate daughter Bianca. She was only 7 years of age and still living at home with her mother Bernardina of Corradis. Many in the court wondered about the political purpose of this announcement and interpreted it as a warning by Ludovico to the young Duke of Milan that Count Galeazzo was aligning himself politically and militarily with Ludovico Sforza through this marriage of convenience. Galeazzo Sanseverino was himself a Sforza, blood-related to Ludovico and Bianca. His grandmother was Ludovico's aunt Elisabetta Sforza, sister of duke Francesco Sforza the 4th Duke of Milan and the first of the Sforza Milanese dukes. The nuptials between Galeazzo Sanseverino and Bianca Sforza were celebrated with great joy on January 10, 1490 in the Sforza Castle after the notary Zunico wrote down their official marriage contract in Vigevano on the 14th of December 1489. Galeazzo pointed out that although they were now married, the consummation would not be scheduled until 20th June 1496 when the girl would be 14 years of age, and that until that time she would remain a virgin in the care of her mother. Many saw this as an opportunity for Galeazzo to continue sowing his oats and furthering his ambitions elsewhere before he needed to demonstrate his jousting skills to Bianca.

Galeazzo Sanseverino was Ludovico Sforza's most favourite knight, and Ludovico treated him as his own son. He was one of the best jousters in Italy, and he rarely lost at any of the great jousting bouts held in Milan, Pavia, Vigevano, and Monza. Depending on his audience, he usually dedicated his fights to Isabella the Duchess of Milan or to Beatrice d' Este or to his young betrothed Bianca. He credited his success to his marvellously trained horses. Galeazzo Sanseverino always maintained that it was his horse's fearless instinct to be at the right place at the right time that was the main advantage that he had over others to win. Leonardo agreed with many others who know something about horses that Galeazzo Sanseverino was one of the best horse trainers who he had ever met. But, there was nobody else in the Duchy of Milan who trained so hard and dedicated himself so much to the sport of jousting. It was his greatest passion. Because of Galeazzo's betrothal to his illegitimate daughter, Il Moro granted his favourite knight many new properties and lands in Milan and Pavia. Galeazzo, a favourite son of Ludovico, was fast becoming one of the richest lords in the Duchy.

The Heralded Rumours of Gian Galeazzo Sforza's Impotency

Overall, the remainder of 1489 progressed happily for the young duke and duchess of Milan without too many incidences, except for the continued rumours spread in the Duchy of Milan and other states of Italy about the duke's impotency. Ludovico and his physicians provided regular news bulletins about the young duke's condition to ambassadors from Naples, Florence, Venice, and Ferrara until they eventually reached the ears of Isabella's grandfather king Ferdinand I of Naples and her father Alfonso. Both Isabella's grandfather and father were highly embarrassed, and they demanded Ludovico to remedy the situation. They even suggested that they would dissolve the marriage immediately, and they thought about offering Isabella to Ludovico if he was still willing to marry her; after all, he had secretly proposed to them in 1487 that he wanted her hand (in order to prevent his nephew Gian Galeazzo from marrying her). But, he was no longer interested in the wife of his nephew Gian because he had negotiated with Ercole I d'Este to marry his virgin daughter Beatrice. The king of Naples was not deterred by Ludovico's refusal letting him know that he still intended to dissolve the marriage between his granddaughter and Ludovico's nephew Gian and to find a more suitable husband for her, somebody like the Emperor Maximilian of Germany who would be able to provide her with children and security. The ambassador of Florence Pietro Filippo Pandolfini reported to Lorenzo de' Medici that Ludovico was confident that Gian Galeazzo was not going to have heirs with Isabella and that he, therefore, would be able to undermine the Neapolitans by interfering in their relationship with the papacy. The ambassador also passed this information on to Leonardo and asked him to keep an eye open on the developments of the marriage between Gian and Isabella and Ludovico's manipulation of Naples and his overtures to the papacy.

Leonardo da Vinci and others believed that Ludovico and his doctors were practicing malevolent sorcery (*maleficium*) on Gian's spirit and body in an attempt to create his impotency and destroy his marriage to the feisty Isabella and have her sent back to Naples. It would be a dangerous game for Leonardo to interfere or advise on the marriage for he knew that the walls have many eyes and ears and that Gian and Isabella were imprisoned in Pavia by Ludovico's agents who watched and recorded their every move. Yet, Leonardo would find a solution and it would start with the Feast of Paradise in honour of the marriage between Gian Galeazzo Sforza and Isabella of Aragon.

La Fest del Paradise and Squaring the Circle, January 1490

Almost a year after Gian and Isabella were wed, Leonardo organised and conducted his legendary spectacular *La festa del paradiso* for them to celebrate their first year of marriage. This spectacle became the talking point of Italy and the rest of Europe for many years there after. He recreated a similar *festa* 26 years later for the marriage between Lorenzo di Piero de' Medici and the French king's niece Madeleine de la Tour d' Auvergne in the gardens and on the grounds of the Cloux Chateau in Amboise in France that I was present at and witnessed in May of 1518.

The *Feast of Paradise* was staged after a night of dancing and feasting at the Castello Sforza in Milan on 13ᵗʰ January 1490. At the stroke of midnight, the duke stopped the music and led his wife and guests to the theatre room to witness Leonardo's latest creation: a revolving stage shaped like an enormous half-egg. The poet Bellincioni recounted the enormous success of the wedding celebration and the performance of *the Feast of Paradise* in his sonetti, canzoni, and capitol that was published in Milan in 1493.

> The guests now streamed into the Sala del giuoco alla pala, which had been arranged for the representation of the Paradiso, by Leonardo da Vinci, the Court mechanician. Then a train of powder exploded, and crystalline globes, like planets, were seen disposed in a circle, filled with water, and illumined by a myriad of living fires sparkling with rainbow colours.

Bernardo Bellincione had written a poem based on Dante's account of *Paradise,* and he persuaded his Florentine friend Leonardo to stage and costume the spoken performance for Gian and Isabella who he believed were now in their own paradise of married bliss. The Duchess Isabella was highly educated by her mother Ippolita Sforza and her tutors in the Greek and Italian classics and especially in the works of Dante's *The Divine Comedy,* as was her husband Gian who was tutored by many including Bellincione about the genius of Dante. They could all recite excerpts from their favourite cantos. Leonardo was easily persuaded to stage the *La festa del paradiso* for he had been long obsessed with solving Dante's mathematical puzzle outlined in the last canto (XXXIII) of *The Divine Comedy.*

> O Light Eternal, who in thyself alone
> Dwell'st and thyself know'st, and self-understood,
> Self-understanding, smilest on thine own!
> That circle which, as I conceived it, glowed
> Within thee like reflection of a flame,
> Being by mine eyes a little longer wooed,
> Deep in itself, with colour still the same,
> Seemed with our human effigy to fill,
> Wherefore absorbed in it my sight became.
> As the geometer who bends all his will
> *To measure the circle, and howso'er he try*
> *Fails, for the principle escapes him still,*
> *Such at this mystery new-disclosed was I,*
> *Fain to understand how the image doth alight*
> *Upon the circle, and with its form comply…*. [S19]

Only a few years previously, Leonardo thought that he had solved the problem on how to square the circle, and he had revealed his solution in his drawings and paintings on a wall of the Church of St. Andrew in Melzo. Then, he wanted to demonstrate how to square the circle by drawing his *Vitruvian Man* using my father as his model of the perfectly proportioned man.

But, before doing so, Leonardo decided to square the circle as a performance in Bellincione's *Feast of Paradise*. The quest for the Duchess Isabella, like Dante's Beatrice, was enlightenment, beauty, eternal light, and love. The solution on how to honour the Duchess Isabella was written in the last six lines of Dante's *The Divine Comedy*.

> But these my wings were fledged not for that flight,
> Save that my mind a sudden glory assailed
> And its wish came revealed to it in that light.
> To the high imagination force now failed;
> *But like to a wheel whose circling nothing jars*
> Already on my desire and will prevailed
> *That Love that moves the sun and the other stars.* [S19]

Circular movement, love, and light. It was so simple, really. Bernardo Bellincioni had already written the words of love that would move the sun and the other stars while the square audience including the Duke and Duchess of Milan sat at the centre of a revolving circle. All Leonardo had to do was to implement his mind's design of the theatre, the set, the actors, the costumes, and the lighting. The theatre would be a circle within circles and squares. Firstly, the stage would be a semicircle, an amphitheatre for the actors to perform their rotating, circular recitations. The mathematician and architect Vitruvius had already pointed out in his writings that a theatre should reflect the heavens and the chant of angels in the harmonies of the spheres within them. Circular motion symbolises faultless activity and therefore the theatre should be conducted in the round. The Duke and Duchess would sit in the centre of the circle and the other guests would radiate out as spokes within a semi-circle as the planets and suns on their circumference would pass by them and disappear at one or other of the corners of the square, and then reappear at one or other of the corners to continue orbiting about the Duke and Duchess who, as the Centre of the Orbits, represented the fusion and energy of the Suns driving the motion of all the planets. Paradise itself would open up to the choirs of the angels, sweet and ample, an angelic harmony of instruments and voices would surround the audience and the Duke and Duchess of Milan. The all-inclusive celestial sight and surround sound within the auditorium would soon ennoble the audience's senses and blur their hold on material reality. The planetary divinities would step out from their predetermined course and recite pretty verses in honour of the princely pair, reminding the audience that Lombardy forever grows better from their virtue and their righteous heritage, the beauty and glory of the Duchy evolving from them, the Duke and Duchess, and their togetherness in marriage. It was all smoke and mirrors and flashing lights in a beautifully constructed celestial dance. The audience was spellbound throughout the entire performance and remained stunned and silent in disbelief for a short time after its conclusion. Then, heartfelt, rapturous applause broke out at a level rarely witnessed at courtly well-mannered performances. This production by Leonardo demonstrated that he was the master of alchemy, fireworks, man-propelled and self-propelled machines, and processions and pageants; a genius who could create massive illusions and theatre in order to mesmerise, entertain, and impress a noble and highly privileged audience in the mystical ways of the world and towards a Golden Age that they were still unaware that they had entered into.

Leonardo's Gift of Erotica to Gian Galeazzo Sforza

Before the Duke and Duchess of Milan returned to Pavia, they invited Leonardo to their rooms for supper and to thank and praise him for the marvellous spectacular that he had prepared for them. After some pleasantries and a discussion about Leonardo's contribution to their wedding ceremony and the Feast of Paradise, the duchess retired to her room while

Leonardo and the duke continued to drink fine red wine together. It was then that the young duke confided to Leonardo about his problem to impregnate the Duchess. His problem was his shyness, fevers, and a weakness to perform in the presence of so many spectators whenever Isabella visited his bed in the presence of all her maids. Leonardo told him that he might have the solution for the Duke, and that he would return within the next quarter of an hour with some gifts from his studio.

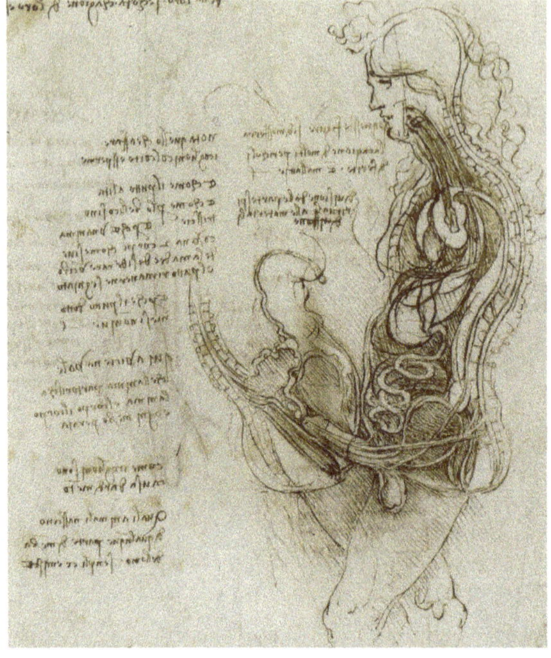

Fig. 39. Leonardo's cross sectional drawing of an act of consummation (copulation).

On his return, Leonardo handed the Duke a box of herbal powder and a folio of drawings. Two spoons of powder dissolved in water were prescribed to be taken a half-hour before the time of intercourse. Leonardo also advised the duke not to take the potions provided to him by his uncle's physicians because they might be designed to dampen his ardour. Leonardo suspected, but did not tell the young duke that Ludovico and his doctors were probably administering him with poisons such as arsenic or other heavy metals to prevent him from impregnating Isabella. Leonardo pointed to his folio of erotic sketches and suggested to the young duke that he and the duchess should play games of sensual eroticism in their own privacy without the presence of observers and attendants. One of the drawings that Leonardo presented to the young duke was an extraordinary anatomical cross section of a couple in the act of sexual intercourse. Gian Galeazzo Sforza was amazed by it. He stared spellbound by its absurdity and anatomical improbability, even though he had been in a somewhat similar situation on occasions with Isabella when nobody was watching them. After a while, he looked at the other sketches, but soon he was back again to stare at the anatomical cross section of the copulating couple. I like this one, Maestro, he said.

Yet, they both knew that the sexual act, the consummation between the duke and duchess had to be observed and recorded by officials before his lordship's reputation of impotency could be fully absolved. The officially recorded consummation came about in April of 1490, and the ambassador of Naples in Milan Giovanni Carafa reported the happy event to the Duchess Isabella's father Alfonso II Aragon of Naples and Duke of Calabria:

> Most Illustrious and Excellent Lord, Most Honourable, my messenger brings you the happy and joyous news that two nights ago your daughter the illustrious Duchess Isabella Aragon of Milan successfully shared the bridal bed with her husband Lord Gian Galeazzo Sforza, the duke of Milan. They demonstrated the indisputable actions of feverish sexual pleasure and were busy throughout the night in successive and successful congress in the duke's bedroom witnessed by her princely relatives and a select number of Ludovico's ambassadors. On receiving the joyous news from his envoys, Ludovico, the duke of Bari, was quick to acknowledge and congratulate his nephew and niece on their royal consummation.

A Visit to Pavia with a Pavilion and Bath for the Duchess, 1490

After the festivities and celebrations of the *Feast of Paradise* in Milan, the Duke and Duchess returned to their court in Pavia, and Leonardo resumed his work on the 'Sforza Horse' as he outlined in his notes. In spring, the architect and mathematician Giacomo Andrea Da Ferrara visited Milan, and Leonardo showed him his drawings of the *Vitruvian Man* and the measurements that he had taken of the *Shroud Man*. They spent a long dinner together discussing mathematical concepts and their applications to painting and architecture. On June 8, the Sienese artist, architect, and engineer Francesco di Giorgio Martini arrived in Milan and visited Leonardo for dinner. He was invited by Ludovico Sforza to advise Giovanni Antonio Amadeo on building the lantern for the *tiburio* of Milan Cathedral that Leonardo had missed out on in favour of Ludovico's preferences. Although Francesco di Giorgio Martini was 13 years older than Leonardo, they shared many interests and were good friends. Like Leonardo, Francesco di Giorgio Martini was interested in architecture and military engineering, and he wrote a *Treatise on Civil and Military Architecture* that greatly influenced his younger admirer. Then, Ludovico Sforza and the young duke of Milan invited Leonardo and Francesco di Giorgio Martini to Pavia to provide advice on their project to rebuild the Cathedral at Pavia. With their expenses to be paid by the Works Department of the Pavia Cathedral, Leonardo and Francesco di Giorgio Martini and a group of engineers and helpers set out together on horseback on June 21, 1490 for Pavia. They stayed at the Inn of the Saracen where they met with Donato Bramante who was in charge of rebuilding the Pavia Cathedral.

Bramante and Leonardo stood in the piazza in front of the cathedral, and they looked back at a bronze equestrian statue known as the *Regisole*. Bramante told him that the statue was ancient and that King Charlemagne of France had moved it to Pavia from Ravenna. Leonardo, thinking of his design for his Sforza monument, studied the action of the bronze horse before them and told Bramante, *'the movement more than anything else is deserving of praise. The imitation of antique works is better than that of the modern. Beauty and utility cannot go together as may be seen in fortresses and in men. The trot has almost the quality of a free horse. Where natural vivacity is lacking it is necessary to make accidental liveliness.'*

After much discussion about the renovations to the cathedral, Bramante took Leonardo and Francesco di Giorgio Martini on a tour of the buildings and architecture of Pavia. Leonardo later noted, *'I have watched the repair of part of the old walls of Pavia, which have their foundations in the banks of the Ticino. The piles there were old and were of oak as black as charcoal, those of alder had a red colour like Brazil wood; they were of great weight and hard as iron, without blemish.'*

Leonardo visited the anatomy department at the Medical University of Pavia and undertook some drawings of human dissections including a woman and infant who had died before childbirth. He also met with the Duchess and Duke of Milan who invited him to their Castle to reward him for his *Feast of Paradise* and his aphrodisiacs. They introduced Leonardo to their magnificent Sforza library in one of the towers of the castle. More than one thousand books and manuscripts were stored in a large vaulted hall, stacked in bookshelves that lined the walls as high as the ceiling with a central table also stacked with many manuscripts and maps. The library's greatest prize was a copy of Virgil's *Aeneid* with marginal notes in the poet Petrarch's own hand when he was in charge of the library. Leonardo was introduced to the contemporary book curator, and he quickly befriended him to find out what marvels were housed in this particular room. Leonardo skimmed through some of the manuscripts on the table, and this immediately stimulated him to want to return and further feed his hunger for the knowledge contained within this library. He wrote in his notebook, *'try to get Vitolone* (Witelo, a Silesian optical theorist of the thirteenth century) *which is in the library of Pavia and treats on mathematics. In Vitolone there are 805 conclusions about perspective and optics.'* And so, he requested the Duke and Duchess that they grant him permission to return again and stay on for a longer time in Pavia to explore the library and undertake a few architectural projects for them and the Duchy. Francesco di Giorgio Martini and Leonardo returned to Milan after three weeks in Pavia, but Leonardo was back in Pavia to source the many rare and valuable books and manuscripts on the arts and sciences at the Sforza library, explore the architecture and buildings of Pavia, and look with great happiness at the belly of Duchess Isabella that was growing healthily everyday during her highly visible pregnancy.

The simplicity and beauty of the Sforza-Visconti castle in Pavia greatly impressed Leonardo as it does any person who has visited and seen it at close hand. Built in 1360 by Galeazzo II Visconti and located to the north of the city of the Ticino River, it is one of the most notable structures in the city that befits the history of the ancient Visconti/Sforza nobility. Surrounded by walls with ditches and three drawbridges to access different doors into the city and the adjoining Visconti Park, it has four large towers five stories high (including a covered battalion), 264 battlements all around the castle on top of two stories (upper and lower levels) of a square construct with large mullioned windows. It is built of reddish bricks enclosing a beautiful interior garden in the shape of a square that contains a large fishpond. The nature and terrain of the adjoining outside park includes forests, meadows, ponds, and water from the Vernavola and Carona canals, and it has a host of animals of different species such as bears, lions, monkeys, tigers, a leopard, an elephant, and crocodiles for hunting or for observing in viewing enclosures. This park also houses a hunting lodge called Mirabello where the young duke enjoyed staying overnight to drink, sing, and dance with his hunting parties.

The interior of the Pavia castle is equipped to house a large number of the people of the court, and it has all the basic facilities needed for daily life. The lower and upper floors of the four sides of the castle all have a portico (undercover hall) between the central garden/courtyard and the eleven vaulted rooms accessible through adjoining chambers. The portico at the lower level is open to the courtyard, and the ground floor has the cleaning and cooking staff with the laundry, bathhouses, kitchens, bakery, and butcher. The upper portico overlooks the courtyard and is bricked in to provide a closed interior space for the courtiers. It serves as a passage between the rooms and a dining venue for the ladies, and it also houses some of the guards and servants. The upper floor with additional kitchens was reserved for the household of the duke and duchess, the Chancery staff, and other serving members of the court.

The duke and duchess and their personal entourage had their own rooms located away from each other. The duke's apartments were in one of the towers, whereas the duchess had her apartments on the upper floor of the west wing locked off from those of the men. The other tower rooms until recently held the prison, treasury, library, and the Privy Chancery. The stables were beneath the women's wing on the western side of the castle. The halls and chambers within the castle are all vaulted and painted with historical and contemporary hunting paintings. The roof is azure with a variety of animals in gold paint to which Leonardo contributed, especially lions, leopards, tigers, hounds, boars, monkeys, horses, and stags. A large hall facing the park to the north has beautiful frescoes painted by Pisanello with scenes of fishing and hunting and tilting parties with the dukes and duchesses overseeing the celebrations.

During his time at the Castello in Pavia in 1490, Leonardo designed and built a beautiful enclosed pavilion for the Duchess in the middle of her husband's Labyrinth where she and her ladies-in-waiting could go and rest from the heat or bath in an enclosed pool that had hot and cold running water. Leonardo proposed this project with intended fun and grace because he enjoyed pleasing the Duchess. The pavilion is a polygon with 16 sides surrounded by a moat with water. It is composed of a central room with a marble bath rimmed by a railing and columns that support the architrave. The central bathroom is ringed by eight small octagonal dressing rooms alternating with small triangular rooms where the ladies could store their belongings and assorted items, handbags, fans, mittens, etc. It stands within a loggia beneath a dome with a large skylight divided into segments by ribs with a triangular eye at the beginning of each segment. Leonardo envisaged it as the grand bathhouse for the Goddess Diana and her Pavian nymphs and modelled it on the circular church of Santa Maria in Praticha. He gave the bathroom hot and cold water that allowed the Duchess and her nymphs to select the water temperature with a few handles and the slight adjustment of female and male screws. He occasionally observed them bathing on the pretext of having to adjust or improve the plumbing and design.

The Little Devil (Salai or *Il Salaino*) Joins Leonardo's Studio Household, 1490

When in Pavia, the young Duke presented Leonardo with the full ownership of one of his vineyards located outside the Porta Vercellina in Milan within close walking distance of the Church of Santa Maria delle Grazie and near the properties and mansion of Galeazzo Sanseverino. The young duke wanted Leonardo to paint a mural of the *Last Supper of Jesus* at the Church of Santa Maria delle Grazie and to feature him as the young disciple John. He awarded the vineyard to Leonardo on condition that he accepted the tenant Pietro di Giovanni and his family as the caretaker of the vineyard and his son Gian Giacomo Caprotti di Oreno as his assistant. Leonardo obliged the young duke and accepted the gift and agreed to mentor the boy Gian Giacomo Caprotti di Oreno who apparently was a handful for all who knew him. The 10-year-old Gian Giacomo joined Leonardo's workshop as an apprentice, but he quickly earned a reputation as a glutton and a thief after stealing a silverpoint from Leonardo's assistant, the painter Marco d' Oggiono. Consequently, Leonardo called the young boy 'the little devil' (*Il Salaino*) or Salai. The young ward eventually grew to accept his nickname as an endearing badge of honour, and he went on to use the name Andrea Salai as his painter's signature. He remained with Leonardo until his mentor's last year of life, a time when he could no longer watch Leonardo's health deteriorate. And so, he left Leonardo in France and returned to the vineyard in Milan that had been gifted to Leonardo by the young duke of Milan Gian Galeazzo Sforza and that Leonardo had left for him in his last will and testament.

The following are some of the notes I found in Leonardo's manuscripts referring to Salai.

On St. Mary Magdalene's day [22nd July] 1490 Giacomo came to live with me, when ten years of age. Thief, liar, obstinate, glutton. The second day I had two shirts cut out for him, a pair of hose, and a jerkin, and when I put aside money to pay for these things he stole it from the wallet, and it was never possible to make him confess, although I was quite certain of it—lire 4. The day after I went to sup with Giacomo Andrea, the other Giacomo ate supper for two and did mischief for four, as he broke three flagons, spilled the wine, and after this came to sup where I was entertaining. On the seventh day of September he stole a stile worth 22 soldi from Marco who was staying with me. It was of silver and he took it from his studio, and when Marco had searched for it a long time he found it hidden in the box of Giacomo— lire 1 soldi 2. On the 26th day of January 1491, when I was in the house of Messer Galeazzo da Sanseverino to arrange the festival for his tournament, and certain footmen had undressed to try on some of the costumes of the savages which were to appear at the festival, Giacomo went to the wallet of one of them as it lay on the bed with other clothes, and he took out whatever money he found there - 2 lire and s. 4. Item, when I was in the same house Maestro Agostino of Pavia gave me a Turkish hide in order to make a pair of boots; this Giacomo stole it from me within a month and sold it to a cobbler for 20 soldi and with this money by his own confession, he bought aniseed comfits.

Tying the Knot Between the Sforza and Este Families with a Strategic Double Marriage

With the approaching birth of the heir of the Duchy of Milan to Isabella and Gian Galeazzo Sforza the 6th Duke of Milan, there was enormous pressure on Ludovico Sforza to relinquish his rule over Milan and his nephew. But, Ludovico had no intention of abdication, a decision that would lead to the eventual unhappy and tragic consequences five to eight years later for most citizens of Milan. Speculation of Isabella Aragon Sforza's pregnancy in August of 1490 had already spurred Ludovico to quickly proceed with his plans to marry Beatrice d' Este, and a flurry of arrangements were made for a date in late 1490 or early 1491 that would be astrologically propitious. After much deliberation, the wedding date of the 16th January 1491 was chosen. Ludovico now had to hurry with proceedings because there was great pressure on him to have his own legitimate heirs if he wanted to successfully usurp his nephew and take over the Duchy of Milan.

Ludovico originally intended to marry Beatrice's elder sister Isabella d' Este, but her father Ercole I d' Este the Duke of Ferrara married her to Francesco II Gonzaga, a condottiero and Marquess of Mantua. To cement an alliance between the Este and Sforza families, Ludovico instead was betrothed to Beatrice. On the day of her marriage, Beatrice was 16 years of age and 23 years younger than the Duke of Bari. Like her older sister Isabella d' Este, Beatrice was educated in the classics and the arts and taught to converse with and to entertain nobles from the most splendid courts of Italy and Europe. Many regarded Beatrice to have been one of the most beautiful and accomplished princesses in Italy during her marriage to Ludovico, first as the Duchess of Bari and later as the Duchess of Milan. I have added two pictures of her elegance, one with her husband and her children kneeling before Mary and Jesus painted by Bernardino Zenale (Fig. 47), and the other, her posthumous portrait painted by Bernardino de Conti (Fig. 40) that was heavily influenced by Leonardo da Vinci's portrait of the Mona Lisa. Leonardo also painted a few portraits and murals of Beatrice, but in general he preferred to concentrate on the Duchess Isabella and a few other of his favourite sitters, much to the annoyance of Ludovico.

January 1491 was the month and the year that Ludovico Sforza married Beatrice d' Este and his niece Anna Sforza married Alfonso I d' Este in a double marriage in the Duchy of Milan in attempt to cement the bonds between the Sforza and Este families and the duchies of Milan and Ferrara. Leonardo's role in Ludovico's marriage to Beatrice was more subdued than the one he had for Gian and Isabella, the Duke and Duchess of Milan. Ludovico Sforza preferred that his trustworthy and honourable ministerial adviser and secretary Bartolomeo Calco prepare the marriage arrangements and celebrations with all the appropriate royal symbols and expectations of an alliance between the Sforza of the Duchy of Milan and the Este of the Duchy of Ferrara, Modena, and Reggio, places that were located south of the Po River along the borders between the Duchy of Milan and the Republic of Florence and the Papal States. The double marriage was highly strategic and symbolic and therefore, it required all the correct courtly procedures of state to show off its magnificence and significance. These princely marriages, pageants, and celebrations in Milan were renowned not only for their pomp and splendour, but also for their orderly organisation, protocols, rights of precedence, seating arrangements, and ranks of processional participants conducted in a dignified and decorous manner, completely in contrast to the chaotic events often held in the Duchy of Ferrara. Ludovico did not trust Leonardo's surprises and his tendency for the abstract and the unusual that some lords and ladies had difficulties in understanding. He was determined that his wedding with Beatrice and that of his niece Anna Sforza to Alfonso I d' Este would be no less ordered and structured than any of the other previous spectacular Milanese princely events of his ancestors. So, Leonardo was given kitchen duties to help organise the feasts and prepare for the post wedding entertainments, especially for the jousting spectaculars. Ludovico and his father-in-law Ercole I d' Este were both robust fighting men who preferred to celebrate with the manly sports rather than those classical and obtuse tales about the Gods and Planets that Leonardo was likely to present them with. If the tales were going to be about Gods then let them be the masculine ones like those about Mars, Mercury, and Aries that are firmly grounded in combat rather than about those sissy goddesses, full of light and love and obscure Florentine verse.

Fig. 40. Portrait of Beatrice d' Este *by Bartolomeo Veneto.*

Beatrice's wedding party departed from Ferrara on 29th December 1490. Among the party were her mother Leonora Duchess of Ferrara and her brothers Ippolito the Archbishop of Esztergom in Hungary and Alfonso who was to be wed to Anna Sforza, sister of the Duke of Milan and daughter of the assassinated Duke Galeazzo Maria Sforza. Because the River Po was frozen, they rode in sledges and carts as far as Brescello. From there, they navigated the Po in a fleet of boats and barges and three bucentaurs for four or five days until they reached Piacenza where they rested for a day. Later, they met with Galeazzo Visconti Sanseverino and his company of troops who were there to escort them up river to Pavia. They reached Pavia on a Sunday afternoon where Ludovico with his carefully selected company of Milanese lords and gentlemen including my father and his brother Beltrame met them at sunset on the banks of the river Ticino. Then, with much fanfare, the bridal party was escorted to the warmed rooms of the Castello for a welcomed and joyous reception. Now, in the warmth and luxury of the castle, the bride and her travelling companions could rest and recover from the cold and fatigue of their long journey from Ferrara.

After long consultations for a day with the court physician and astrologer Ambrogio da Rosate, the wedding ceremony was held in the chapel of the Castello on Tuesday the 17th of January 1491, a propitious day to also celebrate Mars. Those present included the young duke Gian Galeazzo Sforza, Niccolo da Correggio, Galeotto Prince of Mirandola, Rodolfo Gonzaga, the four Sanseverino brothers, Leonora the Duchess of Ferrara and her daughter Isabella d' Este the Marchioness of Mantua, the young Don Alfonso, his uncle Sigismondo, and a select retinue of Ferrarese officials, courtiers, and ladies. The duchess Isabella who was heavily pregnant and expecting her child any day soon waited for the bride and groom's arrival in Milan where the official festivities were yet to be celebrated. The official proclamation was made in Milan the next day, and the magistrates of the different cities in the duchy as well as the duke's ambassadors at foreign courts were duly notified. *'The nuptial benediction was pronounced, and the act of espousals confirmed by the ring which Signor Ludovico placed on the bride's finger, and that night the marriage was consummated.'*

Next morning, after Ludovico happily fulfilled his marriage vows, he left for Milan to complete the arrangements for the bride's reception to be held during the following week. He was determined to honour his nuptials and leave nothing undone for his bride and guests. His chief commissioner Ambrogio Ferrari commanded that all painters and artisans including Leonardo, Bernardino da Rossi, Buttinone di Treviglio, Treso di Monza, Bramante, and the

Predis brothers be at hand to decorate the city and the ducal rooms of the Sforza Castello. From summer to winter, troops of painters, goldsmiths, embroiderers, and architects decorated the suite of rooms in the Rocco (inner citadel) of the Porta Giova and the Corte Ducale and the *Sala della palla*, the spacious hall with the vaulted roof on the first floor of the Castello. Leonardo and his assistants painted the ceiling of the *Sala della palla* in azure and embossed gold to imitate the starry sky while the walls were hung with canvases, arms, and heralds of the heroics and victories of past glories of the Visconti, Sforza, and the Este dukes and condottieri. It was here, in this place, that the elaborate German and Italian dances and spectacular entertainments were held to celebrate the two marriages between the Sforza and Este's families. At the entrance of the Great Hall and under a triumphal arch, the effigy of the illustrious Condottiero Francesco Sforza sitting on a horse stood as a smaller replica of the monumental masterpiece that Leonardo had already constructed in clay and was ready to caste in bronze. It stood there to commemorate and celebrate the enormous and heroic achievements of Francesco Sforza as the father of Ludovico and the grandfather of Gian Galeazzo Sforza who was soon to follow him in ruling Milan.

While Ludovico returned to oversee proceedings in Milan, Beatrice and her bridal party including her young brother Alfonso stayed on in Pavia to visit the sights of the cloisters of Certosa, the parks and gardens, and to relax in readiness for their travel to Milan a few days later. They left Pavia on Saturday the 21st with the escort of a large contingent of Captain Galeazzo Sanseverino's troops, stayed overnight at Binasco, and arrived next day in Milan. The heavily pregnant Duchess of Milan Isabella of Aragon was escorted in her carriage from the basilica of Saint Eustorgio to the outer gate of the Porta Ticinese to warmly greet her young cousin who was now recognised and entitled as the Duchess of Bari and Ludovico's official bride. Isabella and Beatrice were cousins, and they spent their childhood together in Naples under the care of their grandfather King Ferdinand I, and his second wife, Joanna of Aragon. Although Beatrice was younger than Isabella the Duchess of Milan by about five years, they had regularly corresponded with each other and were good friends. Now, together again, they shared the carriage to the gate of the inner wall where Ludovico and his nephew Gian and more than a hundred trumpeters and escorts waited to accompany them through the assembled crowd and past the magnificent decorations to the piazza outside the Castello. Here, under a grand portal, the duchess-mother Bona of Savoy and her two daughters Bianca Maria and Anna Sforza received Ludovico's wife Beatrice and her brother Alfonso with much pomp and ceremony. Following the French king's request to Ludovico and the Milanese council, Bona of Savoy was permitted to stay on in Milan for another two years after her son's marriage to bear witness to her daughter Anna's marriage to the heir of the house of Este and to cordially welcome the boy's mother Duchess Leonora to the Sforza castle.

The following day, the young prince Alfonso d' Este and the princess Anna Sforza were married in the ducal chapel, but deferred their final nuptial benediction until they returned to Ferrara in February. But, while in Milan together, the sumptuous trousseau, jewels, and magnificent presents of both brides were displayed in the Sforza Castello for the pleasure of the courtiers, ambassadors, and royal visitors who came to pay their homage to the newly weds. There was the grand ball, *festa per lé donne*, at the *Sala della palla* where more than two hundred Milanese ladies of high rank attended. But, best of all were the jousts, and the crowning event was the *Giostra* on the 26th of January 1991. On the day of the grand joust, Leonardo attended the house of Galeazzo Sanseverino to help him to prepare for the festival and tournament, *La Festa Della Sua Giostra*, in order to further honour the wedding of Ludovico Sforza and Beatrice d' Este. Leonardo and Galeazzo Sanseverino were still good friends, and Leonardo wanted to please him as best he could. I have Leonardo's notes and sketches of the costumes and masks that he designed for the attendant warriors and soldiers to wear at the intended joust and extravaganza. Leonardo also noted on one of the accompanying sheets his ideas for the casting of the 'Sforza Horse' monument. Strangely, it is a horse without a tail.

The jousts are always magnificent events, and *La Festa Della Sua Giostra* that was held on the great piazza in front of the Castello was no exception. In fact, it was very special. At this tournament the knights entered the lists in companies, clad in fancy costumes, and bearing the symbolical devices of the knights, houses, and cities from whence they came. The Mantuan troop with Alfonso Gonzaga at their head arrived first. They were composed of twenty horsemen clad in green velvet and gold lace, bearing golden lances and olive boughs in their hand. Then came Annibale Bentivoglio the young husband of Lucrezia d' Este with the Bologna knights, riding beside a triumphal carriage drawn by stags and unicorns carrying the badge of the House of Este. Gaspare Sanseverino followed them with his band of twelve riders in black and gold Moorish dress bearing Ludovico's symbol of the Moor's head on their helmets and white doves on their black armour. Last of all, came a troop of wild Scythians, mounted on Barbary steeds, galloping, whooping, and hollering across the piazza before halting in front of the ducal party. They suddenly discarded their disguises and stood there in their magnificence with Galeazzo Sanseverino the captain of the Milanese armies at their head. He planted his golden lance in the ground, and a giant Moor from his troop advanced to the front of them all and recited a poem in honour of Duchess Beatrice. These Scythian disguises worn by Galeazzo Sanseverino and his companions were designed by Leonardo da Vinci, and I have the drawings of the savages and masks on a number of pages of his sketch books.

After this initial pageant, the serious business of the *Giostra* began, and lances of the tilting-matches crashed heavily onto the shields, armour, knights, and horses for three days. As usual, Galeazzo Sanseverino was the champion of all the tournaments. Leonardo often liked to tell the story about how one of Galeazzo's opponents tried to provoke him by holding up his shield and shouting out, 'alas, your tool is too small for so large a business as jousting with me.' Galeazzo ignored him, and in the ensuing joust, he knocked his opponent flying from his horse to land heavily onto the ground well covered in horseshit. While the knight lay dazed and battered on the ground with his legs lifted to the heavens as if he was trying to ride off on an invisible horse into the ether, Galeazzo rode up to him and said, 'alas, my tool is still much too long and strong for your arsehole and your horse, fanforone.' And with that, he trotted off to be awarded his prize from the princess Beatrice d' Este. Yes, Galeazzo Sanseverino was the foremost knight of Milan who distinguished himself beyond even Ludovico's expectation on this day when he received the *pallium* of gold brocade from the bride's own hand. Other knights who distinguished themselves and received honourable mentions and rewards from the Duke of Bari and the Duke of Milan for their bravery and perseverance were the young Annibale Bentivoglio from Bologna who badly wounded his hand but continued to fight in a number of losing bouts, the Marchesino Girolamo Stanga who was one of Beatrice's most devoted servants, Niccolo da Correggio who stood out in his suit of gold brocade, and one or other of the Sanseverino brothers. Leonardo in the meantime was busy in the kitchen and dining rooms preparing for the celebratory nights' banquets.

On the final day, Gian the young Duke of Milan presented a splendid tribute to all who had participated in the *Giostra* thanking all the knights for their valour and unsurpassed skill and bravery in the tournaments. The ducal speech was applauded and cheered by all the knights, but it did not impress Ludovico the Regent of Milan for he thought that the celebrations should have been much more about him, the groom. With the final celebratory banquet at the Castello, the wedding festivities were brought to a close, and they were unanimously pronounced to have been a brilliant success. Leonardo da Vinci, of course, played no small part in their overall success and he was congratulated by many of the participants and guests for his magnificent banquets and spectacular costumes for the masquerades.

The Celebrated Birth of the Little Duke Francesco II Sforza, 30th January 1491

A year and a half after his marriage to Isabella, Gian Galeazzo Sforza Duke of Milan finally disproved the odious rumour about his impotency when his wife Isabella happily gave birth to a healthy boy, their 'Little Duke' (Il Duchetto) Francesco II Sforza on the 30th January 1491. Little did they realise that tragedy was awaiting them four years later, and that it would follow their 'Little Duke' for the remainder of his life.

Anna Maria Sforza's Triumphant Reception in Ferrara

Two days after the birth of the Duke and Duchess of Milan's son on the 30th of January 1491, the Duchess Leonora took leave of her daughter Beatrice and her son-in-law Ludovico and her niece Isabella Duchess of Milan, and she set out on her homeward journey with her son Alfonso and his bride Anna. The newly weds were escorted by two hundred Milanese gentlemen, Anna's brother Ermes Sforza, and the Count of Caiazzo Gian Francesco Sanseverino past Pavia to embark on the bucentaurs that would take them back along the River Po to Ferrara.

Much has been written about the spectacle of IL Moro's wedding to Beatrice and therefore I refrain from writing any more about it. However, I add a worthy note about Anna Maria Sforza's reception in Ferrara after her wedding to Alfonso in Milan that my father attended without my mother because she was six months pregnant and not well enough to travel and accompany him. His mother-in-law Caterina Visconti who had been Anna Sforza's tutor and lady-in-waiting for seven-years was invited to accompany the travel party as a representative of the Sforza court, but she elected to stay in Milan with her pregnant daughter. According to my father and a few other Milanese reporters, the triumphal entry of Anna and Alfonso into the walled city of Ferrara on 12th February 1491 was a spectacular and well-organised event. The bride and groom were carried by forty doctors of law and medicine from the University of Ferrara in a triumphal carriage covered by an immense *baldacchino*. Their citizens welcomed the procession consisting of some 4,000 participants and 200 musicians into the walled city with enormous happiness and enthusiasm. Although my father and the other Milanese expected a disordered affair, it was well organised with no squabbling or fighting between the officials that was a common sight with previous Ferrarese events. Apparently, the Duke and Duchess and the officials of Ferrara had learnt much from attending the Gian and Isabella wedding in Milan a few years previously, and they intended to at least match the minimal requirements of previous Milanese examples. However, some organised confusion did eventuate towards the end that was typically Ferrarese when the procession reached the last of the magnificent triumphal archs and entered the piazza located between the cathedral and the ducal palace. Here, a thousand cheering citizens dressed in masks and carnival costumes and bearing torches and flags had gathered to enthusiastically greet the young married couple, their future duke and duchess of Ferrara. When the bridal couple and the *illustri* mounted the steps in a driving snowstorm to enter the palace, the gathered mob broke through the security guard, and with spontaneous acts of joy, they seized and destroyed the empty triumphal carriage and *baldacchino* in their desire for a celebratory souvenir. Secure from the celebrating mobs, the nuptial mass was held in the family chapel, and the banquet was in the *sala grande* of the palace, and by all accounts including those of my father, the *festa all' antica* was a resounding success.

My Celebrated Birth: Little Count Giovanni Francesco Melzi, 20th April 1491

I was born on April 20th, 1491, Count Giovanni Francesco Melzi, later to be known as Cesco Melzi or the 'Little Count'. It was a few months after the birth of the 'Little Duke' Francesco II

Sforza, and we grew up together as friends until, when at the age of nine years, he was exiled to France by the French king Louis XII. The city festivities and celebrations were not as great for me as for the 'Little Duke', but Leonardo visited my mother and father and me to see my little face the day after I was born and to congratulate and celebrate with them on my successful and healthy birth. He was pleased and honoured to be one of my nominated godfathers. 'We'll make a great artist of him,' he told my parents.

Travels to Lake Como and Bormio in the Lombardy Alps, 1492

A year after my birth, my father accompanied Leonardo to the Lake Como region on some civil engineering and reconnaissance projects for Ludovico Sforza and his nephew Gian Galeazzo Sforza the Duke of Milan. They visited Vercellina, Valtellina, Valsassina, Bellagio, and Ivrea. Many years later, I found some notes about their travels in one of Leonardo's notebooks. These notes left an impression on me as much as these regions always had on him for they formed the background to so many of his paintings to the day that he left us:

Above Lake Como in the direction of Germany lies the valley of Chiavenna, where the river Mera enters the lake. Here the mountains are barren and very high with huge crags. In these mountains the water birds called cormorants are found; here grow firs, larches and pines, and there are fallow deer, wild goats, chamois, and savage bears. One cannot make ascents there without using hands and feet. In the season of the snow the peasants go there with a great trap in order to make the bears fall down over these rocks. The river runs through a very narrow gorge: the mountains extend on the right and the left in the same way for a distance of twenty miles. From mile to mile one may find good inns there. Higher up the river there are waterfalls six hundred braccia high which are very fine to see, and you may find good living at four soldi for your bill. A large quantity of timber is brought down by this river.

Valley of Trozzo: In this valley fir pines and larches grow plentifully; and from here Ambrogio Ferrere has his logs brought down.

At Bellagio: Opposite the castle of Bellagio is an insignificant stream, which falls from a height of more than a hundred braccia from the spring where it rises sheer into the lake with inconceivable din and uproar. This spring flows only in August and September.

The Voltolina: The Voltolina as has been said is a valley surrounded by lofty and terrible mountains; it produces a great quantity of strong wine but has so great a stock of cattle that the peasants reckon that it produces more milk than wine. It is this valley through which the Adda passes which first flows through Germany for more than forty miles. In this river is found the grayling, which feeds on silver of which much is to be found in its sand. Everyone in this district sells bread and wine, and a jug of wine is never more than a soldo, veal is a soldo the pound, and salt ten denari and butter the same and eggs a soldo for a quantity.

At Bormio: At the head of the Voltolina are the mountains of Bormio, which are terrible and always covered with snow. Here ermines breed. At Bormio are the baths; eight miles above Como is the Pliniana, which rises and falls every six hours, and as it rises it supplies two mills with water and there is a surplus, and as it falls it causes the spring to dry up for a distance of more than two miles. It is in this district that a river falls with a great impetus through a mighty chasm in the mountain. These journeys should be made in the month of May, and the largest bare rocks which exist in these parts are the mountains of Mandello near to those of Lecco and Gravidonia; towards Bellinzona thirty miles from Lecco are those of the valley of Chiavenna; but the greatest is that of Mandello, which has at its base a gully towards the lake that descends two hundred steps, and here at all seasons there is ice and wind.

In Vol Sasina: Vol Sasina runs in the direction of Italy. It has almost the same shape and characteristics. The mappello grows here plentifully: there are great floods and waterfalls. In Vol Sasina between Vimognio and Introbbio on the right hand where you enter the road to Lecco you come upon the Trosa, a river, which falls from a very high rock and as it falls goes underground and so the river ends there. Three miles farther on you come to the buildings of the copper and silver mines near to the district known as Prato San Pietro, and the iron mines, and various strange things. The Grigna is the highest mountain in these parts and it is without any vegetation.

Birth of Ercole (Maximilian) Sforza, Son of the Duke and Duchess of Bari, 25th January 1493

Now happily married to the young and beautiful Beatrice d' Este for two years, Ludovico realised he needed sons, and he needed them quickly to successfully retain his rule over Milan and to silence the continuing complaints and looming competition of the young Duke and Duchess of Milan. Gian was now approaching 23 years of age, and the Duchess Isabella continually reminded him that he was the legitimate Duke of Milan, and that he was of rightful age and ready to rule. It would be difficult for Ludovico to stop him without having a legitimate heir of his own. And so, Beatrice provided Ludovico IL Moro with an heir Maximilian (formerly Ercole) Sforza on the 25th January 1493, and a second son Francesco II Sforza on 4th February 1495. Ludovico would make sure that it was his two sons and not the son of Gian and Isabella who would become the future dukes of Milan.

Their first child, a fine healthy boy, received the name of Ercole to honour his maternal grandfather the Duke of Ferrara, but he was afterwards renamed as Maximilian when the Holy Roman Emperor became his godfather after his marriage to Bianca Sforza, the niece of Ludovico. The birth of Ercole was an auspicious event hailed with much public rejoicings. The bells rang, and solemn processions were held for six days, and many thanksgivings offered up in all the churches and abbeys of the Duchy.

Marriage Between Emperor Maximilian of Germany and Bianca Sforza, 30th November 1493

Soon after the birth of his son Ercole, Ludovico arranged to marry off his niece Bianca Maria Sforza (the sister of the Duke of Milan Gian Galeazzo Sforza) to the Holy Roman Emperor Maximilian I.

Maximilian and his father Fredrick III, together, were the Holy Roman Emperors of Germany. They were constantly at war with France and their kings Louis XI and Charles VIII over the Duchy of Burgundy and disputed French territories that Maximilian had inherited from his wife Mary the Duchess of Burgundy after she died from a riding accident in 1482. In order to strengthen his relationship with Maximilian I and Charles VIII, Ludovico offered to mediate as a peacemaker between the German and French kings. He wanted the friendship of the two kings in order to win their support with his aim to usurp Gian's dukedom and become the Duke of Milan in place of his nephew. So, in 1492, he charged his ambassador Belgiojoso to visit Charles VIII and his court in France in order to broker an alliance with Milan and a peace settlement with Maximilian I. At the same time, he sent my father and the diplomat Erasmo Brasca to Germany to discuss with Maximilian I the possibility of a three-way alliance between Milan, France, and Germany.

Ludovico successfully won over the two kings and began to set his schemes into motion. Charles VIII as monarch of the House of Valois had a long-standing claim to be the rightful monarch of the Kingdom of Naples instead of King Alfonso II of Naples because Rene of Naples who was Duke of Anjou and Lorraine and also King of Naples had left the Neapolitan throne to Charles VIII's father King Louis XI of France. Ludovico, in order to oppose and upset Isabella the Duchess of Milan, supported the French king's claim for Naples and secretly offered him the right of passage through the Duchy of Milan if the king desired to invade Naples. At the same time, he encouraged the Treaty of Senlis in Oise in May of 1493 between France and Germany that ceased all hostilities between the Houses of Habsburg and Valois and that returned the Duchy of Burgundy and its city Dijon into French hands while allowing Maximilian I of Habsburg to retain the other disputed territories including Artois and the County of Flanders.

Then, in the middle of 1493, Ludovico convinced the widower Maximilian with a rich dowry of 400,000 ducats to marry his niece Bianca Maria Sforza, the sister of Gian Maria Sforza the Duke of Milan. This marriage would assert Maximilian with the right to be the Imperial Overlord of Milan and add to his other titles of Holy Roman Emperor, German King, Archduke of Austria, and Duke of Burgundy. For this marriage, Ludovico extracted a secret promise from the Emperor that he would grant him the investiture of the duchy of Milan as soon as the King of the Romans (Germans) was married to Bianca Sforza. This was what Ludovico wanted more than anything else; he wanted to be the fully sanctioned Duke of Milan invested by the Holy Roman Emperor. Previous Emperors had formerly granted the investiture of Milan to the Visconti dukes of Milan, but not to the previous Sforza dukes Francesco, Galeazzo or Gian who were elected from father to son by popular election and had never been granted investiture by the Holy Roman Emperor. Ludovico wanted to be the first. Otherwise, without the investiture, the Duchy of Milan as a fief would be rightfully returned to the Holy Roman Empire. Indeed, Ludovico saw the current Duke of Milan Gian Galeazzo Maria Sforza as the real usurper because the Emperor had not yet officially approved his investiture. Of course, the Milanese council and nobles would not support this interpretation of the rights of the Duchy that Ludovico had whispered into the Emperor's ear so it needed to be kept a secret for now. My father, who was the new Count Palatine of Insubria and who officially represented the Holy Roman Emperor's interests in the Duchy of Milan from 1488, was privy to this secret between the Emperor and Ludovico, and he later shared it with Leonardo.

My father and Leonardo travelled to Hungary in 1485 on behalf of Gian the young Duke of Milan and Ludovico the Regent of Milan to formalise the engagement between Bianca Sforza and Janus Corvinus son of Matthias the king of Hungary. But, due to the connivances of Queen Beatrice of Naples who was a member of the Neapolitan House of Aragon and the wife of King Matthias, the formal marriage never happened. Instead, eleven years later, in 1496, Janus married Beatrice de Frangepan of Croatia. Bianca Sforza, on the other hand, who was widowed at age ten and previously left alone at the altar twice, was finally ready to be married at the age of 22 years to the 35-year-old Maximilian I and destined to become the Duchess consort of Austria, Queen consort of Germany, and the Empress of the Holy Roman Empire.

The formal arrangements for the marriage were made so that a wedding by proxy would be held in Milan at the Duomo on the 30th November 1493 with Bianca and the Emperor's proxies in attendance while her husband Maximilian I would remain in Germany for security reasons because of the recent death of his father Fredrick III (19th August 1493). His Majesty was in mourning and therefore would wait for the arrival of his bride for their formal marriage and consummation to take place in Innsbruck on 16th March 1494.

Beatrice d' Este, the wife of Ludovico Sforza the Duke of Bari, wrote to her sister Isabella a month after the proxy wedding ceremony of her niece Bianca Maria Sforza to Maximilian I the Holy Roman Emperor. I have a copy of this historic letter given to me by Isabella d' Este in exchange for one of Leonardo's paintings that was in my possession.

Very illustrious Lady and my dear sister,
I told you some time ago that I would relate to you in detail the triumphal ceremony

that took place at Milan for the marriage of the Most Serene Queen of the Romans. Although I certainly gave orders to my secretary to send you this account, yet since you write me that it has never reached you, the blame must be laid on the Secretary and you must excuse me for my apparent negligence. The marriage took place on the last day of last month, and in preparation for the solemnisation, a porch had been erected before the principal church in the city of Milan, with columns on each side bearing a violet canopy embroidered with doves. Inside the Church, the aisles were draped with brocade as far as the choir, in front of which had been erected a triumphal arch on massive pillars. This was painted all over, and in the centre could be seen a figure of the Duke Francesco on horseback, with the ducal arms above and those of the King of the Romans [Maximilian]. This triumphal arch was square in shape and decorated with pictures of old-time ceremonies. The imperial insignia and my husband's coat of arms were placed on the side facing the High Altar. On the further side of the arch were steps leading to a big stand erected in front of the High Altar. On the left was a small stand decked with gold brocade, where were the Embassies and on the right, a stand decked with silver brocade, and behind these stands, seats draped and arranged in tiers for the Councillors and other noblemen and gentlemen. At the ends of the choirs were two raised platforms, one for the singers, and the other for the trumpeters and musicians, and between the two were seated the Doctors of Law and Medicine, with their caps and cloaks fringed with fur, each placed according to his degree. The Altar itself was sumptuously decorated with silver vases and with images of the saints in silver, which you must have seen at the Rocchetta [a courtyard within the castle] when you were at Milan.

The street leading to the Cathedral was magnificently decorated. There was a series of columns garlanded with ivy the whole distance from the ramparts of the Castello to the end of the place, and between these columns garlands of branches bore cartouches with ancient emblems, and round shields with the imperial arms and those of our house. Above the street from the Castello to the Cathedral were stretched flags of the Sforza colours. In front of many doors, the flagstaffs were decked with creepers and green foliage, in such wise that one seemed to be in the month of May. On both sides of the street, the houses were decked with satin, with the exception of those houses that have recently been decorated with the frescoes that are now being made on the dwellings of Milan, and which are no less handsome than tapestries. At about half-past nine on the morning of that day, the reverend and magnificent Ambassadors of the King of the Romans rode to the church, escorted by the Marquis Ermes, the Count of Caiazzo, the Count Francesco Sforza, the Count da Melzo, and Messer Ludovico de Fojano, and took their seats on the grandstand, in the little box on your left as you enter, this being considered as the place of greatest honour, being on the same side as the pulpit. At ten o'clock, Her Most Serene Highness mounted into the triumphal chariot, which our most dear Mother of revered memory gave me when I was at Ferrara, and that was drawn by four white horses.

The Queen wore a toilette of crimson satin embroidered with stripes of gold and covered with precious stones. Her train was of immense length, as also her hanging sleeves whose shape made them appear like two wings, and these produced a splendid effect. Her headdress was composed of magnificent diamonds and pearls, and to add to the impressiveness of the occasion, Messer Galeazzo Pallavicino carried her train, and the Counts Conrado de Lando and Manfredo Torriello each carried one of her sleeves. Before the bride walked all the chamberlains, courtiers, officers, gentlemen, feudatories, and last of all the councillors. The Queen was seated in the middle of the chariot, with the Duchess Isabella on her right, and with me on her left. The said Duchess wore a camora of crimson satin, with gold cords, worked on it, just the same as on my camora of grey material that you must remember having seen in my wardrobe. And as for me, I wore a camora of violet velvet with a cape, and embroidered on it interlaced chains in massive enameled gold, the background in white and the chains in green so as to create the right effect—which chains were half an arm high from the ground. Likewise there were chains on the bodice in front and behind, and the sleeves were attached with the same chains. The camora had several linings of cloth of gold, and over all the collar of Saint Francis made of big pearls, and at the end instead of the ornament, a fine balas ruby without leaves.

On the other side of the chariot were Madonna Fiordelise (a natural daughter of the Duke Francesco Sforza), Madonna Bianca (the natural daughter of Ludovico the Moor), wife of Messer Galeazzo, and the wife of the Count Francesco Sforza. Behind followed the Ambassadors sent by His Most Christian Majesty the King of France to do honour to the wedding. Then came the envoys of the different Italian States, according to their rank, with the Lord Duke and my husband on horseback. Behind followed about twelve chariots bearing the most noble damsels of Milan specially selected and invited to assist at the ceremony, and the Queen's ladies all wearing the same uniform costume, that is to say, camoras of tan satin and cloaks of pale green satin. The Duchess Isabella's ladies and my own were likewise in chariots, and when we reached the Cathedral in that order, the shops and windows all along the way were decked with satin draperies, and so packed with men and women that it would have been impossible to gauge the crowds who gathered at every corner of the streets.

When we had arrived at the door of the Cathedral, we got down out of the chariots and advanced to the steps of the stand where the Ambassadors of the King of the Romans came forward to meet the Queen and lead her to her place on the stand in front of the high altar. Then we occupied all the seats which had been reserved for us; that is to say, that the Ambassadors mounted into the stand decked with cloth of gold, the queen was conducted to the stand decked with cloth of silver between the French Ambassadors, whilst behind them were seated the envoys of the other powers, the Duke and my husband, the Duchess and I. The other relatives of the bride occupied a row of seats further down, and the centre of the stand was filled with a great concourse of ladies. Beside the Queen, councillors, feudatories, and other courtiers, officers and chamberlains occupied the rest of the seats. As for the crowds, the Church, despite its dimension, could not hold them all.

When we were all in our places, the very reverend Archbishop of Milan made his entry in full dress with his priests in their usual vestments and commenced the celebration of the Mass with the most solemn ceremonial, to the sound of trumpets, flutes, and organs, joined to the voices of the choir of the chapel who regulated their singing from the time of Monsignor. Hard by the pulpit, two of the priests of the ordinary of the Cathedral offered incense, one to the Ambassadors of King Maximilian, and the other to the Queen, the Duke and Duchess, and to my husband and me, who were sitting on the opposite side. When the time for it came, the Blessing was given by the Bishop of Piacenza to the representatives of the King and by the Bishop of Como to us others who were in the other stand.

After mass had been celebrated with the greatest solemnity, the Queen rose from her seat between the Ambassadors of His Most Christian Majesty and accompanied by the Duke and my husband, the Duchess Isabella and me, and followed by all the Princes of the Blood, advance towards the Altar. The Ambassadors of King Maximilian came forward in their turn, and we all stood before the Altar where Monsignor the Archbishop celebrated the marriage, and the Bishop of Brixen first handed the ring to the Queen and then, assisted by the Archbishop, placed the crown on her head, which act was heralded by great fanfares of trumpets, ringing of bells, and firing of cannon. The said crown was of gold encrusted with rubies, pearls, and diamonds, and constructed in the shape of small arches intercrossing. On the top was an image of the terrestrial globe, surmounted with a little Imperial Cross, after the model given by the Ambassadors, according to their Sovereign's instructions. After this, each of us went in procession to the door of the Cathedral, the Feudatories mentioned above bearing trains and sleeves. There the women as well as the men mounted on horseback, and an awning of white edged with ermine was made ready, under which the Queen rode, preceded by the Ambassadors and all the Court, headed by the Duke and my husband. At the side of the Queen rode the Ambassadors of the King, her husband, the Bishop of Brixen being on her left outside the canopy; and in this order the long procession started back to the Castello. The canopy was carried the whole of the distance by Doctors in their robes, as has been mentioned above, and behind the Queen rode the Duchess and myself, followed by relatives, courtiers, and guests, all on horseback. Then came the Queen's Ladies, the duchess' and mine, all sumptuously dressed and giving a splendid effect, but the fairest of all was the Queen with the Imperial crown on her head. Nothing but cloth of gold or silver was to be seen and the people of less estate wore crimson velvet, so that the toilettes were a wonderful sight, without mentioning the countless chains of gold worn by the cavaliers and others. All those who were present agreed that they had never seen so magnificent a spectacle, and the Ambassador of Russia, who was numbered amongst them, declared that he had never witnessed such an extraordinary display of pomp. The Nuncio of his Holiness the Pope said the same thing, as well as the Ambassador of France, who declared that, although he had been present at the Coronations of the Pope and of his own King and Queen, he had never seen anything more splendid. Your Excellency may judge from that what a wonderfully pleasant and glorious wedding this was. Everyone in the crowd was shouting with joy, and continued until we reached the Castello of Milan, where the procession broke up and the crowd dispersed. Many times during the ceremony I regretted your absence, and since my desire could not be satisfied, I thought it would be an excellent plan if I wrote to you the description of it all by my own hand.

As ever, I commend myself to your Highness, Your sister, Beatrix Sfortia Vicemoes Estensis Duchissa Bri. Viglevani, XXVIIII December 1493 [S20]

The Duchess Bona of Savoy, shedding many tears of joy, welcomed her daughter's marriage with a grand festival held in the Castello during the next two days. There was the usual jousting tournament with the grand prize once again won by the grandest jouster of them all Galeazzo Sanseverino. Much feasting and dancing, and a grand display of fireworks followed. *So many torches and lights illumined the darkness of night, that all Milan blazed as if the city were on fire.*

Then, before the celebrations had even settled, it was time for the new queen of Germany to start on her journey across the Alps to Innsbruck to meet with her husband the Emperor king waiting patiently for her arrival. This would be a most difficult journey because it was already high winter with large snowfalls and many snowstorms reported in the Alps. The new queen was to be attended and protected by Maximilian's ambassadors, her brother Hermes Sforza, her cousin Francesco Visconti-Sforza - the bishop of Milan, the poet Gaspare Visconti, the jurist Giasone del Maino, as well as Erasmo Brasca - the special envoy to the King of the Romans, my father - Count Palatine to the Romans and Milan, Ambrogio de Prédis (instead of Leonardo) - the court painter, and a large suite of ladies of the queen's choosing. Gian and Isabella - the Duke and Duchess of Milan, Ludovico and Beatrice – the Duke and Duchess of Bari, and Bona of Savoy, all accompanied Bianca as far as Como where the bishop and his clergy led her in state to the cathedral for celebratory prayers and a solemn thanksgiving service. The queen and the German ambassadors spent the night in the episcopal palace while the other princes and princesses were entertained in the houses of distinguished courtiers in the town. Next morning, the bride farewelled her family and boarded a richly decorated barge to be rowed across lake Como by forty sailors while her suite followed in thirty smaller boats, painted and decked out with laurel boughs and tapestries. It was a beautiful morning, the lake was covered with glittering sails, the shores were crowded with people, and the air was filled with the joyous sounds of music. The bridal party spent the night at the Marchesino Stanga's castle in Bellagio, and then, next morning, they sailed off again towards the upper end of the lake. However, the weather changed suddenly, and they encountered a violent storm that scattered the fleet in all directions. By the grace of God, the queen and her escorts survived the tempest, and after being tossed about on the waves for several hours, the queen's barge managed to pull back and find safety at Bellagio once again.

Thereafter, the journey was no easier, and the crossing through the mountain passes that divided the Valtellina from the Tyrol was particularly difficult with the continuing bad weather. The rough mule-track over the Alps with the precipitous cliffs near Nombray filled the Milanese ladies with terror, and Bianca complained bitterly of the hardships that she had to endure. The ambassador Erasmo Brasca wrote to Ludovico:

> The queen conducts herself well on the whole, but often complains that I deceive her, by telling her, each morning when she mounts her horse, that she will not find the road so rough today, and then, as ill luck will have it, it turns out to be worse than ever. [S7]

Fig. 41. Portraits of Bianca Maria Sforza, the Holy Roman Empress and Queen of Germany by Ambrogio de' Predis.

Finally, on the 23rd of December, the queen and her attendants reached Innsbruck where they were kindly received by Maximilian's uncle the Archduke Sigismund of Austria and his wife with whom they spent Christmas and the winter days dancing and playing parlour games while Ludovico's ambassador Erasmo Brasca went on to meet the King of the Romans in Vienna. Then, in no great rush, Maximilian arrived eventually at the castle of Hall in Innsbruck on the 9th of March to meet with his bride and to consummate his marriage *'to the confusion of all our enemies'* as Brasca put it triumphantly in writing to his master the following morning. This union, according to Erasmo Brasca and Ludovico's friends and foes alike, was acknowledged to be a masterstroke of diplomacy, but in the end, it was destined not to prove a very happy one for either Bianca or Maximilian. From the very first moment that Maximilian laid eyes on his bride of 21 years of age who was thirteen years younger than himself, he was critical of her, and he told Erasmo Brasca that Bianca was as fair as his first wife Mary of Burgundy, but inferior in wisdom and good sense, and he hoped that she might improve in time. He treated her kindly to begin with, but before long, he began to find fault with her extravagant spending habits and annoying behaviours such as eating her meals on the floor instead of at the table. Moreover, she was prone to intrigue and quarrels with her ladies and royal staff, and Maximilian found her presence wearisome, and he tended to leave her mostly to herself. His hopes for an heir with Bianca were never realised, and she lived a very dull and solitary life in her castle in Innsbruck.

Often left alone in the vast, gloomy castle of Innsbruck, Bianca pined for the bright and sunny villas and palaces of Milan, and she often wrote affectionate letters to her uncle, begging him for portraits of himself with Beatrice, as well as for the silks and feathers, the jewels and perfumes with which her thoughts were always busy. She loved her uncle, and she proved to be a most loyal friend in his darkest days when his children lived in exile with her at Innsbruck. Yet, she was greatly saddened by her husband's neglect, and her health gradually deteriorated until she died in Innsbruck in 1510. Her bronze effigy that is robed in rich brocades that she loved so much still adorns her sumptuous mausoleum where she was buried in the Franciscan church of Innsbruck.

Fig. 42. Portraits of Maximilian I the Holy Roman Emperor by Ambrogio de' Predis, and his Queen Bianca Maria Sforza by Bernhard Strigel.

A summary of the important marriages in Milan attended to by Leonardo da Vinci:

1. The marriage between my mother Tommasina della Torre and my father Gerolamo Melzi in May 1488.
2. Gian Galeazzo Sforza Duke of Milan to Isabella of Aragona Princess of Naples, daughter of King Alfonso II of Naples and Ippolita Maria Sforza, eldest daughter of the 4th Duke of Milan, Francesco Sforza (15th Feb., 1489). Birth of Francesco Sforza Count of Pavia and heir to the Duchy of Milan, 30th January 1991. Birth of Bona Sforza on 2nd February 1494.
3. Marriage contract between Galeazzo Sanseverino and Bianca Sforza in Vigevano 14th December 1489. Wedding consummation rescheduled for 20th June 1496.
4. Duke Ludovico Sforza of Bari married to Beatrice d' Este (16th January 1491). Anna Maria Sforza married Beatrice's brother Alfonso I d' Este, future duke of Ferrara (21st January 1491). Ludovico and Beatrice's issues are Maximilian Sforza on 25th January 1493 and Francesco II Sforza on 4th February 1495.
5. Emperor Maximilian of Germany married Bianca Sforza, 30th November 1493.

CHAPTER 10

Auguries. The Death of the Magnificent Florentine in 1492, and the Passing of Leonardo's Mother, 1494

I have from an early age abjured the use of meat, and the time will come when men such as I will look upon the murder of animals as they now look upon the murder of men.

— Leonardo da Vinci

Death of Lorenzo, the Magnificent, 9th April 1492

A few days before Leonardo's fortieth birthday, he received the news that Lorenzo di Piero de' Medici from the noble House of Medici had died on the 9th of April at his family villa of Careggi. The Signoria and council of Florence issued the following decree to their ambassador in Milan:

> Whereas the foremost man of all this city, the lately deceased Lorenzo de' Medici, did, during his whole life, neglect no opportunity of protecting, increasing, adorning, and raising this city, but was always ready with counsel, authority and painstaking in thought and deed; shrank from neither trouble nor danger for the good of the state and its freedom..... it has seemed good to the Senate and people of Florence.... to establish a public testimonial of gratitude to the memory of such a man, in order that virtue might not be unhonoured among Florentines, and that, in days to come, other citizens may be incited to serve the commonwealth with might and wisdom. [S21]

Leonardo sat alone in the Duomo in meditation to ponder his time and relationship with Lorenzo de' Medici. Some saw Lorenzo de' Medici as a merciless tyrant, whereas others considered him to be an enlightened and honourable ruler. He inherited power from his father at the tender age of twenty years and consolidated control of the republican government for himself by restructuring the Signoria, the family banks, and trading houses, and establishing new alliances and dissolving old ones. He assured his popularity with his citizens by feeding them with lavish spectacles and festivals. He was cunning and prudent, brutal and magnanimous, and surrounded himself with writers, artists, and philosophers, and established in his gardens the School of Platonic Scholars. He also made enemies who conspired to kill him because of his political and financial ploys and intrigues and aggrandisement.

Lorenzo had done much in Florence for the art of poetry and sculpture, and a little for painting and drawing. Banking, finance, and trade were successful sectors for him, but soon after his death, it became known that the Medicis were bankrupt. What caught Leonardo's eye was Lorenzo's growth as a diplomat after the Pazzi Conspiracy and his troubles with Pope Sixtus IV who died in 1484. The art of diplomacy probably started in December 1479 when Lorenzo decided to go to Naples to confront the King of Naples in a diplomatic mission at the time when the King of Naples had declared war against him and Florence. Lorenzo returned to Florence in April 1480 with a peace treaty and the withdrawal of the King of Naples's troops from the Republic of Florence. On returning to Florence, he immediately restructured the constitution government with new councils and branches. Since the council was filled with Lorenzo's sycophants, the effect of the constitutional change was to make his tyranny more obvious to his detractors. Under his rule, however, the prosperity of Florence grew, primarily through banking and commerce. Not the least of Lorenzo's contributions to this prosperity was the peace that his diplomacy from 1480 until his death maintained between Florence and the rest of Italy. He developed a foreign policy aimed at maintaining equilibrium and peace between the Italian states and of keeping the other major European states such as France and the Holy Roman Empire's Habsburg rulers out of Italy. He also encouraged the first permanent embassies amongst the states of the Italian peninsula in order to monitor compliance with the terms prohibiting the support of exiled dissidents.

Leonardo was three years younger than Lorenzo, less privileged, less formally educated, but much handsomer, artistic, and musical. They shared a love for horses, music, poetry, learning, and beautiful women, but their different characters and social standing kept them from engaging with each other on a regular basis. Many thought that Leonardo hadn't been as well treated or respected by Lorenzo, the Magnificent, certainly not as well as the other Florentine artists in his stable, the likes of Botticelli, Michelangelo, Perugino, and Ghirlandaio. Apparently, Lorenzo had never offered Leonardo a single, full-scale commission. Yet, Lorenzo was sensitive to Leonardo's legitimacy and needs, and he knew that Leonardo was more likely to thrive in Milan in the service of the Sforza than under the more restrictive and demanding expectations of the Florentine Republic and its more competitive, conservative, and religious society. Leonardo needed to be protected from his father's excesses and his envious enemies in Florence. So, Leonardo was in Milan largely because Lorenzo had sent him there to seek the support of the Sforza for the Medici Family and the Republic of Florence. Possibly, Leonardo hadn't grasped this at first, but he grew to appreciate Lorenzo much later when he returned to live in Florence for six or seven years after the demise of the theocratic rule of the Dominican prior Girolamo Savonarola. Leonardo, in the end, saw Lorenzo as an enlightened diplomat who gave him his opportunity for greatness in Milan and who provided him with an introduction to his sons who would sponsor him in his later years in Rome. *'The Medici made me and now they want to destroy me,'* was how Leonardo finally remembered Lorenzo and his sons.

The death of Lorenzo, Gian Galeazzo Sforza's godfather, was very dangerous for the young Duke of Milan because it suddenly opened up the possibility of his assassination by Ludovico. With no protection from his dead godfather and the Government of Florence, the secret murder of Gian by his uncle Ludovico looked likely. Bona of Savoy pleaded with Leonardo to take care of her son Gian from the forces that she now was sure would begin to undermine the young duke and attempt to stop him from becoming the sole ruler of Milan and his Duchy in a year or two. Leonardo knew that he had little or no power to protect the young duke, and that his friend Galeazzo Sanseverino was now completely in the power of Ludovico IL Moro Sforza. Leonardo reflected on Lorenzo's achievements, and he now saw himself very much as a powerless diplomat of the arts, architecture, and sciences with little or no influence in the dark arts of political intrigue and government, and this was due in no small measure to the death of his Florentine mentor Lorenzo.

The Passing Away of Leonardo's Mother, June 1494

When Leonardo was 41 years old, his mother Caterina at the age of 59 years arrived in Milan to stay with him from 16th July 1493 until her death on 16th June 1494. Her husband Achattabriga di Piero del Vacca was dead and her three daughters and younger son were married and living with their own families. She was unwell with malaria and dying, and she wanted to confess and say her final goodbyes to Leonardo, her first-born. She wanted to apologise to him for her neglect that was forced upon her by the Vinci family patriarchs and her husband, but he, Leonardo, was the one that she always loved the most. She wanted to tell him that she loved him, and that she had come to reveal secrets about her life and her Armenian origins, her abduction from Antalya, and her slavery as a servant for the wealthy Florentine Vanni di Niccolo di Ser Vann family who became bankrupt and indebted to Leonardo's father the notary Ser Piero di Antonio da Vinci. Caterina told Leonardo that it was the wealthy Marchionni family in Florence who were involved in the slave trading operations in Kaffa on the Crimean peninsula and in Lusignan Cyprus for domestic servants who had first abducted and enslaved her. She told him that she loved his father because he had freed her from slavery, and he helped her in her new life in Vinci even while she was married to Achattabriga.

Some of Leonardo's strange ideas and practices stemmed from his mother's belief in a corrupted form of Adoptionism and Catharism that Christ is a man and therefore is the adopted and not the natural Son of God. The Roman Church of Saint Peter condemned Adoptionism and Catharism as heresy. The Cathars were a Christian sectarian movement that thrived in Armenia, Bulgaria, southern France, and northern Italy until it was almost wiped out by the Crusades and the persecutions and inquisitions of the 13th Century. Caterina's parents were followers of the Paulician movement in Armenia. They believed in the dualism of Marcionism (a branch of Gnosticism), the doctrine that there are two Gods, an evil God of life as we know it and a good God of death, whereby the former is the creator of evil in this world and the latter presides over the good world after death. They taught Caterina that Jesus was not the true son of Mary because the good God could not have taken flesh and made him into a man. Jesus Christ was Jesus of Nazareth, a simple Jewish peasant born of flesh who claimed that he was the Messiah, and that he wanted to overthrow the Romans and oust them from Israel, the kingdom of God. Jesus was punished and crucified by the Romans and the collaborative ruling Jews for the serious crime of claiming to be the King of the Jews and for recruiting supporters and followers to spread sedition and zealotry and to raise arms against the Roman occupation. Jesus believed that it was the sacred duty of all Jews to free their promised land from Roman rule and occupation. The Romans placed a plaque (*titulus*) under Jesus's wooden cross detailing the crime for which he was crucified. '*Jesus – King of the Jews*'. His crime: '*sedition - claiming kingly rule.*' He was killed for inciting armed rebellion and claiming the mantle of being the king and messiah of the Jews. But while dying on the cross, Jesus of Nazareth saw the light of the good God, and he was saved by his resurrection into Heaven (the good world). He was forgiven by Rome for his sins and his sedition against the Roman rulers to become Jesus Christ, the adopted, enlightened Son of God, and the holy symbol of the Roman Christian Church and his evangelising followers.

Caterina's parents taught her to honour the Gospel According to Luke and the letter of St. Paul and to reject the Old Testament and the sacraments, the false worship, and the hierarchy of the established church of Saint Peter in Rome. She taught Leonardo from a young age that John the Baptist was the true prophet who preached the word of God, Jesus was his follower, and that Paul (Saul) of Tarsus, after his vision of Jesus on the road to Damascus, taught the pure form of Christianity. 'We're saved by Faith (and Love), alone.' She often reminded Leonardo that John the Baptist was a man sent from the good God to bear true witness to the light. Jesus of Nazareth was the 'false messiah' who perverted the teachings entrusted to him by John the Baptist. The worship of John the Baptist in the Republic of Florence was perfectly safe because he was the patron saint of Florence and the symbol of moral rectitude and political correctness on whom the Florentines built their economic fortune and good government. His image was stamped on the Florentine gold coin, the *fiorino d' oro*, since 1252, the Florentine coin of European commercial exchange with a value of one lira or 20 soldi or 240 denari. The feast day to celebrate St. John the Baptist in Florence with parades and folkloric events and flag bearers showing off the city's symbol of the bright red *fleur-de-lis* is June 24th. When Leonardo painted his version of the John the Baptist pointing his finger up into heaven, it was likely to have been the image that he imagined that his mother would have wanted him to paint.

She was by no means a practicing Cathar, for it was extremely dangerous or almost impossible for her to be one in a small village like Vinci where the residents were all orthodox Roman Catholics, and they never would have allowed her to express her sacrilegious beliefs. But, she had no fear to instil some of her Cathar beliefs into her son while he was a young boy running wild in the fields and valleys of Vinci. Some of these dangerous beliefs were with him all his life and some of them he depicted in his religious art and writings. We should never write down or teach the ideas of Catharism for it is sacrilegious, but here are some of the things Catherine taught Leonardo to ponder about all his life. She was anti-sacerdotal, and she rejected the sanctity of marriage (although she was forced to marry Achattabriga against her wishes). She abstained from all animal food because killing any life was abhorrent. She believed in reincarnation (continuous resurrection) and that all living things by their very nature suffered in the real world. Like many other Cathars or Gnostics, she assigned a greater importance to the role of Mary Magdalene in the spread of early Christianity saying that Mary was more important to pure Christianity than that of the founder of the Roman Church, Saint Peter. For Mary Magdalene was the disciple who Jesus loved more than any of his other disciples. She was the apostle to the apostles who attended to Jesus at his crucifixion and was the first to witness his resurrection. One way or another, Mary Magdalene became an important pictorial theme for Leonardo and his studio painters Andrea Solario and Bernardino Luini and other followers like Giovanni Pedrini Giampietrino.

From the time that Leonardo's father first freed Catherine from the servant's chains of the Ser Vann family, she wore an ornate Armenian Cross around her neck. For her, the Armenian Cross represented her lost world, the four corners of the earth and the teachings of the four Gospels. Leonardo designed a knotted version of the cross as a four-leafed-clover that he occasionally painted as a decoration into the dresses of some of his female portrait sitters. The Armenian Cross is also present, but invisible, in his sacred geometry of the *Vitruvian Man*.

Leonardo was neither a Cathar nor a Gnostic, yet, he respected his mother's beliefs, and he never argued or debated with her about religious matters. He told her that the sciences were the laws of God and that these laws were immutable, repeatable, predictable, and discoverable. Because we were creatures of God, we could never attain the full knowledge of Our Maker and much would remain a mystery or miracle to our minds. But, with God's gift of reason, we can wonder and discover the beautiful and simple logic of His laws. In truth, Leonardo was a Deist, and he favoured the simple and rational theology of ancient times such as Heraclitus's *Logos* (cosmic logic and reason) and Plato's *Demiurge* (the Creator and creation). He rejected the revelations, doctrines, and authority of the Church, and instead, he used his own reason and observations of the natural world to accept the existence of a single creator of the universe. For Leonardo, the Universe was God and True Knowledge was His Scientific Laws. The mysterious changes and contradictions were manifestations of His creative Nature that could be elucidated from seeing the right evidence and information. He believed that God could be experienced only through reason, the senses, and understanding the nature of the universe, and not through the ignorant teachings of others, either the current or the ancient. The priesthood and the church were the enemy of reason and true knowledge because they peddled falsehoods, deceptions, and mythologies, and like parasites, they lived off the people by keeping them fearful, delusional, and ignorant.

Caterina lived the remainder of her life in Milan for eleven months under the loving care of Leonardo and those doctors who he knew and came to treat her. She tried to cook, clean, and darn his clothes and those of his assistants, but she was too fatigued and ill for most of the time to be of much help. She died (after a seizure and coma) in his presence at his home in the Parish of the Saints Nabore and Felix, Porta Vercellina, on 26th June 1494, and he made the following material account of her death in his diary:

Expenses for Caterina's ~~death~~ entombment

For 3 pounds of wax	s. 27
For the bier	s. 8
Pall over the bier	s. 12
Carriage and placing of a cross	s. 4
For the bearers	s. 8
For 4 priests and 4 clerks	s. 20
Bell, book, sponge	s. 2
For the gravediggers	s. 16
For the dean	s. 8
For the licence	s. 1
Doctor	s. 5
Sugar and candles	s. 12
	———
	s. 123

His mother's death cost him a total of 123 soldi. After her death, he was inspired to write a novel about her life and her Armenian roots, but changed the theme to one less about her and more about Armageddon, climate change, the deluge, earthquakes, and the promised-land. He entitled it, the *Prophet of Mt. Taurus*. He wrote a few introductory and dispersed chapters and then abandoned it.

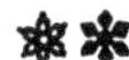

CHAPTER 11

Ludovico Sforza's French Alliance, and the Suspicious Death of Gian Galeazzo Sforza, the Sixth Duke of Milan, 1494

Again, the lion covers over its foot tracks, so that the way it has gone may not be known to its enemies. Thus it beseems a captain to conceal the secrets of his mind so that the enemy may not know his purpose.

— Leonardo da Vinci

Ludovico IL Moro Sforza Betrays His Marriage Vows to Beatrice in Favour of the Beautiful Cecilia Gallerani

Soon after Ludovico Sforza and Beatrice d' Este were married, the regular reports back to Beatrice's mother in the Duchy of Ferrara about her daughter's happiness were highly positive. One of the letters to Beatrice's mother read:

> Most Illustrious Madonna and Dear Marchesana, Since I have remained here after your Highness's departure from Milan, continually in the company of your sister, the illustrious Duchess of Bari, and of her husband, Signor Ludovico, I will no longer delay to discharge my duty in sending you some comforting words as to the well-being and happiness of the said duchess. I cannot express how happy she is to see herself every day more affectionately caressed and petted by her husband, who seems to find his sole delight in giving her every possible pleasure and amusement. It is indeed a rare joy to see them together and to realise what cordial love and goodwill he bears her. God grant it may last long! And I felt that I must write this good news to your Highness, knowing that it would give you especial satisfaction. I will only add that the air here seems to suit her particularly well, and that she is certainly very much improved and stronger in appearance, and seems every day to grow more beautiful. I beg of your Highness to commend me to Madonna Beatrice and Collona.
>
> Your Highness's servant, Polissena d' Este. From Milan, 12th of February, 1491. [S7]

The young duke of Milan Gian also wrote to Beatrice's mother in praise of her daughter's marriage to his uncle:

> I cannot sufficiently express how much joy this marriage has given me, and how glad I am to see the singular virtues and talents of Madonna la Sposa. She has provided great happiness to my uncle, which increases my own joy, and together we are blessed to have renewed a strong alliance between our two houses. For by means of this marriage, besides the two sisters which God had already given us, we have now gained a third, whom by God's grace we shall not love less than the two who are ours by nature. [S7]

But, this happiness was false and not as it seemed. A few months after the marriage between Ludovico and Beatrice, a strong and unhappy turbulence descended on and whirled throughout the Sforza court in Milan. Ludovico had resumed his long-standing affair with Cecilia Gallerani (Fig. 31), and she was soon to bear him a child. Beatrice found out soon enough, and her immediate response was to lock herself in her chambers and refuse entry to her husband or his servants. Ludovico realised he had lost her affection and that it threatened an important alliance between the Sforza and Este and that his continued liaison with his mistress could cause a distressing scandal that could seriously upset his future plans. He set out to remedy the misunderstanding. Every day, he sent Beatrice pleading messages of love and forgiveness while at the same time he promised to have his mistress married off or sent to a convent. Instead, he chose to have the pregnant Cecilia marry one of his most loyal servants Count Ludovico Bergamini of Cremona who accepted to care for Ludovico's mistress and child, born on the 3rd of May and named Cesare. Ludovico presented his mistress with a sumptuous trousseau and his stately Palazzo del Verme on the piazza of the Duomo in Milan where they continued their discreet liaisons. Cecilia, nevertheless, lived harmoniously with her husband in Cremona or country villa where she regularly held learned entertainments with her friends including Leonardo da Vinci. In the meantime, Ludovico's imploring messages of love and forgiveness worked their magic, and Beatrice allowed him entry back into her bedchamber. He espoused his words of undying love, and they were soon seen together again as the most loving and accommodating couple in the court.

In April, Beatrice wrote a letter to her sister Isabella in Mantua.

> I am now here at Villa Nova, where the loveliness of the country and the balmy sweetness of the air make me think we are already in the month of May, so warm and splendid is the weather we are enjoying! Every day we go out riding with the dogs and falcons, and my husband and I never come home without having enjoyed ourselves exceedingly in hunting herons and other water-fowl. I cannot say much of the perils of the chase, since game is so plentiful here that hares are to be seen jumping out at every corner so much so, that often we hardly know which way to turn to find the best sport. Indeed, the eye cannot take in all one desires to see, and it is scarcely possible to count up the number of animals that are to be found in this neighbourhood. Nor must I forget to tell you how every day Messer Galeazzo and I, with one or two other courtiers, amuse ourselves playing at ball after dinner, and we often talk of your Highness, and wish that you were here. I say all this, not to diminish the pleasure that I hope you will have when you do come by telling you what you may expect to find here, but in order that you may know how well and happy I am, and how kind and affectionate my husband is, since I cannot thoroughly enjoy any pleasure or happiness unless I share it with you. And I must tell you that I have had a whole field of garlic planted for your benefit, so that when you come, we may be able to have plenty of your favourite dishes!
> Ex Villa Nova, 18 Martiji, 1491. [S7]

All seemed lovey-dovey and playful between Ludovico and Beatrice as they enjoyed their time together attending hunting-parties and sharing their thrilling adventures with the Duke and Duchess of Milan and their premier knight the Captain-general Galeazzo Sanseverino. Ludovico would betray Beatrice again for another (Lucrezia Crivelli) with tragic consequences for his broken hearted wife on the third day of the New Year in 1497. But, I leave this matter for later.

Ludovico Sforza Plots Against the Duke and Duchess of Milan

It was soon after the birth of his first healthy son on 25th January 1493 that Ludovico began to seriously plot against Gian and Isabella in order to gain a stranglehold over his rule of the Duchy of Milan. He thought it should be easy. Kill Gian and blame his death on his life-long illnesses, or better still, on his wife Isabella of Naples the Duchess of Milan. Hadn't he already successfully killed enough of his family and in-laws to get to where he was now, the Regent of the Milan Duchy? Why stop now? One more death and he could easily be the new Duke of Milan.

Isabella the Duchess of Milan sensed the danger from Ludovico, and she worked hard on her husband to try and persuade him to confront the Privy Council and to demand his birthright to rule the State, to be the arbiter of war and peace, bestow the honours and rewards, collect the taxes, listen to petitions, and keep the public money in his own hands. It was easy to rule, and he was now of the rightful age to sit on the throne. But, Gian Galeazzo remained afraid of his uncle and did not want to confront him. This frustrated the Duchess of Milan, and she secretly complained to her father Alfonso and to her grandfather the King of Naples about her husband's plight and that Ludovico refused to step aside and to allow her husband to rule the Duchy of Milan. She wrote the following secret letter to her father that had escaped Ludovico's censors demanding that he help her and his son-in-law to relegitimise command of their rightful dominion:

In the Castello of Milan,
   This 7th day of April, 1493.
     Illustrissimo e Eccellentissimo Signor, mio Padre. It is now five years since you married me to Gian Galeazzo in the full belief that in due time he would succeed to the crown of his father and sit upon the throne of Galeazzo and Francesco Sforza and of his Visconti ancestors. Now, Gian is of full age and is a father himself, but he is still kept as a child; he has never been put in command of his dominions, and even his food and clothing are doled out to him by Ludovico and his Ministers. It is Ludovico who rules the State, who is the arbiter of war and peace, who bestows honours and rewards, who collects the taxes, listens to petitions, and keeps the public money in his hands. He has absolute rule, while we have no friends or money and are merely his subjects. It is Ludovico, and not Gian Galeazzo, who is the acknowledged ruler of this realm. It is he who dismisses Governors from the castles, and puts his own minions in their place; the army is his, the magistrates are his servants, and his word is law. He, in short, is the real Duke of Milan.

     A son has recently been born to his wife and all the world declares that this child will soon be named Count of Pavia and, as his heir, will succeed to the Dukedom.

     At his birth he received royal honours, while my husband and son are treated with contempt, and it is at the peril of our lives that we remain beneath the roof of this Castello, from which Ludovico would expel us in his envy and hatred; he would leave me widowed and forlorn, without help or friends. Yet, I have not fallen so low but that I still have courage and spirit; and our people look upon us with pity, and think of him with hatred and malediction, for he has robbed them of money and land to satisfy his grasping desires. I am trampled on with humiliations, for I am but a woman, and cannot hold my own. I have no one to consult, for our very attendants are in his service.

     But, if you can be moved by your paternal piety, by your love for me, by my just tears, by the magnanimity of a King ... I pray you to deliver your son-in-law and your daughter from this shameful servitude, and restore to them their rightful dominion. If you will not help us, I would rather die by my own hands than bear this tyrannous yoke and suffer in a strange country under the eyes of a rival. [S16]

Ludovico soon received correspondence from Isabella's father and the Court of Naples about Isabella's complaints questioning his reasons for not allowing his nephew to rule Milan in his own right. He realised that he had to act quickly to prevent the legitimate Duke and Duchess of Milan from gaining the upper hand. He had to usurp total control from Gian. First, he needed to discredit the Duchess of Milan. Without any hard evidence in hand, he accused her of attempting to murder his son-in-law Galeazzo Sanseverino with a deadly poison in the shape of a mysterious white powder. Isabella protested bitterly against the unfounded accusation. This false accusation was eventually ignored when the powder was revealed to be refined sugar that had no harm on any of the farm animals or servants that ingested it. Ludovico, however, never withdrew his accusation nor apologised to the princess for his libel.

Instead, he intensified his plot to form a secret alliance with the Holy Roman Emperor Maximilian I who he thought might be interested in conquering Naples to gain a foothold into Italy. He strengthened the alliance by convincing the Emperor to marry his niece and the young duke's sister Bianca Maria Sforza. He told everybody in Milan that he had successfully fulfilled his dead brother's wishes by marrying off all of his legitimate children Gian Galeazzo, Bianca Maria, and Anna Maria and thereby had strengthened their royal bloodlines. The nobles of Milan were pleased with him and his achievements, and they were ever more malleable in his hands. With a strong alliance and financial inducements, Ludovico had already received the promise of an officially sanctioned investiture of the Duchy of Milan from the Holy Roman Emperor, something that the previous Sforza dukes had never been granted. He was now firmly on track to usurp the Duchy, something that he desired more than pure gold, great wealth or even his own good name.

Ludovico's Alliance with the French Against Naples, 1494

By the end of spring in 1494, Ludovico Sforza was immensely pleased with himself. Firstly, he had married off his niece Bianca Maria Sforza to the Holy Roman Emperor who was now his ally and who would soon grant him the official title of Duke of Milan when the time was propitious. The new queen of the Holy Roman Empire was writing to him regularly and reaffirming her love and appreciation and support for him. Secondly, his young wife Beatrice was a smashing success in the courts of Milan and Venice where the ruling class seemed to have no objections to him and her becoming the new Duke and Duchess of Milan when the time was propitious. Thirdly, he now had his own heir Ercole (soon to be renamed Maximilian Sforza), to convince the nobles and merchants of Milan that he and his son should be the rightful Dukes of Milan. Fourthly, his son in law Captain-General Galeazzo Sanseverino had returned to Milan in April from his two-week mission to Lyon in France where he had successfully confirmed an allegiance with King Charles VIII to allow the French king passage through the Duchy of Milan on his way to invade the Kingdom of Naples. The French king was so impressed with Captain General Galeazzo Sanseverino's diplomacy and feats of bravery, skill, and horsemanship at jousting that he rewarded him with the French order of St. Michael and shared his domestic favourites with him at his private apartments. Fifthly, Ludovico assured the French king that Maximilian the Emperor of the Holy Roman Empire would not oppose his designs upon Naples.

Ludovico still had a number of thorns jabbing at his side that he needed to remove or to attenuate as soon as possible. Firstly, his niece the Duchess of Milan Isabella of Aragon continued complaining to her father Alfonso the recently crowned King of Naples and to anybody else who would listen to her that he, Ludovico, had usurped her husband's throne and refused to let him rule the Duchy of Milan. Secondly, the King of Naples who had recently declared to support Gian Galeazzo Sforza and his daughter Isabella of Aragon as the true rulers of the Duchy of Milan was sending messages and annoying Ludovico about a need for him to step down. Thirdly, the Church of Rome under Pope Alexander VI had now sided with Naples and was resistant to any proposed invasion by the French via Milan or elsewhere. Fourthly, Piero de' Medici the new ruler of Florence was intent on siding with Naples against Milan and to support his father's godson Gian Galeazzo Sforza to immediately ascend the throne and rule the Duchy of Milan in his own right.

The biggest concern for Ludovico was with the king of Naples who together with the rulers of Rome and Venice had already known before the marriage between Maximilian and Bianca in 1493 that the Holy Roman Emperor had promised him the investiture of the Duchy of Milan. This was seen as an insidious betrayal, and it alone was reason enough for Alfonso of Calabria, Ludovico's brother-in-law, to raise forces and declare war against him in defence of the rights of his daughter Isabella and his son-in-law Gian Galeazzo Sforza. Alfonso had previously encouraged his father King Ferdinand I to make peace with Pope Alexander VI in order to form an alliance with the Pope's forces against Milan for the rumours were already strong by October in 1493 that Ludovico had organised an alliance with the French to invade Naples. However, King Ferdinand I of Naples, the grandfather of Isabella the Duchess of Milan, waivered and avoided a declaration of war against Milan, and instead, he tried to appease Ludovico and encouraged him to break his alliance with France. Then, on the 25th of January 1494, a few days before a scheduled meeting in Genoa to discuss terms with Ludovico of a possible settlement, King Ferdinand I died of fever. Alfonso, Isabella's father, who hated Ludovico and felt completely betrayed by him, replaced his dead father as the king of Naples and immediately argued for war against Ludovico. He realised Ludovico had capitulated to Charles VIII and that a French invasion with the assistance of Milan was inevitable and soon forthcoming. To counter the possibility of an invasion, Alfonso formed alliances with the Borgia Pope Alexander VI and Piero de' Medici of Florence for Piero's father Lorenzo de' Medici had been a loving godfather of Gian Galeazzo Sforza and always wanted him to be the rightful ruler of Milan. By the end of May in 1494, Alfonso of Naples declared war against Milan, seized Ludovico's principality of Bari, prepared a naval fleet to attack Genoa, and had his army join forces with the papal land forces in preparation to march through Romagna to invade Milan.

Yet, none of these political machinations or preparations of war appeared to outwardly fluster Ludovico and his court in Milan. They still had their gay hunting-parties at Vigevano and the usual festivities, occasional lavish dances, and indulgent dinners at the Sforza Castello of Milan. Ludovico continued to engage Bramante and Leonardo on building and artistic projects at the Santa Maria delle Grazie, the Dominican church that was his personal favourite retreat. This church, where Leonardo would later paint the *Cenacolo (Last Supper)* on the refectory wall, was intended to be the burial site for Ludovico and his family, and so, he continued his special interest in its development, decoration, and renovations.

The Highly Suspicious Illness of Gian Galeazzo Sforza, the Sixth Duke of the Duchy of Milan

During this time of spring leading into summer, the Duchess of Milan Isabella of Aragon trapped in the verdant gardens, immense parks, and luxurious rooms of the Castello in Pavia continued espousing her husband's right to be the true and only ruler of the Duchy of Milan. However, the young Duke Gian Galeazzo Sforza responded weakly to her counsel and pleas, and he refused to confront his uncle. Leonardo da Vinci saw Gian's nature as that of a gentle and generous lamb whereas others saw him as weak and indulgent and not fit to rule the Duchy of Milan. Moreover, over the summer, Gian had taken to having fits and dizzy spells that had affected his riding and hunting and socialising, and he was often bed ridden to overcome unspecified and undiagnosed fevers.

Isabella told everybody who would listen that her husband was being poisoned and that he needed protection from Ludovico and his officials, but Ludovico's courtiers dismissed her protests and replied that his uncle would never undertake such a heinous crime and instead would always protect Gian with his own life. The courtiers even spread rumours that the illnesses were the result of Gian's licentious ways. Leonardo wasn't convinced by such rumours for he had experienced similar lies about himself previously in Florence that had led to the unfounded charges of sodomy against him by the Officers of the Night that were eventually dismissed. Nevertheless, the accusations were an unsettling attempt to discredit him and other de' Medici supporters as forerunners to the eventual assassination attempts against Lorenzo de' Medici. Leonardo and his supporters at the time believed that all those charges were connected and that they involved the Pazzi family and the agents of Pope Sixtus IV. In this regard, Leonardo and Isabella knew exactly what the real motives were behind the unfounded rumours by Ludovico's minions in Milan about the poor health of Gian Galeazzo Sforza, for these rumours were impacting negatively on Gian Galeazzo's fitness to legitimately rule Milan in his own right. Leonardo had urged Gian to be more proactive with his uncle and demand from him more time to engage in the affairs of state. Gian agreed, but always backed off when his uncle told him that the time wasn't appropriate because the Tarot cards were against him and that the following year was much more propitious for both of them and everybody else. Leonardo, like others, saw that Gian was too afraid of his uncle to confront him directly or to organise allies to overthrow him. He was a shaky, timid lamb in front of a hungry, ruthless lion.

Gian Galeazzo was always considered to be unusually prone to illness, but in the summer of 1494, he reached new heights of poor health. He suddenly was met with a series of recurring cyclical fevers. This led to a flurry of correspondence between Ludovico and his physicians who had been sent to Pavia to monitor and care for the betterment of the young duke's health. Their explanation for his sudden deterioration in health was his poor physical constitution, unhealthy diet, and bad planetary influences and conjunctions. However, others saw it for what it really was. It was the young duke's natural physical response to the ingestion of poison. The young duke's symptoms of excessive fever, sweating, vomiting, convulsions, cramping, and seizures pointed to the obvious, that it was his own body's response to fighting off the poisons that were being secretly administered to him. The continuous purging and blood letting was weakening him, but at the same time the expulsions of the poisons from his body were keeping him alive. It seemed that the physical constitution of the young duke was not so easy to kill off as the assassins had expected and hoped for. Yet, apart from Isabella Aragon the Duchess of Milan nobody else had the courage to accuse Ludovico and his doctors directly with their suspicions of attempted murder.

In their correspondence and public declarations, Ludovico and his doctors continued to espouse great concern for the young duke's health. They also continuously highlighted how the young duke forever defied their advice and had developed a habit of excessive unhealthy eating and drinking that was detrimental to his recovery.

One of Ludovico's physicians wrote to him:

> Most Illustrious and Excellent Lord, Most Honourable, I have attended to the health of Our Lord the Duke with your other physicians as you, your Most Excellent Lord, has commanded us to do so in your letters. His Highness the Duke has expelled an emesis of putrid choleric matter and bloodied yellow pus. He has a severe fever and has complained of painful and extended liver and stomach that react violently when pressed with the hand. We have treated him with different pills and useful medicines provided to us by the Most Honourable Ambrogio Varesi and they have worked wondrously well as we had hoped. Although His Highness has been obedient in receiving his medication, he has refused to follow our advice on eating and insists on too much drink and dining with the Duchess. We have hidden his wines from him for they are the cause of his many health problems as are the mysterious reasons of the heavens and the planets. At this hour he sleeps and we hope that with God's help he will recover and be better again.

This flurry of concern during 1494 by Ludovico and his doctors that they greatly cared for Gian Galeazzo's physical recovery was highly suspicious to Ludovico's critics who believed that the young duke would not last out the year. Leonardo initially thought that Gian's misdiagnosis and treatment by Ludovico's doctors was making him physically sick. However, when the young Duke's health deteriorated even further over the next few months, Leonardo suspected that the Duchess Isabella was right in her accusations, and that the young Duke was indeed being slowly poisoned by his minders. Leonardo tested some of Gian's food for the presence of poison by feeding portions to his pet mice, yet the mice showed no evidence of being harmed. If Gian was being poisoned then it was not by way of his meals, but was probably by way of the doctors' specialist treatments given to him by the seemingly concerned Ludovico.

Ludovico Sforza's Invitation to the French King Charles VIII to Invade Naples Through the Duchy of Milan

Whether or not Ludovico was poisoning Gian or simply had seen that the Angel of Death was hovering above the young duke's head, he now took this moment of enhanced confusion and weakness in the Duke and Duchess's household as his best opportunity, against their protests, to encourage Charles VIII to invade Naples. Charles VIII needed little encouragement from Ludovico for his own courtiers had strongly urged him to invade Italy and recapture his heraldic rights to rule Naples. Etienne de Vesc reminded Charles VIII that with the death of Rene of Naples and the extinction of the House of Anjou it was he, the French king, who was now the rightful heir to the Angevin titles to the Kingdom of Naples. Charles agreed and charged de Vesc with the preliminary arrangements for the invasion. Louis Duke of Orleans was another French proponent who encouraged Charles VIII to invade Italy. Louis wanted to have the Duchy of Milan for himself. He considered it to be his rightful inheritance because his paternal grandmother Valentina Visconti was the daughter of Gian Galeazzo Visconti, the first Duke of Milan and Isabella, a daughter of King John III the Good of France. When Valentina married Louis's grandfather Louis de Valois, Duke of Orleans, she received as a dowry the County of Vertus and the city of Asti with the sums of 450,000 florins in cash and 75,000 florins in jewellery. In addition, it was stipulated in her marriage contract that in the absence of male heirs in the Visconti line, then she, Valentina, would inherit the Visconti dominions including the Duchy of Milan. Thus, according to the Duke of Orleans and the Valois House, it was their House and not the Sforza House who were the rightful owners and rulers of the Duchy of Milan. Louis of Orleans hoped that if Charles VIII was successful in his invasion of Naples then he might be granted the rule of the Duchy of Milan. Many a keen critic of Ludovico Sforza could see that he was playing a highly dangerous game that could be harmful to himself and his family by encouraging the French to invade the Italian peninsula. They believed that Louis Duke of Orleans was next in line to be the French king, and that if Charles VIII should die prematurely then Louis would definitely invade Milan and overthrow the Sforza house.

For now, the Duke of Orleans crossed the Alps on the 10th of July with the advanced guard of Charles VIII's French army and arrived at his own city of Asti, the fief that was part of the dowry of his grandmother Valentina Visconti. Three days later, Ludovico Sforza betrayed all of Italy and met with the Duke of Orleans at Alexandria for a council of war. They discussed the naval preparations being made at Genoa against a possible invasion from Naples. The duke of Orleans requested and received a loan of sixty thousand ducats from Ludovico who watched his rival with suspicious eyes. Ludovico's first impression of Louis was not a favourable one, and he wondered then and there whether his gamble to ally himself with the French was a gross mistake. He decided he would need to be extremely watchful of the Duke of Orleans who after his interview with Ludovico at Alexandria rode on to Genoa to prepare the French fleet to oppose Alfonso's brother Federigo who had already set sail to attack Genoa. During the next few weeks, the Neapolitan forces attacked Porto Venere and Rapallo, but were repulsed by the Genoese and French troops who were supported by a strong Milanese contingent marshalled by the Sanseverino brothers Fracassa and Antonio. They forced Federigo's fleet to seek refuge at the harbour of Leghorn and then to sail back to Naples to defend the city and harbour against a forthcoming French attack.

While Ludovico prepared for war against Naples, Leonardo was commissioned to paint murals of horses within some of the Sforza Castello rooms where visitors were likely to be entertained or allowed to lodge. While in one of these rooms in the Sforza castle on the 27th of July, Leonardo looked out of the window and sketched what he saw of the proceedings in the piazza below him where Ludovico handed the baton of command to Captain-General Gian Francesco Sanseverino the Count of Caiazzo who was the appointed head of fifteen hundred foot soldiers and light cavalry who were ready to join the French army and march into Romagna and challenge the forces led by Ferdinand II the Duke of Calabria. Three of the captain-general's younger brothers were each in charge of their own cavalry divisions, and they were present at the hand-over ceremony in their full armour and colours ready to ride in support of their elder brother. Galeazzo Sanseverino, on the other hand, was ordered to remain in the outskirts of Milan with a few thousand foot soldiers and one troop of light cavalry in case that the Duke of Orleans decided to spring a surprise attack on Milan from Asti.

Ludovico Welcomes the French Presence to Lombardy and Milan

After receiving sufficient funds and loans from his allies to pay his troops, king Charles VIII left Lyon and crossed the Alps to arrive at Asti on the 9th of September where he was met by Ludovico and his father-in-law Ercole d'Este of Ferrara and his son-in-law Galeazzo Sanseverino. The magistrates and citizens welcomed the French king with much pomp and ceremony as their liege lord. Two days later, Ludovico's wife Beatrice d' Este and his daughter Bianca, wife of Galeazzo Sanseverino, also arrived at Asti accompanied by a choir of singers and musicians and eighty ladies to entertain the 24-year-old king who was much impressed by the Duchess of Bari and her ladies-in-waiting. On the other hand, the ladies of Milan were surprised by the king's appearance for as Charles's ambassador to Venice Commines wrote of him, 'he was little in stature and of small sense, very timid in speech owing to the way in which he had been treated as a child, and as feeble in mind as he was in body, but the kindest and gentlest creature alive.' Nonetheless, Beatrice and her ladies were charmed by the king's attention, his familiarity, affectionate nature, and genial manners.

A grand fete was arranged the next day, but the king couldn't attend for he had fallen ill with a bout of fever and was indisposed for the next fortnight. He recovered sufficiently to leave Asti on the 6th of October to visit the Marquis of Montferrat in Vigevano where Ludovico and Beatrice met with him once again and honoured him with a splendid reception, banquet, and a boar-hunt. On the 13th of October, Charles entered Milan with Ludovico and Beatrice to spend a night at the Sforzesca Castello. Here, he met Leonardo who provided him with a tour of the rooms and frescoes and showed him the clay model of the equestrian statue still waiting to be modelled in bronze. Next day, Leonardo was among the official party to visit the Sforzesca farmlands, Ludovico's vast family farm complex outside Vigevano, to show the French king where the Sforza agricultural industries were cultivated on such a splendid scale. Here, they saw the spacious buildings and the stables of mares and stallions that were bred and reared under Galeazzo Sanseverino's care; the pastures with their many buffaloes, oxen, and cows, the many sheep and goats; and the large dairies, where butter and cheese were made on an industrial scale.

Ludovico wanted Charles to stay a few days longer at the Sforza castle, but the French king insisted that he wanted to visit his cousin Gian Galeazzo Sforza the Duke of Milan and his aunt Bona of Savoy who were residing at the Castello in Pavia. The young king was concerned about the absence of the Duke and Duchess of Milan from proceedings on his entry into the Duchy of Milan, and he wanted to confirm their well being for himself. Bona of Savoy was the king's aunt, for his mother Queen Charlotte of Savoy was Bona's sister. This made Gian Galeazzo Sforza his cousin. Bona and Charlotte were sisters along with 17 other siblings, of which 14 had survived at birth. Their mother was Anne of Cyprus and Duchess of Savoy who bought the Shroud of Turin in 1452 (the year of Leonardo's birth) from Jeanne de Charny in exchange for the castle of Varambon. Years later, the Holy Shroud was deposited in the vault of the castle of Chambéry where Leonardo examined it when he visited Bona of Savoy in 1486.

The French King Visits the Deathbed of the Sixth Duke of Milan, His Cousin Gian Galeazzo Sforza

Ludovico Sforza hoped that the French king would not visit his cousin on his deathbed and instead would bypass Pavia on his way to Piacenza where most of his troops were stationed waiting for his arrival, but this was now impossible to avoid. He immediately sent messengers to the officials in Pavia for them to prepare for the king's visit. He also sent Galeazzo Sanseverino and Leonardo to Pavia to meet with the Duke and Duchess of Milan and prepare them for the King's visit for he believed that his son-in-law and the maestro had a friendly and calming effect upon them. At the time of King Charles's entry into the Duchy of Milan, the Duke and Duchess of Milan and their children were occupying their rooms in the Castello of Pavia. During the last few weeks, Gian Galeazzo was seriously ill and unable to leave his bed, even though he wanted to meet and welcome the French king in Asti. Both his wife Isabella and his mother Bona unremittingly attended to the sick prince, and Isabella hardly ever left his bedside for she dearly loved him. Ludovico was worried about the king meeting with Isabella because the French king was on his way to overthrow her father King Alfonso from the throne of Naples and possibly kill him and the rest of her family. Isabella was distressed, and under such circumstances would she greet the French king cordially or at least with royal or diplomatic restraint? Ludovico prayed that night that Isabella Duchess of Milan would be overcome by a fit of ardent fervour and attempt to stab the French king in order to prevent him from invading Naples. On the other hand, he did not want her to complain to the French king that he was plotting to kill the duke in order to usurp his duchy.

The French king arrived in Pavia with Ludovico on the 15th October where the clergy and professors of the university had gathered to hail the king's presence in long harangues and complimentary speeches under triumphal arches. Although lodgings were prepared for the king in the city, His Majesty insisted that he stay at the Castello itself where he could meet with his cousin the Duke of Milan. Ludovico obliged, but first showed the king the library and other treasures of his ancestral palace and took him out hunting in the park and a visit to cloisters of Certosa before returning to the Castello for a banquet.

Next morning, Ludovico led the king and his small entourage to meet the Duchess Isabella with her young son Francesco at the portico of the Castello where she immediately threw herself on her knees before the French king and begged him to have pity upon her father and brother and to spare them and the House of Aragon. Although the king was touched with compassion by the grief of the unhappy duchess and spoke a few consoling words and promised her that her son was as dear to him as his own son, he apologised that it was now too late for him to give up his expedition to Naples. He then requested that Ludovico be gracious and permit him to privately visit his cousin in the presence of Isabella and some members of his entourage for he did not want to trouble them much more in their time of great worries. Ludovico stepped aside and allowed Isabella to escort the king to see her husband in his sickbed. There, the king met with his aunt Bona of Savoy who welcomed him effusively and then immediately accused Ludovico of poisoning her son. The king said nothing in response because he did not want to displease Ludovico, his ally. Instead, he asked his aunt to lead him to her son's bedside and introduce him for they had not seen each other for a number of years.

Gian Galeazzo Sforza was slightly older than his cousin the French king, and despite being close to death's door, the young duke looked angelic and in wonderment while propped up in his bed with the help of pillows and his wife's arms. The cousins exchanged genuine praise and love for each other, and then, the king with great thoughtfulness allowed the young duke to ask questions and lead the conversation. They spoke of generalities and of their love of horses, dogs, and falcons with no mention of the oncoming war with Naples, and the young duke apologised a number of times asking the king to forgive him for not being able to leave his sickbed and escort him throughout his duchy. When the young duke was visibly fatigued, the king asked him to allow his accompanying doctor Theodore Guainiero of Pavia to examine him in case he might be able to assist in some way. The king's cousin replied that yes he would hold out his tongue for the surgeon to examine it, but that he already had many cures and opinions that were most unhelpful. The king's doctor took the pulse of the young duke, examined his eyes, the inside of his mouth, and the tips of his fingers and finger nails, tapped his chest, smelt his breath, massaged his feet, and then allowed him to lie back on his pillows to rest. The king took hold of his cousin's hand and bid him to rest comfortably and recover quickly. He bent and kissed the young duke's brow and told him that he would be leaving Pavia for Piacenza early next day and that he would be praying for him to recover quickly from his illness. The king bowed to his aunt and her daughter-in-law thanking them for allowing him to see his cousin, and then, he bid them farewell. Once they were out of earshot of any of the Sforza family, the French king's doctor confided to the king that he had detected signs of poisoning in the sick duke's face and body, and that he had not much more time to live. It was too late for antidotes, and it was unlikely that he would last the night.

Next morning, on the 17th of October, Charles and Ludovico attended mass in the chapel of the Castello, and they left Pavia for Piacenza to join the waiting French army to prepare for their invasion into the Tuscan territory. On arriving in Piacenza, they learnt that their opponent the Duke of Calabria already had been defeated in two engagements by the forces of the Count of Caiazzo and the French under d'Aubigny, and that he and his army were in full retreat back towards Naples.

The Death of Gian Galeazzo Sforza, the Sixth Duke of Milan, Aged 25 Years, October 1494

Four days after Charles and Ludovico's departure from Pavia, Gian Galeazzo's condition suddenly worsened after his morning meal of chicken-broth, raw eggs, pears, and wine. The meal and wine seemed to induce within him excessive fever, sweating, vomiting, convulsions and cramping, seizures, and a coma, finally resulting in his death in the morning of the 21st of October.

A few days before Gian Galeazzo's death, the attending physicians Nicolo Cusano and Gabriele Pirovano wrote to Ludovico Sforza to inform him of his nephew's condition:

> Most Illustrious and Excellent Lord, Most Honourable, His Highness the Duke woke in distress in the late hour of the day after his meal of eggs and chicken broth and some sleep. He looked pale and weak and complained of pain and bloat in the region of his liver, stomach, and intestines that were extended and sensitive to the touch. He passed wind from his mouth and other orifices, and we heard the noise of water that moved in the region of his liver, spleen, and intestine. We attempted to settle him with some broth and medicines but this seemed to aggravate his condition further, and he complained of a sense of suffocation. We have now reached the end of our remedies, although we will continue caring for him for as long as we can. Even with medicine, we can see the sign of power of evil of itself and in the terrible influence of the heavens. His time looks near, and the Illustrious Duchess is much distressed and calls for others including Leonardo the Florentine to come and treat her husband. If it is not in our power to restore his

health, we will inform you immediately of what ensues and make the appropriate provisions – God forbid - when we seen clear signs of him dying.

Gian Galeazzo Sforza the sixth duke of Milan at 25 years of age died without fear or complaint in the presence of his wife, two children, mother, his confessor, his attending doctors, his favourite servant named Dionigi Confanerio, and Leonardo da Vinci the Florentine who the young duke loved so much as his surrogate father, tutor, and entertainer. While his mother Bona of Savoy openly wept, his wife Isabella the Duchess of Milan maintained her composure and allowed her children to kiss their father goodbye while she recited a prayer to his Saviour to forgive their indiscretions and allow them to meet again in heaven. Before she ushered her children away from their dead father's room, she asked Leonardo to accompany her to the children's room. There, out of earshot of her children, she asked Leonardo to secretly remove some of her dead husband's body parts and analyse them for the presence of arsenic for she was convinced that he had been poisoned during the course of his medical treatment by one or all of the four doctors who had cared for him. Leonardo assured her that he would do his best and returned to the duke's room with the pretext that the duchess had requested him to sketch his face and to prepare a death mask. When he was alone with the body, Leonardo surreptitiously removed some of the duke's tonsil, a salivary gland, a skin biopsy, hair samples, and a fingernail and a toenail and wrapped them in a clean cloth to hide them from prying eyes. He quickly prepared a death mask from bees-wax that Isabella had given him, made some quick sketches, and thanked the corpse of the young duke before him for all his generosity and friendship during the fourteen years since they first met in Milan when he, Leonardo, had given the young duke the gift of the lyre from his godfather Lorenzo de' Medici of Florence. He said his tearful goodbye to the dead duke, and he left the room just before the monks and doctors descended onto the body to wash and prepare it for travel and a state display in Milan.

A week later, back in Milan, Leonardo conducted alchemy tests on Gian Galeazzo's hair and tissues samples using ingenious concoctions and dyes that showed that these tissues and those of poisoned animal tissues that he used as positive controls contained deadly amounts of arsenic whereas those of negative controls from animal tissues and those of his assistants and himself had not. In his secret and illegal examination of Gian Galeazzo's body, Leonardo discovered the cause of death, but decided to keep it a secret even from the dead duke's wife Isabella. He believed his evidence was too great a danger to her and her children, and it was best that she did not know about it. Justice would have to be served in other ways than by public exposure that would not work in his or her favour. Ludovico was far too powerful and dangerous, and he could easily extinguish them all.

Gian Galeazzo Sforza was a favourite subject among the court painters of Milan including Leonardo, Ambrogio de' Predis, Marco d' Oggiono, and Giovanni Antonio Boltraffio. The young duke was accessible, handsome, and amusing. He treated all those who he loved with great tenderness and respect, the same way as his horses, greyhounds, and falcons. He loved his uncle Ludovico much more than his uncle could ever love him. This was Gian's tragedy for if he was more ambitious, cunning, and wary of his uncle then he might have outlived him, as he should have if proper justice existed.

Leonardo, Ambrogio de' Predis, and Marco d' Oggiono together painted two posthumous portraits of Gian Galeazzo Sforza that warrant a few comments because the young Duke's portraits are often not recognised for who he is. In one portrait (Fig. 43), Gian Galeazzo Sforza is dressed in blue and black, the colours of his uncle Ludovico IL Moro Sforza who usurped his crown of the Duke of the Duchy of Milan. Gian Galeazzo looks forlorn and melancholic as if he has lost something that he knows that he will never retrieve.

Fig. 43. Portrait of a sad and dead Gian Galeazzo Sforza wearing the colours of his uncle Ludovico IL Moro Sforza painted by Leonardo da Vinci and Marco d' Oggiono.

He holds a message in his right hand on which it is written and that we can clearly see, *1494, AR, ANO,* and *20*. Gian Galeazzo died of poisoning on the 21st October in 1494, and it was the year that the French king Charles VIII visited him a few days before his death. *AR* is a Latin abbreviation for *Anno Regi* (Year of the King), *ANO* is Latin for 'the other person or party', and the number 20 was the day of the month that Gian Galeazzo was born and close to the day of his death. Many had thought that he died on the night of the 20th of October.

The *ANO* can also be interpreted as the last three letters of Milano in Italian, that is, the portrait is of the Duke of Milano. Leonardo also added the same Vinci knotted bows to his jacket that he and his assistants had presented in their earlier paintings of the young duke of Milan as *St. Sebastian* (Fig. 32).

Fig. 44. Portrait by Leonardo da Vinci and Ambrogio de' Predis of a sad and dead Gian Galeazzo Sforza painted in his heraldic colours of red, green, and brown.

In accordance with numerological meaning, those born under the influence of the number 20, incarnate for 'Universal Service', that is, to serve souls who are ailing and are in need of help. However, such individuals are also easily influenced, emotional, crave beauty, harmony, and love, and often, they are not able to cope with stress that can upset their balance and lead to illness. Leonardo saw the good nature of Gian Galeazzo Sforza, and he was upset by his suspicious death.

The other portrait of Gian Galeazzo Sforza by Leonardo and Ambrogio de' Predis portrays him in his own heraldic colours of green and red and with his glistening golden hair (Fig. 44). A tinge of green is reflected in Gian Galeazzo's face and eyes, and it is the colour of arsenical dyes. The Latin inscription on the painting is in honour of his life. It is *Vita, si scias uti, longa est*, meaning *Life, if you know how to use it, is long enough*. It was a saying of Senaca the younger, one of Gian Galeazzo's favourite Roman philosophers.

Some years later, the scene of Gian Galeazzo Sforza's death in the presence of his family or during the French king's visit became a favourite theme of a few well-known painters. Also, Bernardino Luini, the great disciple of Leonardo, used Isabella, Gian, and Leonardo as his models in many of his magnificent paintings. Here, I add just two of the Luini paintings that feature Isabella as *Madonna with Child*, Gian as *St. Sebastian,* and Leonardo as *Saint Roch* with Gian's unfettered white dog. Saint Roch is the patron saint of dogs, falsely accused, and bachelors, and he is invoked against the plague and storms.

Fig. 45. Gian Galeazzo Sforza (St. Sebastian) and Isabella of Aragon (St. Mary and child), the Duke and Duchess of Milan, with Leonardo da Vinci (Saint Roch) by Bernardino Luini. The unchained dog is the symbol of Gian Galeazzo Sforza and his family.

CHAPTER 12

The Investiture of Ludovico Moro Sforza the Seventh Duke of Milan, Betrayer and Usurper, and the Tragic Death of His Wife Beatrice

He who offends others, does not secure himself.
— Leonardo da Vinci

Ludovico's Good News – the Duke Is Dead

Ludovico was in Piacenza on the 20th of October when he received word from a courier that his nephew was dying. He immediately set out for Pavia and on the way received the message that he had been waiting for … THE DUKE IS DEAD. Back in Pavia, he briefly visited the corpse of his nephew and gave orders that the body be transferred as soon as possible to the Duomo of Milan. His nephew's 4-year-old son Francesco II Sforza was now next in line to inherit the title of Duke of Milan, and he needed to stop the boy's investiture as soon as possible. Without any further delay, Ludovico hastened to Milan to win over the ownership of the prize he coveted most, the title of the Duchy of Milan.

On arrival at the Castello in Milan, he immediately gathered together a few of his most loyal friends and courtiers to the great hall of the Rocchetta to inform them of his nephew's lamentable death due to a long period of sustained weakness and fever. He reminded them that his nephew's 4-year-old son Francesco would be proclaimed duke in his father's place, and he asked them emphatically if that was what they really wanted for Milan. Ludovico's prefect of the Treasury Antonio da Landriano jumped to his feet and responded passionately to his illustrious lordship's question pointing out that now in these troubled and dangerous times of war, it was not the proper time to have a 4-year-old child or his mother at the helm of the state.

'Since the death of your brother and Gian Galeazzo's father Galeazzo Maria Sforza, we have had no duke but you to govern us, and you alone among our princes can grasp the ducal sceptre with a firm hand.'

The small gathering applauded the sentiment and called on Ludovico to undertake the burden of sovereignty and to ascend the ducal throne in place of the 4-year-old Francesco Sforza and Isabella Aragon Sforza as the Regent for the sake of the people whom he had hitherto ruled so well and wisely in his nephew's name. They agreed to summon the councillors, magistrates, and chief citizens of Milan to a meeting on the following day to appoint and install Ludovico Maria Sforza, Il Moro, to be the Seventh Duke of Milan.

The historian Guicciardini later wrote of the meeting,

> It was propounded by the principals of the Counsel, that, in regard of the greatness of that estate and the dangerous times prepared now for Italy, it would be a thing prejudicial that the son of Gian Galeazzo, having not five years in age, should succeed his father, and therefore, as well as to keep the liberties of the State in protection, as to be able to meet with the inconveniences which the time threatened, they thought it just and necessary—derogating somewhat for the public benefit, and for the necessity present from the disposition of the laws--as the laws themselves do suffer to constrain Ludovico, for the better stay of the commonwealth, to suffer that unto him might be transported the title and dignity of Duke, a burden very weighty in so dangerous a season; with which

180

colour and honesty giving place to ambition, the morning following, making some show of resistance, he took upon him the name and arms of the Duke of Milan. [S7]

Another wrote,

Thus, while the dead prince lay before the high altar of the Duomo for three days, clad in the ducal cap and robes, with his sword and sceptre at his side, and his white face exposed to view, Ludovico Sforza without any opposition was proclaimed duke instead of his nephew's son, and, clad in a mantle of cloth of gold, rode that afternoon through the streets of the city, and visited the church of S. Ambrogio, to give thanks for his accession to the throne. The ducal sword and sceptre were borne before him by Galeazzo Visconti, the bells were rung, and the trumpets sounded, while the people hailed him with shouts of Duca! Duca! Moro! Moro! With this, Milan had sealed its fate against good fortune and honest leadership. [S7]

Accession to the Throne: I Will Be as I Wish

Despite his accession to the throne, Ludovico refrained from calling himself Duke of Milan until he had received the proper imperial privileges confirming his election and granting him the investiture of the duchy. The Holy Roman Emperor Maximilian had already granted Ludovico the desired investiture for himself and his sons, but the diploma was granted on the 5th of September at Antwerp more than a month before the death of Gian Galeazzo with the stipulation that it was not to be announced until after the Feast of St. Martin (11th November). The published date of the 5th of September was now an embarrassment for Ludovico, clearly revealing his rotten ambition and betrayal of his nephew the 6th Duke of Milan. Ludovico wanted the diploma redated so that it appeared to have been prepared after Gian Galeazzo's death. Accordingly, he ordered his most trusted agent Mapheo Pirovano to inform Maximilian and his wife in Antwerp that Gian Galeazzo's death was on the 21st of October and to ask for the prompt redating of his coveted privileges.

Mapheo, We have written this evening to Germany to inform the Most Serene King of the Romans of the death of the illustrious Duke, our nephew, and must now send you to state our case *viva voce* to his Majesty, desiring him to give effect in our person to the ducal privileges, which he never consented to give our nephew, in consequence of the wrong which the emperor supposed to have been done him by our father and brother, in holding the duchy without any concession from the imperial authorities. And therefore the said king has conceded these privileges to us, as being innocent of this fault, and as having claims to the title by reason of our maternal descent, but has desired that these privileges should not be made public before the next feast of St. Martin, and before this date will not fix the time and place for the expedition of the said privileges. The approach of this time, the fact that this death has compelled us to take up the succession, have impelled us to send an envoy to the said king, and for this purpose we have made choice of yourself, being persuaded that your faithfulness and prudence will be equal to the gravity of this emergency. And so I desire you to start with the utmost speed, and not to rest till you have found his Majesty, and our councillor and ambassador Messer Erasmo Brasca, to whom you will explain the reason of your coming, and having through his means obtained an audience of his Majesty, you will pay him our dutiful respects, and, after delivering your credentials, by virtue of them will proceed to tell him how immediately after this death the chiefs of the State and of the people of this city approached me to offer their condolences in the customary manner, and signified their fears and anxieties as to the succession. One and all, speaking in the name of the State, declared that they would have no lord but ourselves, and entreated us with earnest words to accept this dignity, saying that if we refused they would not be content and would have to consider some other mode of action. After this has been explained to the king, you will tell him that, seeing on the one hand the conditions imposed by his Majesty respecting the privileges, which we do not intend to infringe, and on the other the dangers that might arise if the State were left without a lord until the time fixed for the promulgation of the privileges, and being further aware that the people of Milan set the example and draw after them all the rest of the State, we have chosen to accept the burden they offer us, and have ridden through the town in order to satisfy the wishes of the people. And this we have done, in order not to leave the State and city in doubt as to the last duke's successor, without taking either title or armorial bearings, lest we should incur the same blame as that illustrious lord our father. Thus, solely to prove that the State is not left without a lord, and at the same time not to infringe the conditions attached to the privileges, we have taken this name of duke, and will inscribe our name as *Ludovicus Dux* in letters and other documents, without specifying of what place we are duke, so as to observe the commands laid upon us by his Majesty not to publish the privileges before the feast of St. Martin. The full form, which we intend to adopt at the said feast will be signified to him after this feast, when we shall adopt the style of *Dux Mediolani* in accordance with this command. But we will abstain from publishing the privileges until we have the approval of the said Majesty, which we hope to obtain as soon as the term, which he fixed, shall expire.

And you will also tell his Majesty that the publication of these privileges carries with it the investiture and enjoyment of the temporal possessions of the duchy, and therefore, as our procurator, you will ask for this investiture with all respect and submission. And you will beg his Majesty to send us an ambassador to declare that he places us in possession of the duchy, in order that he may give the world an outward demonstration of the act that he has already done in private. This, we beg to assure his Majesty, shall ensure a perpetual obligation on our part and that of our posterity towards his Majesty, who may count on the fidelity of this State in all contingencies, most of all in the affairs of Italy, where no State can be greater or of more importance than this one, which has the same influence in Italy as he has in Germany. And since the form of investiture has been given this summer to the Treasurer of Burgundy, you can obtain it from him by means of Messer Erasmo, and we will afterwards send you the imperial mandate that you may arrange this. As to the form of delivery of the temporalities, we desire to follow that which was employed in the cases of former dukes, which we will seek out and let you have. To this effect, you will negotiate with the Most Serene King of the Romans, making use of the advice of Messer Erasmo, in order to obtain this concession in the manner that we devise.

You will also visit our niece, the Most Serene Queen, and condole in our name on the duke's death, which is a common cause of grief to both of us, and will recommend our affairs to her, begging her Majesty to assist you, and to employ great warmth and fervour in addressing the Most Serene Lord her husband.

Milan, 22nd October, 1494. [S7]

Ludovico urged Mapheo to present the enclosed petition to Maximilian without delay.

Mapheo, We enclose the petition for the investiture, and have today sent you money and horses. There is nothing more to say, excepting to urge you once more to use all diligence to seek out His Serene Majesty, and with the help of Erasmo leave nothing undone that may induce him to grant the investiture without delay, and at the same time send back with you persons empowered to put me in possession of the temporal possessions of the duchy. Without these two things, all that has been done till now will be of no avail. [S7]

On the evening of the 27th, the body of the young duke, after lying in state for several days before the high altar in the Duomo of Milan, was buried in the vault of his ancestors with the greatest pomp and honour.

The Duchess of Milan Isabella of Aragon, her children, and her mother-in-law Bona of Savoy were missing from the congregation for they were too distraught to leave Pavia to attend their lord's burial in Milan. Before they knew what had happened, his body was transported from Pavia to Milan, and he was quickly buried and out of their and the peoples' sight. Leonardo as the young duke's tutor was permitted to attend the burial, and as he stood on the periphery of the congregation he wondered about his own security and safety and possessions, and whether the gifts that he had received from the young duke would now be taken away from him by the new Duke of Milan. One such gift was the vineyard and adjoining house that were just a short distance down the road from where he would paint the *Last Supper* at the Santa Maria, which was to become a special project about the betrayal of the young, dead duke who lay buried before him.

The day after his nephew's entombment, Ludovico, the new duke of Milan, joined the French king in his camp under the walls of Sarzana. He was greatly surprised to find that Piero de' Medici the son of Lorenzo de' Medici and staunch ally of Naples had suddenly surrendered to king Charles and the French without a fight, and that he had promised them free passage through Tuscany. Ludovico, on the other hand, was appalled by this turn of events because now that he had the Milanese dukedom in his grasp he wanted the French army's progress to be compromised and halted. He also sensed that there was a general acceptance in the French army that it was he who had hastened his nephew's demise and this deepened the distrust that was already present between him and the French. Charles VIII believed in Ludovico's guilt, although he did not show or express this outwardly because he still needed the duke as his ally. Ludovico stayed with the French for only a few days, and on the 3rd of November after gaining the French king's support for the renewal of the investiture of Genoa that had been previously granted to his nephew Gian Galeazzo Sforza for the payment of 30,000 ducats, he returned to Milan with the bulk of his army. Only his son-in-law Galeazzo Sanseverino and Duchess Beatrice's brother Ferrante d' Este with a troop of fifty horses remained in the French camp, and they were the only Italians seen to be riding in the royal procession with king Charles when he made his triumphal entry into Florence.

On the 6th of November, Ludovico returned to Milan and joined his wife and infant son for a well-earned rest and a quiet celebration at Vigevano. A week later, when he was back at the Castle in Milan, he recalled the Milanese troops from Romagna because, according to him, their presence was no longer required in the war effort against Naples. Outwardly, Ludovico showed the face of neutrality, but inwardly, he now was considering betraying the French because of his fear of the Duke of Savoy who was still in Asti with his mind set on overthrowing Ludovico and taking over the Duchy. But first, Ludovico wanted the widowed Isabella, her children, and her mother-in-law the Bona of Savoy back behind the fortified walls in Milan with him where he could keep a close watch on them. He especially wanted Bona of Savoy the aunt of Charles VIII out of Pavia where she might stir up anti-Ludovico forces to overthrow him as Duke of Milan in favour of her four-year-old grandson Francesco II Sforza the Duke of Pavia. Ludovico wanted to bask in his dukedom with a much greater sense of security knowing that Isabella and Bona would not conspire to try and overthrow him.

The Former Duchess of Milan Grieves Her Losses

After her husband's death, Isabella the former Duchess of Milan shut herself up in her rooms in Pavia and in deep mourning refused to leave. Ludovico sent his councillors to offer their condolences and invited her and her mother-in-law to come to Milan in his name and those of all the people, assuring her that she and her children would be treated safely and with due honour, and that they would retain possession of their ducal residence in the Castello. While gratified with this news and the benign attention from Ludovico, she still refused to move from the castle in Pavia. Then, on the 6th of December, after much cajoling from Ludovico and from her cousin Beatrice the new Duchess of Milan and their diplomats and officials, Isabella of Aragon relented and summoned up the courage to return to Milan where she was received by Ludovico, her cousin Beatrice, and their court jester Barone, and given her rooms in the Castello where she and her now deceased husband had formerly resided. The following is Chiara Gonzaga's, the wife of the Duke of Montpensier, account of the meeting in a letter that she sent to her sister-in-law the Marchioness of Mantua Isabella d' Este.

> Last night the Duchess Isabella arrived in Milan, and our duchess went to meet her, two miles outside the town, and directly they met, our duchess got out of her chariot and entered that of Duchess Isabella, both of them weeping bitterly, and so they rode together towards the Castello where the Duke of Milan met them on horseback at the gate of the garden. He took off his cap, and accompanied them to the Castello, where they alighted, and placing Duchess Isabella between them, our newly elected duke and duchess accompanied the former duchess to her old rooms. When they reached these rooms they sat down together, and the Duchess Isabella could do nothing but weep, until at last the duke spoke to her, and begged her to calm herself, and be comforted, with many other similar words. Dear friend, the hardest heart would have been melted with compassion at the sight of her, with her three children, looking so thin and altered by her grief, wearing a long black robe like a friar's habit, made of rough cloth, worth fourpence the yard, and her eyes hidden by a thick black veil. Certainly I, for one, could not help crying, and if I had not restrained myself, I should have wept still more. [S7]

Bona of Savoy who had accompanied Isabella to Milan was also given her own rooms in the Castello for a year before the duke moved her out to the old palace of Corte Vecchio near the Duomo because her apartments in the Castello were required by the court officials, and they needed to remove her to stop her from spying on them within the castle walls. A year later, Bona left Milan for good and returned to France where she lived at Amboise until the end of 1499. When she returned to her native land of Savoy, she died at Fossano on the 23rd November 1503.

Duke Ludovico Rebrands His Duchy

By the end of 1494, Ludovico had achieved all that he had ever wanted. He had at last attained the object of his greatest ambition, and at the age of 42 years, he was sitting on his father's, brother's, and nephew's throne as the 7th Duke of Milan. But, by the year's end, the gossip abroad was rife about how he, Il Moro, had contrived to murder his nephew the young duke of Milan in order to seize the throne and crown. In Florence and Venice, it was no secret that Gian Galeazzo Sforza, the unhappy duke, was poisoned by his uncle. The moment of his death helped to confirm their suspicions and gossip. It was all too opportune, too prompt, and too exact with Ludovico's plans to seize the crown, which belonged to the young Gian Galeazzo and his son Francesco II.

Ludovico was obsessively impatient to extinguish from Milan all the coins that carried the image of his nephew's head as the 6th duke of Milan. Only a few months after the death of Gian Galeazzo Sforza and a few weeks before Christmas, new coins of authority were issued to the bankers, shopkeepers, and street dealers of Milan. Ludovico Sforza's head as the seventh duke of Milan was engraved on thousands of copper, bronze, silver, and gold coins. Most good thinking citizens suspected that these coins already had been minted well before the death of Gian Galeazzo Sforza.

The gold testone, a double ducat, fewer in number than the other metal coins, is particularly impressive. I have four of them in my collection. Ludovico's head is held high, haughty, and proud; he is conscious of his power and defiant of his betrayals. The inscription on the portrait side is *LVDOVICVS • M • SF • ANGLVS • DVX • MLI* (*Ludovicus Maria (Moro) Sforza Anglus, Duke of Milan*). On the reverse side, he rides his galloping horse, wearing his armour, and plumed crown with sword raised in his right hand. Inscribed around the coin's periphery is the Latin text *PP • ANGLE • Q3 • CO • AC • IANVE • D • 7C* (*Count of Pavia and Angera and Lord of Genoa and 7th Duke of Milan*).

The humanitarian Giorgio Valla had a very strong opinion on how Gian Galeazzo Sforza had died when he wrote from Venice to his friend General Gian Giacomo Trivulzio in France reminding him of how he had predicted Gian Galeazzo's death by murder twelve years before.

> I believe that you are now informed of the well-known fact, how Gian Galeazzo, the Duke of Milan, is dead, and how Ludovico Sforza has been acclaimed by his court to be the new duke. Do you remember how I foresaw this occurrence twelve years ago? Remember when Giovanni Marliani treated the disease of Duke Gian Galeazzo, and I revealed to him that the Duke was poisoned and would have died if not treated correctly. Without me knowing it, Giovanni informed Ludovico who summoned me to his castle and after dismissing all witnesses he asked me what I thought about the duke. When I answered that the duke's illness would have killed him and that the future Duke of Milan would have been him, Ludovico, he answered me by saying 'It will be as I wish.' He ordered me to keep this matter to myself, and so I discussed this only with you. You told me, 'Ludovico is a good man, and that he would never proclaim himself duke.' Now you know what has happened and why it was safer for me to leave Milan in 1485 and find solace in Venice. Give some attention to those things that I said in other letters for it will not be long before the name of the Sforza will be wiped out from Lombardy.

Twelve years prior to Gian Galeazzo's death, Giorgio Valla was in the position to reveal Ludovico's devious schemes. Valla was the professor of rhetoric at the University of Pavia and a student of Giovanni Marliani who was the ducal physician attending to Gian Galeazzo's illness in 1483. It was at the time that Ludovico claimed ownership of his nephew's life, when he had become the official guardian of the young duke of Milan. Giorgio Valla was a supporter of Bona Savoy and her secretary Cicco Simonetta who was executed by Ludovico Sforza when he overthrew them to gain power in the city and take over the guardianship of the young duke of Milan. With the execution of Cicco Simonetta, Valla accepted the fate of those who were close to Bona and her secretary, and so in 1485 he opted to leave the duchy for safer havens. The Venetian Senate employed him to teach in the city's schooling system, and it was where he remained in exile until his death in Venice in 1500.

Although Ludovico was aware of the offensive accusations against him of murdering his nephew the 6th Duke of Milan, he denied all such intention or possibility. According to him, in a letter to the Bishop of Brixen, he had no knowledge of the seriousness of Gian Galeazzo's illness until the very last few days.

> The three doctors who treated Our Illustrious nephew informed us that his illness was light and curable. I did not neglect visiting him when I had the opportunity, and I fulfilled my duty as a father by encouraging the doctors to take good care of him. The Christian King of France and other French noblemen had access to him in Pavia and they saw him with their own eyes, and if they wish to admit the truth, they certainly cannot deny that he died of natural causes. Nothing was more alien from our nature than the thought of plotting the death of our nephew, to whom we always bestowed paternal charity.

Ludovico IL Moro Sforza believed that like a lion he had covered his tracks exceptionally well, and that nobody could prove that he was complicit in the murder of his nephew who, so he professed righteously, he had loved and cared for so exceptionally well.

Betraying the French King

On the 30th of December in 1494, the French king and his troops entered Rome by the Flaminian Gate, and he rode in triumphal procession along the Corso with Cardinals Giuliano delle Rovere and Ascanio Sforza at his side. Pope Alexander VI fled from his rooms in the Papal palace to shelter at the fortified Castello Sant' Angelo while king Charles took up his abode in the palace of San Marco from where he dictated terms of peace to the frightened pontiff. The victorious French king convinced the Pope to sign a treaty with him on the 15th of January for the crown of Naples to be bestowed upon him and the chief Papal fortresses to be surrendered into his hands until his return. Four days later, king Charles paid homage to His Holiness before the College of Cardinals and was embraced and welcomed by the Pope as a principal of the Church. A week later, king Charles left Rome and set out at the head of his army on the march to Naples. King Alfonso of Aragon on hearing the news that the Church and king Charles were allies abdicated his crown in favour of his son Ferdinand II, and he left Naples to Sicily to wait for the outcome of the French attack.

On the 4th of February, the new Duchess of Milan Beatrice gave birth to a second son, Francesco, another healthy boy for Ludovico. The celebrations were magnificent, but short-lived, for the news reached the Sforza court in Milan that the King of France had entered Naples and had been crowned King of the Sicilies in the city's cathedral on the 22nd of February. The young king of Naples Ferdinand II who was the brother of Isabella Aragon Sforza the deposed Duchess of Milan had fled Naples to Ischia with the rest of his royal family. This news threw a gloom over the celebrations in the Sforza Castello, and all the pleasure and feasting of the Carnival, all the mirth of the dancing and feasting, faded away. The new Duchess of Milan Beatrice d' Este thought sadly of her cousin Ferdinand, the chivalrous young king who was a favourite with all his kinsfolk, and his sister, the now widowed Isabella Aragon Sforza former Duchess of Milan, shed bitter tears over this fresh sorrow in regard to her Neapolitan family. Ludovico with the upmost royal hypocrisy told Isabella that he still held her in high regard, and therefore he would on her behalf drive the French out of Italy, and that *'you see how little the king has followed my advice and how cruel and insolent he has shown himself. These French are bad people, and we must not allow them to become our neighbours.'*

On the evening of the 27th of February, while the bells of the Milanese churches rang to honour the French king's triumph, Ludovico sent for the Venetian ambassadors to inform them that he was ready to betray the French king. With the loss of Naples to the French, he was ready to do whatever the Republic desired of him to combat any further advancement by the foreign invading force with whom he had been previously in league. The duke felt unsafe while Louis of Orleans remained at Asti, and he declared that he was ready to place himself at the head of a league for the defence of Italy. The League of Venice was formed on March 31 with the representatives of Pope Alexander VI, the King of the Romans (Germany), the King and Queen of Spain, the Signoria of Venice, the Duchy of Mantua, the Republic of Florence, and the Duke of Milan, and it was solemnly proclaimed on the 10th of April, Palm Sunday, in a procession of the nations' flags, colours, and banners on the Piazza of St. Mark in Venice. The new Duke of Milan had now betrayed the French, and they would forever hate him for it.

Meanwhile, the French king was living the high life in the gardens and palaces of Naples, entertained by daily jousts, banquets, and licentiousness, unaware of Ludovico's betrayal. His fun was somewhat disrupted when he received messages from his Ambassador to Venice Commines about the formation of the League of Venice, and that Ludovico had sent Galeazzo Sanseverino with his troops to Asti on the 19th of April to demand that the Duke of Orleans surrender the town and drop his claim to the title of Duke of Milan. The Duke of Orleans immediately responded to declare that Asti formed part of his heritage, and that he was ready to defend it to the last drop of his blood against Signor Ludovico or any other foe who might dare to enter; and he sent an urgent appeal to the Duke of Bourbon for reinforcements. Thus, a stalemate was reached, Sanseverino and his army camped outside the city ready to cut off supplies and prevent reinforcements from entering the beleaguered city.

But, when the news of these events reached the ears of the French king, he finally realised that Ludovico Sforza had betrayed him, and that he had raised a formidable opposition against him. In between his continued celebrations, the French king prepared to leave Naples with the bulk of his army and march northward to Rome. He left Naples on the 20th of May leaving behind the Duke of Montpensier with a few hundred French troops and a few thousand Swiss mercenaries to defend his newly conquered kingdom. He entered Rome by the Latin gate on the 1st of June. The French king's retreat from Naples allowed King Ferdinand II to return to Calabria to recruit fighters to join him under the banner of the house of Aragon and win back Naples.

The Investiture of Lord Ludovico Sforza by the Grace of God and the Will of His Caesarean Majesty Maximilian, Emperor-elect and Chief of the Holy Roman Empire, May 1495

At last, in Milan, the long-promised privileges for the duke and duchess of Milan had arrived from Emperor Maximilian's envoys. After attending high mass at the Duomo during the festival of S. Felicissimo on the 26th of May 1495, Lord Ludovico Sforza was solemnly proclaimed Duke of Milan, Count of Pavia and Angera, by the grace of God and the will of his Caesarean Majesty Maximilian, Emperor-elect and chief of the Holy Roman Empire.

> The imperial delegates, Melchior, Bishop of Brixen, and Conrad Sturzl, Chancellor of the King of the Romans, first read aloud the privileges in their master's name, and then invested Ludovico with the ducal cap and mantle, and placed the sceptre and sword of state in his hands. Giasone del Maino, the celebrated Pavian jurist, recited a Latin oration, after which the duke, accompanied by the imperial ambassadors, and followed by the duchess and a brilliant suite of courtiers and ladies, rode in procession to the ancient basilica of S. Ambrogio to return thanks for his accession. Then, the whole company returned, 'with immense rejoicing and triumph,' to the Castello where a series of splendid fetes were given in honour of the occasion, and rich presents were made to the imperial ambassadors and court officials. [S7]

Two days afterwards, another imposing ceremony was held in the Castello when the heads of houses from the different quarters of the city were assembled and each citizen in turn swore fealty, first to Duke Ludovico and afterwards to Duchess Beatrice whom, in the event of his own death, he had appointed to be the regent of the State and the guardian of their sons.

The 26th of May was the proudest day of Ludovico's life, for although he was the seventh Duke of Milan, he was now the first Sforza proclaimed to be so by the Holy Roman Emperor. This was the official investiture that he had dreamed off and possibly killed for. But, his exaltation was shattered by the end of the month when resting at Vigevano after the triumphant celebrations in Milan, he received word that Louis the Duke of Orleans had left Asti with his army and captured Novara, a city between the rivers of the Sesia and the Ticino only a day's ride from Milan. The citizens of Novara being disaffected by Ludovico for reasons of his growing oppressive exactions had with no hesitation opened their gates to the French duke. On receiving this news, the recently crowned Duke of Milan suddenly was seized by an irresistible panic, and he retired from Vigevano, first to Abbiategrasso, east of the Ticino river, and then to Milan where he took refuge in the Castello with his wife and children.

According to many of those working or living in the Sforza Castle at the time, including Leonardo and my father, Ludovico had isolated himself in his rooms for two weeks with illness and nervous exhaustion leaving his 20-year-old wife Beatrice Duchess of Milan to rule the city. It was she who showed the courage and presence of mind to call together the ruling noblemen of Milan to organise the appropriate measures to defend the Castello and city. She asked Leonardo and Bernardino del Corte the Governor of the Rocca to fortify the Castello and make it an impregnable citadel for it *held her and her husband's treasure and jewels together with all his most precious possessions.* It was on the 22nd of June that my father in the company of the Venetian general Bernardo Contarini at the head of several thousand Greek Stradiots returned to Milan from their patrols of the Adda River to defend the duke and duchess and its citizens. Their arrival to defend the Sforza castle was much heralded, and it roused Ludovico from his fear and lethargy to soon recover his health and nerve and take control of the defence of his city and domains. He immediately called for help from Maximilian who had long-promised him a contingent of Swiss and German troops. Soon after the return of my father to Milan, Ludovico's fortunes changed again for the better.

The French Retreat

The French king was still in Rome, but becoming more concerned with the thought of an attack from the League of Venice. He decided it was time to return to France and confront the League forces with his army wherever they may lie in wait for him. The return back to France wasn't going to be easy for him. He knew that Ludovico and his allies would block his passage through the Duchy of Milan and the other states of Italy on his way from Rome. His previous allies were now his enemy; many of them were waiting for him on the bank of the Taro River at the village of Fornovo near Parma in Romagna. It was here, on the 6th July 1495, that he fought his greatest and most difficult battle of the campaign with 12,000 of his men against the League's army of 25,000 men led by the Duke of Mantua Francesco Gonzaga. With the ensuing battle, the League lost 2,000 men - mostly Venetian reservists, and the French king lost 1,000 of his soldiers as well as most of his hard earned booty. The League suffered many casualties, and they could not prevent Charles and his army from crossing the Italian lands on their way back to France. Exhausted by the fighting, king Charles and the remainder of his tired army reached the safety of Asti on the 8th of July. Commines the king's ambassador to Venice wrote the following in his published history:

God Himself was our guide and led us home with honour, as that good man Fra Girolamo of Florence had foretold. But, as he said truly, we were made to suffer for our sins, for we were in sore need of food, and so great was our want of water that men drank of the ditches along the road; but no one was heard to complain, although it was the hardest journey I ever took in my life, and I have had many bad ones. [S7]

The day before the French king reached Asti, King Ferdinand II was welcomed back to Naples by his subjects. One by one, the castles in the neighbourhood surrendered to him, their rightful king, forcing Montpensier and the remnants of his force to retire into the wilderness of Calabria. The news in Milan of King Ferdinand's return to Naples was presented with great joy to his cousin Beatrice the Duchess of Milan and his sister Isabella the former Duchess of Milan. Ludovico could now concentrate and present all his attention to removing Louis of Orleans from Novara and sending him over the Alps back to France. A week after the battle of Fornovo, General Gian Francesco Gonzaga and the remains of his League army now reduced to 20,000 men were sent to lay siege to Novara. Maximilian's contingent of Swiss and German troops joined them, and the Sanseverino brothers were already stationed at the outskirts of the city. The garrison of the besieged city was seven thousand strong and well provided with arms and ammunition, but with dwindling supplies of food. A council of war was held on the 5th of August and Ludovico's recommendation was adopted to blockade the town instead of attacking it. The duke and duchess of Milan reviewed the entire army outside the walls of Novara where Gonzaga's troops and the German and Swiss reinforcements numbered upwards of forty thousand men. The parade of troops on chargers in glittering armour, the marching infantry, Stradiots armed with lances, Venetian cross-bowmen, and light cavalry passed by Ludovico mounted on his horse and the chariot of Duchess Beatrice to the sound of trumpets, beating drums, and martial music. It was a spectacular sight for all to see. However, Galeazzo Sanseverino received a sharp rebuke from his anxious father-in-law Ludovico for wearing the French armour of the knight of the Order of St. Michael while bearing the ducal banner with the figure of a Moor holding an eagle in one hand and strangling a dragon with the other. At the end of the magnificent parade, the Duke of Milan embarrassed himself in view of the Duke of Orleans when he fell from his horse and soiled his rich clothes in the dark brown mud and manure. The Neapolitan chronicler, Jacopo d'Atri, wrote, *'this fall was held to be an evil omen, and was remembered afterwards by many who were present that day.'*

Louis of Orleans and his famished soldiers may have laughed when they saw Ludovico fall into the mud and horse shit, but they were now more concerned about their own need for reinforcements and supplies for they were on the brink of starvation. The king of France, after rest and recovery in Asti and then later in Turin where he stayed with Blanche of Montferrat the regent and Duchess of Savoy, gathered together his troops and a league of 12,000 Swiss Cantonese friendly to France, and they advanced to Vercelli in the Duchy of Savoy to set up camp. It was September, and he was ready to advance and relieve Louis of Orleans at Novara. Except for Louis who very much wanted to take on Ludovico and exact his revenge, both the French and the Italian generals and diplomats were tired of the warfare, and they were ready to negotiate a quick settlement. The Italians demanded the unconditional surrender of Novara while king Charles VIII of France asked for the restitution of Genoa, an ancient fief of the French crown. Nothing was concluded, but a truce was agreed upon after a number of prolonged conferences. Finally, against the advice of Louis of Orleans and the French king's ally the condottiero Gian Giacomo Trivulzio, Charles agreed to Ludovico's terms, and Louis of Orleans evacuated Novara on the 26th of September with an escort from the Marquis of Mantua and the Count of Caiazzo. Thousands had died in Novara from illness and starvation, but this unphased Louis of Orleans who swore that he would return all the way to Milan and become their new duke in the very near future. On the 9th of October, a separate settlement was concluded between the King of France and the Duke of Milan ignoring the interests of the other powers. Charles recognised the right of Ludovico to Novara, Genoa, and Savona, and he renounced his support of his cousin's claims to Milan. In return, the Duke of Milan promised not to assist King Ferdinand II with troops or ships, renounced his claim on Asti, and agreed to pay the Duke of Orleans 50,000 ducats as a war indemnity and to cancel Louis's debt still owing to him of 80,000 ducats. Immediately after the peace agreement was signed, Charles VIII left Vercelli, crossed the Alps with the remnants of his army, and reached Lyons on the 7th of November. Although the Venetians were not sorry to see the French leave the Italian peninsula and cross the Alps back to France, they were highly indignant with the Duke of Milan's breach of faith in concluding a separate peace without their involvement, and they expressed strong words to the effect that he could no longer be trusted. This contemptuous disregard for his allies, this new betrayal, would come back to haunt him years later when he needed them again to protect him from a new French attack led by a new French king who was none other than Louis the Duke of Orleans.

Ludovico Sforza's Family Altarpiece with Virgin and Child and Church Saints

Christmas of 1495,

> … was celebrated with great joy and splendour at the court of Milan. After the troubled times of the last twelve months and the dangers which had threatened the very existence of the State, and brought the noise of war to the gates of Vigevano, peace and tranquillity were once more restored, and another era of unclouded prosperity seemed about to dawn. Now that Gian Galeazzo was dead, and Louis of Orleans had once more crossed the Alps, there was no one to dispute Ludovico's title or to prevent his son from eventually succeeding him on the throne. Once more he and Beatrice were free to devote themselves to the encouragement of learning and poetry, of painting and architecture, to watch Bramante and Leonardo at work, or read Dante and Petrarch together. [S7]

In that winter of joy, Bernardino Zenale and Leonardo began to paint a highly stylised altarpiece for Ludovico IL Moro Sforza with him and his family portrayed as the masters of Lombardy. The altarpiece can be seen at the monastery of S. Ambrogio *ad Nemus* that is located in the park and forest outside the city's northwest wall and within a short walking distance of the Castello Sforzesca.

The painting was commissioned by Ludovico as a political propaganda piece to show off the pomp and power of his rank with his huge ducal chain hung prominently around his neck and across his chest. The benevolence of the Madonna and the Christ-child and the Saints are displayed towards him for his religious piety and the future of his dynasty and heir. In this painting, in a style reminiscent of Giovanni Ambrogio Bevilacqua, the Madonna and Child are enthroned in the centre of the picture; the four Fathers of the Church, Ambrose, Augustine, Jerome, and Gregory, stand on either side; and in the foreground, kneeling at the foot of the throne are the Duke and Duchess of Milan with their two sons, Maximilian and Francesco. The Christ-child turns towards Ludovico and St. Ambrose the protector and patron saint of Milan who with a whip in his left hand lays his protective right hand on the shoulder of the duke, as he, clad in rich blue brocades and wearing a massive ducal gold chain round his neck, clasps his hands together in righteous prayer. And the gentle Madonna stretches out her left hand lovingly towards Beatrice who kneels at her feet, Beatrice with the snake-like long coil of twisted hair behind her head and back, pearls on her head and neck, and her favourite knots of ribbons fluttering from her shoulders and falling over the velvet stripes of her yellow satin robe. Close at her side is the swaddled infant prince Francesco Sforza with his baby face (born 4th February 1495); while Maximilian Sforza the handsome little Count of Pavia and the future duke of Milan (born 25th January 1493) is kneeling at his father's side. The golden richness glistens about them.

Fig. 47. Madonna and Child with St. Ambrose, St. Augustine, St. Jerome, and St. Gregory, in the presence of Ludovico and Beatrice, Duke and Duchess of Milan, with their two children. Monastery of S. Ambrogio ad Nemus.

But, look closer at the painting and you will see unusual coded details and the influence and hand of Leonardo at work. Look at the left hand of the Madonna stretched out towards

Beatrice. The little finger of Madonna that is pointing towards the Duchess Beatrice is bent almost at right angles. This is an obvious sign of betrayal and that a full blessing cannot be administered – it is broken. Is the Christ-child blessing or admonishing Ludovico the Duke of Milan? The face of the winged angel hovering above St. Gregory's cross and Ludovico's head and holding onto the crown of power looks very much like it is the face of the betrayed and dead Gian Galeazzo Sforza. Also, the face of the Madonna looks like that of the betrayed and sad former Duchess of Milan Isabella Aragon Sforza, the widow of the Gian Galeazzo Sforza. Her eyes are hooded and puffed from grieving, her mouth is sadly sagging. She sits on the throne placed on steps that are decorated with her Aragona emblem, the head of a bull. None of the saints are smiling. They look away from Ludovico and Beatrice and their children. They seem disapproving of Ludovico trying to legitimise his rule over Milan, knowing that he has usurped the legitimate heir Francesco Maria Sforza on the death of his father Gian Galeazzo Sforza. This is a coded painting disapproving of Ludovico rather than celebrating and honouring him.

Bernardino Zenale was a Milanese painter and architect born in Treviglio in 1460. He trained with Vincenzo Civerchio and often worked with a fellow painter Bernardino Butinone. Years later, he struck up a friendship with Bernardino Luini and soon became another follower of Leonardo da Vinci. Looking at his altarpiece painted to honour Ludovico and his family you can see Leonardo da Vinci's subtle influence especially in the faces of the Virgin and some of the saints, and in the complicated pose of the Christ-child and his mood of authority and reverence.

The Holy Roman Emperor Maximilian I Visits Lombardy and Other Italian States

The year 1496 was one of much needed rest, recreation, and recovery for all who were still in Milan including the ducal court. The state coffers had been majorly drained during the previous years because of the large amount of finances spent on the armies and instruments of war and the rewards, settlements, and inducements paid to an ever-growing and ever-changing list of allies and army generals. For my father, the Count of Melzi, the year started with his immediate recall to Ludovico's court to help him with the arrangements for the Emperor Maximilian to visit Milan and Italy. Ludovico felt he needed to reward the German king for his war support and for granting him the official ducal investiture. In addition, his niece Bianca the Queen of Germany was pestering him regularly for an invitation to return to her beloved Milan and Italy in the company of her husband. But, most of all, he was worried by rumours that the king of France was gathering together a new force with the aim of a second French expedition to win back Naples from King Ferdinand II. He needed the Emperor Maximilian as his ally to curb the French king's ambitions. I was now 5 years old, and I would on occasions accompany my father to the court meetings where I would sit with my pad and crayons that Leonardo had given me to draw whatever subject caught my eye or mind's fancy. By mid-March, Ludovico and my father had sent Marchesino Stanga across the Alps to invite Maximilian to Lombardy to help and provide a balance of power between Venice and Florence in their fight over the ownership of Pisa. The Emperor was flattered by the invitation, but stressed that due to his lack of money Duke Ludovico would need to cover all his and his party's travel expenses in Italy.

And so it was that on the 5th of July, the Duke and Duchess accompanied by my father, Leonardo, Galeazzo Sanseverino, courtiers, diplomats, and soldiers set out to journey up to lake Como to Bormio in Valtellina to the mountains of Tyrol where they had arranged to meet with the Emperor who was travelling south from Innsbruck. The Emperor arrived at the Abbey of Mals on the 20th of July 1496 with what he described as his hunting party; 100 foot soldiers bearing long lances, 50 German lords on horseback with falcons on their wrists, a troop of servants and pages in imperial liveries of red, white, and yellow, and a long procession of ladies and lords and their attendants. The Emperor arrived on horseback dressed in a hunting-garb of a grey cloth tunic and black velvet cap with a lion's skin wrapped around his hips. Here, I add what the Venetian ambassador's secretary Conrad Vimerca reported on the meeting at the Abbey of Mals.

His Majesty alighted with an eagerness, which seemed to me only too great, and went upstairs, where he found the duke alone with the duchess, and spent half an hour in close and affectionate intercourse with them both. Afterwards they all three attended mass in the neighbouring church, and his Majesty appeared, leading the duchess with his right hand and the duke with his left, with such demonstrations of love and familiarity as can hardly be described. All three then rode on horseback to the emperor's lodgings at Colourno (Glurns), some eight miles distant, where his Majesty entertained the duke and duchess and their entire suite at dinner under a pavilion, which had been erected under the trees. His Majesty insisted on both the duke and duchess washing their hands with him in the same bowl, and, sitting down between them at table, himself helped first one, then the other, from the endless variety of dishes spread out before them. All this he did with an ease and kindness beyond anything that I have ever seen in royal personages. Each time the duke spoke he took off his cap, and his Majesty did the same. After dinner they remained for some while in pleasant conversation, and then rode all three together to another place called Mals, one mile further off, his Majesty bearing all the expenses of the entertainment. Tomorrow night they will remain together here, and there will be some time for discussion. I am quite sure, after this that we shall see his Majesty in Italy next August, and this you may hold to be absolutely certain. As for the King of France, they do not even mention his name or think of him any more than if he did not exist. [S7]

A few days later, a conference was held between the Emperor, the duke of Milan, and the ambassadors to form a new League between the Pope, the king of Spain, the king of England, the Venetian Republic, and the duke of Milan. At this meeting, Emperor Maximilian was promised a subsidy of 16,000 ducats in order to cross the Alps with an army and compel the Florentines to give up Pisa and Leghorn. While the Emperor considered his options and commitment to the new League, he, his wife, and the Duke and Duchess of Milan and their retinue travelled together in the region of the Lombardian Alps on hunting parties to Bormio and Tirano before they separated on the 10th of August to return to their respective homes to prepare for the Emperor's visit to Milan as soon as he was able.

And so it was that a few weeks later, the Emperor re-entered Lombardy to meet with Ludovico in Como and later travel together to the Duke's favourite summer palace in Vigevano where the Duchess Beatrice and her children waited for their arrival. Along the way, the Emperor inspected some of his properties and farmlands that were managed by my father in his capacity as the Emperor's and the Duke's Count Palatine. Once they reached Vigevano, the Emperor relaxed in the company of the Duke's family for the next three weeks and participated in a succession of fetes and hunting parties including a hunt for a leopard. According to my father, it was in Vigevano that the Emperor begged both Ludovico and Beatrice that their eldest son, Ercole, bear his name Maximilian. And so it was that Ercole henceforth became known as Maximilian Sforza. It was also a name that my father would give to one of my younger brothers.

It was in Vigevano that Ludovico and the Emperor received the news that Isabella Aragon Sforza's brother Ferdinand II the king of Naples after a short illness had died at Somma Vesuviana on 7th September 1496. He was 27 years old, recently married to his cousin Joanna of Aragon, but he left no heirs. Back in Milan, Isabella Aragon Sforza added another great sorrow to her life.

The Emperor left Vigevano on 23rd of September to sail with his fleet from Genoa in order to secure Pisa's independence for the League against the Florentine claims. He landed at Pisa on the 21st of October, but for various reasons, he was not able to win over Pisa or Leghorn from the Florentine forces and was soon back in Pavia and Lombardy by the 2nd of December.

Before the Emperor arrived back in Pavia, he was informed that the Sforza's were in mourning because the Duke's daughter Bianca who was married to Galeazzo Sanseverino had only a few weeks previously died in childbirth (22nd November). The Duke and his son-in-law were inconsolable as was the Duchess for she counted Bianca as one of her very dearest friends. Nevertheless, although the duke and duchess were in deep mourning, they together with a small suite of courtiers travelled from Milan to Pavia to receive their illustrious kinsman when he arrived there from Sarzana.

Maximilian behaved with great consideration, and he showed his deepest sympathy to his distressed relatives. Instead of making a public entry through the city, he entered the Castello through a private gate and spent the evening alone with the Duke and Duchess and the little Count of Pavia in gracious condolence and understanding and prayer. Next day, he informed his officials that it was unwise for him to visit Milan or remain any longer in Italy, since the Imperial Diet of Augsburg was about to meet, and he was anxious to be back in Germany. On the 4th of December, he attended a solemn requiem mass for the lamented princess Bianca in the Duomo of Pavia, and in the afternoon, he rode out to the Certosa with Ludovico who showed him all the wonders of that famous church and abbey. On the 6th, the duke took his wife back to Milan to rest for she was with child again, while the Emperor rode out to the ducal villa of Cussago and later on to Groppello to meet again with Ludovico on the 11th. Here, they shared their fond farewells, and the Emperor rode out on his journey to cross the winter Alps, while Ludovico returned to Milan to join the company of his new mistress Lucrezia Crivelli who was a new and young lady-in-waiting to his wife the Duchess Beatrice. My father accompanied the Emperor to Bellagio and Marchesino Stanga's castle that overlooked the lake at Como. Here, they parted company after the Emperor had instructed my father to sell off a number of his properties in Lombardy for a good price. The Emperor had become concerned that his properties might be confiscated from him if the French decided to invade Lombardy as was strongly rumoured at the time, and it was considered it would be better for him to sell them off now than fight for them at a later time. It would be my father's duty to Maximilian to find the buyers and sell at a good price.

The Venetians were exceedingly upset with the outcome of the Emperor's and the League's unsuccessful Pisa adventure. They blamed Ludovico Sforza for the failure of the Pisa expedition and the lack of support for them from the Emperor. Malipiero who accompanied the Venetian fleet that sailed with Maximilian against Leghorn wrote the following comments.

> Things go badly for the Signory at Pisa and the cause of this is Ludovico Duke of Milan…. His pride and arrogance are beyond description. He boasts that Pope Alexander is his chaplain, the Emperor Maximilian his condottiere, the Signory of Venice his chamberlain, since they spend their money largely to attain his ends, and the King of France his courier, who comes and goes at his pleasure. Truly a fearful state of things! [S7]

And Marino Sanuto of Florence remarked,

> The Duke of Milan is one of the wisest men in the world, but his success has rendered him very ungrateful to Venice, whose secret enemy he will always remain. He made a great mistake in allowing the Duke of Orleans to escape from Novara, and some day he will be punished for his bad faith. For he never keeps his promises, and when he says one thing, always does another. All men fear him, because fortune is propitious to him in

everything. But, none the less, I believe that he will not continue long in prosperity, for God is just, and will punish him because he is a traitor and never keeps faith with any one. [S7]

Although the Emperor had originally intended to visit Milan, and a triumphal arch in the Roman style had been ordered by the duke and built by Leonardo and his team, the visit never happened. My father had no explanation for why this never occurred other than that the Emperor did not want the League to accuse him of favouritism for only visiting Ludovico's Ducal city. However, other chroniclers were less kind and suggested that Ludovico wanted to save the Emperor when in Milan from the embarrassment of seeing or meeting with the Duchess Isabella's son Francesco II Melzi the 'Little Duke' who was the real Duke of Pavia and rightful heir to the crown and Duchy of Milan.

The Shocking and Unexpected Death of Beatrice the Duchess of Milan, 3rd January 1497

Ludovico still felt triumphant and joyful about his own accomplishments soon after the Emperor had left Lombardy back over the Alps to return to Augsburg in Germany before Christmas. He had accomplished more than he had expected in the last two years. He now wanted to relax and enjoy his Christmas festivities with his pregnant mistress Lucrezia Crivelli and his pregnant wife Beatrice. He had met and fallen in love with Lucrezia when she had accompanied his wife Beatrice as her lady-in-waiting to meet with the Holy Roman Emperor in the Italian Alps. His infatuation was instantaneous, and he provided Lucrezia with her own private rooms at the Sforza castle where he visited her more often than he did to see his own wife. Although the affair was discrete and hidden from Beatrice, the Duchess found out about it by mid November, and she demanded hysterically that Ludovico remove Lucrezia from the castle. But, he ignored her, causing her much greater distress. The pregnant Duchess felt that her husband had suddenly abandoned her. Many saw it as another one of his many betrayals. She felt further distressed and abandoned when her closest friend Bianca Sforza died unexpectedly in Vigevano on the 22nd of November due to complications during child-birth.

From then on, the courtiers often saw the Duchess in tears and wondered if they were caused by her husband's neglect or by her grief for the death of Bianca. Day after day, she paid long visits in prayer and in tears to the tomb where the duke's daughter was laid to rest at the Church of S. Maria delle Grazie (Saint Mary, Our Lady of Graces). Then, on Monday, on the second day of the New Year, 1497, she passed through the Porta Vercellina and visited the Church of S. Maria delle Grazie for the last time. She greeted Leonardo who was in the Church refectory still working on his great fresco of the *Last Supper*. She called him down from his scaffold and told him how much she was looking forward to seeing his finished painting, which was only recently started and still missing the figures of Jesus, Judas, and many of the apostles. She told him that she could guess where Leonardo would place Judas at the table of Jesus, and she suggested whom he should look like for the model of the betrayer lived close to her in the Sforza castle. She then gave Leonardo a discreet kiss and asked him to accompany her to Our Lady's altar where she prayed for the repose of Bianca's soul. Leonardo and the Duchess also moved across to the tomb being constructed by Cristoforo Solari for her and her husband where she stayed to pray again. After her prayers and with tears in her eyes, she bid Leonardo farewell wishing him well in his future employ with her husband the Duke IL Moro. Then, she left with her small group of ladies-in-waiting and returned to the Castello. It was the last time that Leonardo saw the Duchess alive. Back in her rooms in the Rocchetta, the Duchess was suddenly taken ill at eight o'clock in the evening. Three hours later, she gave birth to her stillborn son, and half an hour after midnight, her own spirit left her and she soon passed away. She was not yet 22 years of age.

This sudden, unexpected death of the Duchess was a shock to all in Milan and most of all for her husband Ludovico. By all accounts, horror and confusion reigned in the Castello of Milan for the next few days. The duke's grief was said to be beyond belief, but he still managed to send a grieving message to his brother-in-law Francesco Gonzaga.

> Most Illustrious Relative and Dearest Brother, My wife was taken with sudden pains at eight o'clock last night. At eleven she gave birth to a dead son, and at half-past twelve she gave back her spirit to God. This cruel and premature end has filled me with bitter and indescribable anguish, so much so that I would rather have died myself than lose the dearest and most precious thing that I had in this world. But great and excessive as is my grief, beyond all measure, and grievous as your own will be, I know, I feel that I must tell you this myself, because of the brotherly love between us. And I beg you not to send any one to condole with me, as that would only renew my sorrow. I would not write to the Madonna Marchesana, and leave you to break the news to her as you think best, knowing well how inexpressible her sorrow will be.
>
> Lodovicus M. Sfortia, Anglus Dux Mediolani. Milan, January 3, 1497, 6 o'clock. [S7]

When the Duke recovered briefly from his own bitter anguish, he arranged for his beloved's funeral. She was taken from the Castello in a long procession of mourners by the light of a thousand torches to her last resting-place under Bramante's cupola at the Church of Our Lady (Santa Maria delle Grazie). My mother, father, grandmother, and Leonardo were in the procession to the church, but they never talked about it in any detail. A number of ambassadors and chroniclers published their accounts of the sad occasion.

The Ferrarese ambassador Antonius Costabilis wrote in part,

> The obsequies that followed were celebrated with all possible magnificence and pomp. All the ambassadors at present in Milan, among whom were one from the King of the Romans, two from the King of Spain, and others from all the powers of Italy, lifted the corpse and bore it to the first gate of the Castello. Here the privy councillors took the body in their turn, and at the corners of the streets groups of magistrates stood waiting to receive it. All the relatives of the ducal family wore long mourning cloaks that trailed on the ground, and hoods over their heads. I walked first with the Marchese Ermes, and the others followed, each in his right order. We bore her to Santa Maria delle Grazie, attended by an innumerable company of monks and nuns and priests, bearing crosses of gold, of silver and wood, infinite numbers of gentlemen and citizens, and crowds of people of every rank and class, all weeping and making the greatest lamentation that was ever seen, for the great loss which this city has suffered in the death of its duchess. There were so many wax torches it was marvellous to see! At the gates of Santa Maria delle Grazie, the ambassadors were waiting to receive the body, and, taking it from the hands of the chief magistrates, they bore it to the steps of the high altar, where the most reverend cardinal-legate was seated, in his purple robes, between two bishops, and himself said the whole Office. And there the duchess was laid on a bier draped with cloth of gold, bearing the arms of the house of Sforza, and clad in one of her richest camoras of gold brocade. My dear lord, besides the extraordinary demonstrations of grief which have been shown by the whole people of this city, and by the women quite as much as by the men, which may well be a great consolation to your Excellency, I must tell you how above all others, Signore Messer Galeazzo di Sanseverino has both by his words and deeds, as well as by his demonstrations of sorrow, given admirable expression to the affection which he had for the duchess, and has taken care to make known to every one the virtues and goodness of that most illustrious Madonna. All of which I have felt it my duty to tell your Excellency, in the hope that it may help to alleviate your sorrow, praying

you to maintain the same fortitude that you have always shown hitherto. To whose favour I ever commend myself, Your Excellency's servant, Antonius Costabilis, Milan, January 13, 1497. [S7]

Somebody else wrote,

On Wednesday, the 4th of January came the news of the death of Beatrice, Duchess of Milan. And the duke was very sad, and so were all the people. And on the 12th, Duke Ercole attended an Office said for the repose of the late duchess in the church of the Dominicans, which was all hung with black, and all the clergy, magistrates, and courtiers were there, carrying lighted torches; all the people wore black, and the shops were closed as if it were Christmas, and more than 400 Masses were said for the repose of her soul, and 660 candles were burnt that day. It was a fine day, but a great quantity of wax tapers was used for this funeral service. As for the Duke of Milan, I will say nothing, because the things he does sound incredible to those who have not seen them. Certainly the extraordinary honours, which he pays his dead wife, show how dearly he loved her. She has left him two little sons. And all Ferrara sorrows for her death, and I saw many weeping. And so goes this ribald world. [S7]

So, the year 1497 began with great tragedy for Ludovico, the 7th Duke of Milan. Whether or not he foresaw his own future with any trepidation is uncertain, but the portents were not good. Despite the great sorrow felt for the death of the Duchess of Milan, many felt little sympathy for the Duke. They felt that he had betrayed his wife Beatrice and too many others in his greedy grab for the throne of Milan. Ludovico IL Moro Sforza had coveted the title of the Duke of Milan since the assassination of his brother Galeazzo Maria Sforza on the 26th December 1476; he rushed onto the throne in too much of a hurry immediately after the death of Gian Galeazzo, the sixth duke of Milan. He showed the young duke Gian Galeazzo Sforza too little respect both before and after his death in his rush for the coveted title of the dukedom of Milan and its fiefdoms. Ironically, Ludovico's standing in the world diminished rather than grew after his investiture with the royal titles given to him by the Holy Roman Emperor Maximilian I on the 26th of May 1495. Instead, Ludovico Sforza became better known as the betrayer. He betrayed his family, his dead brothers, his sister Ippolita Maria Sforza and her daughter (his niece) Isabella of Aragon, his nephew the Duke Gian Galeazzo Sforza, his sister-in-law Bona of Savoy, and his wife Beatrice d' Este. Moreover, he betrayed Naples, Rome, Florence, and Venice, indeed all of Italy and France; and the Venetians and the French were not about to forgive him for his betrayal of their alliances. Ultimately, as the double-dealing prince and regent, he betrayed himself, Milan, and Lombardy.

CHAPTER 13

Leonardo's *Last Supper*, Coded Messages, and Allegories of the Dark Beast of Milan

LIES. The mole has very small eyes and it always lives under ground; and it lives as long as it is in the dark, but when it comes into the light it dies immediately, because it becomes known; -- and so it is with lies.
The perception of the object depends on the direction of the eye.

— Leonardo da Vinci

Leonardo's *Last Supper*: Painting a Memorial to the Betrayal of the Sixth Duke of Milan, the Young Lord Gian Galeazzo Sforza

After the death of Gian Galeazzo Sforza in October of 1494, Leonardo was unsure about his own future in Milan. Gian as the young duke of Milan had treated him well with various commissions and provided him with land and a house outside the Porta Vercellina only a few streets away from the Church of Santa Maria delle Grazie. He also provided Leonardo with servants including Salai and his father, stipends for his assistants and artists, donations for the upkeep of his studios, and helped Leonardo to pay for the bronze to be used for the equestrian sculpture of Francesco Sforza. Now with the death of Gian, Ludovico - the new duke of Milan - without informing Leonardo - simply gave away all the bronze for the statue to his father-in-law Ercole I of Este to build a cannon against his perceived fear of an attack from the French. Leonardo was devastated for he suddenly realised that the statue might never be completed now that Gian Galeazzo Sforza was no longer alive to support him. Another project that Gian had wanted Leonardo to start with his full support was a large fresco of the *Last Supper of Jesus* at the Church of Santa Maria delle Grazie. They had talked about it often, and even a month before his fatal illness Gian had indicated that the documents for the commission were already drawn up for Leonardo to read and sign. However, Leonardo never saw those documents either before or immediately after Gian's death, and he wondered how he and his studio would fare with the loss of one of his most generous benefactors. Yet, Ludovico's son-in-law Galeazzo Sanseverino was still a great supporter and friend of Leonardo, and he strived with the assistance of Ludovico to keep Leonardo busy through the years of 1495 and 1496. Together, Galeazzo Sanseverino and Ludovico commissioned Leonardo and the Florentine monk Luca Pacioli to publish a great work on the mathematics and logic of perspective called *De Divina Proportione,* and Ludovico sought to fulfil Gian's wish for Leonardo to paint the *Last Supper of Jesus.*

Ludovico Sforza decided in March of 1495 (just before his investiture as the first Duke of Milan to be sanctioned by the Holy Roman Emperor in May 1495) to honour the vision of his nephew and let Leonardo paint the *Last Supper* on a wall at the Santa Maria della Grazie. He thus ordered the Benedictine monks to formerly commission Leonardo for this task in the refectory of the church. And so it was that Leonardo, although depressed by the loss of his bronze for the equestrian statue, was commissioned to undertake one of his greatest projects ever and accomplish a result that would immortalise him as one of the greatest artists who had ever lived.

Matteo Bandelli, the court historian and friend of Leonardo, wrote much about Leonardo's initial procrastination on how he spent more time constructing his scaffolds, eating, and drinking in the refectory than actually preparing the wall or drawing and painting on it.   To the great annoyance of the monks, Leonardo disturbed their access to the dining room and kitchen of the refectory for two years before any of his images were painted on the wall.

In April of 1496, the Prior of Santa Maria delle Grazie wrote to Ludovico:

> My Lord, it is over twelve months since you despatched Master Leonardo to perform this commission and in all that time not one mark has been made upon our wall. And in that time, My Lord, the cellular of the Priory show vast depletion and now are nearly dry, for Master Leonardo insists all wines be tried until the right one for his masterpiece arrives – he will not have it other … My Lord, I urge you hasten Master Leonardo in performance of his work, for now his presence, and of his band as well, does threaten us with penury. [S22]

Nine months later, in January 1497, Raymond Perault Bishop of Gurk visited the refectory after attending mass for the deceased Beatrice Duchess of Milan and sent a letter to his superiors in Innsbruck saying,

> Master Leonardo has drawn a cartoon of some pillars and the outline of a table on his wall and below it built a platform with one long table on it; and to this table do his several helpers – who I conjectured would be employed in mixing colours – brings food and jugs of wine which master Leonardo looks at and re-arranges before he makes a drawing of – and then he bids all eat and drink. And this, the Prior so told me, has been how it was since commencement of the exercise. Master Leonardo showing no interest only for the contents of his table and still yet none for the persons seated at it. [S22]

And what of the foods on the painted table on the wall? Only bread rolls, mashed turnips, and slices of eels accompanied by empty wine glasses and jugs.

The gestation of Leonardo's *Last Supper* began in 1480 in Florence with his drawings of Jesus with one hand over his heart and his head leaning away to one side. As first conceived in Florence, the word **'betrayal'** reverberates throughout the Milan painting. In Florence, the theme was the deadly papal plot to murder the de' Medici brothers, whereas in Milan it is the murder of Gian Galeazzo Sforza. Although the underlying theme is betrayal by murder, the painting at the Santa Maria delle Grazie is obviously one of resignation to destiny: '*One of you will betray me.*' Ludovico's culpability in the death of Gian (John) is simply portrayed by the dark, swarthy, almost black features of the bearded Judas seated to the right of Jesus (does Jesus represent Leonardo?) and the young, blond, and innocent Gian (John) Galeazzo Sforza characterised as the Apostle John dressed in greenish blue and red looking away, but reaching out and almost intimately touching Jesus's (Leonardo's?) right arm. Ludovico as Judas is coveting and reaching out for Gian's bread roll. In between Gian and Ludovico is Francesco Maria Sforza the 4th duke of Milan, father of Ludovico and grandfather of Gian. The *Last Supper* is a clear political statement for those who can read the codes and symbols. Many of the Apostles are dressed in green, red, and gold, the heraldic colours of Gian Galeazzo Sforza the 6th Duke of Milan. Others are in blue and brown, the heraldic colour of Ludovico Sforza the Governor of Milan.

Leonardo's use of perspective is genius in the way he used it to deflect our attention away from the cowering, shadowy Judas (Ludovico Il Moro Sforza) to the more upright, taller, and brighter figures to his left and to the right of Jesus. The vanishing point takes our attention first to the central figure of Jesus, and then, the brighter white wall directs us to the questioning and disturbed group of Apostles seated to the left of Jesus who turns his head and leans a little towards them. Then, our gaze eventually turns away from them and towards the other two groups of Apostles to the right of Jesus, first to the three standing figures at the very end of the table before we follow their gaze and the horizontal hands pointing back towards Gian (who looks away from Jesus) and the central figure of Jesus. We almost totally overlook Judas whose head and shoulders are at a slightly lower position, below the horizontal, than any of the other figures in the painting. Thus, on first observations, it is difficult to see and immediately connect with Judas who is diminished and half hidden from our minds. Our attention is first drawn to Jesus and the other Apostles. It takes some contemplation and effort for our mind to see and calculate the location of the shadowy Judas and to read the political narrative that this dark, sombre figure provides. Ludovico Sforza would have looked at and studied the painting many times because he dined at the refectory with the apostles and monks twice a week, and undoubtedly, he would have attempted to decipher Leonardo's codes and symbols.

Fig. 48. The Last Supper *by Leonardo da Vinci at the monastery of Santa Maria delle Grazie.*

Yet, it was impossible for Ludovico Sforza in his situation at that time to accuse Leonardo of painting a seditious attack against him, against his very royal person the Duke of Milan as invested to him by none other than his Caesarean Majesty Maximilian, Emperor-elect and Chief of the Holy Roman Empire. After all, Jesus's betrayal by Judas is one of the foundation blocks of the Church, and any accusation by Ludovico that Leonardo's painting was a seditious attack against him would have been derided and interpreted as the paranoia of a deluded Duke who had lost his mind and ability to properly guide Milan in a rational manner. Instead, according to many of Leonardo's followers, Ludovico hired his Dominican agents at the Church to slowly and secretly destroy the painting by having them regularly wash the egg tempera painting with abrasives and solutions in the hope that it would degrade the undercoat and make it appear as if natural degradation had occurred due to poor preparation of the wall (coated and sealed with plant resins) by Leonardo's assistants. This destructive work by Ludovico's agents was so effective that a few years after Leonardo completed the painting, the degradation and the damage was visible for all to see. The French king Louis XII when he first saw it in 1499, said, 'it looks very old.' Because of this rapid deterioration to his painting at the monastery in Milan, Leonardo secretly re-painted the *Last Supper* onto canvas with my and others' assistance (Fig. 132) when he was in Rome in the years 1513 to 1516. In his Rome version, Leonardo introduced the sacrificial lamb as his central theme and as a symbol of Gian's demise, the sacrificial lamb served up on an oval platter and placed before Jesus (Leonardo da Vinci) and Judas (Ludovico Moro Sforza). By then, Ludovico Sforza was dead and no longer a threat to Leonardo or to anybody else.

Fig. 49. Leonardo's sketch of the Last Supper *of Gian Galeazzo Sforza, the sixth duke of Milan.*

In early 1516, the same year that Leonardo da Vinci and I left for Amboise in France, Salai and I arranged on behalf of Isabella Sforza Aragon the Duchess of Bari to commission the painter Nicola Mangone of Caravaggio to paint a cycle of frescoes at the church of Saint Maria Annunziata of Abbiategrasso in remembrance of her deceased husband the young duke Gian Galeazzo Sforza who had been born in Abbiategrasso on the banks of the Naviglio Grande. Among the subjects chosen for the walls and vault of the refectory was the subject of the *Last Supper* in the style of Leonardo's depiction of Gian Galeazzo. If you visit the church, you will see the painted figure of Gian Galeazzo dressed in green and red seated with his eyes closed and his head resting on the shoulder of Jesus (Leonardo) with the plate of a decapitated lamb before them. The dark, swarthy face of Judas (Ludovico) turns away from them and directly stares out at us, daring us to think, '*and so, Ludovico, you are the dark betrayer of goodness, wisdom, and light.*' Thus, Nicola Magone of Caravaggio well understood Leonardo da Vinci's narrative of Ludovico the betrayer when painting his version of the *Last Supper*. He completed his fresco in 1519, the year that Leonardo da Vinci died in Amboise in France. To commemorate Leonardo, he painted with Salai's assistance the distinctive tangles and knots of Leonardo da Vinci's geometric patterns into the sockets of the south wall of the church.

The painter Nicola Mangone of Caravaggio had looked at and modified a drawing of the *Last Supper* by Leonardo. In this drawing by Leonardo, you can see Gian Galeazzo Sforza the young duke of Milan, his head and chest slumped forward on the table as if he was dead after having being poisoned by his uncle Ludovico Sforza who sits on a stool in front of him coveting the dukedom. The others stand about the table confused by what has happened.

Leonardo's Academia and the *Divine Proportion* by Luca Pacioli

In 1490, when Leonardo and Bramante travelled to Pavia together to inspect the Duomo, a small debating group of teachers and professors was formed at the university around Leonardo's lectures on art, music, architecture, and perception. The young Duke Gian, when he heard about this assembly of disputations from Leonardo for the first time, told him that he wanted to sponsor similar events two or three times a year with him and/or Ludovico in attendance. Thus, this gathering of artists, poets, architects, and musicians became know as *Academia Leonardo* with Leonardo acting as their chairman. This organisation gradually grew with the added involvement of writers, poets, artists, musicians, architects, engineers, and mathematicians and the sponsorship of other nobles including Galeazzo Sanseverino who became one of their most enthusiastic members. Those among the list of Milan's better known academicians of good standing were the court poet Gaspare Visconti, Antonio Fileremo Fregosa, Bernardo Bellincioni, Cornellio Balbo, Ambrosio Archinto, Bernardo Aretino, Donato Bramante, Cristoforo Foppa (known as Caradosso), and musicians Gaspare Werbecke, Janes da Legi, Pietro da Legi, and Antonio Pagano Perino, among many others. Some of the debates centred about one group's passion for Petrarch (supported by Visconti and Sanseverino) and another group's preference for Dante (supported by Bramante, Leonardo, Bellincioni, and other Florentines).

At one of the debates held at the Castello in Milan in the presence of Galeazzo Sanseverino and his father-in-law Ludovico, Leonardo presented a dispute about divine numbers and the falsehood of contemporary astrology informing the gathering that many of his own mathematical ideas had stemmed from those of the Franciscan friar Luca Pacioli who had published a book on mathematics for Venetian school boys. Luca Pacioli also invented and published double-entry bookkeeping for accounting and business, that is, assets equal liabilities and equity. Galeazzo Sanseverino decided then and there that he and Ludovico should invite this Grey Friar to Milan so that he could teach them and others about accounting, mathematics, and the divine proportions. Moreover, they wanted this friar to write a book on the subject and have Leonardo illustrate the various geometric shapes. And so it was that Luca Pacioli arrived in Milan in 1497 at the invitation of Galeazzo Sanseverino and the duke of Milan Ludovico Sforza, and he stayed there until he and Leonardo left Milan together in 1499.

When Luca Pacioli was in Milan, he attended a number of debates and discussions of the *Academia Leonardo* and marvelled at Leonardo's prints of the interwoven knots advertising his meetings. In the introductory chapter of his book *De Divina Proportione*, Luca Pacioli alludes to one such meeting saying that he attended a praiseworthy and scientific duel that took place in February 1498 at the Castello Sforza with some of the city's most important scholars, theologians, and astrologers in attendance. This debate or disputation became known as '*duello scientifico*'. It included, among many others of Ludovico's courtly entourage, Ambrogio Varesi da Rosate, Gabriele Pirovano, Nicolo Cusano, and Aloiso Marliani who were the four physicians who were constantly at the bedside of Ludovico's nephew Gian Galeazzo Maria Sforza the young Duke of Milan until his death at the end of 1494. Varesi and Pirovano were also the Duke's 'celestial' astrologers and astronomers who considered themselves superior to scholars like Pacioli because they believed that they could use mathematics to decode the future. Yet, Pacioli as he alluded to it in his *De Divina Proportione* considered the likes of Varesi and Pirovano as tainted mathematicians who relied too much on outmoded and often incorrect data of the ancients such as Ptolomy, Albumasar, and others, and consequently, too often made inaccurate and damaging predictions. One of the disputations that Pacioli had with the limited astrological mathematicians was that mathematics was superior to all other arts and sciences and that the art of science should hinge upon the *Quadrivium*, that is, *Arithmetica* and *Geometria*, *Astronomia*, *Musica*, and *Perspectiva*. Leonardo supported his friend's arguments and further argued that,

> No human investigation may claim to be a true science, if it does not pass through mathematical demonstrations; and if you would say that those sciences, which begin and end in the mind possess truth, this is not conceded, but denied for many reasons. The

foremost reason is that such mental discourses do not involve experience, and nothing renders certainty of itself without experience.

Leonardo preached that painting being based on the prime principles of mathematics and geometry is a *scientia* (science) and therefore superior to other art forms such as poetry, which in agreement with Luca, he criticised to be, *'vague fables and other ridiculous and false facetie and also phony and incredible poetical inventions that are just hazy concepts that please the ear.'* Both Leonardo and Luca were treading on shaky ground for they were openly claiming that painting was part of pure science (vision and experience) like mathematics and therefore superior to astrology and poetry that were imprecise and phoney, but on which the Duke of Milan Ludovico Sforza had come to rely on far too much in his private, political, and social decisions. Their argument for mathematics and reason was viewed with outrage by some of Leonardo's critics at the Sforza court.

This debating dual or *duello scientifico* about the superiority of painting over poetry mainly between Leonardo and the poets of the court of Ludovico became legendary in the Italian and continental artistic circles and cemented Leonardo's reputation as a skilled and persuasive orator and debater, something that had been long held among his colleagues of the *Academia Leonardo*. It also cemented Leonardo as the Master Entertainer for he provided great drama, logic, passion, and emotion at these disputations and debates. Moreover, this debating dual that Luca Pacioli had witnessed and participated in led Leonardo to write and publish (posthumously) his book about the sciences and the arts that he entitled *Paragone*. Both his debating duals and his book were different forms of the same argument that painting was a science and that the eye was the prince among the senses that therefore privileged painting over all the other arts. His rhetoric, dialectic, and scholastic argumentation incorporated his interest and expertise in anatomy of the brain, perspective, optics, psychology, and his own experience and mastery in the arts and sciences. Leonardo argued that painting follows the principles of natural philosophy and that anybody who dismisses painting as a lesser art than any other therefore scorns natural philosophy and Nature. To know more about Leonardo's thoughts about the arts, science, medicine, philosophy, painting, sculpture, music, and poetry, I recommend my reader to access and read a copy of *Paragone*, the book of Leonardo's that I helped to compile, edit, and first publish in summary form in 1542, twenty-three years after his death and ninety years after his birth. By the time I had published this book, Leonardo's method of disputation was becoming the norm of scientific and academic teaching methods.

Stringing Knots

How long and straight is a piece of string? According to Leonardo's string theory, matter and the universe can be envisaged as solitary or multiple pieces of open and closed string, intertwined, interconnected, and attached at particular points or nodes of overlap. Thus, his drawings of elaborate knots became the symbols of his debating society that covered a wide range of subjects and included a wide variety of artists, poets, scientists, politicians, and musicians. These drawings, like his debates, were encompassed together with one end (birth) and the other end (death) of the looping, knotted circle joined together within an ever changing (infinite) circular field. Leonardo could see a variety of pathways, dimensions, and communities in his elaborate tying together of knots. This idea was seen not only as an elaborate decoration for his society, but also as a radical view of cosmology, phenomenology, nature, and landscapes. Since it was debated as a novelty and an amusement, it was rarely viewed as sacrilege by the church. It was seen more as mathematical phenomenology than as a philosophy. What fascinated Leonardo about his circular constructs was, (1) the mirror symmetry he saw wherever he chose to section objects along their diameter through the centre of the circle, and (2) whether he could construct algebraic formulas to solve the meaning of these symmetries in terms of duality and the relationship between these different geometric objects.

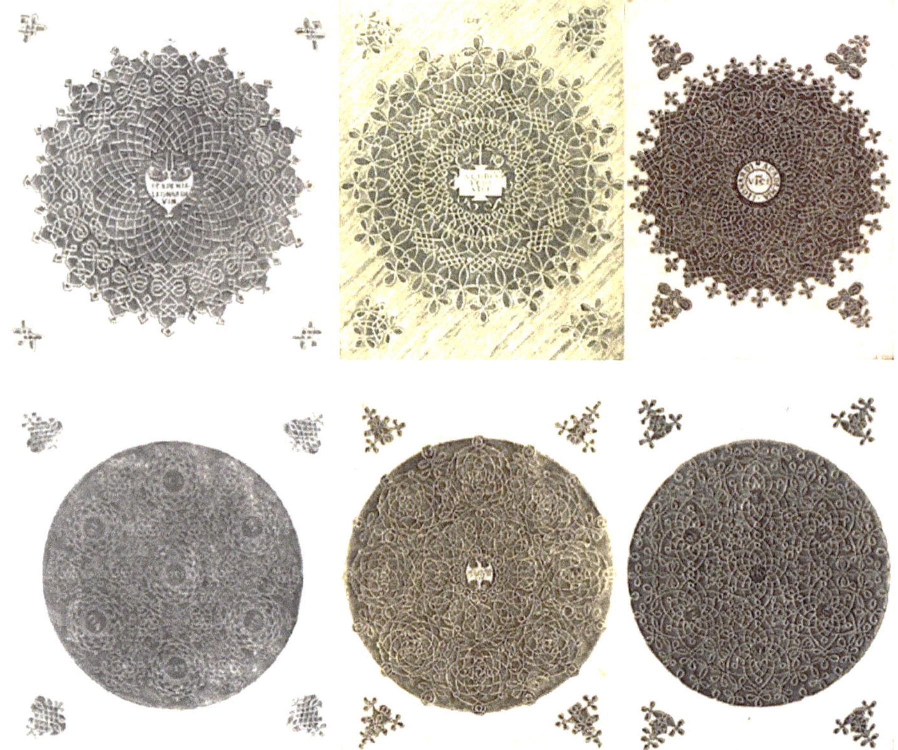

Fig. 50. Leonardo's Fantasia, *the published knot images.*

Here, I show you six of Leonardo's elaborate knots known as Leonardo's *'Fantasia'* that he used to advertise his Academia, and I must let you consider them and decide for yourselves on their meaning. He had them engraved on copperplates and printed on linen or paper and hung as banners when the debates were in progress.

The Completion of the *Divine Proportion* by Luca Pacioli, 1498

Initially, Luca Pacioli produced three illuminated presentation copies of his *De Divina Proportione* in folio size before the end of 1498. He dedicated and provided one copy to Ludovico Sforza Duke of Milan and provided another copy to Galeazzo Sanseverino condottiere of Ludovico's army and 'second to none in military prowess and a keen imitator of our own disciplines.' Leonardo who added sixty geometric figures to each of these gift copies received the third copy. In his later edition of 1509, Luca Pacioli wrote by way of an introduction,

> A work necessary for all clear-sighted and inquiring human minds, in which everybody
> who loves to study philosophy, perspective, painting, sculpture, architecture, music, and
> other mathematical disciplines will find very delicate, subtle, and admirable teaching and
> will delight in diverse questions touching on a very secret science.

A dedication in the first chapter included a few pages praising Leonardo's skill as a sculptor and painter referring especially to his equestrian monument to Francesco Sforza and his two

204

frescoes at Santa Maria della Grazie including that of the finished *Last Supper* on the refectory wall. It is interesting that of the few Sforza court figures mentioned in the dedication chapter, Pacioli also includes the names of the four physicians/astrologers who were constantly at the bedside of Ludovico's nephew Gian Galeazzo Maria Sforza the young Duke of Milan when he died suspiciously in October of 1494. It is intriguing that Leonardo suspected that all four of them colluded to poison the young duke. In fact, Leonardo had evidence that Gian Galeazzo Sforza was poisoned by arsenic. He had conducted alchemy tests on samples of Gian Galeazzo Sforza's hair and tissues and found that these tissues contained deadly amounts of arsenic, whereas those of negative controls had not. Arsenic mixed with a solution of copper salts at the boil turn into a green precipitate. Leonardo also strongly suspected that Galeazzo Sanseverino was complicit in the plot to murder Gian Galeazzo Sforza. He revealed his suspicions in an amazing portrait of Luca Pacioli and Galeazzo Sanseverino who sponsored Pacioli's the *De Divina Proportione*.

The Portrait of Luca Pacioli and Galeazzo Sanseverino among the *Geometric Elements* and Coded Messages

In the painting by Giovanni Antonio Boltraffio and Leonardo of the *Geometric Elements*, Friar Luca Pacioli looks out into the middle distance oblivious to our presence or to the person beside him. Galeazzo Sanseverino looms menacingly at the side of Luca, staring at us directly, daringly, guiltily, and conspiratorially with a block of yellow and black arsenic ore slipping out of his sleeve below his left elbow onto the red (spilt blood) 'family tomb' of Gian Galeazzo Sforza that has a large block of a dodecahedron solid on it. The dodecahedron has 12 flat faces each composed of pentagons (5 edges), 30 edges and 20 vertices. It is pentagonal both inside and out. The dodecahedron has many fascinating properties, but here as a composite of pentagons, we can see that it possibly represents Galeazzo Maria Sforza (the murdered 5th Duke of Milan) who is the brother of Ludovico Sforza (the usurper and the 7th Duke of Milan) and the father of Gian Galeazzo Sforza (the murdered 6th Duke of Milan). The dodecahedron like the murders of the two dukes weighs down heavily on the Sforza family tomb, for the assassination of Galeazzo Sforza at Christmas time in 1476 and the elimination of Gian Galeazzo Sforza in October of 1494 finally led to the reign of Ludovico Sforza as the 7th Duke of Milan in 1495.

A remarkable thing about Leonardo's geometric elements in the painting is that he shows his underlying interest in the transformation of rectilinear shapes. Only he and Luca knew that he had used three-dimensional geometry to transform a dodecahedron into a cube by using four clear and easy steps. First, he cut the dodecahedron into 12 equal pyramids with pentagons at their base. Next, he cut each of the 12 pyramids into five smaller pyramids with triangular bases to produce 60 pyramids of equal size. Then, the triangular base of each pyramid was used to form a rectangle of equal area. Finally, he stacked the 30 rectangular pyramids into a cube that had the same volume of the dodecahedron. Then, he reversed the process by starting with a cube and ending with a dodecahedron. In this way, Leonardo had transformed one body shape into another body shape without either diminution or increase of matter, and he demonstrated the principle of conservation of mass and/or volume. The cube, rectangle, triangular base, pentagonal base, dodecahedron, and pyramid are all shown in the painting of his geometric elements that depicts the theme of transformation of forms.

Apparently, Galeazzo Sanseverino and Gian Galeazzo Sforza looked alike in some portraits, and a few people who I know who have seen this painting of geometric forms have mistakenly thought it is Gian Galeazzo Sforza and not Galeazzo Sanseverino who stands with Luca Pacioli. However, Leonardo presents Galeazzo Sanseverino with his red and white dynasty colours on his shirt and sleeves, and so we know who he is.

In 1496, while working with Luca Pacioli on his book *De Divina Proportione*, Leonardo began to paint a portrait of the two men standing beside an image of a hanging rhombicuboctahedron, a distorted polyhedron half–filled with liquid. Here, Leonardo had some fun showing off the complexity of geometry using the symbols of spheres and polyhedrons. Luca Pacioli points to the Euclidian sphere, the flat circle, and the triangles contained within it. Euclidian geometry is simple, spherical, flat, and old school. The polyhedron hanging from the ceiling represents distortion and non-Euclidian geometry, a complex and three-dimensional shape holding together both the elements of air and water. Leonardo espoused the view that unity, whether social, spiritual, material or otherwise was more like a polyhedron than a sphere in that it lacks the simple and beautiful harmony and proportions of a sphere, but still retains the unity of a solid in its multifaceted complexity. While the sphere is homogenous, uniform, smooth, and equal in all its parts, the polyhedron consists of multiple forms, is multifaceted with flat faces, straight edges, sharp vertices, and has variable distances emanating from its centre that provide overall a complex unity within its diversity.

However, the hanging rhombicuboctahedron is more than just non-Euclidian geometry. It contains within it the elements of air and water. The essence of Gian Galeazzo Sforza's character is represented by air that lies on top of the water, but permeates through it. Gian was characterised by Ludovico's astrologers with the numbers three (triangle) and four (square), associated with the third house Gemini and the air sign, and he was viewed to be a weakling who would disassociate like water. Later, the Ludovico propagandists dismissed Gian Galeazzo Sforza as a weak-willed, retard, not fit to rule the Duchy of Milan. Leonardo saw him as a gentle lamb and a caring and thoughtful person who would have been a wise and just ruler.

Within the refractions of the three fragments seen on the upper and lower parts of the rhombicuboctahedron, you can see the images of Gian's three favourite castles located in Milan, Abbiategrasso, and Pavia. They are reflected or refracted in the air and the water. In 1494, Gian was coming of age at twenty-five years, and he was ready by law to take over the Duchy of Milan from his uncle and guardian Ludovico and to rule Milan and its dominions in his own right. According to Leonardo, he was ready, but according to his guardian Ludovico, he was not.

In this portrait, Leonardo has also added a piece of mouldy yellow paper with a black fly and the following encryption:

IACO.B AR.VIGEN / NIS.P.149?

The black fly or a black figure (IL Moro) with arms outstretched above his head distorts the last number so that it is not clear if it is a 6, 5 or 4. What does this code tell us? Try to decipher this code for yourself before I explain some of it for you.

A Platonic dodecahedron with 12 regular pentagonal faces lies on top of a red book that is Luca Pacioli's mathematical textbook as identified by the inscription *LI.R.LUC.BVR* that can be translated as *Liber Reverend Lucia Burgensis*. An alternative interpretation is that it is a red (bloodied) box (*R.LVC/BVR*) holding the secrets of the Sforza court where the letters *BVR* refer to the Latin technical term for a 'family grave' or 'family tomb'.

The black fly on the yellow notepaper beside the red (bloodied) box is a reference to Ludovico IL Moro Sforza the 7th Duke of Milan to whom the author Luca Pacioli dedicated his mathematics book *De Divina Proportione*. Indeed, the black fly is the black prince IL Moro - Ludovico Sforza, the lord of the flies, symbolic of sinister corruption, decay, evil, and death; suspected of killing his nephew Gian Galeazzo the 6th Duke of Milan and usurping his throne. IL Moro was characterised by astrologers with the number five (pentagon), associated with the fifth house Mars (Leo) and the fire sign; an extrovert, impatient, unreliable, adventurous, eclectic, charismatic, and competitive. He is portrayed by the black background, and the solid dodecahedron on top of the red and brown box, and by his son-in-law Galeazzo Sanseverino dressed in red and blackish blue – the symbols of war - blood, fire, and ash.

Fig. 51. Portrait of Fra Luca Pacioli and Galeazzo Sanseverino by Giovanni Antonio Boltraffio and Leonardo da Vinci.

Fig. 52. Detail of the black fly and the cryptogram in the painting of Luca Pacioli and the geometric shapes.

With this clearly in mind, let me now decode the following cryptogram for you: [S23]

IACO.B AR. VIGEN
NIS. P. 149?

I…Illustrious *A*…ugusto *CO*…regent (Illustrious lieutenant and guardian (regent)), Duke of *BAR*i, born in *VIGE*vaNo (and killer of the *VI*th duke *GEN* (Gian Sforza) / *NIS* (killed by the uncle), killed in *P*avia, *149* (the number after the 9 is either a 4 or a 5 that has been slightly smudged or made slightly ineligible by the black figure of the fly below *VIGEN*). This is a clear coded message to those who suspected that Ludovico Sforza IL Moro murdered Gian Galeazzo Sforza 6th Duke of Milan.

Leonardo loved to play with the double meaning of words and codes. Here are another three interpretations of *IACO.B AR. VIGEN*:

(1) *IACO* is *ICAEO* ('Here I am lying ill' or 'here I am dying'). The green table reveals that the *'I'* is Gian Galeazzo Sforza for green was his official colour. He is often depicted wearing green in his portraits and in the Sforza *Book of Hours*, whereas Ludovico is often symbolised by black, blue or brown figures (eg., black background of the painting, Sanseverino's blackish blue coat). The fullstop (.) is his termination, he is finished or killed at the age of 25, killed by the Duke of *BAR*i from Vigevano (*VIGEN*). *NIS*, 'ended' like a boiled or barbecued 'pink-speckled shrimp'. *P* is *Perdidit* (destroyed). *149*4

(2) Il Moro (the **black fly**) is the Duke of Bari (*B AR*) who poisoned his nephew Gian (*GEN*) the 6th (*VI*) duke of Milan and consequently was invested as the 7th Duke of Milan in **1495**.

(3) These sinister meanings were hidden from the vindictive Ludovico who was told that *IACO.BAR.VIGEN* / *NIS.P.149?*, essentially refers to *Illustrious Augusto Coregent*, that is, *BAR*i, *VIGE*vaNo/ followed by *NIS* = born, and *P.* = Pacioli or Painting, commissioned in *1496*. *NIS* also = *Nominatio Imperialis Sfortiae*. In other words, this **P**icture of **P**acioli was commissioned (*Nominatio Imperialis Sfortiae*) in 1496 by Ludovico Moro Sforza, the Illustrious August Regent Duke of Bari who was born Lord of Vigevano.

The menacing looking compass on the green table points to the yellow paper with the secret code (cartouche) that uncle Il Moro killed his nephew Gian. The figure of Galeazzo Sanseverino dressed in blackish blue and red shows him to be a follower of Il Moro (black) with blood (red) on his person, complicit in the 1494 October murder of Gian Galeazzo Sforza now entombed in the red 'family grave' (1494/5/6). Therefore, the shape of the 4, 5 or 6 in 1494/5/6 on the cartouche is purposely ambiguous. The 6 is assumed to be the correct number because 1496 was the year when Ludovico Sforza and Galeazzo Sanseverino first commissioned Luca Pacioli while he was still in Venice. The number 5 is assumed to be correct because it lies beside the polyhedron with the pentagons, and for Luca Pacioli the number 5 was divine because Nature is composed of five elements (earth, water, air, fire, and ether) chosen by God and sufficient to account for all of creation. The year 1495 was also the emblematic year for the investiture of the Moro as Duke of Milan by the Holy Roman Emperor Maximilian who visited Lombardy as the guest of Ludovico so soon after Gian Galeazzo Sforza's death. But, the 4 in 1494 reveals the year that Gian Galeazzo died (October 21) and was entombed when Ludovico immediately inherited the dukedom by acclamation of his ruling council to become the new Duke of Milan, now forever independent of his nephew Gian. Moreover, the 4 for 1494 also stems from the left of the picture with Euclid's 4-sided rectangle (or Gian Galeazzo's tomb) to which Luca Pacioli is pointing with his right hand, and the obvious four-sided squares contained with the rhombicuboctahedron hanging next to him. The year 1494 also was when Luca Pacioli published his book *Summa Mathematica*. Thus, Leonardo intended the 4, 5, and 6 to represent a kind of ambiguous chronological transition from 1494 into 1496. Leonardo saw the transition of 1494 to 1495 as a political and social transformation and a 'desecration of the sacred' at the hands of a dirty black fly, the Prince of

Darkness, yes, Judas - who was no other than his Highness, the Illustrious Ludovico Moro Sforza, the seventh duke of Milan.

The green table from the left side to the right side of the picture as we look at it is a time scale of Gian Galeazzo Sforza's life from 1494 to 1495 from when he was first administered poison (arsenic) until his death in 1494, his entombment (the red box) in 1495, and his permanent removal from the records of Milan in 1496. The correct alchemic mixture of copper and arsenic can produce a green precipitate, the colour of the dyed tablecloth. The black background above the green table is the lingering and oppressive spirit of Ludovico IL Moro, himself pressing down on Gian Galeazzo Sforza's life and erasing it from his presence. Usually, Leonardo liked to add light and airy backgrounds with rocks, mountains, rivers, lakes, and a bluish sky. In this case, however, the background of the painting is black and menacingly sombre.

Across the green bench (Gian Galeazzo Sforza's body) from left to right in the foreground: an eraser (lump of arsenic ore), a set square (planning), a black pencil case lying on top of the green bench (the black Ludovico again pressing down on top of the green Gian as his ruler and murderer), black inkwell hanging (the signing of Gian's death warrant), the compass pointing to the yellow paper with the coded message beside the red book that is the *Somma* published in 1494 (the tomb of Gian Galeazzo Sforza). Galeazzo Sanseverino stands above the compass, the yellowed paper message, and the red book with his hand in a green glove (arsenic and Gian's heraldic colour) showing that he was complicit in the murder of the Illustrious 'Green' Duke Gian Galeazzo Sforza.

Also, we should remember that Gian Galeazzo Sforza with his long blond hair and his light green breast armour was light and airy in physical appearance like the hanging rhombicuboctahedron, whereas his uncle Ludovico Moro Sforza with his black hair and dark skin or as often seen in his brown or dark-blue breast armour was dark and solid like the dodecahedron. Once you know all this, there is complete clarity in the interpretations and attributions whichever way you look at the picture.

What of the letters *R.LUC / BUR* on Luca P's red book? Could it have meanings other than Luca Pacioli's ownership? R = regicide, *LUC* = light, *BUR* = imprisoned? And what of the colours black, green, red, and dirty yellows? Is the dark one (Moro the black fly) imprisoning and killing the light (his nephew) and burying him in the family tomb? There are other symbols and codes to decipher in this amazingly historic picture, but I leave them for you to find and solve.

My father served Ludovico faithfully, and he says that he knew nothing of Gian's murder. Of course, he like others heard the rumours in the courts, cities, and other lands, but he thought of them as unjustified gossip, and he ignored them because he believed that Ludovico did not have the vile heart to murder his nephew. Instead, he believed that the young duke had died of ill health contracted naturally as a consequence of his weak constitution. Leonardo never told my father about his findings, and I only found out about the arsenic from the Duchess Isabella when Leonardo, Salai, and I visited her in Bari, three or four years before her daughter Bona left for Poland to marry the old King Sigmund I.

Leonardo's Allegorical and Political Drawing of the Dark Beast of Milan

Leonardo did not agree with my father about Ludovico's innocence in the demise of Gian Galeazzo. In 1496, after the official investiture of Ludovico as the Duke of Milan by Emperor Maximilian, he presented my father with a red chalk drawing of the beast of Milan sailing his boat of state towards the kingdoms of France and Germany. This allegory of Ludovico sailing up river to sell his Duchy to foreign powers at the expense of Gian Galeazzo and his son Francesco the rightful heir to the Duchy of Milan shows a sailboat on Lake Como with a beast at the tiller in the stern sitting with his right paw on a compass guiding the boat along the Adda River past the Swiss Alps and straight towards a crowned eagle that is perched on a globe on the shore of an European Empire. The mast is the mulberry tree of Ludovico, the two shoots on either side of the tree are his two sons who he hopes will grow up to inherit his Ship of State. The rocky background from which the boat leaves is Italy and the Duchy of Milan. The beast is the symbol of gluttony, rapaciousness, and corruption who has betrayed the army of Charles VIII of France for whom he had previously given access through the Duchy of Milan to allow the French king to claim the throne of Naples. Now, having betrayed the French king and many of his previous allies, the beast is dependent entirely on the support of the Holy Roman Emperor Maximilian I. Where will this lead to?

Fig. 53. Leonardo's cartoon of a beast sailing his ship of state towards a crowned eagle perched on a globe on the shore of his Empire.

CHAPTER 14

Colours and Symbols of the Sforza Books of Prayer. A Prelude to the End of Milan's Ruling Dynasty

I obey Thee Lord, first for the love I ought, in all reason to bear Thee; secondly for that Thou canst shorten or prolong the lives of men.

— Leonardo da Vinci

Sforziada, the Sforza Books of Prayer [S24]

The colour palette that Leonardo chose to tell his story about Ludovico and Gian Galeazzo Sforza in his amazingly symbolic painting of Luca Pacioli and Galeazzo Sanseverino is best illustrated in the Sforziada Book of Prayers commissioned separately by Ludovico Sforza, Bona of Savoy, and her sister-in-law Isabella of Aragon where you can clearly see Ludovico's colours of dark blue, red, brown, and black and Gian's colours of green, red, and gold.

After the 1476 assassination of Galeazzo Maria Sforza the 5th Duke of Milan, his widowed wife Bona of Savoy and the Dowager Duchess of Milan commissioned Giovanni Simonetta to write the history of the Francesco Sforza legacy for her children, especially for her son Gian. Giovanni Simonetta was the brother of Francesco Cico Simonetta who Bona had appointed as the Governor of Milan. Ludovico Sforza in his coup of 1480 falsely imprisoned Giovanni Simonetta and had his brother Francesco beheaded for treason. Nevertheless, Ludovico pardoned Giovanni Simonetta who had completed the commission to write the history and achievements of Francesco Sforza the first Sforza duke of Milan. Ludovico and Bona commissioned the court artist Giovan Pietro Birago to illustrate their book covers and the interior with devotional images. The Sforza Books of Prayer were meant to be a remembrance of the great Sforza deeds and to be used daily as devotional prayer books, and therefore, they were sometimes called the *Book of Hours*. They were small in size for easy transportation and consisted of 500 or more pages of text and illustrations referring to Gospel extracts, Hours of the Virgin, Prayers to the Virgin, Memorials of the Saints, Penitential Psalms, Office of the Dead, the Hours of the Holy Spirit, the Passion Cycle According to St. Luke, and an illustrated liturgical calendar. Giovanni Simonetti wrote the Latin text before 1480, and he had Leonardo's friend Christophoro Landino translate it into Florentine Italian in the 1480s. Soon after, Bona of Savoy was exiled from Milan and dispatched to live in the Duchy of Savoy. Ludovico received the first books of prayer written in Latin, and these featured him on the cover and became known as Ludovico Moro's Sforziada.

Bona was permitted to return to Milan in 1488 to help with the preparation of her son's wedding to Isabella Aragon Princess of Naples. She quickly set about commissioning writers and the artist Giovan Pietro Birago to produce a version of the Book of Sforza Prayers in honour of her son Gian Galeazzo Sforza the 6th Duke of Milan. Antonio Zarotto printed a number of copies on vellum in 1490, and these became known as Gian Galeazzo's Sforziada *Book of Hours*. Bona of Savoy received six copies of the Sforziada illustrated by Giovan Pietro Birago. She kept one copy for herself and presented a dedicated copy each to her son Gian and daughters Bianca and Anna, and a copy each to her brother-in-laws Ludovico and Cardinal Ascanio Maria Sforza.

In 1496, Bona of Savoy finally left Milan forever, and she died in misery and near poverty on 23rd November 1503 at the castle of Fossano, a small town in the province of Cuneo between Turin and Nice; a very sad and unfortunate end to the life of the Duchess Consort of Milan who was the sister-in-law of French King Louis XI, the proud and loving wife of the Milanese Duke Galeazzo Maria Sforza, and the loving mother of Gian Galeazzo, Hermes Maria, Bianca Maria, and Anna Maria. Bona died nine years after the death of her son Gian Galeazzo the 6th duke of Milan, at a time when Louis XII was the ruling king of France and the duke of Milan, and Ludovico Sforza was a prisoner of the French. Leonardo da Vinci told me that he liked and admired Bona greatly as much for her generous heart as for her enormous suffering due to the loss of her son Gian Galeazzo and her daughter Anna, and for her added internal grief that Ludovico Sforza had murdered her son and had got away with it. But, not in the eyes of God. Leonardo would say, justice will be done, and it was.

Fig. 54. Ludovico Moro Sforza's Sforziada Book of Prayers.

Years later, after the death of Gian, Isabella Aragon Sforza commissioned Birago to illustrate her own copy of the Sforziada in memory of her marriage to Gian and her devotion to him and their three children Francesco 'il Duchetto', Bona, and Ippolita Maria Sforza. The original Sforziada books dedicated to Ludovico were eventually taken to France after the French had occupied Milan. These copies ended up in King Francois's royal library in Fontainebleau, whereas Isabella Sforza's book was given to her daughter Bona who took it with her to Poland when she left the Duchy of Bari to marry the old Polish king Sigismund I (1467-1548) in 1518. Moreover, when Bona Sforza was the Polish Queen, she commission her own Sforza Book of Prayers, and she asked me to visit Poland in 1524 to help her miniaturist and decorator Stanislaw Samostrzelnik to illustrate her *Book of Hours* with a few pictorial stories featuring memories of her father Gian and her mother Isabella and her godfather Leonardo da Vinci.

The symbolic colours of Ludovico and Gian are revealed clearly on the covers of the Sforziada books. The colours of Ludovico on his Sforza book cover are deep blues, browns, reds, and blacks. The background colour for his portrait and that of his father Francesco Sforza the 4th Duke (*DUX*) of Milan is dark blue. The side panels are decorated with Sforza and Este symbols. In the right panel, there are two classical bare-breasted sphinxes with the heads and breasts of women and with wings attached to baboon-like bodies. They are bound together supporting the display of a column of Sforza symbols including two Visconti blue serpents that swallow two red human forms while a dwarf holds up Ludovico's royal profile as he admiringly looks across to his father. In the bottom central panel, red-winged putti play mischievously behind Ludovico's new coat-of-arms that is intermixed with the red, white, yellow, and blue of d' Este and Sforza blasons.

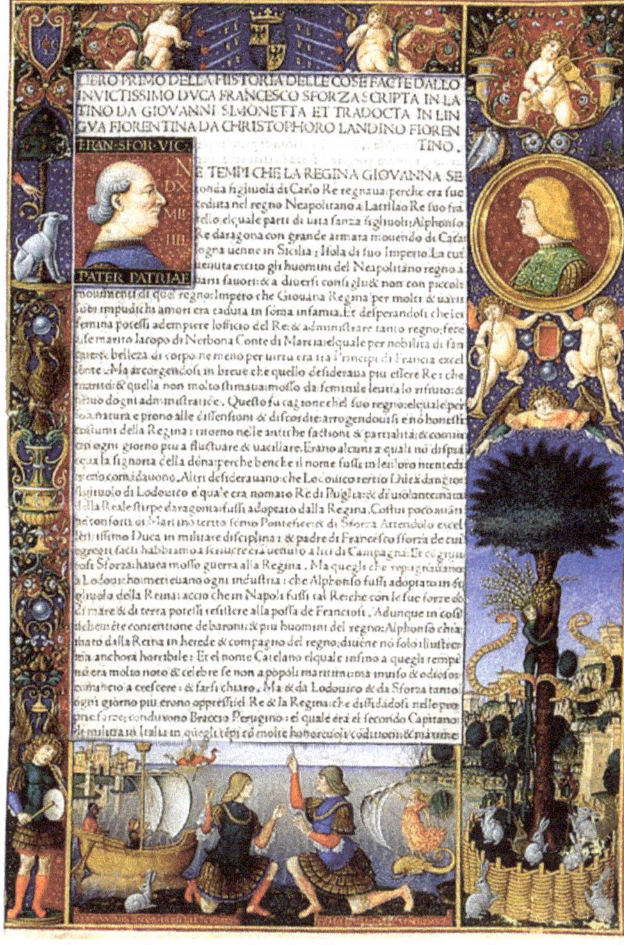

Fig. 55. Gian Galeazzo Sforza's Sforziada Book of Hours.

In stark contrast to the dark blue in Ludovico's Sforziada, Gian's portrait and symbols in his Sforziada Book of Prayers are depicted in green, gold, and red, and there is far less dark blue. He wears his green vest while Francesco and Ludovico wear their blue vests. In the right panel, the green Gian grows out of the soil clinging to his dark brown uncle Moro with the Mulberry tree hairdo. Above them is a portrait of Gian with his beautiful red ruby framed in gold with pearls attached to each of the four midpoints of the perimeter frame. Putti blowing trumpets and playing the violin add musical drama to his portrait. Remember that Leonardo had presented the young duke Gian Galeazzo Sforza with a violin as a gift from his godfather Lorenzo de' Medici and that he was also Gian's musical instructor. Gian loved music, and he was an accomplished musician and an enthusiastic sponsor of court and church choirs, bands, and musical instruments.

In the left panel, we again see Gian the musician beating his drum in time with playing his flute. Above him through the decorations, we come to see his symbol of the unchained dog released from the constraint of the fertile conifer tree. While Gian at the suggestion of Leonardo used the same symbol of the dog and the tree as a previous Visconti duke, he unclasped the collar and unchained the dog. Leonardo told us that dogs are like falcons and need not be chained in captivity. Of course, I am like Gian and all other falcon trainers before and after me who could never completely trust our birds from flying away from us if we ever left them alone, unfed, and unchained. But, while the dog was unchained, the bottom and right panels show that Gian was chained to Ludovico, and his uncle has no intention of ever letting him go. Gian kneels before Ludovico receiving a lecture from him about his grandfather Francesco Sforza. The French king Charles VIII gave Gian Galeazzo Sforza the titles of Genoa as his fief in 1491, and Gian tries to sail away from Genoa against the winds of Fortune, but his uncle Ludovico the Moor is still in charge of the oars. The boat has nowhere to go except back to shore with his uncle in control. We see the letters IOG at the top of the left panel with an L through the heart of the O. The letters IOG are Gian Galeazzo Sforza's initials. The L is Ludovico.

Fig. 56. Isabella Aragon Sforza's Sforziada Book of Hours.

The colours of Isabella's Sforziada, like Gian's (GZ), has more reds and yellows and greens than in Ludovico or Gian's books. She chose the colours red and golden-yellow in the right panel because they are the specific colours of her father and the Neapolitan dynasty of Aragon. Note the adjoining colours of green and red or the green and blue rubies or green, red, and blue in testimony to her husband's position as the 6th Duke of Milan in the footsteps of his father and grandfather. Also, note that her putti are playing musical instruments just as in Gian's book cover.

In the left panel, Gian's various shared ducal symbols rise up from his grandfather's blue vest past his grandfather's portrait (*Dux IIII*) with the blue background until we reach the top panel where the dog and the conifer symbols are serenaded by the putti musicians. One important symbol that is shown in both the right and left panels is the cheesecloth filter being held in both hands. Gian inherited this filter or cheesecloth image from his father and grandfather as a symbol of self-purification. It is their underlying symbol of proper justice and self-rule and avoidance of self-corruption while in their highly privileged position of being the Duke of Milan. Above the cloth, there are two adjoining quivers filled with arrows, the symbols of Gian's favourite saint, St. Sebastian. Ludovico could not use these Milanese symbols at this time because he was Duke of Bari and not the Duke of Milan.

The cheesecloth symbol to strain off the waste and self-corruption that is seen in Isabella's Sforziada is depicted also in other images, such as the one on the covering of Gian's horse as he rides proudly between his father Galeazzo and his uncle Ludovico in a scene that was painted on one side of a Sforza Cassone that was in Isabella's possession.

The bottom panel of Isabella's Sforziada shows political satire at its very best, added with a possible touch of family bitterness and irony at the injustice of Fortuna. This is the scene that Leonardo had helped Birago to create. Isabella and Leonardo knew, as many others did, that Ludovico had killed Gian and usurped his crown with the help of the Sanseverino brothers. Here, in this illustration, we see the crowned Ludovico Moor with his ducal chain of interlocking rings around his neck sitting on top of the stolen throne (the coffin of his nephew Gian Galeazzo Sforza) with blood on his hands (red cloth) while his closest supporters and condottieri, the Sanseverino brothers (Gian Francesco, Antonio Maria, Gaspare, Galeazzo, Federigo and Giulio, red and white were their dynasty colours), and his dark illegitimate daughter Bianca surround him to idolise and protect him with weapons at their side in readiness for more adventures inside and outside of Lombardy. Ludovico's illegitimate daughter Bianca, born to his mistress Bernardina de Corradis, married Galeazzo Sanseverino when she was 7 years old, and she died in childbirth when she was 14 years old in 1496. The fat, black Ludovico, the darkened Bianca, and the Sanseverino brothers stand on top of Gian's green field (they buried him in a green grave of fertile achievements) with blood on their hands just as Leonardo had depicted them in his Fra Luca Pacioli portrait in the *Geometric Elements* (Fig. 51). The artist Giovan Pietro Birago: *PSBR IO. Biragus fecit* signed the front of Isabella's manuscript in 1513 and the bowl in his illustrations at the bottom of the right panel.

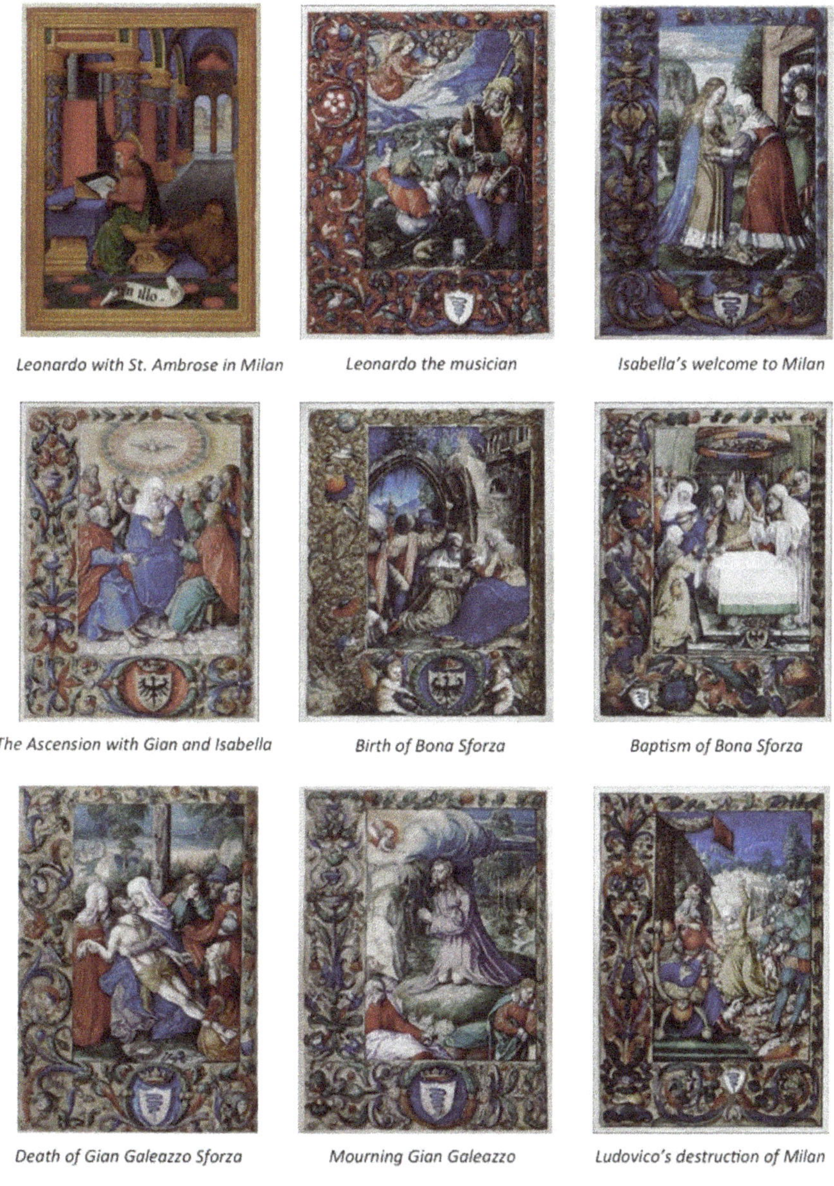

Leonardo with St. Ambrose in Milan — *Leonardo the musician* — *Isabella's welcome to Milan*

The Ascension with Gian and Isabella — *Birth of Bona Sforza* — *Baptism of Bona Sforza*

Death of Gian Galeazzo Sforza — *Mourning Gian Galeazzo* — *Ludovico's destruction of Milan*

Fig. 57. Bona Sforza's Book of Prayers and Remembrances of her father Gian Galeazzo Sforza.

Fig. 58. Leonardo's profile sketch of Bona Sforza (left) and a much later printed woodcarving of her by an unidentified artist as Queen of Poland (right).

The young Bona Sforza inherited Isabella's *Book of Hours* from her mother as a wedding present when she married the Polish king. She showed it to me when I visited her in Masovia in 1549, one year after her husband Sigismund I the King of Poland had died. Their son Sigismund II Augustus had succeeded his father as the new king of Poland. As the Duchess of Bari and the mother of the king of Poland, she greeted me warmly, and we reminisced about her dead mother, sister, and brother and her childhood memories of Milan, which remained vivid to her despite her age. She was only 6 years old when she and her mother left Milan for the Duchy of Bari that they inherited from their nemesis Ludovico Sforza.

As I looked at the miniatures in Bona and Isabella's book, I remembered how I had helped Giovanni Ambrogio de' Predis and Giovan Pietro Birago to engrave and paint miniature landscapes and characters as their part-time apprentice before they died. Leonardo had sent me to their studios to help them with the illustrations, but also to learn drawing, copper engraving, and painting from the two masters of miniature illustration and illumination. I also helped the illustrator Stanislaw Samostrzelnik to decorate his Polish Queen's Sforza *Book of Hours* with narrative miniatures and devotional images of her mother Isabella, her father Gian, and her godfather Leonardo da Vinci in some of the illustrations (Fig. 57).

CHAPTER 15

Leonardo's Liaison with Mona Lisa, the Princess Isabella Aragon Sforza, at the Corte Vecchio in Milan

I love those who can smile in trouble, who can gather strength from distress, and grow brave by reflection.
— Leonardo da Vinci

Leonardo's Studios at the Corte Vecchio

When Leonardo was appointed Painter and Engineer of the Sforza court in 1487, Gian the young Duke of Milan permitted him to establish his own studio and workshops (*bottega*) at the Palazzo del Broletto Vecchio in the centre of Milan. The Palazzo is about 1700 steps (1300 metres) from the Sforza castle (Castello Sforzesco), but in closer vicinity (a few hundred steps) to the workshops of the Duomo where Leonardo constructed his wooden model of the cupola for the cathedral and prepared the displays for the wedding between Gian and his cousin Isabella of Naples. The Palazzo is large and spacious, and it was the former seat of government of Milan for more than a hundred years during the period of the medieval communes and fiefdoms. It was also the former residence of the Visconti family when they were the Dukes and rulers of the Duchy of Milan. After the 4th duke of Milan Francesco Sforza moved his court to the Sforza castle, the Palazzo became a residence for various Sforza family relatives, court officials, and ladies-in-waiting who had not yet established their own private residence. The Palazzo consists of a number of three-storied buildings with hundreds of rooms interconnected by corridors and galleries and inner courts and gardens. It is located opposite the Duomo and is known by many different names including the Corte Vecchio, Visconti Palace, Court Verte, Palazzo Reale or the Royal Palace of Milan.

Leonardo's studio at the Corte Vecchio was modelled on the *bottega* in Florence where he had been apprenticed to the renowned Master Painter, Sculptor, and Engineer Andrea del Verrocchio. In replicating the operation of a *bottega*, Leonardo's studio at the Corte Vecchio was where he would prepare the overall design of a painting and theatrical settings through templates and cartoons and allow his assistants to participate by colouring or decorating the simpler aspects of his work either for commercial or for training purposes. Often, his assistants simply would make copies of Leonardo's original prototypes or paintings as exercises or for sale to certain rich clients or as gifts for favours rendered. Occasionally, he allowed them a free hand to do their own drawings and to use their own methods, styles, and techniques. Although the atmosphere at the studio was joyful and energetic with occasional musical performances and innate chatter, Leonardo always expected his assistants to work hard and quietly to their very best standards. He saw his studio as a commercial enterprise, and he wanted it to run with the best commercial practices employing the most innovative and effective techniques, designs, and styles. By 1494, the same year that the young Duke of Milan died, Leonardo had at least seven assistants in his care and many others who were paying him for short visits and living there or at nearby residences with their own finances, brushes, paints, and provisions. His dependants and assistants at this time were Salai, Marco d' Oggiono, Giovanni Antonio Boltraffio, Tommaso Masini (Zoroastro), Giulio the German, Francesco Napoletano, and

Gianpietro, and they were accompanied by frequent visits and help from Bartolomeo Suardi, Bernardino Luini, Andrea Solorio, Ambrogio de' Predis, and Il Sodoma.

Isabella Aragon Sforza Transfers from the Sforza Castle to the Corte Vecchio, 1497

A few months after the death of Ludovico Sforza's wife, the grieving duke decided to move Isabella Aragon Sforza and her children (except for the eldest boy Francesco who remained in his care) out of the Castle Sforza to the Corte Vecchio and to the former rooms of Bona of Savoy who had left to live in France. Ludovico suddenly could not cope having the sad and resentful Isabella about the place to remind him of his loss of Beatrice. When Ludovico dismissed Isabella Aragon Sforza from her rooms at the Sforza Castle and sent her and her two daughters to live in the old and gloomy apartments at the Corte Vecchio beside the Piazza Duomo, she was at first highly indignant and dismayed that he continued to treat her so meanly and disrespectfully. After all, she was the former Duchess of Milan, and she believed that she was as entitled, as much as he was, to live in the royal rooms of the Sforza Castle. Secretly, she still claimed entitlement to the Duchy of Milan believing that her son was the rightful Duke of Milan.

After the death of Isabella's young husband the duke of Milan in Pavia in 1494, his uncle Ludovico transferred her from Pavia to the more secure domicile at his Sforza castle in Milan where he thought that she the widowed Duchess of Milan would be less threatening to him. Here, he kept a firm eye on her activities and her friends while he usurped her son's throne and became the new Duke of Milan. Isabella stayed in deep mourning for a few years while living with Ludovico and his wife Beatrice at the Sforza castle. But then, after the death of Beatrice in January of 1497, Ludovico wanted her out of his immediate sight at Sforza castle while he went through his own grieving process. Away from the scrutinising eye of Ludovico at Corte Vecchio, Isabella soon found a new freedom and slowly began to find her confidence to socialise happily again with various poets and artists who visited her comfortable salon for receptions and discrete entertainments. She was back in society, still young (27 years of age), intelligent, and well loved for being the feisty widow who had accepted her fate as being *'unique in disgrace by her own hand'*.

Apart from Leonardo and his household of painters, there were regular visits to Isabella's salon from poets, artists, musicians, gentlemen, and clergy including Count Baldassare Castiglione, Franchinus Gaffurius, Cardinal Ippolito d' Este, Ariosto, and Bellincioni who had previously attended many of the Beatrice d' Este's receptions before her untimely and tragic death in January of 1497. Now, within a much more subdued and saddened Milan, the nobles enjoyed to gather again at Isabella Aragon Sforza's salon to talk about the arts, literature, politics, and the programs and subjects that were debated at Leonardo da Vinci's Academia. It was a meeting place that was quickly becoming popular for intellectual jousting and the occasional flirting. Most agreed that Leonardo was winning most of the verbal jousts that he participated in, and they enjoyed their time with him at Isabella's salon.

During the light of day, my mother would assist Isabella in the salon to entertain her guests. My mother was of similar age to Isabella, and they both were still great beauties and very pleasing to the eye of the male visitors. Much news and various events of 1497 and 1498 were discussed openly and with enthusiasm or with great sadness such as was the case on hearing the news of the deaths of notables such as the young Anna Sforza who was the wife of Alfonso of Ferrara and sister-in-law of Isabella Aragon Sforza, the accidental death of the French King Charles VIII in Amboise, and the martyr-death of the prophet Fra Girolamo Savonarola at the stake in Florence. In April of 1498, the unexpected death of king Charles VIII and the accession of Louis XII to the French throne provided much heated discussion at the Isabella entertainments on how the new French king might influence the future stability of

Milan. These entertainments and discussions were pleasing for all who attended until the drums of war with France grew much louder in 1499.

Some of the more popular events in Isabella's parlour were the musical recitals performed by the musicians Josquin des Prez and Franchinus Gaffurius. They performed French chansons and ballads with lute accompaniment in the manner of the Italian frottole. Many of them were comic or amorous with a lighter, homophonic texture and faster tempo (usual in 3/4 or 4/4 metre) than the more serious polyphonic motets of hymns or anthems with counterpoint that did not necessarily always coincide with repeating melodic patterns. Leonardo, Isabella, and their friends also would cross the piazza from the Corte Vecchio to the Duomo where five to fifteen singers would perform the Josquin des Prez and Franchinus Gaffurius's compositions of sacred masses and motets. These performances I can vouch for were a marvellous intermix of Italian and French recipes to stimulate the head, mind, and body with a perfect heavenly sound.

The Sad News of the Death of Anna Maria Sforza – the Beautiful Princess

One week into the month of December of 1497, Isabella Aragona Sforza received the shocking news of the sudden and unexpected death of her sister-in-law Anna Maria Sforza the Hereditary Princess of Ferrara. She died in Ferrara on the 30th of November while giving birth to a healthy son named Alessandro. The sad news of her death spread quickly throughout Milan, and the church bells rang to mourn her loss for the next few days because she was greatly loved and admired by the Milanese. A few months later, the Ferrara poet Antonio Tebaldeo and his Milanese friend the poet Bellincioni visited Isabella Aragon Sforza at one of her salon gatherings, and Tebaldeo recited his sonnet dedicated to Anna Sforza d' Este.

> When Death saw that Moro had closed the passage
> To Charles, who was arming himself again,
> From which the impious one expected much prey,
> She said: I will not leave this man unpunished.
> She wrote it not in dust but on hard stone,
> And, turning with her bow to the city of Ercole,
> Anna (flower of the Sforzas) was taken from us,
> Never under the earth went a body so wearied.
> Not being quite sure of her victory,
> Death, as Anna was beautiful, she was
> Cruel and relentless in the battle.
> To leave Italy to the Gauls was a lesser evil;
> One day she could free herself; but Nature
> Could never hope to make another like her again. [S25]

This poem brought tears to Isabella's eyes for not only did she mourn the recent loss of her sister-in-law Anna, it also brought back instant memories of the heartbreaking loss of her husband Gian Galeazzo Sforza who was the loving brother of Anna. Yet, Isabella's bravery stood tall and strong, and she thanked Tebaldeo for reciting his beautiful poem in honour of Anna and invited him to carry on with his other sonnets of love and the domestic and social activities of the other beloved ladies who were still living in scandal or grace at the time.

Anna Maria Sforza was very pretty and a favourite of the artists in the Sforza court especially among the painters within Leonardo's studio. Her sister-in-law the Duchess of Milan Isabella Aragona Sforza loved her very much, and they kept company together as much as they were allowed, and they remained in constant communication even after Anna moved to Ferrara. Isabella described her as gentle and charming and highly intelligent with a great knowledge of the classics for one so young. Isabella loved and inherited a drawing by Leonardo of Anna reading the verses of Dante.

Fig. 59. The Beautiful Princess Anna Maria Sforza by Leonardo da Vinci.

A few years before Anna Maria Sforza was married to Alfonso d' Este, her brother the young Duke of Milan asked Leonardo and Giovanni Ambrogio de' Predis to provide him with profile portraits of her and her sister Bianca on vellum, which he wished to bind into a small book as a remembrance for his mother Bona of Savoy. Leonardo produced an outstanding profile of Anna Maria Sforza in red and green (livery colours of Gian and the Este) on yellowish vellum to highlight the golden-copper colours of the Este-Sforza Houses of Ferrara and Milan and her golden nature as the Hereditary Princess of Ferrara. He captured the green colour of her dress by mixing his blue chalk on to slightly yellowish vellum. The red, green, and brown of Anna Maria Sforza's dress are the same as the heraldic colours of her brother Gian Galeazzo Sforza the 6th duke of Milan. Her pursed lips refrain from smiling.

Anna looked very much like her aunt Ippolita Maria Sforza (the mother of Isabella of Aragon the former Duchess of Milan), which may not be so surprising to know since they were closely related by blood. It is the distinctive shape of the mouth, the slight over-bite that the Aragon/Sforza women seemed to share. Leonardo derived his study of Anna's profile from the Ghirlandaio frescoes of Giovanna degli Albizzi in the Tornabuoni chapel at the Santa Maria Novella in Florence. He was impressed by Domenico Ghirlandaio's profile portrait of Giovanna degli Albizzi where she is eternally static with her arm, neck, and spine held decorously firm articulating a 'dowry of virtue', piety, and propriety. The inscription dated 1488 (the year of Giovanna's death) behind Giovanna's image indicates that she was the bearer of noble conduct and soul. Leonardo brought the same message to his portrait of Anna Sforza as he remembered a poem by his past Florentine mentor Lorenzo de' Medici:

> Her beauty was wonderful...she was of an attractive and ideal height; the tone of her skin, white but not pale, fresh but not glowing; her demeanour was grave but not proud, sweet, and pleasing, without frivolity or fear. Her eyes were lively and her gaze restrained, without trace of pride or meanness; her body was so well proportioned, that among other women she appeared dignified... and in all her movements she was elegant and attractive;

her hands were the most beautiful that Nature could create. She dressed in those fashions, which suited a noble and gentle lady…. [S26]

The last I saw of the portrait of the young Anna was when it was in the hands of Bona Sforza Aragon the Queen of Poland. The vellum had changed in colour towards a much darker yellow, almost golden. I could see that it had been retouched by another's hand. The profile had been outlined in ink, and some colours painted onto the cheek, neck, and above the eye. The nose was slightly distorted to present a more rounded tip than Leonardo had originally provided, and the contour of the nape of the neck was changed and broadened from its original finer and aristocratic shape. You also can see the shape of her ear in a distorted position beneath slightly transparent strands of hair. Leonardo originally showed off her ear, but this had been changed and covered over. Nevertheless, the portrait still glowed with a life-like intensity before my eyes as I stared at it with enormous admiration and an overwhelming sense of love. The drawing and colours draw out her beauty, sweetness, intelligence, purity, and her tight-lipped stubbornness about the time of her marriage to Alfonso. The profile painted by Ambrogio de' Predis six years later when he was in Ferrara also shows her intelligent beauty, but now without the tight-lipped stubbornness that only Leonardo could show. Two other paintings and drawings of Anna Sforza that highlight her charming beauty were favourites among the collection of Isabella Aragon Sforza.

Anna Maria Sforza was engaged at birth to Alfonso I d' Este who later would become the Duke of Ferrara in June of 1505. She married him on 21st of January 1491 at an age when she wasn't quite 15 years, and her mother Bona of Savoy was there for her marriage. She grew up with a preference for the company of women rather than men, and her constant companion and lover in her early years of marriage was her black maid Salome. She did not consummate her marriage to Alfonso d' Este until six years after her vows when she immediately became pregnant with his child, and she sadly passed away at the age of 21 years as a consequence of giving birth to her son Alessandro. She was buried in the nunnery of San Vito to which she was a benefactor and that stands in the shadows of the Estense palaces in Ferrara. Her death in childbirth essentially marked the end of the alliance between the Sforza and the Este family, and it was a bad portent for Ludovico and his rule as Duke of Milan after 1497.

Alfonso I d' Este later married Pope Alexander VI's beautiful illegitimate daughter Lucrezia Borgia even though he was terribly disfigured by the pox (syphilis). Lucrezia had ten children during this marriage and possibly some others from long standing love affairs with Francesco II Gonzaga Marquess of Mantua and with the poet Pietro Bembo. She died on 14th June 1519 from complications of giving birth to a dead daughter. Pietro Bembo wrote passionate and loving poems to Lucrezia when she lived, and he survived her fevered love and went on to live and remember her for another 28 years, dying at the age of 77 years in 1547. Perhaps, I have digressed a little too much here, and so I will now return to my account of the Leonardo and Isabella friendship.

Leonardo and Duchess Isabella at the Corte Vecchio, 1497 to 1499

Isabella's rooms at the Corte Vecchio adjoined those of Leonardo's at either end of a shared corridor and stair well. She and her girls became Leonardo's regular visitors and models for him and his painters. In a short time, Leonardo and Isabella seemed to have become like husband and wife in their own privacy together and in the company of their closest friends including my mother who was now working as a lady-in-waiting for Isabella. I was taken along as a six-year-old with my mother to play with Isabella's children and their cousins at the Corte Vecchio and at Leonardo's studio where I witnessed their flirtatious friendship blooming.

Leonardo was a great admirer of Isabella of Aragon from the moment he first set eyes on her in Naples in 1488. Her serene beauty and gentle intelligence was everything he admired in a woman. In 1491, she quickly became his idealised Madonna whom he recreated numerous times in his sketches and in his paintings. He spent as much time with her as he was permitted for she was an illustrious princess with young children and courtly duties and a staff to attend to. In contrast, he was only a court painter and entertainer who had to indulge her husband Lord Gian Galeazzo Sforza and his uncle the Duke of Bari Ludovico Sforza. Yet, Leonardo and Gian were good friends, and so he spent considerable leisure time with the young duke and his wife the Duchess Isabella. He prepared their portraits prior to and after their wedding in Milan, staged their wedding procession to the Duomo, and their after-wedding celebrations including the renowned *La fest del paradise*. When Ludovico complained to Leonardo that he was spending too much time at Gian's court and not enough at his own, Leonardo's allegiance was diverted temporarily to the more powerful and influential Ludovico Sforza and his wife Beatrice. But now, Leonardo was refurbishing Isabella's bathroom at the Corte Vecchio like he had at her castle in Pavia and later at the Sforza castle in Milan. He excitedly made notes and drawings about it in his folios:

> Hydraulics: To make water rise and remain upon the ascent! [With drawing of pump]. For the bath of the duchess Isabella; a Spring. Made for the stove or bath of the duchess Isabella; a is in this position because the screw does not turn with its socket. [With drawings]. Water raised by the force of the wind. This syringe has to have two valves, one to the pipe, which draws the water and the other to that which ejects it. Method of making water rise to a height. In this way one will make water rise through the whole house by means of conduit pipes.
>
> KEY OF THE BATH OF THE DUCHESS. Show all the ways of unlocking and releasing. Put them together in their chapter.
>
> BATH: To warm the water of the stove of the duchess add three parts of warm water to four parts of cold water.

She and Leonardo were intimate and secret friends in the period of 1497 to the end of 1499, and according to a few rumours circulating about the city of Milan at the time, they were together as man and wife. Whether true or not, they were certainly good friends, and she and her children became the principal models for him and his painting assistants Giovanni Antonio Boltraffio, Marco d' Oggiono, Bernardino Luini, and Salai who painted many portraits of her and her children. Sometimes, his assistants would include Leonardo, my father, and me in their paintings of Madonna and Child and Family. When Isabella moved into the Corte Vecchio, she was 27 years of age; and of her three children, Francesco was 6 years, Bona was 4 years, and Ippolita was 3 years. Leonardo and his assistants had already painted numerous portraits of them together as Madonna and child when her husband Gian was still alive and living in Pavia and even while she was a widow in mourning and living at the Sforza castle. Yet, undoubtedly, the acquaintance between Isabella and Leonardo intensified the painting duties in the studios of the Corte Vecchio, and it was a happy time for them and their friends, despite the growing tensions of Milanese politics and the talk of war soon emerging between Ludovico Sforza and the new French king Louis XII.

My mother was one of Isabella's ladies-in-waiting, and she assisted her with the care of her daughters. This allowed me and my brother and sister to play with Isabella's daughters on many occasions, and we were good friends. Leonardo's studio and workshop was open to all of us, and Isabella and my mother would often visit him to talk and watch him and the other painters at work. Leonardo was friendly with all the children, and because he was my and Bona Sforza's godfather, he provided us with extra care, attention, and warm affection.

Leonardo produced a series of portraits of Isabella that later became fashionably iconic among the Leonardeschi painters and copiers such as Boltraffio, Bernardino Luini, Raphael, Giampietrino, Titian, Giorgione, Andrea Solari (Gobbo), Ambrogio Bergognone (also known as Ambrogio da Fossano), and others. One much copied style was the three quarter frontal portrait with the regal sitter looking out at the viewer with a sad, accepting or knowing smile. Whether standing or sitting, the face of the Madonna had a long and straight or aquiline nose, wide eyes, and a closed smile ever so slightly turned up at the corners. Often, if the figure is standing or sitting the head might be slightly tilted to one angle and downward. This style of face for either man or woman became the universal image for many of Leonardo's figures and those of his followers. Leonardo's young and mischievous assistant Salai would later parody many of them in a number of his copies or portraits that he sold as original Leonardo's to unsophisticated and unknowing wealthy buyers.

Before they left Milan at the end of 1499, Leonardo commenced a portrait of Isabella that he referred to as his medical portrait. He noticed features in her face and hands that he believed were symptoms of a medical disorder that could lead to obesity and heart problems. He believed that it was a hereditary condition, for example, like consumption, leprosy, gout, and some forms of dropsy, blood disorders, and mental illnesses that are passed on from one generation to the next from either the male or the female. He wanted to record the changes developing on Isabella's face and her body as part of his long-term project to follow the condition in her and her children, but circumstances and events would cut the project short.

Leonardo's *Mona Lisa* [S27]

Leonardo painted a portrait of the widowed Duchess of Milan Isabella Aragon Sforza that he named *Mona Lisa* and that the king of France Francois I greatly admired and eventually owned. I gifted the portrait of *Mona Lisa* to the king who hung it in his bedroom in Fontainebleau. Giorgio Vasari in his book of *The Lives of the Most Excellent Painters, Sculptors and Architects* describes Leonardo's portrait of *Mona Lisa* as follows:

> Leonardo undertook to execute for Francesco del Giocondo the portrait of Mona Lisa, his wife, and after he had lingered over it for four years, he left it unfinished; and the work is today in the possession of King Francois of France, at Fontainebleau. Anyone wishing to see the degree to which art could imitate nature could readily perceive this from the head; since therein are counterfeited all those minutenesses that with subtlety are able to be painted: seeing that the eyes had that lustre and moistness which are always seen in the living creature, and around them were the lashes and all those rosy and pearly tints that demand the greatest delicacy of execution. The eyebrows, through his having shown the manner in which the hairs spring from the flesh, here more close and here more scanty, and curve according to the pores of the flesh, could not be more natural. The nose, with its beautiful nostrils, rosy and tender, appeared to be alive. The mouth with its opening, and with its ends united by the red of the lips to the flesh-tints of the face, seemed, in truth, to be not colours but flesh. In the pit of the throat, if one gazed upon it intently, could be seen the beating of the pulse: and indeed it may be said that it was painted in such a manner as to make every brave artificer, be he who he may, tremble and lose courage. He employed also this device: Mona Lisa being very beautiful, while he was painting her portrait, he retained those who played or sang, and continually jested, who would make her to remain merry, in order to take away that melancholy which painters are often wont to give to their portraits. And in this work of Leonardo there was a smile so pleasing, that it was a thing more divine than human to behold, and it was held to be something marvellous, in that it was not other than alive.

Fig. 60. My copy of Madonna Isabella Aragon Sforza, the Duchess of Milan.

Vasari never saw the original portrait of the *Mona Lisa* and so his description and narrative about this painting is derived from the word of mouth of others including from me. He is wrong about the painting with respect to a number of his incorrect facts. The *Mona Lisa* is not the wife of Francesco del Giocondo of whom I know nothing, although Salai told me that

Leonardo had painted a small portrait in 1504 of a lady for a Florentine silk merchant who was acquainted with his father.

The *Mona Lisa* that I know is the portrait of Isabella Aragon Sforza, the Duchess of Bari, and the widow of the 6th Duke of Milan Gian Galeazzo Sforza. Vasari uses similar words (although with much greater exaggeration and sense of poetry) to those that I used when I showed him my personal copy of the portrait of *Mona Lisa* (Fig. 60). I never mentioned the name Francesco del Giocondo, a person I have no knowledge of. Instead, I told him that it was a portrait of a smiling Isabella de Aragon Duchess of Bari (former Duchess of Milan) and that Leonardo had painted it for his own pleasure. I inherited it, and left it as a gift in the possession of the French king after Leonardo's death. For some reason, Vasari has forgotten this part of my account and chosen not to acknowledge the Duchess Isabella Aragon Sforza as the true sitter for the portrait. It is possible that Vasari mistook the words *la Gioconda* ('the smiling woman') for a person's name or because Leonardo often said *iocondo* ('I will keep') my portrait of *Mona Lisa*. He did keep the *Mona Lisa* with him all his life until the day he died. In France, it became known as *La Joconda* or *La Jocondo*, the smiling woman, and not the actual name of the sitter.

Fig. 61. Raphael's sketched copy of Leonardo's portrait of a Madonna.

The portrait that Francesco del Giocondo obtained of his wife or mistress may have been the one painted by Raphael (Raffaello Santi) who made many copies of Madonnas when he was an apprentice in Leonardo's studio in Florence in 1504 and when they were together again in Rome from 1513 to 1516. Raphael assimilated many of Leonardo's creations into his own portraiture painting as you can readily see in this attached sketch (Fig. 61) and in his later painting that he did of the *Lady with a Unicorn* (Fig. 125).

Leonardo broke many rules and introduced new innovations into his style of portraiture. This style could describe any one of thirty to forty different Madonnas that Leonardo and his assistants had painted during their lifetime. Through the propagation of the good and bad copies of *Madonna Isabella* (*Mona Lisa*) painted by Raphael, Boltraffio, Bernardino Luini, Bernardino de' Conti, Giampietrino, Titian, Giorgione, Andrea Solari (Gobbo), and many others, this style of portraiture in Italy of the three-quarter sitter showing her nature and mood through her expressive eyes and mouth and the delicate fold of her arms and hands is now the new norm of painting. Leonardo brought movement and grace of the soul into his figures, the delicate smiles and gestures that mirror *'the true expression of what passes in the mind of that figure, which he must feel, and that is very important.'*

Those of us who knew Leonardo well know that the *Mona Lisa* is Isabella of Aragon. He has placed the Duchess on a balcony of a castello in the vicinity of the Grigna massif and the villages of Lecco and Mandello on the eastern shore of Lake Como near the source of the Adda River looking back towards the Bergamasque (Bergamo) Alps in northern Lombardy. Leonardo would often stand with Isabella on the roof of the Cathedral or at the top of the towers of the Corte Vecchio, and together they would look north over the rooftops of Milan and at the mountain range of the Grigna ('the grin') where the sun moved the shadows and changed the colours and shapes of the mountain peaks. Occasionally, Leonardo would ask Isabella to stand facing him while he sketched her portrait with the massifs and rocks foreshortened behind her. These drawings were the templates for his painting of the *Mona Lisa.*

Leonardo was fascinated by the Grigna, and he often travelled with my father through the northern mountain regions of Lombardy on the pretext that he was studying the landscape and watercourses for canalisation projects or for inspecting the layout and condition of all the fortifications that bordered Lake Como and along the banks of the River Adda from Mandello and Lecco all the way south to our villa and estate in Vaprio. Isabella had seen the awesome view of the Grigna at close range when she travelled with her husband Gian from Milan to Lecco and Bellagio when they accompanied her sister-in-law Bianca Maria Sforza on her way across the Alps into Tyrol to marry the Holy Roman Emperor Maximilian in Innsbruck in the winter of 1493. Leonardo loved his painting of the *Mona Lisa* for it was a memory of Isabella, Lake Como, and the Lombardy Alps, a holy trilogy that he never forgot. Some who recognised that this was Isabella's portrait mistakenly believed that the background was the Amalfi coast in Naples with the islands of Capri and Ischia in the distance. Leonardo often added an inexact and abstract landscape as an intentional trick to pictorially suggest an association between the Amalfi and Isabella of Aragon, which pleased her ironic sense of humour.

Fig. 62. The Sforza chain of golden interlocking rings on the neckline of the Duchess Isabella Aragon Sforza whom we called the Mona Lisa.

In the portrait of Isabella Aragon Sforza that I have presented here, she is recently widowed. She wears the symbol of her deceased husband's ducal chain of golden interlocking rings, as well as a second layer of loops with clover shaped crosses personally designed for her by Leonardo to represent the emblematic Cross of Jerusalem that she received when she inherited the title of Queen of Jerusalem from her brother Ferdinand II King of Naples and Jerusalem soon after his death in 1496. These symbols are carefully embroidered onto the neckline of her dress. The same golden interlocking rings are clearly visible on the cover of her and Gian Galeazzo Sforza's personal copies of the *Book of Hours* that I reproduced for you in one of my earlier chapters. The Sforza men Gian and Ludovico often wore the ducal chain of interlocking rings around their neck on formal occasions to show to all those present that they were the dukes of Milan (Fig. 55). The ducal chain of golden interlocking rings can be seen in many of Gian's portraits (Fig. 32), and Leonardo carried on this Sforza tradition in his *Mona Lisa* portraits to show her connection to Gian Galeazzo Sforza the Duke of Milan. Also, Gian's personal colours of green, gold, and red (see his *Book of Hours,* Fig. 55) are subtly represented on Isabella's dress to show that she was his wife. However, she still wears the Sforza mourning dress, a modest dress of dark green with two sleeves of red velvet (or lion yellow in some versions) and a veil on her head with a black headdress beneath it to demonstrate that her husband had died recently. Thus, the portrait by Leonardo depicts her during her first few years of mourning when she was only 25 or 26 years of age.

Fig. 63. Leonardo's portrait of the widowed Madonna Isabella Aragon Sforza, the former Duchess of Milan.

Leonardo noticed features in Duchess Isabella's face and hands that he believed were the symptoms of a developing health condition that could lead to obesity and heart problems. He believed this condition was hereditary and that the male and the female of related families can pass it on from one generation to the next. He had made such observations previously of families in Florence and during his dissections of corpses in the hospitals of Florence and Milan.

He began to record the *'fatty'* deposits developing in Isabella's face and hands intending to follow and record the changing features of these *'little hillocks'* as she grew older. Leonardo with the assistance of Salai made two separate copies of the Duchess Isabella, one before the development of the *verruca* or hillock in the corner of her left eye and another after its appearance.

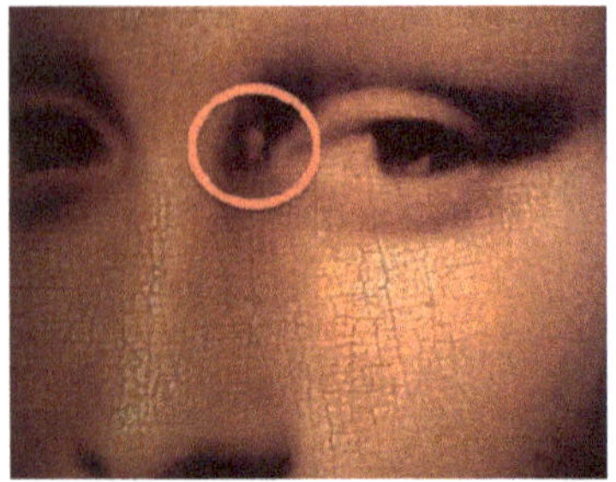

Fig. 64. Detail of the fatty deposit (circled) in the corner of Mona Lisa's left eye.

Also, he highlighted an area of fatty deposits or hillocks near the knuckles of her hand and forefinger. This was an extraordinary observation. Nobody really quite understood what Leonardo was referring to or was so excited about. He saw and recorded something that nobody else could see or wanted to see. Leonardo's friend, a distant cousin of mine, had given this condition the medical name *Xanthelasmoideus tumulus*, which I simply refer to as the 'yellow hillock'. Isabella had many more lipomas about her eyelids as she grew older. I met her in Naples in 1524 when she was 53 years of age. She had become obese and had problems with her heart and blood pressure as Leonardo had predicted. In addition, she was self-medicating herself with mercury to treat the pox. This treatment had blackened the enamel on her teeth, which she scraped off to leave her teeth white, but bare of enamel. I believe that she died of heart failure and mercury poisoning.

Fig. 65. Bona Sforza, Queen of Poland, and daughter of the Mona Lisa.

Isabella's older daughter Bona Sforza the Queen of Poland also developed *Xanthelasmoideus tumulus* and grew obese with age, but at the time of my writing she is still alive, although I believe, unwell, and living in Bari.

Isabella Aragon Sforza was a popular model and many painters who I know painted her iconic image. Here, I want to present a few examples from one Leonardeschi painter Bernardino Luini (1480 to 1532). He was a committed disciple of Leonardo da Vinci and Isabella of Aragon. Although he was ten years younger than Isabella, she became his favourite model for the Madonna images that he continually recreated. Some of his favourite themes were *Virgin with Child and Saints, Salome and the Beheading of John the Baptist*, and he featured Isabella often as *Mary Magdalene*, *St. Catherine* or *St. Anne* or a *Princess* or the *Virgin with St. Sebastian* (Gian Galeazzo Sforza) and with Leonardo as *St. John the Baptist* or *St. Roch*.

Fig. 66. *Lady Isabella Aragon Sforza, the Duchess of Bari, Queen of Jerusalem, former Princess of Naples and Duchess of Milan, with a brown ermine and the golden cross of Jerusalem, painted by Bernardino Luini, 1521.*

I especially like two of Luini's portraits of Isabella. One is where she is the Duchess of Bari with a brown ermine, and she is dressed in the heraldic colours of the House of Aragon. In this portrait of her as the Princess of Naples and the Queen of Jerusalem (the title she inherited from her deceased brother in 1496), she wears and fingers the emblematic golden cross of Jerusalem, and in her right hand she holds a brown ermine, the heraldic symbol of the Kingdom of Naples and the House of Aragon. It is an interesting contrast to Leonardo's the *Lady with the White Ermine* (Fig. 28) and Raphael's portrait of her as the young and beautiful Princess of Naples (Fig. 36).

The other Bernardino Luini portrait I admire of Lady Isabella Aragon Sforza is where she is portrayed as Mary Magdalene in the *Allegory of Modesty and Vanity* (1520), and she wears the heraldic red, green, and brown colours of her deceased husband Gian Galeazzo Sforza. I obtained a loan of these paintings to study and copy, but I was not able to purchase them for my own collection as I had hoped.

Fig. 67. Mary Magdalene in the Allegory of Modesty and Vanity by Bernardino Luini.

Luini was born in Runo near Lake Maggiore, and he first met with Leonardo and Isabella in 1497 before they left Milan at the end of 1499. He later met with Leonardo on numerous occasions in Milan after 1508 and in Rome between 1513 and 1516 where he again met with Isabella of Aragon and with Raphael. He returned to Rome to work on frescoes soon after Raphael's death in 1520 and later he moved to Brera, Legnano, Saronno, and Como, often to paint frescoes on the life of the *Virgin and Christ*.

Leonardo's Symbolic Painting of Isabella Aragon Sforza as *Flora* (*Columbine*), the Goddess of Fertility, Sex, and Flowers

Soon after Isabella Aragon Sforza married the Duke of Milan in February of 1489, her husband was expected to have instantly impregnated her. Yet, the young duchess showed no sign of pregnancy for about one and a half years, and during this time her enemies and especially Ludovico Sforza spread unsavoury rumours that she was infertile or unable to excite her husband or, more likely, that her husband was impotent. These rumours distressed them both because they were greatly attracted to each other, and they spent many blissful moments together on the marriage bed when they were away from various people scrutinising their marital performance. In his despair, the young duke asked his good friend Leonardo to provide him with a solution. Leonardo's solution was simple; it was erotic art and a few glasses of an herbal aphrodisiac. Later, they commissioned Leonardo for a painting of Isabella depicted as *Flora*, the goddess of fertility, sex, and flowers (blossoming). Leonardo loved to draw and paint Isabella's image, and he immediately set himself the task of producing a memorable picture.

Fig. 68. Leonardo's painting of Isabella Aragon Sforza, the Duchess of Milan as Flora, *the Goddess of Fertility, Sex, and Flowers.*

By the time he started the painting of Isabella as *Flora*, she already had given birth in January of 1491 to her first born Francesco, and by late 1493, she was well on her way towards having her second child. Because of the disturbing political climate at the time, Leonardo kept

231

the painting for himself and hung it in his studio at our villa in Vaprio d'Adda. I still have possession of the painting, and many people who have seen it believed that it was my hand that painted it. I did not always correct their error.

The design and balance of the picture is exquisite. Isabella sits in slight counterbalance with a loving smile and her head and eyes turned toward the head of her imaginary child. It is pure illusion as only Leonardo can do it. Instead of a child's head, the fingers of her left hand appear to hold on to the stem of a cluster of columbine flowers, a symbol of fidelity and holiness. Leonardo also has tied a knot around her left wrist as a jest on his own name Vinci (a knot) and a nod to the use of his left hand to paint, draw, and write with. Her right hand holds onto the cuttings of wild jasmine ('the gift from God') with buds and flowers in bloom that symbolise love, romance, beauty, sensuality, motherhood, and purity. This same hand rests on her lap as if she was cradling her stomach because of an early pregnancy hidden beneath her blue cloak. There are anemones in her lap that symbolise a return to new life. The partly illuminated flowers, leaves, ferns, and ivy in the background stand out against the darkness of the wall of stone, and they look mysterious, yet charming. Flowering heads of allium that represent unity, patience, and humility, and chrysanthemums that symbolise happiness, love, longevity, and joy, also blossom behind her shoulders. Her yellow satin blouse decorated with red motifs of bull or devil heads bares the colours of her origin, the yellow and red of the Aragon House of Naples. The red beast head motifs repeated on Isabella's yellow blouse is a jest towards Botticelli's drawings of the three-headed beasts of Hell who chewed up sinners in Dante's *Divine Comedy*. Both Isabella and Gian were Dante scholars and understood and appreciated Leonardo's jest. Positioned between her breasts is Gian's large, square, red ruby that is set in a golden frame surrounded by four pearls between unfolding ferns. It is similar to the red ruby displayed under his portrait on the cover of his Sforziada *Book of Hours* (Fig. 55). The beast's black eye (Ludovico Il Moro perhaps?) looks out from within the ruby. Her blue cloak that also has a Vinci knot tied on its left side is decorated with indistinct clover rings that Leonardo will later modify and include into the dress of the *Mona Lisa*.

This is a remarkable painting, rich in allegory, and it immediately catches the eye and disturbs the senses with pleasure and guilt. I have named it *Columbina* because that is how Leonardo referred to it. The circle of spurs of the flower columbine resembles doves perched around a fountain or as Leonardo preferred to see them - the talons of an eagle. *Columbina* is much different to his painting of the *Mona Lisa*. Isabella is younger and more hopeful as the *Columbina* than she is as the widowed *Mona Lisa* whose son Francesco was being held hostage first by Ludovico il Moro Sforza and then by the French king. *Columbina* is fresh faced and happily expectant cradling her imaginary child to her bare breast not yet filled nor swelled by the heavy milk of late pregnancy and imminent birth. She is the symbol of fertility. Her hair is coloured a distinctive orange/brown just like that of the real Isabella Aragon Sforza (see the Luini painting of Isabella Aragon Sforza as the *Queen of Jerusalem with a Brown Ermine*). This painting of *Flora/Columbina* made Leonardo famous among his acolytes and contemporaries, and many of them like Luini used the face and figure and pose of *Columbina* as their standard template for their depiction of *Madonna with Child* and other themes.

CHAPTER 16

Ludovico Sforza's Demise by a French Takeover, 1498 to 1500

*Those who trust themselves to live near him, and who will be a large crowd, these shall all die cruel
deaths; and fathers and mothers together with their families will be devoured and killed by cruel creatures.
The Duke has lost the state, property and liberty, and none of his enterprises were carried out by him.*

— Leonardo da Vinci

Ludovico Sforza's Last Gasp as the Seventh Duke of Milan, 1498 to 1500

Soon after Ludovico Sforza received his gift copy of *De Divina Proportione* by Luca Pacioli with
Leonardo's illustrations in 1498, he started to worry that the French might compromise his
good fortune, and that he was running short of time to rule his beloved Milan the way that he
really always wanted to. In the year following the death of his wife, another two deaths
occurred that seriously effected the dynasty and destiny of the Sforza family and the future rule
of Milan. Firstly, Anna Sforza who was Ludovico's niece and Gian Galeazzo Sforza's sister
died unexpectedly during childbirth at the age of 21 on 30th November 1497 in Ferrara. This
greatly affected the Sforza and Este alliance because Anna was the husband of prince Alfonso
d'Este, and she had helped to maintain cordial relationships between the two Houses. Soon
after Anna's death, Prince Alfonso renounced Ludovico and became an ally of king Louis XII
of France (and five years later he married Pope Alexander's illegitimate daughter Lucrezia
Borgia). Anna's death greatly upset Gian's widow Isabella Aragon Sforza who very much loved
her sister-in-law and as first cousins they were closer than most. Leonardo remembered her as
a lovely, gentle, and friendly person and a favourite model for the Lombardian and Ferrarese
artists. Secondly, Charles VIII king of France died unexpectedly on the 7th April 1498 at the
age of 27 years after he accidently hit his head on a door beam while watching a tennis match
(*jeu de paume*) at the Chateau Amboise. His 36-year-old cousin Louis Duke of Orleans
succeeded him and began his reign as King Louis XII. Immediately upon his succession to the
throne of France, Louis XII announced his plans for the conquest of Italy and his claim on the
duchy of Milan. He addressed Ludovico simply as Messer (Mister) and entitled himself as King
of France and Duke of Milan.

Even a few months before Charles's death, a French war with Italy was on the horizon
again. Ludovico Sforza sent envoys to Venice in an attempt to win them over as allies against
the likely invasion by the French. Before the Venetians could reply to Ludovico's overtures,
they heard that Charles VIII was dead and that France was now in the hands of Charles's
cousin Louis of Orleans. When this news reached Milan's ruling council they all knew with
certain trepidation that an invasion was imminent from King Louis XII because he had told
them so. By the end of April, both Ludovico and Louis XII were in a scramble to find allies,
Ludovico to defend his status and Louis XII to take it away from him. In the ensuing year,
Louis formed an alliance with Venice at the Treaty of Blois on the 15th of April 1499 where the
Signory agreed to invade Lombardy with 6,000 men for the price of being awarded Cremona
and a share of the partitioning of Ludovico's dominion. Pope Alexander VI also joined France
and Venice as an ally after declaring that the House of Sforza must be swept from the face of
the earth, and so he sent his illegitimate son Cesare Borgia to negotiate favourable terms with
Louis in France. The French king took an immediate liking to Cesare and gave him honours,
money, and an army to lead the invasion of Milan. The king also provided Cesare with the title

of the Duke of Valentinois and arranged his marriage to the beautiful Charlotte d'Albret in Blois on the 10th of May. King Louis XII also won over Francesco Gonzaga of Mantua from the Ludovico camp. On the other hand, Ludovico the Duke of Milan could find no allies in Italy for he had betrayed them all during his previous campaigns, and he now depended entirely on his friend Maximilian I the Holy Roman Emperor and some of his own citizens in Lombardy to defend him and his status. Even Maximilian who was at war with the neighbouring Swiss was in friendly negotiations with Louis of France and wavering about what assistance he could afford for Ludovico.

By most accounts at the time, Ludovico started the New Year in 1498 preparing himself psychologically for his possible demise as the ruler of Milan. He was heavily taxing his citizens and creating a heavy burden for them to the degree that they resented him and wished that he would by overthrown and replaced by a Republic or by anybody who might be more considerate of their needs. Yet, he expected his citizens to remain loyal and defend him and his duchy from any potential invaders from the west (France) or the east (Venice). He also prepared an extensive will fearing that it would not be executed according to his wishes if it fell into the hands of his enemy, the French king Louis XII. Here are a few of the requested items in his will that reveal his insecurity and worries at the time. He wanted his body, the ducal robes, and insignia to be buried on the right-handed side of his wife in the tomb erected by him in the Cappella Maggiore of Santa Maria delle Grazie. There was an endowment to be left for the said convent with a rent of 1,500 ducats so that they may never cease to pray for his soul and that of his beloved lady Beatrice. Seven masses to be said daily for the duke, seven for the duchess, five requiems to be chanted every Tuesday, and the whole office for the dead to be used on the third of every month being the day on which Beatrice died. The amount of 4,000 ducats to be distributed yearly in alms, 3,000 more to pension his old servants, and 5,000 ducats to be paid to each of his illegitimate sons Cesare and Gianpaolo.

Ludovico also added instructions for the Ruling Council to educate and guide his two legitimate sons by proper State administration until his eldest son Maximilian reached the age of twenty; and then that he immediately apply to Maximilian the King of the Romans or to the alternate reigning Caesarean Majesty to be confirmed with the same ducal privileges that had been granted to him; that he reside at the Castello and not travel further than his country houses in Abbiategrasso, Cussago, Monza, Dece, and Melegnano, until he reached the age of fourteen; that he be educated in all branches of religious and secular learning, in good conduct and habits, and in the knowledge of letters, and be entrusted to the best governors and teachers; that he take his place in the council from his earliest years and be gradually initiated into the management of affairs; and that he be taught to deliver speeches and how to receive ambassadors graciously, and receive instruction in all that is necessary to make him a wise and good prince. This illustrates Ludovico's state of mind at this time of his diminishing rule when he refused to consider remarrying because he was still overly distraught by the death of his young wife Beatrice d' Este. Ludovico expected both his boys to manage the inherited ducal stables and chapel choir wisely and not to assume the ducal crown until after he has been laid and buried in his grave and not before.

Yet, apart from his last will and testimony and his preparation for war, Ludovico was still building monuments and decorating the rooms of the Sforza Castello; and the gardens, friary, portico, and cupola, Beatrice's tomb, and the cappella and the interior of the Sante Maria delle Grazie including Leonardo's life-sized portraits of Ludovico and Beatrice and their children on the wall opposite the painting of the *Last Supper of Jesus*. Other instructions issued to his secretary Bartolomeo Calco included that the ducal arms be constructed in gold letters on a marble slab on the Porta Ludovica, together with ten bronze medals bearing the duke's head; and that the following items be completed immediately, the portico of S. Ambrogio, the Strada da Corte, the new gate called the Porta Beatrice in the walls corresponding to the Porta S.

Marco, and that the decorations of the Broletto Nuovo should be finished by August. Surprisingly, Ludovico willed his favourite property the Sforzesca, the vast family farm complex outside Vigevano, in perpetuity to the Church of Santa Maria delle Grazie.

He also must have realised that he hadn't used the talents and skills of his genius Leonardo the Florentine to their true potential because suddenly he requested him to redecorate the rooms within the Castello, strengthen the fortification of the walls and gates of Milan, and draw a map of the city and its precincts and canals both for its defence and as an exercise in town planning.   More importantly for Leonardo, Ludovico at last officially conceded the properties that had been given to him by the previous duke Gian Galeazzo Sforza, and he even added to them by extending the land rights adjoining his vineyard outside the gate of Vercellina near the monastery of Saint Vittore. He promised Leonardo that they would soon find the money for him to complete the Francesco Sforza equestrian statue.

But, his most surprising *'mea culpa'* was to try and restitute Isabella Aragon Sforza for her loss of the Duchy of Milan as the regent for her 8-year-old son Francesco II Sforza, the legitimate Duke of Milan. No, he wasn't about to return the Duchy of Milan back to her son. No, he would die defending his own legitimacy as Duke of Milan before he would ever let go of Milan and his associated titles. Instead, he gave her his titles and deeds to Bari. So with the simple signature from his pen and his ducal stamps, Isabella Sforza of Aragon the former Duchess of Milan was now the Duchess of Bari with an annual revenue of 6,000 ducats in place of her lost dowry. Ludovico Il Moro Sforza also suggested that she and her family board her cousin's ship in Genoa and leave for Naples as soon as possible for it would be unsafe for her and her children to remain in Milan when the French arrived. She ignored his good advice and suffered the consequences when Louis XII took her 9-year-old son away from her to be his life long houseguest at the Château de Noirmoutier. The boy later transferred to Angouleme and died in 1512 at the age of 20 years after falling from his horse while hunting.

By the summer of 1499, everybody in Milan knew that the invasion from the French was inevitable. In July, my mother and I took our leave of Isabella Aragon Sforza at the Corte Vecchio in Milan, and we accompanied my father, Leonardo, and Luca Pacioli to our villa in Vaprio on the Adda River. Leonardo fearing that the French or others might steal or destroy his valuable manuscripts, books, paintings, and sculptures had most of them transferred from Milan to his library, rooms, and studio at our villa in Vaprio. After helping Leonardo secure his belongings, my father returned to Milan, whereas Leonardo and Luca Pacioli and an armed escort accompanied my mother and me and my siblings to Bergamo to stay with her relatives. While Luca Pacioli explored Bergamo and met with the town's clergy and various scholars, Leonardo wandered off to contemplate on his situation and undertake further studies of nature and the flow of waterways in the neighbouring hills and mountains. It was while Leonardo was lost in the mountainous woods that he decided that he would have to leave Milan permanently and accompany his friend Luca Pacioli to Venice via Piacenza and Mantua.

Ludovico's astrologer and physician Ambrogio Varesi of Rosate predicted that they would face a particularly dangerous period from the French army in August, but he was confident that the signs pointed to a victory by Ludovico and his followers in September. By the 31st of August, Ludovico took heed of his astrologer and sent his two sons out of Milan to Como in the company of his brother the cardinal Ascanio Sforza and the cardinal Federico Sanseverino. Lady Camilla Sforza who was the widow of Costanzo Lord of Pesaro was put in charge of the care of Ludovico's two sons. They rode out with an additional eight horses carrying precious jewels and 240,000 gold ducats. A few days later, on the 2nd of September 1499, my father helped to escort Ludovico out of Milan accompanied by Gian's brother Ermes Sforza, Galeazzo Sanseverino, Cardinal Ippolito d' Este, and a few armed horseman to meet with Ludovico's two sons in Como. From there, while my father returned to Vaprio, Ludovico and his party rode over the mountains of the Valtellina glacial valley to Bormio and on to

Innsbruck to stay with his loyal, royal niece the Empress Bianca Sforza who was the wife of Maximilian I the Holy Roman Emperor. Here, Ludovico rested with his two boys and his royal niece and prepared to plot for his return to Milan.

The Italian general Gian Giacomo Trivulzio who was allied with Louis led 15,000 of the King's troops to Asti in May, and then, on the 13th of August, he invaded Lombardy and captured the castle of Annona. On the same day, the Venetians advanced towards the river Adda where my father waited with his small detachment of troops to defend Vaprio and Borromeo castle at Cassano d'Adda. The taking of the city of Milan by the French and their allies was relatively swift. On the 6th of September, Trivulzio and Charles of Bourbon the Duke of Ligny entered the city of Milan by the Porta Ticinese with a hundred horseman and visited the Duomo where the Milanese nobles were waiting eagerly for them to hand over the keys of the city in an attempt to preserve their own rights and privileges. The French and their allies were now both inside and outside the city and in full command except for the Sforza castle, which continued to hold them out for another few weeks. Eventually, the governor and custodian of the Castello, Bernardino da Corte, surrendered to the Duke of Ligny for a large sum of money and privileges for his family and friends. Now, the treasures of the Sforza castle belonged to King Louis and his friends, although the king himself was still in France, in Lyon, waiting for news about the outcome of his attack on Milan.

On September 12th, Ludovico's astrologer and wizard Ambrogio Varesi was captured near Lecco while attempting to flee from Lombardy in the company of one of his sons. He was brought back to Milan where he was imprisoned in the house of Luigi Trivulzio and where Isabella of Aragon visited him and took the opportunity to accuse him of poisoning her beloved husband Gian Galeazzo Sforza. Ludovico's wizard and advisor quickly confessed to the murder in front of a number of witnesses including Gian Giacomo Trivulzio, admitting that he had poisoned Gian Galeazzo Sforza with a syrup provided to him by Ludovico Sforza's chemist and with the full knowledge and specifications from Ludovico Sforza himself. The Duchess Isabella now had the satisfaction that the truth was finally revealed that Ludovico Sforza had indeed murdered his nephew Gian Galeazzo Sforza, the 6th duke of Milan. Now, all she could ask for was that justice be served to at least one of her husband's murderers and that Ambrogio Varesi be punished appropriately before the law and the eyes of God. He was stripped of his fief and possessions, but his life was spared. His defence was that he only followed the orders of his Lord and Master Ludovico Sforza. He was released after a year in prison, and he retired to Corbetta where he later cared for the health of the former canon of the Basilica of Sant' Ambrogio, Pietro Casola. When Maximilian Sforza won back the Duchy of Milan from the French in 1512, he returned to Ambrogio Varesi and his descendants all their confiscated possessions and the fief of Rosate Pieve that had been invested to him originally by the Duke Gian Galeazzo Sforza in 1489. Count Ambrogio Varesi of Rosate, physician to the Sforza, died in 1522, twenty-eight years after he murdered the 6th Duke of Milan Gian Galeazzo Sforza, fourteen years after the death of Ludovico Il Moro Sforza, and two years before the death of Isabella Aragon Sforza, the Duchess of Bari and former Duchess of Milan.

The French king eventually arrived in Milan on the 6th of October 1499 in order to claim and admire the splendour of the Sforza castle. Many of the castle's treasures, the paintings and portraits, statues, wall hangings, gold plates, furniture, tapestries, priceless manuscripts, Greek and Roman antiques, jewellery, and large sums of money had already been stolen by Trivulzio, Ligny, Bernardino da Corte, and the two Milanese governors Francesco Visconti and Antonio Pallavicini weeks before the king's arrival. King Louis XII entered Milan triumphantly dressed in his ducal robes over his suit of royal purple with a brightly coloured peacock feather stuck in his ducal cap. The Cardinals Giuliano della Rovere and Georges d'Amboise rode in front of him, the Dukes of Ferrara and Savoy were by his side, and a large train of ambassadors, princes, and nobles including Francesco Gonzaga, Francesco and Fracassa Sanseverino, Niccolo da Correggio, and Cesare Borgia followed. The procession rode to the Duomo where the king alighted from his horse and entered the spacious interior with the vaulted aisles where many of the Sforza coronations and the glorious weddings had taken place. The king knelt and prayed at the Madonna's shrine for his good fortune and continued future success, and then he self anointed himself as the new Duke of Milan. The procession rode on again along the main street to the sound of trumpets, horns, and beating drums past the goldsmiths, artisans, armourers, and frescoed palaces to the gates of the Castello that once was the proud citadel of the Sforza family and that now he, Louis XII, the King of France, could call his own as the proud grandson of Valentina Visconti and the original owner of the site Galeazzo II Visconti. The French king thought it to be a truly magnificent edifice, as one of scribes wrote:

> … with so many large and beautiful rooms that I lost all reckoning. Without are broad lakes, fair running streams, and bridges. There is a fine large square on the side of the town, and on the other are beautiful meadows and woods and the chateau, where the Moro had his stables, painted with frescoes of different-coloured horses. [S7]

Next day, Louis's retinue including Cesare Borgia, the Marquis of Mantua, and many cardinals and ambassadors accompanied him to attend mass at St. Ambrogio and to visit the church and convent of Santa Maria delle Grazie where they admired Leonardo's *Last Supper of Jesus* and the beautiful tomb of Ludovico's deceased wife Beatrice. The French king so admired Leonardo's *Last Supper* that he wished it could be transferred to France. The Dominican monks and the Italian nobles in his wake reminded their majesty that it was not necessary for him to have it transferred now that he was the Duke of Milan and that he could visit to see it whenever he liked. The king agreed, but was highly disappointed that Leonardo was not present because he thought he might have a few commissions for the Master. The king was also greatly moved by the beauty of the marble figure of Beatrice in repose with her folded hands and the softness of her child-like face, and thus, with great sensitivity, he expressed his condolences to her brothers, Alfonso and Ferrante, and her father, the elderly Duke Ercole, who were there with him in attendance.

Many Milanese patriarchs and celebrities were missing from Louis's celebrations for they had left before the French army had captured the city. Ludovico and his two boys Maximilian and Francesco, Galeazzo Sanseverino, Leonardo, and my father were amongst those who had left the city for safer grounds or to defend their out-lying territories.

The French King Louis XII Adopts Isabella Aragon Sforza's 9-Year-Old Son Francesco II (Il Ducetto) Maria Sforza and Exiles Him in France

Isabella Aragon Sforza (the *Mona Lisa* and Duchess of Bari), against the good advice from Ludovico and her friends including my mother and father and Leonardo, unfortunately decided to stay on in Milan and to meet with the King of France. She wanted to plead with the king for him to restore her son's legitimacy to the ducal title of Milan. Her advisors instead pleaded with her not to be so naive and warned her passionately that the king saw only himself as the rightful Duke of Milan and that he would only recognise and honour his grandmother's (Valentina Visconti's) titles to the Duchy of Milan. Like Ludovico Sforza, he would never recognise or allow her son to have the throne of Milan. In short, she would be placing herself and her son in mortal danger. But, she stubbornly refused to listen to this good advice and instead continued to insist that it was better for her and her son to meet with the king and plead their case. Incredibly, she sent her 9-year-old son unaccompanied to the Castello to meet with king Louis XII. To her shock and dismay, the king refused to allow the young prince to return to her rooms at the Corte Vecchio, and when he left Milan on the 7th of November 1499, he took the boy with him to France. The king eventually made him Abbot of Noirmoutiers where he lived in retirement until, eleven years later, at the age of twenty, he fell from his horse and broke his neck in a riding accident while out hunting in Angouleme.

Fig. 69. Francesco II (Il Ducetto) Maria Sforza,
painted by Giovanni Antonio Boltraffio, 1498/99.

Leonardo's Meeting with King Louis XII and the Commissions for *The Virgin and Child and Saint Anne*

Once Leonardo heard the news of the unfortunate kidnapping of Isabella Aragon Sforza's son by the French king, he immediately left Vaprio and returned to the Corte Vecchio in Milan with Salai and Luca Pacioli to provide the distraught princess with the moral support and comfort that she needed so much. Back in Milan, he found out from officers within the interim government and council that his property and vineyard at San Vittore near the Porta Vercellina had been confiscated and that they were now considered to be French properties and were being used as a camp to billet French troops. Moreover, the French archers had used his monumental clay model of the Sforza horse as target practice and damaged it beyond repair. Salai's father who was the resident caretaker of the vineyard relocated to the Melzi farms near Vaprio, so Leonardo felt that he no longer belonged nor needed to stay in Milan.

Within a day or two of his return to Milan, Leonardo received an invitation from the French king's Secretary Florimond Robertet to attend a meeting and presentation with the French king. The king was most impressed with Leonardo's paintings, and he wanted to meet with the painter and commission some pictures of Madonnas. Leonardo was reluctant to provide his services to the French king and the new interim duke of Milan, but Isabella Aragon Sforza's pleas convinced him to meet and advocate on her behalf. She wanted Leonardo to plead for mercy from the king and have him return her son Francesco to her with the promise that she would leave the Duchy of Milan forever.

The meeting took place a few days before the king's scheduled return to France. The king told Leonardo that he was greatly honoured to meet with the greatest painter of their time and how much he was overwhelmed by the *Last Supper* and his beautiful painting of the *Virgin of the Rocks*. He apologised to Leonardo for the damage to his giant clay horse, and he hoped that Leonardo would be able to restore it to its previous glory. While the king did not have the funds for the restoration of the horse, he wanted to commission Leonardo to provide him with paintings and altarpieces of a Madonna and Child in the presence of her mother Saint Anne. Leonardo was informed that Saint Anne was the patron saint of king Louis's wife Queen Anne Duchess of Brittany and that her Royal Highness desired a votive for the chapel of the Church of St. Anne that she sponsored near the village of Roche-Bernard and attended for prayers and devotions on her travels between Vannes and Nantes in Brittany. Leonardo agreed to the generous terms of the commissions from the king and his secretary. However, he explained to them that he was already committed to return to Florence in order to fulfil commissions that had been arranged there for him. Also, he needed to take care of his father and uncle who were both ill and who wanted him to be back in Florence with them at a time in their lives when they were both old and infirmed, and they were fast approaching their own deaths with unwelcomed anxiety. He told his French Lords that he was obliged to attend to his filial duties and that he would commence his paintings of the Madonnas for them when he was back in Florence. The French king was returning to France and so had no major objections to this proposal and hoped that Leonardo would finish his paintings for him within a year or two taking into account the present upheavals to both of their lives. Leonardo's advocacy on behalf of Isabella Aragon Sforza for the release of her son fell on deaf ears.

Isabella Aragon Sforza and Leonardo da Vinci Bid Farewell and Leave Milan Before Christmas, 1499

As a consequence of his meeting with the French king, Leonardo had no choice but to return to Florence and to visit his father and uncle and inquire into their health. With the help of Salai and Tommaso Masini, he disbanded and paid due reward to his staff and cleaned out his studio and workshops at the Corte Vecchio. Most of his assistants chose to remain in Milan and to join other studios including that of Ambrogio de' Predis, whereas Giovanni Boltraffio accepted sponsorship from the Casio family in Bologna. Leonardo's new student Bernardino Luini decided to travel with Leonardo and his small group to Rome, Mantua, and then to Venice where Leonardo had arranged to meet with his other acolytes for a grand tour of the art works of the city and to discuss with them their need for independence from him and how to best find new commissions and sponsors.

Leonardo's close neighbour at the Corte Vecchio, Isabella Aragon Sforza also gave instruction for all her belongings, except those treasures she valued too highly to part with, to be sold forthwith in preparation for the start of a new chapter in her life far away from the Duchy of Milan. Then, on the 14th of December in 1499, she and her two daughters, together with Leonardo da Vinci, Tommaso Masini, Salai, Bernardino Luini, and Luca Pacioli, left for Pavia as their departure point from Lombardy to travel to other states and dominions. From there, Leonardo's party separated from the Duchess and her children, and they first travelled to Rome and Naples. They were on secret missions for Isabella Aragon Sforza, Cesare Borgia, and Count Louis de Ligny before visiting Mantua at the invitation of Marquess Francesco II Gonzaga and his wife the Marchesa Isabella d' Este on their way to Venice and Bologna. Luini found a sponsor for his work in Treviso and chose to stay there for a few years to further his career as a fresco painter before returning to Milan. The others finally reached Florence on the 24th of April and settled at the cloisters of the Basilica of Santissima Annunziata of the Servite order the Servants of Mary where Leonardo would stay for a while to paint his two masterpieces, the *Virgin and Child with St. Anne* and the *Madonna of the Yarnwinder*.

The unhappy and disgraced Isabella Aragon Sforza and her two young daughters left Pavia down the River Po to visit Isabella d' Este at Mantua for a few weeks over Christmas and the New Year, before they travelled on to Genoa and then, years later, by sea to Naples.

Ludovico's Last Stand, Capture, and Imprisonment. February to April 1500

After King Louis XII left Milan to return to France, the people suddenly decided that they wanted the uncivilised French out of their city. Ludovico who was still in Innsbruck was greatly encouraged by the news that the Milanese wanted him to return and form a resistance force against the foreign occupation. Remarkably, he found sufficient finance, men, and support from Maximilian I and his wife Bianca Sforza and from Swiss bankers to set out from Brixen on the 24th January 1500 in the company of Galeazzo Sanseverino and an army of 10,000 troops in an attempt to regain his city and dominions. He rode into Milan with his army on 5th February 1500 without any substantial resistance and took everybody by surprise including himself, his enemy, and his supporters. He described his success in a triumphant letter to his sister-in-law Isabella d' Este.

> Illustrious Lady and Dearest Sister, On the 24th of last month we left Brixen by the grace
> of God, and crossed Monte Braulio into the Valtellina with a body of Landsknechten.

Monsignore the Vice-chancellor, Messer Galeaz, and Messer Visconti, went on before with the Swiss and Grison infantry, by way of Coire and Chiavenna, and reached the lake of Como on the 30th. Here M. Galeaz fitted out eleven ships, with which he attacked and put to flight the enemy's fleet, and took a fortress occupied by the French. Both the Castle of Bellagio and the town of Torno surrendered to His Reverence, who pushed on with his troops to Como, where he met Monsignore Sanseverino arriving from the Valtellina, and the two cardinals together did the rest. Monsieur de Ligny and the Count of Musocho--Trivulzio's son-- who held the town with 1,500 horse, fled at the approach of the two Monsignori, knowing the feeling of the people, and his Eminence entered Como amidst the greatest rejoicing in the world. M. Galeaz and his light horse pursued the enemy, and Monsignore pushed on towards Milan, hearing from our friends there that his arrival was impatiently desired. On Friday, the last of January, some of the people rose in arms, and M. Gian Giacomo fortified the Corte Vecchio and the Duomo, and, with 2,000 infantry, marched through the streets of the armourers, the builders, and the hatters, to make a public demonstration. But our friends waited, knowing that the right moment had not yet come. On Sunday, the 2nd, the French captains, hearing of the cardinals' approach, and knowing the strong feeling in the city, assembled their troops early on the Piazza of the Castello. Our friends were well prepared, and at the same moment all the bells rang, and the whole city rose in arms. More than 60,000 people attacked the French, and drove them back into the Castello, where they spent the night, without forage for their horses, and on Monday morning, the day before yesterday, they fled from Milan in terror. The bridges had been broken down to hinder their passage, but, luckily for them, the Ticino was low, and they crossed the bed of the river, and retired to Gaiata in safety. And on Monday the Vice-chancellor entered Milan, amidst universal rejoicing, and endeavoured to give chase to the French army, but had not a sufficient number of horses to effect his object.

On Monday morning we reached Como, after taking possession of the castle on the rock of Musso, and were joyfully received all along the lake, by the chief citizens and gentlemen of the district, who came out in boats to meet us. At the gates of the city, the whole population received us with incredible rejoicing and loud acclamations. Yesterday we slept at Mirabello, a house of the Landriani, about a mile out of Milan. All the way from Como crowds of gentlemen and citizens streamed out to meet us on foot or on horseback, in continually increasing numbers, and cries of Moro! Moro! and shouts of joy greeted our steps, whichever way we turned. This morning at sunrise we left Mirabello, and entered the suburb of the Porta Nouva, at the hour indicated by our astrologer, but alighted at Gian Francesco da Vimercato's garden, and waited there a little while to give the gentlemen time to meet us and enter the city.

The two cardinals rode out to meet us, and Messer Galeaz and many gentlemen, with a great number of men-at-arms on foot and horseback, and we marched all through the city and up to the Duomo. All the streets and windows and roofs were thronged with people shouting our name with such rapture that it would be a thing almost incredible if we had not seen it ourselves. And so with universal rejoicing we have returned here, by the grace of God, and already we hear that Lodi, Piacenza, Pavia, Tortona, and Alessandria have driven out the French, and returned of their own free will to our allegiance. The castle of Trezzo has surrendered, and that of Cassano has been fortified in our name by the Marchesino, and all the towns on the Venetian frontier have declared for us, and before long we hope to have recovered the whole state. The Castello here is still held by 300 French soldiers, but it is badly provided with victuals and fuel, and although they have saltpetre, there is no charcoal to make gunpowder, so we are in good hope of recovering the place, but do not mean to let this delay us for a moment in pursuing our victorious course. The enemy is in full retreat, and we mean to drive them back to the mountain passes, and have already sent M. Galeaz early this morning with the infantry, and all the horse that we have, in their pursuit. Monsignore Sanseverino is gone today and we follow tomorrow with all the horse we can collect and a good number of infantry, the better to carry out our plans. We hear that the soldiers, which were in

Romagna, to the number of 250 lances, besides infantry, have been recalled, and have reached Parma, and feel sure that your lord, the Marquis of Mantua, and our other allies will pursue them, and with their help, and the general rising of the people, we trust to obtain complete victory. We tell your Highness these things the more gladly because we feel sure that you have been grieved for our trouble, and will rejoice with us at these fortunate successes. You will forgive me for not writing in my own hand, because of pressing engagements.

LODOVICUS MARIA SFORTIA, Milan, February 5, 1500. [S7]

But, Ludovico's victory, euphoria, and return to Lombardy were short lived lasting only two months. He was captured on the 10th of April 1500 outside of Milan and imprisoned at the citadel of Novara for a week before being transferred over the Alps to Lyon in France where he was paraded on the 2nd of May riding backwards on a mule through the streets to abusive and jeering crowds. His final eight years were spent in the French prisons at Pierre-Encise in Berry and in Lys Saint-Georges, and he died aged 56 years, a penniless prisoner in the dungeon of Loches in Tourine on 17th May 1508. His death was written about, celebrated, and mourned. My father was deeply upset by the death of Ludovico who he had hoped he could free from his French prison some day when the time was right.

Gian Galeazzo Sforza's brother Ermes Maria Sforza, a strong supporter of his uncle Ludovico Sforza, was also captured in Novara. He managed to escape custody and flee to Tyrol and find safety under the protection of his sister the Empress Bianca Sforza the Queen of Germany and live peacefully in Innsbruck until his death a few years later.

Leonardo da Vinci was back in Florence painting at the Basilica of Santissima Annunziata when he received the news of Ludovico's capture and imprisonment by the French. This news was a blow to his hopes of regaining his confiscated house, vineyard, belongings, and other properties. While memories and regrets flooded into his mind about his time with Ludovico in Milan, he jotted down the following notes about his shattered hopes:

The Saletta above ... (left unfinished).
Bramante's buildings ... (left undone).
The Castellano a prisoner ...
Visconti in prison--his son dead.
Gian della Rosa's revenues seized.
Bergonzio--the duke's treasurer-- deprived of his fortune.
The duke has lost state, fortune, and liberty, and not one of his works has been completed.

These last words of Leonardo are an ironic and a fitting epitaph for Ludovico Moro Sforza. But, it was the Roman historian Girolamo Borgia who best summarised Ludovico and his wicked and ruthless thirst for power:

The usurper Ludovico Sforza, the Moor, with the viper as his emblem, revealed his evil intentions, and embraced the field of sin, and tyranny. He attended to the cure of Gian Galeazzo, son of his brother, an innocent youth, and the legitimate prince of Milan, by administering poison to him. Instead of looking after his health and protecting him from harm, he killed him with a poisoned chalice. If he cared for the young duke as he had previously done, then he could have continued to reign without envy and hatred and governed the duchy in the face of his own strong desires. There was nobody who did not condemn this man's great impiety with whatever kind of malignant accusation, denouncing, and loathing of such an incredible, atrocious, and unchristian deed in any man, and particularly in the one who was like a father, a ruler, and the organiser of all things related to the duchy and the world that he ruled as he chose following his own conscience as its governor. Who did not foresee that this violent and miserable crime would fall upon and bring down the same tyrant and his progeny? [S29]

Girolamo Borgia was born in 1479 in Senise (Basilicata) in the Kingdom of Naples, and he wrote his twenty-one books of the *History of the Italian Wars* covering the period from 1494 to 1540s. He was 15 years of age when Gian Galeazzo Sforza died, and he met with me to discuss my time in the service of the French king Francois I and how the Milanese adjusted to Spanish rule. He was curious to know what I knew of the murder of the sixth Duke of Milan and what role his uncle had played in it. I told him all what I knew and I believed. He told me that he had more direct sources than me, the attending doctors, who told him that the young duke was poisoned by Ambrogio Varesi by instruction from Ludovico Sforza and that they were much too afraid of being killed themselves if they stood in the way of divine providence.

As righteous chroniclers and historians and paragons of virtue, we can add many more wrongs and disappointments to those already listed of Ludovico's wrongs and betrayals.

- The overthrow and murder of the Governor Ciccio Simonetta.
- The overthrow and banishment of Bona of Savoy.
- The murder of Gian Galeazzo Sforza to usurp his throne.
- The usurpation of Gian Galeazzo Sforza's son Francesco II Sforza and his right to inherit the title of the Duchy of Milan.
- The house arrest of Isabella Aragon Sforza and her children.
- The premature death of Bianca Sforza, his illegitimate daughter and wife of Galeazzo Sanseverino.
- The betrayal and premature death of his own young wife Beatrice d' Este.
- The betrayal of Milan and its Lords and Citizens.

This is but a short list of his deceitfulness and intrigues, not to mention all his betrayals of his previous allies, the Venetians, the French, the Florentines, the Papal States, the Neapolitans, and even his own people. As a consequence of Ludovico's war with Charles VIII and Louis XII, a whole collection of his most loyal supporters suffered along with him after his defeat, not only to lose their lands and houses, but in some cases also their liberty or even their lives. Leonardo da Vinci the Florentine had his house and vineyards in San Vittore confiscated by the government of the French occupation forcing him to leave Lombardy and look for commissions elsewhere. The French archers damaged beyond repair the clay equestrian statue of Francesco Sforza that Leonardo had constructed during the early 1490s for the Sforza dynasty, and it was left to stand exposed neglected and decaying among the vineyards on his confiscated property at San Vittore. The ducal treasurer Antonio Landriano was mortally wounded by a wild mob on the Duomo Piazza, and Ambrogio Ferrari's house was sacked and destroyed by a mob. Marchesino Stanga lost his house, land, and life while imprisoned in the Castello of Milan. Pope Alexander VI seized Cardinal Ascanio Sforza's palace and treasures in Rome while the cardinal was held prisoner in France in Bourges and before he was released to attend a conclave and elect Pius III in September 1503. Niccolo da Bussola and Jacopo Andrea were arrested and imprisoned by General Trivulzio and then hanged, drawn, and quartered and displayed from the battlements of the Castello in Milan. Caterina Sforza was captured by Cesare Borgia and the French and imprisoned for a year within the walls of the Castel Sant Angelo in Rome before her release and exile to Florence. Many of Ludovico's supporters such as Crivelli, Bergamini, Marliani, and the loyal Visconti took refuge in Ferrara, Mantua, Florence, Venice, and Rome or with the Emperor Maximilian's travelling courts in the Tyrol or his Queen's residence in Innsbruck. Many lost their lands, wealth, and reputation. Some of them eventually were pardoned and returned to Milan and Lombardy, but most of them died in exile. In 1500, the French murdered Giacopo Andrea, the Ferrarese architect who translated the works of Vitruvius for Leonardo.

Others would betray Ludovico and cross sides and escape persecution by the French. The Marquis of Mantua and the Sanseverino brothers Fracassa and Antonio Maria sided with the Venetians, but later returned to support Ludovico in his attempt to regain Milan. Gian Francesco Sanseverino the Count of Caiazzo jealous of the relationship between Ludovico and his younger brother Galeazzo Sanseverino secretly joined the French side. Others to betray Ludovico and join General Trivulzio with the French were Francesco Barnardino, Antonio Maria Pallavicini of Tortona, the Borromeos, Francesco Berardino Visconti (governor), Castiglione, Erasmo, and Bernardino da Corte the governor left in charge of the Sforza fortress, and so many more too numerous to list.

The Count of Caiazzo and his brother Cardinal Sanseverino who now held much influence in the French court successfully persuaded King Louis to pardon all the Sanseverino brothers. Galeazzo Sanseverino stayed loyal to his father-in-law Ludovico right to the end and was in exile in Innsbruck on the periphery of the Empress Bianca's court attempting to negotiate on behalf of Emperor Maximilian for Ludovico's release. The French admired the way Galeazzo Sanseverino stayed loyal to Ludovico to the end, and they never doubted his bravery, horsemanship, and fighting skills, and so they decided to rehabilitate him. After all, he was a French knight of the Order of Saint Michael. Cardinal d'Amboise invited him to Milan and after a summons to the French court his houses and estates and fortune that he had inherited from his dead wife Bianca were eventually restored to him. He soon won royal favour with Louis XII and was appointed Grand Ecuyer de France (Head of the Royal Stables). He accompanied Louis XII to Milan in 1507 and organised the grand jousting tournaments held on the Piazza of the Castello. Galeazzo Sanseverino triumphed once more, and he outlived King Louis and many of his old allies and enemies. He also attended Leonardo's funeral and rode guard of honour in his shiny black armour beside his old friend's funeral carriage in Amboise in 1519.

Machiavelli would see Ludovico Sforza's major failures as vacillation and the inability to honour his word, content the people, keep the allegiance of his nobles, and to maintain a strong and uniform military organisation. He also failed by spending too much time indulging himself and his vassals with intrigues and relying far too much on his astrologers like Ambrogio Varesi who often led him down the wrong paths and into deadly *cul de-sacs*. Interestingly, Machiavelli thought that the Sforza failure was also because of their misunderstanding about fortifications:

> It can be put like this: the prince who is more afraid of his own people than of foreign interference should build fortresses; but the prince who fears foreign interference more than his own people should forget about them. The castle of Milan, built by Francesco Sforza, has caused and will cause more uprisings against the House of Sforza than any other source of disturbance. So the best fortress that exists is to avoid being hated by the people. If you have fortresses and yet the people hate you they will not save you; once the people have taken up arms they will never lack outside help.

PART 2

CONTINUED ... ITALIAN-FRENCH CONNECTIONS

A stone of some size recently uncovered by the water lay on a certain spot somewhat raised, and just where a delightful grove ended by a stony road; here it was surrounded by plants decorated by various flowers of divers colours. And as it saw the great quantity of stones collected together in the roadway below, it began to wish it could let itself fall down there, saying to itself: 'What have I to do here with these plants? I want to live in the company of those, my sisters.' And letting itself fall, its rapid course ended among these longed for companions. When it had been there sometime it began to find itself constantly toiling under the wheels of the carts, the iron-shoed feet of horses and of travellers. This one rolled it over, that one trod upon it; sometimes it lifted itself a little and then it was covered with mud or the dung of some animal, and it was in vain that it looked at the spot whence it had come as a place of solitude and tranquillity. Thus it happens to those who choose to leave a life of solitary contemplation, and come to live in cities among people full of infinite evil.

A rat was besieged in his little dwelling by a weasel, which with unwearied vigilance awaited his surrender, while watching his imminent peril through a little hole. Meanwhile the cat came by and suddenly seized the weasel and forthwith devoured it. Then the rat offered up a sacrifice to Jove of some of his store of nuts, humbly thanking His providence, and came out of his hole to enjoy his lately lost liberty. But he was instantly deprived of it, together with his life, by the cruel claws and teeth of the lurking cat.

A man saw a large sword, which another one wore at his side. Said he 'Poor fellow, for a long time I have seen you tied to that weapon; why do you not release yourself as your hands are untied, and set yourself free?' To which the other replied: 'This is none of yours, on the contrary it is an old story.' The former speaker, feeling stung, replied: 'I know that you are acquainted with so few things in this world, that I thought anything I could tell you would be new to you.'

Man does not vary from the animals except in what is accidental.

— Leonardo da Vinci

CHAPTER 17

Farewell to the Mona Lisa and Self Exile in the New Millennium. The Wandering Years

Those who fall in love with practice without science are like a sailor who enters a ship without a helm or a compass, and who never can be certain whither he is going.

— Leonardo da Vinci

Isabella Aragon Sforza, Former Princess of Naples and Duchess of Milan, Now the *Sou Jure* Duchess of Bari and Princess of Rossano, Leaves Her Former Duchy for a New Life in Naples and Bari

At the end of 1499, Cesare Borgia, the Italian-French condottiero and illegitimate son of Pope Alexander VI, asked Leonardo to accompany the Duke of Ligny on a mission to Rome and Naples with secret messages for the Pope and the King of Naples. Cesare had set his sights on becoming the new administrator of Romagna with French support, and he wanted Leonardo's architectural and engineering assistance to assess the fortifications of the towns and cities that he had set his sights on. Leonardo saw this as an opportunity to meet with Isabella Aragon Sforza in Naples and graciously accepted Cesare's mission, and together with the Duke of Ligny, Salai, Fra Luca Pacioli, Tommaso Masini, and Bernardino Luini set off for Rome and Naples. When in Rome, Leonardo met with Sancha the half-sister of Isabella, and then after a few weeks into the New Year, he travelled with the Duke of Ligny and Bernardino Luini to Naples where he again met with Isabella, the new Duchess of Bari, and her daughters who were staying as guests of Federico, the King of Naples, before embarking on their journey to Bari. In Naples, Leonardo and Bernardino Luini sat with Isabella on a balcony, and they sketched some new portraits of her in front of a mountainous Neapolitan backdrop. They stayed with her for only a few days before travelling with Salai, Fra Luca Pacioli, and Tommaso Masini to Mantua to meet with Isabella d' Este and her husband Francesco II Gonzaga. With new plans in his mind, Leonardo declined Isabella Aragon Sforza's kind offer to take up residence at her court in Bari and told her that he had committed to a number of new contracts in Florence. Also, he was in negotiations with Cesare Borgia and the French for possible future employment. While Isabella was disappointed, she nevertheless realised that Leonardo was still too attached to the cities of Florence and Milan, and that he was unlikely to ever join her in the far out-reaches of the Duchy of Bari on the Adriatic coast. She was right. Leonardo had little interest in the Duchy of Bari, except for the occasional visit. He still had big ambitions to enhance his reputation as a Tuscan/Lombardian painter and an engineer to the powerful rulers rather than reside in a royal court of prettiness with Isabella in Bari. However, he carried his unfinished portrait of her, the *Mona Lisa*, back with him to Florence where he intended to finish it and then undertake a series of new portraits of her as his muse. He continued to work on her medical portrait for the remainder of his life and his memory of her never left him. Isabella also became the favoured model of Bernardino Luini, and he used her image frequently in his paintings of Madonnas and allegorical paintings of interesting and mythological women.

The Duke of Ligny and Leonardo had travelled to Naples to warn Isabella and her uncle of the planned French-Spanish invasion. In the last week of July of 1501, before Isabella and her children could safely depart for Bari, they suddenly were forced to make haste and escape from Naples to the nearby island of Ischia in the company of Isabella of Balzo, the Queen consort of Naples. Her father's uncle, Federico, the king of Naples, was threatened and deposed by invading French and Spanish troops, and King Louis XII of France now laid claim to Naples.

While in Ischia on the 2nd September 1501, Isabella, the Duchess of Bari, dispatched the following imploring letter to King Ferdinand of Spain:

> Sacred Majesty (King Ferdinand II of Aragon)
>
> Kissing the hands of Your Majesty with my public misfortunes, I believe that Your Majesty already knows how after I lost my husband and the State of Milan I also lost both my father and my brother and my son was taken away from me. As a last refuge, following the order of my Majesty S. King Federico, I came to this kingdom with my two daughters where his Majesty King Federico delivered us, and my dowry given to me with S. Ludovico's willingness, the duchy of Bari and the principate of Rossano and the county of Borrello, the kingdom that had belonged to the above mentioned S. Ludovico. I have been sustaining my life and those of my poor daughters with the income from these properties until the present day, but now this other misfortune has occurred with the expulsion of King Federico from the Kingdom of Naples. I, to make offer as an obedient daughter of his Majesty and to not dishonour my debt and to preserve my honour and to not stay in Naples depending on a foreign power, being a young woman and widow, I came here to Ischia with his Majesty King Federico where I am now destitute from every favour and support and from every way of life with my poor daughters. Since all my properties that I had both in Puglia and in Calabria are now under the jurisdiction of Your Majesty, I implore that Your Majesty may consider to have all my properties confirmed and returned to me like I had them in the past so that I can go on living from them without being forced to go panhandling with my two daughters. I trust on the goodness of Your Majesty that Your Majesty will personally provide for me out of pure compassion for what and who I am, I being of the house of Aragona; and for this grace Your Majesty will receive merit from S. God and everlasting glory on earth. I remit myself to Your Majesty who is my most royal and valued relative, and here I present don Antonio de Cardona who in my name will tell you that I continuously recommend you in good grace. In Ischia on 2nd September 1501.
>
> From Your Majesty's obedient servant and great-niece Isabella de Aragonia Sforcia, unique in disgrace by her own hand, Y(Isabella) [S30]

It was only a few months after Isabella dispatched the pleading letter to the king of Spain that tragedy struck her again. Her youngest daughter Ippolita Maria Sforza suddenly became ill and died unexpectedly at the age of eight years. The young girl was engaged to marry Ferdinand, the Duke of Calabria, the son of King Federico and Queen Isabella del Balzo, but instead, he was trapped with her on the island only to watch her die. Isabella of Aragon, Duchess of Bari, was in mourning, and she stayed for another year on the island before leaving and arriving safely in Bari with her grieving nine-year-old daughter, Bona Sforza. In a period of two years, Isabella had lost her youngest daughter to a sudden illness and death, and her son Francesco Sforza was abducted by King Louis XII and exiled somewhere in France. Francesco was now 11 years of age and not permitted to attend his sister's funeral or join his mother to live freely in Bari. Fortune seemed very unkind to Isabella and her children, but now she had the important task to take care of her surviving daughter Bona and also her people of Bari, for their previous duke Ludovico Sforza had long neglected them.

The Story of Isabella of Aragon's Half Sister, Sancha of Aragon, Princess of Squillace

Sancha was the half-sister of Isabella of Aragon, Duchess of Bari, the former consort to the Duke of Milan, Gian Galeazzo Sforza. She was born in 1478, the illegitimate daughter of Isabella's father King Alfonso II of Naples and his mistress Trogia Gazzela. Sancha was eight years younger than Isabella, but they loved each other and forever remained the best of friends. Sancha also had a younger brother named Alfonso III of Aragon who she loved very dearly and took care of him like her own son. Sancha had a strong rebellious streak that upset many of her peers, but she and Isabella rarely quarrelled, and they were very sad when Isabella left Naples in 1489 to marry Gian and live in Milan. Nevertheless, they corresponded regularly describing their adventures, thoughts, and beliefs and the various mishaps that continually confronted them in their life's journey. Isabella shared many of Sancha's stories with Leonardo who was interested to hear all her stories and encouraged her to tell him about all her relationships and adventures when she lived in Naples, Milan, and Rome. He enjoyed relating them to us when we travelled together to Rome in 1513. The following is what he told us about the fascinating Sancha Aragona.

In 1493, when Sancha was 15 years of age, she was engaged and married by proxy to the 11-year-old Gioffre Borgia, brother to Cesare Borgia, and the last illegitimate son of Pope Alexander VI. A year later their marriage was consummated in Naples and witnessed by her father King Alfonso II of Naples and Gioffre's uncle, the cardinal Juan Borgia. In May of 1496, at the insistence of the Pope, they left Naples and moved to live in Rome where at 18 years of age Sancha was greatly admired for her sensuality and beauty by the court of the Vatican, and especially Gioffre's two older brothers, Cesare and Giovanni Borgia. Within the year, she became the mistress of both Cesare and Giovanni while still the wife of Gioffre. Cesare, jealous of his 23-year-old brother's more intimate and frequent relationship with Sancha, stalked and murdered him and disposed his body into the Tibre River on the night of 14th of June 1497. With Giovanni dead, Cesare proposed to marry Sancha and send his brother Gioffre to a monastery. However, his father the Pope intervened angrily and had him engaged instead to Princess Carlotta of Aragon, rather than disrupt the as yet fruitless marriage between Sancha and Gioffre. Bereft at the loss of Sancha as his preferred wife, Cesare instead arranged the marriage of his sister Lucrezia to Sancha's younger brother Alfonso III. In this way, Cesare hoped to remain in intimate contact with Sancha and his sister Lucrezia. Sancha was very happy and pleased with Cesare for the arrangement because Lucrezia was her best friend. In the meantime, the wedding negotiation between Cesare and Carlotta was postponed, and his father the Pope sent him on a mission to France to make arrangements for an alliance with the French king Louis XII. Cesare and Louis immediately took a great liking to each other and became firm friends, and Cesare was rewarded with the title of Duke of Valentinois, and he was married to the king of Navarra's sister, the princess Charlotte d'Albret.

While in France, Cesare and Louis, now the very best of friends, plotted the invasion of the Duchy and city of Milan and the overthrow of Ludovico Sforza, the nemesis of Isabella of Aragon. In addition, Louis wanted Cesare's father the Pope to allow him to invade Naples and overthrow the rule of Isabella's uncle, king Federico of Naples. However, Sancha received word from her sister-in-law Lucrezia who had overheard her father the Pope plotting with his cardinals that Louis XII and Cesare intended to overthrow the King of Naples. This plot angered Sancha greatly, and so she and her brother Alfonso III fled from Rome on the 2nd of August to return to Naples and warn her uncle Federico of the intended invasion. This in turn angered the Pope who threatened to excommunicate Sancha and Alfonso from the church if they did not immediately return to Rome, which, under duress, they did return in December of 1499. By then, the French and Cesare Borgia were already in Milan and planning their campaign to invade Naples. Nevertheless, Cesare wanted Leonardo and the Duke of Ligny to go to Rome to convey his love to Sancha and to tell her that he had no intention of ever harming her or her brother or her uncle, the King of Naples, but that an invasion was imminent. Leonardo felt obliged to also warn Isabella Aragon Sforza of the approaching danger from Cesare and the French.

When Leonardo visited Isabella of Aragon in Naples in late January of 1500, he was accompanied by the Count of Ligny who had a message from the French king for Isabella about her son Francesco who was exiled in France, and the intended invasion of Naples by the French who were concerned with Isabella's continued attempts to find allies for her uncle the King of Naples. The message essentially was that no trouble would come to her or to her son as long as she did not make claims for him to be the Duke of Milan. Also, she should immediately cease requesting Spain for assistance. If she complied with the wishes of the French king, then she would be given safe passage to Bari, and the French were willing to form an alliance with her and provide her with protection if she and her Duchy ever needed it.

In August of 1500, tragedy struck the House of Aragon again when an assassin strangled and killed the young Alfonso III (Sancha's brother and Lucrezia's husband) while he was in his bed still recovering from wounds that he had sustained in a previous assassination attempt only one month before. Lucrezia and Sancha were horrified by the bloody scene, for they had both been purposefully distracted from the bedroom moments before by Cesare Borgia to allow his executioner to murder Alfonso in their absence. Lucrezia had only one year earlier joyfully delivered Alfonso's healthy young son, and she was understandably greatly distressed by the unwarranted murder of her husband whom she dearly loved. The Pope showed no sympathy and instead ordered his daughter to give up her son to adoption because he had arranged for her to remarry, and the infant was an impediment to the new engagement. Lucrezia was now to become the property of Alfonso d' Este who was the widowed husband of Anna Sforza, Gian Galeazzo Sforza's youngest sister. Sancha aggrieved by the murder of her brother offered to take care of his young son Rodrigo of Aragon, and she arranged that Lucrezia could secretly meet with her son away from the watchful eyes of the palace guard, the clergy, Cesare, and her father the Pope. The widespread rumour was that the Pope and Cesare Borgia had ordered Alfonso III d' Aragon's murder because they had allied themselves with France against Naples, and they thought that he might stand in their way.

Cesare Borgia's message to Leonardo and Sancha was confirmed when the French and Spanish armies seized Naples on 2nd August 1501. Isabella the Duchess of Bari who had been residing with the King of Naples in his palace in Naples made her escape to the island of Ischia before the enemy army entered the city. It was in Ischia that Isabella's young daughter Ippolita Maria Sforza suddenly became ill and died at the age of eight years. Isabella stayed on the island of Ischia for another year and then sailed to Bari in late 1502.

Lucrezia Borgia left Rome to marry Alfonso d'Este in Ferrara in early 1502, and Sancha became the official and solitary guardian of her nephew Rodrigo while she remained in Rome with Gioffre and the Pope at the Vatican. However, because of her constant complaints and rebelliousness about the invasion of Naples by the Spanish and the French, her father-in-law Pope Alexander VI in October of 1502 had her imprisoned in the Castel Sant' Angelo in Rome. She stayed in captivity with her nephew Rodrigo for almost a year, at which time she became the lover of her cousin, the Cardinal Ippolito d' Este. With the death of Pope Alexander VI on 18th August 1503, her new lover Prospero Colonna set her free and took her and her 4-year-old nephew to Naples. Prospero Colonna also captured her husband Gioffre Borgia and persuaded him to change his allegiance from the French to the Spanish. After the French conceded Naples to the Spanish on 2nd January 1504, Sancha continued to live with her nephew in Gioffre's palace in Naples, and she began an affair with the Spanish viceroy of Naples, General Gonzalo Fernandez de Cordoba. Then, in May of 1504, Cesare Borgia who was under house arrest in Rome by the order of his old enemy Giuliano della Rovere, now

Pope Julius II, escaped, and he arrived at his brother Gioffre's palace in Naples on the pretext that he had come to reunite with Sancha and to bring gifts for his sister's son, Rodrigo. Instead, Sancha's lover Gonzalo Fernandez de Cordoba arrested Cesare and sent him to prison in Spain. The incorrigible and belligerent Cesare Borgia escaped from his prison in 1507 and joined his brother-in-law King John III of Navarre to assist him in his fight against his old Castilian enemy. When Cesare was in Viana, the Castilians killed him on the 11th March 1507.

All who I had talked to and who knew Cesare thought he was a brave and skilled soldier, but an unscrupulous person with a ferocious and uncontrolled temper. Machiavelli who was in Rome during the latter half of 1502 used Cesare in his historical writings as an example of the most dangerous man of his times who used violence and corruption to acquire a principality by virtue of manipulating others who had more power than he did. Strangely, Cesare employed Leonardo as his military architect between 1502 and 1503, and he provided him with a signed and stamped official passport for unlimited access to inspect and direct all ongoing and planned construction in Romagna. Leonardo's biggest construction for Cesare in that year was the canal from Cesena to the Porto Cesenatico on the Adriatic coast. I never really understood why Leonardo provided his service to Cesare. I assume that he must have had some admirable reasons that were never clear to me. Leonardo said that he left Cesare's service as a protest against Sancha of Aragon's unwarranted imprisonment at the Castel Sant' Angelo, and instead that he joined Machiavelli in Florence to assist him and the Signoria to straighten the Arno River at Pisa in an attempt to end the siege of that city.

Sancha of Aragon died childless in Naples at the age of 27 years in 1506, one year before Cesare's death. Her half-sister Isabella of Aragon, the Duchess of Bari, now 36 years of age, took over the care of their nephew Rodrigo, and he grew up with her in the Bari court. The boy with the titles of Duke of Bisceglie and Sermoneta of the House of Trastamara died due to illness in 1512 at the age of 12 years. His mother Lucrezia Borgia, after she left Rome to live with Alfonso d'Este in Ferrara in 1503, never saw Rodrigo again. However, she paid for his upkeep and his education, and provided him with the best teachers that she could find. After her son's death, she attempted to win over his title to Bisceglie, but before she received it, she died from complications of childbirth in Ferrara on 24th June 1519. She was 39 years of age.

After Sancha died in 1506, her legitimate husband (and Lucrezia's brother) Gioffre married his cousin Maria de Mila of Aragon. They had a son and three daughters, and he retained the title of Prince of Squillace on the Calabrian coast, which he ruled as a feudal vassal of Naples until his death in 1518, one year before the death of his sister Lucrezia.

Leonardo never tired to tell stories and sing songs about the sad sagas of the Sforza, Borgia, and Aragona Madonnas, particularly about the princesses Isabella and Sancha of Aragon, and Caterina and Anna Sforza. Whether true or not, they were enchanting tales that made us grown men laugh and cry about the fortunes and misfortunes of these great beauties.

A Meeting with Isabella d' Este in Mantua, February 1500

Isabella d' Este lived from 1474 to 1539, and she was very well known in Italy as a patron of the arts, leader of fashion, and an influential observer of cultural and political events. She was the daughter of Ecole I d' Este and Eleanor of Naples, and she was the eldest sister of Beatrice d' Este, the wife of Ludovico Moro Sforza, the 7th duke of Milan, and she had four influential brothers. Her brother Alfonso married Anna Sforza, the sister of the Gian Galeazzo Sforza, the 6th duke of Milan. Her grandfather, the father of her mother Eleanor of Naples, was Ferdinand I, the Aragonese King of Naples. This meant that she was a near relation to Gian Sforza, the 6th duke of Milan, and a cousin of his wife Isabella of Aragon. Because Isabella d' Este's sister Beatrice was married to Ludovico she became his very close friend, and she enjoyed following and participating in his intrigues. Gian Galeazzo and his wife Isabella Aragon Sforza were also her friends, and they corresponded with her regularly.

She married Francesco II Gonzaga the marquisate of Mantua who was the Captain General of the armies of the Republic of Venice. He, like his wife, was a patron of the arts, and together they had eight children in a highly productive marriage. He died a number of years before his wife Isabella. He contracted syphilis from his regular relationships with prostitutes and his long and ongoing affair with Lucrezia Borgia.

The Marchesa Isabella had a long-lived passion for collecting treasures from great artists, and she was determined to obtain a beautiful portrait of herself from Leonardo da Vinci. As the sister-in-law of Ludovico Moro Sforza, she visited Milan as his guest on numerous occasions, and she received from him many rare gifts and treasures. She used Ludovico for her benefit during the good times, but abandoned him when he needed her support during the bad times just before his demise. Whenever she was in Milan, Leonardo hid from her for he knew that she had a grasping nature and would constantly pester him for a portrait of herself or have him gift her with one of his beautiful pictures of Madonnas.

Her studiolo and other rooms in the tower of the old Castello di San Giorgio at the Court of Mantua were piled high with treasures of all sorts, shapes and sizes, ancient and contemporary art, statues, cameos, priceless gems, exotic pictures, rare instruments of music, silver lyre of Atalante, furniture and manuscripts, books, and precious classics of all sorts. She pestered the clavichord and lyre maker Lorenzo Gusnasco da Pavia for years in an attempt to obtain one of his beautiful sounding instruments that he had once made for her sister. She also greedily chased after her deceased sister's jewellery, wardrobes, and clothing. Only a year after Beatrice's death, Isabella d' Este wrote to the duke's former mistress Cecilia Gallerani to ask for the loan of her portrait painted by Leonardo's hand. Although Cecilia Gallerani Visconta Bergamina had wronged her sister deeply, Isabella d' Este had no qualms at all to write to her to borrow and admire the portrait of her sister's rival for Ludovico's affection.

> Most Excellent Countess Bergamini, Having today seen some fine portraits by the hand of Giovanni Bellini, we began to discuss the works of Leonardo, and wished we could compare them with these paintings. And since we remember that he painted your likeness; we beg you to be so good as to send us your portrait by this messenger whom we have despatched on horseback, so that we may not only be able to compare the works of the two masters, but may also have the pleasure of seeing your face again. The picture shall be returned to you afterwards, with our most grateful thanks for your kindness, and assuring you of our own readiness to oblige you to the utmost of our power, etc. Isabella d' Este, From Mantua. 26th of April 1498. [S7]

Cecilia sent her picture by courier to the Marchesa Isabella d' Este in Mantua with the following note:

> Most Illustrious and Excellent Madonna and Very Dear Lady, I have read your Highness's letter, and since you wish to see my portrait I send it without delay, and would send it with even greater pleasure if it were more like me. But your Highness must not think this proceeds from any defect in the Maestro himself, for indeed I do not believe there is another painter equal to him in the world, but merely because the portrait was painted when I was still at so young and imperfect an age. Since then I have changed altogether, so much so that if you saw the picture and myself together, you would never dream it could be meant for me! All the same, your Highness will, I hope, accept this proof of my goodwill, and believe that I am ready and anxious to gratify your wishes, not only in respect to the portrait, but in any other way that I can, since I am ever Your Highness's most devoted slave and commend myself to you a thousand times. Your Highness's servant, Cecillia Visconti Bergamina, From Milan, the 29th of April 1498. [S7]

The Marquess Francesco II Gonzaga invited Leonardo to Mantua with the promise of offering him architectural commissions for work in Florence. Isabella Aragon Sforza had been there as a visitor only a few weeks previously for Christmas and the New Year, and when she met with Leonardo in Naples she encouraged him to accept the invitation and visit her cousin in Mantua. And so, he, Salai, Bernardino Luini, Tommaso Masini, and Luca Pacioli visited for a week in late February on their way to Venice (where they stayed from March 8th to 13th). Leonardo presented the Marquess Gonzaga with a washed sketch of his wife painted in red and yellow ochre that neither he nor his wife appreciated, and that they eventually gave away to another patron. Isabella thought that she was more beautiful than she actually was and she disliked the lumpy nose and slack chin that Leonardo had given her. This was an intentionally hurried and bad portrait of her with her hair worn like a helmet and her nose of sufficient size to sniff out very good bargains. But, more unusually for an artist who always preached correct perspective, Leonardo deformed her right arm and hand to make it appear like a grasping, twisted appendage extending out from her right shoulder.

Fig. 70. Leonardo's sketch and painting of Isabella d' Este, 1500.

Leonardo had a strong dislike for Isabella d'Este. He didn't like the way that she kept black children in her court as her slaves and mere curiosities, and that she mistreated her artists. So he had no intention of ever presenting her with one of his very fine portraits. He knew that she had threatened to imprison his friend Luca Liombeni for not having completed the decoration of her *studiolo* in the time that she had specified. According to Leonardo, she was a patron of the arts who could never understand or appreciate the slow and deliberate pace of an artist's work. He made an agreement with her husband for at least one architectural commission in Florence and then made his excuses to leave for Venice.

Before leaving, he'd agreed to present the Marchesa with a painting that he said that he would prepare and send to her from Venice. However, he avoided all her overbearing overtures and constant pestering from her agents over the next few years. In the end, she did give up on him ever providing her with a properly finished Leonardo da Vinci portrait. One of her agents, the rich Florentine merchant Agnolo Tovaglia, wrote to her on 27th May 1504 to diplomatically discourage her from her continual pursuit of Leonardo.

> I have received Your Excellency's letter together with the letter for Leonardo da Vinci, to whom I presented it, urging and counselling him with effective arguments that he should in every way oblige Your Excellency with the painting of the young Christ, according to your request. He promised me he would do it during such hours and occasions as were left to him from the work undertaken for the Signoria here. I shall not be remiss in pressing the aforementioned Leonardo and also Perugino in regard to the other painting: both give fine promises and appear to share a great desire to serve your Excellency, and yet I do not doubt that we shall have a competition in tardiness: I do not know which one in this completion is superior to the other, although I am sure Leonardo will be the victor. Nevertheless, I shall behave toward them with an extreme diligence. [S31]

Fig. 71. Titian's painting of Isabella d' Este, 1516.

Leonardo eventually relented, and he sent her a small portrait that his assistant Salai painted for him in 1507.

Her Excellency, the Marchesa Isabella d' Este eventually won the favour of Titian (Tiziano Vecelli) who made her look the way that she wanted to be portrayed. He completed the flattering portrait in 1516 when she was already 42 years of age, but even he managed to distort the look of her right arm, fingers, and hands.

Fig. 72. Salai's 1507 painting of Isabella d' Este from the sketch by Leonardo, 1500.

A Side Trip to Bologna and a Meeting with Copernicus

In March 1500, on the way back to Florence from studying the paintings of the Bellini brothers in Venice, Leonardo and his small party of travellers visited Bologna as guests of the poet Gerolamo Casio in order to meet up again with his assistant painter from Milan, Giovanni

Boltraffio who had settled there. While staying with Gerolamo Casio, Leonardo and Luca Pacioli were invited to accompany him to attend a farewell dinner for Nicolaus Copernicus who was a Polish student enrolled in a religious law program at the University of Bologna. Copernicus was in his final year of law and preparing to soon attend the University of Padua to study medicine and astrology. The principal astronomer and astrologer at the University was Domenico Maria de Novara, and he shared a house with Copernicus and organised the dinner and invited Gerolamo Casio and his friends. Domenico Maria de Novara issued annual astrological prognostications for the city, forecasts that included all social groups, giving his special attention to the fate of the Italian princes and their enemies. During the night, much of the conversation centred on astrological prognostics, Ptolemy's geocentric astronomy, and Regiomontanus's corrections, and the critical expansions of certain important planetary models. Leonardo, of course, had heard all this before from Ludovico Sforza's physician and astrology, the wizard and necromancer, Ambrogio Varesi. He pointed out to Domenico Maria de Novara that astronomers were still in disagreement about the correct order of the planets, and therefore astrologers could not be certain about the strengths of the powers issuing from the planets to make any accurate predictions.

It was immediately after dinner that Leonardo told them about his belief that the earth and the planets circled the sun, a belief that contradicted the central geocentric dogma of the Church that the earth was the centre of the cosmos, and that the sun and all the planets circled the earth. To think otherwise and contradict the Ptolemy geocentric model was considered sacrilegious and tantamount to insanity. Leonardo pointed out to his audience that his sun-centred heliocentric theory had arisen from his reading of the Muslim astronomer Ibn al-Shatir of Damascus as well as being based on his own observations and calculations that he had made while observing the movement of the planets and the stars from the Melzi tower in Vaprio. Moreover, the heliocentric theory was ancient; the Greek Aristarchus of Samos already had developed it in 310 BC. Leonardo quickly sketched out the reformed models of the Sun, Moon, and planets eliminating Ptolemy's eccentric and equant, but showing the epicycles of planets that he previously introduced to the Sforza audience in his design of the revolving planets in his *Paradiso Fiesta* that celebrated the marriage of Gian Galeazzo Sforza and Isabella de Aragon in Milan in 1490. The fact that Leonardo had raised this heliocentric theory to an astrologer and student of canon law was highly provocative. However, Copernicus was more than just a religious lawyer and cleric, he was also a mathematician, classical scholar, diplomat, artist, amateur astronomer, and critical student of astrology. When Leonardo was leaving the party with Casio and Luca Pacioli, Copernicus approached him and thanked him for his views about heliocentrism for he believed them to be correct from his own limited observations and calculations of eclipses, alignments, and conjunctions of the planets and the stars. Leonardo and Copernicus met again at the University of Padua in 1502. It was in Padua that Copernicus introduced Leonardo to Bartolomeodi Montagnana the Younger who became a renowned scholar and author about syphilis. It was a disease that also caught Leonardo's imagination for intense investigation when he was in Rome in 1513, and that he studied in order to develop his theory of microscopic agents of disease.

I read Copernicus's description in favour of heliocentrism of the solar system in a book, the *Narratio Prima*, published by Franz Rhode, and later in the biography of Copernicus by Georg Joachim Rheticus. Copernicus's publication was filled with numbers, calculations, and mathematical explanations on the workings of heliocentrism that was far beyond my limited understanding. I was amazed that Copernicus had probably learned and developed his revolutionary theory of heliocentrism largely from what Leonardo had told him and directed him towards at their meeting in Bologna. Copernicus never acknowledged Leonardo da Vinci for his discourse on the heliocentric theory that the earth and the planets circled the stationary Sun. Yet, in one of his notebooks amongst his mathematical notes, Leonardo has printed in very clear and large capital letters, THE SUN DOES NOT MOVE. This heretical truth contradicts the teachings of the Bible and the Roman Catholic Church that tells us that the earth stands still and the sun orbits it (from the east to the west as we see it). We find this same claim in Psalm 93:1 and Ecclesiastes 1:5 written as, 'Psalm 93:1: The LORD reigns, he is robed in majesty; the Lord is robed, he is girded with strength. Yea, the world is established; *it shall never be moved*;' and in Ecclesiastes 1:5: 'The sun rises and the sun goes down, and hastens to the place where it rises.'

Here is Leonardo's own love letter to the Sun:

IN PRAISE OF THE SUN. If you look at the stars, cutting off the rays (as may be done by looking through a very small hole made with the extreme point of a very fine needle, placed so as almost to touch the eye), you will see those stars so minute that it would seem as though nothing could be smaller; it is in fact their great distance which is the reason of their diminution, for many of them are very many times larger than the star which is the earth with water. Now reflect what this our star must look like at such a distance, and then consider how many stars might be added--both in longitude and latitude—between those stars which are scattered over the darkened sky. But, I cannot forbear to condemn many of the ancients, who said that the sun was no larger than it appears; among these was Epicurus, and I believe that he founded his reason on the effects of a light placed in our atmosphere equidistant from the centre of the earth. Any one looking at it never sees it diminished in size at whatever distance; and the reasons of its size and power I shall reserve for Book 4. But, I wonder greatly that Socrates should have depreciated that solar body, saying that it was of the nature of incandescent stone, and the one who opposed him as to that error was not far wrong. But, I only wish I had words to serve me to blame those who are fain to extol the worship of men more than that of the sun; for in the whole universe there is nowhere to be seen a body of greater magnitude and power than the sun. Its light gives light to all the celestial bodies which are distributed throughout the universe; and from it descends all vital force, for the heat that is in living beings comes from the soul [vital spark]; and there is no other centre of heat and light in the universe as will be shown in Book 4; and certainly those who have chosen to worship men as gods--as Jove, Saturn, Mars, and the like--have fallen into the gravest error, seeing that even if a man were as large as our earth, he would look no bigger than a little star which appears but as a speck in the universe; and seeing again that these men are mortal and putrid and corrupt in their sepulchres.

New Madonnas, Children, and Animals for the French Royalty and Italian Religious Orders

On his return to Florence in April 1500, Leonardo soon settled into his rooms and studio in the cloisters of the basilica at the Santissima Annunziata that was built by Leon Battista Alberti and completed in 1481 soon after his death. Fra Luca Pacioli and the Servite friars formally organised Leonardo's rooms for him and his two most faithful assistants Salai and Tommaso Masini, and for the portfolios of his drawings of madonnas and children that he had prepared while in his travels to Rome, Naples, Venice, and Bologna. Before leaving Milan in 1499, Leonardo had a secret meeting with the French king Louis XII and Florimond Robertet and gained from them paid commissions for paintings of the *Virgin and Child*. The French king's secretary Florimond Robertet was highly cultivated, exceedingly powerful, and one of the richest men in Europe. He previously served as a diplomat and personal secretary to Charles VIII and now was the secretary and treasurer of king Louis XII. Leonardo could not ignore or turn down either of them too easily. The monks of Santissima Annunziata also had commissioned from him a devotional *Madonna and Infant*. So, Leonardo quickly settled down in his workshop to draw and paint Madonnas, especially his *St. Anne and the Virgin and the Infant Christ with a Lamb* for king Louis XII of France. However, Isabella d' Este still pursued him at this time and over the next few years for her 'promised' painting from him, and she had her own agents out to spy on him.

Fra Pietro de Nuvolaria, the Vice-General of the Carmelite Order, had seen Salai and Tommaso Masini at work and dutifully reported back to Isabella d' Este with the following correspondence:

> Most illustrious and excellent Lady, — I have just received Your Excellency's letter, and will obey your orders with the utmost speed and diligence. But, from what I hear, Leonardo's manner of life is very changeable and uncertain, so that he seems to live for the day only. Since he has been in Florence, he has only made one sketch — a cartoon of a child Christ, about a year old, almost jumping out of his mother's arms to seize hold of a lamb. The mother is in the act of rising from S. Anna's lap, and holds back the child from the lamb, an innocent creature, which is a symbol of the Passion, while S. Anna, partly rising from her seat, seems anxious to restrain her daughter, which may symbolise the Church, who would not hinder the Passion of Christ. These figures are as large as life, but are drawn on a small cartoon, because they are represented either seated or bending down, and one stands a little in front of the other, towards the left. And this sketch is not yet finished. He has done nothing else, excepting that two of his apprentices are painting portraits to which he sometimes adds a few touches. He is working hard at geometry, and is quite tired of painting. I only write this that Your Excellency may know I have received your letters. I will do your commission, and let you know the result very soon, and may God keep you in His grace. Your obedient servant, Fr. Petrus Novellara, Carm. Vic-Gen. Florence, April 3, 1501. [S32]

Ten days later, the Carmelite friar wrote again to tell Isabella the result of his efforts to meet with Leonardo and to see his work:

> Most illustrious and excellent Lady, — This Holy Week I have succeeded in learning the painter Leonardo's intentions by means of his pupil, Salai, and some of his other friends, who, to make them more fully known to me, took me to see him on Wednesday in Holy Week. In truth, his mathematical experiments have absorbed his thoughts so entirely that he cannot bear the sight of a paintbrush. But I endeavoured as skilfully as I could to inform him of Your Excellency's wish. Then, finding him well disposed to gratify you, I spoke frankly to him on the subject, and we came to this conclusion: if he can, as he hopes, end his engagement with the King of France without displeasing him by the end of a month at latest, he would rather serve Your Excellency than any other person in the world. But, in any case, as soon as he has finished a little picture, which he is painting for a certain Robertet, a favourite of the King of France, he will do your portrait immediately and send it to you. I left two good petitioners with him. The little picture which he is painting is a Madonna, seated as if at work with her spindle, while the Child, with His foot on the basket of spindles, has taken up the winder, and looks attentively on the four rays in the shape of a cross, as if wishing for the cross, and holds it tight, laughing, and refusing to give it to His mother, who tries in vain to take it from Him. This is all I have been able to settle with the master. I preached my sermon yesterday. God grant it may bring forth much fruit, for the hearers were numerous. I commend myself to Your Excellency.
> — Frateb, Petrus de Novellara. Florence, April 14, 1501. [S32]

One year later, Leonardo and his assistants were still painting Madonnas and children with and without the company of various animals. The *Madonna Lactans* feeding the Christ-child who holds a red-faced goldfinch in his left hand is my favourite. Leonardo also introduced his first sketches of *Leda and the Swan* to his assistants as he was more often than not thinking of his time with Isabella Aragon Sforza and her court and my mother when he suddenly invoked the symbolism of the swan among the Madonnas for his own amusement and that of his friends. Much of this proposed work of *Leda and the Swan* was interrupted in 1502 and did not come to full fruition until after I joined his illustrious company back in Milan in 1508.

Fig. 73. The Madonna Lactans and Christ-child with a goldfinch *by Leonardo.*

During these early years when Leonardo was back in Florence, he spent much time trying to perfect his drawings and paintings of the *Virgin and Child and St. Anne.* This included an immense (56 in x 41 in) and unfinished cartoon drawing of the *Virgin and Child and St. Anne and St. John the Baptist* that many different artists including Raphael, Michelangelo, Filippino Lippi, Cesare da Sesto, Giovanni Boltraffio, and Bernardino Luini saw and copied and went on to spread Leonardo's fame throughout Italy and the European continent for creating the most pious and sweet Madonnas imaginable. They are iconic and votive images of refined beauty, and they show his great respect and love for the female form and the nature of women whether breastfeeding with child (*Madonna Lactans*) or exposing a breast ready to feed an imaginary child cradled in the expectant mother's arms (the *Columbina*). Leonardo's madonnas fill the picture frames with movement, full-bodied, and refined proportions, their heads turned counter to the body. Often, they are slightly bent to the side to impart an innocent fragility and an anxiety or concern. Their heads have long, straight, and slender noses, half closed dreamy or alert eyes widely spaced, and narrow lips delicately arched into a mysterious half smile revealing a sweet and loving expression (known as the uncatchable smile). The broad, high foreheads of his beautiful Madonnas with their long hair parted in the middle are classically Leonardesque. The reddish coloured hair of his Madonnas, Saints or Angels usually inform us that we are looking at the amalgamated images of his two most beloved models, Isabella Aragon Sforza and Simonetta Vespucci.

Fig. 74. Leonardo's Virgin and Child with St. Anne *(left) and* Madonna and Child with the Yardwinder *(right).*

Many poets of the Renaissance referred to Leonardo's Madonnas as works of beauty and great symbolism. Here is an example from Leonardo's friend, the Bolognese poet Gerolamo Casio:

> Sonnet about Leonardo da Vinci's painting of St. Anne holding
> In her arms the Madonna who tries to stop
> Her Son from grabbing the lamb.
> Behold, the Lamb of God, said John the Baptist,
> Who entered, and exited the womb of Mary
> With his holy life to guide us
> And our feet to the Heavenly seats

He holds on to the immaculate Lamb and cries out
That he will sacrifice himself to the world.
His mother holds him back not wishing
To see her Son's destruction, nor her own.
Saint Anne, as if she knew
That heavenly Jesus was formed in our human shape
To wipe away the original sin of Adam and Eve
Tells her daughter with pitiful Zeal,
To drive away her fear
For He and His immolation
Is ordained by Heaven. [S33]

Fig. 75. Leonardo's unfinished cartoon in charcoal, and black and white chalk of the Virgin and Child with St. Anne and St. John the Baptist *(instead of a lamb).*

CHAPTER 18

Romagna Campaign with Cesare Borgia, the Illegitimate Son of Pope Alexander VI, and Other Fortification Commissions

When besieged by ambitious tyrants I find a means of offence and defence in order to preserve the chief gift of nature, which is liberty; and first I would speak of the position of the walls, and then of how the various peoples can maintain their good and just lords.

— Leonardo da Vinci

War in Romagna with Cesare Borgia, 1502 to 1503

Leonardo's paintings of Madonna and Child were interrupted in June of 1502 when Niccolo Machiavelli visited his studio and requested that he attend the Signoria and hear an important proposal from them for his service. The Republic had been in correspondence with Cesare Borgia who had requested their support and permission to conquer and unite the territories of Romagna. Cesare proposed to the Signoria that a Florentine ambassador accompany and advise him on his territorial ambitions. Also, he had requested the Signoria to provide him with the illustrious Leonardo da Vinci to be one of the members of the Florentine ambassadorship to assist him with fortifications in the Romagna territories. If Leonardo accepted to act on behalf of the Signoria as their agent in the service of Cesare Borgia, they would richly reward him and also offer him art commissions fully paid by the Signoria. And so, Leonardo once again entered into the world of territorial political intrigue, this time involving a variety of independent states and fiefs of Romagna.

Ever since the Frankish kings Pepin the Short and Charlemagne the Great captured Italian territories from the Lombardian kings in their conquests of 714 to 814 AD, the Papacy has always claimed the Lombardian territory of Romagna that extended south-east of the Po River ranging from the Tyrrhenian Mountains in the north-west to the Adriatic Sea in the east between the Reno and Silaro rivers. The Frankish kings gifted these and other eastern territories to the Papacy of Rome, a gift that became known as the Donation of Pepin. However, the Popes were not able to reign effectively over the extensive and distant mountainous territories of Romagna, and over time they fragmented into independent city states, small fiefdoms, counties, and marquisates controlled by their own fortified townships, villages or rocca (fortified stronghold) and ruled over by feudal lords, condottieri, bishops, and cardinals who desired their own fiefdoms. The major towns and villages of the Romagna fiefdoms were located south east of Bologna (another papal fiefdom) and included Ravenna, Rimini, Cesena, San Marino, Forli, Faenza, and Imola. Like previous popes, Cesare Borgia's father Pope Alexander VI claimed dominion over the Romagna because of the Donation of Pepin. In order to regain control of the fragmented Romagna territories, the Pope formed an alliance with the French king Louis XII on proviso that while the French would rule Milan and Naples, he and his son Cesare Borgia would receive their support to conquer and unify all the territories of Romagna for the Papacy. The French king agreed to support them with their ambitions for Romagna, but only after he had first secured Milan.

By 1500, the 26-year-old Cesare Borgia had received many of the things that he most desired: a reputation as a formidable military leader, his own French estates, and a beautiful French wife. Now he had assurances from the French that they would help him to capture all the territories of Romagna and recognise his self-proclaimed title of the Duke of Romagna. By

261

the end of 1499, he succeeded in gaining Imola and Forli, the two fiefs that were in the possession of Caterina Sforza who was the Countess of Forli and the Lady of Imola. Although she resisted Cesare bravely for a few months in her fortress of Ravaldino in Forli, by January 1500, Cesare and the French had overwhelmed and captured her. Cesare's father the Pope imprisoned her at the Castel Sant' Angelo in Rome, but the French chivalrously released her from prison on the 30th June 1501 while they were marching to Naples, after which she soon retired with her children to Florence.

In the meantime, Cesare Borgia's progress through the Romagna region was impeded by strong resistance from the duke of Urbino, Guidobaldo da Montefeltro, who prevented him and the French marching through his duchy on their way to conquer the city of San Marino and Rimini. However, in June of 1502, Cesare Borgia successfully forced the duke to flee from Urbino after another treacherous act of negating on all his promises that he solemnly had made to the duke. In an attempt to dispose of the duke of Urbino forever, Cesare requested Florence to support him in his claim for Urbino and the other fiefdoms of Romagna and Marche. The Florentine Signoria were highly concerned by Cesare Borgia's expansionist plans, and they decided to send a diplomatic team to Urbino that included Machiavelli and Leonardo da Vinci as observers to obtain more precise details of the Borgia intentions. The Florentine Signoria appointed Machiavelli to be their official commissioner to the Borgia court, while Cesare independently recruited Leonardo to be his chief engineer of fortifications in order to immerse him deeper into his conspiracies.

Soon after a number of intense meetings with the Florentine diplomats, Cesare was recalled to Pavia by the French king who became worried by the outbreaks of resistance occurring in Lombardy. While in Pavia with the French, Cesare prepared a passport for Leonardo to allow him entry into any area of Romagna with his full support and official signature. The passport was dated 18th August 1502, and it was accompanied by this glowing command from Cesare:

> Cesare Borgia of France by the grace of God Duke of Romagna and Valentinois, Prince of Andria, Lord of Piombino. Also, the Gonfalonier of the Roman Holy Church and Captain General. To all our lieutenants, castellans, captains, condottieri, officials, soldiers, and subjects, who are presented with this document: You are hereby ordered and commanded on our behalf to allow our most excellent and well-beloved friend, the architect and engineer general Leonardo da Vinci, the bearer of this pass, who has received our commission, to inspect all the places and fortresses of our states for their maintenance, and provide him with all such assistance as the occasion demands and his judgement deems fit. He shall be given free passage and be relieved of all public tax both for himself and for his companions, and he shall be welcomed amicably to inspect, measure, and examine whatever he wishes. For this purpose you are to provide him with as many men as he requests, and grant him all the help and favour that he may demand, for it is our will that every engineer in our dominions shall be bound to consult with him and conform with his advice. Let no man dare to do the contrary, if he does not wish to incur our wrath. [S31]

Leonardo was already in the services of Cesare Borgia since July, and he needed an official document to wave at checkpoints and roadblocks and into the faces of the officious or suspicious sentries and officials who obstructed him during his inspections. This passport provided him and Salai with enormous power and favour, for all who looked upon it knew that if they disobeyed Cesare Borgia's orders they were condemned to great punishment, prison or death. Salai now 22 years of age was Leonardo's sword and shield, and he knew how to fight. While Cesare was in Pavia consulting with the French and preparing a passport for his chief engineer, Leonardo had already embarked on his tour of Romagna, and he jotted down in his notebooks some of the days and places that he had visited on his inspections:

30 July - the dove-cote at Urbino.
At the foot of the Apennines, the shepherds make peculiar large cavities in the mountains in the form of a horn, in which they place a real horn. The small horn then combines with the shape of the cavity to form a huge horn, which makes a very loud noise.
1 August - in the library at Pesaro.
8 August - make harmonies out of the different falls of water as you saw in the fountain at Rimini.
10 August – At the Feast of San Lorenzo at Cesena.
15 August – St Mary's day at Cesena.

On the 21st of August, a courier from Cesare Borgia in Pavia presented Leonardo with his travelling passport with a clear warning to the commanders and citizens of Romagna that he, Leonardo, must be treated with favour and respect unless he, the commander or citizen, wishes to incur Cesare Borgia's wrath. The work of Cesare's most favoured engineer, Leonardo, was physical and strenuous, always on the move between occupied cities and towns, fortresses and castles, and long tracks between suspicious, uncomfortable inns with unforgiving early starts, hot days, and late nights. Accompanied by his two assistants, Salai and the newly recruited bodyguard il Fanfoia, Leonardo tracked, measured, paced backwards and forwards, and observed the structure of fortresses while they were watched by the suspicious menacing eyes of armed sentries and their hired cutthroats. Yet, Leonardo at the age of 50 years set about his task with great exuberance, although knowing that he was assisting his employer in the destructive acts and violence of war, *the most brutal madness there is.* In between the inspection of defences and fortresses he still found the time to visit libraries, sample the grapes, inspect the dove coves and fountains, and observe the peasants and villagers and their creative ways of generating new sounds using the forces of wind and nature herself. But, he knew that he was there principally to provide advice to Cesare and his lieutenants. Fra Luca Pacioli, in one of his accounts, included this description of Leonardo with the Borgia troops:

> One day Cesare Valentino, Duke of Romagna and the present Lord of Piombino, found himself and his army at a river which was 24 paces wide, and could find no bridge, nor any material to make one except for a stack of wood all cut to length of 16 paces. And from this wood, using neither iron nor rope nor any other construction, his noble engineer made a bridge sufficiently strong for the army to pass over. [S10]

Not quite the story of the 'loaves and fishes' or the 'parting of the Red Sea', but near enough.

In his notes Leonardo wrote a few reminders to himself.

> See that the escape passage does not lead straight into the inner fortress, otherwise the commander will be overpowered, as happened at Fossombrone.

Provided the following recommendations,

> To order and manufacture the powerful cannons of the French caliber in order not to rely on the French provision.

Criticised the design of the local carts with two small wheels in the front and two high ones behind, which is *'very unfavourable to their momentum because there is too much weight on the front wheels'* and *'the chief realm of idiocy.'*

Admired an entrance to a fort,

>6 September – At Porto Cesnatico, the way in which bastions ought to project beyond.

And watched a battle and a retreat,

>11 October – At the sacking of the fortress of Fossombrone.
>15 October – Retreat from Fossombrone and overwhelmed with Don Michele at Calmazzo.
>20 October – At Imola (with Machiavelli).

By mid September, Cesare had established his headquarters in Imola and assembled his troops with a plan to invade Bologna even though it was already a papal state. Cesare wanted to depose Giovanni Bentivoglio because the Pope had accused him of despotic and corrupt rule of the papal fiefdom, but he held off waiting for his father's permission to launch the attack. This planned attack was abandoned when Cesare received word from his spies that there was to be a retaliation against him from the Magione alliance made up of Ermes Bentivoglio of Bologna, Vitellozzo Vitelli of Citta di Castello, and Paolo Orsini. So, Cesare abandoned his planned attack and instead called on his generals and engineers to strengthen the defences of Imola. He instructed Leonardo to construct a map of the city and the country around it. Leonardo and his assistants paced out the streets and the defensive walls, and he sketched the layout of the small city as if he was observing it from above like a bird. Imola within its walls was less than a mile long and half a mile wide. Cesare's new artillery had arrived from the foundry at Breccia, and he wanted Leonardo to advise him on the best positions for his cannons and mobile precision artillery and explosive projectiles to defend them against an imminent attack.

Using his various measuring machines such as a quadrant, hodometer, calculator, and a magnetic compass on a surveyor's table, as well as his own strong legs, Leonardo paced out and measured Imola to produce a beautiful bird's eye view of the city and the surrounding territories. The map of Imola is delicately coloured showing the city walls in silvery grey, the moat and river in blue, red roofs, and yellow public places. The city is contained within a great circle divided into sixty-four degrees, and Leonardo noted the distances of Imola to Bologna, Castel San Pietro, Forli, and Bertinoro according to the points of the compass. He prepared a number of copies of the map and presented one to Cesare Borgia and retained a souvenir copy to present to Caterina Sforza when they met some time later in Florence. In another series of maps, he showed the roads and streams near Castiglione and Montecchio with distances marked out in the braccia units. Another map showed the whole river-system of central Italy (north to the left and south to the right) with the Mediterranean coast from Civitavecchia to La Spezia (a distance of 170 miles or 274 kilometres) and to the Adriatic coast at Rimini. This map rivals his beautiful map of Vol di Chiana that he prepared for Cesare during his travel through Arezzo to Urbino.

The attack on Imola by the Magione forces never eventuated for they were disrupted by the rumour that a large French force was approaching to free Cesare Borgia from the siege. As a consequence, Cesare Borgia negotiated a pact with Orsini and Vitellozzo to provide him with military services and to abandon their former alliance with Duke Guidobaldo. In this way, Cesare's forces double-crossed and ousted Duke Guidobaldo from Urbino, and Cesare established his own rule there, allowing him and his army to leave Imola and head east towards Cesena and the Adriatic against the order of the Pope who was by now greatly annoyed by the cost of maintaining his son's expensive campaigns in Romagna.

Before the siege of Imola, Cesare Borgia had appointed Antonio Sansavino as 'President of the Romagna' to establish a just and cohesive government to unite the citizens in a way that had not been seen previously since the disintegration of the Roman Empire. It seemed that most of Romagna welcomed the Borgia rule because Sansavino introduced an efficient, enlightened, and centralised administration to the region. Machiavelli disagreed that it was a just or cohesive government because he thought that Borgia allowed too much unruly behaviour from the French and Spanish occupation forces that he didn't allow in the citizens that they were supposed to be protecting. Nevertheless, most would agree that Cesare Borgia and Antonio Sansavino had unified Romagna with an efficient government established from the capital of Cesena.

By 12th December 1502, Cesare and his army had reached Cesena on the Savio river south east of Forlì where he took up residence and declared it to be the capital of his Romagna dukedom. He had captured the entire area of Romagna for himself and the Pope and now he looked forward to rest and take stock of his gains and losses. On the 14th of December, Leonardo and Machiavelli joined him in Cesena to listen to his intended plans for Romagna. He told them that his rule was guaranteed by a treaty with his father the Pope, the King of France, the Signoria of Florence, and Cardinal Giambattista Orsini who had initially opposed Cesare, but had now joined him as his supporter. On the 20th December, the French troops of more than 3,000 men left Cesena to march back to Milan because it was evident that Cesare Borgia no longer had the funds to pay them. His father's coffers had run dry.

On the 31st of December, Cesare declared that he wanted revenge against his enemies, the Orsini brothers (Paolo, Giulio, and Francesco), Vitellozzo Vitelli, and Oliverotto da Fermo. Cesare met them at Senigallia on the Adriatic in the Marche region to reconcile with them, and then in his typical way, he betrayed and wreaked his revenge upon them. Leonardo and Machiavelli were present, and they saw the bloody vengeance that Cesare and his troops dispensed against his enemies. Cesare entered Senigallia on the morning of 31st December, and Machiavelli wrote a dispatch the following day:

> The sack of the town continues although it is now the 23rd hour. I am much troubled in my mind. I do not know if I can send this letter having no one to carry it. It is my opinion the rebels will not be alive tomorrow.

Vitellozzo and Oliverotto were strangled the same night. The three Orsini brothers were hanged at the Castel del Pieve a few weeks later. The senseless killing revolted both Leonardo and Machiavelli. The previous sacking of the fortress of Fossombrone a few months ago resulted in the unnecessary loss of too many lives, and now the same was happening in Senigallia. After the remorseful rebels in Senigallia had let Cesare and his army entry into their town in good faith, it was pure treachery by Cesare to murder them in cold blood as he did.

Yet, Leonardo thought that by strengthening the fortresses, and improving roadways and canals, he was helping to secure the citizens' wellbeing. His insider information was also helping Machiavelli to protect the interests of Florence against Cesare Borgia's possible plans to expand his war into the Republic's territories. The continued war and sieges were a worry for Leonardo and Machiavelli, but neither of them dared to show their concerns to Cesare. By mid January in 1503, Cesare Borgia had captured Siena, and Leonardo wrote in his notebook, *'14th January – Siena, church bell, 10 braccia in diameter, remember the way it moved and how its clapper was fastened.'*

On 20th January, Machiavelli told Cesare Borgia that the Signoria had recalled him back to Florence and that they would replace him with another ambassador. He thanked Cesare with great sincerity for his kindnesses and interesting discussions and was relieved to hurriedly exit the Borgia camp and return to Florence with his life intact.

By the end of January, Cesare Borgia's ailing father, Pope Alexander VI, summoned him to Rome for support and consultation, and Leonardo and Salai travelled to Rome with him and his entourage. By the end of March, Leonardo, il Fanfoia, and Salai left the service of Cesare Borgia with a large payment as their reward for services rendered, and by April 1503, they were back in Florence ready to spend some of their well-earned money.

Despite conquering Romagna, Cesare Borgia's fortunes soon changed for the worse when two events led to his downfall. First, the Spanish forces turned against the French in the month of May in 1503 and drove them out of southern Italy. Cesare accepted the French defeat in Naples calmly for he was still in control of the Romagna and receiving financial support from his father and the papal purse. Then, the second event occurred in Rome that proved disastrous for him. He and his father became violently ill on the same day. While Cesare recovered, his father Pope Alexander VI died due to bad wine or poison on August 18. With the death of his father, Cesare's power-base of papal influence was shattered and his greatest supporter was gone. Cesare Borgia who still had power in Rome to influence the choice of the new Pope then made the biggest mistake of his life by supporting the wrong man for the papacy. The new Pope, Julius II, was Cesare's betrayer. He thanked Cesare for his support, but then, as a sworn enemy of the Borgia, he refused to recognise Cesare's title of the Duke of Romagna and demanded the restitution of his dominions. With the loss of support from the papacy and from the governments across most of Italy including Romagna, Florence, and the new Duchy of Milan, Cesare Borgia sought safety in Naples. Instead of refuge, he was arrested there and exiled to Spain as their prisoner. After escaping from prison, he died as a mercenary in 1507 at the age of thirty years in the Kingdom of Navarre in Basque country. It was the passing of another despot and tyrant during the times of Leonardo da Vinci.

Back in Florence, Machiavelli wrote the following about Cesare Borgia in chapter 7 of his book *The Prince*:

> Those who solely by good fortune become princes from being private citizens have little trouble in rising, but much in keeping atop; they have not any difficulties on the way up, because they fly, but they have many when they reach the summit….
>
> Concerning these two methods of rising to be a prince by ability or fortune, I wish to adduce two examples within our own recollection, and these are Francesco Sforza and Cesare Borgia. Francesco, by proper means and with great ability, from being a private person rose to be Duke of Milan, and that which he had acquired with a thousand anxieties he kept with little trouble. On the other hand, Cesare Borgia, called by the people Duke Valentino, acquired his state during the ascendancy of his father, and on its decline he lost it, notwithstanding that he had taken every measure and done all that ought to be done by a wise and able man to fix firmly his roots in the states which the arms and fortunes of others had bestowed on him.….
>
> Alexander VI, in wishing to aggrandise the duke, his son, had many immediate and prospective difficulties. Firstly, he did not see his way to make him master of any state that was not a state of the Church; and if he was willing to rob the Church he knew that the Duke of Milan and the Venetians would not consent, because Faenza and Rimini were already under the protection of the Venetians.….
>
> For he had killed as many of the dispossessed lords as he could lay his hands on, and few had escaped; he had won over the Roman gentlemen, and he had the most numerous party in the college. And as to any fresh acquisition, he intended to become master of Tuscany, for he already possessed Perugia and Piombino, and Pisa was under his protection. And as he had no longer to study France (for the French were already driven out of the kingdom of Naples by the Spaniards, and in this way both were compelled to buy his goodwill), he pounced down upon Pisa. After this, Lucca and Siena yielded at once, partly through hatred and partly through fear of the Florentines; and the Florentines would have had no remedy had he continued to prosper, as he was prospering the year that Alexander died, for he had acquired so much power and reputation that he would have stood by himself, and no longer have depended on the luck and the forces of others, but solely on his own power and ability.….

> When all the actions of the duke are recalled, I do not know how to blame him, but rather it appears to me, as I have said, that I ought to offer him for imitation to all those who, by the fortune or the arms of others, are raised to government. Because he, having a lofty spirit and far-reaching aims, could not have regulated his conduct otherwise, and only the shortness of the life of Alexander and his own sickness frustrated his designs…..
>
> He who believes that new benefits will cause great personages to forget old injuries is deceived. Therefore, the duke erred in his choice, and it was the cause of his ultimate ruin.

I find Machiavelli's view of Cesare Borgia intriguing for two reasons. First, his book *The Prince* is an attack on the Church of Rome and a plea for us to break our reliance on the Church, God, and Fortune, and he argues that instead we should create better conditions to organise and manage our civil life free of tyrants. Second, although Borgia was a representative of the papacy acting through his father Alexander VI, Machiavelli, like Leonardo, seems to have had an enthusiastic respect for him. According to Machiavelli, Borgia lost his power more to back luck than to poor judgment. His only bad judgment it seems was that when he was recovering from illness he didn't rise up against his enemy Pope Julius II (Giuliano della Rovere), but instead lazily supported him with the predictable treacherous consequences. Machiavelli believed that Cesare had the great opportunity to rid Italy from the evils of the Church by killing his father and by eliminating the College of Cardinals. Instead, Cesare squandered that opportunity when it arose and as a result the Church ruined him.

Machiavelli first met Cesare Borgia when he was sent by Florence on his mission to engage with King Louis XII of France for 6 months in 1500. Thereafter, he was sent by the Florentine council to continually negotiate with Cesare Borgia to maintain good relations with Florence from June 1502 to January 1503. Machiavelli and Florence were wary about the Borgia ambitions to conquer Florence. Machiavelli therefore became good friends with Cesare in order to examine his mind and interests. He was in Rome before the election of Pope Julius, and this is what he says in *The Prince* of his meeting with Cesare Borgia at the time:

> On the day that Julius II was elected, he told me that he had thought of everything that might occur at the death of his father, and had provided a remedy for all, except that he had never anticipated that, when the death did happen, he himself would be on the point to die.

I disapprove of Machiavelli's endorsement of Borgia's tactics, including deceit, brutality, and the betrayal of his own agents. He is much too enthusiastic for my liking in his endorsement of a cruel prince. And like Leonardo, I disagree with Machiavelli that cruelty is often better than mercy to preserve the peace and order of the state and that a prince needs to be deceitful when circumstances call for it. Both Cesare Borgia and Ludovico Moro Sforza failed in their rule of their dominions because of their deceit and treachery, and they would have been more successful if they were more temperate and in less of a hurry to fulfil their blind ambitions. But, then, we all know that time and deception waits for no man.

And what of Leonardo – what was his fascination with Cesare Borgia? When Leonardo was back in Florence, he and Machiavelli had many discussions about the Lorenzo de' Medici's art of diplomacy in comparison to the Ludovico Sforza's dictatorial and deceitful rule of the Duchy of Milan. Ultimately, Leonardo was an architect and engineer greatly interested in fortification and the art of defence to protect its citizens. He related to Machiavelli that his initial intention in Milan was to write and illustrate a book on the *Art of War* with his collaborators Galeazzo Sanseverino and Pietro Monte, a book that never came to fruition. Now, he and Machiavelli talked about the possibility of collaborating together on such a book. And so, when the Florentine council was preparing to send Machiavelli to negotiate with Cesare Borgia, he suggested to the Signoria that Leonardo should join him. Leonardo jumped at the opportunity for he was becoming bored in his painter's studio, and he wanted to once again test his skills and provide his credentials on engineering and fortifications. Cesare Borgia had already contacted him on more than one occasion requesting advice about such matters. He and the French commanders all knew that Leonardo had helped the Sforza's strengthen the main castle in Milan and other regions of Lombardy including the forts along the Adda River that bordered with the Republic of Venice. Thus, Leonardo was Cesare Borgia's favourite candidate to advise him about military engineering. Machiavelli convinced Leonardo that he would find Cesare to be an alluring prince, *'a man of splendour and magnificence'*, albeit a challenging and ruthless one. It is clear from the travelling document written for Leonardo by Cesare that they struck up an immediate and mutually respectful friendship. Leonardo was attracted by Cesare's vibrant personality and strong intelligence, a person who could express his ambitions with enthusiasm and great reason. Leonardo loved to travel and visit new places, and so Cesare's offer to tour the territories of Romagna and Marche was an opportunity he could not resist. Leonardo's companions, Salai (aged 23 years) and il Fanfoia (aged 28 years), encouraged him for they were equally enthusiastic for the opportunity of adventure at little or no financial cost to themselves. But, probably more than not, Leonardo was really there to spy for Machiavelli and the Florentine Signoria in order to protect his family and their interests in Florence and in Vinci. Moreover, Cesare and the Republic of Florence paid Leonardo a substantial amount of money for his role in the Romagna campaign, and he was able to recoup some of his losses from the French occupation of Milan.

The Siege of Pisa

Before Leonardo could settle down in Florence into a comfortable routine of painting his Madonnas again, Machiavelli and the Signoria of Florence commissioned him to advise them on fortifications and river hydraulics in their conflict with the government of Pisa. Since Pisa reclaimed their independence from the Florentines with the help of Charles VIII of France in 1494, the Florentines continually attempted to reconquer Pisa, but without any success. Pisa was again under siege from the Republic of Florence, and Machiavelli wanted Leonardo's advice on how to divert the Arno River out of and around the city of Pisa. If this could be done successfully then the Florentine troops could starve Pisa of its main resources, and the city might finally fall under their control.

Leonardo obliged to help them in June of 1503 by travelling to the Florentine headquarters at the Pisan front in the company of five of his assistants on white horses and a loud piper leading the way at a total cost to the Signoria of 56 lire and 13 soldi. When they reached their destination, Leonardo inspected the sieged city and the layout of the river that ran through Pisa all the way to their harbour on the Tyrrhenian Sea. He calculated, measured, and drew maps and took long walks around various locations outside the city. He established his camp at a hilltop, a Pisan fortress called *La Verruca* (the Hillock) that was captured by the Florentines. Leonardo wandered about and sketched its appearance and layout. To the great annoyance of the fort commander Pier Tosinghi, Leonardo advised him on how to repair and better fortify *La Verruca* against a Pisan attack. After a one-month stay on the remote crag overlooking the Arno valley, Leonardo concluded that the Arno River could be diverted around Pisa to the marshes of Stagno towards Liverno, but that it would be more economical to bypass the fortified city by building a canal. Either way, it would cost a lot of time and money with the possible loss of many lives. He provided his suggestions and estimated costs in a written report with illustrations and calculations. This included a painted map of the Arno River from its source and tributaries passing through Florence and Pisa with the mountains coloured brown and the rivers and lakes coloured blue. The camp commander Francesco Guiducci passed on his communication to Machiavelli suggesting that the discussion about Leonardo's plan was heated and not fully supported:

> Yesterday Alessandro degli Albizzi together with Leonardo da Vinci and certain other were there, and they studied the plan with the commanding general, and after much discussion and considerable difference of opinion they reached the conclusion that the work would be very suitable, whether it actually succeeded in turning the course of the Arno or only went as far as the construction of a canal that would at any rate prevent the hills from being menaced by the enemy. [S31]

Fortifications and Architecture at the Harbour Citadel of Piombino

Towards the end of 1504, Leonardo was fed up with the planning and preparation of his cartoons for painting a mural in Florence and accepted an architectural commission from the Duke of Piombino, Jacopo IV, d'Appiano d' Aragona, to examine and advise on the improvement of his fortifications. The duke had returned to Piombino only in 1503 after having been two years in exile because Cesare Borgia and Pope Alexander VI had conquered and occupied his territories. Now that the Pope was dead and Cesare Borgia was recovering from illness, Jacopo was back in Piombino requesting Leonardo to help him to strengthen his defences against potential new invasions. Leonardo looked forward to this commission because Piombino is a harbour citadel located on the coast opposite the island of Elba directly south west of Florence. It borders the Ligurian and Tyrrhenian Seas. As usual Salai and il Fanfoia, Leonardo's sword and shield, travelled with him to assist with the measurements and the maps. They stayed in Piombino for most of November and December. Apart from solving the architectural problems for the duke, Leonardo also spent time drawing sailing ships that were entering the harbour and manoeuvring into different positions depending on the direction of the wind, as well as writing numerous notes about the form of the currents, winds, and navigation. As Leonardo stood on top of the castle wall at Populonia and looked out over the sea towards the island of Elba, he jotted down a remembrance, *'when I was once in a place on the sea, at an equal distance from the shore and the mountains, the distance from the shore looked much greater than that from the mountains.'*

Isabella, the Duchess of Bari, now the former Duchess of Milan, had recommended Leonardo to the Duke of Piombino because Jacopo IV d' Appiano d' Aragona was married to Donna Vittoria who was the daughter of the Duke of Amalfi and of Maria of Aragon, the daughter of King Ferdinand Aragon of Naples. Therefore, Isabella was Donna Vittoria's aunt, and she was at the Jacopo and Donna Vittoria's court for a short visit while Leonardo was there. They spent a few days together before she returned to Naples to negotiate with the then ruling Spanish governor Gonzalo Fernandez de Cordoba about her rightful status as the Duchess of Bari, Princess of Rossano, and Queen of Jerusalem.

CHAPTER 19

Back Home in Florence, World Maps, and the *Battle of Anghiari*

The knowledge of past times and of the places on the earth is both an ornament and nutriment to the human mind.

— Leonardo da Vinci

Leonardo's Land Purchase from an Uncle and Flying High in Fiesole

On the 13th of July 1503, Leonardo purchased a plot of land beside the walls of the hillside town of Fiesole where he intended to build a house and workshop with beautiful views overlooking Florence only 8 km south below him. A few months later, he purchased an olive grove and more land that he intended to develop into splendid gardens adjoining his previous purchase. Whenever Leonardo was residing in Florence and its surrounds, he regularly visited his step-uncle Alessandro Amadori in Fiesole. Alessandro Amadori was the Canon of Fiesole, and it was he who assisted Leonardo in the purchase of the properties in Fiesole. Alessandro Amadori was the brother of Albiera di Giovanni Amadori who was the first legitimate wife of Leonardo's father. She was childless, and before her untimely death in 1464 at the age of 28 years (when Leonardo was 12 years old), she had treated Leonardo as her very own son, and he loved her and her brother in return.

Alessandro Amadori also acted as an agent for Isabella d' Este, and he wrote to her the following letter in May 1506 after he had offered her his service when she visited Florence in March in an attempt to purchase a Leonardo artwork:

> Your Illustrious and Gracious Excellency.
>
> Here, in Florence, I act at all hours as the representative of Your Excellency, with Leonardo da Vinci, my nephew, and I do not cease to urge him by every argument in my power to satisfy the desire of Your Excellency, and paint the figure for which you asked him, and which he promised you several months ago, in the letter that I showed Your Excellency. This time he has really promised me that he will soon begin the work and satisfy your wish, and desires me to commend him to your favour. And if, before I leave Florence, you will tell me whether you prefer any especial figure, I will take care that Leonardo satisfies Your Highness, whom it is my greatest wish to oblige. I visited Madonna Argentina Soderini this afternoon, and she was glad to hear from me that Your Highness had reached Mantua safely. I gave her Your Highness's messages, and she sends the enclosed note in return.
>
> May God prosper Your Excellency.
>
> May 3, 1506, Alessandro Amadori, Canon of Fiesole [S32]

The Canon of Fiesole was no more successful in eliciting a small painting from Leonardo da Vinci's hand for Isabella d' Este than any other of her numerous agents.

It was in Fiesole at the nearby Monte Ceceri, a sandstone hill, where Leonardo, Salai, Il Fanfoia, and Tommaso Masini (Zoroastro da Peretola) conducted their flying machine experiments in a number of field trials. Leonardo's painting assistant and master of metal works Tommaso Masini was strapped hanging in a prone position on the flying machine and launched into the air from the edge of a quarry on Monte Ceceri. He soared magnificently like

270

an eagle and glided one kilometre towards the Arno River before crash landing at Camerata and breaking his leg. Nobody else had the courage to repeat Leonardo's flying experiment, although Leonardo thought that the first test flight was a great success despite Tommaso's complaints of a broken leg, numerous bruises and abrasions, and a partial loss of memory. When Tommaso regained consciousness from his crash landing he had no memory of his flying experience or why he was lying on the hard and rocky ground feeling battered and bruised. Leonardo said that despite the crash it was all for a worthwhile cause – allowing man to fly, although a few of his assistants, including Tommaso, did not necessarily agree with him. They preferred to keep their legs firmly on the ground.

Leonardo's flying angel Tommaso Masini was an artisan who prepared colours for Leonardo's paintings and metals for his sculptures from their earlier days together in Florence. He was born 1462 (ten years younger than Leonardo) in the village of Petatola between Florence and Prato and joined Leonardo's workshop as his servant in 1478. Tommaso was a magician, a jester, chemist, master metallurgist, and a vegetarian, and he was very brave. He brewed strange concoctions, kept rare reptiles, and painted odd animals with grotesque faces. He travelled as an 18-year-old with Leonardo to Milan in 1480 in the company of Atalante Migliorotti (musician and poet), and they stayed working together until Leonardo left Florence in 1508. I replaced Tommaso when Leonardo returned to Milan to work for the French governor Charles d' Amboise. Tommaso travelled with us to Rome in 1513 and again with the poet Giovanni di Bernardo Rucellai in 1516 soon after Leonardo and I had left the city to return to Milan. Tommaso died in Rome in 1520, a year after Leonardo's death in Amboise in France.

Florentine Master Painters' Reunion and the Death of Filippino Lippi, April 1504

After his participation in the Romagna and Pisa campaigns, Leonardo was keen to reopen his workshop and rooms that he had previously rented at the cloisters of the monastery of Santissima Annunziata and settle into a calm and creative period of painting again. With a considerable amount of money in hand, Salai and il Fanfoia were spending large and buying expensive clothes and jewellery, while Leonardo was concentrating on purchasing property and farm land on the outskirts of Florence, and the tools and equipment, pigments, and the ephemera and plethora of requirements for his workshop. Apprentices and masters in painting regularly visited Leonardo's studio to see what the maestro was producing. Ridolfo Ghirlandaio, Andrea del Sarto, and Raphael were among the young artists who often visited Leonardo's studio to copy his Madonnas, and other paintings and preparatory drawings that he had on display.

Ridolfo Ghirlandaio was the son of the Florentine master painter Domenico Ghirlandaio who died in 1494. Being less than 11 years old when his father died, Ridolfo trained with the master painter Fra Bartolomeo. Leonardo greatly admired Domenico Ghirlandaio's portraits and frescoes, and so he and Ridolfo would often tour the churches and palaces in Florence to look at Domenico's works. Leonardo especially liked the *Apotheosis of St. Zenobius* in the Sala del Giglio, the *Last Supper* in San Marco's refectory, the *Adoration of the Shepherds* at the Sassetti Chapel, and the *Birth of Mary* at the Tornabuoni Chapel that he had not seen before because he was in Milan when they were produced. Both Ridolfo and Fra Bartolomeo were friends of Raphael, a young painter who came from Perugia and trained with Perugino who had workshops in Perugia and Florence. Leonardo was on friendly terms with Perugino who like Leonardo was once an apprentice of Andrea del Verrocchio, and so they and the young painters all exchanged ideas and shared materials in a spirit of friendly cooperation.

Andrea del Sarto was apprenticed to Piero di Cosimo who painted large mythological and allegorical subjects and fantasia, until Piero was influenced by the preacher Girolamo

Savonarola and changed to painting religious works of saints, martyrs, and visitations. It was Piero di Cosimo who Leonardo disliked because he had painted a portrait of Simonetta Vespucci as *Cleopatra* wearing a necklace of asps. Piero now spent more time on designing pageants, carnivals, and triumphal processions for the youth and clergy of Florence than on religious paintings. Andrea del Sarto went on to develop his own style, and with the help of Leonardo, the Servite monks employed him from 1509 to 1514 to paint a series of frescoes, nine or more, at the Basilica della Santissima Annunziata. He painted the *Adoration* and the *Annunciation* and visited France in 1518 to honour Leonardo.

In his free time, Leonardo would visit the workshops of his old friends Lorenzo di Credi and Sandro Botticelli who like Leonardo were apprentices and assistants of Andrea del Verrocchio. Lorenzo di Credi inherited Verrocchio's workshop after his death, and Leonardo was curious to see how things had changed since he left Florence in 1480 to live and work in Milan. Lorenzo di Credi first influenced Leonardo da Vinci, and in later years, it was he who was greatly influenced by Leonardo. Lorenzo di Credi has a large output and among his works were the *Annunciation, Madonna with Child, Adoration of the Shepherds,* and *Madonna and Saints* that were greatly influenced by Leonardo. Lorenzo di Credi's portrait of Caterina Sforza is eye catching, and it has a strong resemblance to Leonardo's portrait of the *Mona Lisa.*

Leonardo was especially keen to visit Botticelli whose paintings had influenced him greatly when he was a student with Verrocchio. Sandro Botticelli was born in 1445 and most of his works were produced between the years of 1470 and 1500. His output after 1503 was slim. He was now 58 years of age and not in the best of health. He'd also become a follower of the preacher Girolamo Savonarola and was greatly disturbed by the preacher's execution in 1498. When Sandro and Leonardo met in 1503, they reminisced about old times. Leonardo told him how much he admired Sandro's portraits and his paintings of *Madonnas* and *St. Sebastian* and that his favourite was still the *Adoration of the Magi* of 1475. Sandro laughed and told Leonardo that he so admired Leonardo's *Annunciation* that he became totally obsessed with it and had painted more than three or four similar versions for his clients and for himself.

The other painter that Leonardo liked to meet and talk with about art, history, and science was Filippino Lippi who completed his apprenticeship in the workshop of Botticelli in 1472. Filippino Lippi was the son of the master painter Fra Filippo Lippi to whom Botticelli was apprenticed. Fra Filippo Lippi and Botticelli were the catalysts for the Florentine golden age of painting. When Filippino Lippi was working on the painting of the *Deposition* for the Santissima Annunziata Basilica, he often would visit Leonardo in his nearby studio, and then they would go together to visit Botticelli and try to lift his flagging spirits. Filippino told Leonardo that Sandro Botticelli had been accused of sodomy in November of 1502, and although the charge was eventually dismissed, Botticelli was still badly affected by it. Leonardo shuddered at the thought that these slanders were still rife in Florence.

In January of 1504, Lady Caterina Sforza invited the painters Leonardo, Perugino, Botticelli, Lippi, and di Credi to a small and intimate gathering at the Villa Medici di Castello where she resided with her children and grandchildren. The meeting was referred to as the Florentine Master Painters' Reunion, and she said that she wanted to take this opportunity to meet and celebrate the art and science of painting with her favourite Florentine painters because such opportunities were rare. Botticelli, Leonardo, and di Credi had painted her portrait, and the others had worked on the frescoed decorations of Lorenzo de' Medici's villa. They all knew and loved Caterina Sforza, the former Lady of Forlì and Imola, and they were enormously pleased to attend and honour her invitation. She had married Giovanni de' Medici il Popolano in 1497, had a son with him, and then, she was soon widowed when he died in 1498, and consequently, he was not able to protect her from capture and imprisonment by Cesare Borgia and his father Pope Alexander VI. When she was released from prison in Rome in 1501, she settled in Florence to live in the villas of her deceased husband Giovanni de' Medici il

Popolano. Their son Giovanni (later to be known as the condottiere Giovanni dalle Bande Nere) inherited the Villa Medici di Castello from his father, and Caterina was his and the villa's strict and litigious guardian. The villa is in the hills outside Florence, and it was once a country residence of Lorenzo and Giovanni di Pierfrancesco de' Medici. Moreover, it now housed a few masterpieces by Sandro Botticelli, Leonardo, and di Credi. The Florentine Master Painters Reunion had come to see and admire Botticelli's the *Birth of Venus* and *Primavera*, Leonardo's the *Lady and the Ermine,* and the unveiling of di Credi's portrait of the *Lady of Forli* (known also as *La dama dei gelsomini*). Caterina and her guests enjoyed a stroll in the beautiful garden, which ran from the villa up the gentle slope towards the mountain. She wanted Leonardo to design the waterworks for her garden with fountains and running streams. The painters and Caterina enjoyed their day reminiscing about their youth and the political intrigues that they had survived, and they also critically discussed the current trends in painting and the rise of the younger Florentine talents such as Ridolfo Ghirlandaio, Andrea del Sarto, and Raphael.

Filippino Lippi died a few months after the Florentine Master Painters' Reunion at the Villa Medici di Castello and long before he could complete his painting of the *Deposition* for the Santissima Annunziata church. On the day of his burial, all the 110 master workshops of the city closed as a mark of respect to honour him and his beautiful works. Large wakes were held at Perugino's workshop, Botticelli's workshop, and at the Piazza del Duomo. The *Deposition* that Filippino Lippi began in 1503 was completed by his workshop successor Perugino in 1507. Perugino's effort, however, was deemed a failure due to the painting's lack of innovation and originality, and in great shame, he abandoned Florence and retired to Perugia.

The Death of a Father, July 1504

Leonardo received word of his father's death while preparing his preliminary drawings at his workshop for a new commission to paint a battle scene on one of the walls of the Sala del Gran Consiglio in the Palazzo Vecchio. In an unexpected, shocked reaction, he wrote the following in his notebook:

> On 9th July 1504, Wednesday, at the seventh hour, died Ser Piero da Vinci, notary at the Palazzo del Podesta, my father, at the seventh hour, being 80 years old, leaving 10 male and 2 female children.

Leonardo was filial, and as the eldest son he greatly loved and respected his father who had been married three times and produced many children. But, father and first son were completely different from each other in character and in deed. Leonardo was the illegitimate son, and he spent most of his childhood and youth living in the care of his grandfather and his uncle Francesco in Vinci. Later, when he was employed in Verrocchio's workshop in Florence in the 1470s, Leonardo spent considerably more time in the company of his father and his first two stepmothers, but saw very little of them or their children after he had moved to Milan in 1482. On his return to Florence in 1500, Leonardo visited his father on only a few occasions, and he had little or no interaction with his much younger brothers and sisters for whom he had little affection. He attended his father's funeral and the wake with his uncle Francesco, and he mingled quietly with his brothers and sisters and nephews and nieces who had gathered for the day of remembrance and mourning. His father was a notary and lawyer who specialised in arranging marriages and wills and became comfortably wealthy living in Florence and its surroundings. He'd grown powerful through his dealings with important bankers and merchants, and he climbed the social scale and accumulated a considerable number of assets and properties that now had to be shared out amongst his 12 children. Strangely, as a lawyer and notary, Leonardo's father had not prepared a will for his estate, but instead, he had left three of his sons who also had become notaries to divide out the inheritance equally to all of his children including Leonardo. The brothers passed on nothing of their father's estate to Leonardo because he was the only illegitimate son and not necessarily entitled by law. The disputation with his brothers would bother him for the next four years.

The Sea-God Neptune

Giorgio Vasari wrote in his *Life of Leonardo da Vinci*:

> Leonardo then made a picture of Our Lady, a most excellent work, which was in the possession of Pope Clement VII; and, among other things painted therein, he counterfeited a glass vase full of water, containing some flowers, in which, besides its marvellous naturalness, he had imitated the dew-drops on the flowers, so that it seemed more real than the reality. For Antonio Segni, who was very much his friend, he made, on a sheet of paper, a Neptune executed with such careful draughtsmanship that it seemed absolutely alive. In it one saw the ocean troubled, and Neptune's car drawn by sea-horses, with fantastic creatures, marine monsters and winds, and some very beautiful heads of sea-gods. Fabio, the son of Antonio, presented this drawing to Messer Giovanni Gaddi, with the following epigram:

> > Virgil and Homer both depicted Neptune,
> > Driving his seahorses through the rushing waves.
> > The poets saw him in their imaginations,
> > Vinci with his own eyes; rightly vanquished them.

> The fancy came to him to paint a picture in oils of the head of a Medusa, with the head attired with a coil of snakes, the most strange and extravagant invention that could ever be imagined; but since it was a work that took time, it remained unfinished, as happened with almost all his things. It is among the rare works of art in the Palace of Duke Cosimo, together with the head of an angel, who is raising one arm in the air, which, coming forward, is foreshortened from the shoulder to the elbow, and with the other he raises the hand to the breast.

Fig. 76. Leonardo drawing of the sea-god Neptune *in charge of his seahorses.*

Leonardo had a great love for the sea, and he wrote this ode to Neptune:

O powerful and once living instrument of constructive Nature, thy great strength not availing thee, thou must need to abandon thy tranquil life to obey the law which God and time ordained for all-procreative Nature! To thee availed not the branching, sturdy dorsal fins wherewith pursuing thy prey thou wast wont to plough thy way, tempestuously tearing open the briny waves with thy breast.

O how many times the frightened shoals of dolphins and big tunnyfish were seen to flee before thy insensate fury; and thou, lashing with swift, branching fins and forked tail, didst create in the sea sudden tempest with loud uproar and foundering of ships; with mighty wave thou didst heap up the open shores with the frightened and terrified fishes, which thus escaping from thee were left high and dry when the sea abandoned them, and became the plenteous and abundant spoil of the neighbouring peoples.

O Time, swift despoiler of created things! How many kings, how many peoples hast thou brought low! How many changes of state and circumstance have followed since the wondrous form of this fish died here in this hollow winding recess? Now, destroyed by Time, patiently it lies within this narrow space, and, with its bones despoiled and bare, it is become an armour and support to the mountain, which lies above it.

O how many times hast thou been seen amid the waves of the mighty, swelling ocean, towering like a mountain, conquering and overcoming them! And with black-finned back ploughing through the salt waves with proud and stately bearing!

Leonardo presented the finished drawing of the sea-god *Neptune* to his friend Antonio Segni, the master of the papal mint for Pope Julius II. I have a copy of Leonardo's drawing of *Neptune* in my possession. At the top of the drawing Leonardo has written the words, '*lower the horses*'. His painting of *Medusa* is in the possession of the former governor of Florence Pietro Soderini.

World Map on an Ostrich Egg and Globe Gores [S34]

Since Leonardo's travels on the Vespucci trading ships in 1476, his old Florentine friend Amerigo Vespucci had set sail to the Americas from Spain and Portugal in the footstep of Columbus on three or four different occasions in the years between 1499 and 1502. He had written accounts of his travels to Piero Soderini, the governor of Florence, and to Lorenzo di Pierfrancesco de' Medici, cousin of Lorenzo de' Medici, providing them with maps and vivid descriptions. They in turn approached Leonardo and asked him to provide them with a map of the world based on Vespucci's descriptions and previous maps of the world that they had available in their libraries. For the next five years, Leonardo worked on producing a number of different world maps, and with Tommaso di Giovanni Masini they constructed the sculpture of a world map on an ostrich egg (a sphere) that they used to cast copper globes the size of a small melon (11 cm in diameter and 2 mm thick). They first made plaster copies of each half of the ostrich egg and then painted the inside of the plaster models with a copper paste. Here is Leonardo's recipe for preparing the copper paste.

TO DISSOLVE COPPER
Dissolve the copper with these waters and then evaporate it so that it becomes like paste or mustard, and daub it over your figure and polish it well with a brush and dry it; then cover it with earth out of doors and make a great fire in such a way that the copper between the two layers of earth becomes united, or mix this copper with quick-silver.

Leonardo first produced a world map from his readings of the geographical books and the maps provided to him by Piero Soderini. It was an isometric octant world map projected onto eight spherical-geometrical triangles. I have at least eight other isometric global projections that he left me in his notebooks and sketches. He learnt to draw them from his friends, the cartographers Paolo Toscanelli and Donnus Nicolaus Germanus, and from his meetings with sailors and Islamic scholars of the Middle East during his travels to escape the confines of Florence. Leonardo had produced the maps as eight equilateral triangles to cover a sphere and use them as guides for engraving the continents and islands onto the ostrich egg. He laid these maps over the two separate halves (the northern and southern hemispheres) of the egg, and Tommaso meticulously engraved the lands through the map and onto the egg and labelled them with their topographical names. Then, with the assistance of a magnifying glass, they carefully engraved the curved and swirly lines of the ocean currents to look like sinews and muscle fibres intertwining. It is a dark-indigo-blue, living ocean connected to white mountainous continents, grey islands, and sailing ships, and sea creatures. Leonardo had calculated the diameter of the world to be 7000 miles, so 1 cm is 636.4 miles (1024 km) on his 11 cm ostrich egg globe.

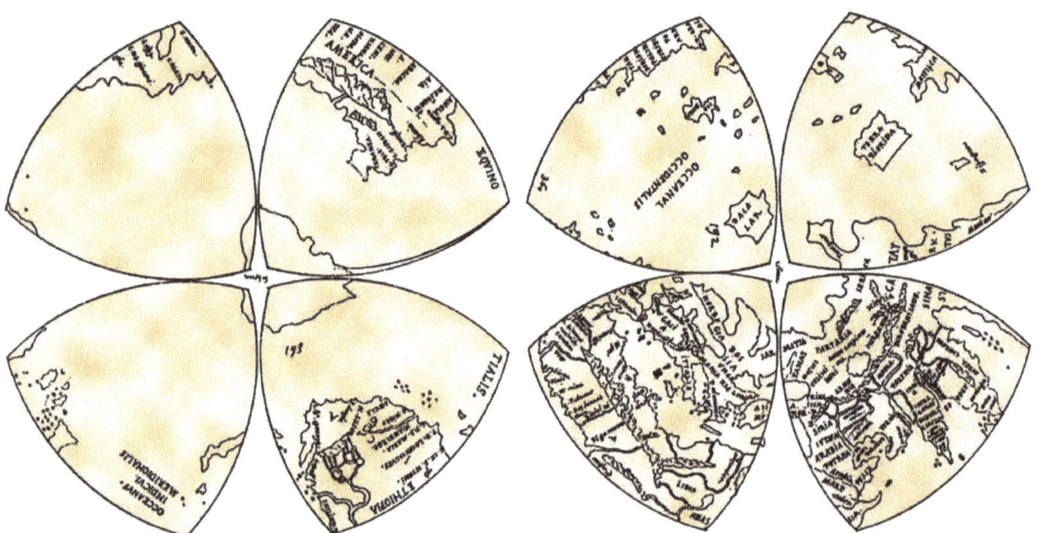

Fig. 77. Leonardo da Vinci's world map (mappa mundi) drawn as gores depicts the southern and northern hemispheres with the polar landmasses and the islands of the Americas.

According to Leonardo, the globe on which we live is a living thing in its own right.

> The globe is an organism. Nothing originates in a spot where there is no sentient, vegetable, and rational life; feathers grow upon birds and are changed every year; hairs grow upon animals and are changed every year, excepting some parts, like the hairs of the beard in lions, cats, and their like. The grass grows in the fields, and the leaves on the trees, and every year they are, in great part, renewed. So that we might say that the earth has a spirit of growth; that its flesh is the soil, its bones the arrangement and connection of the rocks of which the mountains are composed, its cartilage the tufa, and its blood the springs of water. The pool of blood which lies round the heart is the ocean, and its breathing, and the increase and decrease of the blood in the pulses, is represented in the earth by the flow and ebb of the sea; and the heat of the spirit of the world is the fire which pervades the earth, and the seat of the vegetative soul is in the fires, which in many parts of the earth find vent in baths and mines of sulphur, and in volcanoes, as at Mount Aetna in Sicily, and in many other places.

Leonardo and Tommaso made a number of the copper casts of the ostrich egg globe and gave them out to their friends and to some people of importance in Florence and Milan. The governor of Florence Piero Soderini, the banker and politician Lorenzo di Pierfrancesco de' Medici, and the governor of Milan, Charles of Amboise, and the French king's secretary, Florimond de Robertet, were much pleased with their New World globes. Marco d' Oggiono and Salai often painted the ostrich egg globe or its copper copy being held in the left hand of a Christ like figure who was based in part on Leonardo da Vinci's painting of the *Salvator Mundi*.

Fig. 78. Two paintings by Marco d' Oggiono of a male model holding the ostrich egg globe or its copper version.

The *Battle of Anghiari*, a Heroic Mural for the Palazzo Vecchio (1503 to 1506)

In November of 1503, a few months after advising Machiavelli and the Signoria about the best course of action for the diversion of the Arno River, Leonardo received and accepted a commission from them to paint a battle scene on one of the walls of the Sala del Gran Consiglio in the Palazzo Vecchio. This was to be a monumental battle scene between the Milanese and the Florentines staged over a bridge in Anghiari on June 29, 1440. Leonardo had written down in one of his notebooks an abbreviated account of the battle as translated from the works of the historian Leonardo Dati, and he also had instructions given to him from the Signoria and Machiavelli about what they wanted to see. His plan was to paint a triptych starting with the commander of the Milanese forces Niccolo Piccinino presenting an oration to his troops on the left side of the wall, then the Milanese army approaching in a cloud of dust towards the bridge defended by the Florentine troops, then the desperate battle scene between the adversaries, men on horseback, and men fallen to the ground trampled by horses in the central portion of the wall; and finally, towards the right side of the wall, the Florentine victory scenes and trophies being presented to the Patriarch of Aquileia, the papal legate who was in charge of the Florentine and Papal forces winning against the Milanese invaders and Florentine rebels. The observer on entering the Sala del Gran Consiglio and looking along the whole length of the wall would have the illusion of taking part in the battle.

To accomplish this immense task, Leonardo decided that he would first draw three main cartoons onto paper in his workshop, next transfer the drawings to the wall, and then colour inside the outlines with oil paints. To allow him to prepare his cartoons in privacy, the Signoria arranged for the papal reception room, the Sala del Papa, in the monastery of Santa Maria Novella to be his workshop that he could close and lock away his inspirations from prying eyes and mischievous spies. Leonardo's general philosophy was to never let anybody see what he was painting until it was finished. In this way, he could continually change the scenes, images, and colours without too much interference or opinions from others. Leonardo was living comfortably with sufficient money to spend on his friends and assistants, and he was in no hurry to leave the Santa Maria Novella. However, the Signoria was becoming concerned about the slow progress. Consequently, the elected gonfalonier Piero di Tommaso Soderini and the priors of Florence met officially with Leonardo on May 4, 1504 to determine why, despite the scaffolding covering the wall, nothing had yet been painted on it. He promised them that he would complete the painting by February 1505 without fail otherwise they could seek restitution from him.

Battles Within Battles: Leonardo da Vinci Versus Michelangelo in the Dual of the Painters

One year after Leonardo had started work on his cartoons of the *Battle of Anghiari,* he heard from Machiavelli that the Signoria had granted Michelangelo a commission to paint a battle scene on the wall opposite to the one that was set aside for his painting. The Signoria were setting up an artistic dual. Apparently, Michelangelo had taken great exception to the Signoria granting Leonardo the commission for the painting at the Palazzo Vecchio and for not having considered him for the work. He'd complained to the Signoria that while he'd been working hard for Florence and the Republic for the past twenty years, Leonardo on the other hand was back in Florence for only three years after a twenty-year absence and was unjustly awarded the commission. To stop Michelangelo's continuous complaints, the Signoria awarded him the commission for a picture on the opposite wall, a picture of the *Battle of Cascina.* The subject suited Michelangelo perfectly because it was about an incidence in 1368 when Pisan troops attacked a group of Florentine soldiers relaxing and bathing in a river. This permitted Michelangelo to paint his favourite subject, naked muscular men bathing. Although the two painters worked on opposite walls from each other, they never engaged in any friendly conversation. Michelangelo worked angrily as if he was in combat with Leonardo, constantly mumbling about how it was unlikely that the so-called master would ever be able to complete his painting on time.

Michelangelo resented Leonardo's acclaim and celebrity, but most of all he hated Leonardo for his paragone that painting and painters were superior to sculpting and sculptors. Leonardo had once said during one of his academic debates in Milan that:

> The only difference between painting and sculpture is that the sculptor accomplishes his work with the greater bodily fatigue, and the painter with the greater mental fatigue. This is proved by the fact that the sculptor in practising his art is obliged to exert his arms and to strike and shatter the marble or other stone, which remains over and above what is needed for the figure which it contains, by manual exercise, accompanied often by profuse sweating, mingled with dust, and transforming itself into dirt; and his face is plastered and powdered with the dust of the marble, so that he has the appearance of a baker, and he is covered with minute chips, and it appears as if snow had fallen on him, and his dwelling is dirty and full of chips and the dust of stone.

The description of sculptors looking like bakers or pastry cooks covered in flour was widely quoted by the painters in Florence, and Michelangelo having no sense of humour was highly offended by Leonardo's effeminate sentiment. In addition, he held Leonardo personally responsible for having his statue *David* positioned at the Ringhiera where people gathered to complain outside the palace and not where he wanted it to stand on the Piazza del Duomo outside the entrance of the cathedral. In fact, Leonardo had little or no authority in deciding where it was to be placed, other than that he was one of twenty-eight members of the artists' committee that made suggestions for the best position. *David* was Michelangelo's crowning achievement and symbol of the overthrow of tyranny - the tyranny of the Medici, the tyranny of Savonarola, the tyranny of the tyrannical everywhere. David was the resurrection of the dead, the emblem of the Republic, and Michelangelo believed that his *David* needed to be placed in a position to be constantly admired and marvelled at. Leonardo along with a few others including Botticelli suggested that it would be best situated on a parapet in the Loggia, while the people of Florence wanted it at the Piazza della Signoria. The Signoria had the final say, and on January 25, 1504, they had it positioned at the Ringhiera. Nevertheless, Michelangelo claimed that it was all Leonardo's fault that the *David* statue wasn't located where he wanted it to be in the Piazza del Duomo.

One time when Leonardo was discussing the poetry of Dante with a group of gentlemen near the Palazzo Spini, he cheekily asked for an opinion from Michelangelo who was passing by them at that very moment. The group and Leonardo acknowledged Michelangelo to be a competent poet and an authority on Dante, and so they asked him to contribute his opinion. Michelangelo on hearing Leonardo's question turned towards him and shouted out angrily: '*You are the one who made a design for a horse to be cast in bronze and shamefully failed. And worse, those Milanese idiots believed in you!*' And with that, he immediately disappeared from view leaving Leonardo feeling highly embarrassed. And yet their antagonism towards each other did not stop them from occasionally painting opposite each other at the Palazzo Vecchio. Leonardo never finished his painting by February 1505 as he had promised. Neither did Michelangelo, and he left Florence in 1505 to live and work permanently in Rome.

Michelangelo di Ludovico Buonarroti Simoni was 23 years younger than Leonardo and felt superior to him as an artist. When Michelangelo was 13 years of age he was apprenticed to Domenico Ghirlandaio, and at 15 years of age in 1490 he was invited to attend Lorenzo de' Medici's Neo-Platonic Humanist academy where the greatest writers, philosophers, and artists of the day attended to debate Platonic teachings. He could not accept hearing the accolades about Leonardo from other people at these or other meetings, and he was often acerbic. The young apprentice sculptor Pietro Torrigiano permanently disfigured Michelangelo's nose during one of their highly heated debates about Leonardo's worthiness and high standing as an influential Italian painter and sculptor. According to Benvenuto Cellini, the prominent Florentine sculptor, artist, soldier, and musician who was born in 1500, Torrigiano had told him many years later about his incident with Michelangelo:

> This Michelangelo Buonarroti and I, when we were boys, used to go into the Church of the Carmine to learn drawing from the chapel of Masaccio. It was Buonarroti's habit to banter on all those who were drawing there; and one day, among others, when he was annoying me, I got more angry than usual, and clenching my fist, gave him such a blow on the nose, that I felt bone and cartilage go down like biscuit beneath my knuckles; and this mark of mine he will carry with him to the grave. [S35]

Soon after the incidence of the broken nose, Torrigiano left for Rome where he felt a little safer to be away from Florence because Michelangelo was extremely angry and vindictive and a particular favourite of Lorenzo de' Medici. While Torrigiano was in Rome, he assisted Pinturicchio to decorate the private apartments of Pope Alexander VI. Michelangelo moved to Rome in the summer of 1496, and while he was there for the next four years, at the age of 21 to 24 years, he produced his masterpiece, the *Pieta*, the polished marbled flesh of Mary and Jesus that he created from a formless block of rough stone. Nobody could deny its immense beauty nor could they not praise its artistic perfection, not even Leonardo nor Torrigiano.

Large crowds gathered at the Palazzo Vecchio in the hope of seeing the two great artists cross paths and throw paint and paintbrushes at each other in their fight to depict the best battle scenes from the past. But, they rarely saw the two of them in action. Guards were stationed at the doorways to Sala del Gran Consiglio, and they only allowed certain authorities and the two painters and their personal assistants to pass in and out of the grand hall on the occasions that they were there to paint. For most of the time, the two painters worked different days and hours and avoided each other while setting up the scaffolds and preparing the walls in readiness for their paintings. Most of the time, they prepared their cartoons in the privacy of their own workshops before they were ready to transfer the prepared images to their respective walls.

Eventually, Leonardo finished his drawings and moved the large masses of illustrated paper from his workshop at the Sala del Papa in the monastery of Santa Maria Novella to glue them to the wall of the Sala del Gran Consiglio in the Palazzo Vecchio. Then, disaster struck:

> On the 6th June 1505, a Friday, at the stroke of the thirteenth hour [at 9 am] I began to paint in the palace. At the moment of putting the brush to the wall the weather changed for the worse, and the bell started to toll, calling the men to the trail. The cartoon came loose, the water poured down, and the vessel carrying it broke. And suddenly, the weather worsened still more and a very great rain came down till nightfall. And it was as dark as night.

There was an immense storm and flooding in Florence. The change in weather and humidity liquefied the paste that attached the immense cartoon to the wall, and it slid down the wall and fell into a wet heap on the floor. Leonardo stood at the top of the scaffold in dismay watching his drawing disappear from view. It was a dark and gloomy day on the 6th June 1505.

Fig. 79. Copy of scene from Leonardo da Vinci's painting of the Battle of Anghiari.

By the end of summer in 1505, Michelangelo finished his cartoon of the *Battle of Cascina*, but he never transferred it to the wall of Sala del Gran Consiglio. Soon after, he moved to live and work in Rome. Although it took Leonardo another year to recover from the Florence inundation and complete his painting after his promised deadline to the Signoria, at least he now had the excuse of Nature's intervention interfering with his intended timetable.

After Leonardo finished his first panel, many travelled out of their way to visit Florence to see the outcome of the personal battle between the two painters. All agreed that the battle for the standard by Leonardo was a masterpiece, and it enhanced his reputation over Michelangelo as the better painter. In general, what people saw was Leonardo's superiority in draftsmanship in human and animal anatomy and for evoking emotion, complexity, and action. Leonardo's grappling horsemen, two against two, are full of twisting, turning figures in the horrible ferocity and agony of a battle to the death. The horses and human bodies are interlocked with savagery and fear contorting their faces. In comparison, Michelangelo's beautiful nudes of lumpy, muscular figures at the *Battle of Cascina* are emerging indulgently from the River Arno. There are no horses, no horrors, and no fear of impending death from war. It's a group of self-contented pederasts eagerly attending an orgy and occupying themselves in a bewildering array of over-staged masculine mannerisms at a Roman hot-bath orgy. It is immensely ironic that Michelangelo considered Leonardo an effeminate artist who spent his life painting the mysterious and beautiful faces of women, while Michelangelo spent his very long life painting and sculpting naked youths. It has come to pass in recent times that some art historians incorrectly claim that Leonardo was a pederast and a sodomite, whereas Michelangelo who outlived Leonardo by 45 years was a man's man only interested in naked youths and highly muscled men for art's sake. I know that the reverse was true. Michelangelo was the pederast

and sodomite, whereas Leonardo was a gentleman of the highest order and neither a pederast
nor a sodomite.

In accepting the dual against Michelangelo to paint their assigned battles in the public
forum, Leonardo fulfilled one of his beliefs that:

> A good painter should depict the fury of a battle and that a poet should write about it, and
> that they might be put in public where many people could see them and then we would see
> where the witnesses would look more, where they would give the most praise and which
> would satisfy them more; certainly the painting would please more, being more useful and
> beautiful.

Isabella d' Este travelled to Florence in March 1506 to see Leonardo's wall painting with a
high hope of also meeting with him. She looked with wonder and admiration at Leonardo's
decoration on the wall of the Council Hall in the Palazzo. But, he was unavailable to meet with
her. He was away, residing with friends at his property in Fiesole. Instead, she met with
Leonardo's uncle Alessandro Amadori and convinced him to act as her agent to try and
procure one of Leonardo's paintings. In addition, she met with Madonna Argentina, the wife
of the Signoria's Gonfalonier Piero Soderini, and requested the sculptor Filippo Benintendi to
model a silver effigy of herself to be placed in the Gonzaga chapel in the church Santa Maria
dell' Annunziata. Because it was her first ever visit to Florence, she toured the main sights of
the city, the Duomo and Campanile of Giotto, the workshop of Leonardo's old master,
Verrocchio, now run by Lorenzo di Credi, various churches, banks, and palaces along the Arno
river, and the many frescoes and paintings of those Florentine artists from whom she had
commissioned works for her private collection. She wasn't in Florence for much longer than a
few weeks before she was summoned back to Mantua because of an outbreak of the plague.
She didn't stay there for more than a month before the plague forced her and her children to
leave and spend the next few months at their summer retreat at the villa of Sacchetta.

Fig. 80. Michelangelo's cartoon of the Battle
of Cascina.

Leonardo's painting of the
Battle of Anghiari was not plain
sailing. He was interrupted in his
preparations many times by other
requirements and unfortunate
events such as the death of his
father in June of 1504. In
November 1504, Machiavelli sent
Leonardo to advise Jacopo IV
Appiani on his fortifications and
water supplies at the port city of Piombino, south of Pisa. Machiavelli hoped that this would
calm and compensate Leonardo for the decision by the Signoria to appoint Michelangelo to
paint the wall opposite to him at the Sala del Gran Consiglio. Leonardo spent a month with the
lord of Piombino providing him with inspections and advice on the drainage of the marshes
and the strengthening of fortifications before returning to Florence a little better refreshed
after mourning the death of his father and recovering from his disappointment of having to
compete with Michelangelo at the Sala del Gran Consiglio.

Michelangelo never lost his hostility to Leonardo even many years after Leonardo's death.
Some years after I published Leonardo's thesis on painting, the historian Benedetto Varchi
contacted me in regard to Michelangelo's response to the argument that was presented about

the insufficiency of sculpture as art. Benedetto Varchi had written to Michelangelo asking for his opinion on the continuing debate about painting versus sculpture, 28 years after Leonardo's death. Varchi sent me a copy of Michelangelo's response knowing that Michelangelo had never read any of Leonardo's writings and never would.

Michelangelo (1547):

> No painter ought to think less of sculpture than of painting, and similarly no sculptor less of painting than of sculpture. By sculpture I mean that which is fashioned by the effort of cutting away, that which is fashioned by the method of building up being like unto painting. It suffices that as both, that is to say sculpture and painting, proceed from one and the same faculty of understanding, we may bring them to amicable terms and desist from such disputes, because they take up more time than the execution of the figures themselves. If he who wrote that painting is nobler than sculpture understood as little about the other things of which he writes – my maidservant could have expressed them better. [S36]

CHAPTER 20

Leonardo's Family and Florentine Disputes, and His French Recall to Milan

The tears come from the heart not the brain.
Nothing is so much feared as Evil Report.
Wherever good fortune enters, envy lays siege to the place and attacks it; and when it departs, sorrow
and repentance remain behind.
The memory of benefits is a frail defence against ingratitude.

— Leonardo da Vinci

The Royal Invitation from the French King to Return to Milan, September 1506

After completing the painting of the central portion of the *Battle of Anghiari* early in August of 1506, Leonardo abandoned the remainder of the project in favour of a commanding invitation from Charles d' Amboise, the Viceroy of Milan, acting on behalf of the French king Louis XII. The French wanted him to return to Milan for three months to undertake a few projects for the king. The commission of two separate little devotional Madonnas was in the offering. Without receiving permission from the Florentine Signoria to leave, Leonardo was welcomed back in Milan by Charles d' Amboise with great friendliness and honour. The king was still in France, and so the Governor of Milan invited Leonardo to stay with him in his own villa in San Babila, and he immediately commissioned from him an equestrian statue and architectural plans for a new suburban palace and gardens. He also wanted one or more erotic paintings from Leonardo to hang in his villa. This was the time that Leonardo began to think about illustrating the myth of *Leda and the Swan* and possibly painting a nude of *Mary Magdalene*.

The Florentine Signoria however became indignant that Leonardo had left Florence before completing his contract with them for the *Battle of Anghiari*, and they soon demanded his immediate return to Florence. They had already paid Leonardo a considerable sum of money for the wall painting, and they expected him to be back in Florence within the month to complete it. They were incensed when he had not yet returned by October, and they sent a damning letter about him to Charles d'Amboise.

> Leonardo has not comported himself toward this Republic as he should have done, for he has accepted a goodly sum of money and has done very little of the great work he should have done, and out of love for Your Highness has indeed comported himself like a debtor. We demand that there should be no more extensions, for his work must satisfy the general body of our citizens and we cannot dispense him from his obligations without failing in our duty. October 9, 1506, Pietro Soderini, Perpetual Gonfalonier of the Signoria of Florence. [S31]

Leonardo was back in Florence by late December mainly to care for the well being of his dying uncle. Charles d'Amboise soon sent a letter to the Signoria thanking them for allowing Leonardo to remain in Milan longer than they expected.

The excellent works that your fellow citizen Master Leonardo da Vinci has left in Italy, and most especially in this city, have led all those who have seen them to feel a singular affection for their author, and this is true even among those who have never set eyes on him. For ourselves, we confess we must be counted among those who loved before he was personally known to us. And now, since we have employed him here and made trail of his many virtues, we seen in truth that his renown in painting is obscure compared with the great merit he has achieved through the other great virtues he possesses. We desire to confess that with his accomplishments in architecture and drawing and other matters relating to our governorship, he has satisfied us in such a way that we are not only content with him but have conceived an admiration for him. And therefore, since it has pleased you to let him remain here through all these days to our gratification, it would seem ungrateful if we did not tender you our thanks on his return to his own country.

We therefore thank you warmly as possible; and if a man of such genius may be recommended to his fellow citizens, we assure you that you can never do anything to augment his fortune and comfort, and to honour him, without giving us as well as to him the most singular pleasure and putting us under the greatest obligation to Your Magnificences. December 6th, 1506. Charles d' Amboise. [S31]

The Death of Leonardo's Loving Uncle Francesco and Conflict with His Brothers over His Inheritance

Fig. 81. Leonardo's portrait of his uncle, Francesco da Vinci.

Leonardo's uncle Francesco died early into the new year of 1507, only a month after Leonardo had returned to Vinci from his six-month sojourn in Milan. The main reason he had previously returned to Florence in 1500 was to care for his uncle in his old age, right to the very end of his life. A few days before his uncle's death, Leonardo sketched a loving portrait of him in red chalk that many today mistakenly believe is Leonardo's self-portrait before his own death in 1519. No, it isn't Leonardo. I have often corrected this mistaken belief by the likes of Giorgio Vasari and others. It is a portrait of his beloved uncle Francesco da Vinci drawn in 1507, a few days before his death. The difference between uncle and nephew is evident in the different shape of the nose, mouth, and unkempt eyebrows, and the age that they died, Francesco da Vinci died at 81 years of age, and his nephew, the maestro, Leonardo da Vinci, at 67 years.

The death of Leonardo's uncle Francesco da Vinci soon led to an unsavoury dispute between him and his half-brothers about the uncle's inheritance. The uncle was childless, and he always favoured Leonardo and left everything to him. Francesco's nephews united together to contest their uncle's last will and testament, and this legal disputation would take up much of Leonardo's time and energy for the next two years.

Leonardo's Recall to Milan by the French King Louis XII, 1507

Soon after Leonardo attended his uncle's funeral in Vinci, the Florentine Signoria received a letter from the French king Louis XII requesting that he return immediately to Milan.

> To our very dear and great friends, allies and confederates, the Princess and the Perpetual Gonfalonier of the Signoria of Florence. Louis, by the grace of God King of France, Duke of Milan, Duke of Genoa, etc.
>
> Very dear and great friends. Because we have an urgent need of Maestro Leonardo da Vinci, painter of your city of Florence, and because we desire from him some work by his hand upon our arrival in Milan, which, God willing, will take place shortly, We therefore affectionately request that you will make it possible and that you will be pleased to let the aforementioned Maestro Leonardo remain in our service for a while until he has finished the work that we desire him to do.
>
> Therefore, putting aside any other letters you receive, instruct him not to make any move until we arrive in Milan, and while he is waiting for us, we shall inform him concerning the work we desire from him. Make it especially clear that he must not leave the aforementioned city until our coming, as we already have explained to your Ambassador, telling him to write to you about the matter; and in doing this you will be giving me great pleasure.
>
> Very dear and great friends, may our Lord have you in his keeping. LOUIS [S31]

The French king *inter alia* the Duke of the Duchy of Milan was now in a serious dispute with the Florentines for the services of Leonardo da Vinci. He wanted Leonardo back to complete his painting of *Our Lord the Christ with Sphere* (the *Salvator Mundi*). This dispute amused Leonardo no end, and he may well have been guilty of playing off one side against the other. Leonardo was back in Milan by mid January to prepare for the return of the French king in April of 1507 when Louis XII arrived there with his large contingent of troops and a large number of his courtiers to the highly decorated city. Cheering crowds greeted the French king, and he attended many celebrations, pageants, jousts, and parties held in his honour. The Marquis of Mantua, Francesco II Gonzaga, who had joined forces with the French king to quell a Florentine inspired uprising in Genoa, was invited to Milan to be awarded the title of Grand Master of the Order of St. Michael. His wife Isabella d' Este accompanied him for she was keen to return to Milan and meet the French king and visit the great halls of the Rochetta where her sister Beatrice had danced and dined as the Duchess of Milan with her husband, the former duke of Milan, Ludovico Sforza. She wanted to pay her respects and prayers to the memory of her sister at her tomb in Santa Maria delle Grazie. Isabella wrote about her impressions of Milan and her meeting with the French king in a letter to her sister–in-law Elisabetta Gonzaga who was still in Urbino at the time:

> Since Your Excellency went to Rome and Rome came to Urbino, I have never ventured to rival the grandeur of your court, nor to pretend that I have seen as many rare and excellent things as you have done, but have looked on in silence and not without hidden envy at Your Highness. But now that I have been to the first and noblest court in Christendom, I can boldly not only challenge you, but compel you to envy me. A few weeks ago, I was summoned by my illustrious lord to Milan to pay homage to His Most Christian Majesty, and arrived there on the vigil of Corpus Christi. After dinner, as I was about to go and pay my respects, I received a message from him, desiring me to go to the lists on the Piazza where the Giostra was being held. So I went there at the stated hour and found His Majesty, who came to meet me on the steps and received me with the greatest courtesy possible. All the Milanese ladies were present and the Princess of Bisignano, as well as all the barony and nobility of France and the great lords of Italy, the Duke of Savoy, the Marquises of Mantua and Montferrat, and all the castellans of the Milanese towns, and the

ambassadors of every power in Italy. The French lords are so numerous that it would be impossible to name them all. But I must mention the Duce de Bourbon, our nephew, a tall youth of handsome and majestic appearance, who closely resembles his mother (Chiara de Montpensier) in complexion, eyes, and features. If the Roman Court is marvellous for its ceremonial and order, that of France is no less amazing and extraordinary for confusion and disorder — so much so that it is quite impossible to distinguish one man from another. It is also certainly remarkable for its freedom and absence of etiquette. In this court, for instance, cardinals are not treated with any greater honour than chaplains are in Rome. No one gives place to them or pays them any respect, from the king downwards. His Majesty, however, is always most courteous and respectful to all who presume to approach him, and above all to ladies, always rising from his seat and lifting his cap to show them honour. Thrice over he came to visit me in my lodgings. The first time, when I happened to be dining with Signor Zoanne (Gian) Giacomo Trivulzio, he waited more than half-an-hour for my return, and each time he remained no less than two or three hours, conversing on different subjects with the greatest friendliness in the world, neither did he fail to speak honourably of Your Highness in the course of conversation. Madonna Margherita di San Severino (sister of Emilia Pia), the Contessa di Musocho, and sometimes the Princess of Bisignano, who are well versed in the French language, were our interpreters. In spite of repeated efforts, I never succeeded in finding His Majesty in the Castello, saving one day when he invited me to a public banquet in the Rocchetta, where the Princess of Bisignano and I had the honour of sitting at his table. We danced in an informal manner both before and after supper. His Majesty danced with me, and the Cardinals Narbonne, San Severino, Ferrara, and Finale, who were present at the banquet, were constrained by him to dance, much to our amusement and diversion.

I will not write about the public spectacles held on the Piazza, because I know that they will have been fully described by your ambassador. Certainly I have seen better-managed jousts, but I never saw, and do not think that, in all Christendom, it would be possible to see, a greater number and variety of people! Most of them were nobles — not only those of Milan, which must be the first or second largest city in the world, but the whole court of France and most of the courts of Italy were here assembled, so that Your Excellency will understand how proud and glorious a sight it was! The assembly was a much larger one than we could have seen at the king's own palace in France, because the lords who followed him to Italy do not reside at court, and if they are occasionally present at some solemn ceremony, we should not have seen all the people and nobles of Milan, and indeed we may say of Italy, since the gentlemen and citizens of many different cities came to witness these spectacles.

O how great was my happiness! And how it makes me rejoice every time that I remember it! Only think what it would be if Your Signory were here and we could communicate by word of mouth! I have written all this to deliver myself from the sin of envy, and also to describe a thing, which is excellent in spite of its disorder. I am sure that the Roman court is not to be compared with the French court, where the temporal and spiritual are united. If Your Excellency could have seen the procession of Corpus Christi set out from the Duomo with little enough order — first the clergy, then an infinite number of Swiss guards with halberds on their shoulders, behind them the Gentlemen of the Guard, battle-axes in hand, and after them under a *baldacchino* borne by the chief lords came the Legate of France bearing the Body of Christ, followed by the king, with seven Cardinals and all the barony of France and Italy, and people of Milan and the neighbouring towns — it would have seemed to you the finest spectacle which you had ever witnessed! It is true that Your Signory may say, 'I have seen Rome'; still you must confess that you saw it undone and in ruins. But I have seen Genoa, Florence, and Milan, which in our age are no less worthy of admiration in their most triumphant days. I will not deny that I have a great wish to see Rome, not for the sake of the court and the different nations who are represented there, for I could not look upon anything finer than what I have seen here, but in order to visit the antiquities and famous ruins of Rome and to realise what the triumph of a victorious Emperor must have been.

But this occasion has not been entirely without Roman ceremonies, since at the entrance of my friend, the Most Reverend Cardinal and Legate of S. Prassede, he was received by the Legate of France and eight Cardinals, all the orders of clergy, and singers, with great magnificence, because His Most Reverend Signory holds the rank of the Pope whom he represents, so that I may say I have seen both the Pope and the Roman court. Afterwards I paid His Signory two visits at his lodgings, where I was most lovingly received, embraced, and honoured, and was able to realise the splendid state of the Cardinals who live in Rome. This impression was confirmed by the visit which I received from Cardinal de Rouen and all the other Cardinals attached to this court, who came in a body, not to pay me honour, which would not have been suitable on their part, but merely to show me courtesy. I might go on and describe all the separate visits which I received from Italian and French lords and Milanese ladies, as well as from the King and the Cardinals, but this and all the rest I will leave to Your Signory's imagination, lest I give you too much reason to envy me.

I' Mantua, July 7, 1507. [S32]

I received a copy of the above letter from Elisabetta Gonzaga when I visited her in her refuge in Ferrara in 1524. She was with little money and wanted me to find her a buyer for her portrait that was painted by my dear friend Raphael in about 1504.

I have added Isabella d' Este's written account of her visit to Milan here because I think it captures very poetically the spirit of the times when the French king was in attendance in Milan at that time. I remember seeing her at the castle and thinking to myself how happy and beautiful she looked. I was 13 years of age, and my father and Leonardo who was then painting a portrait of the king honoured me with an introduction to Him, the French Duke of Milan. I remember fondly the dizzy and glorious sights of all the different visitors and courtiers and how joyous it all was with the number and variety of people in our beautiful city that was still recovering from the damages of the French invasion of 1499. I believe Isabella d' Este's words have captured the happiness of the city at the time of her visit to meet the French king. Galeazzo Sanseverino was back in the city in the service of the king, and he once again was winning jousts for the pleasure of the citizens, and not just for the Este or the Sforza. Leonardo was here to prepare the decorations and feasts for the French king and his honoured guests and to undertake new architectures and surveys of the cities, canals, and town planning. It is no wonder that he was in no hurry to return to Florence to service the dull and serious Signoria of Florence. Although Leonardo intended to stay in Milan and take on the wonderful opportunities on offer to him, he suddenly left and returned to Florence in September to fight a litigation battle brought against him by his brothers who contested the inheritance that he had received from his uncle Francesco.

Legal Disputations and a Lack of Brotherly Love, 1507 and 1508

When Leonardo's uncle Francesco da Vinci died in January of 1507, he left all his estate to Leonardo da Vinci, his nephew whom he loved like he was his own son. The estate included a property in Santa Croce near Vinci, where Leonardo when he was a child and a youth had grown up with his uncle, aunt, and grandfather, happily running about and exploring the property at his leisure and pleasure. Now his angry brothers who received nothing contested their uncle's will believing that they were entitled to a share of the estate that was left to Leonardo who, after all, was illegitimate and had spent twenty years in Milan contributing little to the upkeep of their father's families. Leonardo, on the other hand, believed that his half brothers had totally ignored their uncle and had been nasty to him, and it was one of the reasons why he had returned to Florence to better care for him. He was incensed by their claims and action, and he was determined to justify his uncle's bequest and also to claim a share of his father's estate. In one of his notebooks Leonardo wrote a very strange dialogue between himself, his father, and his brothers about his uncle's inheritance.

> You wished the utmost evil to Francesco and have let him enjoy your property in Santa Croce during your life; to me you do not wish a greater evil.
>
> To whom have you wished better? To Francesco or to me? To you he wishes it, and he gives mine after me so that I cannot dispose of my inheritance according to my wish, because he knows that I cannot alienate my heir. He wishes then to demand from my heirs and not as Francesco, but as one entirely alien, and I as one entirely alien will receive him and his.
>
> Have you given such money to Leonardo? No. Oh what excuse whether feigned or true will you be able to give for having drawn him into this trap, except to take him and his money. And I will not say anything to him as long as he lives. You do not wish therefore to repay the money lent on your account to his heirs; but you wish that he should pay over the revenues that he has from this possession.
>
> Oh why do you not allow him to enjoy them during his life, since afterwards they would return to your children, and he cannot live many years?
>
> If then you take into account that I may do that, you will wish that I was the heir, because I should not be able as heir to demand from you the moneys, which Francesco had given me.

Leonardo had no intention of losing his father's or his uncle's inheritance, and he decided to fight his brothers with tooth and nail to the bitter end. But the stumbling block that he had in front of him was that three of them had followed in the footsteps of their father and had become successful notaries and lawyers themselves. He had to contest all three of his brothers who had vast experience in litigation and the court processes. On the other hand, he loathed lawyers, courts, legal matters, and litigation - it was an anathema to his artistic temperament.

The litigation started off very badly for him, so to counter his brothers' effectiveness he decided to recruit important people on his behalf. These people were the young cardinal Ippolito d'Este, the French king Louis XII and his secretary Florimond Robertet, the viceroy of Milan Charles d'Amboise, and Machiavelli and his secretary Agostino Vespucci, and finally and most effectively, the de' Medici brothers, and especially Giovanni di Lorenzo de' Medici, the future Pope Leo X of Rome.

The following are some of the letters presented to the Florentine Signoria on Leonardo's behalf in 1507. First, the king's letter countersigned by Florimond Robertet.

> To our very dear and great friends, allies and confederates, the Perpetual Gonfalonier and the Signoria of Florence. Louis, by the Grace of God King of France, Duke of Milan, Lord of Genoa.
>
> Very dear and great friends. We have been informed that our dear and well-beloved Leonardo da Vinci, our painter and engineer in ordinary, has some dispute and litigation pending in Florence against his brothers over certain inheritances; and inasmuch as he could not devote himself properly to the pursuit of the said litigation by reason of his continual occupation in our entourage and in our presence; and also because we are singularly desirous that the said litigation should be brought to an end in the best and briefest delivery of justice as soon as possible: for this reason we willingly write to you on the matter, requesting that you do indeed bring the said dispute and litigation to an end with the best and briefest delivery of justice as possible; and you will be giving us a very agreeable pleasure in doing so. Very dear and great friends, may Our Lord have you in his keeping.
>
> Given in Milan, on the XXVI day of July.
> LOUIS   Robertet [S31]

When Leonardo found out that it was Raphaello Hieronymo who was going to preside over the lawsuit, he wrote a letter to their mutual friend the Cardinal Ippolito d' Este:

> Most Illustrious and Most Reverend, My Unique Lord, The Lord Ippolito d'Este, Cardinal of Ferrara, My Supreme Lord, Most Illustrious and Most Reverend Lord.
>
> A few days ago I arrived here from Milan, and learning that one of my elder brothers refuses to carry out the provisions of a will made three years ago when my father died; and also, and no less, because I would not fail in my own eyes in a matter I esteem most important, I cannot forbear to request of your most reverend Highness a letter of recommendation and favour to Ser Raffaello Hieronymo, at present one of the most illustrious members of the Signoria before whom my case is being tried; and more particularly His Excellency the Gonfalonier has laid the matter in the hands of the aforesaid Ser Raphaello to the end that his Lordship may be able to reach a decision and bring it to completion before the Feast of All Saints.
>
> Wherefore, my Lord, I entreat you, as urgently as I know how and am able, to write a letter to the said Ser Raphaello in that skilful and affectionate manner that you know so well, recommend to him Leonardo Vincio, Your Lordship's most abject servant, as I call myself and always wish to be: requesting him and urging him not only to do me justice but to do so with propitious urgency; and have not the least doubt that, from the many reports that have reached me, Ser Raphaello, who is most affectionately disposed toward your Highness, will bring the matter *ad votum*. And this I shall attribute to the letter of your most Reverent Highness, to whom once more I commend my self. *Et bene valeat.*
>
> Florence, 18th September 1507
>
> E.V.R.D. Your most humble servant, LEONARDUS VINCIUS, Pictor [S31]

Yet, the litigation carried on for another half year and involved correspondence from many of Leonardo's supporters who attempted to sway the Florentine court in favour of Leonardo. His brothers were canny and determined, and they fought hard to keep the matter in the courts in an attempt to win a favourable outcome for themselves. Eventually, in March of 1508, when Leonardo's friends the de' Medici brothers exerted their power to have the litigation thrown out of court and for his uncle's will to be properly executed in full for Leonardo, the chief of the brothers Ser Giuliano hastily concluded a settlement in favour of Leonardo and the estate of the dead Francesco. Leonardo always told his brother Ser Giuliano that when he died he would pass on his Fiesole property and a sum of money to his much younger surviving brothers. Leonardo expressed the following in his last will and testament that I executed in 1519:

> You and your brothers have been willed to be heirs of a sum of money held in the hands of the treasurer of Santa Maria Nuova in the city of Florence. The aforesaid Maestro Leonardo has deposited in Santa Maria Nuova in the hands of the Camarlingo 400 gold scudi in marked and number notes, bearing interest at 5 per cent, which on the 16th October will have been there for 6 years, and also there is a property at Fiesole which he desires to be distributed among you. The transference of the property and willed sum from the treasurer to you will be arranged by me, the Testator, and the treasurer of Santa Maria Nuova over the next year. After one year's grace I as his lawful executor will contact you with the appropriate letters and documents for you to procure and receive your rightful entitlements from the treasurer of Santa Maria Nuova as deemed in your brother's last will and testament.

Dissections and Anatomy in a Winter of Discontent, January to March of 1508

As far as Leonardo was concerned the painting for the *Battle of Anghiari* was truly finished at the end of 1507. All his assistants except for Tommaso had moved on elsewhere, and Salai and il Fanfoia had stayed on in Milan. His rival artists, Michelangelo and Raphael, were both in Rome. Leonardo himself was thinking of the best ways to return permanently to Milan, but he still was waiting to settle the legal dispute with his brothers in Florence. He paid some new temporary assistants to move all of his belongings from the Sala del Papa in the monastery of Santa Maria Novella (Nuova) to various properties and his new workshop at Fiesole. He turned his mind back to science and began a new notebook on the study of bird flight – he wanted to write and publish his codice on the flight of birds. He'd also informed the nuns at the hospital of Santa Maria Nuova in Florence that he wanted to stay there to continue his anatomical studies. So in the winter of late 1507 the nuns arranged adjoining rooms for him at the hospital. One room was where he could stay and sleep overnight or when he was tired and needed to rest away from the stench of the cadavers. The other room was where he could perform his dissections without disruption. Leonardo regarded that his anatomical studies were his most important contributions to knowledge and the betterment of mankind, and he always appreciated the help of the nuns of Santa Maria Nuova for him to achieve these goals.

> I reveal to men the origin of their first or perhaps second cause of existence. Would that it might please our Creator that I was able to reveal the nature of man and his customs even as I describe his figure.

And are the nature and customs of man all that different from animals? If we were originally derived from animals such as the apes on earth then apparently these differences are not so great on closer inspection.

> In fact **man does not vary from the animals except in what is accidental**, and it is in this that he shows himself to be a divine thing; for where nature finishes producing its species there man begins with natural things to make with the aid of this nature an infinite number of species; and as these are not necessary to those who govern themselves rightly as do the animals it is not in their disposition to seek after them.

Although Leonardo had already dissected many cadavers of humans and animals in previous years starting in Florence at the hospital of Santa Maria Nuova in 1476, this was the first time he was dissecting to discover the cause of a man or child's death. Now, for the first time, he had the opportunity to undertake comparative anatomy studies of the cadaver of an 100-year-old man and a 2-year-old boy immediately after their deaths.

> And this old man, a few hours before his death, told me that he lived a hundred years, and that he did not feel any bodily ailment other than weakness, and thus while sitting upon a bed in the hospital of Santa Maria Nuova at Florence, without any movement or sign of anything amiss, he passed away from this life. And I made an autopsy in order to ascertain the cause of so peaceful a death, and found that it proceeded from weakness through failure of blood and of the artery that feeds the heart and the other lower members, which I found to be very parched and shrunk and withered; and the result of this autopsy I wrote down very carefully and with great ease, for the body was devoid of either fat or moisture, and these form the chief hindrance to the knowledge of its parts.
>
> The other autopsy was on a child of two years, and here I found everything the contrary to what it was in the case of the old man. The old who enjoy good health die through lack of sustenance. And this is brought about by the passage to the mesaraic veins becoming continually restricted by the thickening of the skin of these veins; and the process continues until it affects the capillary veins, which are the first to close up altogether; and from this it comes to pass that the old dread the cold more than the young, and that those who are very old have their skin the colour of wood or of dried chestnut, because this skin is almost completely deprived of sustenance. And this network of veins

acts in man as in oranges, in which the peel becomes thicker and the pulp diminishes the more they become old. And if you say that as the blood becomes thicker it ceases to flow through the veins, this is not true, for the blood in the veins does not thicken because it continually dies and is renewed.

I am not a physician nor an anatomist, but I do know that by dissecting the very old and the very young, Leonardo discovered that death was caused in the old by the thickening of the arteries and the veins, and that this in turn affected the nutritional well being of the vital organs, like the heart, the lungs, the spleen, and the liver that declined in efficiency and consequence due to a lack of the proper spread of nutrition throughout the body. He already knew that the heart was a muscle and that its beating pumped the blood as pulsating waves through the arteries and veins by means of contractions and expansions, and that this finding was profound and meaningful in its own right. He also knew that the blood in man and animal was always renewed, it had its own cycle of death and rebirth possibly through processes originating in the bone marrow. But, nobody I know in the world of medicine has yet brought to our attention that the movement of the nutritious elements of blood through the veins and arteries declined in old age because of blockages caused by the thickening of the blood vessels. This is an unbelievable revelation that no others have yet comprehended properly.

In proportion as the veins become old they lose their straightness of direction in their ramifications, and become so much the more flexible or winding and of thicker covering as old age becomes more full with years.

You will find almost universally that the passage of the veins and the passage of the nerves are on the same path, and direct themselves to the same muscles and ramify in the same manner in each of these muscles, and that each vein and nerve pass with the artery between one muscle and the other, and ramify in these with equal ramification.

The artery and the vein which in the old extend between the spleen and the liver, acquire so great a thickness of skin that it contracts the passage of the blood that comes from the mesaraic veins, through which this blood passes over to the liver and the heart and the two greater veins, and as a consequence through the whole body; and apart from the thickening of the skin these veins grow in length and twist themselves after the manner of a snake, and the liver loses the humour of the blood which was carried there by this vein; and consequently this liver becomes dried up and grows like frozen bran both in colour and substance, so that when it is subjected even to the slightest friction this substance falls away in tiny flakes like sawdust and leaves the veins and arteries.

And the veins of the gall and of the navel, which entered into this liver by the gate of the liver all remain deprived of the substance of this liver, after the manner of maize or Indian millet when their grains have been separated.

The colon and the other intestines in the old become much constricted, and I have found there stones in the veins which pass beneath the fork of the breast, which were as large as chestnuts, of the colour and shape of truffles or of dross or clinkers of iron, which stones were extremely hard, as are these clinkers, and had formed bags which were hanging to the said veins after the manner of goitres.

Many years later, when I worked for Leonardo, one of my duties was to help him rewrite his anatomical and medical notes in preparation for them to be published into a large and comprehensive book. One of my favourite passages was his comparison of the heart and vessels proceeding from the heart with the roots and ramifications (branching) of plants. To my simple mind this reads more like poetry than science.

The heart is the nut which produces the tree of the veins; which veins have their roots in the dung, that is, the mesaraic veins, which proceed to deposit the blood they have acquired in the liver from which afterwards the upper veins of the liver are nourished. The plant never springs from the ramification for at first the plant exists before this ramification, and the heart exists before the veins. All the veins and arteries proceed from the heart; and the reason is that the maximum thickness that is found in these veins and arteries is at the junction that they make with the heart; and the farther away they are from the heart the thinner they become and they are divided into more minute ramifications. And if you should say that the veins start in the protuberance of the liver because they have their ramifications in this protuberance, just as the roots of plants have in the earth, the reply to this comparison is that plants do not have their origin in their roots, but that the roots and the other ramifications have their origin in the lower part of these plants, which is between the air and the earth; and all the parts of the plant above and below are always less than this part which borders upon the earth; therefore it is evident that the whole plant has its origin from this thickness, and, in consequence, the veins have their origin in the heart where is their greatest thickness; never can any plant be found which has its origin in the points of its roots or other ramifications; and the example of this is seen in the growing of the peach which proceeds from its nut as is shown above.

Leonardo's heart-felt efforts for his anatomical drawings and commentaries on the dissections of the old man and young child fill entire notebooks with soulful love about the mysteries of all life. He generally worked alone for long days and long nights talking to himself or to the dearly departed before him while he performed the dissections, notes, and drawings in either a hot or cold room depending on the time of day, sparing others from the uncomfortable sight of the corpses *'quartered and flayed and horrible to behold.'* Occasionally, his faithful servant Agnolo Benedetto assisted him and kept him company in the ghostly atmosphere and death stench of the morgue exchanging thoughts about the purpose of creation and the frailty of the mortal coil.

And you who say that it is better to look at an anatomical demonstration than to see these drawings, you would be right, if it were possible to observe all the details shown in these drawings in a single figure, in which, with all your ability, you will not see nor acquire a knowledge of more than some few veins, while, in order to obtain an exact and complete knowledge of these, I have dissected more than ten human bodies, destroying all the various members, and removing even the very smallest particles of the flesh which surrounded these veins, without causing any effusion of blood other than the imperceptible bleeding of the capillary veins. And as one single body did not suffice for so long a time, it was necessary to proceed by stages with so many bodies as would render my knowledge complete; and this I repeated twice over in order to discover the differences.

But though possessed of an interest in the subject you may perhaps be deterred by natural repugnance, or, if this does not restrain you, then perhaps by the fear of passing the night hours in the company of these corpses, quartered and flayed and horrible to behold; and if this does not deter you then perhaps you may lack the skill in drawing essential for such representation; and even if you possess this skill it may not be combined with a knowledge of perspective, while, if it is so combined, you may not be versed in the methods of geometrical demonstration or the method of estimating the forces and strength of muscles, or perhaps you may be found wanting in patience so that you will not be diligent.

Concerning which things, whether or not they have all been found in me, the hundred and twenty books, which I have composed will give their verdict 'yes' or 'no'. In these I have not been hindered either by avarice or negligence but only by want of time. Farewell.

In spring, after the winter dissections, Leonardo wanted to organise his vast array of notebooks and manuscripts in some sort of meaningful order with the thought of publishing his findings and discoveries and having his drawings printed from copper engravings with the help of the engraver and sculptor Giovanni Francesco Rustici who was residing in the house of Piero di Braccio Martelli.

> Began in Florence in the house of Piero di Braccio Martelli, on the 22nd day of March 1508: This will be a collection without order, made up of many sheets which I have copied here, hoping afterwards to arrange them in order in their proper places according to the subjects of which they treat; and I believe that before I am at the end of this I shall have to repeat the same thing several times; and therefore, O reader, blame me not, because the subjects are many, and the memory cannot retain them and say 'this I will not write because I have already written it'. And if I wished to avoid falling into this mistake it would be necessary, in order to prevent repetition, that on every occasion when I wished to transcribe a passage I should always read over all the preceding portion, and this especially because long periods of time elapse between one time of writing and another.

Leonardo was at the Martelli house to enlist the service of Giovanni Francesco Rustici for his bronze sculpture of *Hercules* to be displayed in the garden of Pier Francesco Ginori. Rustici was a master of works in terracotta and also of gilt-bronzed base-relief plaques, statues, and fountains, and he could easily prepare copper engravings. Together they created small bronze statues of galloping horsemen and recreated the *Battle of Anghiari* in bronze because Leonardo knew his painting at the Palace Vecchio would not last long. Rustici again enjoyed having his master's help in sculpting horses as he did with his sculpted group in bronze of *St. John the Baptist Preaching to Levite and a Pharisee*. These three marvellous bronzes sculpted by Leonardo and Rustici are now displayed above the north door of the Baptistery of Florence. St. John is the patron saint of Florence and building, and naturally, he is the central figure in the troika of saints. Rustici and Leonardo enjoyed their time together for Rustici was an irreverent and boisterous wit as Leonardo was when they both shared a cup of wine. Rustici was a member of the Company of the Saucepan and the Company of the Trowel, a group of artists who organised fantastic banquets in Rustici's house. Approximately, eight years after Leonardo died in France, Rustici left Florence and also went to work for king Francois I of France. He died in France at Tours in 1554 after eighty years of a good and productive life.

***

With the litigation settled in his favour, Leonardo felt unneeded in Florence and was ready to return to the service of Charles d'Amboise in Milan. The Viceroy had treated him with great respect and friendliness and promised him the return of his Milan properties that had been confiscated from him when the French had first invaded the city in 1499. But, he needed to check with the Viceroy that his promises still held true.

He wrote to my father requesting assistance from somebody to help him to cope with the French and their language and to help him to reorder his notes and drawings into cogent preparations for publication. He needed a replacement for his long time servant Tommaso who wished to remain in Florence. He needed a young, energetic secretary, a gentleman, somebody like me, if my father would allow it. He also wrote the following letter to Charles d'Amboise inquiring whether the French would return to him his properties and grant him his promised canal rights if he were to return to Milan.

Leonardo's letter to Charles d'Amboise, the French Governor of Milan:

> Magnifico Signore mio, the love Your Excellency has always shown me and the benefits I constantly received from you I have hitherto possibly failed you.
> I suspect that the poor return I have made for the great benefits that I have received

from your Excellency, may have made you somewhat indignant with me, and thus it is that I have written so many letters to your Lordship and have never had a reply. I now send Salai to you, to explain to your Lordship that I am almost at the end of the lawsuit that I have had with my brothers, and that I expect to find myself with you this Easter, and to bring with me two pictures of the Madonna, of different sizes, which have been made either for our Most Christian King, or for whomsoever your Lordship pleases. I should be very glad to know on my return there where I am to take up my abode, as I would not give any more trouble to your Lordship; and also, as I have been working for the Most Christian King, whether my salary is to continue or not.

I am writing to the President about that water which the King granted me, and of which I was not given the possession, because at that time there was a shortage in the canal by reason of the great drought, and because its outlets were not being regulated; but he gave me a definite promise that when this was done I should be put in possession, so that I beseech your Lordship not to be unwilling now that the outlets are regulated to remind the President of my suit, namely that I should be given possession of this water, for when I am established there I look forward to constructing machines and devices which should be a source of great pleasure to our Most Christian King. Nothing else occurs to me. I am always at your commands.

Florence, April 1508

E.V.R.D. Your most humble servant

LEONARDUS VINCIUS Pictor

Farewell Dinner with Niccolo Machiavelli

On his last night in Florence, Leonardo attended a private dinner with his friend Machiavelli to thank and honour him for his assistance during the last five or six years of his stay in Florence. He much appreciated Machiavelli's help with various commissions and presented him in gratitude with the gift of two beautiful equestrian sculptures, one a rearing horse and the other a copy of the horse that he designed for the Sforza family in honour of Francesco Sforza. Machiavelli was a great admirer of Francesco Sforza, the fourth duke of Milan, and liked to talk to Leonardo about the duke's achievements. During the past month, Leonardo had stayed in the company of the Florentine sculptor Giovanni Francesco Rustici at the villa of Piero di Braccio Martelli and helped him with the design and production of the equestrian sculptures. Leonardo now wanted more information from Machiavelli about the current rulers of Milan, Louis XII the French king and *inter alia* the Duke of Milan, Charles d'Amboise the governor of Milan, and the French knights La Palice, Gaston de Foix, Louis II de la Tremoille, Bayard, Yves d'Alegre, Lautrec, and other favourites of the king such as Florimond Robertet, Bartolomeo de Cavaleris, and Monssignor Rohan, and scores of others. Machiavelli knew them all very well because he had been in their service in France when he was the envoy of the Florentine Republic on at least two different occasions. He had even ridden into Milan as a diplomatic observer when the French king first entered the city in 1500. Machiavelli had also introduced Leonardo to Charles d'Amboise and Count of Ligny, when Leonardo undertook the secret mission for the French and Florentine alliance against Romagna about the time he left Milan with Fra Luca Pacioli and Salai. Machiavelli, born in 1469, was 17 years younger than Leonardo, but his maturity and cunning belied his years. Also, he was seven years younger than king Louis XII, but understood him well enough and considered him a good friend.

Niccolo Machiavelli had a long and interesting history in public life as an officer of the Florentine Republic. He was appointed secretary and second chancellor to the Florentine Republic in 1498 at the age of 29 years. During his time in office, he accompanied a number of diplomatic missions to King Louis XII in France. His first mission was for six-months in 1500 when he befriended Georges d'Amboise, the Cardinal of Rouen. His other mission to the court of Louis XII in France was in 1504. Thus, Machiavelli knew something about the French court that Leonardo wanted to tap into.

They talked long into the night about the French conquests and their arrogance and claims on Italy and other matters. Niccolo told Leonardo that he was particularly interested in the Sforza rule of Lombardy and how Francesco Sforza was a model leader of a state. He compared how Francesco Sforza became a prince by his own strength and kept his state, whereas Cesare Borgia became a prince by his father's influence, and, despite his best efforts, could not maintain his state after his father's influence failed. He asked Leonardo for his opinion of Ludovico Sforza and how he thought his rule compared to that of his brother Galeazzo. Leonardo replied carefully and diplomatically without vexation praising all the previous rulers of a city where he now intended to spend the remainder of his life, even if it was to be ruled by the French. He then changed the subject and preferred to reminisce about his time and friendship with Lorenzo de' Medici and praise the virtues of 'Magnifico' as a splendid ruler of the Republic of Florence and as a highly regarded diplomat of Italy.

Machiavelli who already had published a number of impressive political and historical discourses told Leonardo about his plans to write and publish further discourses on modern tyrannical rule and tyrants and a series of books on the modern history of Italy and the rise and governance of the Florentine Republic. He pointed out to Leonardo that he would be highly critical of the Roman Catholic rule and their corruption of the political and social systems.

As the night wore on into the very late hours Machiavelli turned his attention to Leonardo's unique position as a court painter and engineer general of fortifications and how in these positions he could garner important political information for the Florentine Republic. He thanked Leonardo for all the information that he had previously provided them. Indirectly, he was asking Leonardo to act as a spy for him on behalf of Florence and the Florentine Signoria. This shocked Leonardo because he never envisaged himself to be a spy or a secret agent for any state or government official including Machiavelli. A messenger? A diplomat? Yes - he had been an envoy and a diplomat for many people on many occasions, and he saw nothing wrong or contradictory with that role or that of his work as an artist, a scientist, an engineer, an entertainer, a consultant or an advisor. But, a spy, in the pay of a secret government agency!!! No. Never. He wondered what information he might have given to Machiavelli to allow him to think that he would want to act for him as a secret agent. No. He wouldn't entertain such an impure thought. Instead, Leonardo saw himself more as a priest at the confessional who would never divulge or share with others the secrets and gossip that he heard from his clients. Whatever was shared between him and the client would stay between him and the client. He believed in confidentiality. Without it, he would lose the trust of his clients and their commissions. Confidentiality and integrity were integral to his beliefs and actions.

Before Leonardo could answer no to being a spy, Machiavelli already became more specific. He asked Leonardo to report to him directly with any information that he might be able to glean from the French about their intentions for Genoa and Pisa. The Florentine Republic was still intent to invade and annex Pisa, and Machiavelli wanted to know what the French mood would be if they did so. In regard to Genoa, it was more about what allies the French would retain to maintain their hold on the harbour town. Florence still had their eye on Genoa as a prize that they would try to take from France when the time was right. To keep his peace with Machiavelli on his last night in Florence, Leonardo absentmindedly returned to the subject of the French and those who he was most likely to encounter and deal with on his return to the city of Milan.

After Leonardo left Florence, Machiavelli held his post in the Signoria for the next four years. He continued to publish discourses on various political and historic subjects and travel on missions to different territories on behalf of the Florentine Republic. Then, something happened in April of 1512 that he didn't anticipate. Florence was invaded by the Papal led

Spanish forces. The Perpetual Gonfalonier Piero Soderini was ousted from his exalted position into a life of exile in Rome, and the entire Signoria was overthrown. Machiavelli was ousted from the Chancery in November, and in February 1513, he was arrested, tried for conspiracy, tortured, and imprisoned for two months. On release, he retired to his farm at Sant' Andrea in Percussina, seven miles south of Florence to farm, meditate, and write more books and discourses on history, politics, war, and the Italian language.

Fig. 82. Niccolo di Bernardo dei Machiavelli *by the painter Santi di Tito.*

A few years after I had returned from France in 1522 to live in Vaprio on the Adda River, I began to correspond with Niccolo Machiavelli about the French-Italian Wars. This was a few years before King Francois I of France was captured and imprisoned by the Spanish in 1525. When Francois I was released from prison by the Spanish king and Holy Roman Emperor Charles V on the 17th March 1526, both Machiavelli and I sent him our congratulatory messages as soon as we heard that he was safely back in France. I stayed in regular touch with Machiavelli until his death in 1527, the same year that the Medici were expelled from Florence, and a new Republic and constitution was adopted.

CHAPTER 21

Milan's French Kitchen, 1508 to 1513

From the beginning of the canal of Brivio to the mill of Travaglia is 2794 trabochi, that is 11176 braccia, which is more than 3 miles and two thirds; and here the canal is 57 braccia higher than the surface of the water of the Adda, giving a fall of two inches in every hundred trabochi; and at that spot we propose to take the opening of our canal.

— Leonardo da Vinci

Milan and Lombardy: Under French Occupation from 1499 to 1512

When Leonardo returned to Milan in 1508, the city no longer had the *joie de vivre* and sparkle it enjoyed before the French invasion of 1499. After eight years of French occupation, Milan was run down, unkempt, depressed, and expensive. The streets and shops were dirty with many more beggars on the corners and drunken French soldiers lounging about inside and outside the many taverns. The prostitution that once had been discrete was now rampant, overt, and present in the opens streets and town squares. Few French in Milan could speak Italian, and few Italians spoke French, so there were continual misunderstandings and unnecessary violence. Many of Leonardo's favourite waterways and canals were in major disrepair, and while in the outskirts of the city, he saw that the once thriving farms were well below the expected levels of production and often left untended or neglected. A few years before the French occupation, Milan was the richest city in Europe, thriving in agricultural production and various manufacturing industries. According to the citizens of Milan, the lands of the duchy belonged as much to them as to the duke, and they were proud to maintain its wellbeing. In the past, most of the citizens had lived comfortable and prosperous lives, the city was clean, well maintained, and there was no shortage of work, business, good food, art, festivities, and lively entertainment. However, much had changed for the worse under the French occupation.

It took a while for the Milanese to realise that things had changed, and that they were now under direct French rule with a French flavour and tepid cuisine. The leading civic families expected that Milan would become an autonomous republic and hold authority over all the territories that had been governed previously by the Sforza, and that they now would pay only a small annual tax to the French king. A few cities in the duchy, such as Pavia, wanted their own autonomy.

However, the French king had other ideas. He installed himself as Duke of the Duchy of Milan and also declared himself Duke of Genoa from the very beginning of his occupation. To reiterate to the citizens who was the boss of Milan, he introduced gold and silver coins of himself that bore an image of his profile on one side of the coin (*LVDOVICVS • DG • FRANCOR (VM) • REX* [*Louis by the Grace of God, King of the Franks*]) and St. Ambrose on the other side with words to the effect that he was the Duke of Milan (*MEDIOLANI DVX*). The portrait-bearing coins of previous dukes and duchesses of Milan were quickly removed from public circulation. Those coins that were bearing the images of Duke Galeazzo Maria Sforza, the Regent Bona of Savoy, the young prince regent and Duke of Milan - Gian Galeazzo Sforza, and his guardian and uncle Ludovico Sforza, the Duchess Beatrice d' Este, and other combinations of the Sforza family were melted down to their base metal or stored in vaults to be traded secretly among the entitled and rich collectors. The French king hoped to forever exorcise the Sforza name and swamp Milan with coins bearing his own image and his name as the King of France and the Duke of the Duchy of Milan.

Fig. 83. The testone of King Louis XII, Duke of Milan, with Saint Ambrose on horseback.

The French Cardinal Georges d' Amboise, guided by the authority of the king of France, initially instituted a parliamentary Senate of seventeen Italian members with a presiding French chancellor to supervise the civil administration of the whole duchy. As in the French provinces, the head of the financial administration was the General of Finances. Military matters were the responsibility of the Lieutenant General or Governor who would also be the most important political authority in the duchy with powers analogous to those of the French provincial governors. Trivulzio was appointed the Lieutenant General, but the Milanese citizens greatly resented his appointment because they regarded him as a traitor and not their equal. So, the French king had to send him back to France and replace him with a governor better suited for the people. Because of constant incursions from the North by German and Swiss mercenaries and various rebellions across Lombardy, the parliamentary Senate was soon abandoned for a strong military government that was run by French marshals, nobles, and captains, and other army officers in charge. The Corte Vecchio (Royal Palace), where Leonardo once had his apartments and workshop, became the administrative centre for the French to rule over the city and the communes. When in Milan, King Louis stayed at the Sforza castle, and it was also the residence of many of his French marshals. Large numbers of French troops were left in the duchy, together with 10,000 Swiss mercenaries loyal to the French king. Only Frenchmen, and no Italians, were now appointed at the highest level of the reorganised government, and Charles Chaumont (II) d' Amboise was appointed the Governor of Milan in 1503 to represent his king and govern the duchy until his death in 1512.

King Louis's declared intention from the beginning was that the cost of his Italian campaign would be paid for entirely by the Milanese, especially to punish them for their brief rebellion and for permitting the return of Ludovico Sforza in the year of 1500. The indemnity to the city of Milan was 800,000 ducats. Other cities that had supported the Sforza rule also were obliged to expiate their crime by paying large indemnities. Louis and his entourage had little sympathy for the aspirations of the Milanese citizens, and he provided generous grants of estates to many of his French nobles and commanders, even if they had no intention of permanently settling there because they were constantly homesick and wanting to return to their own French homelands. When the properties of the Milanese rebels were assigned to the French, it was on condition that they resided there for at least two or three years. If they wanted to sell the property and return to France, then they could sell only half and forfeit the rest. Both the French and Italian beneficiaries of these grants generally preferred to sell as soon as possible and convert their newly gained properties into cash. Thus, the marketeering in the property of the rebels was a thriving business and at a low enough price that most of the confiscated properties finished up back in the hands of the Milanese rebels and their relatives.

Urban billeting of French troops was another cause of grievance for the Milanese citizens because of the swaggering arrogance of French soldiers rejoicing in their easily gained occupation. Disciplinary edicts and exemplary executions had some effect, but resentment among the Italians and French festered. Living in the presence of French troops was a vexation because, even when not campaigning, they often robbed and mistreated the civilians. The French soldiers like other foreign occupying forces expected the people in the towns and countryside to provide them with billets, food, drink, fuel, and other provisions, and to supply them with money for their pay as well. Townsmen were not accustomed to having large numbers of soldiers living amongst them, and so they resented their presence all the more.

By 1508, the king needed more money to prepare for a new campaign against the Republic of Venice that would later become known as the War of the League of Cambrai. He still controlled the Duchy of Milan and the Duchy of Genoa, but he now wanted to gain more Italian territories especially from the Venetians. So, most of the Lombardians, with high taxes imposed on them, resented the presence of the French king and his countrymen.

Melzi Life Under French Occupation

Since the year of 1500, my father and the House of Melzi found favour with the French rule, and they were permitted to retain all their properties without being overly overtaxed. My father helped the French emissaries to negotiate an alliance with Maximilian I for the partitioning of Naples between them and Spain. He also received favour from them for patrolling and protecting the Adda River from any further encroachment from Venice. My mother and I spent time between our fortified villa in Vaprio and our apartment in Milan. I was in the phase of my education where I received strong tutoring from my French teachers into the French ways of speaking, writing, cultural nuances, and government administration. My Latin lessons and those on civic law and foreign languages continued to be relentless. The French administrators and my parents continually tried to persuade Leonardo to return to Milan, but he resisted their advances until the French governor of Milan signed a decree to finally restore to him his vineyard at San Vittore near the Porta Vercellina, which had been expropriated from him during the fall of Milan in December 1499.

Leonardo's New Secretary and Painting Assistant

I was 17 years old in 1508 when I joined Leonardo's service as his assistant and student in painting. Because I spoke, read, and wrote perfect French, I provided him with bilingual secretarial skills and helped to manage his correspondence and letters. Another major task was to help him with the organisation of his writings and drawings, his manuscripts, notebooks and novels, and to assist him with the preparation of his thesis on painting and other works for publication. Apart from these duties, I was to assist him, Salai, and other artists with their paintings. My father had written a severe and binding contract with Leonardo on my behalf. It was agreed that my father would pay for my upkeep and salary, and, in exchange, my father and I would inherit Leonardo's library, manuscripts, notebooks, correspondence, paintings, and other works of importance after his death as stipulated in the contract. This was a satisfactory contract for Leonardo to sign because my father's villa and estate in Vaprio was also a secure home away from home for him while he was travelling or when he was living at his other temporary residencies in the city of Milan. In Vaprio, he had his own room, library, and studio in the Melzi tower, and he could come and go whenever he pleased as a member of our family. I was his godson, and he cared for me with the love of a tolerant and just father. He had no other heirs who he much cared for other than his ward Salai and one or two of his servants who he considered to be part of his immediate family. Although I spent much time with Leonardo in his rooms and studios, I also had my own rooms in my parents' apartment near the Sforza castle outside the Porta Nuovo where I could indulge myself with my own interests, riding, hunting, and especially participating in the art of falconry. At times, like Salai, I frustrated Leonardo with my inattention or neglect to detail. I found the following two amusing entries in one of his notebooks while I had been translating them:

Good day to you, Messer Francesco. God knows why, when I have written you so many letters, you have never made me a single reply. Just wait until I come to you, by God, for I will make you write so much that you will perhaps be sorry for it.

Dear Messer Francesco, I am sending Salai to you in order to learn from his Excellency the President what conclusion has been reached in the matter of the regulation of the water, since at my departure the order for the outlets of the canal had been set in hand; because the illustrious President promised me that my claim should be settled so soon as ever this adjustment had been made. It is now a considerable time since I learnt that the canal was set in working order and likewise its outlets, and I wrote immediately to the President and to you, and then repeated my letters, but have never had any reply. Will you therefore have the kindness to write and inform me what has taken place, and unless it is actually on the point of settlement, will you for my sake be so kind as to exert a little pressure on the President and also on Messer Girolamo da Cusano, to who please commend me, and also offer my respects to his Excellency?

I am happy to report to you as I did to Leonardo that I settled the matter with the President and his assistant by early 1509, so that Leonardo was soon able to take possession of his allocated amount of canal water at San Cristoforo, and that the outlets were set in perfect working order for him to make a healthy profit for his household.

For the Maestro's fifty-seventh birthday, Salai, Bernardino, Giovanni, and I presented him with a copy of his portrait. When he left Milan in 1499 his dark hair and beard had begun to turn grey. Now, back from 8 years in Florence, it was more white than grey, and he preferred to wear caps and hats than have his head uncovered. He was still an impressive and handsome man, but looked like the wizard Merlin from the ancient tales of Geoffrey of Monmouth.

Christ as *Salvator Mundi* and the Divine Proportions

Back in Milan, Leonardo finally unveiled his painting of the *Salvator Mundi,* ready to be presented to his client King Louis XII of France. He had been working on it for more than twenty years, ever since he first saw the face of the holy *Shroud Man* in Chambery in 1486. Now that he had a client for his painting, he could show it off to his friends and the World.

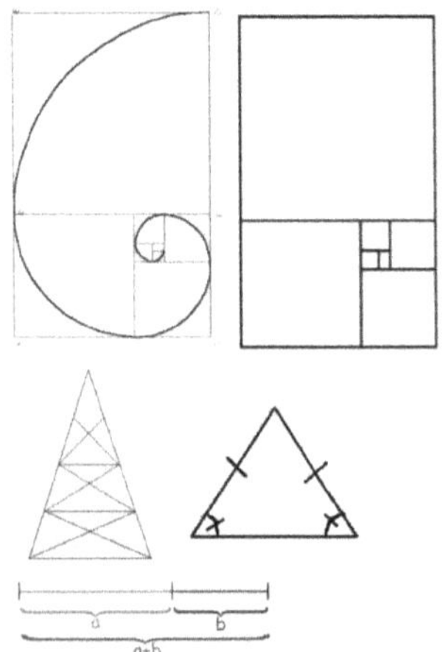

Fig. 84. Images of the golden spheres, golden rectangles, golden triangles and a calculated golden mean.

The Maestro handed me a book entitled *De Divina Proportione* that he had published with his friend Luca Pacioli and told me to read it and then to copy his painting of Christ and to find the divine proportions in the composition. It is another masterpiece in composition using the divine proportions or the golden elements that Luca Pacioli described in his book that Leonardo had illustrated for the Duke of Milan, Ludovico Sforza. We already saw the divine proportions used most effectively in his paintings of the *Last Supper,* his portraits of the *Mona Lisa,* and the drawings of *Vitruvian Man* to create balance and harmony in the images.

The golden proportion is a number for quantities a and b where if $a > b > 0$ then $a + b$ is to a as a is to b. This number is 1.618 or *Phi,* and it is known also as the golden mean.

The dimensions of the *Salvator Mundi* painting measure 25.8 inches by 17.9 inches and nearly every inch of it has examples of golden proportions in its composition as golden rectangles, spheres, and triangles. A large golden sphere encompasses the entire *Salvator Mundi* painting. It starts near the centre of the globe in the left hand of Christ and curves around to the bottom of the painting, up past the raised right hand and curves back, up towards the central line of the painting above Christ's head. The golden triangles are obvious in the embroidered bands, shaped like Xs, across the chest of his vestment. Another more subtle and unseen triangle runs through the line of the equator of the sphere starting at the lower forefinger, up to the outside corner of the left eye, then along the second line from the left eye to the centre of the palm of the raised right hand, and then down along the third line from the right hand to the bottom of the sphere in the left hand. The golden rectangles with the golden ratio of 1.613 (*Phi*) are seen everywhere in the painting starting with the height of head, the width of the hand, the height of the orb, and the height and width of the embroidered emblems. Look closely at the interweaving of the golden elements in the patterns of the embroidered emblems on the chest bands or measure the width of the jewel in relation to the width of the medallion to calculate the divine proportions. He even gave divine proportions to the three reflected dots of light in the transparent orb. No wonder it took him twenty years to create this masterpiece.

Apart from the hidden mathematics in the painting that can be measured with callipers and a ruler, the message in the image is deceptively simple. It is Christ (God the Son) offering a blessing and showing an orb representing his dominion over heaven and earth (the universe). However, as I already mentioned previously, the face and colour of Christ is strongly influenced by the image of the Face of Christ on the *Shroud of Chambery*. The embroidered emblems on the costume are shaped like St. Andrew's Crucifixion Cross, the X that Leonardo had previously painted in the fresco of the church of St. Andrew in Melzo. The patterns of embroidery include the boxed Xs that he had painted into the *Lady with the Ermine*. The orb in Christ's hand is a globe representing the entire universe as described in Plato's *Timaeus*. God (divine creation or nature) made the universe a circle, invisible, formless, and immune from all variation. Leonardo did not support Plato's doctrine of the universe, but he used the clear globe to illustrate the Christian conception of the universe.

In 1509, Leonardo took me to Turin to see the *Shroud Man,* and I believe it is the miraculous image of Christ. It took me many more years with the help of Salai and a few others to finish my copy of *Salvator Mundi,* but with a few touches from Leonardo I sold it quickly to a rich French client. Many painters in Milan copied Leonardo's painting of Christ as *Salvator Mundi* before it was transferred to the French king, and I have yet to see any that reflect the genius of the original.

Resolution of the *Virgin of the Rocks* Disputation

On April 25, 1483, eight years before I was born, Leonardo and the brothers Evangelista and Giovan Ambrogio de' Predis signed a long and detailed contract with the members of the Confraternity of the Immaculate Conception for a sumptuous altarpiece that was to include the *Virgin of the Rocks* as its main panel in their chapel in the church of San Francesco Maggiore in Milan. It was finished and installed in the chapel on December 8, 1488, the Feast Day of the Immaculate Conception. A few years later Leonardo and Giovan Ambrogio de' Predis complained to Ludovico Sforza 'Il Moro' that the Confraternity had grossly underpaid them for the panel *Virgin of the Rocks* and the two flanking paintings of angels. The Confraternity had paid them the 800 lire for their costs, but not the final 1,200 lire for completion and delivery as stipulated in the contract. In his complaint, Leonardo stated that none of the members understood the art of painting '*because a blind man cannot judge colour*' and asked that their criticisms be dismissed and that the painting be reappraised. The Confraternity had a host of dissatisfactions with the painting including that the holy mother and child didn't have haloes over their heads to depict their holiness and that there was an absence of the use of golden brocade as requested. Leonardo would not accept any of their complaints – he was a social realist painter and not of the old school that separated the saints from the people, and so, he refused to make any changes to his masterpiece.

The Confraternity in turn refused to pay the final amount until the painting was finished according to their stipulations. On March 9 and June 23, 1503, the notary for the Confraternity of the Immaculate Conception met and produced a report that sided with the Confraternity that the *Virgin of the Rocks* was unfinished. In 1506, while in Florence, Leonardo in a highly litigious mood requested Giovan Ambrogio de' Predis to appoint independent arbitrators to resolve the dispute over the price of the *Virgin of the Rocks* altarpiece. Giovan Ambrogio de' Predis reached an agreement with the Confraternity of the Immaculate Conception that he and Leonardo would finish the incomplete *Virgin of the Rocks* altarpiece in two years for a fee of two hundred lire *imperiali.* Leonardo was unsatisfied with this agreement and a new arbitrator was appointed to reassess the offer. Then, when Leonardo returned to Milan in 1508, he and Giovan Ambrogio de' Predis received permission to remove the *Virgin of the Rocks* altarpiece so that de' Predis could copy it under Leonardo's supervision to allow them to sell the original version with the proceeds of the sale to be divided equally between them in good faith and without fraud. The newly copied version with the saintly haloes was to be given back to the Confraternity as their altarpiece for their chapel in the church of San Francesco Maggiore. Leonardo helped Giovan Ambrogio de' Predis with the copy and allowed him to paint in the haloes over the heads of the Virgin, infant Jesus, and infant John the Baptist. Also, the wings on the Angel's back were made more distinctive in the copy than the original, and John the Baptist was provided with a cross. Leonardo sold the original version of the *Virgin of the Rocks* to King Louis XII of France who was more than happy to pay him and Giovan Ambrogio de' Predis a handsome sum. Finally, on October 23, 1508, Giovan Ambrogio de' Predis received two payments of one hundred lire *imperiali* for the new *Virgin of the Rocks* copy, and Leonardo, after a payment dispute of twenty-five years, signed off on the final settlement of the Confraternity's debt for their *Virgin of the Rocks* altarpiece. O! Hallelujah.

In the Service of Charles II of Amboise, 1508 to 1511

Fig. 87. Charles II of Amboise, the French Governor of Milan from 1503 to 1511.

A few months after arriving back to Milan from Florence, Leonardo heard from the French governor Charles of Amboise that the former duke of Milan, Ludovico Moro Sforza, had died in his prison in Loches, France on the 27th May. Ludovico and Leonardo were born in the same year of 1452, and their paths had intertwined for better or for worse for twenty years, and Leonardo had managed to outlive and forgive him. Leonardo and my father held a personal remembrance for Ludovico in their chapel in Vaprio for they both felt that overall IL Moro personally had treated them well enough during their twenty years or more in his service at the Sforza court.

The French viceroy and governor of Milan, Charles of Amboise, had convinced Leonardo to return to Milan with the promise of the return of his properties and the vineyard at Saint Vittore and an honorary position of *'our dear and good friend Leonard de Vinci, our painter and engineer'*, with a large salary and a role as advisor to the ruling inner cabinet. Leonardo had written in his 1508 notebook,

> The salary I received from the King from July 1508 to April next 1509 was first 100 scudi, then 100, then 70, then 50, then 20, and then 200 francs at 48 soldi the franc.

Charles of Amboise made no great demands of Leonardo other than request an architectural design for a small palace, the *palais de luxe*, and to provide him with advice on matters of art and canal building. King Louis XII also gifted Leonardo the right to twelve inches of water from the Canal Santo Cristoforo for his own usage.

The French governor wanted Leonardo to design his *palais de luxe* not only to please himself, but also the many women who he expected would be visiting or living with him. He wanted an elaborate façade and ornamental stairwell and rooms that were water cooled in the heat of summer. He ordered a secret fountain for his garden that could be turned on 'should anyone wish to give a shower bath from below to the women or others who should pass there.' He also wanted netting over the walking garden to prevent songbirds from escaping, and commissioned erotic art and murals to be displayed in some of his rooms of pleasure.

> The front -a to m- will give light to the rooms; -a to e- will be 6 braccia -a to b- 8 braccia -b to e- 30 braccia, in order that the rooms under the porticoes may be lighted; -c to d to f- is the place where the boats come to the houses to be unloaded. In order to render this arrangement practicable, and in order that the inundation of the rivers may not penetrate into the cellars, it is necessary to chose an appropriate situation, such as a spot near a river which can be diverted into canals in which the level of the water will not vary either by inundations or drought. The construction is shown below; and makes choice of a fine river, which the rains do not render muddy, such as the Ticino, the Adda and many others. The construction to oblige the waters to keep constantly at the same level will be a sort of dock,

as shown below, situated at the entrance of the town; or better still, some way within, in order that the enemy may not destroy it.

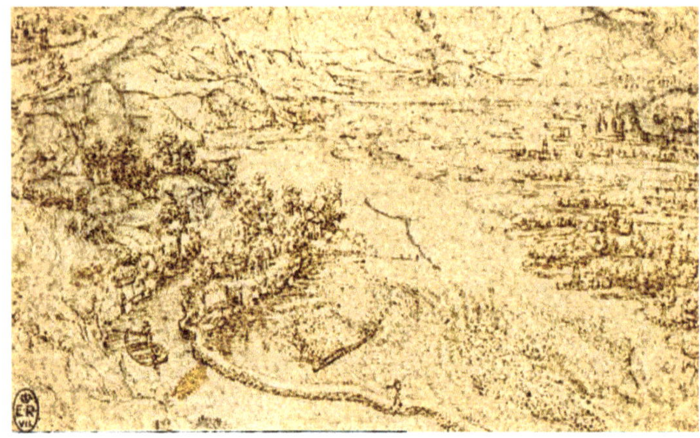

Fig. 88. A boatman on a canal in the Adda River valley.

Leonardo, now 56 years old, was happy to be back in Lombardy with a considerable degree of freedom and little expectation from the French rulers. He travelled continually, including to Savoy and Pavia, visited country estates, sailed the rivers, and often stayed with my family at Vaprio d' Adda. There, he wrote and painted at leisure and without constraint and began his manuscript of 12th September 1508 on the study of water. He intended to write 15 chapters on the strange nature of water in the rain, sea, springs, rivers, canals, waterfalls, currents, eddies, pumps, and irrigation, and how to divert the flow of rivers and why the banks of rivers crumble. While Leonardo was in Vaprio, he and I began to paint a huge fresco of a *Madonna and Child* on the ground floor wall of the Melzi villa facing the entrance where people could see it from the canal walkways as they passed by below.

Leda and the Swan, *Mary Magdalene*, and a *Palais de Lux* for the French Governor

The French governor of Milan, Charles of Amboise, was a man with a strong sexual appetite. When he asked Leonardo for a few erotic and exotic paintings to decorate his Villa where he loved to entertain the ladies of the court and those willing ladies who he attracted from elsewhere, Leonardo showed him a number of sketches of an erotic nature that pleased him. I asked Leonardo how or why he thought that *Leda and the Swan* would titillate Charles of Amboise. He told me that when Charles d'Amboise had asked him one time about bestiary and erotica in art, he'd been thinking at that very moment about the unusual way that swans became airborne running on the surface of the water or along the ground, and then once they were airborne, how they flew with their long necks extended out in front of them. He then made the obvious phallic connection and remembered seeing engravings and an erotic copy of a Roman marble sculpture of *Leda and the Swan* that had been attributed to the antiquities. He knew from the verses in *Metamorphoses* by Ovid that Zeus, the powerful god of the sky and thunder and the king of the gods at Mount Olympus, had transformed himself into a swan in order to seduce and rape the beautiful Leda, Queen of Sparta, while she lay with her husband, King Tyndareus of Sparta. As a consequence of the coupling, Leda produced four children from two eggs; Helen of Troy, Clytemnestra (future wife of Agamemnon), Castor, and Pollux. In his own mind, Leonardo suddenly saw the French rulers, like Charles d'Amboise and king Louis XII, as Zeus-like-figures disguising themselves as swans to rape Milan and Lombardy. He considered the possible consequences of the image and thought that this was the perfect metaphor for an erotic painting for the French Governor of Milan.

The bizarre irony of the paintings of *Leda and the Swan* was their holy/unholy comparative connection to Leonardo's paintings of the *Madonna and Child*. In the former case, Leda gave birth to her hatchlings in eggs after being impregnated by a God (Zeus) disguised as a swan. In the later case, according to Christian doctrine, the Holy Spirit (God disguised as a spiritual dove) impregnated the Virgin Mary, and she gave birth to Jesus, the Son of God. In both cases, the mythical subjects were about transformation and impregnation by birds.

Fig. 90. Correggio's seated version (1530) of Leonardo's Leda and the Swan (1506).

Leonardo began his studies and drawings for *Leda and the Swan* in 1506 with a painting of Leda sitting nude on the ground with her children. He followed this up in 1508 with Leda standing nude and cuddling the Swan and looking down demurely at her two sets of twins being hatched out of two separate eggshells. In the far background, we see the town of Vaprio and the Melzi villa. These two paintings formed the basis for the many copies that were produced by his pupils and assistants, including me, that set a trend for leading artists such as Raphael, Michelangelo, and Antonio Allegri da Correggio to try and outdo the Maestro.

Another painting that Leonardo started and then had Salai and Bernardino Luini finish for him were two beautiful portraits of the bare breasted *Mary Magdalene* for Charles d' Amboise's *palais de luxe*. Although Leonardo presented Charles of Amboise with many architectural plans, the *palais de luxe* was never built. The French governor of Milan died from sexual over-exertion in his bed on 10th of March 1511 at Correggio.

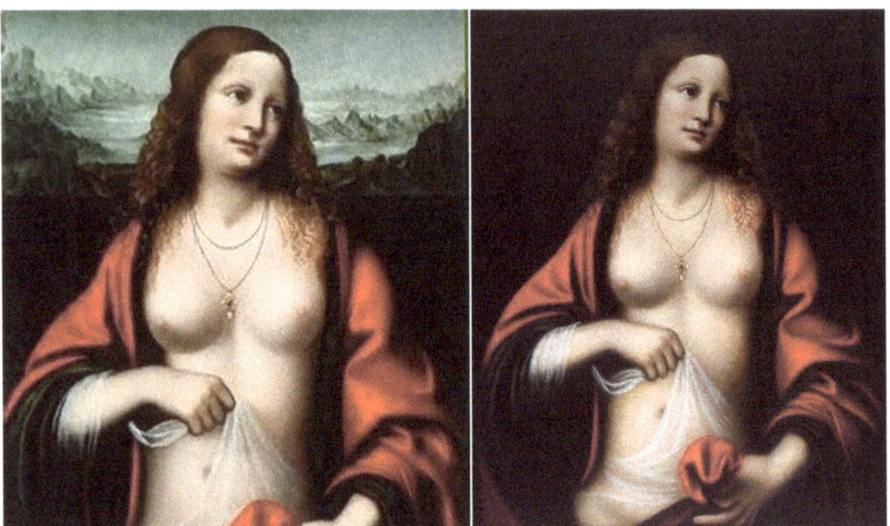
Fig. 91. Mary Magdalene *by Leonardo, Salai, Giampietrino, and Bernardino Luini.*

Leonardo's Return to Anatomical Studies of Conception, Birth, and Death

The painting of the hatchings in the *Leda and the Swan* series rekindled Leonardo's interest to undertake and finish his dissection and anatomical studies on human pregnancy and birth. He was able to achieve this between 1510 and 1512 by collaborating with Marcantonio della Torre, the professor of anatomy at the University of Pavia, who was a distant relative of my mother. Unfortunately, Marcantonio della Torre died of plague in 1512, and Leonardo was not able to use the help of the professor of anatomy to prepare and publish his *Atlas of Anatomy*. The genius of Leonardo came forth in his innovative studies and drawings of human and animal anatomy that were derived from his philosophy and understanding of art, engineering, architecture, and cartography. He began slicing sections of the brain and staining them with different dyes to reveal never before seen structural patterns. However, his human anatomy studies were interrupted again when the new French-Italian wars intervened on Milan in the year of 1512.

Leonardo's New Patron, Gian Giacomo Trivulzio, Governor of Milan

Soon after death of the French governor of Milan Charles d' Amboise in 1511, the young knight Gaston de Foix replaced him as the new governor. However, he was killed a year later while in his golden armour and in pursuit of a rebellious Spanish infantry unit at the battle of Ravenna on 11th April 1512. Leonardo's friend, the Italian condottiero, Gian Giacomo Trivulzio, was appointed the Governor of Milan in place of Gaston de Foix in May of 1512 as a reward for his war service to France. Trivulzio belonged to one of the most powerful noble families of the Sforza duchy, and he possessed major feudal holdings in Lombardy. He shared most of his childhood with Ludovico's brother, Galeazzo Maria Sforza, and served him as a military captain when Galeazzo was the 5th duke of Milan. His amicable relationship with Ludovico Sforza deteriorated into open antagonism after Galeazzo Maria's assassination, Cicco Simonetta's execution, and Bona of Savoy's exile, and he left Lombardy thereafter to enter for a few years into the service of King Ferdinand I of Aragon in Naples. With the death of

Ferdinand I in 1494, Gian Giacomo Trivulzio transferred his service over to the French kings Charles VIII and Louis XII who appreciated his knowledge of Milan's military capabilities and its surrounding geography. Louis d' Orleans became king in May 1498, and he immediately began referring to himself as duke of Milan and sought the military skills of Gian Giacomo Trivulzio to invade Milan.

Fig. 92. Gian Giacomo Trivulzio's Heraldry portrait as Governor of Milan with his French Medal of the Order of Saint Michael.

A few years earlier, Ludovico Sforza had confiscated Trivulzio's lands and possessions, and the French king promised Trivulzio that they would all be returned to him when he and his French troops ousted Ludovico from Milan. Ludovico placed images of Gian Giacomo Trivulzio hanging by one foot from a post on every street corner in Milan to show his citizens that his former condottiero was now a traitor. Gian Giacomo Trivulzio had a strong incentive to oust Ludovico from Lombardy and avenge the deaths of his friends including Galeazzo Maria Sforza and his son Gian Galeazzo, and to win back his confiscated lands and possessions. On the same day that Ludovico Sforza left Milan for the safety of the Swiss Alps in 1499, Gian Giacomo Trivulzio with a small French army entered the city through an undefended gate, and next day, the patriarchs and merchants surrendered the city to him and the French king.

Fig. 93. Leonardo's study for the Trivulzio equestrian monument.

Gian Giacomo Trivulzio was unpopular with the citizens of Milan. However, Leonardo came to know him as a friend and often stayed at his house as a guest and received various commissions from him. One particular commission for Leonardo was to draw up the architectural plans for a splendid palace that was to be better than the one that Trivulzio had confiscated from Galeazzo Sanseverino. Another commission requested that Leonardo design and construct a splendid sepulchral monument dedicated to Trivulzio, his magnificent self. It was to be a giant-sized columned monument in the church of San Nazaro with Trivulzio riding a horse on top of a high column and also with him recumbent on a marble tomb below. The column would be highly decorated with festoons and trophies and bound slaves showing off his conquests. Leonardo was drawing horses again as he once had done for Gian Galeazzo Sforza and Ludovico Sforza when he constructed the greatest equestrian monument ever to be built of clay in Milan. Now, with fresh enthusiasm, he again was drawing rearing horses, some with raised forelegs, and yet others trampling fallen soldiers. Leonardo charged Trivulzio the sum of 2,000 ducats for the materials, and the treasury of Milan that was at the governor's disposal paid Leonardo this amount to purchase his materials.

As the Trivulzio monument was about to be built, Leonardo's plans were suddenly thwarted again. Trivulzio was Governor of Milan for only a few months before he was forced to leave Milan and retreat to France in exile. Before the construction of the monument even started, the citizens of Milan overthrew Trivulzio and replaced him with Ludovico's son, the 19 year-old Maximilian Sforza, who with a small army of Swiss troops backed by Pope Julius II had returned to take over the city on 29th December 1512. Trivulzio fled back to France and never returned to Milan, not until he was a corpse. He lived long enough in France to see Maximilian Sforza overthrown by the French three years later. He advised a new French king, Francois I, not to cross through the main passes in the Alps where the Swiss and main Papal forces would be waiting for him, and instead to invade Italy and enter Lombardy through the river valley of the Stura and then head north east towards Turin. Leonardo met Trivulzio in France in 1517 and then again a few days before his death in Chartres in 1518. Trivulzio's corpse was transferred to the sarcophagus in a chapel wall in the Church of San Nazaro Maggiore in Milan.

Collapse of French Rule and Installation of Maximilian Sforza as the New Duke of Milan on 29th December 1512

Since the Milanese victory in 1500, the French were involved in two clear conflicts in Italy. The first was the War of the League of Cambrai (1508-1510) that was a successful attack on Venice by a French alliance that included the Holy Emperor Maximilian of the Romans, Pope Julius II of Rome, and Ferdinand II Aragon of Spain. The second was the War of the Holy League (1510-14) when the Pope turned against the French and successfully ended the rule of France over Milan and its duchy. When Louis first invaded and won Milan from Ludovico Sforza in 1500, he had granted Venice the eastern part of the Duchy of Milan, but he soon reclaimed it for himself. The official War of the League of Cambrai began with the French declaration of war against the Republic of Venice on 7th April 1509. The Pope joined the French side on 27th April to defeat the Venetians at Agnadello (14th May 1509). In the aftermath of that defeat the Venetians withdrew from most of their outlying posts and entered into peace negotiations with the Pope giving him some of their minor cities. This effectively ended the War of the League of Cambrai. The Pope was then more worried about the danger of French domination in Italy, and in February 1510, he formed a new Holy League with the Venetians against the French who successfully defended his attack against them in Genoa. At this stage, the Pope lacked other allies and became vulnerable to a defeat when a French army invaded Bologna late in the year. However, in early 1511, he successfully defended the French attack on Bologna and led an attack on Mirandola, an outlying fortress of Ferrara. The French under Charles II d' Amboise, and with the assistance of Alfonso I d' Este, Duke of Ferrara, struck back, and captured Concordia and Mirandola, defeated a Papal army at Casalecchio (21st May 1511), recaptured Bologna, and in December defended a Swiss attack against Milan. Leonardo commented about this Swiss attack on Milan in his notebook:

> On the tenth day of December at nine o'clock in the morning the place was set on fire. On the eighteenth of December 1511, at nine o'clock in the morning, this second conflagration was started by the Swiss at Milan, at the place called DCXC.

The Pope's only real success of the year came in October when the Spanish (Ferdinand II of Aragon) joined the Holy League. The fortunes of the Holy League changed at the start of 1512 when the Venetians recaptured Brescia and Bergamo east of the Duchy of Milan, and the Spanish and Papal armies successfully attacked Bologna and Ferrara. The French had a brief comeback under Gaston de Foix. He raised the siege of Bologna, defeated the Venetians at Isola della Scala, captured Brescia, and then besieged Ravenna. The Holy League attempted to lift the siege, but suffered a heavy defeat in the resulting battle of Ravenna (11th April 1512).

The death of Gaston de Foix at the battle of Ravenna ended the French comeback and none of his replacements were up to the task to fight against the Pope's allies. In August of 1512, the French were forced to abandon Milan, which fell to the Swiss in the company of Ludovico Sforza's son, the 19-year-old Maximilian Sforza.

The complete French collapse in Lombardy by the 29th December 1512 was so unexpected that it took the Holy League completely by surprise. Soon the members of the League were fighting amongst themselves, and they were in disagreement on what territories should be included in the duchy of Milan and who should govern there. The provisional Milanese government in the absence of the French argued for the same borders as those under Ludovico Sforza and the installation of Ludovico's 19-year-old son Maximilian Sforza as their independent duke. The Holy Roman Emperor and King Ferdinand II of Spain disagreed. However, the Swiss asserted their right as the victors in the field, and they were intent on securing the territorial, financial, and commercial fruits of victory. So, they made a treaty of perpetual alliance with the provisional Milanese government. The cantons undertook to support Maximilian Sforza as duke in return that he pay them a pension of 40,000 ducats a year and confirm their possession of Lugano, Locarno, and Domodossola. In addition, the Swiss merchants were to be exempt from tolls from their borders to the gates of Milan. Maximilian Sforza agreed, and he was installed as the new Duke of Milan with no experience or real desire to govern. The young duke was more interested in enjoying himself with the pleasures of life than in the serious business of government. His subjects watched him squander most of the revenues that his allies and protectors left to him, and they were soon disenchanted and embittered by his behaviour and indifference.

In February 1513, Pope Julius II's life ended, and he was replaced as pontiff by Giovanni de' Medici who took on the title of Pope Leo X. Much younger than Julius, Pope Leo's fixed purpose was to strengthen his family's position in Florence and to dictate Florentine foreign policy. He almost lost a key ally when Venice agreed to a new alliance with France. The new allies then invaded Milan, but the French suffered a heavy defeat at the battle of Novara (6th June 1513), which was a major success for the Swiss pike men and Maximilian Sforza and a disaster for the French forces. The Venetians who had now sided with the French were eventually forced to retreat into their home territory when they suffered a heavy defeat at the Imperial hands of the Holy Roman Emperor at La Motta Vicenza (7th October 1513).

After Gian Giacomo Trivulzio's retirement from Milan in August 1512, Leonardo considered discretion was the better part of valour, and he and his household of Salai, Battista, and il Fanfoia retired from the city to join my father on his estates in Vaprio. Leonardo considered Maximilian Sforza to be a mindless puppet of the Swiss mercenaries, and because he and my father had been in the service of the French in Milan, they both decided it was safer to stay away from the city while Maximilian Sforza and his Swiss friends were attacking and looking for retribution and arresting many perceived enemies as French collaborators. Strangely, just as Milan and the Duchy of Lombardy fell back into Sforza hands, so the de' Medici won back the Republic of Florence. It was like old times again, with the Sforza ruling the Duchy of Milan and the de' Medici ruling the Republic of Florence and forming friendly alliances with each other. In Florence, Leonardo's friend, Niccolo Machiavelli, was deprived of office in 1512, and he was imprisoned for a few months in 1513 before being released into retirement at his estate at Sant' Andrea in Percussina.

Back to Vaprio on the Adda River

With Maximilian Sforza's rooms and offices set up at the Corte Vecchio while the French garrison still occupied the Sforza castle, Leonardo and his servant Battista de Vilanis stayed with us at our home in Vaprio while his assistant Salai chose to live with his father at

Leonardo's vineyard at Santa Vittore. Leonardo resided in his rooms at one of the towers of our house where he stored many of his treasures and possessions and had good views of the Adda River and the territory about him. While he was there, he began a series of new anatomical studies concentrating on dead dogs and oxen. '*Look at the dead dog, its lumbar region, the diaphragm and motion of the ribs,*' he wrote in his 1513 notebook. He sketched our house and once again prepared architectural plans to transform it into a palace. At the top of one page of his notebooks, he wrote the date January 9, 1513 with drawings of the Trezzo castle. This castle was located a kilometre north of us at the bend of the Adda River and up stream of the Brembo River. One week earlier we sat in his workroom watching the Venetians bombard the castle while he calculated the location of their gun emplacements from the trajectories of their cannonballs. The Venetians captured the castle a few days later and used it as a base to drive deeper into eastern Lombardy in their attempts to recapture Bergamo, Lodi, Brescia, Caravaggio, Crema, and Cremona from the Duchy of Milan. They were at war with the Swiss and the German Imperial forces, and they were using the chaotic times as an excuse to regain as much territory as they possibly could east of the Adda River from the Duchy of Milan. They mercifully chose to bypass Vaprio and Canonica and ignored us, although their troops continually scouted the borders of our properties and territories to the great concern of my father and his family.

Fig. 94. Sketch by Leonardo da Vinci of a barge crossing the Adda River near Vaprio.

CHAPTER 22

Leonardo's Apocalyptic Novel of the Deluge: *The Prophet of Mt. Taurus*

Of the men who are there some must have fallen to the ground and be entangled in their garments, and hardly to be recognised for the dust, while those who remain standing may be behind some tree, with their arms round it that the wind may not tear them away; others with their hands over their eyes for the dust, bending to the ground with their clothes and hair streaming in the wind.

— Leonardo da Vinci

Doom and Gloom

Soon after Leonardo's mother died in Milan in 1494, his thoughts turned towards writing an account of her life. Then, on further reflection, he decided it would be better to write a novel about a Prophet of Light rather than a whole biographical story about his mother. However, there were so many prophets of doom and gloom in Italy at the turn of the century in 1500 when Leonardo was 48 years old that his own thoughts turned to the end of the world believing nothing lasts forever and that there is continuous birth, death, and renewal, and then the final end. And so, he prophesied climate change and the end of life, as we know it.

> Of the end of the world. The watery element remaining pent up within the raised banks of the rivers and the shores of the sea, it will come to pass with the upheaval of the earth that as the encircling air has to bind and circumscribe the complicated structure of the earth, its mass which was between the water and the fiery element will be left straitly compassed about and deprived of the necessary supply of water. The rivers will remain without their waters; the fertile earth will put forth no more her budding branches; the fields will be decked no more with waving corn. All the animals will perish, failing to find fresh grass for fodder; and the ravening lions and wolves and other beasts, which live by prey will lack sustenance; and it will come about after many desperate shifts that men will be forced to abandon their life and the human race will cease to be. And in this way the fertile fruitful earth being deserted will be left arid and sterile, and through the pent up moisture of the water enclosed within its womb and by the activity of its nature it will follow in part its law of growth until having passed through the cold and rarefied air it will be forced to end its course in the element of fire. Then, the surface of it will remain burnt to a cinder, and this will be the end of all terrestrial nature.

Back in Florence in 1504, Leonardo started to reflect on the sermons from the religious prophets of the time, men with vivid and violent imaginations and convictions like Fra Francesco di Montepulciano and Savonarola. He called them the Doom and Gloom Brigade. Pity, mercy, a world destroyed, and ruination were their catch cries. Leonardo believed that the World had a finite time, and he reasoned it would eventually fall into ruin as part of the natural processes of physics. Although the secular people and peasants of the ruled world were subjected to constant preaching about doom and gloom, the rulers of the world were enjoying their hunting and hawking parties and entertaining each other in their sumptuous villas with feasts and festivities as if totally unaware of these prophecies of doom. And so, Leonardo decided to write a novel about doom and gloom with a happy ending.

The Prophet of Mt. Taurus

On his return to Vaprio in 1508, Leonardo began to outline his novel and to illustrate some of his visions of destruction with the earth in a state of convulsions from ferocious winds, earthquakes, and rockfalls, and men and women caught in a maelstrom of horror.

THE DIVISIONS OF THE BOOK
The preaching and persuasion of faith.
The sudden inundation down to its end.
The ruin of the city.
The death of the people and their despair.
The pursuit of the preacher, and his liberation and benevolence.
Description of the cause of this avalanche of the mountain.
The havoc that it made.
The avalanche (the destruction by snow).
The finding of the prophet.
His prophesy.
The inundation of the lower parts of western Armenia, the channels in which were formed by the cutting of Mount Taurus. How the new prophet showed that this destruction occurred as he had foretold according to his prophecies.

Fig. 95. My painting of Leonardo da Vinci for his 60th birthday in April of 1512.

Here are some excerpts from the novel:

Description of Mount Taurus and of the River Euphrates. To the Devatdar of Syria, lieutenant of the sacred Sultan of Babylon: The recent unforeseen event, which has occurred in these our northern parts which I am certain will strike terror not only into you but into the whole world shall be revealed to you in its due order, showing first the effect and then the cause. Finding myself in this part of Armenia in order to discharge with devotion and care the duties of that office to which you have appointed me, and making a beginning in those parts which seem to me to be most suitable for our purpose, I entered into the city of Calindra which is near to our borders. This city is situated on the sea-coast of that part of the Taurus range which is separated from the Euphrates and looks westward to the peaks of the great Mount Taurus. These peaks are of such a height that they seem to touch the sky, for in the whole world there is no part of the earth that is higher than their summit, and they are always struck by the rays of the sun in the east four hours before day. And being of exceedingly white stone this shines brightly and performs the same office for the Armenians of these parts as the beautiful light of the moon would in the midst of the darkness; and by reason of its great height it outstretches the highest level of the clouds for a space of four miles in a straight line.

I am not justly to be accused of idleness, O Devatdar, as your strictures seem to intimate, but your unbounded affection which has caused you to confer these benefits upon me has constrained me to employ the utmost care in seeking out and diligently investigating the cause of so momentous and so startling an occurrence, and for this time was necessary. In order now to make you well acquainted with the cause of so great an effect it is necessary that I shall describe the nature of the place, and then I will proceed to the event, by which process I believe you will be fully satisfied. I will omit any description of the shape of Asia Minor, or of what seas or lands they are which determine the aspect of its surface, knowing as I do your diligence and care in your studies to be such that you will already have acquired this knowledge. I pass on therefore to furnish you with an account of the true shape of Mount Taurus, which has been the scene of so surprising and destructive a catastrophe, for this may serve to advance our purpose.

It is this Mount Taurus which, according to many, is said to be the ridge of the Caucasus, but, wishing to be quite clear about this, I set myself to interrogate some of the inhabitants of the shores of the Caspian Sea; and they inform me that although their mountains bear the same name these are of greater height, and they confirm this therefore to be the true Mount Caucasus, since Caucasus in the Scythian tongue means 'supreme height'. And in fact nothing is known of the existence either in the east or the west of any mountain of so great a height, and the proof of this is that the inhabitants of those countries which are on the west see the sun's rays illuminating part of its summit for a fourth part of the longest night, and similarly with the countries which are on the east. This peak is visible from a great part of the west illuminated by the sun after its setting during the third part of the night. And it is this, which among you in calm weather has formerly been thought to be a comet, and seems to us in the darkness of the night to assume various shapes, sometimes dividing into two or three parts, sometimes long and sometimes short. And this proceeds from the fact that the clouds on the horizon come between part of this mountain and the sun, and by their cutting these solar rays the light of the mountain is broken by various spaces of clouds and therefore its brightness is variable in shape. The shadow of this ridge of the Taurus is so high that in the middle of June when the sun is at the meridian it reaches to the borders of Sarmatia, which are twelve days' journey, and in mid-December it extends as far as the Hyperborean Mountains, which are a month's journey to the north. And the side that faces the way the wind blows is full of clouds and mists, because the wind which is cleft in twain as it strikes against the rock and closes up again beyond it, carries with it in this way the clouds from all parts and leaves them where it strikes, and it is always full of thunderbolts through the great number of clouds which are gathered there, and this causes the rock to be all fissured and filled with huge debris.

This mountain at its base is inhabited by a very opulent people; it abounds in most beautiful springs and rivers; it is fertile and teems with everything that is good and especially in those parts which have a southern aspect. After an ascent of about three miles, you come to where begin the forests of great firs and pines and beeches and other similar trees; beyond for a space of another three miles you find meadows and vast pastures, and all the rest as far as the beginning of the peak of Taurus is eternal snow, for this never disappears in any season, and it extends at this height for about fourteen miles in all. From the point where the peak begins for about a mile the clouds never pass, so that they extend for about fifteen miles with a height of about five in a straight line. As far beyond or thereabouts we find the summit of the peaks of Taurus, and here from about half way upwards we commence to find the air grow warm, and there is no breath of wind to be felt and nothing can live there very long. Nothing is brought forth there except some birds of prey, which nest in the deep gorges of the Taurus and descend below the clouds to seek their prey upon the grassy hills. It is all bare rock from above where the clouds are, and the rock is of a dazzling whiteness, and it is not possible to go to the lofty summit because the ascent is rough and dangerous.

People were to be seen who in a state of great excitement were bringing together all sorts of provisions upon vessels of all descriptions hastily put together as necessity dictated. The gleaming of the waves was not visible in the parts that reflected the dark rain and the clouds. But where they reflect the flashes produced by the thunderbolts, as many gleams were seen caused by the images of these flashes as were the waves that reflected them to the eyes of the spectators. And then the deluge struck us. The inundation of the lower parts of western Armenia, the channels in which were formed by the cutting of Mount Taurus. And certainly I for my part cannot imagine that since first the elements by their separation made order out of chaos, they can ever have united their force or rather their frenzy to work such destruction to mankind, as has now been seen and experienced by us; so that I cannot imagine what could further increase so great a misfortune as this that we have experienced in a space of ten hours. First we were assailed and buffeted by the might and fury of the winds, and then followed the avalanches from the great snow-covered mountains which have choked up all these valleys, and caused a great pan of this city to fall in ruins. And, not content with this, the tempest has submerged with a sudden deluge of water over all the lower parts of the city; and beyond all this there was added a sudden storm of rain and a furious hurricane, laden with water, sand, mud, and stones all mingled together with roots, branches, and stumps of various trees; and every kind of thing came hurtling through the air and descended upon us, and finally a great fire, which did not seem to be borne by the wind but as though carried by thirty thousand devils has burnt up and destroyed all this country and has not yet ceased. And the few of us who remain are left in such a state of dismay and fear that, like those who are half-witted, we scarce dare to hold speech one with another, but giving up even the attempt at work we stay huddled together in the ruins of some of the churches, men and women small and great all mingled together like herds of goats; and but for certain people having helped us with provisions we should all have died of hunger. Now you can understand the state we are in; and yet all these evils are as nothing by comparison with those that threatened us within a brief space of time.

I know that you as a friend will have a fellow feeling for my misfortunes, even as I in my former letters have shown myself glad at your prosperity. As I have in my letters rejoiced with you many times over your prosperous fortunes so I know now that you as a friend will share my sorrow at the miserable condition to which I am reduced; for the fact is that in these last days I have had so many anxieties, so many fears, dangers and losses, as have also the wretched country-folk, that we have come to envy the dead.

Writing like a novelist, Leonardo tried to convince us that these imaginary things really happened. He then came to the realisation that there was little variation in the theme of imminent destruction and that, indeed, there had to be some hope for the story to be appealing. He had entered into a dark place, the world of doom, gloom, destruction, and damnation of an apocalyptic storm and found it difficult to exit and find the brighter light leading to hope and a greater optimism. Indeed, in Dante's *The Divine Comedy* there was the faith and hope that one would survive and transverse from the inferno into a divine light. Could Leonardo bring us back from his dark misery, back into the light of eternal hope?

A Gallery of Sketches and Paintings of Apocalyptic Storms

Unsatisfied with the poetry of his words, Leonardo turned to illustrating the horror of the deluge with drawings of how the storm and the waves might look like.

He drew hurricanes sweeping across the earth, trees bent to the ground, men and horses thrown down or tumbling headless in the sky. I had never seen such drawings of terror and destruction and violent movement, distorted human and animal shapes and total destruction plucked out of nightmares.

Here are some of Leonardo's images and suggestions for painting an apocalyptic storm:

Fig. 96. Leonardo's gallery of tempests.

HOW TO REPRESENT A TEMPEST. If you wish to represent a tempest consider and arrange well its effects as seen, when the wind, blowing over the face of the sea and earth, removes and carries with it such things as are not fixed to the general mass. And to represent the storm accurately you must first show the clouds scattered and torn, and flying with the wind, accompanied by clouds of sand blown up from the sea shore, and boughs and leaves swept along by the strength and fury of the blast and scattered with other light objects through the air. Trees and plants must be bent to the ground, almost as if they would follow the course of the gale, with their branches twisted out of their natural growth and their leaves tossed and turned about. Of the men who are there some must have fallen to the ground and be entangled in their garments, and hardly to be recognised for the dust, while those who remain standing may be behind some tree, with their arms round it that the wind may not tear them away; others with their hands over their eyes for the dust, bending to the ground with their clothes and hair streaming in the wind. Let the sea be rough and tempestuous and full of foam whirled among the lofty waves, while the wind flings the lighter spray through the stormy air, till it resembles a dense and swathing mist. Of the ships that are therein some should be shown with rent sails and the tatters fluttering through the air, with ropes broken and masts split and fallen. And the ship itself lying in the trough of the sea and wrecked by the fury of the waves with the men shrieking and clinging to the fragments of the vessel. Make the clouds driven by the impetuosity of the wind and flung against the lofty mountaintops, and wreathed and torn like waves beating upon rocks; the air itself terrible from the deep darkness caused by the dust and fog and heavy clouds.

Fig. 97. Leonardo's depiction of Aiolos, the Greek God of Winds.

TO REPRESENT THE DELUGE. The air was darkened by the heavy rain whose oblique descent driven aslant by the rush of the winds, flew in drifts through the air not otherwise than as we see dust, varied only by the straight lines of the heavy drops of falling water. But it was tinged with the colour of the fire kindled by the thunder-bolts by which the clouds were rent and shattered; and whose flashes revealed the broad waters of the inundated valleys, above which was seen the verdure of the bending tree tops. Neptune will be seen in the midst of the water with his trident, and let Aeolus with his winds be shown entangling the trees floating uprooted, and whirling in the huge waves. The horizon and the whole hemisphere were obscure, but lurid from the flashes of the incessant lightning. Men and birds might be seen crowded on the tall trees which remained uncovered by the swelling waters, originators of the mountains which surround the great abysses. Let the dark and gloomy air be seen buffeted by the rush of contrary winds and dense from the continued rain mingled with hail and bearing hither and thither an infinite number of branches torn from the trees and mixed with numberless leaves. All round may be seen venerable trees, uprooted and stripped by the fury of the winds; and fragments of mountains, already scoured bare by the torrents, falling into those torrents and choking their valleys till the swollen rivers overflow and submerge the wide lowlands and their inhabitants. Again, you might have seen on many of the hilltops terrified animals of different kinds, collected together and subdued to tameness, in company with men and women who had fled there with their children. The waters which covered the fields, with their waves were in great part strewn with tables, bedsteads, boats, and various other contrivances made from necessity and the fear of death, on which were men and women with their children amid sounds of lamentation and weeping, terrified by the fury of the winds which with their tempestuous violence rolled the waters under and over and about the bodies of the drowned. Nor was there any object lighter than the water which was not covered with a variety of animals which, having come to a truce, stood together in a frightened crowd--among them wolves, foxes, snakes, and others--fleeing from death. And all the waters dashing on their shores seemed to be battling them with the blows of drowned bodies, blows, which killed those in whom any life, remained. You might have seen assemblages of men who, with weapons in their hands, defended the small spots that remained to them against lions, wolves, and beasts of prey who sought safety there. Ah! What dreadful noises were heard in the air rent by the fury of the thunder and the lightnings it flashed forth, which darted from the clouds dealing ruin and striking all that opposed its course. Ah! How many you might have seen closing their ears with their hands to shut out the tremendous sounds made in the darkened air by the raging of the winds mingling with the rain, the thunders of heaven, and the fury of the thunder-bolts. Others were not content with shutting their eyes, but laid their hands one over the other to cover them the closer that they might not see the cruel slaughter of the human race by the wrath of God. Ah! How many laments! And how many in their terror flung themselves from the rocks! Huge branches of great oaks loaded with men were seen borne through the air by the impetuous fury of the winds. How many were the boats upset, some entire, and some broken in pieces, on the top of people labouring to escape with gestures and actions of grief foretelling a fearful death. Others, with desperate act, took their own lives, hopeless of being able to endure such suffering; and of these, some flung themselves from lofty rocks, others strangled themselves with their own hands, others seized their own children and violently slew them at a blow; some wounded and killed themselves with their own weapons; others, falling on their knees recommended themselves to God. Ah! How many mothers wept over their drowned sons, holding them upon their knees, with arms raised spread out towards heaven and with words and various threatening gestures, upbraiding the wrath of the gods. Others with clasped hands and fingers clenched gnawed them and devoured them till they bled, crouching with their breast down on their knees in their intense and unbearable anguish. Herds of animals were to be seen, such as horses, oxen, goats, and swine already environed by the waters and left isolated on the high peaks of the mountains, huddled together, those in the middle climbing to the top and treading on the others, and fighting fiercely themselves; and many would die for lack of food. Already had the birds begun to settle on men and on other animals, finding no land uncovered which was not occupied by living beings, and already had famine, the minister of death, taken the lives of the greater number of the animals, when the dead bodies, now fermented, where leaving the depth of the waters and were rising to the top. Among the buffeting waves, where they were beating one against the other, and, like as balls full of air, rebounded from the point of concussion, these found a resting place on the bodies of the dead. And above these judgements, the air was seen covered with dark clouds, riven by the forked flashes of the raging bolts of heaven, lighting up on all sides the depth of the gloom. The motion of the air is seen by the motion of the dust thrown up by the horse's running and this motion is as swift in again filling up the vacuum left in the air which enclosed the horse, as he is rapid in passing away from the air. Perhaps it will seem to you that you may reproach me with having represented the currents made through the air by the motion of the wind notwithstanding that the wind itself is not visible in the air. To this I must answer that it is not the motion of the wind but only the motion of the things carried along by it, which is seen in the air.

DESCRIPTION OF THE DELUGE. Let there be first represented the summit of a rugged mountain with valleys surrounding its base, and on its sides let the surface of the soil be seen to slide, together with the small roots of the bushes, denuding great portions of the surrounding rocks. And descending ruinous from these precipices in its boisterous course, let it dash along and lay bare the twisted and gnarled roots of large trees overthrowing their roots upwards; and let the mountains, as they are scoured bare, discover the profound fissures made in them by ancient earthquakes. The base of the mountains may be in great part clothed and covered with ruins of shrubs, hurled down from the sides of their lofty peaks, which will be mixed with mud, roots, boughs of trees, with all sorts of leaves thrust in with the mud and earth and stones. And into the depth of some valley may have fallen the fragments of a mountain forming a shore to the swollen waters of its river; which, having already burst its banks, will rush on in monstrous waves; and the greatest will strike upon and destroy the walls of the cities and farmhouses in the valley. Then the ruins of the high buildings in these cities will throw up a great dust, rising up in shape like smoke or wreathed clouds against the falling rain; But the swollen waters will sweep round the pool, which contains them striking in eddying whirlpools against the different obstacles, and leaping into the air in muddy foam; then, falling back, the beaten water will again be dashed into the air. And the whirling waves which fly from the place of concussion, and whose impetus moves them across other eddies going in a contrary direction, after their recoil will be tossed up into the air but without dashing off from the surface. Where the water issues from the pool the spent waves will be seen spreading out towards the outlet; and there falling or pouring through the air and gaining weight and impetus they will strike on the water below piercing it and rushing furiously to reach its depth; from which being thrown back it returns to the surface of the lake, carrying up the air that was submerged with it; and this remains at the outlet in foam mingled with logs of wood and other matters lighter than water. Round these again are formed the beginnings of waves which increase the more in circumference as they acquire more movement; and this movement rises less high in proportion as they acquire a broader base and thus they are less conspicuous as they die away. But if these waves rebound from various objects they then return in direct opposition to the others following them, observing the same law of increase in their curve as they have already acquired in the movement they started with. The rain, as it falls from the clouds is of the same colour as those clouds, that is in its shaded side; unless indeed the sun's rays should break through them; in that case the rain will appear less dark than the clouds. And if the heavy masses of ruin of large mountains or of other grand buildings fall into the vast pools of water, a great quantity will be flung into the air and its movement will be in a contrary direction to that of the object which struck the water; that is to say: The angle of reflection will be equal to the angle of incidence. Of the objects carried down by the current, those, which are heaviest or rather largest in mass will keep farthest from the two opposite shores. The water in the eddies revolves more swiftly in proportion as it is nearer to their centre. The crests of the waves of the sea tumble to their bases falling with friction on the bubbles of their sides; and this friction grinds the falling water into minute particles and this being converted into a dense mist, mingles with the gale in the manner of curling smoke and wreathing clouds, and at last it, rises into the air and is converted into clouds. But, the rain, which falls through the atmosphere being driven and tossed by the winds becomes rarer or denser according to the rarity or density of the winds that buffet it, and thus there is generated in the atmosphere a moisture formed of the transparent particles of the rain, which is near to the eye of the spectator. The waves of the sea which break on the slope of the mountains which bound it, will foam from the velocity with which they fall against these hills; in rushing back they will meet the next wave as it comes and after a loud noise return in a great flood to the sea whence they came. Let great numbers of inhabitants - men and animals of all kinds - be seen driven by the rising of the deluge to the peaks of the mountains in the midst of the waters aforesaid.

Fig. 98. A part of Leonardo's gallery of the Deluge.

THE DIVISIONS. Darkness, wind, tempest at sea, floods of water, forests on fire, rain, bolts from heaven, earthquakes, and ruins of mountains, overthrow of cities. Whirlwinds, which carry water-spouts and branches of trees, and men through the air. Boughs stripped off by the winds, mingling by the meeting of the winds, with people upon them. Broken trees loaded with people. Ships broken to pieces, beaten on rocks. Flocks of sheep. Hail stones, thunderbolts, and whirlwinds. People on trees, which are unable to support them; trees and rocks, towers and hills covered with people, boats, tables, troughs, and other means of floating. Hills covered with men, women and animals; and lightning from the clouds illuminating every thing.

OF DEPICTING THE NATURAL PHENOMENA. The tremendous fury of the wind driven by the falling in of the hills on the caves within--by the falling of the hills which served as roofs to these caverns. A stone flung through the air leaves on the eye, which sees it the impression of its motion, and the same effect is produced by the drops of water, which fall from the clouds when it rains. A mountain falling on a town, will fling up dust in the form of clouds; but the colour of this dust will differ from that of the clouds. Where the rain is thickest let the colour of the dust be less conspicuous and where the dust is thickest let the rain be less conspicuous. And where the rain is mingled with the wind and with the dust the clouds created by the rain must be more transparent than those of dust alone. And when flames of fire are mingled with clouds of smoke and water very opaque and dark clouds will be formed.

Fig. 99. Leonardo's drawings of the debris and dead bodies of horses and men after the deluge.

Resolution?

According to Leonardo, his prophet, like himself, was a man of faith, and a hydraulic engineer who foresaw the deluge that scattered and destroyed the city and drowned most of the people. He solved the problem of the inundation from reoccurring again for future generations by draining the waters through a tunnel in the Taurus Mountains. It is a story with a scientific happy ending.

As a young boy in Vinci, Leonardo had seen the destructive power of wind and water, and he would say, *'I have seen movements of the air so violent as to carry away immense forest trees and whole roofs of great palaces.'* Hence, it wasn't too difficult for him to imagine the destructive forces of a super storm that involved hurricanes, deluges, avalanches, and firestorms, for he had seen them.

In one picture of his deluge series, the storm is breaking over a town and the mountains are crumbling while to one side of the picture a group of men surround a prophet with their hands upraised to the heavens, and on the other side a fireball descends on a different group of men kneeling and praying as the flames engulf them. Leonardo sketched images of the annihilation of men by nature while at about the same time he looked out of the window of his room in the tower at the Vaprio mansion where he resided, and he could see in the distance the Venetians bombarding the castle of Trezzo at the bend of the river. The Venetians captured the Visconti/Della Torre castle of Trezzo from the French, Milan was returned to the Sforza rule, and Leonardo was a troubled person. What was his future in Vaprio and Lombardy, he wondered?

Hope and a New Migration

The French returned to Milan in May 1513 in an attempt to overthrow Maximilian Sforza, but in June they were heavily defeated at the battle of Novara and permanently ousted from the Lombardian kitchen. With the recapture of Milan by Maximilian Sforza and his Swiss allies, the last of the French marched out of the Sforza castle with their raised flags and handed the fort back to the Sforza dynasty in September 1513. Leonardo was more than 61 years of age. He was feeling old and tired. His fingers were gnarled, and he needed a set of reading and writing glasses.

There was continued war, skirmishes, and changing and unpredictable diplomacy between the Pope, the Milanese, the French, the Germans, the Spanish, and the Venetians. It looked like it would never end. He abandoned his plan to complete his novel on the *Prophet of Mount Taurus*, leaving the bundle of hand written pages of the manuscript in a box in his room at the Melzi Tower, and instead, he accepted the generous offer from his new sponsor, Giuliano de' Medici, the Pope's brother, for paid employment in Rome. There was a bright light and a greater hope at the end of the tunnel after all. All roads lead to Rome.

CHAPTER 23

A Roman Sojourn

I left Milan for Rome on the 24th day of September 1513, with Giovanni, Francesco di Melzi, Salai, Lorenzo, and il Fanfoia.

— Leonardo da Vinci

A Roman Holiday. Three Years in Rome

The de' Medici brothers Giuliano and Giovanni became the new rulers of Florence after overthrowing the Florentine Republican Government in September of 1512. When Giovanni was elected Pope Leo X on the 9th March 1513, his younger brother Giuliano de' Medici became the solitary ruler of Florence. In September 1513, when I was 22 years of age, Leonardo at the age of 61 years was invited to Rome by Giuliano de' Medici and his brother Pope Leo X with full sponsorship to be an artist-in-residence at the luxurious Bellevere Palace. Leonardo could not refuse such a tempting offer to leave Lombardy while it was in the hands of the young Maximilian Sforza, and so Salai, Lorenzo the Florentine, Giovanni Tommaso Masini, il Fanfoia, and I helped him pack, and we all departed from Milan to go to Rome on September 24, 1513. The painter Lorenzo Lotto who had come from Bergamo to visit Leonardo and show him some of his paintings accompanied us on our travels. He was a former apprentice of Leonardo's in Florence, and he previously worked in Rome (1508 to 1510) to decorate the papal apartments before he left there to live and work in the Marche where he painted the six-panclled *Recanati Polyptych* at the church of San Domenico. He now wanted to return to his old haunts and evaluate the new developments in the Eternal City. I looked forward with anticipated fascination to experience the intrigues and hallowed halls of Rome where Michelangelo, Raphael, Donato Bramante, Il Sodoma, and Luca Signorelli were in residence.

Leonardo's Rome According to Giorgio Vasari

Leonardo went to Rome with Duke Giuliano de' Medici, and knowing the Pope to be fond of philosophy, especially alchemy, he used to make little animals of a wax paste, which as he walked along he would fill with wind by blowing into them, and so make them fly in the air, until the wind being exhausted, they dropped to the ground. The vinedresser of the Belvedere having found a very strange lizard, Leonardo made some wings of the scales of other lizards and fastened them on its back with a mixture of quicksilver, so that they trembled when it walked; and having made for it eyes, horns, and a beard, he tamed it and kept it in a box, but all his friends to whom he showed it used to run away from fear.

He used often to have the guts of a wether completely freed of their fat and cleaned, and thus made so fine that they could have been held in the palm of the hand; and having placed a pair of blacksmith's bellows in another room, he fixed to them one end of these, and, blowing into them, filled the room, which was very large, so that whoever was in it was obliged to retreat into a corner; showing how, transparent and full of wind, from taking up little space at the beginning they had come to occupy much, and likening them to virtue. He made an infinite number of such follies, and gave his attention to mirrors; and he tried the strangest methods in seeking out oils for painting, and varnish for preserving works when painted. He made at this time, for Messer Baldassarre Turini da Pescia, who was Datary to Pope Leo, a little picture of the Madonna with the Child in her arms, with infinite diligence and art; but whether through the fault of whoever primed the panel with gesso, or because of his innumerable and capricious mixtures of grounds and colours, it is now much spoilt. And in another small picture he made a portrait of a little boy, which is beautiful and graceful to a marvel; and both of them are now at Pescia, in the hands of Messer Giuliano Turini. It is related that, a work having been allotted to him by the Pope, he straightway began to distil oils and herbs, in order to make the varnish; at which Pope Leo said: 'Alas! This man will never do anything, for he begins by thinking of the end of the work, before the beginning.'

There was very great disdain between Michelangelo Buonarroti and him, on account of which Michelangelo departed from Florence, with the excuse of Duke Giuliano, having been summoned by the Pope to the competition for the facade of S. Lorenzo. Leonardo, understanding this, departed and went into France, where the King, having had works by his hand, bore him great affection; and he desired that he should colour the cartoon of S. Anne, but Leonardo, according to his custom, put him off for a long time with words.

Thus wrote Giorgio Vasari in *Lives of the Most Eminent Painters, Sculptors, and Architects* about Leonardo's stay in Rome. Perhaps, some of the above is true, yet his time in Rome was influential if not brilliant. Maybe, Leonardo left nothing substantial to posterity in Rome, but his presence was enough to inspire others to leave something of him in their works. Raphael immortalised him as Plato in his painting of the *School of Athens* in the Stanza della Segnatura in the Apostolic Palace. Even Michelangelo who had no great love for Leonardo left an image of him for future generations to ponder. Leonardo had commenced his paintings of *Saint John the Baptist,* and many in Rome's painting circles came to admire these pictures and the *Mona Lisa* for their beauty and grace and to learn more about his unique painting techniques. He met with a number of his old Florentine and Milanese friends including Bramante, Il Sodoma, Antonio Cordini, Baldassarre Turini, Giulio Romano, Antonio Segni, and Piero and Francesco Soderini. The Florentine Signoria had elected Piero Soderini a Gonfalonier for life in 1502 when Leonardo was there, but now poor Piero was an exile in Rome after his overthrow by the Medici family in 1512. Leonardo renewed his Florentine friendship with Raphael who often visited our studio to make copies of Leonardo's *Mona Lisa* and his other Madonnas. On a few occasions, the *Mona Lisa* herself, Isabella Aragon Sforza, the Duchess of Bari, came from Bari and Naples to visit Leonardo and me in Rome and to model for Raphael and other painters in their studios. In this way, I became a close friend of Raphael and spent much time with him in his studio and at his home where he resided with his mistress Margherita Luti. As an agent to the painters, I obtained some originals and copies of Raphael's paintings including the incredible one of his half naked mistress depicted as *La Fornarina*. When Leonardo saw it, he said that he wished he'd done a similar portrait of Simonetta Vespucci.

One night, Raphael, Bramante, Leonardo, and I snuck into the empty Sistine chapel to admire the completion of Michelangelo's painting of the *Book of Genesis* on the ceiling above us. It struck me as a marvel in its size, narrative, colour, and perspective, but as usual we thought that his naked figures, especially the women, were lumpy and overly muscular, but fitting for him and some of his friends at the Vatican. On another day, we all went to see the ancient statue of *Laocoon and His Sons*. These marble figures are slightly largely than life size, and they represent the Trojan priest Laocoon and his sons Antiphantes and Thymbraeus being attacked by sea serpents. Their horrified expressions and contorted bodies are a marvel to behold, and Leonardo kept returning to sketch them on numerous occasions. The statue of *Laocoon and His Sons* was discovered and excavated as a single intact piece in 1506 on the Esquiline Hill in Rome, and it was recognised immediately as the Laocoon sculpture that was described by Pliny the Elder as the masterpiece from Rhodes. Nobody knows how it arrived at the excavation site, but some have suggested that it belonged to Emperor Nero when he built his mile long Golden House (*Domus Aurea*) after the fires of Rome, and it was where Pliny the Elder saw it displayed in the palace of Titus Flavius Vespasianus some years later. We also visited the Pope's zoo garden and met with his white elephant named Hanno.

Hanno, the White Elephant

Hanno arrived in Rome in 1514. He was 4 years old and sent from Lisbon by the king of Portugal as a gift for Pope Leo X. He became a great favourite of the papal court and was a feature in many processions. The Pope kept him like his large pet dog, initially in an enclosure in the Belvedere courtyard, but later moved him to his own elephant building between St. Peter's Basilica and the Apostolic Palace, near the Borgo Sant' Angelo. Pasquale Malaspina commemorated his presence in Rome in a poem:

> In the Belvedere before the great Pastor
> Was conducted the trained elephant
> Dancing with such grace and such love
> That hardly better would a man have danced:
> And then with its trunk such a great noise
> It made, that the entire place was deafened:
> And stretching itself on the ground to kneel
> It then straightened up in reverence to the Pope,
> And to his entourage. [S37]

Hanno fell ill and died on the 8th June 1516 with the distressed Pope at his side. Hanno was interred in the Cortile del Belvedere at the age of seven years. The Pope himself composed the epitaph:

> Under this great hill I lie buried
> Mighty elephant which the King Manuel
> Having conquered the Orient
> Sent as captive to Pope Leo X.
> At which the Roman people marvelled,
> A beast not seen for a long time,
> And in my brutish breast they perceived human feelings.
> Fate envied me my residence in the blessed Latium
> And had not the patience to let me serve my master a full three years.
> But I wish, oh gods, that the time which Nature
> Would have assigned to me,
> And Destiny stole away,
> You will add to the life of the great Leo.
> He lived seven years
> He died of angina
> He measured twelve palms in height.
> Giovanni Battista Branconio dell'Aquila
> Privy chamberlain to the pope
> And provost of the custody of the elephant,
> Has erected this in 1516, the 8th of June,
> In the fourth year of the pontificate of Leo X.
> That which Nature has stolen away
> Raphael of Urbino with his art has restored. [S37]

Leonardo thought that the death of Hanno was an omen because it was only a few months earlier that he had been dismissed from Rome by the Pope. The news of Hanno's death prompted Leonardo to make the following comment about elephants in his notebook.

The huge elephant has by nature what is rarely found in man; that is Honesty, Prudence, Justice, and the Observance of Religion; inasmuch as when the moon is new, these beasts go down to the rivers, and there, solemnly cleansing themselves, they bathe, and so, having saluted the planet, return to the woods. And when they are ill, being laid down, they fling up plants towards Heaven as though they would offer sacrifice. -- They bury their tusks when they fall out from old age. Of these two tusks they use one to dig up roots for food; but they save the point of the other for fighting with; when they are taken by hunters and when worn out by fatigue, they dig up these buried tusks and ransom themselves.

They are merciful, and know the dangers, and if one finds a man alone and lost, he kindly puts him back in the road he has missed, if he finds the footprints of the man before the man himself. It dreads betrayal, so it stops and blows, pointing it out to the other elephants who form in a troop and go warily. These beasts always go in troops, and the oldest goes in front and the second in age remains the last, and thus they enclose the troop. Out of shame they pair only at night and secretly, nor do they then rejoin the herd but first bathe in the river. The females do not fight as with other animals; and it is so merciful that it is most unwilling by nature ever to hurt those weaker than itself. And if it meets in the middle of its way a flock of sheep it puts them aside with its trunk, so as not to trample them under foot; and it never hurts any thing unless when provoked. When one has fallen into a pit the others fill up the pit with branches, earth, and stones, thus raising the bottom that he may easily get out. They greatly dread the noise of swine and fly in confusion, doing no less harm then, with their feet, to their own kind than to the enemy. They delight in rivers and are always wandering about near them, though on account of their great weight they cannot swim. They devour stones, and the trunks of trees are their favourite food. They have a horror of rats. Flies delight in their smell and settle on their back, and the beast scrapes its skin making its folds even and kills them.

When they cross rivers they send their young ones up against the stream of the water; thus, being set towards the fall, they break the united current of the water so that the current does not carry them away. The dragon flings itself under the elephant's body, and with its tail it ties its legs; with its wings and with its arms it also clings round its ribs and cuts its throat with its teeth, and the elephant falls upon it and the dragon is burst. Thus, in its death it is revenged on its foe.

Rome and Leonardo as I Saw Them

On first arriving in Rome, Leonardo and Giovanni Tommaso Masini immediately went to see Donate Bramante to find out what progress he had made on the construction of the new St. Peter's Basilica. They stayed with Bramante for a few days while Salai, il Fanfoia, Lorenzo the Florentine, and I remained at Belvedere Palace preparing, cleaning, and refurnishing our apartments and studios. Pope Julius II had commissioned Bramante in 1503 to rebuild St. Peter's Basilica in the shape of a centralised Greek cross with four great chapels filling the corner spaces between the equal transepts where each one would be capped by a small dome surrounding the great dome over the crossing. The great dome was designed to be like the Pantheon; constructed in tufa concrete and raised like a drum above ground by four massive piers with a wall pierced by windows and an encircling peristyle. The cornerstone of the first of the great piers of the crossing was laid on 17th April 1506, and by the time that we were there the four central pylons had been built and the walls of the Basilica had reached the top of them. But, the further construction of the Basilica halted when Bramante died on the 11th March of 1514. The recently elected Pope Leo X organised a committee of architects to reassess the progress and provide new proposals for its continuation. Leonardo, Raphael, and Michelangelo were part of the committee and they proposed a longitudinal plan closer to the ecclesiastic tradition, while Baldassarre Peruzzi and Antonio da Sangalio favoured the original central plan. There was very little progress on the Basilica for the next forty years, not until Pope Paul III commissioned Michelangelo to finish the project. The building was completed in 1560 and the construction of the dome followed thereafter.

During our first few weeks in Rome, we and Leonardo tracked down and looked at the art of his Florentine friends, Sandro Botticelli, Melozzo da Forli, Fran Angelico, Benozzo Gozzoli, Luigi Vivarini, Bartolomeo di Tommaso, Perugino, Ghirlandaio, Bernardino Pinturicchio, Piero della Francesca, Vivarini, Lorenzo Lotto, and many others such as Raphael's assistant, Giovanni da Udine. This was my first visit to Rome, and I was excited and overwhelmed by the experience and its history and the old ruins. I looked everywhere for the remaining evidence that it was the centre of the Roman Empire and the birthplace of modern Christianity, the Church of Saint Peter. Salai and I visited the usual tourist sights, the Forum, the Seven Hills, the Imperial Palace of Augustus on top of the Palatine Hill, the encampment of Romulus and Remus, the remnants of the palaces and gardens of the Caesars and Emperors (Hadrian's Villa, Villa dei Quintili, Ostia Antica, etc.), the Pantheon, the Colosseum, the Circus Maximus, the Citizens' Markets, the Baths, the taverns, and eateries, and pleasure houses, the Vatican, and St. Peter's Basilica. We had much to do everyday, looking through the different churches' treasures and the commissioned art works of the many past artists. I was busy also with translating Leonardo's treatise on painting.

Over the next few years, Leonardo had a major falling out with his German neighbours who he accused of stealing his mirrors and glass grinders and designs. He complained bitterly about them to the Pope's secretary and the Belvedere Palace attendants who did nothing to right his wrongs, and so he jotted down his frustrations into his notebooks. In this and the next year, he wrote drafts of letters to Giuliano de' Medici that described his quarrels with his German assistant, Giulo the iron worker, and Giovanni degli Specchi, a German mirror maker in the Pope's and Giuliano de' Medici's employ.

    My Most Illustrious Lord and Dearest Father,
        On the last of the past month I had the letter you wrote to me which in a brief space caused me pleasure and also sorrow. I was pleased at learning from it that you were in good health, for which God be praised. I was filled with sorrow at hearing of your discomfort.
        So greatly did I rejoice, most illustrious Lord, at your much wished-for restoration to

health that my own malady almost left me. But I greatly regret that I have been unable to satisfy the desires of your Excellency, entirely through the malice of that German rogue, as regards whom I have left nothing undone which I thought might give him pleasure. And firstly because I invited him to take up his abode and have meals with me, so that I could always see what work he was doing and could easily correct his errors, and moreover he would acquire Italian and so be able to speak it easily without an interpreter, and most important of all the moneys due to him could always be paid before the time, as always has been. Then he asked that he might have the models finished in wood just as they were to be in iron, and wished to carry them away to his own country. But this I refused, telling him that I would give him a drawing of the width, length, thickness, and outline of what he had to, and so we remained at enmity.

The second thing was that in the room where he slept he made himself another workshop with new screw-vices and instruments, and he worked there for others. Afterwards he went to dine with the Swiss of the Guard where there are plenty of idlers, but he beat them all at it. Then he used to go out and more often than not two or three of them went together with guns to shoot birds among the ruins, and this went on until the evening.

Finally, I discovered that it was this master Giovanni who made mirrors who had brought all this about and this for two reasons; first because he had said that my coming here had deprived him of the countenance and favour of your Lordship which always is of great honour to me and which I cherish, and the other reason is because he says the room of this iron-worker would suit him for working at mirrors, and he has given proof of this, for besides setting him against me he has made him sell all his effects and leave his workshop to him, and he has established himself there now with a number of assistants making many mirrors to send to the fairs. I believe that he would gladly deny if it were not that I had the signature witnessed by the hand of the interpreter. And as I saw that he would not work for me unless he could not find any work to do for others, and that he sought for this diligently, I urged him to have his meals with me and to work with his files near to me, for besides this being economical and good for his work it would help him to acquire Italian; and so he always promised to do but he was never willing to do it. ... So two months passed and the thing still went on, until one day happening to find Gian Niccolo of the Wardrobe I asked him whether the German had finished his work for Il Magnifico, and he told me that it was none of it true because he had only given him two guns to clean. After this when I expostulated with him he left the workshop and began to work in his own room, and wasted a lot of time in making another vice and files and other instruments with screws, and made shuttles there to twist silk and gold, which he hid whenever any of my people went in, and this with a thousand oaths and revilings, so that none of them were willing to go there any more.

I have satisfied myself that he accepts commissions from all and has a public shop; for which reason I do not wish that he should work for me at a salary, but that he should be paid for the works that he does for me; and since he has a workshop and house from the Magnifico he should be obliged to give precedence to the works for the Magnifico before all.

Leonardo's knight, Salai, occasionally threatened to kill the Germans, but that did nothing to discourage them from exploiting Leonardo's objects and good will. In general, Salai was more interested in his own adventures, and he spent considerable amounts of time and money in the taverns, baths, and brothels selling fake copies of Leonardo's paintings, especially the *Mona Lisa*, at exorbitant prices. This led him into fights and insults about art and money and forced Leonardo to ask il Fanfoia to accompany Salai in his wanderings in order to keep him out of trouble.

Most of the time, Leonardo was busy with his own paintings and his various projects on the science and engineering of glass lenses, working obsessively on preparing and experimenting with concave and convex mirrors. He wanted to construct magnifying glasses and tubes to present to the Pope as a way to look at objects that were far away whether they were on the land, sea or in the heavens as if they were close up before his eyes. He was particularly excited about magnifying unseen miniscules in water, puss, and blood. *'This is the real world of aliens,'* he'd say as he showed me creatures wriggling in drops of water through his magnifying glass, creatures that were invisible to my naked eye. *'Extraordinary,'* was all I could say. But, I was more interested in keeping the company of Raphael and his friends, and I tended to ignore Leonardo much more than I should have.

While in Rome, Leonardo lost interest in creating new paintings and sculptures and instead pursued esoteric subjects such as making lenses and mirrors that were of no interest to the Pope who already had a group of German mirror makers staying with him in the Belvedere. Leonardo's attitude annoyed Leo X who wanted him to be continuously gainfully employed producing works of art for him, his family, and the Vatican. But this wasn't to be. Instead, it seemed to some, like Giorgio Vasari had written, that Leonardo squandered his three years in Rome on trivialities and squabbles with foreigners and officials. As usual, Leonardo kept himself busy with his own interests rather than those of Pope Leo X. Nevertheless, the Pope and his brother Giuliano de' Medici sent Leonardo, Salai, and me on a number of diplomatic missions. In September of 1514, we visited Parma and travelled along the river Po on our way to study the harbour and archaeological ruins at Civitavecchia. Here, Leonardo considered re-establishing and renovating the ancient canal system that was deteriorating between the harbour and Rome.

Raphael of Urbino (1483 to 1520)

I spent more time with Raphael and his two assistants Giovanni da Udine and Giulio Romano than I did with Leonardo who constantly reminded me that I was ignoring and falling behind in my translation of his *Treatise on Painting* and his writings concerning the *Paragone*. I was eight years younger than Raphael, but we took an immediate liking to each other. He soon had me seated in his studio to paint my portrait as the young dandy gentleman from Milan. Salai and I spent long hours with him and his assistants talking about his frescoes on the walls at the Apostolic Palace, and we had great fun designing and preparing his cartoons for the *Fire in the Borgo* and the *Liberation of Saint Peter.* I also helped him a little with some of his erotic frescoes for the Pope's treasurer and banker Agostino Chigi at his villa in Trastevere on the west bank of the Tiber river.

Raphael loved to party and have affairs with beautiful young women. He had a magnificent collection of erotic art and created his own folio of erotic drawings of many ample *potta spalancata* that I copied meticulously into my own collection. Here, we looked for sexual and artistic variety, varying the posture, the angle of vision of the sexual organs in relation to the display and gesture of the limbs before, during, and after copulation or sexual intertwinement. Raphael showed me some of Leo X's collection of erotica including Giovanni da Udine's stucco relief in the Pope's Vatican Loggia of a winged female nude spreading her legs widely to reveal her vulva in a ribald genital display. On many occasions, Raphael was required to help prepare the Pope's banquets that almost always ended up as highly debauched affairs. While Leonardo attended occasionally, he seemed to have lost total interest in the behaviours of excessive drinking, irreverent womanising, and watching the sodomisation of young boys. Raphael told me that the Pope had overt homosexual tendencies, although he never displayed such behaviour in public. At his banquets however, the Pope permitted such behaviour and watched it with much amusement. A number of his cardinals were much more brazen, and they could be seen buggering young attendants in the dark recesses of the banquet room.

Raphael and I were very much heterosexual, and we preferred to have our parties with young, nubile dark-eyed women. While Salai and il Fanfoia joined us in our debauched activities, Leonardo usually turned a blind eye with occasional warnings about the dangers of the French pox. He wanted us, for our own protection and that of our sexual partner, to wear penis protectors (condoms) that he had made from the guts of sheep or pigs. But, he also put these condoms to other uses as attested by Giorgio Varasi in *The Lives of Artists*:

He used often to have the guts of a wether completely freed of their fat and cleaned, and thus made so fine that they could have been held in the palm of the hand; and having placed a pair of blacksmith's bellows in another room, he fixed to them one end of these, and, blowing into them, filled the room, which was very large, so that whoever was in it was obliged to retreat into a corner; showing how, transparent and full of wind, from taking up little space at the beginning they had come to occupy much, and likening them to virtue.

Leonardo preached sexual moderation, and he reminded us that as artists we were better off to be voyeurs than perpetrators of debauchery. He reminded us about those who were disfigured by the pox and asked whether we wanted to change our good health and looks to suffer instead from the monstrosity of the sexual disease. I heeded Leonardo's good advice and therefore avoided the pox and other sexually transmitted diseases. He was studying the causes of the French pox intensely and was wondering about what was contained within the pustules of those with the pox, and how the disease was transmitted from the genitals to other organs including the face and the brain. He had developed magnifying glasses that he used to try to identify and classify the miniscules or corpuscles within the pus and blood of diseased people and animals. This was proving dangerous work for him because his views about these microscopic agents of disease were displeasing the protectors of the church doctrines. In truth, it was his obstreperous and quarrelsome neighbour in the Belvedere, Giovanni degli Specchi, a manufacturer of mirrors, who, jealous of Leonardo's influence with his patron, reported Leonardo's studies of anatomy and unspeakable substances to the Pope in order to have him punished or dismissed from Belvedere.

Raphael is well known for his beautiful pictures and portraits of Madonnas. Most of them are based on Leonardo's pictures that he had seen when they were both together in Florence.

Raphael copied every picture of Leonardo's Madonnas that he could find. He even used Isabella, Duchess of Bari, as one of his own models. Leonardo had no objections to Raphael's use of his designs and concepts, and he unashamedly encouraged him to do so saying that this should be the new trend in female and male portraiture. And so it was. Giorgio Vasari recognised the influence of Leonardo on Raphael's Madonnas and wrote the following in his *Life of Raffaello da Urbino (Raffaello Sanzio), painter and architect:*

> For, after seeing the works of Leonardo da Vinci, who had no peer in the expressions of heads both of men and of women, and surpassed all other painters in giving grace and movement to his figures, he was left marvelling and amazed; and in a word, the manner of Leonardo pleasing him more than any other that he had ever seen, he set himself to study it, and abandoning little by little, although with great difficulty, the manner of Pietro, he sought to the best of his power and knowledge to imitate that of Leonardo. But for all his diligence and study, in certain difficulties he was never able to surpass Leonardo; and although it appears to many that he did surpass him in sweetness and in a kind of natural facility, nevertheless he was by no means superior to him in that sublime groundwork of conceptions and that grandeur of art in which few have been the peers of Leonardo. Yet Raffaello came very near to him, more than any other painter, and above all in grace of colouring.

Fig. 104. Raphael's fresco, the Knowledge of Causes *(also known as* the School of Athens*), with the two central figures of the young and old Leonardo da Vinci representing Aristotle and Plato.*

In the fresco *Knowledge of Causes* (also known as the *School of Athens*), Raphael used Leonardo as his model for the central two figures Plato and Aristotle in his painting of the ancient artists, philosophers, and scientists gathered together at the Lyceum (based on Bramante's first design of St Peter's Basilica). Plato and Aristotle stand together as mirror images at the centre of the painting. Plato points to the heavens while Aristotle points down towards the ground. They are surrounded by numerous figures; scholars, thinkers, artists, mathematicians, and philosophers, who are in ardent thought or discussion. What Raphael had not realised in his representation was that Leonardo saw himself more closely aligned with Aristotle than Plato. Although as a youth, Leonardo followed the Florentine obsession with Platonism, as he became more mature, he shifted to Aristotle's views and immersed himself in empirical studies and in the natural sciences, and he adopted the view that the mind only fully develops because of experience and perception. Many of Aristotle's views on the natural sciences are the foundations underlying Leonardo's works on physics, geology, engineering, biology, zoology, logic, ethics, theatre, music, rhetoric, politics, and government. When I pointed this out to Raphael, he said, *'that's duality. He is both. It's Leonardo the younger and Leonardo the older, together, they are the yin and yang, the complementary opposites of each other, the spiritual and the material, exactly how I see him now.'*

Fig. 105. Detail of Raphael's fresco. Leonardo da Vinci as Aristotle (right) and Plato (left).

Leonardo, of course, was greatly pleased and honoured to be depicted and given such eminence and prominence in Raphael's painting of the 'visualisation of knowledge.' The painting shows the joy of participating in mathematics, science, discussion, and debate in the pursuit of knowledge in the style of those who attended Leonardo's Academy of Milan. Apart from Plato and Aristotle, there is Socrates, Chrysippus, Xenophon, Aeschines, Epicures, Euclid, Pythagoras, Diogenes of Sinope, Plotinus, Apelles, Ptolemy, Sodoma, and Hypatia, among the others. Averroes (Ibn Rushd), the Muslim polymath philosopher, astronomer, and mathematician, is depicted wearing a turban (crouching down in the lower left behind Hypatia in the white robe). Michelangelo is depicted in the foreground as the mournful Heraclitus. Hypatia (lower left, standing), the only female at the Lycium and the head of the Neoplatonic school of Alexandria (she was murdered by Christian zealots), is blond and slightly disguised in a white robe because the Pope ordered Raphael to have her removed from the gathering. Raphael included himself standing on the right side of Sodoma (lower right), and he looks out at us in the style of Botticelli. Raphael gave me a list of who is who in the fresco, but the list is far too long for me to detail here.

I was greatly saddened to leave the company of Raphael when it was time for Leonardo, Lorenzo, Tommaso, Salai, and me to return to Milan. Raphael died in Rome at the age of thirty-seven years in 1520, one year after Leonardo's death when I was still in France and in the service of king Francois I. He was buried with great honour in the Pantheon. Raphael's death at such a young age was considered by many to be tragic because it was thought that if he had lived to a ripe old age his legacy would have surpassed that of Leonardo and Michelangelo in the arts. Here is what Giorgio Vasari wrote in his introduction to the Life of Raffaello da Urbino (Raffaello Sanzio), painter, and architect:

> How bountiful and benign Heaven sometimes shows itself in showering upon one single person the infinite riches of its treasures, and all those graces and rarest gifts that it is wont to distribute among many individuals, over a long space of time, could be clearly seen in

the no less excellent than gracious Raffaello Sanzio da Urbino, who was endowed by nature with all that modesty and goodness which are seen at times in those who, beyond all other men, have added to their natural sweetness and gentleness the beautiful adornment of courtesy and grace, by reason of which they always show themselves agreeable and pleasant to every sort of person and in all their actions. Him nature presented to the world, when, vanquished by art through the hands of Michelagnolo Buonarroti, she wished to be vanquished, in Raffaello, by art and character together. And in truth, since the greater part of the craftsmen who had lived up to that time had received from nature a certain element of savagery and madness, which, besides making them strange and eccentric, had brought it about that very often there was revealed in them rather the obscure darkness of vice than the brightness and splendour of those virtues that make men immortal, there was right good reason for her to cause to shine out brilliantly in Raffaello, as a contrast to the others, all the rarest qualities of the mind, accompanied by such grace, industry, beauty, modesty, and excellence of character, as would have sufficed to efface any vice, however hideous, and any blot, were it ever so great. Wherefore it may be surely said that those who are the possessors of such rare and numerous gifts as were seen in Raffaello da Urbino, are not merely men, but, if it be not a sin to say it, mortal gods and that those who, by means of their works, leave an honourable name written in the archives of fame in this earthly world of ours, can also hope to have to enjoy in Heaven a worthy reward for their labours and merits.

Mirrors, Lenses, and Solar Reflectors

Mirrors, lenses, vision, and light were of great interest to Leonardo that stemmed from his young days in Verrocchio's workshop in Florence. Since then, he had undertaken anatomical studies of the bovine and human eye and found that the lens of an eye is globular and centrally placed, and that it is responsible for the reversal of the image seen in the eye. He wanted to know how the inverted image of the eye was righted. He wrote the treatise '*Dell' Occhio*' on the anatomy of the eye in relation to the formation of images and visual perceptions and the mechanics of inversion, refraction, and reflection using the eye's lens. He also wrote about the *camera obscura* as an eye and how to make glasses (*ochiali*) and how we can use them to improve our vision. His notebooks contain innumerable drawings of machines and their parts related to making mirrors and lenses. He designed lamps with magnifying lenses placed in front of lighted candles for nocturnal illumination. He designed and built a magnifying tube of lenses to scan the heavens and to see the moon large:

> If you wish to prove that the moon appears larger than it is when it reaches the horizon, you take a lens convex on the one side and concave on the other and place the concave side to your eye and look at the object beyond the convex surface; and by this means you will have made a true imitation of the atmosphere which is enclosed between the sphere of fire and that of water, for this atmosphere is concave towards the earth and convex towards the fire.

Like others at the time and now, Leonardo wore eyeglasses with convex lenses for *presbyopia* (long sightedness) and used magnifying crystal lenses for reading and for studying minute objects and their patterns. He liked to make his own spectacles with brass support and riveted handles to wind around his ears. He has numerous sketches of men's faces with eyeglasses and has drawn Ludovico IL Moro, Duke of Milan, holding glasses to his eyes to banish Slander fed by Envy with Justice before him in her black robe. His aim in Rome was to further improve the quality of lenses and mirrors for visualisation and perspective. In this regard, he tried to design and wear water-filled lenses to improve his vision by using the refractive properties of the water.

This experiment never developed beyond wearing these contact lenses strapped to his face for a few weeks with various people including us, his immediate family, gawking at him for wearing an unusually grotesque facial mask as if he was plague doctor. Leonardo had more success with grinding mirror lenses for short and large focal lengths and make looking glasses to enhance vision for him and for others. If you look at Raphael's portrait of *Pope Leo X* you will see that the Pope holds a concave lens to improve his vision for reading that was made and gifted to him by Leonardo da Vinci.

Leonardo also explored the use of lenses and mirrors as an aid for design of buildings and for perspective painting, although he was critical of their use for perspective painting in his *Treatise of Painting*, stating that it was preferable for the artist to train his own eye rather than use trickery. However, he never completely condemned the idea of using mirrors, lenses, and other visual aids as tools for constructing perspective.

> Perspective comes into action when judgement is lacking with respect to things that diminish. The eye can never be a true judge for determining with certainty the closeness of one thing compared to something else when the top of the second thing appears to the eye of the observer to be placed at the same level, unless by the use of the intersection, mistress, and guise of perspective.

For most of the time, Leonardo was more concerned with the burning properties of concave mirrors rather than their imaging properties. His patron Giuliano de' Medici was a member of the Medici family textile trade, and he wanted to improve their techniques for dyeing wool and other fabrics and materials such as silk and animal skins. Leonardo was to help him to improve these dyeing techniques as an important step in the Medici manufacture and trade in textiles. Leonardo believed that he could improve the process by heating his boiler dyes using highly polished mirrors that would reflect the heat of the sun. Leonardo explained to his patron that the concave mirrors are converging mirrors that reflect light, and therefore, the sun's heat rays would heat and solder objects by reflection (burning mirrors). The heat reflected from the sun to a focal point that could be used to boil fluids or melt dyes or solder metals depending on the distance of the focal point and the shape of the curve of the mirror. The burning mirrors promised to speed up the heating process that was essential to dissolving dyes and improving their interaction with the wool, silk, and other fabrics. He had already tried to use large glass magnifying lenses for the boiling processes, but they had proved rather inefficient. He hoped that burning concave mirrors made of brightly polished ceramics (or copper, or bronze, or silver) would reflect and concentrate the sun's light at a specific focal distance into a heat source more effectively.

> One wonders whether the pyramid of solar rays, as reflected by a burning mirror, can be condensed to bring so much power to one single point, and whether it acquires more density than the air that sustains it. With this burning mirror one can supply heat for any boiler in a dyeing factory. And with this a pool can be warmed up, because there will be always boiling water.

To keep his designs secret, he placed Salai, il Fanfoia, and me in one studio to draw and paint while he worked in the other studio to construct the burning mirrors and lenses. However, he hired two German mirror makers as his assistants in order to help him prepare the concave heating mirrors. Because his new assistants were unreliable, Leonardo in the end had to invent and build his own machine to grind mirrors or lenses into a concave shape. This was a breakthrough because the concave lenses, in addition, could be made and used as looking glasses to enhance vision. He showed Giuliano de' Medici his drawings and mathematical calculations and explained that he could provide him with prototypes of the burning mirrors within a year.

As usual, Leonardo became easily sidetracked. He suddenly wanted to make convex lenses to converge light rays and to magnify objects at a distance. Also, he believed that he could magnify invisible objects in drops of water by combining two converging convex lens within a tube with a concave mirror for imaging purposes. Therefore, after a year, the burning mirrors and experiments were progressing far too slowly, and Leonardo had me writing out his excuses and sending them in a letter to his patron Giuliano de' Medici. He blamed his two German assistants and accused them of delaying his work, stealing his ideas, and setting up their own mirror workshop.

> I can no longer make anything secretly because of him [the German mirror-maker], for the other is always at his elbow, since the one room leads into the other. But his whole intent was to get possession of these two rooms in order to get to work on the mirrors. And if I set him there to make my model of a curved one he would publish it.
>
> Afterwards he wanted to have the models made in wood, just as they were to be in iron, and wished to take them away to his own country. But this I refused him, telling him that I would give him, in drawing, the breadth, length, height, and form of what he had to do; and so we remained in ill will.

On some hot and sunny days, Leonardo would gather us together, pack up his mirrors, and take us out to a vacant field with a small pond that was absent of inhabitants. Once there, he would instruct us on how to unpack his mirrors and put them together in any particular shape that he wanted them to be. He would cover his mirrors with opaque material, and then, after placing his targets at calculated positions, he would uncover his mirrors, adjust their angles, and watch them burn or boil the intended targets. More often than not, the wooden or fabric target would be set alight by the mirrors and burn away to his great delight. Sometimes, his targets were metal objects of copper, bronze or silver or containers with solutions of dyes, and if they were seen to sizzle, burn, boil or transform, he would shout out with great enthusiasm and perform little jigs of joy. Another time, he set up a collection of his burning mirrors on a high stand built around a small pond and watched the reflection of the sun boil the waters of the pond at different positions. We would repeat this exercise over and over while he sketched and calculated the changes in the temperature of the pond. All these outings and experiments dwindled in number soon after the death of Louis XII in January 1515, and they stopped entirely after the death of Giuliano de' Medici in March 1516.

Alchemy: the Chemical Arts

Leonardo was an expert in alchemy and the chemical arts. He debated the pros and cons of alchemy a number of times at the academies in the late 1480s and the early 1490s. He condemned alchemists if they tried to distort the relationship between art and nature or claimed to have invented new materials not seen in nature.

> Man is involved with things produced by nature and she does not change the ordinary kinds of things which she creates in the same way that from time to time the things which have been created by man are changed; and indeed man is nature's chief instrument, because nature is concerned only with the production of elementary things, but man from these elementary things produces an infinite number of compounds, although he has no power to create any natural thing except another like himself, that is his children. And of this the old alchemists will serve as my witnesses, who have never either by chance or deliberate experiment succeeded in creating the smallest thing which cannot be created by nature; and indeed this generation deserves unmeasured praise for the serviceableness of the things which they have invented for the use of men, and would deserve them even more if they had not been the inventors of noxious things like poisons and other similar things which destroy the life or the intellect; but they are not exempt from blame in that by much study and experiment they are seeking to create, not, indeed, the meanest of nature's products, but the most excellent, namely gold, which is begotten of the sun inasmuch as it has more resemblance to it than to anything else that is, and no created thing is more enduring than this gold.

Leonardo believed that alchemy was an important activity if it contributed to genuine knowledge and improved the condition of man. He noted somewhere that alchemy, *'which deals with simple products of nature and whose function cannot be exercised by nature itself, because it has no organic instruments with which it can work, as men do by means of their hands, who have produced, for instance, glass, etc.'*

Ever since Leonardo helped his grandmother pickle foods and assisted his uncle to distil oil and ferment wine, he was interested in the art and practice of alchemy. He practiced the chemical arts (distillation, fermentation, etc.) as an activity and technology whenever he produced glues, varnishes, solvents, pigments, waxes, soldering materials, and other substances for painting, sculpture, architecture, engineering, and goldsmithing. He designed and built furnaces for casting and metallurgy, alembics for distillation, boilers for the dyeing of cloth, and bellows to fire the furnaces and boilers. In my opinion, the greatest of his alchemic inventions were his different types of paper, the unbreakable glass (*vetro assottigliato*), and a transparent film to protect the surface of objects that he called unbreakable tissue glass (*vetro pannicolato infrangibile*) that could be easily cut and adhered to the surface of any object. I know this because I was there when he invented them in a workshop outside our villa in Vaprio d' Adda that he furnished with furnaces, ovens, and alembics. It was there that he conducted his chemical and metallurgical experiments on amalgams, varnishes, and solvents in privacy, away from the prying eyes of the French government administrators who were ruling in Milan. He wrote in his notebooks of 1508 to 1510:

> ...and so one must take the membranous glass that I have invented, and with egg white or some other transparent and viscous liquor attach this glass.
>
> This very thin glass can be cut with scissors, and when placed over gilt or otherwise coloured bone inlay, you can cut it with a saw together with the bone and then fit the whole into place, and it will retain its lustre and not be scarred nor worn away when touched with the hand.

Of his invented paper, he wrote:

> Opaque white paper is very beautiful when it is made of mixture and stained arum milk. And after this paper is made, it is wetted and folded, and wrapped any which way, and mixed with the mixture, and left to dry like that. But if you break it at random before you wet it, like lasagna, and then wet it and wrap it, and afterwards put it into the mixture and leave it to dry, that, will be good. Also, if this paper is coated with opaque white, and transparent, and sardonyx, and then wetted so that it will not have corners, and then wrapped in strong transparent, and, when it is firm, cut it so that it is two fingers thick, and leave it to dry. Again, if you make an opaque pattern with sardonyx and dry it, and then put it between two sheets of papyrus, and break the inside using a wooden mallet or your fist. Then open it with diligence, keeping the lower sheet firmly level, so that the broken pieces do not become separated ….

He also invented concoctions for health and beauty that I am not privy to divulge for commercial and safety reasons.

Piss, Pus, and the French Pox (Minute Worms or Spirals)

While in Rome, Leonardo returned to his anatomical and medical studies. His attention turned to the diseased bodies and the corpses of people with the pox, known as the French disease (*morbus gallicus*). This was an epidemic disease that began when the French and king Charles VIII invaded Naples in 1494. The French called it the Italian disease because it spread quickly from Naples to France. It was rife in Milan, Venice, Ferrara, Florence, and Rome. Within a period of twenty years, it had spread quickly across Europe to Germany, Hungary, Poland, Spain, the Netherlands, and England. The physician Girolamo Fracastoro provided the name *Syphilis* for the spreading disease in his poem of 1530 entitled *Syphilis, sive morbus gallicus*. He honoured the French disease with the story of *Syphilis*, the shepherd boy in Hispaniola, who together with the inhabitants of the countryside, was punished with the venereal disease by the Sun God Apollo who the shepherd had offended greatly. The symptoms were horrible and painful with physical disfigurement. It was a pestilence that caused itching, penile chancres, crippling pain, bloody sores, pustules, mouth ulcers, haemorrhoids, burning urine, fever, hair loss, deafness, blindness, and in some cases a quick death. Pustules often covered the entire body from head to toes causing the flesh to fall from the person's face and result in a painful death within a few months.

The physicians generally agreed that it was contagious (a contagion) and transmitted by sexual contact. Some believed it was an ancient disease related to leprosy whereas others claimed it was a new disease or a mixture of several different diseases introduced by sailors returning from their explorations of the New World. A few claimed that it was the disease of cannibalism introduced during the war between France and Italy in 1494/1495 when the camp sutlers and victuallers secretly cooked up dead soldiers as meals for those still living and hungry in the army camps. Others claimed it was the result of sexual intercourse between a leprous knight and a courtesan, couplings between men and monkeys, leper's blood mixed with wine, poisoned wells, or the Moors' revenge for being forced out of Spain in 1492. The prevailing academic explanation was that the pestilence was caused by the malevolent conjunction between Saturn and Jupiter. The church called it for what it really was; the growth of heresy and the decline of public morality, God punishing humanity for its sins, transgressions, depravity, and prostitution. If prayer was an insufficient treatment then the French pox was seen as a pollutant that needed to be expelled from the body by exorcism and purging. The treatments given by physicians were large doses of mercury, arsenic, sarsaparilla, and violent purgatives such as soldanella and the herb *Hyssopus* to cleanse the body of its contagions. As

Leonardo often told us, a fun night with Venus could lead to a lifetime of sorrow with Mercury.

A few of Leonardo's friends and acquaintances in the courts of Italy contracted the French pox, among them were Lucrezia and Cesare Borgia, Alfonso d' Este, Pope Julius II (Guiliano della Rovere), Lorenzo di Piero de' Medici - the Duke of Urbino, Francesco II Gonzago - the Marquis of Mantua, and Isabella of Aragon - the Duchess of Bari. Francesco Gonzago and Isabella Aragon Sforza had an affair on the island of Ischia in January 1510 when they attended the marriage between Vittoria Colonna and Fernando Francesco d'Avalos. I know this because Vittoria Colonna wrote about it in one of her letters to me after I had met her a number of times in Rome when she visited her friends Raphael and Michelangelo. She was a year younger than me, and we corresponded about art and her poetry and her friends on a number of occasions before her death in 1547 when she was 56 years of age. I know that the Emperor Maximilian, Francois I, and Henry VIII also had syphilis. Some of the diseased wore masks, others displayed their disfigurement as a badge of honour. Miraculously, Cesare Borgia was cured of his French disease after an epiphany and violent illness in Rome in 1503.

Leonardo having seen a number of his friends disfigured by this agonising disease believed that there was some living agent that was responsible for its spread, and that its transmission could be stopped between copulating couples simply by the male covering his penis with a condom. In his mind's eye, he envisaged that it was something like a tapeworm contracted from undercooked or raw meats or other worms contracted from water or foods. In the case of pox, however, the contaminants were produced in males and females during sexual intercourse and were spread by the body fluids. Leonardo kept his hypothesis secret because it was one that some powerful people had deemed to be blasphemy.

Nevertheless, he believed the pox was transmitted by living corpuscles – living objects smaller than worms and that these living particles were invisible to the naked eye, but that they could be seen when magnified with a group of his lenses placed in a brass or copper tube. Leonardo had told me years later when we were in France that these living corpuscles or spirals were like the intestinal worms in that they could be introduced into the body by contamination, in this case not by the diet or unboiled drinking water, but by a contaminated body fluid. Such body fluids, contaminated by living foreign corpuscles and produced by the male and female urinary or sexual glands during sexual congress, could then be passed between the copulating individuals. He further believed that once the contamination was present in the urinary and genital tissues of an individual, it could be easily passed on to other parts of the body by way of the circulating blood stream or even by the array of neural pathways connecting the urinary and genital tracts to other organs of the body, such as the skin and the brain. These contagions could then reproduce and grow in great numbers at these newly contaminated sites like any other living thing wanting to procreate, and if not controlled, they would become transformed in the pustules and eat away the flesh. Nice idea, but how do you test and prove it to be true in order to convince the physicians, academicians, and clergy that those microscopic living things of the mind actually exist?

Leonardo began collecting the urine of sufferers in order to examine their cloudy particular contents (stained or unstained) after he had filtered them through a linen cloth and transferred them across to one of his inventions, the transparent tissued-glass (*vetro pannicolato*) that he could easily cut and adhere to any surfaces of any configuration or texture. This was his highly transparent film (varnish) that he had prepared while he wasted the Pope's time by '*distilling oils and herbs, in order to make the varnish.*' He removed samples of pustules and contaminated body fluids from the corpses and stained them with different dyes in an attempt to discover what corpuscles and/or spirochetes were responsible for this and other contagious diseases. Leonardo's big secret project in Rome was his use of magnifying instruments to test his corpuscular theory of contagions and disease. The German mirror maker Giovanni degli

Specchi had a strong inkling about these studies, and he tried to defame Leonardo by complaining to the Pope about this sacrilegious behaviour of desecrating corpses instead of consecrating them. He wanted Leonardo's apartments.

The Death of King Louis XII of France, 1ˢᵗ of January 1515

Leonardo wrote in a notebook:

> Il Magnifico Giuliano de' Medici set out on the ninth day of January 1515 at daybreak from Rome, to go and marry a wife in Savoy. And on that day came the news of the death of the King of France.

The French king Louis XII who was born 27ᵗʰ June 1462, died on 1ˢᵗ of January 1515 after a severe bout of gout. He had only recently married his third wife Mary Tudor of England, the sister of the future king Henry VIII, and he expired and died from over exertion in the bedroom. She was 19 years of age and beautiful, and he was 53 years old with gout. This was what we were told by Leonardo's sponsor Giuliano de' Medici some months after he returned from France where he married the dead king's niece Filberta of Savoy.

Fig. 107. Louis XII, King of France (1498 to 1515), King of Naples (1501 to 1504), and Duke of Milan (1500 to 1512), born June 27, 1462 and died January 1, 1515.

Louis XII died 9 years after the title of Father of the People was conferred upon him in 1506, despite his acknowledged military and diplomatic failures. His unexpected death made us reflect on his legacy for Milan. He launched a successful war against Milan in 1499 and he became Duke of Milan in 1500. A year after the death of Ludovico Sforza in 1507 in a French prison, Louis XII launched the third Italian war (1508 to 1515) with the assistance of his most gallant, good knight, Chievalier de Bayard, in order to expand his territories further outside of Lombardy into Venetian territory. Pope Julius II supported Louis XII, and they formed an alliance known as the League of Cambrai with Maximilian I, the Holy Roman Emperor, and Ferdinand II of Aragon, King of Spain to curb the Venetian influence in the north of Italy and to regain the fiefs of Rimini and Faenza that the Pope had lost to Venice in 1503. The League against Venice quickly expanded to involve the Duchy of Ferrara, the Republic of Florence, the Duchy of Milan, England, Scotland, and the Swiss. During the first two years of the war, Louis XII occupied Venetian territory as far to the east as to Brescia. The Cambrai alliance collapsed in 1510 because of disagreements and growing friction between the Pope and the king of France. The Pope instead allied himself with the Venetians in the new alliance of the Holy League, and they drove the French out of most of Italy in 1512. The Pope's Swiss forces combined with the Venetian army and by

August 1512 had forced the Governor Gian Giacomo Trivulzio out of Milan, allowing Maximilian Sforza to be proclaimed Duke with their support. The French were forced to withdraw across the Alps, and Maximilian Sforza was back in Milan as their new duke. However, the Venetians and the Pope soon fell into dispute, and the Venetians allied themselves again with the French and Louis XII on 23rd March 1513. By the end of September 1513, Leonardo, Tommaso Masini, Salai, and I had left Vaprio and Milan to live and work in safety in Rome. We were there in January 1515 when we heard that Louis XII's young nephew, Francois I of the Angouleme branch of the House of Valois, had replaced him on the throne.

This was Niccolo Machiavelli's assessment of King Louis XII's initial adventures into Italy (1499 to 1504) that he published in *The Prince*, Chapter 3.

> King Louis was brought into Italy by the ambition of the Venetians, who expected by his coming to get control of half the state of Lombardy. I don't mean to blame the king for his part in the scheme; he wanted a foothold in Italy, and not only had no friends in the province, but found all doors barred against him because of King Charles's behaviour. Hence he had to take what friendships he could get; and if he had made no further mistakes in his other arrangements, he might have carried things off very successfully. By taking Lombardy, the king quickly regained the reputation lost by Charles. Genoa yielded, and the Florentines turned friendly, the Marquis of Mantua, the Duke of Ferrara, the Bentivogli (of Bologna), the countess Forlì, the lords of Faenza, Pesaro, Rimini, Camerino, Piombino, and the people of Lucca, Pisa, and Siena all sought him out with professions of friendship. At this point the Venetians began to see the folly of what they had done, since in order to gain for themselves a couple of districts in Lombardy, they had now made the king master of a third of Italy.
>
> Consider how easy it would have been for the king to maintain his position in Italy if he had observed the rules [of not worrying about weaker powers, decreasing the strength of a major power, not introducing a very powerful foreigner in the midst of his new subjects and taking up residence among his new subjects and/or setting up colonies], and become the protector and defender of his new friends. They were many, they were weak, some of them were afraid of the Venetians, others of the Church, hence they were bound to stick by him; and with their help, and he could easily have protected himself against the remaining great powers. But no sooner was he established in Milan then he took exactly the wrong tack, helping Pope Alexander to occupy the Romagna. And he never realised that by this decision he was weakening himself, driving away his friends and those who had flocked to him, while strengthening the Church by adding vast temporal power to the spiritual power, which gives it so much authority. Having made this first mistake, he was forced into others.
>
> To limit the ambition of Alexander and keep him from becoming master of Tuscany, he was forced to come to Italy himself in 1502. Not satisfied with having made the Church powerful and deprived himself of his friends, he went after the kingdom of Naples and divided it with the king of Spain (Ferdinand II). And where before he alone had been the arbiter of Italy, he brought in a rival to whom everyone in the kingdom who was ambitious on his own account or dissatisfied with Louis could have recourse. He could have left in Naples a caretaker king of his own, but he threw him out, and substituted a man capable of driving out Louis himself. If France could have taken Naples with her own power, she should have done so; if she could not, she should not have split the kingdom with the Spaniards. The division of Lombardy that she made with the Venetians was excusable, since it gave Louis a foothold in Italy; the division of Naples with Spain was an error, since there was no such necessity for it. When Louis made the final mistake of depriving the Venetians of their power (who never would have let anyone else into Lombardy unless they were in control), he thus lost Lombardy.

The New French King, Francois I

The new French king Francois I was 21 years of age (born 12th September 1494) and three years younger than me. King Louis XII was his cousin and father-in-law, for Francois had married king Louis's daughter Claude a few months before his death. Claude was the Duchess of Brittany, and her mother was Anne who was the previous French Queen and who had been married to Maximilian I, the Holy Roman Emperor, and later to King Charles VIII, before she married Louis XII. Queen Anne died on the 9th January 1514 just one year before the death of Louis XII. After her death, Louis XII married Mary Tudor, the sister of Henry VIII of England, in Abbeville, France, on 9th October 1514. He died less than three months after he married Mary, reputedly worn out by his exertions with her in the bedchamber. Their union produced no children.

Both Francois I and his wife Claude had legitimate claims to the duchy of Milan because like Louis XII they were the direct descendants of Valentina Visconti who had lawfully inherited the Duchy of Milan in 1387. Francois I as Duke of Valois was the first King of France from the Angoulême branch of the House of Valois. His father was Charles, Count of Angoulême, his mother was Louise of Savoy, and he had an elder sister Marguerite who became princess of France, Queen of Navarre, and Duchess of Alencon and Berry. His father Charles was a grandson of Valentina Visconti, and he died on 1st January 1496 when Francois was only a little older than one year of age. His mother Louise of Savoy was a great influence on his life, and she ruled as regent of France when the Spanish imprisoned him between 1525 and 1526.

Louise of Savoy was born at Pont-d'Ain, the eldest daughter of Philip II, Duke of Savoy, and his first wife, Margaret of Bourbon. Her father's sister was Bona of Savoy, the mother of the 6th duke of Milan, Gian Galeazzo Sforza, and therefore Bona was her aunt. Louise excelled in politics and diplomacy, and she was greatly interested in the advances of arts and sciences in Renaissance Italy. She made certain that Marguerite and Francois were strongly educated in the spirit of the Italian Renaissance, and she specifically taught them Italian and Spanish. Francois was highly intelligent and an excellent student, and he grew up to learn and speak fluent French, Italian, German, Spanish, and Hebrew. When Francois became king of France, he named his mother Duchess of Angoulême. Like his mother, he had a great interest in Italian art, science, and humanism, and he especially wanted Leonardo da Vinci to join their court and his circle of influence in France.

A New French-Italian War (1515-1516)

The advent of Francois I to the throne at 21 years of age brought much hope for France's political, military, and moral revival. One of his first decisions was to appoint his mother's friend Antoine Duprat as his chancellor with instructions to provide the legal authority and the finances to launch a major military expedition into Italy and remove Maximilian Sforza from his rule of Milan and reclaim the duchy as a possession of the French crown. This required not only a vast sum of money for the army and munitions, but also a large number of administrators to provide governance after the victory. The king was quick to enlist others for his campaign, anybody who had a good knowledge of the Italian geography, their laws, and culture. Among them were Odet de Foix (viscount of Lautrec), Menaud de Marthery, Jean de Pins, Galeazzo Sanseverino, Chievalier de Bayard, Jean de Selve, La Palice, Robertet, the Italian lord Theodore Trivulzio, and the Spanish engineer Pedro Navarra. The exiled Italian condottiero and former Governor of Milan, Gian Giacomo Trivulzio, advised Francois to avoid the usual passages through the Alps where the Swiss and papal forces would be waiting for him, but to have one army cross the normally unused Col d' Argentiere and another army advance along the coast towards Turin and Genoa. This strategy proved successful. In September 1515, Francois won a decisive victory at the battle of Marignano over Maximilian Sforza and his Swiss allies. The Duchy of Milan was won and returned to a new French monarch's hands.

The French chancellor Antoine Duprat chose French senators with experience and learning and an interest in Italian affairs, and he reorganised the Parliament and administration of Milan. Jean de Selve was chosen vice-chancellor of Milan, and Odet de Foix was the Governor of the Senate. Senator Jean de Pins was sent to Rome by Antoine Duprat to organise a mid-December meeting between Pope Leo X and King Francois I in Bologna that later become known as the Concordat of Bologna. This historic agreement conferred upon Francois the authority to appoint individuals of his choice to more than 600 ecclesiastical positions in France and broaden his taxation base to raise much needed revenue.

With the treaties of Noyon and Brussels in 1516, the territories of Italy were redrawn back to the status quo of 1508 at the time when Louis XII had ruled the Duchy of Milan. Now it was the new king of France, Francois I, who claimed the Duchy of Milan as his own. We all wondered whether the overthrow of Maximilian Sforza in Milan would mean that we could return safely to the city. The answers then were unclear, a mixture of definite and indefinite replies, a yes, a no, and much doubt.

In Florence with Pope Leo X and Giuliano de' Medici

We entered Florence on 30th November 1515 to celebrations and festivals in honour of the Pope's return to the city of his birth, for he was the first Medici to have been elected as the head of the Roman Church. The Florentines had worked hard to provide their Pope with a splendid reception. The decorations erected along the streets were magnificent, and the city gate was transformed into a spectacular entrance leading to a king's palace. Vast sums of money were expended to employ thousands of workers to construct the beautiful and lavish gilded decorations to honour the head of the Christian Church. We participated in some of these celebrations, but I was more interested for Salai, Tommaso, and il Fanfoia to show me the sights of Florence including Michelangelo's statue of *David* and Leonardo's frescoes of the *Battle of Anghiari* at the Palazzo Vecchio. They also accompanied me to the outskirts of the city to Leonardo's vineyard in Fiesole and to the top of Magno Cecero from where Tommaso Masini (Zoroastro da Peretola) had launched himself in Leonardo's flying machine and glided one kilometre towards the Arno River before crash landing at Camerata and breaking his leg. Salai asked me to test the new version of the flying machine, but I declined his kind offer. While in Fiesole, I met with some of Leonardo's brothers and sisters and nephews and nieces. They seemed a little rude and grasping and not very much to my liking.

We joined Leonardo to stay overnight with Niccolo Machiavelli who was in exile on his farm in Percussina near San Casciano in Val di Pesa. Machiavelli had retired there after the Medici family had regained the Florentine city-state from the Republic, and he was dismissed from office in 1512 and imprisoned for a few months. He was disappointed that Leonardo was in the employment of the Medici and Pope Leo X. '*You would do better to work for the French,*' he said. They discussed the patronage with little animosity, and Machiavelli told us about the political and historical treatises he was writing. I was intrigued by his thoughts about the Sforza and their rule of Milan. He reiterated that he had no involvement in the overthrow of the Medici by the Republicans, and that he hoped that they would forgive him.

Leonardo met with his patron Giuliano de' Medici to arrange and construct his newly polished ceramic mirrors around each of five large cauldrons that were being used outdoors to dye fabrics. These mirrors were to be used to heat the cauldrons as part of the dyeing process. The hot water baths for dyeing the wools were maintained well below boiling, although an

occasional simmer within the silk baths seemed acceptable. The heat mirrors were arranged in such a way that three or four assistants could move the angle of the mirrors every half hour or hour to account for the movement of the sun. They provided about 4 or 5 hours of optimum heat per day, but other fuels were required when the mirrors were not operational such as during cloudy days or at night. Leonardo told his patron that he could construct mirrors with improved heating power and efficiency when he returned to Rome, but for now these prototypes would suffice as an alternative to using the more expensive and cumbersome wood, hay, and oil mixtures as his heating source.

Fig. 108. Raphael's portrait of Pope Leo X's brother and Leonardo's patron Giuliano de' Medici, Duke of Nemours.

Giuliano de' Medici had recently married Filberta of Savoy, the stepsister of the king's mother Louise of Savoy, and he was invested with the title of Duke of Nemours by the French king. Filberta's father was king Francois's grandfather Phillip II, Duke of Savoy, and her mother was Claudine de Brosse of Brittany. Interestingly, the previous Duke of Nemours was Gaston of Foix, the French military commander who was killed in the Battle of Ravenna on 11th April in 1512 while fighting the Spanish Papal forces for king Louis XII when he had been just elected as governor of Milan. Giuliano de' Medici, the new Duke of Nemours, told Leonardo that he was planning to build a textile factory in Nemours beside the river Loing. He wanted Leonardo to accompany him there as his chief architect and advisor and to help him to design and build the factory required for a textile industry. Nemours is located south of Paris and 30 km south of the King's forest and chateau in Fontainebleau. Leonardo replied that he would consider his Lordship's offer, but that maybe he was now too old to make such a move so late in his life. He was concerned that he would not live long enough to see the end of such a project.

In Bologna with Pope Leo X and the King of France Francois I

After a week in Florence, we accompanied the Pope to Bologna in order to meet with King Francois I. It was December, and the French king was there to negotiate a treaty with the Pope in the wake of his famous victory at Marignano and his recapture of Milan in September. The Pope's entry into Bologna was met with little fanfare and no signs of joy. The people of Bologna still resented papal rule and the expulsion of the previous ruling family, the House of Bentivoglio, in 1506. The magistrates presented a paltry wooden cross to the Pope to kiss and only one *baldachino* of silk covered his large head. The Pope was unmoved by the petty slights and performed the Sacrament with a broad and cheerful smile for all to see. In contrast, the French king entered Bologna the next day on December 11 to large cheering crowds packed together like dazzling dark clouds of starling birds, twisting and surging backwards and forwards in mesmerising murmurations. The king was dressed in black velvet embroidered by silver, riding high on his magnificent white stallion. He was escorted by his bodyguard of 300 French archers and two cardinals through the packed streets decorated with garlands, ivy, and colourful tapestries hanging from the balconies, all the way to his apartments in the Papal palace where he was met by all the Cardinals in their violet liveries. The king was allowed to rest in the afternoon on the day of his arrival before his first audience with Pope Leo at nine o'clock that night.

When they met, the king was dressed in a robe of figured cloth gold lined with sable, whereas the Pope wore his Papal tiara on his head, and he was fat and heavily weighed down by his vestments. The king genuflected three times, kissed the Pope's toe, and then they embraced and kissed each other on the mouth. The crowd cheered with emotion on seeing these two great men, one 22 years of age and the other at 40 years, taking such a liking to each other. After some further exchange the King finally sat beside the Pope and to one side of the Cardinals. Then, to the great amazement of all those who were in attendance to see the marvellous spectacle, Leonardo presented the French king with a mechanical lion that walked forward, growled, and then opened its chest to reveal a cluster of lilies, the *fleur-de-lis*, an emblem of the House of Valois. The king was greatly impressed by the symbolism of this mechanical lion because he immediately saw that the lion represented Pope Leo (or Leonardo the lion) opening his heart to the French king (as depicted by the *fleur-de-lis* in the lion's chest), a powerful gesture for a union between France, Florence, and Rome, and between the French king and the Medici Pope.

The king and Leonardo had a quiet conversation for five to ten minutes that I was not privy to. Apparently, the king told Leonardo about his love for the painting of the *Last Supper* and invited him to France to work for the House of Valois. He asked Leonardo to help him build new towns and castles in the Loire Valley and to design and manage the building of his mother's new castle in Romorantin where he wanted to also establish his own permanent residence. Leonardo listened with interest and then graciously excused himself by pointing out that he was in Rome in the employment of the Pope and his brother Giuliano de' Medici, Duke of Nemours, who was the Governor of the Republic of Florence. Nothing was resolved at that moment about the invitation, so the king thanked Leonardo for his gift of the mechanical lion and said that he would take it back with him to France as a wonderful memento of his visit to Bologna.

I was greatly impressed by the figure and bearing of the French king. He was three years younger than me, well dressed, immensely tall (over 6 feet tall), athletic, energetic, and cultured (spoke Italian and many other languages). He wore his black hair long, and he had an elongated and pronounced masculine nose on a handsome smiling, oval shaped face. Eventually, he would gain the affectionate title of Francois of the Large Nose (*François au Grand Nez*) amongst his citizens of France, which amused and never bothered him. His bearing was most regal and anybody who saw him would immediately guess that he commanded the greatest of royal rank and privilege. Some already were calling out and comparing him to Charlemagne of France.

The Pope and the French king spent the next few days together in long and secret discussions and attending mass. When we were in France one year later, the king told Leonardo and me what some of his discussion was about with the Pope when they were in Bologna. Apart from arranging the Bologna Concordat agreement, they made a pact that the king would help the Pope's brother Giuliano de' Medici hold on to his rule over Florence and assist his nephew Lorenzo de' Medici to become the Duke of Urbino. As part of this friendship with the Pope, Francois I also invested Giuliano de' Medici with the title of Duke of Nemours, a peerage that had formerly belonged to Gaston de Foix who was killed at the Battle of Ravenna outside of Milan in 1512. Then, on the 22nd February 1515, while the king was at his court in France, he presided over the marriage of Giuliano to his half-aunt Filberta of

Savoy, the daughter of his grandfather Philip II, Duke of Savoy, and step-grandmother Claudine de Brosse of Brittany. Now it was the turn of Lorenzo de' Medici, Florentine ruler-in-waiting, to reciprocate and to show his friendship and loyalty to the French king. The Duchy of Urbino lay to the east of the Republic of Florence, and it had belonged to the House of Montefeltro before falling into the hands of Cesare Borgia from 1502 to 1508 and later into those of the della Rovere papal family. Now, with the support of the French king, the Medici family wanted the Duchy for themselves. In addition, the king had previously written to Lorenzo about a future betrothal, '*I intend to help you with all my power. I also wish to marry you off to some beautiful and good lady of noble birth and of my kin, so that the love which I bear you may grow and be strengthened*'. And so it was that the French king arranged the marriage of Lorenzo to a rich and distant relative of his, Madeleine de La Tour d'Auvergne, scheduled for Amboise in 1518. The Pope and his brother Giuliano wanted to be friends with the French king, and so they also encouraged him to consider employing Leonardo for the position of Master of Entertainments, a position that he had previously held in the court of Ludovico Sforza. The king told Giuliano de' Medici and the Pope that it was up to them to see that Leonardo accepted his invitation to join him and his court in France.

The French king was accompanied to Bologna by his mistress Marie Gaudin rather than by his wife Claude who remained in France in Blois. The mistress had a number of diplomatic tasks to perform and one of them was to attract the attention of the Pope and help him make decisions that favoured her good king. She was a beauty with a womanly-shaped figure and round wide eyes, gold coloured hair, and refined features within an oval-shaped face. I found her a little too mousy looking for my taste, but she successfully attracted the attention of the Pope with whom she shared her charms. The Pope responded by presenting her with an expensive large diamond ring that forever became known as the 'diamond Gaudin.' Marie was the king's first official mistress whom he was willing to share with others in exchange for diplomatic favours. She was the daughter of the Mayor of Tours and d'Agnes Morrin, and she already was married for five years to the Lord of Gilvray, Philibert Babou, with three sons. Philibert, of course, received many charges and honours from his king including a charming chateau in Bourdaisiere for allowing Marie to be not only the king's mistress, but also to share her bed with Pope Leo X, Pope Clement VII, and the Holy Roman Emperor Charles V. Marie was greatly privileged, and she went on to give birth to eight children including three daughters who later would become great French beauties, and like herself, the renowned mistresses of great lords and kings.

While the Pope and the French king spent their time together in secret discussions and various other shady dealings, we wandered the streets and canals of Bologna with Leonardo sketching and taking measurements while he told me about his previous visits there with Salai. They had been to Bologna in March 1500 with Luca Pacioli and Giovanni Boltraffio as a guest of the poet Gerolamo Casio when they met with the Polish student Nicolaus Copernicus, and Leonardo described his theory of a heliocentric solar system. They returned to Bologna with Cesare Borgia during his Romagna campaign of 1502 when they built bridges across the rivers for Cesare's unsuccessful invasion of the city. It had been a feudal city under the rule of the Bentivoglio family for sixty years until Pope Julius II and his Papal troops conquered it in 1506.

Bologna is a beautiful city located between the Savena, Aposa, and Reno rivers and on the Via Aemilia, a Roman road that was built from Rimini to Piacenza in the Emilia-Romagna region in 187 BC. The city has one of the most complex canal and waterway systems in Europe. The hydraulic system that derives its energy from the canals to run the numerous textile mills and transport vessels completely fascinated Leonardo who was happy to be back studying them again. Bologna also has the oldest university in Italy (founded 1088) where the poet Dante attended as a student. It has the longest and loveliest porticoes of all the towns of Italy and their wings, like that of a giant protective bird, spread out between the large towers and a sprawling piazza. Pope Leo X loved to visit this papal city, and it was a fitting location for him to meet with the French king and to negotiate the Concordat of Bologna.

We also attended a banquet with the king's Chamberlain and Grand Squire of France, Galeazzo Sanseverino, and some other French marshals and officials who we knew in Milan. Chievalier de Bayard was there, and he was the greatest of the knights amongst them. He had participated with varying success in a succession of Italian battles between 1502 and 1512; Canossa, Garigliano, Genoa, Agnadello, Padua, Ferrara, Brescia, and Ravenna, and he had even fought at the Guinegate-battle of Spurs in Pas-de-Calais as part of the Italian-English wars in 1513 and in many more battles later on while in the service of King Francois I. Monsieur Galeazzo Sanseverino was surprised how much I had grown and he asked me what manure Leonardo was growing me on to have me sprout so quickly. It was at this meeting that Sanseverino told Leonardo that he and his friends had persuaded the French king to invite him to France to work for the king as his court engineer. Leonardo was greatly flattered, but he was now 63 years of age growing tired with no intentions of travelling and working in France. He graciously thanked Sanseverino and all those present for their consideration, kindness, and patronage, and he reminded them that he was now residing and working in Rome under the patronage of the Pope and his brother, the Duke of Nemours.

The Bologna meeting ended on the 15th of December, and King Francois and his court of officials and marshals and troops returned to Milan where the king elected Odet de Foix as the Governor of the Duchy of Milan. Odet de Foix had participated in many of the French campaigns in Italy for Louis XII when he was Knight of the Order of St. Michael, governor and admiral of Guyenne (region that encompasses Bordeaux in France), and lieutenant-general of the king's armies in Italy, and then as Marshal of France in 1511. Left for dead on the field of the battle of Ravenna in 1512, Odet de Foix recovered from his serious wounds and became the governor-general of Guyenne in the same year. Now, in 1516, he was the new governor of the Duchy of Milan. His sister Francoise was soon to become the king's second official mistress. After having established stable governance in the duchy of Milan, both the king and his chancellor left on the 8th of January to return to France.

Pope Leo X's Dismissal of Leonardo da Vinci from Rome, 1516

We returned to Rome while the Pope accompanied his brother Giuliano de' Medici back to Florence to test Leonardo's heating mirrors. Unknown to us, Bologna would be the last time Leonardo saw his Florentine patron alive. Sadly, Giuliano de' Medici died in Fiesole near Florence on the 17th of March 1516. When Leonardo heard about the death, all he could repeat to himself was 'the Medici made me and now they want to destroy me'. Giuliano de' Medici, the Duke of Nemours, had supported us for three years in Rome, but now with his death, it seemed inevitable that the Pope no longer would bother to support us in the same way that his brother had done.

A few days before his birthday in April of 1516, Leonardo was called to an audience with the Pope.

The Pope said, Leonardo, I have called you here to warn you to leave the Holy City at once, before the next full moon. Unless you have left by then, you will be arrested as a heretic and disbeliever. You will be charged with:

1. Preaching heliogeometricism,
2. Developing spyglasses and magnifying glasses and dabbling with the occult,
3. Preaching theories that miniscules spread disease and pestilence, which is an unholy, irrational, and unscientific perspective.

4. Your obsession to work on cadavers, bodies of the dead, is unnatural and obsessive and unholy in Rome where we give the dead their proper honour and right for a spiritual opportunity to meet and make peace with their Maker.

My brother Giuliano, God bless his soul, loved you as he did me, and he wanted me to guarantee a future for you in Rome, but I cannot do this for you, My Son. I cannot give you any further favours, rooms, and commissions. I can only give you my advice to leave Rome as soon as you can with my prayers and with the blessing of God and Our Savoir, Jesus Christ. I can only provide you with short-term protection here and hold back my prosecutors for a few weeks at most, before they demand that I allow them to draw up your arrest papers.

You are fortunate, Leonardo, for God has intervened on your behalf at just the right time.

I received a letter from Francois I, the King of France, dated 14th March, 1516, requesting that I provide him with my permission to grant you free passage to visit and honour him at his residences in France.

I want no trouble with this young king who now controls the territory of Milan, and for all I know, covets control of Rome, the Vatican, and the Holy See. I foresee, after speaking with my Lord above, that I have no choice other than that I implore you, Leonardo da Vinci, to take immediate leave of Rome and accept the French king's request. The Christian king wishes that you provide him with your service immediately in the capacity of his Chief Painter and Engineer. He will pay generously for your service. He feels that you are ignoring his invites because I am holding you back, possibly even imprisoning you in Rome. Heaven forbid – as if I would do such a despicable act.

Leonardo, in all honesty, you are past your use by date here in Rome. I can no longer accommodate you. I need your apartments for younger more active men. I have Raphael and all his assistants here to help me with our decorations. They are Giovanni Francesco, II Bologna, Perino del Vaga, Pellegrino da Modena, Vincenzio da San Gimignano, and Polidoro da Caravaggio and others. They provide beautiful portraits and narratives for my cardinals and me, and you provide us with nothing. You are no longer of any service to me or to the Vatican and yet you occupy our space. You don't paint, you don't sculpt, you upset my visiting jewellers and mirror makers from Germany and Switzerland, you constantly annoy Michelangelo, pestering to see his paintings and sculptures, and you are frankly not in the best of health. I cannot give you and your assistants any further pensions. You must go and seek other favours. What have you to say?

Leonardo's head was bowed, and he was visibly shaken by the Pope's chastisement. He hadn't anticipated such a cruel attack from his Pope, the brother of his recently deceased mentor the Duke Giuliano de' Medici. It was already evident to all of us before this meeting that Leonardo had lost favour with the Pope, but to be accused of heresy by the Pope with a possible arrest and trial in the next few weeks was totally unexpected. How could it be possible that matters had got so bad for Leonardo in Rome that he was threatened with imprisonment, or worse, to be burnt at the stake for his ideas about beauty and the truth? This was stunning, hurtful, and inconceivable.

A bemused Leonardo raised his head and looked at the Pope seated in his throne of the God's messenger and he said, Holy Father, I did not realise that I had shamed myself to such an unimaginable degree in Your Holy eyes. Holy Father, I seek your forgiveness.

The Pope responded immediately, tersely:

You will find my forgiveness, Leonardo da Vinci, only after you have left Rome. Again, I advise that you leave Rome, the Italian peninsula, and accept the French King's invitation to serve him faithfully in Amboise with my complete and total blessing. It will be the best for all three of us. You could be useful to me by serving the French King and letting me know what his intentions and interests are for us in Italy, Rome, and the Holy Empire. We could all benefit from this and form a nice alliance together.

I will be happy to serve my brother's memory and give you official leave from Rome and provide you with protection to travel safely to France in the Pope's name.

I will be happy to reply to the King granting his request and letting him know that you and I have come to an agreement, and that you will be in France before the end of summer.

You have too many enemies in Rome, Italy, the northern borders, and Spain to remain here safely without being attacked or arrested. It is in your very best interest to leave quickly and quietly. Speak Leonardo da Vinci.

Thus, spoke Leonardo: And what of my followers, students, and friends, Your Holiness? Are they safe?

There was a slight pause as the Pope studied Leonardo's sincerity.

Yes, Leonardo. As long as they do not provoke us with your libertine thoughts and heretical opinions, and that they stay rigidly within their artisanship and God-given gifts only. I have much to do here, things to build to the Glory of God, and I have not enough time on this Earth, as it is true for any mortal, even a Pope. Your painters and technicians, if they wish, can stay in the Vatican and Rome by transferring to the studios of my artists. You have one month to organise your matters before you leave and only ten days to give me your answer in regard to His Majesty's invitation. I cannot leave his request and communication with me unanswered. You can take Count Melzi with you and one or two other servants of your choice, if this pleases you. If you accept the King's invitation, I expect to receive reports from you and Count Melzi on a regular basis. Think about it carefully and without any further delay, Leonardo da Vinci. I want you to meditate about this and then confess your sins to Bishop Arturo before you leave Rome. He will await your visit on Friday and give you further instruction. You may come forward Leonardo da Vinci and kiss my ring. I wish you God's grace and safe travel for we will not see each other again in this mortal world.

Leonardo, arose from his chair, knelt before the Pope, and kissed the holy ring on his outstretched hand. He then rose to his feet, backed away, and while his head was bowed, he said, I thank his Holiness for his indulgence, his and his family's support, and I hope that I will leave his Holy Eminence and the Holy See with their occasional good thoughts of me, and that the eminences will forgive me in their prayers to Our Lord for my past misdeeds and blind unawareness in my pursuit of God and the truth about His natural world. God is Great. I hold his Holiness's brother, his Lordship and Eminence Giuliano, Duke of Nemours and Governor of the Republic of Florence, firmly in all my prayers and will forever thank him for his generosity. I thank his Holiness for his most considerate warning and for allowing me another chance to continue on with my flagging life with the support of the Holy Christian Empire and the French King. I thank you, your Eminence, and God for your consideration, for God is great.

Leonardo raised his head to look at the Pope for one last time and wait for the dismissive wave of his hand.

The Pope looked at me and at Leonardo and said:

Maestro Leonardo da Vinci and Count Francesco Melzi. The Holy Pope and God thank you for your attendance, and you both have instruction to leave by way of the vestibule where the secretary will provide you with a copy of the French King Francois the First's letter to the Pope and further written instruction from the Church and the Pope for your visitation to the French King. We also remind you Maestro Leonardo da Vinci that you are required to visit Bishop Arturo on Friday at 11 in the morning for your confessions and religious instructions. You are now free to leave.

With that final farewell from the Pope, the Swiss guard, dressed in red, banged his halberd on the ground, and a curate suddenly appeared out of the closet and led Leonardo and me from the meeting into an adjoining office where we received a copy of the French King's letter to the Pope, instructions from the Church and the Pope regarding our visit to the French King, our dismissal notices from the Bellevere Palace, and instructions on what we were permitted to take and not take with us after an exhaustive and thorough audit.

When we returned to our apartments at Bellevere Palace all we could hear Leonardo repeatedly say was '*the Medici made me and now they have destroyed me*', while we looked about us to see what needed to be packed. Soon after, we decided it was time to return to Milan. But, it was not really the end for Leonardo, not just yet. He had another three good years ahead of him in France with king Francois I.

A Few Words About Pope Leo X

Pope Leo X lived for 46 years, and he was the Pope for eight of them. His life ended after a sudden illness and fever on 1st December in 1521, two and a half years after Leonardo's death. He was a highly duplicitous Pope and generally disliked by many statesmen and leaders who dealt with him. However, he was a generous Pope to the poor providing lavishly to many charities, he was a great patron of the arts, and he borrowed and spent heavily on himself and others, especially on some of his most favourite relatives. The construction of St. Peter's Basilica slowed under his reign, but he was generous with his support for Michelangelo and Raphael. He oversaw the signing of the Concordat of Bologna between himself and Francois I on 18th August 1516 in order to regulate the relations between the French Church and the Holy See. The Concordat allowed the Pope to collect income from his Church in France and permitted the French king to nominate the appointments of French archbishops, bishops, abbots, and priors, and thus control the personnel of the French Catholic Church. However, Pope Leo X was and continues to this day to be strongly criticised for not silencing Martin Luther and not stopping the protestant reformation. His nephew Lorenzo de' Medici became the Duke of Urbino and the new governor of the Republic of Florence. He died on 4th of May, 1519, two days after Leonardo da Vinci's death and 22 days after his daughter Catherine de' Medici was born (13th April 1519). Catherine married King Francois's son Henri II, and she became Queen of France in 1547.

CHAPTER 24

Leonardo's Final Farewell to Milan and Vaprio d' Adda

By making the canal of Martesana, the water of the Adda is greatly diminished by its distribution over many districts for the irrigation of the fields. A remedy for this would be to make several little channels, since the water drunk up by the earth is of no more use to any one, nor mischief neither, because it is taken from no one; and by making these channels the water which before was lost returns again and is once more serviceable and useful to men.

— Leonardo da Vinci

Light and Dark and Shades of Grey and John the Baptist as Leonardo's Alter Ego

In April of 1516, Leonardo, Salai, and I were back in Vaprio. My mother was excited to see us. My brothers and sisters had grown into adults. Leonardo settled into his Vaprio rooms and studios, and he was glad to be back. He returned to his studies of geology, geography, anatomy of animals, reading, writing, painting, and recovering from a slight paralysis to his right arm that he had contracted in Rome. Salai settled in his house at the vineyards outside the Porta Vercellina in Milan and occasionally visited Vaprio to model for Leonardo for his portraits that later would be referred to as *John the Baptist*. After abandoning his deluge drawings and writings about the *Apocalypse*, Leonardo turned his attention to painting portraiture and his inner self in the form of *Gabriel* or *John the Baptist*. It was based on a painting of an angel that he had already painted in Florence and Giorgio Vasari described in his *Lives of Artists*,

> The head of an angel, who is raising one arm in the air, which, coming forward, is foreshortened from the shoulder to the elbow, and with the other he raises the hand to the breast.

Leonardo finished his painting of *St. John the Baptist* on June 24, 1518 in France. He jotted down the date in his notebook, *'June 24, St. John's Day, 1518 at Amboise, in the palace of Cloux.'* It was the Feast Day of St. John the Baptist in Florence, for he was the patron saint and greatly celebrated in that city with feasts, festivities, parades, costumes, bonfires, fireworks, holy masses, and baptisms. John the Baptist who lived in the woods eating berries and bark and in the desert wearing nothing but a camel skin cloak was a hero for Leonardo as well as for most other Florentines.

John the Baptist preceded Jesus, and in essence, he was the first messenger of God announcing the forthcoming arrival of Jesus, and he even baptised him. Jesus was a follower of John the Baptist.

Leonardo was like John the Baptist in the sense that he felt he was preaching in the wilderness in regard to his scientific findings and his prophecies of the apocalypse. Moreover, John the Baptist, like Leonardo, *'was not the light'*, but he *'came as a witness, to bear witness to the light, so that through him everyone might believe.'* Leonardo, like John the Baptist, was the *'bringer of light,'* a man with a *'burning and shining light,'* lighting the way through darkness and ignorance towards new paths of enlightenment. And like many of the great prophets before him, Leonardo was a vegetarian with humble attitudes to life and great respect for the suffering of his fellow man. The *Prophet of Mount Taurus* in Leonardo's novel was likely to have been modelled on John the

Baptist who lived on locusts and wild honey and sought salvation by baptising with water. In contrast, Jesus was baptised with the fire of the Holy Spirit.

Fig. 109. Leonardo's angel pointing the way out at the crossroads. France is that way.

John the Baptist was a symbolic figure in a number of Leonardo's paintings of himself in transition or caught on the edge of conflict. Towards the end of his life, Leonardo finished two beautiful paintings of *John the Baptist* on the theme of light and darkness and sitting in the shadow of death. One is modelled on how he remembered himself in his youth as a herald sitting expectantly on the edge of a ridge or a divide in the wilderness and the finger of his right hand, like an arrow or a torch, pointing to our right into the darkened edges of the forest shadows and shades of grey. At his feet are the wild flowers, the hellebore, the nightshade, the anemone, and strawberries. In the background to our left, we see the sunlight, the meadows, and valleys of the Adda River, and storm clouds gathering over the distant mountains and possibly heading towards the familiar peaks of Mt. San Martino and the Grigna ranges at lake Lecco. This painting is his self-contemplation about the deluge, the coming storm, the darkness, and his imminent death. Leonardo has come to the crossroads and has met up with the beautiful herald of 'deathly direction' who is pointing the way into the shadow of death. Ironically, Leonardo left his beloved Vaprio and died in Amboise at a place later known as the Le Clos-Luce, that is, the House of Light, fulfilled and much appreciated at the end of his life. Although this painting is the herald at the crossroads of death, some have labelled this painting as *Bacchus (Dionysus)*, the God of wines and vines. If so, then Leonardo forgot to add his favourite wines to the picture.

The other painting of the *Herald* pointing the way out of this life and into another world is a hybrid portrait of Salai, Isabella Aragon Sforza, and Leonardo himself. The solitary finger pointing to heaven is saying, '*this is me (you), I am (you are) the one leaving this world into the next. You are leaving one world of light and darkness into another one, don't be afraid.*' As John the Baptist said '*I bear witness to light*', so does Leonardo. This is a painting about light and darkness, almost monochromatic, with no need for extraneous colours. The image is seen as if it had been painted in the flickering candlelight. It is the last vision of seeing an angel before the flame is snuffed out.

It is a beautiful painting, and it changes in the light like a flame or a flickering fire, the longer you look into it the more changes that you see in it and in your own mind. I see the figure as an immense bird about ready to take off and soar into the heavens, with both joy and despair conveyed in the expression of the face, the muscular turn of the shoulder, and the upward sweep of the arm and the hand. '*Catch me if you can*'.

Leonardo has given the *Herald* the cheeky smile and the beautiful curly hair of Salai. The 'little devil', thief of coins and drawing pens, is pointing up to the heavens with a chortle. This painting by Leonardo is the one most often referred to as *Saint John the Baptist*, and it is the one that Salai made the most copies to sell as his own works. Many people find this painting highly ambiguous and disturbing. Some have told me that they believe that Leonardo is giving them 'the disrespectful finger,' as offensive as the '*gesto dell' ombrello*'. Heaven forbid. Such a thought would never have crossed the Maestro's mind.

The Upraised Index Finger

The upraised index finger meant many things to Leonardo. It was highly contradictory. First and foremost it was a painting device, a finger to the viewer letting him know that he was looking at a moment in time, frozen, infinite, with no living action (like the moment of death). Hence, pointing to the heavens is letting the viewers know that they are looking at a painting that is infinite, saintly, but materially dead, inanimate, a corpse, out of reach of the living, like being out of reach of heaven when one's feet are planted too firmly on the ground, on earth, stuck like glue in the physical plane. The finger is also the more obvious symbol of a saint or a layperson pointing to heaven, to the Lord above, a symbol of the character's urge to be pure in body and spirit. It is also a joke, a profundity, a male erect penis, the passion of the priest and the holy man's desire to rise up and go to heaven. One or two priests, devote holy men, had returned Leonardo's paintings of the Madonna back to him because they could not pray before her without becoming sexually aroused. Thus, he loved this joke of showing the erect finger pointing to heaven. His assistant Salai made great fun of it.

Another meaning for the raised finger is Platonic. Leonardo was well versed in the teachings of Plato from his days in the Medici school of Platonian scholars and poets. The upraised finger is the Platonian symbol of reaching for the great elements of heaven, such as goodness, harmony, love, universal knowledge, etc. Ironically, Leonardo was better balanced than Plato, for he was also Aristolian, a follower of many of Aristotle's scientific principles, grounded in earthly inquiry, observation, and scepticism. In this regard, the upraised index finger to heaven is also an intellectual and a scientific question, a sign of authoritative teaching. Is there really a heaven that we aspire too, up there amongst the planets and the stars?

Fig. 111. Leonardo's Herald *pointing to the sky and ready to fly.*

Another meaning of the raised index finger, one that nobody would ever guess, except for his very best friends and devoted students; the upraised forefinger shows his desire to fly, yes to fly like a bird, up there in the air, up into heaven, like Icarus with his bird's wings of feathers and wax. Leonardo had spent much of his life studying the flight of birds, insects, and bats. He invented machines for flying, contraptions like thc ornaithopter that by hard peddling would flap the man-made wings, balloons that would float away into the sky, and the parachute, a device that would allow a man to float from the heavens back down to earth without damaging himself. I can now hear him in heaven instructing somebody or other who is disappointed about some turn of events in their life by telling them about how a bird lands: '*Watch how a bird puffs himself out like a parachute before he lands on his bent legs to absorb the impact and then straightens himself out once he realises he is safely back on the ground.*'

The upraised, pointed index finger also had the obvious biblical Christian connotations for St. John in traditional religious paintings. It denotes the coming of Christ. Leonardo was not surprised that some of his critics claimed that the upraised finger was his acceptance of homosexuality. 'See this upraised finger pointed up at God and the heavens, it really means he's a pederast.' Leonardo scoffed at that vulgar and incorrect interpretation of course, but he knew that he would always carry that accusation from those pederasts who forever wished that he was more like them.

Fig. 112. Leonardo's naked ego pointing at his emblem of the sword and spear (paint brush) as an X, the diagonal cross.

Some of Leonardo's characters were not always pointing up to Heaven, but instead were pointing out to the side at somebody, usually at a beautiful woman, for he was a devoted Marian. I point up and point across, but never down, he said. My father hated me pointing. He thought it was vulgar. 'People never point in polite company. Only the patricians point to condemn, and the uneducated point to mock or to express their vulgarity' Pointing, he said, 'look as his codpiece, it's sticking out of his pants.' Or, 'look over there, she's showing her pudendum to the whole street while she's having a piss. I'll shove my extended finger in it. I know she wants it.'

Leonardo was a magician. He was an illusionist, and many of his paintings and messages are puzzles or distortions. Often there is no specific message, just an illusion or a symbol to play with. Gone are the haloes, the holy golden crowns of radiating light of divine grace, purity, honesty, and saintliness from the souls of his Saints, although he loved them all. Why distort the painting with a golden crown or halo? Instead, why not just simply paint an upraised finger, or a mysterious symbol, or a medical problem, such as a fatty wart above *Mona Lisa's* eyelid, or a fatty deposit on the extended forefinger of her right hand, or the hernia in the groin of the *Vitruvian Man*? Yes, paint an interesting physical symbol that may have real meaning to somebody long after the artist has passed away.

CHAPTER 25

A French-Italian Welcome in Amboise, 1516

In many cases one and the same thing is attracted by two strong forces, namely Necessity and Potency. Water falls in rain; the earth absorbs it from the necessity for moisture; and the sun evaporates it, not from necessity, but by its power.

— Leonardo da Vinci

The King's Sweet Invitations

While we were in Vaprio recovering from our sojourn in Rome, the new French governor of Milan, Odet de Foix, and his right hand man Menaud de Marthery, bishop of Tarbes, continuously sent messages to us from the king inviting the presence of Leonardo to his court in France.

Dear Maestro,
 Come join us here in our French Kitchen. I have prepared a great workshop and kitchen for you at Le Cloux, the house of Light. It is very pretty. You will like it. Bring your paints, books, inventions, and best friends at once.
We will hang around and feel the cool breeze from the River, brouiller the stew, build castles, fly kites, admire, and smell beautiful things, and cultivate our friends with kitchen staff at hand, in heavenly grace together.
I will pay you, Count Francesco and Master Battista and Peiro Salza the amounts and stipends that we agreed on in this and our previous discussions and our latest correspondence that you acknowledged for as long a time as you want. We guarantee you again with this document.
Come, Mon Piere. We are waiting for you with great eagerness. Come and join our happy world, for we are blessed.
Your loving son and patron
Francois de Valois. Roi de France

Leonardo reread the King's latest letter to us and finally relented, saying that he had no choice but to accept His Majesty's invitation and authority and go to Amboise. In the end, the sweet nature of the young French king won Leonardo over to his side. Leonardo was tiring of the relentless invitations from the French king, the veiled threats from the French Governor of Milan, the constant talk of war and doom in Italy, and all the growing Milanese intrigues and dissatisfaction. The French king wanted Leonardo to be in attendance at his court to design at his leisure and pleasure a new palace for his mother and replace her old residence at Romorantin. After completion of the Romorantin project, a new hunting lodge would be required at Chambord. The king offered Leonardo the title of 'Premier Painter and Engineer and Architect of the King', a generous retainer, an annual salary of 1000 crowns (ecus d'or) per year for two years for Leonardo, 800 crowns for me, and a one time donation of 100 crowns for Salai, and comfortable private accommodation at the Chateau du Cloux, a stone's throw from the king's own residence in Amboise. The accommodation was excellent, with eight large rooms, servants' quarters, a private chapel, a helical stairway, and a large private garden. It was once the French king's own private residence when he was a boy, and he had lived there with his mother and sister. And so it was that Leonardo relented to the king's wishes and agreed to travel and live in Amboise and to help the king build his canals, a dream city, and an opulent palace in Romorantin, the home of the king's mother Louise of Savoy. And Salai, Battista, and I agreed to join him on his new adventure. After presenting our acceptance letter, we spent a few days in communication with the French Governor of Milan to finalise our travel arrangements from Milan in Lombardy to Amboise in France.

Crossing the Alps on the Road to Amboise in France

In October of 1516, we packed our horses and mules, said our farewells to my parents and their staff, and set off from my home at Vaprio d' Adda to Turin as the first resting point in our long track across the Alps to our final destination at Amboise in France. Leonardo was 64 years of age and not in the best of health with a slight limp and some minor difficulties in the use of his right arm. During the past twenty years, Leonardo's life had become a mixed soup, a minestrone, a stew of Italian and French left overs, and promising new endeavours. Caught up in French and Italian intrigues, he was often undecided what to do. Now that he accepted the French king's invitation, we had a plan and prospects ahead of us, and he was determined to cross the Alps into the Duchy of Savoy and embrace and experience the culture of the French. We were duty bound to help the French king build his canals and windmills from Tours to Lyon and to construct the king's ideal city at Romorantin. In between, we would assist the king with his entertainments in Amboise, at his royal residence on the banks of the Loire River, 17 kilometres east of Tours and south west of Blois and Orleans.

For Salai, Battista, and me, this was just another great adventure that we were about to share with Leonardo. Our travels were going to be long and tiring, but hopefully relatively uneventful. Leonardo was keen to protect his paintings and his bundle of manuscripts, notebooks, and drawings. He intended to finally organise his treatise on anatomy. With him in his leather saddlebags were his *Mona Lisa*, *St. John the Baptist*, the *Virgin and Child With St. Anne*, and various Madonnas, as well as his notes and sketchbooks, his manuscripts, and a lifetime's worth of writings and jottings.

To cross the Alps, we took the Mont Cenis Pass into Savoy along the Maurienne valley following the course of the Arc River, before descending down into Grenoble and then Lyon, and finally reaching the Loire Valley and Amboise by following the river Cher. There, Leonardo would be welcomed 'with open arms' and appointed 'First Painter, Engineer, and Architect of the King', and paid the princely retainer of one thousand crowns a year.

In crossing the Alps, we settled on a route from Milan to Turin and Rivoli (four days travel) and then to Susa (one day). At Rivoli we met with our French escort Monsieur le Ventie who was charged by the king to guide us through the passes of the Alps with a mounted guard of five. We rested and fed our horses and mules at Susa for two days while our guide organised our supplies and sent his advance guard to Mont Cenis. Monsieur le Ventie had organised farm and safe houses and inns for us to stay at while we crossed through the pass of Mont Cenis rather than taking the more dangerous Bardonecchia pass. We all realised that either passage was going to involve a number of days of arduous riding and test our and Leonardo's stamina. Leonardo had already covered this route in the past, and also a more northerly one when he had crossed the Alps with my father to Chambery to see the Shroud and meet with Bona of Savoy in 1486 and again in 1507/8. So, he had good memories of the route and was not intimidated by it. In those previous times, he had explored Monte Rosa and Mont Blanc to the north of our intended passage, a route that regrettably we would bypass on this occasion. Monsieur le Ventie told us that we would travel 30 to 50 km per day with rests when required. Leonardo calculated that our travels from Milan to Amboise would take us a month or a little longer. He was in no rush and looked forward to a leisurely pace with some opportunity to explore.

After Susa, we entered the difficult phase of the Alps, ascending through the Cenis valley, passing by the beautiful Lake Cenis, and joining L'Arc River at Mont Cenis (Lanslevillard/Lanslebourg). The source of L'Arc is in the Graian Alps, and it flows into the Isere River on the Savoy side of the Alps. The Isere River originates in the Graian Alps to the north of the Arc River and winds its way south through Grenoble to join the Rhone River near Valence. I marvelled at the Cenis with its brilliant blue lake and the mighty massif that formed the high mountain pass between the Cottian and Graian Alps. Leonardo reminded us that the French kings Charlemagne and Pepin had crossed here during their war against Astolphus, the King of the Lombards. Charlemagne's son Louis le Debonnaire founded a hospital on the plain of Cenis for the local villagers and the travellers who might be in need of treatment or recovery. It is likely that Hannibal and his army of elephants used this route in their attack on Italy and Rome before Christ was born; and some say that Julius Caesar crossed here in his fight against the Gauls. The French know this passage across the Alps between Savoy and Italy much better than the Italians, with the exception of Leonardo and my father and now me, and therefore, they use it more often than any of the other nationals.

From Mont Cenis, we followed the river L'Arc to Modane via the hamlet of Bramans and went further along the Maurienne River valley through the hamlets and communities of Saint-Michel, Saint-Jean, and La Chambre, and to Aiguebelle where the L'Arc meets with the L' Isere River. The scenery was stunningly beautiful, and we forever needed to encourage Leonardo from stopping to admire the panoramic views and to continue riding with us to our next stop over. He drew maps and the flow of the rivers, and he estimated distances and directions and took other measurements that he thought might be useful for King Francois I. There was great danger that we might be caught in the freezing nights without adequate cover and warmth and lose ourselves or our mules and horses to bad weather conditions that were waiting for the unwary. It was fortunate for us that the weather was mild during our travels through the Alps, and that we survived without any major incidence all the way to Aiguebelle where one of our guards fell ill with consumption, and we needed to leave him there to recover in the home of a local doctor.

Once we reached Aiguebelle, Leonardo sat high on his horse and pointed towards the north-eastern mountain peaks and told us about how he and my father had bypassed the base of Mont Blanc and scaled Monte Rosa in 1486 after they had visited Bona of Savoy. He said that while he was in the Alps, he looked at the dark blue sky above him and realised that its gradation in blue is due to the reflection of the sun light by the amount of atoms or moisture in the air.

> I say that the blue which is seen in the atmosphere is not its own colour but is caused by warm humidity evaporated in minute and imperceptible atoms on which the solar rays fall rendering them luminous against the immense darkness of the region of fire that forms a covering above them. And this may be seen, as I myself saw it, by anyone who ascends the Monte Rosa, a peak of the Alps that divides France from Italy.... The same occurs with atmosphere, which excessive moisture renders white, while little moisture acted upon by heat renders it dark, of a dark blue colour. . . . If this transparent blue were the natural colour of the atmosphere it would follow that wherever a greater quantity of the atmosphere intervened between the eye and the element of fire the shade of blue would be deeper; as we see in blue glass and in sapphires, which are darker in proportion as they are thicker. But the atmosphere in such circumstances acts in exactly the opposite way, since where a greater quantity of it comes between the eye and the sphere of fire, there it appears much whiter. This happens towards the horizon. And the less the extent of atmosphere between the eye and the sphere of fire of so much the deeper blue does it

appear, even when we are in the low plains. It follows therefore, as I say, that the atmosphere assumes this azure hue by reason of the particles of moisture, which catch the luminous rays of the sun.

He told us about a terrible flood that had once happened on the slopes of the mountains, not long ago when a hidden lake burst out of a glacier and the water ran out towards the valley where a number of villages and hamlets were flooded and hundreds of people were drowned. Many years later, I found a comment about such an incident written in one of Leonardo's notebooks and wondered if it referred to the Glacier de Tete Rousse:

> That there are springs which suddenly break forth in earthquakes or other convulsions and suddenly fail; and this happened in a mountain in Savoy where certain forests sank in and left a very deep gap, and about four miles from here the earth opened itself like a gulf in the mountain, and threw out a sudden and immense flood of water, which scoured the whole of a little valley of the tilled soil, vineyards, and houses, and did the greatest mischief, wherever it overflowed.

I supposed that this incident was the inspiration for his deluge drawings and paintings, and possibly, even his apocalyptic novel, *The Prophet of Mt. Taurus.*

Having crossed the Alps and the Maurienne valley, we changed course after Aiguebelle and followed the L' Isere River southwest to Grenoble where we stayed at an army barrack for a few days to recover from our gruelling travels from Milan. After a welcomed few days rest in Grenoble, we turned west to the Rhone River and travelled north via Vienne to Lyon. Leonardo's old friend Count Galeazzo Sanseverino, from their Ludovico Sforza days in Milan, was waiting to greet us in Lyon, and he said that he would accompany us as our guard all the way to Amboise. Before our previous guide Monsieur le Ventie was dismissed from our service, I paid him a generous gratuity and took his particulars for possible future work, for he was an excellent and experienced guide and a good companion who possessed a great warmth of character and tolerance for any straggler in his care.

Our new escort Galeazzo Sanseverino was known in the French court as Galeas de Saint-Severin, Grand Ecuyer de France and knight of Saint Michael. Previously, he had been in the service of Ludovico Sforza, the Duke of Milan, both as his son-in-law and his condottiero, until the duke was captured and imprisoned by the French in 1500. Galeazzo Sanseverino also was captured and imprisoned by the French in the same year after the Battle of Novara, but he was pardoned by Louis XII because of a substantial ransom paid by his brothers, and because the previous king Charles VIII had awarded him in 1494 with a knighthood, the Order of Saint Michael. Now, as he had been for Louis XII, Count Galeazzo Sanseverino was Francois's Grand Ecuyer (Grand Squire). Leonardo had resided in Sanseverino's palace in Milan at various times in the 1480s and 1490s and used his collection of horses to model the planned equestrian statue in memory of Francesco Sforza, and they shared many adventures and philosophical debates. In 1504, Sanseverino moved permanently to France where he was appointed firstly as a councillor of the state, and then as king Louis XII's chamberlain and given the castle of Mehun-sur-Yevre located between Bourges and Vierzon.

Sanseverino was six years younger than Leonardo, and they still regarded each other as long time friends and harboured no animosity towards each other about their past histories or the fate of Ludovico Sforza. Galeazzo Sanseverino was now a chivalrous servant of the French kings, and he was one of a number of advisors who had suggested that Leonardo should be appointed to the French court as King Francois's chief architect, painter, and philosopher. They were joyful to see each other and ready to share time together again drinking red wine and reminiscing about their old times in Milan. The Grand Ecuyer de France, who was still regarded as the best horseman in Europe, arrived with a sudden flamboyant rush, grabbed me by my shoulders, and hugged me vigorously shouting, 'you've grown so tall, little one. Tell me, what is the maestro feeding you? It can't be that old stale minestrone and beans of his, can it?' And so, we rested in Lyon for a few days while Sanseverino regaled us with stories about the French court and the charm of the young king, his mother, and sister. Amboise is definitely the place to be, he told us.

From Lyon, we travelled for two weeks with Galeazzo Sanseverino and his guard to Clermont and Bourges, resting a few days at the Sanseverino's castle in Mehun-sur-Yevre, and on to Vierzon, Blois, and finally to Amboise. It was already one week into November when we arrived in Amboise at dusk with the Chateau du Cloux lit up by lanterns, candles, and burning torches. A small staff of eight servants were at hand to help us unpack our mules and horses and to move our belongings into the safety of the grand hall. A light dinner was prepared for us while we were escorted through the Chateau by the cameriere (valet) and each of us, Leonardo, Battista, Salai, and I, assigned to our own bedrooms.   Our rooms and beds were already prepared for a night's sleep, a fire was burning in Leonardo's bedroom while I and the others had a small wood stove heating our rooms. Sanseverino stayed with us for supper and soon after excused himself saying that the king and the queen mother would be visiting us at mid-day, so that we all had better get some rest. And so it was that we all retired to our rooms to recuperate before daybreak.

Chateau du Cloux

I woke with the roosters crowing, dogs barking, and the hens clucking and scratching outside my window. It sounded as if those hens were inside my head. It was still dark, and I soon fell back to sleep for another hour or two before I was woken by a servant who entered my room, drew the curtains wide to let the morning light stream in, and told me that the maestro wanted me up to clear my baggage from the reception room as soon as possible.   Once up and dressed, I visited Leonardo's bedroom where Salai was helping him rearrange the furniture more to his liking with the comforts of a small studio. I greeted them both and asked Salai to help me to transfer my belongings to my room, which he agreed to do only after much encouragement from Leonardo who said that the king was visiting us at mid-day and that we should have all our clutter out of sight. Having moved my valuables to my own room, Salai and I explored the various other rooms within the house that was to be our new home. Apart from the cellars, an attic, kitchen, and the servants' quarters, we counted eight large rooms and a small private chapel. Seeing the bareness of the chapel, I guessed that Leonardo soon would have Salai and me covering its walls and the ribbed vault with colourful frescoes. The two main floors were connected by a helical stairway at their centre. Outside, there was a large garden on the south side sloping down into the woods leading to the river L'Amasse, and there were various outhouses grouped together with nearby vegetable plots and a vineyard.   The chateau building was U shaped with the entrance or central part running at an angled west-east direction, and the two flanking parts running at an angled north-south direction. It was constructed of pink brick and white sand stone facings with two pointed square towers at each end. A covered battlement, running in a more or less southerly direction, connected one side of the house with the southern watchtower. The battlement walk became a grandstand or loggia for the court and its ladies to gather and watch the feasts, tournaments, and other celebrations that would be beautifully organised by Leonardo for the king and his courtiers.

The young king arrived (he was 22 years of age) with three of his courtiers. He greeted us joyfully in perfect Italian (with a slight French accent), and he inquired about our health and the events and opinions of our travels. He immediately called Leonardo 'Mon Pere' or 'Papa' and these honorary titles stuck with him for the remainder of his life in France. The king told us that he had spent his childhood in this house, and that he had run around and played in these grounds with his sister and friends. One of these friends, Robert de La Marck, Seigneur of Fleuranges, was there with him as the captain of his Swiss Guards. Robert called himself the 'Young Adventurer' and told Leonardo that he much admired him as a painter, engineer, wizard, and philosopher. He would later become a Marshal of France, and he always remained close to the king and the House of Valois. All of the king's other friends and playmates from his time in Amboise became his courtiers or soldiers and were bestowed with various privileges. We met them later one by one at various functions and meetings. There was Guillaume Gouffier de Bonnivet who had once tried to seduce the King's sister Marguerite in her bedroom and was now the king's Grand Admiral of France. The others were Anne de Montmorency, the future Constable of France, Marin de Montchenu, the king's Grand Chamberlain in charge of the Bedchamber and Master of Ceremonies, the greedy Philippe Chabot, future Admiral of France and governor of Burgundy, and Jacques I of Montgomery, lord of Lorge and Bourgbarre, and now captain of the king's guards. The latter once set the young king's hair on fire and almost killed him in a prank gone wrong, and yet he escaped punishment without even a reprimand. The king was exceptionally generous, loyal, and forgiving to most of his friends from his boyhood days in Amboise.

Fig. 113. *Chateau du Cloux.*

We walked along a pathway through the nearby woods with dense foliage and across the wooden bridge over the narrow free-flowing Amasse River to view the brick dovecote that houses a thousand pigeon-holes for as many birds. These birds are cherished here for they provide the court and servants with eggs for omelettes, feathers for coats, cushions and quilts, meat for human and falcon consumption, and they are reliable couriers to transport information and messages on their ringed feet between the towns and palaces. They are the symbol of the Holy Spirit, and pigeon pairs are often given as gifts to kings and Lords visiting Amboise or the Loire valley. Furthermore, their guano provides highly valued fertiliser for the vineyards. The Holy Spirit provides divine revelation, and Leonardo felt that he no longer had need for the two wings of faith when he had so many of these birds in hand. It was reason that allowed the human spirit to rise above the mundane in search of truth. Leonardo loved these birds because he could watch them fly and behave nicely or badly with each other while he was close at hand. They had no fear of Leonardo even though he had the occasional pigeon egg for breakfast or lunch.

When we gathered before the Priory of Saint Esprit (Holy Spirit) at the south-eastern end of the grounds of the chateau, the king outlined for us the history of the du Cloux. This property was first the domain of Lord Sulpice III of Amboise who sold it to the Bernardine monks of Monce in about 1214. Next, King Louis XI's kitchen-hand and counsellor Estienne le Loup acquired the Domaine du Cloux from the monks and built the present-day residence with the fortified wall, defensive towers, and postern (a door in a defensive wall). When he fell out of favour, he was obliged to relinquish his property to the king. After the death of Louis XI, King Charles VIII inherited the chateau and property, and it became his and his wife's favourite summer residence that the king called his 'pleasure dome'. In 1492, the king constructed the private chapel for his wife Anne of Brittany who spent much time there in prayer for her four dead children, all of whom had passed away from various illnesses in their infancy. Above the door of the oratory, the king had his craftsmen carve into the stone the coats of arms of the kingdom of France and the Duchy of Brittany, which Anne of Brittany had brought with her into Charles VIII's kingdom.

After Charles VIII's death, king Louis XII made the Domaine du Cloux available to Francois's mother Louise of Savoy and his elder sister Marguerite of Navarre. And so, it was here, at the Chateau of du Cloux, that Francois, duke of Angoulême, spent his early boyhood years surrounded by an adoring mother and sister. His friend and courtier Robert de La Marck described how he and his majesty would play ball games, tennis and bowls, and practice archery in these same gardens and woods. They trained in the art of combat, jousting, and playing war games, while Francois's sister Marguerite of Navarre stayed indoors, reading the classics and writing her own poetry and stories.

The king listened and laughed at La Marck's stories and then invited us all to join him for a banquet at the Royal Castle of Amboise and to meet with his mother and sister who were waiting patiently for our arrival. The king's sister Marguerite of Navarre was most erudite and a lover of art, music, and theatre, and she wanted to meet the legendary Leonardo da Vinci. Looking northeast, we could see the king's palace looming large on a high parapet above us. The king's castle and fortress was built on a high rocky spur located between the Loire River on the northern slope and the Amasse River to the southwest.

The King's Residence, the Palace Amboise

We left the Chateau du Cloux and ascended a steep path bordered by lilies and with a wooden balustrade to assist us with the climb to the Porte des Lions (Lions Gate) located at the southwest wall of the Royal Castle. Both Leonardo and I had good views from our bedroom windows of the palace escarpment, the huge towers, and the bridge that led to the fortress gateway. We stood on the palace parapet and looked down from the Tower Heurtault over the moat to where we could see our new residence, the Chateau du Cloux, nestled in the ravine below us.

The palace grounds were impressive. To the north of the Tower Heurtault and the Oratory of Anne of Brittany (Chapel of Saint-Hubert) were the Royal Apartments, one in the Gothic style and the other in the Italian style. On the eastern side, to our right, was the church of Saint-Florentin. It was at this church that Louis XI instituted the chivalric Order of Saint-Michael to confirm and honour the loyalty of the awarded knights to their king. Galeazzo Sanseverino, Cesare Borgia, Gian Giacomo Trivulzio, and Francesco II Gonzaga are four well-known Italians who were awarded the Order of Saint-Michael. On the eastern side of the Royal Apartments were the parterre formal gardens, landscaped by Italian gardeners and designed by the monk Fra Pacello da Mercogliano whom King Charles VIII had brought over with him from Rome. He also was a hydraulic engineer who was responsible for moving the water from the Loire River up the cliff face to the gardens on top of the palace parapet. Leonardo later helped him design automated pumps that were driven by the power of the strong current of the River. To the south of the gardens, the king maintained a menagerie where he caged his wild animals such as bears, lions, leopards, and raging bulls that could be heard roaring with their displeasure. On the western side, at right angle to the Gothic wing, was a long line of apartments that housed the courtiers, clergy, servants, officials, and army personal. There were more than ten thousand people that lived and worked on the palace grounds.

Fig. 114. My sketch of the view of Amboise Castle as seen from the window of Leonardo's bedroom at the Chateau du Cloux.

The king invited us into the Gothic wing, and we walked through to the battlements of the Tour des Cavaliers (or Tour des Minimes) that overlooked the Loire River and presented outstanding views of the valley. This tower was the original entrance into the castle from the ground below, and it housed an internal spiral ramp (3 metres wide, 50 metres tall) that allowed horsemen, carriages, and soldiers to enter the castle at different levels of the battlements and deliver provisions. Looking west, we had an excellent view of the façade of the Gothic apartments with their beautiful, highly decorated balconies and stone windows. While we stood on top of the tower battlement overlooking the Loire river and the valley below us, the King pointed in the direction of Tours to the west and to Blois and Orleans to the north east and told Leonardo that he wanted him to assist his engineers and architects to build a series of canals and waterways between these towns. King Francois I's ambition was to fulfil the vision of Charlemagne and build a canal that would link the Loire that runs across the country from eastern Burgundy to western Nantes on the Atlantic with a canal to the Saone-Rhone River that goes all the way down to the Mediterranean. It was planned to be a 'two-ocean canal' that would drain the marshlands and transport goods, supplies, and services to help with developing and improving industry, manufacturing, and agriculture. But, with a single sweep of his arm, he let us know that he first wanted waterways linking Tours with Amboise, Blois, Orleans, Romorantin, Vierzon, and Bourges. Leonardo knew that this task was immense and could easily collapse into failure for any one of a hundred different reasons.

Meeting the French King's Wife, Sister, and Mother

We returned to the beautiful and expansive Sales des Etats with its mighty tapestries and wall hangings in the Gothic wing, and I peered out through the northern windows to admire the Loire River and the Island of Amboise below us. The king called us over to a southern window and pointed to the Italian wing that was on the eastern side and at a right angle to the Gothic wing. He told us that he intended to build a third story with rooms in the roof that would be fully decorated in the Italian style with pilasters, stringcourses, and cornices between the dormers. We entered the Italian apartments to meet with the King's consort Claude the Queen of France, as well as with the king's mother Louise of Savoy, and the king's sister Marguerite of Angouleme. They were waiting patiently for us at the banquet hall. After all the correct and polite introductions, we were ushered to our seats in readiness for the meals that were prepared and waiting for us. The king sat between his wife and sister while his mother sat beside the king's wife. Leonardo sat opposite the king's mother, I sat opposite the king's sister, the Queen's chamberlain sat opposite the Queen, Robert de La Marck sat opposite the King, and Salai was placed before one of the pretty ladies-in-waiting. Most of the other ladies-in-waiting and courtiers had their own separate banquet table along the length of the opposite wall facing us, and they came and went as was their want. Guards and servants stood in little groups on all sides of the banquet room with another servery and warming kitchen nearby. During this meal, we learnt much about the Queen Mother and her daughter, for they were generous with tales about their personal lives and those of the King and Queen of France.

Louise of Savoy, the Queen mother and Duchess of Angouleme, sat opposite Leonardo at the banquet table and engaged him in conversation quite coquettishly. In appearance, now at the age of forty, she was classically French, slight and wiry with thick dark hair, a white face, and black-buttoned eyes. She dressed like a nun and exuded a nervous energy and an iron will. She spoke Italian in a lilting French accent with an upturned laugh whenever she found something amusing. She enjoyed her wine, and she told us that she was born in 1476 at Pont-d' Ain in the region of the Rhone-Alps, northwest of Chambery and halfway between Lyon and Geneva; and that she was the eldest daughter of Philip II Duke of Savoy and his first wife Margaret of Bourbon. She was 12 years old when she married Charles d' Angouleme, sixteen when she gave birth to her daughter Marguerite, and eighteen for the birth of Francois who was only 2 years old when his father died at the age of thirty-seven in 1496. Louise never remarried, and she devoted herself to raising and educating her children. She was always greatly interested in the arts and sciences of Italy and personally taught her children Italian and Spanish and made sure that they were strongly educated in the spirit of the Italian Renaissance. She said that her king, her son, was an excellent student as a boy, highly intelligent, and with his phenomenal memory, he had no trouble to learn and to speak fluent Latin, Italian, Spanish, German, and Hebrew. She always knew that her son would one day be elected King of France, and despite the availability of many suitors, she remained a widow in the service of her son, 'my King, my Lord, my Emperor, my son, His Majesty, the King.' She showed Leonardo a medal that she had made for her son when he was 10 years old with a portrait of his head on one side and a salamander on the other. The salamander was both her and her son's symbol, she said, a fabulous creature that thrives amid fire. It was a symbol that reflected their survival through a number of serious fires during Francois's reign for the next fifteen years of her life.

Louise of Savoy was the niece of Bona of Savoy and therefore the cousin of the 6th duke of Milan Gian Galeazzo Sforza, and she knew the whole, tragic story of his murder by Ludovico Sforza; and she was one of the many French nobles who cheered when Il Moro was paraded as a prisoner through the streets of Lyon. She still remained in correspondence with her deceased cousin's wife Isabella Sforza Aragon, the Duchess of Bari. She asked Leonardo to tell her about their time together in Milan and Pavia before he and Isabella left in 1499 with the successful invasion of Louis XII. Leonardo told Louise of Savoy that her cousin Gian Galeazzo Sforza was a highly talented musician with a great sense of fun and who showed great sensitivity with animals, especially his dogs, birds, and horses. He was like Saint Francis of Assisi, and he would have been a marvellous and just ruler of Milan if Fortune had been kind to him. Also, he would have been a loving and loyal ally of his Majesty Francois I, the King of France. Marguerite, the king's sister, thought this description by Leonardo was very funny, and she dug her elbow deep into her brother's side and said, 'if his Lordship the Duke Gian Galeazzo Sforza had lived then you would not have had any need to invade the Duchy of Milan.' At this, Leonardo stopped reminiscing and allowed his French hosts to continue talking amongst themselves.

The king's sister Marguerite of Angouleme was attractive and fascinating in her own right — she was tall and slender, with brown hair, hazel eyes, a beautiful mouth, and a long aquiline nose. Her eyes sparkled with intelligence and sensitivity. She was called the 'pearl of Valois'. I sat opposite her and studied her features as a portrait painter would when he knows that he will be asked to paint her and her brother's portrait. She asked me about my family and background and what my relationship was with Leonardo. She was interested in my father and grandfather being the Count Palatines of Lombardy and wanted to know what their obligations were to the Holy Roman Emperor Maximilian and his ancestors. I answered as diplomatically as I could without revealing too much sensitive information about the properties and towns that the Emperor owned and that were managed by my family. Marguerite, like her mother and brother, enjoyed to converse and tell entertaining stories. She was one year younger than me, and I confess without any shame or guilt that I fell in love with her the moment I sat down across the table from her. Her brother the king told us that his sister was an accomplished poetess and that she had began to write stories about the courts and towns of his domain much in the vein of Boccaccio's stories in the *Decameron*. Boccaccio was her favourite writer, and she also loved the verses of Dante, although he, the king, was himself not very partial to the Dante stories. He enjoyed Boccaccio; although he much preferred the French lyrical poets, and he composed a few verses of his own. He then asked his sister to recite one of her stories from her writings, and she obliged us and her brother by telling us a tale about when her brother at the age of fifteen first fell madly in love with a maiden who charmed his eyes and intoxicated his senses. The maiden was the stepdaughter of his butler, and she lived in his chateau. Marguerite told it charmingly and with humour, and she left us with a few subtle clues to let us know that the story was about her brother. The king's wife Claude revealed no emotion during the telling of Marguerite's tale.

I recently obtained a published copy of Marguerite's stories in a printed book entitled *Heptameron* or *Eighty Stories*. The story she told us at the banquet is one of these published stories. As I write my memories of Leonardo, three of his main French characters, the French king Francois I, and his mother, and sister, like him, have all passed away. The French king died in 1547, his mother in 1531, and his sister in 1549. They all left a marked legacy on their people and helped to develop the artistic and intellectual culture of France that is now so admired by all of Europe. Here, I reprint the story that Marguerite told us at the banquet table about her brother, the king. She entitled the story *The virtuous resistance made by a young woman of Touraine causes a young Prince who is in love with her, to change his desire to respect, and to bestow her honourably in marriage*. This was tale number *forty-two (XLII)* in her published collection of eighty stories that was entitled simply as *Heptameron*:

In one of the best towns of Touraine lived a lord of great and illustrious family, who had been brought up from his youth in the province. All I need say of the perfections, beauty, grace, and great qualities of this young prince is, that in his time he never had his equal. At the age of fifteen, he took more pleasure in hunting and hawking than in beholding fair ladies. Being one day in a church, he cast his eyes on a young girl who, during her childhood, had been brought up in the château in which he resided. After the death of her mother, her father had withdrawn thence, and gone to reside with his brother in Poitou. This daughter of his, whose name was Françoise, had a bastard sister, whom her father was very fond of, and had married to this young prince's butler, who maintained her on as handsome a footing as any of her family. The father died, and left to Françoise for her portion all he possessed about the good town in question, whither she went to reside after his death; but as she was unmarried and only sixteen, she would not keep house, but went to board with her sister.

The young prince was much struck with this girl, who was very handsome for a light brunette, and of a grace beyond her rank; for she had the air of a young lady of quality, or of a princess, rather than of a bourgeoisie. He gazed upon her for a long while; and as he had never loved, he felt in his heart a pleasure that was new to him. On returning to his chamber, he made inquiries about the girl he had seen at church, and recollected that formerly, when she was very young, she used often to play in the château with his sister, whom he put in mind of her. Her sister sent for her, gave her a very good reception, and begged her to come often to see her, which she did whenever there was any entertainment or assembly. The young prince was very glad to see her, and so glad that he chose to be deeply in love with her. Knowing that she was of low birth, he thought he should easily obtain of her what he sought; and, as he had no opportunity to speak with her, he sent a gentleman of his chamber to her, with orders to acquaint her with his intentions, and settle matters with her. The girl, who was good and pious, replied that she did not believe that so handsome a prince as his master would care to look upon a plain girl like herself, especially as there were such handsome ones in the château that he had no need to look elsewhere; and that she doubted not he had said all this to her out of his own head and without orders from his master.

As obstacles make desire more violent, the prince now became more hotly intent on his purpose than ever, and wrote to her, begging her to believe everything the gentleman should say to her on his part. She could read and write very well, and she read the letter from beginning to end; but for no entreaties the gentleman could make would she ever reply to it, saying that a person of her humble birth should never take the liberty to write to so great a prince; but that she begged he would not take her for such a fool as to imagine that he esteemed her enough to love her as much as he said. Moreover, he was mistaken if he fancied that because she was of obscure birth, he might do as he pleased with her, and that to convince him of the contrary, she felt obliged to declare to him that, bourgeoisie as she was, there was no princess whose heart was more upright than hers. There were no treasures in the world she esteemed so much as honour and conscience. And the only favour she begged of him was, that he would not hinder her from preserving that treasure all her life long, and that he might take it for certain that she would never change her mind even though it were to cost her, her own life.

The young prince did not find this answer to his liking. Nevertheless, he loved her but the more for it, and failed not to lay siege to her when she went to mass; and during the whole service he had no eyes but to gaze on that image to which he addressed his devotions. But when she perceived this, she changed her place and went to another chapel, not that she disliked to see him, for she would not have been a reasonable creature if she had not taken pleasure in looking on him; but she was afraid of being seen by him, not thinking highly enough of herself to deserve being loved with a view to marriage, and being too high-minded to be able to accommodate herself to a dishonourable love. When she saw that in whatever part of the church she placed herself, the prince had mass said quite near it, she went no more to that church, but to the most distant one she could find. Moreover, when the prince's sister often sent for her, she always excused herself on the plea of indisposition ... [S38].

I have cut short the transcription of her tale because it wanders on for another three or four pages before reaching its conclusion. I included a portion of it here so that you might, like I do, appreciate the style of her thoughts, mind, and ability to write and tell a tale of those lives about her. But, in short, Marguerite goes on to tell us that the prince, her brother, contrives to fall from his horse in front of the butler's house in the hope that his daughter, the young Maid, will come to comfort him. Instead, despite frantic pleas, she ignores him. After many other bribes, threats, and countless ruses, he failed to overcome her virtue. In the end, the prince relented graciously and permitted his butler's daughter to marry a member of his household, presenting her with other gifts even to this day.

At the end of the story, we all applauded Marguerite for her telling of the charming tale and because the king loved to hear nostalgic or chivalrous stories told about him by his sister. She recited and wrote many more bawdy tales about her and her brother's court, but generally refrained from revealing too much about the king's own bawdy adventures. I enjoyed reading the tales that she told in her book the *Heptameron* that was first published in 1549, the same year as her death. In some of the stories, I could guess immediately whom it was about, whereas in others I know not who they are even after consulting with my friends in the present French court of king Henri II. For example, I know that story number *IV*, *The ill success of a Flemish gentleman who was unable to obtain, either by persuasion or force, the love of a great Princess*, features the incorrigible and licentious Admiral Guillaume Gouffier, Seigneur de Bonnivet, and his attempted rape of Marguerite. Other stories attack the clergy and friars and describe the cruelty of the Duke of Urbino, the spurning of King Charles's love for a foreign Countess, the revenge of King Alfonso's wife on her husband's infidelity, Lorenzio de' Medici's protection of his sister's honour, and Admiral Bonnivet's continual sexual adventures, and so on, including some of her own personal observations and adventures.

While we were at the banquet table, the king's wife Claude, the Queen of France and Duchess of Brittany, sat next to the king's mother and hardly spoke a word to us. She had only two weeks early given birth to her second daughter Charlotte, and she still looked tired from the experience. Louise of Savoy answered on her behalf and told us that Claude had married her son in May 1514 four months after her mother Anne of Brittany, the Queen of France, had died. Her father King Louis XII of France died six months later on the 1st of January 1515, the same day of the month that Louise of Savoy's own husband Charles of Orleans died in 1496. And so, the married cousins Francois and Claude became King and Queen of France, and it was the third time that a Duchess of Brittany was also Queen of France. They had their first child with the birth of Louise on the 19th August 1515 (she died two years later in September of 1517).

At 17 years of age, Queen Claude was short, looked plain and unassuming, and she appeared to have a hunched back. She was a little like her mother-in-law in looks, with a prominent nose, dark piercing eyes, and small mouth. Although she was not a favourite of portrait painters, I found her very charming in her shy beguiling manner. I found out in later years that her sister-in-law Marguerite was in direct competition with her, and that she did not take kindly to her and often treated her harshly and rudely. Of course, Leonardo and I tried to stay out of the family politics and feuds, although Salai was scurrilous at times in his conversations with Claude and Marguerite who were both enchanted by his unusual good looks. The Queen's chamberlain sat opposite Claude and made sure that she was not bothered by the idle chat at the banquet. Claude was the first to leave the banquet table and retreat to the comfort of her rooms with her ladies-in-waiting including the very beautiful English lady Anne Boleyn who later went on to marry the English king Henry VIII. It was rumoured that Francois was having an affair with this English lady, although the king had at one time admitted to Leonardo that although he had an interest in the lady, he had not succeeded with her in the bedroom. She was pure, he said. Henry VIII married her in 1533 and then executed her in 1536 for high treason including adultery, incest, and plotting to kill the king. Francois could never understand such unchivalrous behaviour, even if Anne Boleyn had plotted to murder the king. He was always most tolerant of women, even though in later years he grew to consider most of them to be fickle.

Francois remained married to Claude for ten years until her death from illness in 1524, and together they had seven children, one of whom, Henri II, became the king of France after Francois's death in 1547. Henri II married Catherine de' Medici in 1533 in order to maintain a strong Italian cultural influence in the French court. But, that is a different story to this one that I tell about Leonardo da Vinci because she was born in Florence on 13th April 1519 only twenty days before the death of Leonardo in Amboise.

We dined all afternoon and well into the evening after the sun had set at which time the Queen mother dismissed us, and we were permitted to return to our rooms at the Chateau du Cloux. Leonardo was visibly exhausted, and I was ready for a soak in a warm bath while I reflected on what I had learnt about the French royal family.

The King's French Kitchen and His Italian Family Connections

Ever since Leonardo first arrived in Milan in 1480, he unwittingly became embroiled with the French because of his connection to the Sforza, the Visconti, and the Sanseverino who all had blood and cultural ties to the French kings, Charles VIII, Louis XII, and Francois I, through their own blood ties to Valentina Visconti and Charlotte of Savoy. King Charles VIII's mother was Queen Charlotte of Savoy who was the sister of Bona of Savoy who was married to

Galeazzo Maria Sforza the 5th Duke of Milan. The Duchess of Orleans Valentina Visconti was the daughter of the first Duke of Milan Gian Galeazzo Visconti, and she gave issue to Charles, Duke of Orleans, father of King Louis XII, and Jean, Count of Angouleme, grandfather of King Francois I. Roberto Sanseverino d'Aragona, the father of Galeazzo Sanseverino, was the son of Elisabetta Sforza, sister of Francesco Sforza, the 4th Duke of Milan and therefore a cousin of Galeazzo Maria Sforza, the 5th Duke of Milan. Thus, it was inevitable that discussions and influences about the Milanese and Sforza courts often would turn to the French and their Milanese Italian connections. Once Charles VIII, Louis XII, and Francois I invaded Italy and visited or ruled Milan, Leonardo was captured by the flavours and smells of their French kitchen. In honour of his connection with these leading French chefs, Leonardo devised two distinct French-Italian menus for Louis XII and Francois I. One of the hors d'oeuvres was cooked snails returned to their shells and covered in a hot sauce of garlic, thyme, parsley, mint, and basil ground in olive oil, and the other was barbequed frogs' legs lightly sprinkled with royal golden bread crumbs. And now, he was in the service of the French king in Amboise instead of the Medici in Florence or the Sforza of Milan, something that he never expected would happen when he first embarked from Florence to Milan on a simple diplomatic mission to honour the House of Sforza.

The Tour of Chinon, Tours, Blois, and the Loire Valley

During the first ten years of his reign, king Francois usually stayed in Amboise castle for only a few weeks or up to a few months at a time before moving on to his next castle, village, town or city in the many different provinces of his kingdom. He adopted King Louis XI's preference for a royal progress rather than remaining bound to a single castle or town. In this way, he and his court ceaselessly travelled the roads of France that were white with dust in summer and black with mud in winter. There were as many as 18,000 people who accompanied him, his lords and ladies, officials of the realm, merchants, clergy, jesters, musicians, courtesans, and at least 3,000 troops. Most were on horseback, but carriages and litters carried those who no longer could or would ride horses or mules. A baggage train followed behind with the long line of servants and supplies; food, wine, furniture, tapestries, and tents. They wandered along beside the rivers' banks from town to town, from village to village, from chateau to chateau, from forest to forest, pitching large highly inconvenient tents and living like gypsies. When picnicking beneath the trees, the tables were set for thousands and the great lords' were well supplied and lacked for nothing. The king's household was highly ordered hierarchically during these royal processions. First, the Grand Master and his staff of maîtres d'hotel and private secretaries; next the Grand Chamberlain in charge of the Bedchamber; the Grand Esquire, Galeazzo Sanseverino, master of the horses and carriages; then the Grand Huntsman and Grand Falconer; the Grand Almoner in charge of the royal chaplains; and the many functionaries in charge of Government departments such as the Constable of France and the Admiral of the Navy and Merchant Ships, and the many gentlemen-in-waiting forever ready to be called upon to serve the king. At the rear were the carriages carrying the women of entertainment, the lower level courtesans, and village girls who were there to provide the men with company during the night. This was how I saw and accompanied my French king during my six years of service in his court as his Milanese advisor, chamberlain, and falconer when he visited many parts of his kingdom, travelling to Normandy and Picardy in 1517, Anjou and Brittany in 1518, and Cognac, Charente, and Augouleme in 1520. Whenever he entered a town, there were always parades, banquets, and jousting to celebrate his joyous entry. His wanderings, however, centred mainly in the Loire Valley and between the castles, villages, and towns within the domains of Touraine, Orleans, and Paris.

The king's main palaces in the Loire Valley were located in Tours, Amboise, Blois, Romorantin, and Fontainebleau, and he often had to travel to Paris to attend the central judicature (the Great French *Parlement* of Paris) that was stationed there with sixty or eighty councillors who administered judicial and financial affairs. However, he had a moveable parliament and various ruling councils in all the provinces that he visited to administer the law and collect taxes. His Constable (chief military officer) and Chancellor stayed with him most of the time even when he was travelling between different provinces. I very much wanted to learn the main differences between French and Italian rule at the different councillor levels. Leonardo, on the other hand, was more interested in meeting with the architects, artists, and engineers and inspecting the layout and services within the townships such as Tours, Blois, Romorantin, and Paris.

Two weeks after we had arrived in Amboise, king Francois sent us down the Loire by the Queen's river barge to visit Nantes in Brittany and Tours in Touraine. Claude the Queen of France who was also the Duchess of Brittany had elected to remain in Amboise with her two daughters and to recover from her exhausting ordeal of giving birth to Charlotte only a few weeks earlier. Although it was only 25 km between Amboise and Tours, the Queen still felt weak in body and was unable to travel with the King to Tours, but she would travel the five-hour trip by royal barge (35 km or 7 leagues) to meet him for Christmas at the Blois Palace in the territory of Loire-en-Cher in the Duchy of Orleans.

The Queen's Duchy of Brittany was a medieval feudal state that existed since the year of 939 AD, and it bordered the Atlantic Ocean in the West, the English Channel to the north, the Loire River to the south, and Normandy, Touraine and Anjou and other French provinces to the east. The Loire River has its source in the Massif Central near the Alps west of the valley of the Rhone, and it travels 1,012 km (629 miles or 310 leagues) to the Loire estuary in Brittany and exits from its mouth into the Atlantic Ocean. The king requested Leonardo as his canal builder and waterways engineer to travel the 300 km down the Loire River from Amboise to Nantes in Brittany and inspect its situation and various tributaries, the flow, the harbours, the river traffic, and fortifications, and then, after a week or so, to return and stay with him for a few days in his palace in Tours to talk about the canalisation of his provinces for transportation, farming, and light industries.

It was mid November when we sailed down the Loire past Nantes and all the way to Saint-Nazaire at the mouth of the river in Brittany and then back up again to Tours. The king's friend Guillaume Gouffier, seigneur de Bonnivet, accompanied us as the Admiral of the Fleet, and he gave us lengthy explanations about the history of the regions. He talked about the feudal lords and their ownership of the castles and chateaux, the people and their farms, and the industry of the communities who lived and worked along the banks of the river among the wooded regions. It was mainly fishing, dairy farms, crop farming, and wine country, but other industries were visible along the banks such as the silk farms and factories set up at the time of King Louis XI's reign. While they moved down river, Guillaume Gouffier, seigneur de Bonnivet, revealed to Leonardo that it was he who had signed the king's letter that was sent to his ambassador in Rome and delivered to Pope Leo X with the royal invitation for Leonardo to visit France. It was dated March 14, 1516, and it said:

> I beg you to urge Master Leonardo that he should come to the King's presence, as he is expected by this Lord's great devotion and is wholeheartedly assured that he will be most welcome both by the King and by the Madame his mother.

While we were on our return to Tours, Leonardo asked the Admiral if we could navigate the Vienne River, a tributary of the Loire River, and visit the inn where Joan of Arc stayed in Chinon to meet with Charles VII who later became the king of France after her victory against the English at the siege of Orleans. When Leonardo was a boy in Vinci, a neighbour of his had told him about the heroic adventures of Joan of Arc and her fight to oust the English from Orleans, and he admired and was entirely captured by her brave exploits and martyrdom. The Admiral was raptured by Leonardo's request and immediately agreed. He said that they would stay the night at the large castle on the banks of the river and make their pilgrimage from there in the morning to the inn on the little street where Joan waited to meet the future French king and convince him of her visions and her mission from God. Although she was burnt at the stake on the 30th May in 1431 as a heretic by pro-English and Burgundian clerics, she had paved the way for total victory by the French over the English. However, it was twenty-two years after her death that the hundred-years' conflict between the House of Plantagenet (rulers of the Kingdom of England who also laid claim to the French throne) and the House of Valois (rulers of the Kingdom of France) finally ended.

Fig. 115. Map of the Rivers Loire, Vienne, and Cher, and the main towns in the Loire Valley.

This was a moving visit for me to see where Joan of Arc had first met Charles VII because although I knew her story, I had never given much thought to her martyrdom and the injustices that were levelled against her. Now, being present amongst her worshippers, I was greatly touched by her incredible faith and bravery against the cruelty of the English and her French Burgundian rivals. She was executed by burning in Rouen at the age of nineteen while tied to a tall wooden pillar, and she perished heroically with her faith and her belief still fully intact. An appellate court later declared her innocent, and she was martyred on 7th July 1456. For Leonardo, it was another example of human treachery, and it reminded us of his theme of betrayal in the *Last Supper of Jesus* on the refectory wall of the Convent of Santa Maria delle Grazie in Milan. I was surprised by his sympathy and knowledge of Joan of Arc. I wondered if he had a drawing or painting of Joan of Arc in his mind as we drunk a few wines in the Inn of Joan of Arc and discussed the purpose of her trial and why nobody had stood up to condemn the proceedings and the verdict against her. The massive and grand Chateau de Chinon where we stayed on the banks of the Vienne River is also historic as the former residence of the English king Henry II (in the year 1154). The French king Charles VII installed his court there in 1425, just four years before the 17-year-old Joan of Arc had visited him in 1429 and then commanded his French army for a year before her capture and trial by the Burgundian forces that had allied with the English.

After returning to Amboise, we then embarked with the royal court to spend Christmas in Blois. The king wanted to show Leonardo his renovations on the castle's new wing that he called Francois's Italian wing. After several inspections, Leonardo drew plans for the king to build an outside staircase where the guard could parade and salute him as he rode into the courtyard. The king immediately incorporated it into his plans, and it was completed and built two years later for him and Leonardo to be saluted together by the guard on the day of its official opening. While we were on our first visit to Blois, we participated in all the Christmas pageants and festivities at the royal court and grew to learn more about the king's wife, sister, and mother who were central to all the activities even during the sporting contests and jousts. The king particularly enjoyed all the physical activities including wrestling, the running and jumping races, combats with wooden sticks, and all sorts of competitions that I had not seen before. I was invited to participate in the combats, but declined and said that I needed to preserve my hands and fingers for painting and drawing, although I was happy to give my legs some exercise in the running races. I was best at playing the game of blind man's buff with the ladies and children of the court, and when blind folded, I could easily recognise my favourite ladies by their distinctive perfumes and giggles.

Leonardo played the violin and sang some Florentine songs. He still had a brilliant singing voice and as usual his pitch was perfect, and he charmed all the ladies with his singing, playing, and story telling. The Queen mother and her daughter spent considerable time with him discussing various aspects of art and court life. The daughter would excuse herself from time to time whenever the male courtiers would invite her to join them for a dance or a game that interested her. The court of king Francois made Leonardo and me very welcome, and we felt happy to be here in the French presence, although like the king himself, we had a yearning to be back in Milan. Salai already hinted to Leonardo that a year was all he could take in Amboise, and that he would need to return to Milan for a short period to check on his father and sisters' welfare.

Louise of Savoy told Leonardo about her vision for Romorantin. Her favourite castle was located there, and she had convinced her son the king of France that it should be rebuilt, redecorated, and become the permanent home of the French royal court. It was her idea that Leonardo should design the royal palace for her, and so, she wanted the Maestro to accompany her there in the New Year.

Planning the Failed Construction of the Royal Palace in Romorantin [S39]

The king invited Leonardo to France to help him build his principal residence in Romorantin and a hunting lodge in Chambord within the rectangle of residences that he already had in place between Tours, Amboise, Blois, and his mother's residence in Romorantin that had been built in 1450. Each of the king's palaces in the Loire valley were separated from the other neighbouring one by a few days of travel. Along with Romorantin, the king wanted Leonardo to construct a network of canals or waterways and watermills between the wooded regions from Tours to Lyon for farming and textile manufacture.

Romorantin is in the Loire valley on the Sauldre River close to where it enters the River Cher that leads to the Loire River. It is located between Blois and Bourges and is a full days ride or more than a 24-hour walk from Amboise (71 km or 15 leagues). Leonardo was already informed about the Romorantin project when he and the king had first met in Bologna in 1515 and later by correspondence when Leonardo was still in Rome. The king had told Leonardo that he wanted him, and only him, to build the '*città ideale*', a city organised around and on the water so modern that nothing like it had ever existed before. The city's designs and engineers would manage the proper flows of water, air, energy, animals, and people in contradistinction to the usual '*vast agglomeration of people, packed one on top of the other like goats in a herd, which fill all corners with their smell and spread pestilence and death.*' People would commute via canals and the widespread thoroughfares that could be easily cleaned by Leonardo's special automated devices. Underground conduits would bring in drinking water along one side and evacuate the excrement via a sewer system along the other side of the thoroughfares. The horses would be housed and fed in automated stalls. Modern windmills would irrigate the surrounding farmlands, and the wool factories would be fully mechanised and energised by water mills. The marshlands between Amboise and Romorantin would be drained and transformed into irrigated farmland. The magnificent new palace would rise from the centre of the city on the riverbank and be designed in the French and Italian style with French good taste and flamboyance, and with the style and intelligence of the new-age Italian architecture. Leonardo intended to construct a chateau with a square keep on a central plan, with four round corner towers and a double spiral staircase at its heart leading out to a central court that would be substantially different to those at Blois, Amboise, and Fontainebleau. He had in mind twin palaces and twin parks and a grandiose three-story chateau with stylistic features. In addition, he planned to develop a new, geometrically laid-out town with a practical system providing drainage.

> The water may be dammed up above the level of Romorantin at such a height that it will work many mills in its descent. The river at Villefranche may be led to Romorantin, and also the people who live there; and the timber that forms their houses may be taken on boats to Romorantin, and the river may be dammed up at such a height that the water can be led down to Romorantin by an easy slope.

The plan for the Romorantin Palace was magnificent and complicated, and it had already began before the arrival of Leonardo da Vinci in 1516, as instigated by the king's mother Louise of Savoy, the Duchess of Angouleme. She convinced her son, the king, that they first had to build the cobbled thoroughfares from Romorantin to Amboise and Blois for easy access for the workers' carts and the royal carriages to stop them becoming bogged in the mud during and after every rainfall. This construction began in March and by the summer of 1516 a new road was built from the Pont au Loup in Romorantin for a 10-km distance on the road to Blois with over 2,000 cartloads of stone.

In January 1517, a few months after arriving at Amboise, Leonardo, Salai, and I were in Romorantin measuring, inspecting, sketching, planning, walking, talking, and pacing out the distances. We placed long vertical sticks in the ground to allow us to survey and measure the layout of the twin palaces. Each three-story palace measured 144 metres long by 96 metres wide. Leonardo's plan was to combine the twin palace on the water to accommodate the court with modern stables, a hunting pavilion, and a canal system with windmills involving the town in a major development plan. It was to stand on the north bank of the Sauldre River beside Louise of Savoy's old castle that was built in 1450. The two courtyards for the palace were each measured at 120 by 80 brasses, i.e. 73 metres by 49 metres. The façade of the royal palace was to have a large block of windows arranged in tiers facing onto the Sauldre River and be twice the width of the courtyard. The moats were measured 24.5 metres in width. The quadrilateral palaces would have corner towers and a forecourt flanked by stables and two round fountains on either side of the courtyard. A flight of steps from the west wing that was for the King's family and his friends and his guard were drawn out down to the river where pavilions could be arranged to watch the water jousting. A long avenue lined with some fifty houses on each side and a central church was planned to extend from a colonnaded square and the palace. Stables and additional pavilions were to be built on the south bank as well. The royal residence within the palace was to have a long dormitory for all the king's courtesans and mistresses to spend their time there together as one big and happy family. In the forest to the north of Romorantin, Leonardo intended to build a hunting lodge as an octagonal building with eight paths shaped into a giant star. It was to be a fantasyland.

Fig. 116. Leonardo's drawing of the elevation of the palace of Romorantin.

In the period between January of 1517 and April of 1519, Leonardo and I visited Romorantin on numerous occasions to oversee the project. This city of ten thousand people had now become one immense construction site, busy with rumbling stone-laden carts, and hundreds of bustling workers who Leonardo knew all by name. In two years, we had huffed and puffed our way about the building sites. The foundations were laid, and the walls of the new castle erected to a height of ten feet above the ground in the gardens of the old castle on the north bank of the Sauldre River. And then, it all stopped suddenly with the death of the Maestro in May of 1519. The workers laid down their tools and mourned his death, and they never again recommenced their work on his ideal city.

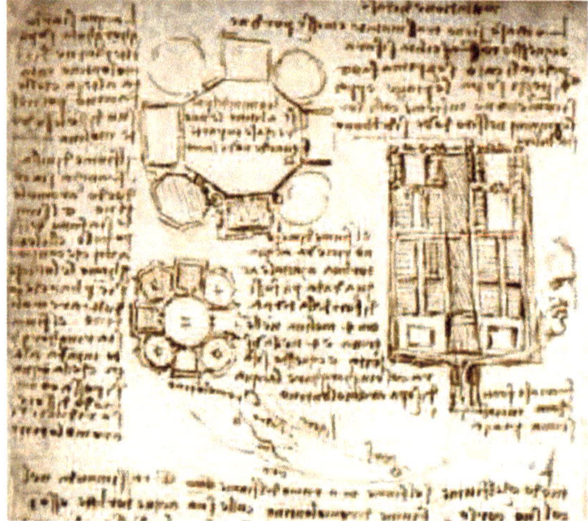

Fig. 117. Leonardo's plan for the twin palaces on the canals.

The new palace, town, and canal system needed Leonardo's vision and energy to drive it to completion. The king could not find anybody to replace Leonardo with the Romorantin project, and so he became disillusioned about its enormous expense and doubtful completion. Instead, he turned his attention elsewhere. First, he completed the Italian wing at Blois castle with Leonardo's magnificent exterior staircase. Then, he turned to his Italian architect Dominique de Cortona to complete the Chambord Chateau that was smaller, cheaper, and less ambitious in scope (with no new town or canal system) than Romorantin. When Dominique de Cortona was in Amboise in April 1518 to organise a festival to celebrate the baptism of the Dauphin, he met with Leonardo, and they planned a model for the construction of the hunting palace of Chambord. The building of the Chambord Chateau began in September 1519 a few months after the death of Leonardo, but its completion was interrupted many times mainly because of the French king's imprisonment in 1525 and his continual wars with the Holy Roman Emperor Charles V.

I attended the French king's funeral in 1547 and later visited the Chambord chateau to see if it had any similarity to the Romorantin plan. Although not fully finished, it was already impressive in its grandeur and majesty. The central keep is a cruciform enclosed by a square with outer wings and four corner towers as planned by Leonardo. The hallmark at the centre of the cruciform is a double spiral staircase, less ambitious than Leonardo's quadruple staircase that was much too difficult for them to implement without his exact measurements. Some of Leonardo's other inspirations that I noted were the Milanese and Bergamese architectural embellishments such as the rooftop minaret towers, cylindrical staircase towers, a central lantern-tower, decorated niche chimneys, and scallop-shell pediments with ornamental vases on the attic windows built to provide an illusion of a soaring city skyline. And there, in the central vestibule with the double spiral central staircase, was an oval shaped vaulted ceiling just as Leonardo had planned them in some of the rooms of the Romorantin Palace. The Chambord hunting lodge is intensely masculine with delightful pockets and niches of femininity. I could see the spirit of Leonardo rushing about me at Chambord, glowing with his wild smile before resting and sketching out some new modification that he intended to improve on.

Visitors and Friends at the Chateau du Cloux

Most of Leonardo's time in France was spent between the leisure and pleasure at Cloux in Amboise and the more stressful management of the building construction at Romorantin. He was most comfortable at the Chateau du Cloux and its beautiful gardens and with the occasional visits to the castle across the moat to meet and consult with the king and his court whenever they were in attendance. The number of visitors who came to meet with Leonardo while he lived in Amboise was very large, and as his secretary, I had to busily schedule the meetings and manage his time and correspondence. It would take me more than a page to list all of his visitors, but I will provide you with a short selection to indicate their diversity.

Amboise's had a strong community of Italian friars, monks, and artisans, many who were brought over by the last three French kings. There were soldiers, artists, humanists, engineers, craftsmen, masons, painters, goldsmiths, cabinet-makers, tailors, musicians, and gardeners who had come to work in the Amboise court. There was the architect Domenico da Cortona, the artist Francesco Primaticcio (Le Primatice), Leonardo's previous assistants Andrea Solario and Marco d'Oggiono, the painter Guido Mazzoni (Modena), the gardener Pacello da Mercogliano, and the sculptor Geraloma da Fiesole. Many of them wanted to meet with Leonardo because they knew him or because he was simply a legend in their eyes, the sculptor who had constructed the largest clay model of a horse that had ever been built, twenty-four to thirty feet high, and it was destroyed by the neglect of his Lord, Ludovico Sforza.

Galeazzo Sanseverino, the king's Grand Ecuyer of France who could testify about the Sforza clay horse, was a regular visitor to the Cloux. He and Leonardo fished and lunched and drunk wine and nibbled on bread and cheese and had long talks about the past and the present. Even the disgraced former Governor of Milan Gian Giacomo Trivulzio who was exiled in France considered Leonardo as his friend and often visited him in Amboise. Trivulzio died on the 5th of December 1518 (only five months before Leonardo), and a few weeks later, I accompanied Leonardo in our slow journey to Arpajon, a small village south of Paris, for him to pay his last respects before Trivulzio's body was transferred back to Milan.

Many Cardinals, Bishops, Lords, and Ladies came from all over to look at and admire Leonardo's paintings that were displayed in the reception room as well as in some of the other rooms of the Cloux. They saw the *Mona Lisa* and accompanying Madonnas, a portrait of *Isabella d' Este – the Duchess of Mantua* (Leonardo had relented and allowed Salai to paint her portrait under his guidance), a portrait of Galeazzo Sanseverino, a copy of *Virgin of the Rocks*, early versions of *Flora* and *Leda and the Swan*, the *Face of Christ* (or *Salvator Mundi*), *Saint Anne and Child, Saint John the Baptist,* a painted copy of the *Last Supper,* and various cartoons and sketches by him, Salai, and me were also on display. Leonardo finished a final version of *Saint John, the Baptist* on the 24ᵗʰ of June 1518, although he displayed the painting on many occasions long before it was finished. *Saint John* was essentially his last painting, although he continued to help me to work on *Flora* in the image of Maturina to the day that he died. Leonardo's friend from Rome and Naples the Cardinal Luigi (Louis) of Aragon visited him in October 1517, and Giorgio Vasari wrote about our meeting with him in his chapter on the *The Life of Leonardo da Vinci*. I told him about the Cardinal's visit, so I will not bother to contradict what he wrote.

Leonardo's previous Milanese assistants Marco d'Oggiono and Cesare da Sesto visited him to pay their respects and to show him some of their recent paintings. The Maestro was pleased with their development and output, and he praised them greatly. Many other Leonardeschi, such as Bernardino Luini, Andrea del Sarto, Andrea Squarzzella, and Andrea Solario, and Raphael's assistants Giulio Romano and Giovanni da Udine travelled to France to meet with Leonardo before his death, and there were also the artists and painters from the Netherlands, Flanders, and Germany, such as Joachim Patinir, Hans Holbein, the elder and younger, and Albrecht Dürer who stayed with Leonardo in Amboise for a day or few weeks. The king tried to coax many of them to stay on in France and paint for him and his court. This prompted Leonardo to tell us on one occasion that *'in the conception and design of religious subjects I was so perfect that many people tried to take the spirit of those figures which I had previously drawn.'*

The king's artist Jean Clouet was also a regular visitor to Amboise to meet and talk with Leonardo and request tips on drawing and painting. Clouet was more interested in drawing and sketching than painting, and he tried to develop Leonardo's style of drawing portraits with lines, outlines, shading, and diagonal cross-hatching. Leonardo encouraged him to use red and black chalk on white paper and taught him how to use the silverpoint pen, a prerequisite for any future painter. Clouet and I worked together to paint the portraits of the king and his sister Marguerite. While Clouet spent his time mostly on the king's portrait, I concentrated more on Marguerite, spending as much time as I was allowed in her lovely company.

The Coronation of the Queen of France

In May of 1517, we were invited to Paris to attend the coronation of Claude of Brittany as the Queen of France. The king was very fond of his wife for she by the age of 17 years had already provided him with two beautiful princesses Louise and Charlotte, and she was an excellent and loving mother. Although plain in face, she possessed a sweet and melancholic expression, and she had become a princess with a charming manner, unfailing kindness, and one who was known to adore her husband. Because she was so well liked by all in her court for her agreeable nature, she soon became known simply as 'The Good'. And now, she was to be rewarded for her goodness, for she was to be consecrated and crowned as the Queen of France in the north of Paris at the Basilica Cathedral of Saint-Denis that was decorated with the heraldry of Brittany and France. Accompanied by Francoise d'Alencon, the Duchess de Vendome, and the king's sister Marguerite, the demure wife of the French king entered the church wearing a mantle of royal blue, lined and bordered with ermine, over a silver robe with a coif of white silver and an ermine surcoat of gold. She was anointed Queen of France with the crown of Charlemagne held over her head by three Dukes while her husband, the king, sat before her with beatific contentment expressed on his face. Next day, the King and Queen entered Paris together with great celebration and rapturous cheering from their subjects. With her new golden crown on her head and wearing her majestic silver and gold skirt encrusted in pearls, diamonds, rubies, and emeralds, the new Queen of France presided over a few rounds of jousting and then an evening of banqueting and dancing. Leonardo, Salai, and I partook in the festivities at the gathering with more than 2,000 lords and ladies and gentlemen in attendance. Leonardo attracted his own small band of followers, for he was already a legend in France. He looked elegant and highly distinguished at the banquet with his long white beard and his long black and crimson frock. All he needed was a long pointed hat and a staff, and then I could have called him Merlin, the wise and prophetic magician after Robert de Boron's poem of the same name.

The courtiers of Francois and Claude loved to dance in the Italian style. Leonardo and I watched with fascination as well as occasionally participating in the spectacle. For, although I had not mentioned it before, Leonardo was very light on his feet (despite a slight limp) and enjoyed to partake in a *contrapasso, riverenza, trabucchetto,* and *ripressa* or display a few jigs in a series of *seguito, passo,* and *spezzato,* and various other dance steps. I watched him do so with Isabella Sforza Aragon at the Corte Vecchio when I was only a six- to eight-year-old boy in Milan.

Tragedy struck the King and Queen on the 21st September 1517 with the death of their firstborn Louise, who was only 2 years of age. The child was sickly for her entire few years of life, and the Queen attended her first child's funeral knowing that she was again pregnant. On the 28th February 1518, Queen Claude gave birth in Amboise to their first son. The king described his son as '*a beautiful Dauphin who is the most beautiful and puissant child one could imagine and who will be the easiest to bring up.*'

Entertainments, Masquerades, and Parades, 1517 and 1518

Leonardo had noted that when children play they often enjoy skipping, an activity that is quickly lost in adulthood, and is replaced by the more taxing and complicated activities of dance and sex. So in his middle age, Leonardo began to experiment with skipping. He would skip two or three minutes every day for three or four times a day. Usually, he would perform this activity alone or only in the presence of his closest friends, but now and then strangers and servants would see him skipping in public, and on these occasions, most people would look away in embarrassment. Leonardo found the activity of skipping like meditation. It would lighten his heart and takeaway his darkest thoughts and obsessions that might have been dominating his thought processes at that time. A few minutes of skipping were enough to recalibrate his mind and body and start things anew, he was refreshed. Yes, he was well aware that in order not to look too silly or insane, he had to perform this activity away from prying eyes. He kept up this activity into his last months of life and even had the French King skipping about with him once or twice in their drunken nights together.

The masquerades are a favourite form of activity with people in parades, festivals, and entertainments. Masquerades are an opportunity for symbolism, satire, and falsehood. The Lords and Ladies of the world greatly enjoy their courtly costume parties and masquerade balls. The mask is a symbol for deception, hypocrisy, mystery, and lies, and a joyful attempt to conceal the truth about oneself in a ritualised setting and time period that is relatively safe and amusing. It is used to frighten enemies, contain identity, and hide the ego. It is a highly popular and acceptable pretence and an opportunity to use the imagination to create mystery, and for a short while, it allows a person to become somebody else behind the mask. Leonardo was an expert in the design and creation of festival costumes, illusions, and masques, and he enjoyed participating in them and creating chimerical monsters as curiosities.

The king requested Leonardo to plan the celebrations for the christening of his son Francois the Dauphin and the wedding festival of Lorenzo di Pietro de' Medici and Madeleine de La Tour d'Auvergne at Amboise. And so it was that from 1517 to the end of his life in 1519, Leonardo produced and organised balls, banquets, masquerades, festivities, spectacles, tournaments, and other games and indulgences that involved special effects, fireworks, water displays, wild animals, lavish sceneries, and various other special theatrical displays to thank and honour the king of France for his benevolence.

The first major entertainment that Leonardo was responsible for was held on the 1st of October 1517 in Argentan, located 41 leagues (200 km) from Amboise, where the king held a party for the Duchess of Nemours, the widow of Leonardo's previous patron Guiliano de' Medici. For this event, Leonardo recreated his mechanical lion of Bologna that the king struck with a rod and released the spray of *fleur-de-lis* hung together on sky blue paper. He also released flying balloons and introduced an array of different coloured lights and shadow puppets during the Italian dancing, which confused many of the dancers.

The two most important events in 1518 were the christening of the king's son Francois on the 25th April and then the wedding festival of Lorenzo di Pietro de' Medici and Madeleine de La Tour d'Auvergne scheduled at Amboise from the 3rd to the 6th of May. This was during Easter and just before Amboise's Festival Season and soon after Leonardo's own birthday on April 15. However, Leonardo collapsed and was suddenly taken ill on the day after his birthday celebrations. He felt a pain in his heart and a weakness in his right arm and thought that his death was imminent. He recovered after a few days bed-rest, yet realised that his end was near. While he was in bed, I followed all his instructions to prepare for the celebrations of the Royal baptism. When he was up and about again, I accompanied him to meet with the Royal notary of Amboise, Monsieur Guglielmo Borian, to prepare Leonardo's last will and testament. He believed it was time to officially document his bequeathments to Maturina, Battista de Vilanis, Salai, his brothers, and me, and to the churches of Amboise.

For the occasion of the christening of the King's son, Leonardo designed a triumphal arch surmounted by a column upon which stood a naked figure bearing a banner depicting lilies of France on the right and a dolphin on the left. On one side of this arch was a salamander, the emblem of the Valois sovereign with the motto 'I feed thereupon and I extinguish it', and on the other side was an ermine 'Rather death than tarnish'. The courtyard of the castle was filled with pavilions, each lit with a thousand candles. The outside walls of the Dauphin's chamber were hung with tapestries depicting heroic tales from antiquity. A high bridge decorated with Turkish carpets and dolphin ornaments and lit by great candles on gold plates crossed from the dauphin's chamber to the church. The procession accompanied by the beat of a 100 drums moved across the bridge to the church. The two Italian nobles who accompanied the Dauphin were the Marquis of Mantua Francesco II Gonzaga and Lorenzo de' Medici who was the Pope's nephew and the Dauphin's godfather. The French king had made a pact with Pope Leo X in Bologna in December 1515 that his nephew would become the Duke of Urbino and marry a rich and beautiful, noble French lady. Now, the Duke of Urbino was in Amboise as the Dauphin's godfather to marry Madeleine de la Tour d'Auvergne, the king's cousin. The Dauphin was christened Francois by Cardinal de Boisy, and the Kings-at-Arms stood at attention and shouted out 'Vive Monseigneur le Dauphin.' After the baptism, it was time for the sumptuous banquet, masquerades, music, and dancing. Bayard then knighted the infant before his mother took him away to rest in her chambers.

A few days after the christening of young Francois II, Leonardo organised the pageants and entertainments for the marriage between Lorenzo Piero de' Medici and Madeleine de la Tour d'Auvergne. Their wedding was sumptuous and as with the other French festivities, Leonardo featured dancing in the Italian style and masquerades in a prominent and spectacular way. Seventy-two ladies were disguised in Italian, German, and other fashionable costumes, and their shapes were richly displayed in elegant sheer silk chiffon and beautiful bright colours to the king's great delight. The King gave his cousin Madeleine 10,000 gold coins, while Lorenzo offered rich gifts in return to the highest of France's nobility.

Then, on the 15th May of 1518, the court attended a new feast at Amboise where Leonardo designed a spectacular siege on the castle square with an assault of a mock castle to celebrate the victorious Battle of Marignano. This battle was King Francois's legendary victory over the Swiss and Milanese forces in September 1515. The mock fortress was built with lengths of fabric nailed to a wooden structure with a scaffold at the top of the battlements where many costumed soldiers fired burning scraps of cloth and paper at their attackers, accompanied by deafening sounds of arquebuses (hand cannons) and mortar fire. When the lead actor, dressed as the French king in bright shining armour, finally won his victory over the enemy, he knelt before a shiny cross and received the enemy's flag as a symbol of their surrender. A thousand cheers accompanied by a hundred beating drums and many more trumpets exploded into a single frightening cacophony while balloons filled the sky and then slowly fell on the square, bouncing in all directions, providing great delight to one and all in attendance. This was something new and most ingenious, yet it was not the end. An unexpected finale followed.

A group of dancers masquerading as a menagerie of wild animals entered the arena shouting and making extraordinary noises. They were followed by a half naked Diana the Huntress accompanied by her band of nymphs, young maidens, wearing very short transparent skirts, their long legs painted provocatively in white, black, and sparkling colours. Diana the Huntress continually leapt about the arena firing off glowing paper arrows from her golden bow that gradually killed off most of the human animals with only a few escaping into the shadows. The nymphs picked up these dead animals from the ground while at the same time revealing their naked derrieres to the great shock and excitement of the Lords and Ladies in the galleries.

The mandatory banquet and dances followed the performances, but the Lords of the King's court could not stop talking about the maidens' glorious legs and derrieres that they had witnessed not long before. The Ladies were all relieved that they had worn their long gowns to the feast and maintained their courtly composure while under extreme provocation from their Lords. In private, they wondered what the reason was for their king to have over excited his Lords with such unusual ardour by staging Diana the Huntress and the nymphs running about half-naked at the conclusion of the battle. The maidens' legs and derrieres seemed to distract attention away from the glory of the French king. But, the king was delighted as much as his lords because he loved the hunt, and Leonardo had organised another triumphal and spectacular celebration.

Leonardo was exhausted, but he still had another pageant to organise in June. It was to be his last. On 17th June 1518, he held an open-air special event at the Chateau du Cloux at nightfall. It was a repeat of the Feast of Paradise that he had staged previously in Milan in 1491 to celebrate the marriage between the Duke Gian Galeazzo Sforza and the Princess Isabella of Aragon. It was Leonardo's simulation of a starry firmament in honour of King Francois I and Queen Claude. The Milanese nobleman Galeazzo Visconti described the event as follows:

> The day before yesterday, the most Christian King gave a banquet at a wonderful feast, as you will see from what now follows. The place was Le Cloux, a most beautiful and grand palace. The paved courtyard was covered with sky-coloured cloth. Then there were the principal planets, the sun on one side and the moon opposite, which was a wonder to behold. Mars, Jupiter, and Saturn were set in their order and right place, with the twelve celestial signs. Around the courtyard, top and bottom, there was a circular colonnade, which was decorated with the same blue cloth and stars. The architraves were decorated with crowns of ivy climbing with festoons. The cobbled threshold was covered with tautened expanses of cloth bearing the motto of the most Christian King; and on one side, but outside the square of the courtyard, which measured approximately sixty spans in length and thirty spans in width, was the ladies' stand, adorned with cloth and stars. There were four hundred and two-branched candelabras, so illuminated that it seemed the night were chased away. [S40]

Galeazzo Visconti seemed unaware at the time of writing to his friend that it was Leonardo da Vinci who had organised the entire spectacle including the banquet, masquerade, and dancing that followed based on the one that the maestro had first staged twenty-seven years previously. Neither Leonardo nor I had met with Visconti, so I'm not sure how he received an invitation to the event or whom he accompanied there. I had befriended the recipient of Visconti's letter when I was back in Milan, and he showed me a copy of his letter, which I have transcribed here into my story of our time in France.

Fig. 118. Leonardo's sketch of an old man reflecting on his life and watching the turbulence of water flow around obstacles.

The continuous staging of the events from April until mid June in 1518 completely exhausted him, and so he needed a month to recover before he would consider any further projects. Essentially, his condition worsened over the coming months. His energy and constitution weakened, and he now needed my assistance and that of a walking stick. In Milan, I had drawn a portrait of Leonardo to present to him as a gift to celebrate his sixtieth birthday when he was in full bloom and still healthy. Now, at 67 years of age, he was no longer the spritely man who I had known him to be, and I could see that his spirit was dying before my very eyes.

CHAPTER 26

Fair and Gallant Ladies

It had long since come to my attention that people of accomplishment rarely sat back and let things happen to them. They went out and happened to things.
And unhappy women will, of their own free will, reveal to men all their sins and shameful and most secret deeds.
How women should be represented in modest attitudes, their legs close together, their arms folded together, their heads bent and inclined to one side. How old women should be represented with eager, vehement, and angry gestures, like the furies of Hades; the movement of the arms and the head should be more violent than that of the legs. Little children with ready and twisted movements when sitting, and when standing up in shy and timid attitudes.

— Leonardo da Vinci

For the Love of Our Ladies

The young king had an insatiable sexual appetite, and he loved to pursue the ladies both inside and outside his court. He was a satyr in constant arousal. His young wife Claude who loved him dearly and would go on to provide him with seven children (three sons and four daughters) forever turned a blind and sad eye away from his philandering, bearing his infidelities and indiscretions with dignified resignation until the day she died. The king took little interest in Claude other than as a mother of his children, and he never hid from her or anybody else his great love for the other women that he wanted to have his sexual adventures with. He enjoyed the diversity and sensuality of women and accordingly satisfied his sexual appetites with as many as he could manage. He always had a group of courtesans and prostitutes within easy reach. At times, he suffered from sexual diseases that his physicians seemed to treat successfully into his old age. He regarded pretty women as the greatest works of art, and he expected his courtesans to dress beautifully and to act as graciously and as lovingly as his sister. Whenever he was on a retreat between the different castles and towns of his provinces, he had many hundreds of his ladies and courtesans accompany him. Although he was convinced that the ladies of his court were easily changeable and fickle, he would never accept any slander or rudeness against them, and he insisted that they always be accorded the greatest honour and respect. It was safe and comfortable to be a lady in King Francois's court. His mother and sister were greatly devoted to him, and they had trained him well on how to behave cordially towards Eve's female descendants in his court, even if they were in conflict or jealous of particular rivals and disrespectful among themselves.

When the king visited Leonardo for his late night chats, he often liked to talk about his love of women and his sexual adventures. The king wanted to hear Leonardo's opinion about the beauty of women because he believed that the great artist had an eye and appreciation for beauty, and that he must have had many pretty girls and women clothed and unclothed in his time. The king wondered, what was it about the fickle sex that was pulling a man like himself towards forever wanting to see and taste their forbidden fruit? One woman was never enough for him. Was it the different taste and appearance of their forbidden fruit that drove his hunger and curiosity or something else? Aye, there's the rub. What was it? Perhaps, it's simply the excitement of the chase and the catch, Leonardo suggested. Once you have caught and

375

devoured your prey, maybe your Majesty still feels dissatisfied and unfulfilled because the need for another hunt and conquest lingers on? Your Majesty may need to satisfy his instinct and appetite for the thrill of the chase of new prey. Does the coy rejection produce more excitement than the easy submission?

No, it's more than just the chase to satisfy our appetite, said the king. It's also the peculiar physical interaction between the two different sexes that we enjoy, something that we do not have or feel for our mother, sister or for another man. What could that be?

Indeed, Leonardo had contemplated the same question many times in the past, but now he was unsure how to best answer his king. The birds do it, the bees do it, the dogs do it, the cats do it, all living creatures do it, even plants do it, for some species there is even the right season to do it, that is, to successfully procreate and regenerate the species. The offspring rarely procreate with their parents, although there are exceptions of course. Could he quote a text from the bible? Nothing came to mind. Instead, he said:

> … the art of procreation and the members employed therein are so repulsive, that if it were not for the beauty of the faces and the adornments of the actors and the pent-up impulse, nature would lose the human species.

You are a very wise person, Leonardo. Indeed, you are. We do find the Ladies of my court wonderful ornaments to look at and the best of companions in times of crisis and stress, although their fickleness does disturb us. Without any doubt, the three most pleasant things to look upon and admire in life are a beautiful woman, a fine horse, and a handsome hound.

After the king left us, Leonardo would say to me, be forewarned that this is your sex education on how not to behave so obsessively and promiscuously. His Majesty, the Most Christian King enjoys to subjugate his women to his power and wealth and to use them as his personal property and playthings. His women are only slightly more compliant to his power than the men, but he satisfies his fantasies and male prerogative by governing their actions and appearance. Their claim to autonomy and allure and what they withhold from him is what distracts him and drives his fantasies.

Everybody knew the king's way of life was highly self indulgent and promiscuous. It is written so:

> He rises at eleven o'clock, hears Mass, dines, spends two or three hours with his mother, then goes whoring or hunting, and finally wanders here and there throughout the night, so one can never have an audience with him by day.

The king's sister Marguerite also hinted at her brother's philandering in her 25th tale in *Heptameron*, '*Cunning contrivance of a young Prince to enjoy the wife of an advocate of Paris.*'

In 1518, Francois acquired the second of his great mistresses, Francoise de Foix, sister of Odet de Lautrec, governor of Milan. She was 23 years old and married to Jean de Laval, Sire de Chateaubriant. She was a large, strong, dark woman, demanding and promiscuous, and at the time sleeping with the king's friend Admiral Bonnivet. The king wanted her as his lover and was soon seducing her with increasingly richer gifts and filling her wardrobe and coffers with various privileges and estates. She couldn't resist. She quickly switched from her favourite Bonnivet to the more generous and richer King of France.

The whole court was obsessed with the subject of cuckoldry. Whose wife or mistress was sleeping with whom? The king felt secure in the faithfulness of his devoted wife Claude and laughed about the indiscretions and cuckoldry of his courtiers. Leonardo and I learnt much from the king's late night gossip about his ladies and lords and how the 'tomcats and bitches in heat' prowled the corridors of his castles and palaces at all hours of the day and night.

Indeed, Leonardo did know many women in his time in the courts of various powerful princes, and many of them did pursue him in his better days when he had all his dark long hair intact, his attractive handsomeness, his polite and gentle manners, his athleticism, and beautiful seductive voice. There were only six with whom he had fallen in love and with whom he had contemplated on having a long-term relationship; Selina, Ginevra de' Benci, Simonetta Vespucci, my widowed grandmother – Caterina Visconti, the widowed Isabella Aragon Sforza, and his servant and cook at Cloux, Maturina. However, in the end, because of his circumstances, and his love of and devotion to intellectual matters, and his pursuit of the sciences, and his many other investigative or commercial interests, he never settled down in the company of the fairer sex. Over the years, Leonardo tamed his own sexual hungers through his intellectual pursuits. From what I saw, he was like a monk, mostly absorbed in his studies, paintings, experiments, and architectural problems. I admired his restraint because he had many beautiful women constantly propositioning him. He seemed to have more fun talking to them, sketching and painting them than bedding them. Now as an old man, Leonardo no longer seemed interested in the pursuit of sexual genital bonding or the subject of cuckoldry, although he never lost his sight or interest in beauty and vitality, particularly for the young and the pretty, either men or women. There was no shortage of them in King Francois's court, and Leonardo and I, the King's Painter and his assistant, could stand in the corridors of palaces and chateaux or in the ladies' parlours or sit somewhere in a garden or courtyard on a bench at any time of the day and watch the beautiful people in their refined or garishly multicoloured outfits soaking in and exuding some element or property from the air, light, earth, rain or ether around us that permitted them to neglect our presence and chase their own solitary thoughts and business with little thought as to why they were really there caught up in their own underlying sadness and discontentment. Leonardo watched with melancholy at his own lost youth mirrored back at him by the young and pretty people who passed by him going to somewhere, unaware that their youth and beauty were fading fast. He could never stage a better parade or a masquerade of the youthful and beautiful energy that swirled about him on this very day in the land of King Francois, the First.

> A JEST. A sick man finding himself in *articulo mortis* heard a knock at the door, and asked one of his servants who was knocking. The servant went out, and answered that it was a woman calling herself Madonna Bona (madam Good). Then the sick man lifting his arms to Heaven thanked God with a loud voice, and told the servants that they were to let her come in at once, so that he might see one good (bona) woman before he died, since in all his life he had never yet seen one.

***

Leonardo told me the ways of a woman, explaining to me the hidden messages in his Codex Venus. Learn to cook, he said. Spend time in the kitchen with them. Smell and touch the food as if you are going to eat it raw. Pound and gnaw it in a way that you don't damage or bruise its vital essence. Treat all food like you would treat the woman that you love and treat your woman like your favourite food, for woman will sustain and nurture you in ways that a man never can. He pointed out to me the nodes and points of a woman's constancy and anatomy, telling me to never hurry in love and to always bring a woman down gently and patiently from her ecstasy, for then she can gradually regain control of herself in her own chosen time and achieve an ultimate satisfaction and confidence and a desire for your long term partnership in bed. Use your eyes, voice, mouth, touch, and breath sensibly, he told me. Stay awake so that she can signal to you when it is time for the two of you to relax, to sleep, and perchance to dream.

I have used Leonardo's lessons well with my beloved wife and eternal mistress. I am happy to announce to all that I am happily married with eight healthy children in my family. Each one of them I presented to my wife with the greatest ecstasy while we danced together in full and satisfactory union to the sound of angelic music in the warmth and comfort of our own bed. I am happy to say that I am not a philanderer and remain always faithful to my wife and children.

Fig. 119. Leonardo's painted sketch of a French lily. Serving perfection, light, and life.

It is foolhardy to think that so many biographers, rumour-mongers, and ignorant still label Leonardo and me as homosexual partners. As Salai would say, they have a great big itch in their poop hole. May they all burn in hell with Jacopo Saltarelli - the bum dancer, and his anal accusers for their envy, idiocy, ignorance, skulduggery, and spitefulness.

In my previous chapters, I already alluded to the many gallant women in Leonardo's Italian and French kitchen such as Valentina Visconti, Caterina da Vinci, Simonetta Vespucci, Ginevra de' Benci, Bona of Savoy, Lucia Marliani, Caterina Sforza-Riario, Anna Maria Sforza, Bianca Maria Sforza, Tommasina della Torre, Isabella of Aragon, Beatrice d' Este, Isabella d' Este, Sancha d'Aragona, Lucrezia Borgia, Cecilia Gallerani, Bona Sforza, Francoise de Foix, the Duchesses of Brittany, Louise of Savoy, Maturina, and Marie Gaudin. Here, I reflect on some of those Italian and French ladies who Leonardo and the French king enjoyed to ponder on during their evening fireside chats.

Leonardo loved the gallant ladies, but he had no time or desire for marriage:

Marriage is like putting your hand into a bag of snakes in the hope of pulling out an eel.

Selina

Mon Pere, said the king, my beloved sister Princess Marguerite told you the story about our first love, Francoise, the beautiful niece of our butler. We failed to seduce her, but rewarded her nevertheless with our gallantry. Tell us, you must still remember who your first love was? We would like to know.

Your Most Royal and Christian Majesty, I do remember. I was just a very young boy running wild in the fields of my grandfather's farm in Vinci. I knew nothing nor cared much about the smell, sound, feel, or sight of a girl's 'forbidden fruit', not until I met Selina. I remember her clearly to this very day with a great fondness, Your Majesty.

Selina was Leonardo's first French Italian connection way back in the days of his childhood in Vinci. She lived on a farm next to Leonardo and his grandparents and uncle Francesco. Her father was an Italian soldier and farmer. Her mother was French, small and beautiful, with large dollish blue eyes, and straw coloured hair. Her mother would call out to Selina by her French name Celine, but everybody else in Vinci called her Selina. Uncle Francesco told Leonardo that Selina's mother was a Celtic-Gaul, although most people thought that she was French-Italian.

Selina was a wild child – a few years older than Leonardo. Together, they explored the creeks and caves behind the farm and would strip off their clothes and wade and swim in the water. Leonardo received his first anatomy and sex lessons from Selina. She would sit on a wet rock beside the creek and show him her glistening private area between her legs. You can look and touch, Leonardo. Don't be shy. You are different to me. Come here and see where you are different. She would say, 'come here and see', like an army instructor, and she would show him what was missing between her legs. She would hold his penis until it hardened, and then say, when you grow up to be a man, Leo, you will put your cock inside me here where my finger is and after a lot of rubbing in and out you will squirt a goo inside me, and this goo will travel inside me to my tummy and grow into a baby. The baby will leave my tummy and out of my tunnel here between my legs. Here, Leo take my baby, and she would hand him her imaginary baby taken out from between her legs.

Holding her baby and rocking it in his arms, he would ask her, 'do you mean I just have to piss into your tunnel and you will make a baby?' Don't be so silly, Leo. When you are older you will grow hair on your balls, and your cock will become big and strong. When you want to make a baby with me your cock will stiffen and stick right up like the church tower of the Holy Cross, and you will push it inside my cave and rub it up and down until you release your sticky goo. When your cock is stiff and large like the rock that we are sitting on top of now, then you won't be able to piss because in your great excitement you will only be able to make a messy goo. Now, your cock is small and pretty and soft and smooth like a babies bottom, and you can only piss from it whenever your bladder is full, but it will change for the better when you are a big man.

How Selina knew these things when she was still so young, Leonardo did not know. He never saw her with a man or a boy other than her own father and an occasional field hand. Girls just seem to know about these things long before boys do. Will we become husband and wife, Selina? Leonardo asked her. Off course we will, Leo. You will go off to war, and when you return from fighting we will make many babies together. Selina was short and strong and her breasts were little buds protruding from her chest. I will feed you and my babies with milk from my breasts. When I am a woman, they will be large and full like my mother's and your mother's breasts. You will be very proud of my figure, Leonardo. How do you know these things, Selina? You are like a doctor. My mother told me. She said that my father made lots of goo inside her to make my baby brothers and me. He often walks around our house at night without his clothes on, and before the break of day I've seen his cock raised up to the roof. It is much, much bigger than your sweet little cock, Leonardo.

They would laugh and run off together along the creek, into a small cave or into the surrounding scrub. Sometimes, Leonardo would ask Selina to stand still and cast her shadow against a rock or tree, and he would trace or scratch around the edge of it with a piece of black charcoal, white lime stone or his sharp knife. He would have Selina's outlines spread all along the creek and say, instead of giving you babies, Selina, I have made many shaded copies of you. These are our babies that we can share together. Yes, Leo. Let's get dressed now and run home and eat some of your stepfather's pies that you have brought with you for my mother. Yes, Leonardo and Selina were only silly and innocent children in those days, and the dark and difficult tasks that lay ahead of them were still well beyond their imaginations.

Leonardo often thought long and hard about what she meant when she said that he would make his own sticky goo. He asked his uncle Francesco who confirmed to him that Selina was a good and accurate teacher about goo and babies. She's correct, Leonardo. You'll make your own goo when you grow hair on your balls. Leonardo found out soon enough that he could make his own goo long before he grew hair on his balls, and that his goo was a lot different to his piss.

Selina and Leonardo were good and intimate play friends for a few years. She would teach Leonardo French words and sentences that she had learnt from her mother. Together, they would pretend to be a Lord and a Lady in the French royal court. They would visit each other's houses and relatives in the area, and Leonardo was friendly with her father, mother, brothers, and grandparents. Selina's mother would speak French to Leonardo and Selina. This was to the great annoyance of her husband and her Italian grandparents who thought that French was far too primitive compared to their own expressive country dialect.

One day, almost overnight, Leonardo and Selina's relationship changed. Selina became very modest, always stayed fully dressed and stopped talking about babies. She attended church more often and began to wear a chain and cross around her neck that she would fidget with. They spent less time with each other, and Leonardo was less welcomed at her home. Eventually, they stopped playing together and would only share polite and short exchanges when they passed each other at church or on the street. Selina was 14 years old and had grown into a beautiful woman. She was betrothed and would only see or talk to Leonardo if she was chaperoned by other girls or family. Leonardo saw that Selina's breasts had grown large, and there was no more talk about babies or his penis. Leonardo missed the intimate and joyful company that she had provided him, and he now spent his time alone exploring the creek and fields talking French to himself as if he was a king playing among his shadow drawings of Selina.

When Leonardo was thirteen and Selina was fifteen, she left Vinci to be married to a rich suitor in Florence, a friend of her father's from his war years. There were no goodbyes between her and Leonardo, and he cried a little to lose the company of his best and most intimate friend in Vinci. He later wrote about a strange desire that he remembered that he had when wandering alone among the gloomy rocks of Vinci and coming across the entrance to a great mysterious cavern. I wondered if the strange desire and thoughts of the mysterious cavern was triggered by a memory of his childhood lessons from Selina.

> Unable to resist my eager desire and wanting to see the great ... of the various and strange shapes made by formative nature, and having wandered some distance among gloomy rocks, I came to the entrance of a great cavern, in front of which I stood some time, astonished and unaware of such a thing. Bending my back into an arch I rested my left hand on my knee and held my right hand over my down-cast and contracted eye brows: often bending first one way and then the other, to see whether I could discover anything inside, and this being forbidden by the deep darkness within, and after having remained there some time, two contrary emotions arose in me, fear and desire -- fear of the threatening dark cavern, desire to see whether there were any marvellous things within it.

Some of you may question whether I purposely have misinterpreted the proper context of the cave in jest because you already know that Leonardo had used the dark threatening cavern in his paintings as his main metaphor for images that he conceived with his brain and protected with his skull. So be it. *Que sera sera.*

This reminds me of another of Leonardo's jests.

> A man, seeing a woman ready to hold up the target for a jousting match, exclaimed, looking at the shield, and considering his spear: 'Alack! This is too small a workman for so great a business.'

Mary Boleyn and Diane de Poitiers

Two of the most beautiful of Queen Claude's ladies-in-waiting who caught Leonardo's eye were Mary Boleyn and Diane de Poitiers. Mary was English from Norfolk and Kent, whereas Diane was French from Saint-Vallier in Drome. Both took a great liking to Leonardo, and they would often visit him for quiet contemplation or conversation at Cloux. He was delighted by their charms and good looks. They were educated in the ways of young maids-of-honour to be accomplished in etiquette, dancing, singing, music, and embroidery, and in parlour and outdoor games. In addition, they were taught the skills of archery, riding, hunting, and falconry. Both could read, write, and perform arithmetic calculations and partake in discussions in the classics, history, and theology in their own and a number of other languages. Both were born in 1499, and they were 17 years of age when they first met Leonardo and me. I tried to act like their elder brother or cousin, and I thought wrongly that they were attracted to me.

Fig. 120. A portrait of Diane de Poitiers by Francois Cloux, son of Jean.

Mary Boleyn became King Francois's lover, and he called her my hackney who was fun to ride, possibly an unflattering description you might think. Later, when she returned to England in 1519, she became the lover of King Henry VIII, and her sister Anne became his second wife of the six who he would marry at one time or another. When Francois found out that Mary was sharing the bed of Henry VIII, he described her as 'a great slag, infamous above all.' Leonardo thought that she was rather sweet like a raisin cake with marzipan icing on top.

Diane de Poitiers had a fascinating history. She was married in 1515 at 15 years of age to Louis de Breze, a man 39 years her senior. They had two daughters. Louis uncovered a failed plot by her father against King Francois. After Louis's death in 1531, she became the Mistress of king Francois's son King Henri II. She was 20 years older than Henri II, providing him with wise counsel, and she looked much younger than her years by drinking copious amounts of gold solution. Although much older, she outlived Henri by 7 years.

The Paintings of the *Death of Lucretia* and Other Popular Heroines

When the French king was in Bologna to negotiate with Leo X in 1516, the Pope showed him a painting that he had in his possession of the *Death of Lucretia* painted by Il Sodomo (Giovanni Antonio Bazzi) in about 1513. The king was well educated by his mother and sister, and he knew well the story of the rape and suicide of Lucretia, the legendary heroine of ancient Rome, as told to us by the classical historians, Livy, Pliny, Suetonius, and Publius Cornelius Tacitus. Virtuous and married to the nobleman Lucius Tarquinius, Lucretia was raped by Sextus Tarquinius, the son of the tyrannical Etruscan king of Rome Tarquin. In her despair, she extracted an oath from her father and husband for vengeance against Sexus and the House of Tarquin, and then she committed suicide by stabbing herself. An enraged populace with Brutus leading the way drove the ruling Tarquin families out from Rome.

Lucretia's story of suicide to protect her virtue and depictions of her as a heroic victim have a long painting history with contributions from painters such as Botticelli (the *Story of Lucretia*, and the *Story of Virginia the Roman*), the Leonardeschi painters, Raphael, Titian, Durer, Palma Vecchio, and others. The Pope had paid a large sum for the painting by Il Sodomo, and he was not willing to part with it. King Francois asked Leonardo to provide him with a similar painting. Leonardo was reluctant to do so for he generally stayed away from this theme and preferred to paint his Madonnas as virgins or joyful mothers, as nurturers and not as the victims of lust or power. Instead, he asked his former student and assistant Marco d'Oggiono to provide the king with a painting of the *Death of Lucretia* and another about *Susanna and the Elders*. The story of the attempted rape of Susanna by the Elders is much different in theme to that of Lucretia because she lived, and her justice triumphed over evil. The other heroines depicted escaping from their tyranny by ritual suicide or murder were Virginia and Dido of Carthage. The theme of self-sacrifice by suicide did not appeal to Leonardo because he had too much love for life and the Madonna.

Fig. 121. Lucrezia's death *by Il Sodomo (left) and Marco d' Oggiono (right).*

Leda and the Swan

I already told you in a previous chapter (Fig. 89) about the legend of *Leda and the Swan*, her rape by the God of Gods Zeus and the phallic symbolism of the Swan. I will say that the copy of the painting of *Leda and the Swan* that Leonardo had painted for a previous governor of Milan Charles d' Amboise hung in my bedroom at the Cloux for three years before Salai and I sold it to the French king.

Isabella Aragon Sforza and Leonardo Painted Together as *Salome and the Head of John the Baptist*

A few years after the death of the sixth duke of Milan Gian Galeazzo Sforza in 1494, the duke's widow, the princess Isabella of Aragon, became an intimate of Leonardo. The artists, assistants, and pupils in his studio used them as their models in paintings of biblical stories and Roman mythology. Isabella and Leonardo became the favourite models for the Leonardeschi painters' depictions of them as *Salome and John the Baptist*. She was 27 years of age, and he was still handsome at the age of 45 years of age.

Here is the story of Salome and John the Baptist according to Mark 6:21-29,

> And when a convenient day was come that Herod on his birthday made a supper to his lords, high captains, and chief estates of Galilee; And when the daughter of the said Herodias came in, and danced, and pleased Herod and them that sat with him, the king

said unto the damsel, Ask of me whatsoever thou wilt, and I will give it thee. And he swore unto her, 'Whatsoever, thou shalt ask of me, I will give it thee, unto the half of my kingdom.' And she went forth, and said unto her mother, What shall I ask? And she said, The head of John the Baptist. And she came in straightway with haste unto the king, and asked, saying, I will that thou give me by and by in a charger the head of John the Baptist. And the king was exceedingly sorry; yet for his oath's sake, and for their sakes who sat with him, he would not reject her. And immediately the king sent an executioner, and commanded his head to be brought: and he went and beheaded him in the prison, and brought his head in a charger, and gave it to the damsel: and the damsel gave it to her mother. And when his disciples heard of it, they came and took up his corpse, and laid it in a tomb. [S41]

Fig. 122. Salome and the Head of St. John the Baptist *by Bernardino Luini, faithful pupil, admirer, and copier of Leonardo.*

The Leonardeschi painters, Giovanni Antonio Boltraffio, Bernardino Luini, Andrea Solari (Solario), Salai, Marco d'Oggiono, Giovanni Ambrogio de' Predis, Sebastiano del Piombo, Giampietrino (Giovanni Pietro Rizzoli), and Raphael all had their own versions of *Salome and John the Baptist*, but always with the head of John the Baptist presented to Salome in a charger (service plate). Salome is depicted usually as a pretty virginal whore.

Here, I show you copies of two of my favourites, both by Luini, and a third by Solari. Luini provides a good likeness of Leonardo when he was in his forties. No commentary is necessary. It is a visual experience. Andrea Solari followed suit to produce his interpretations of the *Salome and John the Baptist* theme. The one that I show you has captured the likeness of Leonardo quite well. The painters Bernardino Luini and Marco d'Oggiono both loved Leonardo and Isabella very much and they prepared many images of Christ, and Madonna and Child using Isabella as their Madonna or Magdalene, and idealised versions of Leonardo and/or Gian Galeazzo Sforza as Christ and/or Saint Sebastian. In some of Luini's paintings you will see the images of old men as drawn by Leonardo.

In the painting the *Conversion of the Magdalene from Vanity to Modesty* by Bernardino Luini, you can see my mother Tommasina della Torre as the angel Modesty converting Isabella as the Mary Magdalene from vanity to modesty (Fig. 67).

During the times of painting the series of *Salome and John the Baptist* in the Leonardo workshop at the Corte Vecchio in Milan, the beheading of Leonardo seemed an appropriate sentiment and symbol for him and his assistants to share together. Leonardo was not on the best of terms with the Milan ruler Ludovico il Moro Sforza. He, like his friend Isabella of Aragon, believed that Ludovico had murdered her husband, the previous duke of Milan Gian Galeazzo Sforza, Ludovico's nephew. Leonardo had depicted his suspicions to the public in his portrayal of Ludovico Sforza as the Judas in his painting of the *Last Supper* and as the evil black fly and assassin in the painting *Luca Pacioli and De Divina Proportione*. Also, he resented Ludovico for the way that he treated and imprisoned Isabella and her son Francesco at the Sforza Castle after the death of her husband Gian. On top of these particular resentments was the fact that Ludovico had not paid Leonardo and his assistants for all the works that they had completed during a year of many large contracts. In addition, Ludovico still had not officially recognised Leonardo's ownership of the vineyard that the previous duke Gian Galeazzo Sforza had given him and that was conveniently located outside the entrance of the Vercellina gate. If Ludovico suspected or found out about Leonardo's political satire and criticism of him, then Ludovico could easily have put his head on the chopping block for treason. Leonardo's political sarcasm was a dangerous game. Fortunately for Leonardo, Ludovico had a love and respect for Leonardo's grace, talents, genius, and temperament, and he never suspected that the maestro's paintings were openly criticising and exposing him as a murderer and a tyrant. The French, including king Francois, shared Leonardo and Isabella's belief that Ludovico il Moro Sforza was a treacherous and murderous tyrant, worthy of life imprisonment or death.

Princess Marguerite d' Angouleme, the Sister of the French King

Before completing my service with king Francois and returning to Milan, I finished, with assistance from Jean Clouet, my portrait of the king's sister Marguerite d' Angouleme. I portrayed her in the style of my own self-portrait, sitting and looking out at the viewer knowingly with a parrot on her hand. I believe I may have painted her bird (Fig. 124) a little better than the one in my self-portrait (Fig. 2). While she sat for me, I tried my best to seduce her, but she seemed to prefer other suitors and always spurned my generous offers. She was a year younger than me, and king Louis XII married her off to Charles IV of Alencon by decree in 1511. It was a marriage of political convenience, and they generally lived apart and had no children. Her husband was considered to be a laggard and a dolt until he died in 1525. Marguerite was remarried soon after to Henry II of Navarre, and she gave issue to a boy and a girl. I had little or no communications with her in her later years. She died in 1549 a few years after her brother.

Lady and the Unicorn

When Leonardo and I visited Paris for the coronation of Claude of Brittany as the Queen of France, we were fortunate to see the series of six beautiful tapestries that were woven in Flanders from wool and silk telling us the story of a noble lady with a unicorn and a lion, a symbol of chastity and conjugal fidelity. Antoine II Le Viste, an important member of the Royal court, sponsored the tapestries in 1500. Leonardo was so impressed by the tapestries that he began to sketch his own version of the *Lady and the Unicorn* that he planned to convert into a painting. His model again was Maturina sitting in the garden of the Chateau du Cloux. The painting was never started and therefore never completed. I showed Raphael the drawing that Leonardo had done of the *Lady with the Unicorn* when I returned to Milan after Leonardo's death. He copied it and then painted his own version.

Fig. 125. Leonardo's drawing of the Lady and the Unicorn (left), and Raphael's painting of the Lady and the Unicorn (right).

Fig. 126. Leonardo's sketch of the Last of the Unicorns Beside a Pool of Incontinence.

Leonardo had a story about intemperance and the unicorn that he liked to tell:

> The unicorn, through its intemperance and not knowing how to control itself, for the love it bears to fair maidens forgets its ferocity and wildness; and laying aside all fear it will go up to a seated damsel and go to sleep in her lap, and thus the hunters take it.

Flora

Flora was the goddess of flowers and represented the season of spring and fertility in Roman mythology. For the artists Botticelli and Leonardo and many of her other followers, she was the best symbol for nature, flowers, youth, and beauty. Her licentious, pleasure-seeking festival, the *Floralia*, was held for six days in Rome between April 28 and May 3, and it celebrated drinking, flowers, and renewal during the cycle of life. The festival was first instituted during the times of Christ, and the churchmen of Rome never had the courage to ban her from the cycle of Christian festivals that they oversaw as a tradition for their flocks of sheep, hares, and goats. It was a fun time and even the prostitutes participated by dancing naked and fighting in mock gladiatorial battles. Like most artists, Leonardo loved this festival when enacted with masquerades, mimes, and farces, and women were permitted to cavort half naked or wear outrageous, multicoloured costumes while the men decorated themselves with flowers and garlands. Leonardo encouraged the French king to introduce this festival into his kingdom, but his most Christian majesty told Leonardo that it was unnecessary to introduce such a festival into France because this kind of behaviour already occurred most days and nights of the year in his kingdom.

Fig. 127. My painting of Maturina as Flora, *with some assistance from Leonardo.*

The Festival of Flora and the Florianum temple honoured Flora, the most celebrated prostitute and courtesan that lived in the time of Emperor Galba (soon after Nero). She was the most engaging and successful courtesan who ever practiced harlotry in Rome, and being of excellent noble lineage, she only gave herself to the very best lords, kings, princes, pontiffs, dictators, and the like. She took no payments and declared that she, like all great ladies, only lived for love's sake, to pleasure her lovers and not for avarice. Moreover, it was said that she preferred the older, wiser, and tamer men over the younger, more vigorous, and stupid. She was renowned across the land for her beauty, her fair and gallant bearing and the large number of courtiers, lovers, and great lords that followed her as if they were her slaves. Even the ambassadors from foreign lands who received great pleasure and delight from her love and generosity extolled her virtues and amplified her legendary status across all the lands of the globe. When she died, she gave her wealth to the city of Rome and her people, and in thanks the emperor allowed the Roman men and women to participate in the most lascivious debauchery and licentiousness to celebrate the greatest whore who had ever lived. The more wanton and lecherous the behaviour, the greater was the honour to Flora at her Florianum temple. After hearing the whole story of Flora the harlot, the French King demanded that Leonardo organise the festival of Flora in his court for the very next spring. But, Leonardo became seriously ill in that particular spring, and he was unable to fulfil the King's wishes.

Leonardo's servant and companion, Maturina, was the model for my painting of *Flora*. I intended to present it to king Francois, but Leonardo suggested that we should keep it. King Francois saw it before it was completed, and he told Maturina that Leonardo used her as his muse because she looked like the young Isabella, Duchess of Bari, who had been his muse for many years in Milan. The king said he knew this because he saw the *Mona Lisa* and the other paintings of the princess Isabella including the one that was called *Columbina*.

Maturina's Black Cloak

The King asked Maturina if Leonardo ever made love to her. She admitted that most times he preferred to be her friend and companion and exchange stories about their different lives and relationships. Often they would kiss and caress each other with words of warmth and tenderness and enduring love.

Sometimes, he would become greatly inflamed with an uncontrolled passion and bring her to unimaginable physical and spiritual ecstasy, which would take her many hours to recover from and find her equilibrium and return to her duties and the kitchen. He never loved like a rampaging bull, it was with skill and knowledge that no other man who had her had ever possessed. His lovemaking was an unbelievable experience.

Other times, he would cloak her in his furs, a black cloak, and make gentle love and sketch her awake or asleep in his bed. He knows every part of my body and my responses and vulnerabilities better than I know or ever could imagine, she said. He found regions in me that I never knew I possessed, she told the king who now looked at her with a lecherous eye. He knew the right nooks and crannies, nodes and crevices to prod and caress. He wouldn't tell me how he knew about these regions. He would only say, I went to heaven, hell, and purgatory to find out. In return, I satisfied him the best I could. It is always easy to know when a man is satisfied. It is more mysterious and hidden with a woman. But, he knew every time that I reached the zone of no return. I could never fool him otherwise. He is sensitive to my needs. Sometimes, a woman has no need to be fully satisfied. She has other matters on her mind, and she doesn't want to enter heaven and meet her creator as tempting and attractive as that may be. He is a very special man. I am so grateful to your Majesty for allowing me to serve such a masterful man.

Yes, yes, Maturina. If we cannot have you then it is good that Our Papa has your very special love and beauty. Still, you must tell us another time some of his tricks so we can provide some unexpected magic for our own beloved Francoise, La Mye du Roi. Papa will just simply not indulge us on such matters telling us that each man must find his own way into a woman's heart. Yet, all our poetry and ardour goes to waste if we cannot unlock our sweet heart's glinting treasure.

Thank you, Your Highness. Master Leonardo tells me he is most satisfied and appreciative with the succulent fruits, vital vegetables, and fine spices in my garden. He is a fully committed vegetarian and is forever grateful to God for having finally been introduced to his most beautiful and magical garden, that is what he told me, Your Majesty. Maybe, you could better hone your gardening skills, Your Majesty?

Yes, yes, whatever. Still, it is a master like Papa who should be teaching us these skills instead of hiding them under his mysterious bushel. Still, we hope to have him home soon after his sojourn to Romorantin. I hear it did not all go well there. Much sickness, I believe.

Fig. 128. Leonardo's sketch of a happy Maturina.

Leonardo returned from Romorantin with a fever, and he needed rest and recovery for a number of weeks with Maturina's tender loving care. A few weeks before Leonardo's death, she told him that she was pregnant with his child, and soon after, he asked me to present Maturina with a copy of his painting of *Madonna and Infant* that we had stored safely away in our vault in Vaprio. Soon after Leonardo's death, Maturina was transferred to the king's household in Amboise where she gave birth to Leonardo's daughter Caterina. The king offered to provide Maturina with a chateau in the Loire, but she preferred to stay in the servant's household, live in her cave below the castle and help her sisters run the Tavern Salamander. Her daughter Caterina grew up a bastard just like her father. When the love child of Maturina and Leonardo reached the age of nineteen years, she married the court painter Francois Clouet, the son of Jean Clouet who painted the portrait of King Francois. I still remain in communication with Caterina who visited me in Vaprio only once. We spent a few months together addressing and collating Leonardo's notebooks before she returned to Amboise with my painting of Maturina as *Flora*.

Maturina asked Leonardo whether her facial appearance was similar to that of Isabella, the former duchess of Milan, who was now the Duchess of Bari.

Leonardo looked at her gently and smiled. Maturina, my love, it is extraordinary how much you do look like her, but you are younger, gentler, and less aggrieved with life. I hadn't noticed that before. How did you know about the Duchess? Did Francesco Melzi say something?

No Leonardo. It was the King. He said your portraits of me looked like the Duchess. He said, she was your muse and that you loved her very much. Is he right?

Maybe, he thinks my portrait of *Mona Lisa* looks like you. He must have noticed a similarity between it and Melzi's *Flora*. He will question me about it when I see him again. The painting of *Flora* is yours, Maturina. Please do not give it to the King. It may be best if Francesco Melzi takes it back with him to Lombardy when I give up my mortal soul here in Amboise.

What am I holding in the painting beside flowers, Leonardo?

You are holding my love and my soul, Maturina. Look after it for me, my love.

Maturina remained a court favourite of the King's until she entered a nunnery in 1531. When Leonardo's daughter Caterina was seventeen years old, she joined the court of Francois I's sister Marguerite de Navarre (died December, 1549) and then went on to live with the painter Francois Clouet as his wife. She became an avid art collector, specialising in Madonnas and infants.

A Woman's Body and Internal Organs

Leonardo studied the anatomy and the internal organs of many women including the genitalia, the reproductive system, and the foetus in the womb.

> Then three figures with the muscles and three with the skin, and their proper proportions; and three of woman, to illustrate the womb and the menstrual veins, which go to the breasts. And three you must have for the woman, in which there is much that is mysterious by reason of the womb and the foetus.

The king often looked at Leonardo's drawings of the female anatomy and discussed with him the true essence of a woman. One remarkable and specific anatomic drawing of the exposed cardiovascular system, and the principal internal organs of a woman drew particular attention. Leonardo had prepared this drawing (47.6 x 332.2 cm) in 1509 in black and red chalk, ink, and yellow wash before he undertook his detailed anatomic dissections of a woman's womb. He never explained to the king that in this particular drawing the organs of the womb were based on those of the uterus of a gravid cow that he had dissected prior to undertaking dissections on the corpse of a woman with the help of professor Marcantonio della Torre in 1511 to 1512.

Although the king and Leonardo gave much thought to the true essence of a woman, I believe that they never reached an agreeable conclusion.

> Take a poet who describes the beauty of a lady to her lover and a painter who represents her and you will see to which nature guides the enamoured critic. Certainly the proof should be allowed to rest on the verdict of experience.

And in regard to Leonardo's book of anatomy, he wrote the following:

This work must begin with the conception of man, and describe the nature of the womb and how the foetus lives in it, up to what stage it resides there, and in what way it quickens into life and feeds. Also its growth and what intervals there are between one stage of growth and another. What it is that forces it out from the body of the mother, and for what reasons it sometimes comes out of the mother's womb before the due time.

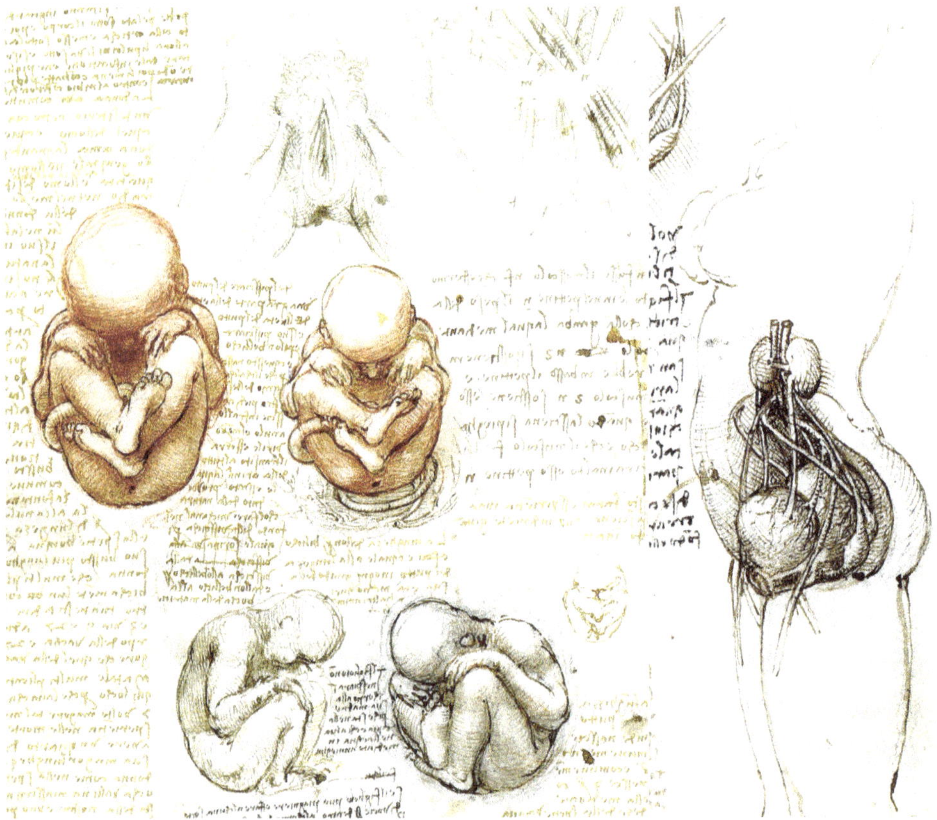

Fig. 129. Leonardo's drawings of foetal positions in the womb and the female reproductive organs shown in profile.

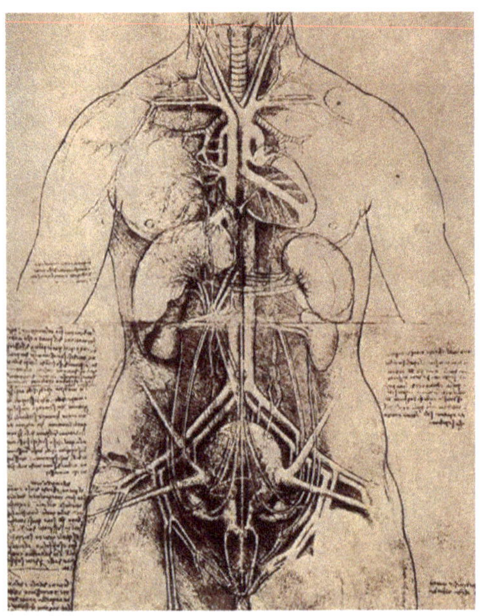

Fig. 130. Leonardo's drawing of the internal organs of a woman showing her with the uterus of a cow.

Leonardo was my godfather, and he treated Salai and me as his sons. I know that he had his own children with noble women out of wedlock, and that he was not recognised to be their father because the nobility at that time considered his social rank too low and unacceptable. Leonardo was a wanderer, a travelling emissary, and an explorer of the arts and sciences, and he had no time to settle with any one lover, wife or family. His life was often unpredictable and left to the fates to lead him wherever his inquiring mind took him. The women who engaged him with physical love knew he was unlikely to remain in their divine presence for long, and that he would soon be seduced by the sciences and his love for Nature and

390

her mysterious ways, and her beautiful and complex forms and forces. He copied down on a folio some memorable words about love by the Roman encyclopaedist Aulus Cornelius Celus:

> The lover is drawn by the thing loved, as the sense is by that which it perceives, and it unites with it, and they become one and the same thing. The work is the first thing born of the union; if the thing that is loved be base, the lover becomes base. When the thing taken into union is in harmony with that which receives it, there follow rejoicing and pleasure and satisfaction. When the lover is united to that which is loved it finds rest there; when the burden is laid down there it finds rest. The thing is known with our intellect.

Isabella d' Este's Fashion Poupee, and the French King's Living Dolls [S42]

One night, king Francois entered Leonardo's reception room carrying a small doll (poupee) in his arms. He placed it upright on a bureau and asked Leonardo if he recognised whose dress the doll was wearing. Leonardo examined the doll briefly and told His Majesty that it was dressed in the fashion of Isabella d' Este, the Marchesa of Mantua. Correct, said the king. The Marchesa sent us samples of her dresses so we can dress our ladies in her style.

The king greatly admired Isabella d' Este's sartorial elegance that flaunted her power and wealth, and she was regarded as Europe's leading fashion expert. He wanted to achieve some of her sartorial style for himself and his country by displaying his court ladies as the most fashionable mannequins in Europe and achieve supremacy over the Italians. But, first, he had to convert the tired French medieval fashions to at least the same level as the Italian stylish ones. The problem was that many of the noble ladies of Italy including Isabella d' Este were secretive about their styles and sartorial inventions in order to maintain an advantage over their competitors. The solution was to have her son Fredrico request her fashion secrets from her on behalf of the king.

Her son Fredrico Gonzaga visited the French king in Milan in 1515 as a 15-year-old to pay homage to the king soon after his unexpected victory at the Battle of Marignano. The king convinced Fredrico to return with him to France as an insurance policy to stop his father from raising troops against them in favour of his alliance with the Pope, Maximilian, the Spanish, or others who might have had their eyes on the Duchy of Milan. Fredrico Gonzaga wrote to his mother on behalf of the Most Christian king to send to him, *'a doll dressed in the fashions of her shirts, sleeves, undergarments, outer garments, dresses, headdresses, and hairstyles …, for he intends to have some of these garments made to give to the women in France.'* The marchesa sent the doll to the king and an accompanying letter that warned him that she was protecting her trademark appearance: *To satisfy the wish of His Most Christian Majesty, we will gladly have a doll made and dressed in all the fashions we wear on our body and on our head, although his Majesty will not see anything new, for the styles we wear are equally worn in Milan by the Milanese ladies.'*

The king held the young Fredrico Gonzaga hostage in France until 1517, and Leonardo and I met him briefly at Fontainebleau and another time in Blois. Leonardo was not a fan of Isabella d' Este because he considered her arrogant, pushy, and devious, and that she flaunted her wealth beyond all good taste and civility. He told the king nothing of his personal thoughts about her in case the king viewed his poor opinion of Isabella d' Este as a criticism of him. Leonardo sensed that the king had brought him Isabella's doll almost as a fetish that he had something of marchesa's personality and essence in his possession, if not the actual body of the woman of his desire. The doll itself was made of cloth and wire frames to support the outfit and a wooden base for it to stand upright on. Without clothing on the body of the doll, one had to have a very fertile imagination to see anything of it that might resemble the marchesa of Mantua. Fashion dolls were usually exchanged between the ladies of the different courts and not between a lady and a foreign king. The women wanted to see the garments and the overall wardrobe designs and feel the texture and shape of the material and not that of the body of the doll.

A few months after Leonardo had seen Isabella's fashion doll, he constructed a beautifully dressed mechanical doll in an Isabella d' Este's headdress and cape of ochre-coloured linen and silk brocade. The doll's head was exquisitely constructed with lovely hooded eyes, strong cheekbones, and an alluring female smile. The internal mechanism enabled the doll to play the lyre and move in time with the music. It was the same size as Isabella d' Este's doll that allowed an exchange of garments. This charming mechanical figure stayed in the possession of the king and his favourite mistresses to the day I left France.

Francois wanted to mould his female courtiers in the image of Isabella d' Este and her fashion doll provided them with her essence. He wanted the polished manners, the intellectual pursuits, and the sexual allure that he heard had prevailed in Mantua. This was a powerful diplomatic weapon that he believed would attract important and influential visitors to his court. Francois coveted feminine beauty in all its forms, and he collected his mistresses like he acquired paintings, sculptures, and other art objects of his desire. The king was generous to his ladies, and he spent large sums of money on their wardrobes and personally selected what they wore right until the day he died. The women in his court were his living fashion dolls who served to display his wealth, good taste, personal desire, and his control over them. He dressed them up, showed them off, and amused himself with them in private. His sister Marguerite de Navarre wrote this about him in her *Heptameron*:

> … a child, depending on his age, loves apples, pears, dolls, and other little things, the most his eye can take in, and perceives wealth as the act of accumulating little pebbles, but as he grows older, he loves living dolls and accumulates the possessions necessary for human life.

I saw his power over his court ladies first hand one night only a few months before I left his service. He had the presence of hundreds of ladies in his court that he forever attended to as his playthings. On this night, he sat five of his male companions and me in the dark behind a lattice screen at the end of a well-lit corridor. We could look out, but it was difficult for anybody looking in from the corridor to see us. He handed us pen and paper and told us that we would gain an excellent view of 12 pieces of his most exquisite artworks, and that we would have to rate each of his items from 1 to 12 ranging from best to worst. We were instructed that we would have a viewing time of five minutes, and that we were not to talk, cough, or make any other noise. He then left us and returned with 12 of his most beautiful courtesans. He instructed them to stand in a line in front of our lattice screen and lift their dresses and underskirts to above their waists and spread their legs wide apart thereby partially exposing their private parts to our view. After a minute or so, he commanded them to turn around and bend over and spread their legs in order for them to expose to our view the totality of their private parts from the rear. I heard a collective gasp, and the breathing behind the lattice suddenly become intense with shock and awe. The temperature of my own body burned a degree or more above normal. I could not believe that this naked act of staged voyeurism and objectification of vulnerable female bodies, twelve in all, was happening in front of me. After a few minutes, the king clapped his hands and commanded his twelve ladies to stand upright and drop their underskirts and dresses and recover their modesty. He then escorted them out from the corridor. I could not understand the purpose of this provocative and unrequested spectacle. None of us had asked for it, and we were all totally surprised by the callousness of what we saw. We were shown the private parts of twelve of his most beautiful court ladies, and before I could regain the control of my senses and thoughts, they were all taken from our view and from any further consideration. I had no specific memory of what I saw and wrote down my ratings as a set of random numbers down the page between one and twelve. This was a blatant display of the king's power over the lords and ladies of his court. They were his possessions, his playthings, and he could strip them of their clothes and dignity whenever and wherever he liked and reveal the private parts of his possessions to his playmates hidden behind a lattice screen. I looked forward to returning to Milan, and I wondered about the sanity of the king who was by then only 28 years of age.

CHAPTER 27

Fireside Royal Chats. Politics, War, Health, and Envy

Science is the observation of things possible, whether present or past; prescience is the knowledge of things, which may come to pass, though but slowly.
It is also good every so often to go away and relax a little for when you come back to your work your judgment will be better, since to remain constantly at work causes you to deceive yourself.

— Leonardo da Vinci

The Amboise Routine

When the king was in Amboise, he led a life of extravagant pleasure. His routine was to rise late between ten and eleven o'clock in the morning, hear Mass, dine for an hour or two in the company of a few of his favourites, have a book read to him for an hour, and then spend another hour or two mainly with his mother or occasionally with his wife. For the remainder of the day, he would go whoring, hunting or play games such as bowls or tennis. After sunset, he would wander about here and there throughout the night or visit Leonardo's kitchen at the Chateau du Cloux for a fireside chat with the maestro in the company of good wine and a few evening snacks.

In contrast to the king, Leonardo liked to rise early, at daybreak, and immediately write some notes and sketch a few ideas before having a bowl of soup and a pigeon omelette. The remainder of the day depended on the previous day's plans or on the occasional whim that suddenly superseded all previous plans and needs. When in Amboise, the young monarch paid Leonardo almost daily visits for the sheer pleasure of conversing with him. At night, the king would take the underground passage that linked the Château with the Royal Castle. Leonardo da Vinci was held in the king's most ardent affection and inspired his deepest, filial esteem.

Although we all knew that we should never discuss the King's temperament, edicts, sexual activity, politics or religion in His Highness's company that was exactly what the king liked to discuss with Leonardo during their fireside chats. The king addressed Leonardo as 'Mon Père' or simply 'Papa', and he never tired of listening to him explaining the subtleties of his philosophy of living forms and his opinions on art, architecture, war, nature, and the divine. This included all manner of subjects such as beauty and proportion, the turbulence of water and air, the formation of rocks and mountains, the origins of fossils and life, and the brain structures that are the seat of the soul and that form the human will. The king also enjoyed telling Leonardo and me about his own life and especially his conquests in love and war.

The King Reflects on War and His Conquest of Milan

All animals are at war with each other. If they're not hunting each other then they're hunting for plants. It's the nature of all living things to hunt and eat for their own survival. Papa, we are constantly at war. It's in our nature. We're forever oscillating between fear and hope. We're forever fearful for our lives, the lives of our family, our tribe, our city, and our country. We need to go to war and to kill to defend our families and our country. We expand our surrounding territories as far as we can to wherever the outer perimeter becomes our first line of defence against invasions. This outer perimeter then becomes permanently ingrained into our normal territory that we need to defend. And so, it is no longer just an outer perimeter. We then need to find and establish a new outer perimeter, and so it goes. We'll stay in Purgatory until we can free ourselves of all of our earthly attachments and bad habits. We will never find peace until we are at the end of our earthly lives, and we are in Heaven with God the Father, God the Son, and God the Holy Ghost, and then we are completely free of our earthly attachments. If we're successful, we will go through the eye of the needle into Heaven, but if we fail, we will tumble into Hell with our attachments and obsessions still intact and forever to be tortured by them. Of course, you know all of this through your Florentine poet Dante who expressed our thoughts so much better than we ever could. But, let me tell you about our war to win back Lombardy with which you may not be familiar, but which we know much about, because it was our first great successful war.

Leonardo had heard the king's arguments about war many times before. He also had seen war during his own lifetime, having participated for Milan in the War of Ferrara (the Salt War) in 1482 to 1484, and then when he served Cesare Borgia and his campaigns in Romagna and Marche. But, Leonardo had to agree with his French king because he was a political realist and realised that the sovereignty of nations, fiefs, kingdoms, and republics forever change depending on the nature of their leaders, governments, dictators, and citizens, and the desires of those near and far who wished to expand on their own possessions and territories and interests. It is like the plants that occupy the different mountains, lakes, rivers, valleys, and fields. They are forever competing, changing, and adapting to different locales depending on the condition and relative wealth of the environment that can or cannot sustain them. And, so it is with humanity and its leadership and its territories. Did not the Romans expand their tentacles from Rome to most territories around the Mediterranean Sea, including Armenia, Babylonia, Judaea, Egyptus, Africa, Hispania, and Gallia, and beyond, as far north west as Britannia and to the south eastern reaches of the Red Sea? Did not the nomadic Mongols expand their reach from the steppes of Central Asia to the inner doors of the Holy Roman Empire and east across all of China to the very edge of the ocean? These and other empires expanded, devoured, and then contracted into a memory of past glories. Yes, this is the nature of man, always dominated by primitive instincts and hunger, unable to be contained by good reason or peace, forever oscillating backwards and forwards like crashing waves on the foreshore of greed, and forever in search for an unfulfilled mystical need to test the doors of death.

The king enjoyed telling Leonardo tales of his war adventures and hunting experiences. Of course, Leonardo had his own adventures of war and hunting that in his old age he neither liked to remember nor wanted to talk about. Nevertheless, he listened to the king with interest and especially to the history of his heroic win over Maximilian Sforza and the Swiss confederation that together were ruling the Duchy of Milan. Soon after his anointment as the fifty-seventh King of France by the Archbishop on the 25th January 1515, Francois brandished the sword of Charlemagne and assumed the title of Duke of Milan. He claimed that he would recapture his rightful territory of the Duchy of Milan in the immortal memory of Valentina Visconti, for his Valois ancestors and for his Kingdom, and the memory of the victories that were won previously by the French kings in Italy. The king was reclaiming his rightful inheritance, and Milan and Italy were at the centre of the civilized world and therefore a great prize for any young and ambitious king who wanted to leave his mark on the world stage. Within months, the Venetians were his allies because they needed his aid against serious attacks from Spain, the Swiss, and the Pope's men.

Before too long, Francois had gathered together 30,000 men. They were a collection of all sorts; 2,500 paid cavalry men from the companies of French soldiers who could still dress in full armour with sword and lance; his body guard of 1,000 noblemen and gentlemen pensioners; 5,000 archers including those from Scotland; and a light cavalry of 1,500 *stradiots* from the Balkans. The foot soldiers consisted of 10,000 Germans wielding Swiss pikes and

carrying matchlock arquebuses, and there were another 10,000 French, half of them from
Gascon and the Basque countries. Then there were 70 great cannons and 300 smaller types
that were rapid reloading and fired shot and exploding cannon balls instead of stones. These
cannon were caste of heavy bronze and pulled along by horses.

The king and his army also had
marshals who were already highly
experienced from previous wars in
Italy during the times of Charles
VIII and Louis XII, and they knew
the lie of the land and the strategies
and tactics of their enemy. There
was Lautrec, la Tremouille, la Palice,
Bayard, and Count Pedro de
Navarro. More importantly, there
was General Gian Giacomo
Trivulzio who warned the king not
to take the usual crossing through
the Alps where he likely would be
ambushed by the Swiss and the
Italians. Instead, Trivulzio suggested
a more southerly route across the
Alps that usually was not taken by
travellers and was more the terrain
of the local shepherds and hunters.

Francois, a king for only six
months, left France in the custody of
his mother Louise, and he embarked from Lyon on the 31st of July to accompany his army,
horses, foot soldiers, guns, munitions, and food supplies across the Alps to Italy. His main
enemy was the Swiss who waited for him at the Alpine passes of Mont-Cenis and Mont-
Genevre. However, the French king heeded the warning of Trivulzio and took a different pass
already prepared for him by Pedro de Navarro with paths, roads, and bridges to smooth the
movements of the carts, wagons, and horses. Nevertheless, the pass they had chosen was
difficult and dangerous and not without incident. The king wrote to his mother in mid August:

> Madame, we are in the strangest country that any man of this company has ever seen.
> But, tomorrow I hope to be in the plain of Piedmont with the troops I command, which
> will please us all as it is troublesome wearing armour in these mountains because most of
> the time we have to go on foot and lead our horses by the bridle. Those who do not see
> it will not believe that anyone could bring over the horsemen and heavy artillery in the
> way we are doing. Certainly, Madame, it has not been without difficulty; if I had not
> come, our heavy guns would have stayed behind. [S43]

The uncomfortable march dragged out over six days before the army reached the relative
safety and stability of the Saluzzo plains on the Lombardian side of the Alps. The crossing by
Francois was hailed as one of the most heroic marches in military history comparable to the

achievement of Hannibal's crossing with his elephants during the ancient days of Carthaginian glory against the Roman Empire.

I listened with awe at the king's descriptions of his army's skirmishes with Italian and Swiss troops on their way to Milan and then their twenty days of negotiations before the start of the battle of Marignano. By September the 8th, the king bribed half of the Swiss army (12,000 men) to return to their homes after signing the treaty at Galarate. The remainder swore that they and Duke Maximilian Sforza would surprise and defeat the king at Marignano. Although the king was not expecting them, he had sufficient defences set up at Marignano and received enough warning from an advanced guard of the approaching enemy to hurriedly prepare for the attack. The king gave us a blow-by-blow account of the ensuing two-day battle sometimes enacting out the fighting. On Friday the 14th September, the second day of the battle, the Venetian light horse and infantry of 12,000 men under the command of Bartolomeo de Alviano arrived to save the king from danger of defeat. After two or three hours of further fighting, the surviving Swiss and Italians retreated to inside the walls of Milan. Next day, the defeated Swiss left Milan and retreated to their Alpine and lakeside valleys. Maximilian Sforza, the former Duke of Milan, realised that without the Swiss to assist him, he had no hope of defeating the French king and his troops, and therefore he accepted the terms of surrender that were offered to him. He could never again claim the Duchy of Milan, and for that he received an indemnity of 30,000 ducats, and annual pension of 36,000 crowns, and a palatial residence in France where he stayed until his death at the age of 37 years in 1530.

The king stayed with the Carthusian monks at the Charterhouse in Pavia until the completion of the surrender. When he received word that the final surrender was accepted and signed, he rode in splendour through the southern gates of Milan with sword in hand on the 16th of October 1515. Dressed in blue velvet, decorated with the golden *fleur-de-lis*, he rode tall at the head of his men-in-arms to the Cathedral to give thanks to God. Over the next few days, king Francois celebrated with the usual feasting, festivals, jousting, and dancing for the citizens of Milan seemed genuinely pleased to have the French king as their new Duke and Ruler. They were pleased to be rid of the Swiss.

Leonardo told us that since he first visited Milan in 1480, there had been at least five leadership coups with accompanying changes in ownerships, taxes, and laws that were difficult for the stability of the city and its citizens. How easy was it for the king to rule Milan from the Loire Valley where it was almost impossible to gauge the mood of the people and their needs? The king's reply was that he trusted his appointed proxies, and that he was ready to send troops to help them if so required. However, Leonardo and I already knew from our friends' letters and visitors from Milan that there was much unhappiness with the corrupt and insensitive French rulers and their overly high taxes.

Sensing a new conflict approaching, Leonardo suggested to the king that his authority and position allowed him to follow the path of peace and diplomacy rather than that of war and conflict. But, if he ever got into serious trouble with his English or European enemies then he should form an alliance with the Sultan of Turkey for his enemies would surely be afraid of an invasion from the Turks and think again about creating any further mischief. This was good advice that assisted the French king a number of times after Leonardo was gone.

Years later, I read the following in Leonardo's notebooks:

> Of the Cruelty of Man. Animals will be seen on the earth who will always be fighting against each other with the greatest loss and frequent deaths on each side. And there will be no end to their malignity; by their strong limbs we shall see a great portion of the trees of the vast forests laid low throughout the universe; and, when they are filled with food the satisfaction of their desires will be to deal death and grief and labour and wars and fury to every living thing; and from their immoderate pride they will desire to rise towards heaven, but the too great weight of their limbs will keep them down. Nothing

will remain on earth, or under the earth or in the waters, which will not be persecuted, disturbed, and spoiled, and those of one country removed into another. And their bodies will become the sepulchre and means of transit of all they have killed. O Earth! why dost thou not open and engulf them in the fissures of thy vast abyss and caverns, and no longer display in the sight of heaven such a cruel and horrible monster.

The King of Beasts. Thou hast described him king of animals, but I would rather say, king of beasts, thou being the greatest—for hast thou not slain them in order that they may give thee their children to glut thy greed with which thou hast striven to make a sepulchre [tomb] for all animals? And I would say still more if I might speak the whole truth. But let us confine ourselves to human matters, relating one supreme infamy, which is not to be found among the animals of the earth; because among these you will not find animals who eat their young, except when they are utterly foolish (and there are few indeed of such among them), and this occurs only among the beasts of prey, such as the lions, and leopards, panthers, lynxes, cats and the like, which sometimes feed on their young; but thou, besides thy children, dost devour thy father, thy mother, thy brother, and thy friends; and not satisfied with this, thou goest forth to hunt on the islands of others, seizing other men and these half naked ... thou fattenest and chasest them down thy own throat. Now does not nature produce enough vegetables for thee to satisfy thyself? And if thou art not content with vegetables, canst thou not by a mixture of them make infinite compounds as Platina wrote, and other writers on food?

Of Catching Lice. And many will be hunters of animals, which, the fewer there are the more will be taken; and conversely, the more there are, the fewer will be taken.

French Platters

The banquets and dinners presented to the king and his attending courtiers were immensely large usually incorporating much wild game and birds from their hunts and fish from their ponds and rivers. Vegetables were an occasional delight more often used for decoration rather than as a food to eat. Herbs and spices depended on the kitchen and the particular tastes of the lords and ladies.

The king would bring game with him from his hunts in the woods and give it to Maturina and Battista to prepare venison, boars, rabbit, bear, vixen, antelope, etc., for his chats with Leonardo. On the other hand, Leonardo was a vegetarian who liked to eat small portions often rather than to sit down for hours filling himself up on heavy fats and meats. Often, Leonardo's own table was as sparse as the one that he painted in his *Last Supper of Jesus* where he had mostly bread rolls, vegetables, fishes, and occasionally, for his meat eating guests, a succulent and juicy sacrificial lamb. Although bird eggs were on his table, the carcasses of birds were rarely there. Leonardo prepared fiddly little platters like snails, cucumber and anchovy biscuits, artichokes, celery, and frog legs in sauces, and soups like minestrone and bouillabaisse, and these things were presented to the French King at their fireside chats where drinking red wine and cognac prevailed. Soups and pasta were Leonardo's favourite foods and minestrone was his preferred vegetable soup with croutons or pasta ears. Here is his recipe for minestrone:

Pasta or rice, two cups of prewashed cannelloni beans, rind of a good cheese, strips of chard, 3 zucchini, chopped carrots (2), diced celery (4 stalks), chopped onions, chopped potatoes if available, salt, garlic cloves, basil, oregano, black pepper, and vegetable bouillon. Saute the garlic, onions, celery, and carrots in olive oil or lard. Add all the other vegetables, pepper and salt, and add a cup of bouillon, and stir gently and frequently. Pour extra bouillon as required. Simmer for 3 hours or until all ingredients merge and are flavoursome in the mouth. Add the beans and pasta (or rice) and simmer for ten minutes before serving. Garnish with basil or oregano and serve with freshly baked bread and a glass of fine wine. Bon appetit.

Leonardo's favourite cookbook was the treatise on Italian gastronomy entitled *On Honourable Pleasure and Health* by Platina (also known as Bartolomeo Platina or Bartolomeo Sacchi). He was given a copy of it by my great grandfather Giovanni Melzi. The book contained, among others, the recipes of the legendary chef Maestro Martino de' Rossi who cooked for Popes and Cardinals. Leonardo enjoyed taking recipes from this book and helping Battista and Maturina prepare meals for the French king when he visited for their fireside chats. Sometimes, to relax the king, Leonardo would charge the meal with a sprinkling of hemp (cannabis) or poppy seeds.

> Hemp seed pottage: Take a *libra* of hemp seeds. Clean well and boil in a pot until they begin to open; and then take a *libra* of white, well-ground almonds, and add to seeds; grind well and add some bread and add to the pea broth made of vegetables, with or without meat for the king.

We introduced the French king to tagliatelle, a pasta dish of long, flat ribbons similar to fettucinne that is made of egg and flour (one egg per 100 g of flour). It was a favourite of Salai, and he made the best sauces and soffritto (mirepoix) that greatly pleased Leonardo. He made the vegetarian version with chopped onion, celery and carrot roasted or sautéed with lard or olive oil for Leonardo, and he added chopped braised meats (beef, veal, pork, bird) for everybody else.

In winter, Leonardo liked to feed the king his minestrone soup saying it was good for his stomach and temperament especially as 'a pick me up' tonic after a long day of lavish banquets. They enjoyed talking about food and the processes of digestion according to Galen's concept of bodily humours and their classification ranging from hot to cold and moist to dry. Most foods should be moderately warm and moist, finely chopped, grounded, pounded, and strained to achieve a good mixture of the ingredients. Colours dominate this classification. For example, egg yolks are warm and moist whereas the whites are cold and moist. Red wine is warmer than white. Leonardo had his own beliefs about food and the ingredients and how they affected our humours. He readily shared them with the king who in return presented Leonardo with a 1486 published edition of the *Le Viandier de Taillevent* with 272 medieval recipes collected around the period of 1320 to 1350 by Guillaume Tirel. '*This is what really good French cooking is, Mon Pere,*' said the king.

Leonardo's Health and Hygiene Advice for the King of France

> Make them give you the diagnosis and treatment for the case from the saint and from the other and you will see that men are elected to be doctors for diseases they do not know.
> To keep in health this rule is wise: Eat only when you want and sup light.
> Chew well, and let what you take be well cooked and simple.
> He who takes medicine is ill advised.
> Beware of anger and avoid grievous moods.
> Keep standing when you rise from table.
> Do not sleep at midday.
> Let your wine be mixed (with water), take little at a time, not between meals and not on an empty stomach.
> Go regularly to stool.
> If you take exercise, let it be light.
> Do not be with the belly upwards, or the head lowered; be covered well at night.
> Rest your head and keep your mind cheerful.
> Shun wantonness, and pay attention to diet.
> It seems to me that coarse men of bad habits and little power of reason do not deserve so fine an instrument or so great a variety of mechanism as those endowed with

ideas and great reasoning power, but merely a sack where food is received and whence it passes. For in truth they cannot be reckoned otherwise than as a passage for food, because it does not seem to me that they have anything in common with the human race except voice and shape. And all else is far below the level of beasts.

If nature has ordained that animals which can move should experience pain in order to conserve those parts which through their motion might diminish or waste; plants are not able to move and therefore do not strike against any objects placed in their way; the feeling of pain is not required in plants and therefore they do not feel pain when they are broken, as animals do.

Lust is the cause of generation, appetite is the support of life, fear or timidity is the prolongation of life, and fraud the preservation of its instruments.

He who fears dangers does not perish by them.

Just as courage imperils life, fear protects it.

Fear arises sooner than anything else.

Every man wishes to make money to give to the doctors, destroyers of life; they therefore ought to be rich.

Learn to preserve your health; and in this you will the better succeed as you shun physicians because their drugs are a kind of alchemy about which there are no fewer books than there are medicines.

Medicine is the restoration of discordant elements; sickness is the discord of the elements infused into the living body.

We are deceived by promises and deluded by time, and death derides our cares; life's anxieties are nought.

That man is extremely foolish who always is in want for fear of wanting; and his life flies away while he is still hoping to enjoy the good things, which he has acquired with great labour.

He who possesses most is most afraid to lose.

O Time, consumer of all things! O envious age, thou destroyest all things and devourest all things with the hard teeth of the years little by little, in slow death. Helen, when she looked in her mirror and saw the withered wrinkles which old age had made in her face wept and wondered why she had twice been carried away. O Time, consumer of all things! O envious age, whereby all things are consumed!

In youth acquire that which may restore the damage of old age; and if you are mindful that old age has wisdom for its food, you will so exert yourself in youth, that your old age will not lack sustenance.

To the ambitious, whom neither the boon of life, nor the beauty of the world suffice to content, it comes as penance that life with them is squandered, and that they possess neither the benefits nor the beauty of the world.

As a day well spent brings happy sleep, so a life well used brings happy death.

Every evil leaves a sorrow in the memory, except the supreme evil, death, which destroys this memory together with life.

Wrongfully do men lament the flight of time, accusing it of being too swift, and not perceiving that its period is sufficient. But good memory wherewith nature has endowed us causes everything long past to seem present.

The *Last Supper* and Portrayal of Lord Ludovico Sforza as Judas the Betrayer

On his arrival into the city of Milan in 1515, the French king was taken to the refectory of the Convent of Santa Maria delle Grazie to see Leonardo's painting of the *Last Supper of Jesus and His Disciples*. He was mesmerised by the brilliance and elegance of its execution. He wanted to meet with the painter and was disappointed that Leonardo da Vinci was in Rome with Pope Leo X. He immediately dispatched emissaries to the Pope in Rome requesting that His Holiness bring Leonardo with him to their scheduled meeting in Bologna. Later on, the French king instructed his engineers to dismantle the painting from the wall of the Convent and transport it to Fontainebleau. His engineers told him that it would be impossible to accomplish moving the wall without destroying the entire painting. So, I must remain the Duke of Milan for as long as God is willing, replied the King. And now, the King had Leonardo in Amboise preparing him supper and talking about the painting and its underlying secret meaning.

Leonardo told the French king that when he was commissioned by Ludovico Sforza to paint the *Last Supper,* his heart and mind were not ready for it. He felt that Ludovico had cruelly betrayed the Duke of Milan Gian and his Duchess Isabella, and that it hurt him bitterly to think about it. It was while pondering the suffering of Isabella and the demise of Gian that Leonardo had his inspiration on how he would represent Jesus and his apostles in the *Last Supper.* He would set the supper in Milan and paint Gian as the young apostle John (Gian), Ludovico as the betrayer Judas, and himself as Jesus, the illuminator. Thus, the *Last Supper* was born politically and was ready to be painted. Yet, Leonardo knew that this painting would be an enormous risk to his own life, more than anything he had ever painted before. It was to be a highly treasonous image, for if Ludovico recognised what Leonardo's painting was really about then Leonardo would be turned into a dead goose. Ludovico would make him suffer even more than he had made Gian suffer near the end of his life.

So, there it was. He would paint the apostle John as the young, illuminous, and beautiful Gian Galeazzo Sforza. Gian was a man of only 25 years of age when he was betrayed and killed by Ludovico and his henchmen. On the other hand, Ludovico IL Moro Sforza would be portrayed as the dark and swarthy betrayer Judas. The people of Milan would see it there before their eyes – the history of Ludovico Sforza as the betrayer of the Duchy of Milan. But, would they recognise it as so? Would they say anything if they did recognise the sacrilegious coded message beneath the obvious depiction of the *Last Supper of Jesus with his Apostles?* It was going to be a dangerous and treacherous path to take to paint the *Last Supper* as Leonardo saw it in the refectory of the Santa Maria delle Grazie to be permanently housed before the supporters of Ludovico Sforza and before his master who he was accusing of treason, betrayal, and murder.

***

In the first year of my commission in the refectory of the Monastery of Santa Maria delle Grazie, I stood and stared at the wall for many hours over many days, looking at the shapes and hidden shadows within the deteriorating plaster to find the best natural design for the end of the room. It must have been like this for hours, for days; because the friars would interrupt me in between their lauds (morning prayers) and vespers (evening prayers), are you all right, maestro? You have been here all day. Would you like a drink, or something to eat, maestro?

No, nothing brothers, I am looking for the essence of the last supper. Bring me some essence.

It was like this throughout the first year and most of the second year as I watched the light change the shape and shading of the shadows, cracks, and stains on the plaster of the refectory wall during different times of the day and the night as the picture slowly unfolded in my mind. First, I saw a brightly illuminated dove hovering with its wings spread out across the wall as if I was seeing the Holy Trinity. There were two adjoining circles on each of the dove's wings with a triangle inside the circle. Then, I saw a table in the shape of a horizontal rectangle below the dove. The design was simple, the hovering dove immediately told me what the *Last Supper* was about, and it was like my last supper during my time in the Sforza Duchy of Milan. Here, your Majesty, I will show you my geometrical design as it evolved.

Leonardo immediately sketched the dove with outstretched wings across a horizontal sheet of paper. He then added a rectangle below the bird and drew two circles in the space of each of the bird's wings. Within each of the circles he drew a triangle.

You see. So easy, so compelling. Now let me show you this pattern on Cesco's copy of the *Last Supper of Jesus with His Disciples.*

I handed Leonardo my copy of the painting on a rolled up canvas. He unrolled it and spread it out putting a heavy object at each end to stop the canvas from rolling up. The King looked over the copy saying, it's a marvel, Papa, but I can't quite see this dove and circles that you've drawn on the paper.

Easy to see, My Most Honourable and Christian Majesty.

Leonardo grabbed a pool of thread from the cabinet, cut an outstretched length into different sizes. He looped the longest piece of the thread into the shape of the dove with wings out-stretched across the painting. The thread was looped to outline and enclose Jesus and most of the disciples. It looked exactly how he had sketched the dove for the King. With the short pieces of threads, he placed four separate circles around each of the three disciples within the area of the spread out wings.

You see. Before I placed a line or any paint on the wall, I already had in my mind the outline of the dove and the four circles above the table. Then, it was easy to fill in the spaces within the circles, the bird and its wings, the table and the other free spaces to give the picture its proper perspective. A smiling Leonardo moved his outstretched hands and fingers across the painting as if he was the gesturing Jesus in the painting.

The King looked at the painting and then at Leonardo, and said, you truly are a genius and a magician Papa, a maestro without any rival to contend with. Isn't this so, count Francesco?

Of course, Your Majesty, I agreed, taking a slight bow before looking across at Leonardo for he obviously wanted to continue with his exposition while we looked at the rolled out copy of the *Last Supper of Jesus.*

Now that I had my design, I saw the story in two different eras, one during the time of Jesus and the other during my time in Milan. Of course most viewers would look at my painting and see the story of the Last Supper of Jesus and His Disciples, and the Holy Eucharist. They will see Christ announcing his betrayal by one of his twelve disciples. Some viewers would immediately identify Judas at the table as the dark, swarthy one with a bag of silver pieces in one hand and the other hand greedily reaching out for a bread roll on the table. Some will see that each of the disciples are organised in groups of three, and that they are further divided into four groups of three. The more mathematically inclined will recognise a geometric pattern and then think of the holy trinity, but four holy trinities and not one. Those who knew their gospels, such as the friars of Santa Maria delle Grazie, told me that each of the four groups cleverly represented the four synoptic gospels told to us by Mark, Matthew, Luke, and John about Jesus at the Last Supper, or according to Paul the Apostle's description of Jesus's Last Supper in the First Epistle to the Corinthians: *The Lord Jesus on the night when he was betrayed took bread, and when he had given thanks, he broke it, and said, This is my body which is for you. Do this in remembrance of me.* Many who saw the painting told me, this scene depicts Luke from 22:20-23 where after the supper Jesus took his cup of wine and said, *this cup is the new covenant in my blood, which is poured out for you. But the hand of him who is going to betray me is with mine on the table. The Son of Man will go as it has been decreed. But woe to that man who betrays him!* The disciples began to question among themselves which of them might be the betrayer. As you can see in the painting, the disciples do react with disbelief and suspicion to the words of Jesus and some already begin to question among themselves their own worthiness before the eyes of God. This is to be human, and Dante depicted beautifully how to be divine in his *Divine Comedy.*

The King nodded his head and said, your story is pictorial, and we can interpret only what we see in your painting and not in your words.

Your Most Illustrious Royal Majesty, you are correct as always. I am but a poor illustrator of the words from the bible. And so it was that some friars, monks, and clergy could relate the figures to certain apostles as I had intended them to be. So, your Majesty, from right to left of

Jesus in the painting, please meet Bartholomew, James Minor, and Andrew in group one; Judas, Peter, and John in group two to the right of Jesus. On the other side of Jesus, please meet Thomas, James Major, and Phillip in group three, and Matthew, Thaddeus, and Simon the Zealot in group four. They are all pleased to give you their blessings, as well as to receive your blessings, your Majesty.

Leonardo bowed respectively on behalf of himself and the twelve Apostles.

Thank you, Papa, but they talked to us already at the Santa Maria delle Grazie about serving and blessing their most recent Majesty king of France and Duke of Milan. What we want to hear is the other level, the secret and personal level that you may have only hinted at in the painting.

Your Majesty! As you decree. After first seeing the dove of the Holy Spirit on the refectory wall, I had a new revelation. I saw myself on the wall as Christ the illuminator at the Santa Maria delle Grazie in Milan. It was a frightening vision. The invisible dove on the wall revealed the truth to me about Duke Ludovico Il Moro as my model for the betrayer. The Duke had betrayed my trust and his nephew's trust. He had poisoned his nephew, murdered his brother, and possibly had his sights set on harming Gian Galeazzo's son the young Francesco, count of Pavia, who was then barely 4 years old and the legitimate hereditary Duke of Milan. I saw the end of the feast on the wall as natural as any supper, the natural supper that the monks and their visitors would see when they entered the refectory to dine. I saw many of Lord Ludovico's betrayals. It happened like a holy revelation, the Eucharist entered me like the bread and wine at the last supper, the Spirit and the Holy Ghost, the dove hovering over the Duchy of Milan. It revealed to me how Ludovico's suppers could sustain the few, but harm the many. I saw what was on the table before Christ and myself and my loved ones. A new war was looming, and I believed your uncle King Louis XII would be involved.

You mean the *Last Supper* is a painting about Duke Ludovico Sforza who in 1508 died a prisoner in my uncle Louis's dungeon at Loches? asked the incredulous young King.

Yes, your Majesty. His Lordship, the Duke Ludovico Sforza is Judas. He looks back towards Gian Galeazzo Sforza and Jesus and out through the windows of the wall behind Jesus at what he covets most, Lake Como and the Alps of Lombardy, two of my symbols for the Duchy of Milan. For many days, I returned to Santa Maria delle Grazie to stare at the refectory wall and through my imaginary windows to see what I could see. I became highly disturbed and excited about what I saw. I wanted to set the *Last Supper of Jesus* in Milan. How can I depict Judas as Duke Ludovico Sforza without him and his apostles recognising the betrayal and lunacy in my work? I stared and stared at the wall for a few hours of each day for months contemplating the true and dangerous purpose of my picture. The monks and the Prior were becoming more and more agitated by my inaction to draw and paint while I considered the wisdom of what I was about to paint on their wall. They were concerned about my mental state and constantly questioning me about my intent. When will you start to work on our wall? They began accusing me of procrastination and other unmentionable sins.

The wall was large in size (460 x 880 cm or 15 x 29 feet). I saw the painting in my mind's eye. I knew what I was going to do. I had no fear of procrastination. My fear was that I would be accused of being a traitor for mocking our illustrious new Duke of Milan, His Lordship Ludovico IL Moro.

I had the picture fully planned now. I would put the table as a horizontal rectangle across the centre of the wall, well above the floor of the refectory. Christ and his disciples would be behind the table facing out and above me as I approached the wall. The disciples would be divided into two halves, one half on either side of Christ, enveloped by wings, spread out from Christ standing radiantly at the centre like a dove, the Holy Spirit, ready to dispense his wisdom to his complacent and inattentive disciples.

When we saw your painting, Papa, one of the friars told us that Jesus is the Sun shining his light onto his disciples with his illuminosity.

Yes, Your Most Gracious Majesty, that is so. You can say that Jesus is the Sun with his apostles revolving around him in God's solar system of enlightenment. I have placed Christ's betrayer on the left side of the picture, but positioned him within reach of Christ's right side. The position of Judas is a break from tradition, possibly even sacrilegiously. Other painters and illustrators always isolated Judas well away from Christ and the other apostles, whereas I intended to place him close to Christ and close to Gian Galeazzo Sforza. Cesco, come here and show His Majesty some of the paintings of the *Last Supper* by other artists.

I slowly flicked through the folio to show the king some copies of the other paintings and the position of Judas. Jesus is always in the centre surrounded by his apostles in a U shaped table. Judas is always isolated lurking somewhere in the periphery and the shadows or seated on the opposite side of the table.

So, your Majesty, Ludovico, that is Judas, he is on the right side of Jesus in my painting, next to his father Francesco, and his nephew Gian is beside me, Leonardo as Christ. As you know, your Majesty, Ludovico poisoned his nephew Gian and was conspiratorial in the assassination of his brother Galeazzo Sforza. Hence, you see Judas's right hand with his bag of silver coins knocking over and spilling the saltshaker, the instrument of his poison. The knife sticking out of Judas's right side is the instrument of Galeazzo's murder. The knife in the unidentified hand sticks out from Judas's side as if it was illusional and not his own hand for Ludovico used other agents and conspirators for his murders. Francesco Sforza points the knife in his hand at Ludovico's three co-conspirators who are responsible for his son (Galeazzo's) and grandson's (Gian's) murder.

The king stood up looking a little confused. But, Leonardo, the dagger is pointing towards the apostles Bartholomew, James Minor, and Andrew. Why is that?

A good observation, said Leonardo. Why point the dagger towards Bartholomew, James Minor, and into the belly of Andrew? Drama. It looks threatening. Tradition tells us that Bartholomew and James were both beheaded. Bartholomew was flayed, skinned alive, and beheaded somewhere in Armenia or the Caspian Sea. James the younger was put to the sword and beheaded by Herod Agrippa King of the Jews during the King's persecution of the Christian church. Andrew was spread eagled, stabbed in the guts, and crucified like our Lord, but at Patras in Achaia.

But, if Judas is Ludovico Sforza then at whom is he pointing his knife? Who is he threatening to harm or kill? My God, exclaimed the King, in genuine horror. He threatens King Charles the VIII of France and his two Italian Generals, Gian Giacomo Trivulzio and Galeazzo Sanseverino (Galeas de Saint-Servin). Is that correct, Leonardo?

He threatens whoever you want them to be, Your Majesty. For me, the hand of Ludovico (Judas the betrayer with the knife) threatens Gian Galeazzo Sforza's relatives from the kingdom of Naples, that is, the three kings of Naples, Ferdinand I, Ferdinand II, and Alfonso II. To the left of Jesus is a group of three representing Charles VIII the former King of France, Charles II the Duke of Savoy, and Maximilian I the Holy Roman Emperor. The group at the far end are the Florentines, Lorenzo de' Medici and my father and uncle who are asking me why did I leave Florence to go to Milan to serve the tyrant Ludovico, who you knew could not be trusted or to keep his word. But, if you like, the groups of three are vacillating or oscillating circles within triangles of the many whom Ludovico betrayed or threatened during his life in Milan.

Who else did Ludovico betray who could be put into any of the places of the betrayed disciples? They could be his wife Beatrice, his father in law the Duke of Este, the Marchioness of Mantua, the Bona of Savoy, the Duke of Montpensier, Roberto Sanseverino, Ferrante d' Este, Cicco Simonetta, and Gian Giacomo Trivulzio, just to name a few. Of course, the

Ludovico Sforza supporters say that I am too harsh and too quick to condemn him, and that he really had not betrayed anybody, and that he was a great ruler of the Duchy of Milan. If you are one of these great Ludovico supporters, then Leonardo, King Francois I, and I totally disagree with you.

Did Ludovico ever suspect that you modelled him as Judas in the painting that he probably saw every day of his life when he went for prayers and contemplation at the Monastery of Santa Maria delle Grazie?

He may have heard rumours, Your Majesty. But I suspect he remained ignorant of the underlying message. Judas was the last figure I painted on the wall. There was great speculation about who that might be. The Prior of the monastery Vincenzo Bendelli wrote to the Duke Ludovico at Easter of 1496 complaining that I was procrastinating and allowing my servants and followers to consume all his food and drink from their cellars and starving his poor Friars. Such arrogance. I saw the letter. I told my Lord Ludovico that I needed the food and drink for my models to properly depict the scene of the last supper, and that I would use the features of the prior for Judas Iscariot. My Lord the Duke laughed and warned me to start to put some marks upon the wall immediately or there would be trouble. In the end, the Prior looked different to Judas.

The features of Judas at the table were the last that I needed to draw on the wall. All the others were there – Jesus and eleven of his twelve apostles were there for all to see. But, only one was missing. Where was Judas? I said I was still looking for my model. I knew it was Ludovico – but how could I portrait him without him knowing and offending him? My solution was to make him dark like Il Moro, but disguise him with a swarthy beard. I wanted to protect myself from the dangerous accusations that Judas looked too much like Ludovico. Soon, I heard rumours that I had found a vicious looking man for my model of Judas. He was a condemned Jew sitting in the Milanese prison with the features of Judas, a dark swarthy man with an unkempt black beard covering a part of his face. I did not deny the rumours.

Finally, when you finished your painting in 1497, what did Ludovico think of it?

The day after I had added my final touches to Judas, Ludovico arrived to view the finished painting. Gian Galeazzo Sforza's widow Lady Isabella Aragon Sforza accompanied my Lord Ludovico. He was still in mourning because only a few months previously his beloved wife Beatrice d' Este the Duchess of Milan had died while giving childbirth. He was distraught for months and only now had allowed himself to be seen in public accompanied by Lady Isabella. They both stood and stared in awe at the beauty of my painting, looking for Judas among the 13 moving figures before them. I manoeuvred myself slightly in front of Ludovico to watch his expressions, to see whether he had recognised himself as Judas the betrayer. I saw the look of awe in the Duke's expression, yet nothing suggested anger. However, I noticed that Lady Isabella's expression had momentarily registered the look of surprise and horror when Ludovico suddenly said, look at Judas, you could recognise him anywhere. Lady Isabella, slightly aghast, looked at Judas and then at me wondering if I had done the unthinkable and portrayed Judas the betrayer as her villainous uncle who had murdered her husband and taken away the Duchy of Milan away from her and her son Francesco, the former Little Duke of Milan. Lady Isabella's beautiful eyes looked away from me and back to the painting on the wall when Ludovico said, he's brilliant, Leonardo. You've portrayed Judas well as the thieving, murderous Jew that he is. Although Judas hanged himself, we will do the favour ourselves to hang that other condemned Jew in our cell. Brilliant, Leonardo. Brilliant. Tell me again who the various apostles are in your picture. Do I recognise any of them? I told the Duke and Lady Isabella the names of each of the apostles in their four groups of three and how you could recognise each of them.

You've excelled yourself, Leonardo, said Ludovico. After all the troubles and accusations of procrastination, the brothers and the Prior have nothing to complain about any more, do they?

They have the best religious painting that has ever been done by anybody anywhere in Italy. They can all thank you and now complete your payments, and you can get on with your other commissions for our rooms, and the portrait of my beloved Princess Beatrice and me and my sons on the opposing wall to the *Last Supper*. And, of course, you can now go ahead and finally complete your Francesco Sforza monument. Surely, it must be ready for its completion. Come, Princess Isabella, let us move closer to the wall and scrutinised the maestro's amazing new painting. Lady Isabella looked at me and gave a wide smile, well done, Maestro. You have given Our Saviour Jesus a beautiful and extraordinary setting. Our Saviour shines out through the wall with great forgiveness in spite of our difficult circumstances and the impending worries ahead of us. With that she and the Duke turned and walked past me to take a closer look at the *Last Supper* glistening with bright, fresh colour, and great meaning on the wall.

To Leonardo's immense surprise nobody seemed to make any connection between the image of Judas and Ludovico. The accepted story to this very day is that an imprisoned Jew condemned to hang was the model for Judas. I had even heard from a number of 'false' witnesses that the condemned Jew met with Leonardo prior to his hanging, and he begged him to intercede on his behalf. Leonardo ignored him saying, I do not know who you are. The condemned man replied, I'm your model, Judas, condemned to die. Leonardo denied ever having met with the condemned Jew.

Fig. 132. A copy of Leonardo da Vinci's painting of the Last Supper.

And so, over the years, the *Last Supper of Jesus* was stared at, admired, and copied by many artists and painters, yet few ever dared to make the connection between Gian as John and Ludovico as Judas in the Duchy of Milan. The hand signs provide additional clues to the identities of the Sforza. Please look carefully. Gian Galeazzo Sforza clasps his hands together, which is the zodiac of a Gemini, his birth sign. Ludovico Sforza is a Leo as indicated by his hands and fingers. The fingers of one hand grasp tightly to his bag of thirty pieces of silver while the other hand is like a claw with his fingers stretching out to grab at a bread roll. Francesco Sforza is on the cusp of Leo and Cancer, one hand holds a dagger the other points in the opposite direction. Leonardo is an Aries, the principal sign of Fire and Enlightment, fiery, headstrong, and opinionated, whereas Jesus is a Pisces with the Element of Water, loving, forgiving, and compassionate. Aries (fire) and Pisces (water) are direct opposites and that is why you see the figure of Leonardo/Jesus dressed in red (fire) and blue (water) with the palm of one hand turned down (the sun, shining its light down onto the earth, the table) and the other turned up (reflection, meditation and evaporation, spreading the element of water through the air).

I already told you in an earlier chapter that Nicola Mangone of Caravaggio painted Leonardo's version of the *Last Supper* in a cycle of frescoes at the church of Saint Maria Annunziata of Abbiategrasso. This was commissioned in 1516 in remembrance of the young duke Gian Galeazzo Sforza who had been born in Abbiategrasso on the banks of the Naviglio Grande. Salai assisted Nicola Mangone of Caravaggio with the painting. Gian Galeazzo Sforza is clearly represented by his green and red colours leaning on the left shoulder of Jesus (or Leonardo if you are a Leonardeschi). Again, Ludovico is portrayed as the dark, swarthy face of Judas the betrayer. Thus, there is a secret society of painters that know the coded story of Leonardo's painting of the *Last Supper,* and they continue to keep it alive as I do by telling you the true story. Sadly, Leonardo's painting is deteriorating badly on the wall of the Santa Maria delle Grazie, and his followers including me have made many copies in an attempt to safeguard the image the best that we can.

Fig. 133. A detail within Leonardo's sketch of the Last Supper *of the sixth duke of Milan Gian Galeazzo Sforza (slumped on the table with his arms in the form of a diagonal cross), Ludovico Sforza as Judas sits on a stool with his extended finger pointed at Gian Galeazzo as if he has shot him with a hand held cannon.*

Leonardo's notes on the *Last Supper* describing the movements of the twelve disciples caught in a moment in time:

One who was in the act of drinking leaves his glass in its place, and turns his head towards the speaker. Another, twisting the fingers of his hands together, turns with stern brows to his companions. Another, with his hands spread out, shows their palms, and shrugs his shoulders towards his ears; his mouth expresses amazement. Another speaks in the ear of his neighbour, and he, as he listens to him, turns towards him, lending him his ear, while he holds a knife in one hand and a piece of bread in the other, half cut through by the knife. Another, in turning with a knife in his hand, has upset a glass on the table. Another lays his hands on the table and looks fixedly. Another puffs out his cheeks, his mouth full. Another leans forward to see the speaker, shading his eyes with his hand. Another draws back behind him who is leaning forward and sees the speaker between the wall and the man who is leaning forward.

It was the twilight hour when the King finished his stories about his uncle Louis XII and the imprisonment and death of Ludovico. The cocks were crowing and horses braying before sunrise. The king rolled up the *Last Supper* and was accompanied by Battista and me through the tunnel back to his chambers in the castle where his mistress Marie Gaudin was waiting for him to wake her and make morning love with a sumptuous breakfast rather than a last supper on his mind.

Maturina accompanied Leonardo to his bedchamber and left him there, alone, in the company of his own ghosts and thoughts of his friends in the *Last Supper,* while she returned to the kitchen to wait for Battista and me. With our return she gave us warm and spicy mulled wine, and she retired to her own bedchamber for a few hours sleep before waking to take on her tasks for the day, still tired, but with a smile on her beautiful face, for she had just heard amazing stories and secrets that she knew were highly privileged, and that nobody else would know about, except her, Battista, Leonardo, me, and the King, and … well …, possibly, her sister and her cat Melody would find out one day.

Gran Cavello. **Leonardo's Colossal Horse**

Birds squat and partially spread their wings in preparation for a take off. Then, they extend them fully upwards and pull them down as they jump up on take off.

To land they spread their wings like a parachute and extend their legs forward to decelerate. Their flapping easily counters the effects of drag and the pull of the earth on their body. They can glide, but if they don't extend their wings, they will drop to the ground like falling stones. Watch them my dear, watch them land and take off above the statue of my horse because they'll teach you how to dance in the sky.

Apart from the *Last Supper of Jesus*, Leonardo's artistry is probably best known for his monumental horse that was destroyed and never caste in bronze. Vasari wrote in his biography of Leonardo da Vinci that,

> …Leonardo proposed to the Duke that he should make a huge equestrian statue in bronze as a memorial to his father; then he started and carried the work forward on such a scale that it was impossible to finish it. There have even been some to say (men's opinions are so various and, often enough, so envious and spiteful) that Leonardo had no intention of finishing it when he started. This was because it was so large that it proved an insoluble problem to cast it in one piece; and one can realise why, the outcome being what it was, many came to the conclusion that they did, seeing that so many of his works remained unfinished.

Michelangelo also mocked Leonardo for not knowing how to caste his giant clay structure. But, Leonardo knew perfectly well how to caste the horse, and he had artisans like Tommaso to help him succeed. The problem was that immediately after the death of duke Gian Galeazzo Sforza, his uncle Ludovico Sforza shipped the bronze for Leonardo's horse down the river Po to his father-in-law Ercole I in Ferrara to be made into a cannon. This was one of the many reasons that Leonardo had grown to disrespect and resent Ludovico Sforza. The giant model of the clay horse was finished and ready to be caste a year before the death of Gian Sforza. The people of Milan saw the model when it was exhibited at the Piazza del Castello before and after the occasion of the marriage of Bianca Maria Sforza to the Emperor Maximilian in November of 1493. It stood twenty-three feet high and weighed nearly 80 tons. After Gian's death in October of 1494, the large amount of bronze acquired by him to caste the horse was given away by Ludovico to his brother-in-law and it was never again made available for Leonardo to complete his big project. Gian was his friend and ally, but Ludovico was his stumbling block if not a direct enemy. The clay model stood neglected and exposed to wind and weather in the castle square and later at Leonardo's vineyard outside the gates of Porta Vercellina between the monasteries of San Vittore and Santa Maria delle Grazie, until the French invasion of 1499 when the French archers used the model as target practice and damaged it beyond repair. Leonardo never saw it again and nobody dared to say that Ludovico Sforza and the French destroyed Leonardo's colossal horse before it could be caste in bronze for posterity. But, those who saw the unfinished clay statue marvelled at its grandeur and beauty, and his reputation as a brilliant sculptor was quickly spread and established throughout Italy and Europe. But, one thing that was rarely mentioned was that the horse never had a rider, the intended rider Francesco Sforza seemed to have been forgotten in favour of just the horse.

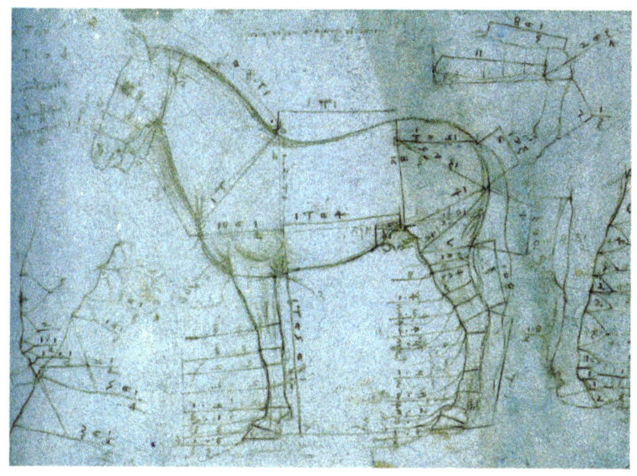

One cold night, Leonardo told the king the history of his horse the *Gran Cavello* while they shared in an ample amount of warmed wine.

When I visited Milan for the second time, it was 1482. I was there on behalf of Lorenzo de' Medici to thank the young duke of Milan Gian Galeazzo Sforza and his uncle Ludovico Sforza the Duke of Bari for their support during his crisis with Pope Sixtus IV. I befriended the young duke and began to give him music lessons. He wanted to play the fiddle, and de' Predis and I used him as our model of the angel musicians for the panels accompanying the *Virgin of the Rocks*. It was at this time that he encouraged me to apply for a position of fortification engineer for the Sforza court. Knowing that I had assisted Verrocchio with his construction of various equine monuments in Florence, he told me about his and his uncle's plan to construct an equine monument to honour his grandfather, the first Sforza to become the Duke of Milan. He helped me write out the following item to add to my application to his Lordship Ludovico Sforza, Governor of Milan:

> Item: I can carry out sculpture in marble, bronze or clay, and also in painting whatever may be done, and as well as any other, be he whom he may. Again, the bronze horse may be taken in hand, which is to be to the immortal glory and eternal honour of the prince your father of happy memory, and of the illustrious house of Sforza.

Although I wasn't appointed as Chief Advisor on Fortifications and Master of Entertainments and Festivities to the Sforza court until my birthday in 1488, I already had began to prepare drawings and small clay models and sculptures of my intended memorial horse in 1483. We finally settled on a plan for a giant horse, measuring 12 braccia (24 feet) in height from the nape to the flat ground. No sculpture of this size had ever been attempted before. I completed the sculpture of the giant horse by the end of 1493 and revealed it for all to see outside the cathedral workshop in Milan for the wedding festivities of the young duke's sister Bianca Maria Sforza to the Emperor Maximilian in November.

I was ready to cast the bronze horse with the assistance of Tommaso Masini da Peretola (Zoroastro) towards the end of 1494. At first, I thought I would cast it in a pit on its side, but then we decided to do it upside down. I had the hoists, braces, and pit built and was ready to do the moulding and casting in a few separate stages. I needed half a boatload of plaster and 100 tons of bronze. The young duke Gian Galeazzo Sforza had secured the bronze for me, and I was in the process of building the four furnaces I needed to liquefy the bronze and the pit to hold the mould. I planned to do the casting in one day. But, as you know, it was never cast. The duke of Milan Gian Galeazzo Sforza died in October, and one month later his uncle Ludovico sent the bronze that had been set aside for me to his brother-in-law in Ferrara to build a giant cannon and one or other smaller sister cannons in preparation for their war against the French. His Lordship Ludovico Sforza had betrayed me, and the wonderful memory of his father and his nephew.

The king nodded. Yes, I remember when Ludovico Sforza was paraded manacled in chains and riding backwards on a mule through Lyons when many in the crowd jeered and accused him of killing his nephew, the Duke Gian Galeazzo Sforza.

Balestrieri Guasconi summed up the tragedy of the Sforza Memorial Horse when he said:

> Leonardo had laboured for sixteen continuous years on the construction of a colossal statue. But the ignorance and negligence of some who by failing to acknowledge virtue show that they do not value it, allowed it to be shamefully ruined, for I remember - and I cannot speak of it without grief and indignation - so noble and masterly a work made a target for the Gascon bowmen.

After the young duke told him about his desire to have a monument constructed in the memory of his grandfather, Leonardo did write a method for his indirect casting in 1485, ten years before he was ready to caste the Sforza equestrian monument:

> You should touch the plaster, which will be sufficiently cool and thick, and pour what remains into the mould filling it with plaster and then take apart the mould and push the rods through piercing the wax and plaster; and then re-clean the wax using your method; after which place it in a wooden box and form over it a plaster mould leaving vents and a mouth for pouring; through that mouth, turning the form upside down when it is red hot, the wax contained inside can exit, and the vacuum it leaves behind can be filled with your molten material, and the casting will be hollow. But to avoid the disintegration of the plaster during reheating, put inside it that you know.
>
> THE MOULD FOR THE HORSE. Make the horse on legs of iron, strong and well set on a good foundation; then grease it and cover it with a coating, leaving each coat to dry thoroughly layer by layer; and this will thicken it by the breadth of three fingers. Now fix and bind it with iron as may be necessary. Moreover take off the mould and then make the thickness. Then fill the mould by degrees and make it good throughout; encircle and bind it with its irons and bake it inside where it has to touch the bronze.
>
> OF MAKING THE MOULD IN PIECES. Draw upon the horse, when finished, all the pieces of the mould with which you wish to cover the horse, and in laying on the clay cut it in every piece, so that when the mould is finished you can take it off, and then recompose it in its former position with its joins, by the countersigns. The square blocks _a b_ will be between the cover and the core, that is in the hollow where the melted bronze is to be; and these square blocks of bronze will support the intervals between the mould and the cover at an equal distance, and for this reason these squares are of great importance. The clay should be mixed with sand. Take wax, to return [what is not used] and to pay for what is used. Dry it in layers. Make the outside mould of plaster, to save time in drying and the expense in wood; and with this plaster enclose the irons [props] both outside and inside to a thickness of two fingers; make terra cotta. And this mould can be made in one day; half a boatload of plaster will serve you.

I left copies of these and other notes on the construction of the mould for Leonardo's horse in the hands of the king in case he ever wished to construct an equestrian monument to himself or to one of his forebears. Although Leonardo always intended to place a statue of Francesco Sforza on top of the horse, he never left any notes on how he would do this.

The Unspeakable Accusation Against Leonardo

Mon Pere, we recently received a letter from Michelangelo, again, graciously declining our invitation to join us here in the Loire. He says he cannot join us while you are here. He has accused you of being a convicted pederast. What does he mean by this accusation, Mon Pere?

Your Most Royal Majesty, he is my enemy and not my friend. He suffers from envy, and he wishes that I were a pederast, just like him. He slanders me at every opportunity for he is envious of my standing and achievements, and he cannot forgive me for rating the art and science of painters' superior to those of sculptors. I say that the painter has a greater scope intellectually to interpret and represent the world than does the sculptor. Any slight meditation on this question immediately reveals that my reasoning is true. I do not deny that sculpture and the carving of objects is a great art or skill, I simply argue that painting and drawing is a superior art and skill if done properly.

But sculptures last longer than paintings and therefore could claim superiority in the antiquities.

Yes, but the surviving paintings and frescoes tell us more about the ancient peoples and their community and way of life than does any armless *Venus* or the perfectly intact marble statue of *Laocoon and His Sons*. Moreover, the very best of the chiselled sculptures have never been able to perfectly capture the look of the eye, the window into the soul that a portrait painter must always try to achieve to show us the true nature of his sitter.

Be that as it may, Papa, do reveal to us whether or not you were convicted of pederasty?

No never, Your Majesty. Long ago in Florence in 1476, I, together with three of my acquaintances, were accused anonymously in a letter of being in the service of a well-known homosexual and dullard by the name of Jacopo Saltarelli.

Francesco will pour us more wine and you will tell us what happened that you were so accused. We listen with bated attention. Go ahead, Papa.

I was accused in an anonymous letter that was sent to the Officers of the Night to have been in the service of Jacopo Saltarelli who sold his sexual favours to any available bidder. The Officers of the Night were the Church's vice squad in Florence. The anonymous scoundrel in his letter accused me of requesting wickedness from the said Jacopo who had previously been before the court for the same said offence. As in France, Your Majesty, the crime of homosexuality in Florence is punishable by excommunication, large fines, long prison sentences, exile or even by death, burnt at the stake.

In my Kingdom, Papa, we used to brand the sodomites with the fleur-de-lis. Under my leadership, we have stopped that practice as a misuse of the fleur-de-lis.

Indeed, Your Majesty. It is no laughing matter to be accused of participating in such wickedness. As Your Majesty knows, I could be easily accused of being an ascetic or a monk, but never a homosexual. Please ask, Francesco, Salai or Battista. They can vouch for me for they see how I live from day to day. As an ascetic with a love for the aesthetic, I am interested equally in man and woman because together they are the whole that make up humanity. I cannot discriminate between the two for they are the right and left side of humanity who fill my canvas and my interest in the arts and sciences. If you should look upon a human foetus before it is born during the first three to four months of pregnancy, it is neither a female nor a male for it displays no sexual organs. You could never guess what sex it will be born, at least not until it is five months or more in the womb.

Interesting, but go on and tell us about your accuser and accusation. We are intrigued.

The anonymous letter sent to the prelates and the magistrates of the city accused not only me as a companion of Jacopo Saltarelli – it also accused three others, a goldsmith, a tailor, and my friend Leonardo Tornabuoni. We were all supporters of de' Medici family, and Lorenzo Magnifico de' Medici believed that it was an enemy of his, a banking family who supported the Pope, who tried to discredit us because Leonardo Tornabuoni was his relative. Leonardo Tornabuoni's uncle was the Medici banker Giovanni Tornabuoni, and his aunt was Lucrezia Tornabuoni, the wife of Piero di Cosimo de' Medici who was the son of Cosimo de' Medici, and she was the mother of Lorenzo il Magnifico, the ruling Lord of Florence who was married to Clarice Orsini from the noble family of the Orsini family of Rome. According to Lorenzo de' Medici, after the attempt on his life in 1478, he extracted a confession from a Pazzi member that one of his secretaries had sent the unsigned accusation to the Officers of the Night and the prelates of the Palazzo Vecchio.

Were you summoned to the courts to testify against this perfidious accusation?

Yes, we went before a magistrate at the Palace of the People. The court dismissed the false and scurrilous accusation immediately because the perfidious accuser had not signed his letter and nobody knew who he was, and there was no evidence or supporting witnesses against us. The accusation was dismissed, and the court provided us with letters of apology.

A strange and unjust accusation, Papa!

Those were the times in Florence, Your Majesty. If you were disliked because of envy or had enemies for any other reason, then, you were often accused of homosexuality or bestiality or participating in wickedness or the art of witchcraft. This was a powerful way to discredit you.

Is it possible that a cuckold accused you for revenge?

That possibility did cross my mind. Perhaps it was Ginevra de' Benci's husband or Lucrezia Vespucci's husband? But then I thought, why would a cuckold also include the other three if he is just attacking me? I think his Lordship, Lorenzo de' Medici, was right. It was an attack on his nephew and on the others and me because we were his good friends.

And what of the homosexual, Jacopo Saltarelli? Did you know him?

Everybody in Florence knew of him and his wicked reputation. He was very open in his proclivity for flagitious things. He used to frequent the restaurant that Botticelli and I serviced on the Ponte Vecchio. We called our restaurant the Three Snails, very French we thought. We often had rowdy crowds, and I would experiment as a cook by providing them with various unusual entertainments and exotic foods instead of the usual porridge that they were used to. Jacopo Saltarelli and his ilk were occasional visitors, disturbing our clientele with offers of prostituting their bodies for a cheap financial exchange. On their last visit to the Three Snails, Jacopo was particularly vociferous, disturbing, and abusing our clientele, and particularly me and Sandro. Five or six of our friends threw him and his obnoxious friend Corrado out into the street. In fact, some of them had dragged him into a dark corner of the square, stuck him upside down into a metal bin, and somebody had written pederast on his naked arse that was visible to any passers-by. They left him so, stuck upside down in the bin displaying his naked arse to the world, a very well labelled arse, while they returned well satisfied from their wicked deed to the Three Snails for a night of revelry. I heard later that a passer-by had stuck a sunflower stem up Saltarelli's arse in an attempt to beautify the stench and the foul display. We never saw Jacopo Saltarelli or his friends back at the Three Snails ever again, and we never gave it another thought, not until about three months later when I and the other three were arrested to stand before a magistrate accused of a public disturbance and sodomy. I was outraged because I immediately thought that I had guessed who our accuser was. I thought incorrectly that it was Ginevra de' Benci's husband. He had a bone to pick with us all. He hated us. He especially hated my portrait of Ginevra and that she still loved me. She wrote me love poems describing her ardour for me. I thought that he had reaped his revenge on us all. But this incidence was never raised in the court, so I realised the accuser was somebody else.

What you experienced is nothing unusual, Papa, said the King. *We all have accusers spreading malicious lies about us behind our backs. They know the consequences if they accuse their king with their lies to our face. They think it's safer for them to do so behind our back, forgetting that we have our informers tracking their lies, and I can assure them that they will not go unpunished.*

It's so, Your Highness, said Leonardo. I had no such luxury of support in Florence and could only live and act on my wits and my reputation. My reputation was somewhat debauched by the accusation of being a sodomite. I learnt later that Michelangelo took great pleasure in calling me the great sodomite behind my back. If I'd known about his treachery then I would have busted his nose. He seemed to gain great pleasure from having his nose constantly broken. He thought it gave him his manly pugilist's look that attracted the young boys to him.

And what of the Three Snails? asked the King. Tell us about the Three Snails. What menus and entertainments did you provide to your customers? Ah, you'll have to recreate some of these menus for us on some evenings when we visit. We'd like to know what it was like to drink and eat at the Three Snails.

Envy and the Cruelty of Nature

While Leonardo was well known and well liked by many in the artistic and engineering circles, some also despised him because of his successes. Leonardo felt that he had been attacked by the sin of envy from a number of different fronts, particularly from Michelangelo. He heard much spiteful ridicule from Michelangelo and other artists who were pleased that he failed to caste his giant horse. Leonardo was very sensitive to the sin of envy, and the kite was the symbol of envy. He wrote into his notebook the following items:

> ENVY. We read of the kite that, when it sees its young ones growing too big in the nest, out of envy it pecks their sides, and keeps them without food.

> This writing distinctly about the kite seems to be my destiny, because among the first recollections of my infancy, it seemed to me that, as I was in my cradle, a kite came to me and opened my mouth with its tail, and struck me several times with its tail inside my lips.

He was writing metaphorically about his destiny that he would be forever burdened by the sin of envy against him. While this may have been an impediment to him, as it was for many others because jealousy is universal, his genius overcame many such obstacles on his way to his many successes.

Leonardo was a pessimist who saw and questioned the cruelty of Nature:

> O Nature! Wherefore art thou so partial; being to some of thy children a tender and benign mother, and to others a most cruel and pitiless stepmother? I see children of thine given up to slavery to others, without any sort of advantage, and instead of remuneration for the good they do, they are paid with the severest suffering, and spend their whole life in benefitting those who ill treat them.

CHAPTER 28

Leonardo's Philosophies and His Studies of the Brain and the Soul, Mechanics, and the Pyramidal Law of Nature

Consider now, O reader! What trust can we place in the ancients, who tried to define what the Soul and Life are— which are beyond proof—whereas those things which can at any time be clearly known and proved by experience remained for many centuries unknown or falsely understood.

— Leonardo da Vinci

Man of God, Reason, and Experience

Giorgio Vasari wrote in his *Lives of the Artists* that Leonardo's,

> … cast of mind was so heretical that he did not adhere to any religion, thinking perhaps that it was better to be a philosopher than a Christian.

Leonardo was a seeker of truth and knowledge through his own experience and not necessarily the teachings of others, especially the revelations of the so-called messiahs. He believed in a supreme creator (Deus, God) who (that) does not intervene in the universe. Thus, he rejected the authority of the church and revelations of messiahs and prophets as a source of religious knowledge, and he concluded that reason and observation of the natural world were sufficient to determine the existence of a single creator of the universe that (who) was a non-interventionist. He believed that cognition, reason, and the soul were intrinsic elements of the non-interventionist creator, and that experience provided the authority to make the correct judgments and to know the true from the false. Supernatural interpretation of events such as miracles were either misguided translations of natural events that could not be easily explained because of the lack of proper information or knowledge or they were superstitions, myths, and stories selfishly created by the church or clergy to maintain their power and dominance over the ignorant. He did not believe in the faith driven religions that are based on the revelations of a messiah or persons with a direct connection to the voice of God, Jesus or other prophets. He told us that Judaism, Christianity, and Islam were not God-made creations, but they were Man-made creations (revelations) to serve certain men's own political self-interests and those of their evangelists for personal gain and the class interest of the privileged priesthoods. He believed that the religions of our day were corruptions of an original, pure religion that was simple and rational in ancient times such as Heraclitus's *Logos* or Plato's *Demiurge*. Leonardo was a questioner and truth seeker, and he deplored the atrocities of the Church officials who devoted much of their time and service to burning heretics, torturing witches, terrifying illiterate congregations with hellfire sermons, and stealing from them their pitifully little earnings by selling indulgences. He cast doubt on the power of the Church to remit punishment for sin.

We had many debates about theology and the universe during our fireside chats, and the King and I raised many arguments and straw dogs to try and contradict Leonardo's position, but he, somehow, always had an answer to our objections. The king was particularly interested in the German theologian, Martin Luther's *95 Theses or Disputation on the Power of Indulgences* that he had nailed onto the door of the All Saints' Church in Wittenberg in 1517. The king, like his sister Princess Marguerite, was a rebel who questioned the wisdom of some of the church's

414

teachings, and how it was similar or different to other religious philosophies. They both dabbled with and listened to the Reformationist teachings of Luther and his followers. The king and his sister were questioners and Protestants at heart. The king enjoyed debating with Leonardo on the subject of God and the purpose of our existence for he was aware about his own highly privileged position in the eyes of God and those of his people, and although still young, he had faced up to his own fallibility and mortality in his battles to capture Milan.

Leonardo was anticlerical and anti-sacerdotal and liked to poke fun at silly religious beliefs and practices. He retold us the following jest that he wrote in one of his notebooks:

> A priest going the round of his parish on Saturday before Easter, sprinkling holy water in the houses as was his custom came to a painter's room and there sprinkled the water upon some of his pictures. The painter turned round, somewhat angered, and asked him why this sprinkling had been bestowed on his pictures; then the priest said that it was the custom and that it was his duty to do so, that he was doing good, and that whoever did a good deed might expect a return as good and better; for so God had promised that every good deed that was done on earth shall be rewarded a hundredfold from on high. Then the painter, having waited until the priest had walked out, stepped to the window above, and threw a large bucket of water on to his back, saying: Here is the reward a hundredfold from on high as you said would come from the good you did me with your holy water with which you have damaged half my pictures.

A short collection of some of Leonardo's other criticisms of the clergy:

> (Of Priests who say Mass). There will be many men who, when they go to their labour will put on the richest clothes, and these will be made after the fashion of aprons.
> (Of Friars who are Confessors). And unhappy women will, of their own free will, reveal to men all their sins and shameful and most secret deeds.
> (Of Churches and the Habitations of Friars). Many will there be who will give up work and labour and poverty of life and goods, and will go to live among wealth in splendid buildings, declaring that this is the way to make themselves acceptable to God.
> (Of Friars, who spending nothing but words, receive great gifts and bestow Paradise). Invisible money will procure the triumph of many who will spend it.
> (Of Priests who bear the Host in their body). Then almost all the tabernacles in which dwells the *Corpus Domini*, will be plainly seen walking about of themselves on the various roads of the world.
> (Of the Religion of Friars, who live by the Saints who have been dead a great while). Those who are dead will, after a thousand years be those who will give a livelihood to many who are living.
> (Of Children who are suckled). Many Franciscans, Dominicans, and Benedictines will eat that which at other times was eaten by others, who for some months to come will not be able to speak.
> (Against friars). And many have made a trade of delusions and false miracles, deceiving the stupid multitude.
> (Of Crucifixes, which are sold). I see Christ sold and crucified afresh, and his Saints suffering Martyrdom.
> (Pharisees). That is to say, friars.
> (Of Christians). Many who hold the faith of the Son only build temples in the name of the Mother.

One night, I wrote down this strange conversation after the king asked Leonardo, *what is Islam?* Just another faith-based religion dependent on the revelations of a messiah or the disciples of a messiah, a more modern version of Judaism and Christianity for the tribes wandering the deserts and oases of the East, was Leonardo's reply. The mystery is the how and not the why. Why do the haves have it? If my dog had different legs and paws, more like our very own, then maybe he could stand and walk like us and use his hand to pick the apple from a low hanging branch without the need to jump and try to bite it from the tree. But, is it not interesting to ask how the dog has legs like a dog and not like a human? If you know the how, then you know the why. If you ask the question, how has the dog developed legs like a dog and not like a human, then you will have the answer as to why the dog has doglegs. If we know how we developed to walk upright on two legs instead of on all fours like the dog and other animals then we would have a much better idea about why we walk on two legs instead of four. It is better to use your own reason and to understand the certainty of knowledge instead of believing the revelations, myths, and stories of others.

So why are we here, roaming the Earth as we do? asked the King.

We are here to serve the one and only God who created the universe and then no longer intervened in its processes. In the classics, the various other Gods themselves have come after creation, so, according to the classics, without a rational mind who really knows truly when or why - the world, existence, creation - has arisen? The real question is how are we here and not why are we here? If God made us, who made God? Is he infinite? If he is infinite, why has he bothered to make us finite and mortal and similar and different to the apes and other animals in that they also have a head with a brain attached to a nervous system, ears, nose, eyes, mouth, stomach and intestine, head, anus, and genitals, all the basic structural necessities to live a short life? Why are we born and why do we die, while our descendants like our ancestors procreate and live for a while and then die in this ever changing, strange, swirling dance that we call existence? And then, there is extinction, when all that we know or have known comes to a total end. Are we accidents or are we made for a purpose? I believe that we are made to wander and wonder and to serve and love God and the Universe.

Yes, but how and why? What is the reason for that? Do we serve to love Him, how? What is better, is it to murder, kill, and steal or is it to love and serve all men and other creatures at the risk of losing your own life?

When you contemplate God and the Universe carefully with a clear mind then you can do whatever your conscience and intuition tells you because they will be harmonised as one. Go ahead, your Majesty, please try.

We sat in silence for a while in our own private meditation, and then Leonardo spoke and continued on about learning to substitute our desire and anger with the right intentions of goodwill and compassion to make us better humans:

> You will never have a greater or lesser dominion than that over yourself… The height of a man's success is gauged by his self-mastery; the depth of his failure by his self-abandonment… and this law is the expression of eternal justice. He who cannot establish dominion over himself will have no dominion over others.

Abstain from lies, slander, gossip, and harsh language that hurt others; be mindful, loving, kind, honest, compassionate, and respectful; and abstain from taking life:

> He who does not oppose evil… commands it to be done. I have been impressed with the urgency of doing. Knowing is not enough; we must do.

He urged us to become vegetarians like him and his mother:

> I have from an early age abjured the use of meat, and the time will come when men such as I will look upon the murder of animals as they now look upon the murder of men… and that his body will not be a tomb for other creatures.

He also told us that you can't always get what you want, and it is better to go with the flow because life is about the senses, feeling, and suffering, and that we often bring this suffering to ourselves because we want something that we often cannot have. Life always brings unwanted change, illness, unhappiness, and eventual death:

> As you cannot do what you want, want what you can do. I love those who can smile in trouble, who can gather strength from distress, and grow brave by reflection. 'Tis the business of little minds to shrink, but they whose heart is firm, and whose conscience approves their conduct, will pursue their principles unto death.

Leonardo encouraged us to forever pursue knowledge for it was a great thing to understand yourself, your fellow man, and the Universe:

> Iron rusts from disuse; stagnant water loses its purity and in cold weather becomes frozen; even so does inaction sap the vigour of the mind. So we must stretch ourselves to the very limits of human possibility. Anything less is a sin against both God and man. Many have made a trade of delusions and false miracles. Where there is shouting, there is no true knowledge.
>
> Those who try to censor knowledge do harm to both knowledge and love because love is the offspring of knowledge, and the passion of love grows in proportion to the certainty of knowledge. The more we know about nature, the more we can be certain of what we know, and so the more love we can feel for nature as a whole. Of what use are those who try to restrict what we know to only those things that are easy to comprehend, often because they themselves are not inclined to learn more about a particular subject, like the subject of the human body. And yet, they want to comprehend the mind of God, talking about it as though they had already dissected it into parts. Still, they remain unaware of their own bodies, of the realities of their surroundings, and even unaware of their own stupidity. Along with the scholars, they despise the mathematical sciences, which are the only true sources of information about those things, which they claim to know so much about. Instead, they talk about miracles and write about things that nobody could ever know, things that cannot be proven by any evidence in nature.
>
> I reveal to men the origin of the first, or perhaps second cause of their existence. Lust is the cause of generation. Appetite is the support of life. Fear or timidity is the prolongation of life and preservation of its instruments. Our life is made by the death of others. In dead matter insensible life remains, which, reunited to the stomachs of living beings, resumes life, both sensual and intellectual. **Motive power** [energy, force, movement, constraint] **is the cause of all life**. Learning acquired in youth arrests the evil of old age; and if you understand that old age has wisdom for its food, you will so conduct yourself in youth that your old age will not lack for nourishment.

Leonardo based his beliefs and knowledge on the experience derived from his senses and reason, not from faith.

> The senses are of the earth; reason stands apart from them in contemplation. Wisdom is the daughter of experience.
>
> It seems to me that all studies are vain and full of errors unless they are based on experience and can be tested by experiment, in other words, they can be demonstrated to our senses. For if we are doubtful of what our senses perceive then how much more doubtful should we be of things that our senses cannot perceive, like the nature of God and the soul and other such things over which there are endless disputes and controversies. Wherever there is no true science and no certainty of knowledge, there will be conflicting speculations and quarrels. However, whenever things are proven by scientific demonstration and known for certain, then all quarrelling will cease. And if controversy should ever arise again, then our first conclusions must have been

questionable. Although nature commences with reason and ends in experience it is necessary for us to do the opposite that is to commence with experience and from this to proceed to investigate the reason.

Study the science of art. Study the art of science. Develop your senses— especially learn to see. Realise that everything connects to everything else. Anyone who conducts an argument by appealing to authority is not using his intelligence; he is just using his memory. I am well aware that because I did not study the ancients, some foolish men will accuse me of being uneducated. They will say that because I did not learn from their schoolbooks, I am unqualified to express an opinion. But, I would reply that my conclusions are drawn from first-hand experience, unlike the scholars who only believe what they read in books written by others.

Although I cannot quote from authors in the same way they do, I shall rely on a much worthier thing, actual experience, which is the only thing that could ever have properly guided the men that they learn from. These scholars strut around in a pompous way, without any thoughts of their own, equipped only with the thoughts of others, and they want to stop me from having my own thoughts. And if they despise me for being an inventor, then how much more should they be despised for not being inventors but followers and reciters of the works of others. When the followers and reciters of the works of others are compared to those who are inventors and interpreters between Nature and man, it is as though they are non-existent mirror images of some original. **Given that it is only by chance that we are invested with human form, I might think of them as being a herd of animals.** Man discourseth greatly, and his discourse is for the greater part empty and false; the discourse of animals is small, but useful and true: **slender certainty is better than portentous falsehood.**

First, I shall test by experiment before I proceed further, because my intention is to consult experience first and then with reasoning show why such experience is bound to operate in such a way. And this is the true rule by which those who analyse the effects of nature must proceed: and although nature begins with the cause and ends with the experience, we must follow the opposite course, namely, begin with the experience, and by means of it investigate the cause.

If you find from your own experience that something is a fact and it contradicts what some authority has written down, then you must abandon the authority and base your reasoning on your own findings. But, remember, the greatest deception men suffer is from their own opinions.

Did Leonardo believe in God? Yes, he did, but only in a noninterventionist God who created the Universe. Here are some comments in his notebooks that refer to God:

Good Report soars and rises to heaven, for virtuous things find favour with God. Evil Report should be shown inverted, for all her works are contrary to God and tend toward hell.

O you who look on this our machine, do not be sad that with others you are fated to die, but rejoice that our Creator has endowed us with such an excellent instrument as the intellect.

If the Lord—who is the light of all things—vouch safe to enlighten me, I will treat of Light; wherefore I will divide the present work into 3 Parts . . . Linear Perspective, The Perspective of Colour, The Perspective of Disappearance.

We may justly call . . . painting . . . the grandchild of nature and related to God.

We, by our arts may be called the grandsons of God.

Fame alone raises herself to Heaven, because virtuous things are in favour with God.

Genesis and Noah's Deluge

Every schoolboy in Europe has learnt the story of creation in the Bible as Genesis: *And so it was, the beginning and the end of genesis, all in seven days.* Leonardo said that the description of the creation of the heavens and the earth and all living things in seven days was complete and utter nonsense, like many of the miracle stories in the Bible. He reckoned that the universe and all living things created by God had evolved over a time period beyond our imagination. He also questioned the veracity of the biblical story of a one-year long flood that allegedly 'covered the highest mountains' all around the world. This is what he wrote about Noah's flood in his notebook:

> Here a doubt rises, and that is: whether the Flood which came at the time of Noah was universal or not. And it would seem not, for the reasons, which will now be given. We have it in the Bible that this deluge lasted 40 days and 40 nights, of incessant and universal rain, and that this rain rose to ten cubits about the highest mountains in the world. And if it had been that the rain was universal, it would have covered our globe, which is spherical in form. And this spherical surface is equally distant in every part from the centre of its sphere; hence the sphere of the waters being under the same conditions, it is impossible that the water upon it should move, because water, in itself, does not move unless it falls; therefore how could the waters of such a deluge depart, if it is proved that it has no motion? And if it departed how could it move unless it went upwards? Here, then, natural reasons are wanting; hence to remove this doubt it is necessary to call it a miracle to aid us, or else to say that all this water was evaporated by the heat of the sun.

Leonardo believed that the Earth was very much older than what the Bible and the Roman Catholic Church taught us. The evidence for his belief came from the location of fossil shells, rock and mountain formations, and the movement of the waters in the rivers, streams, lakes, seas, and oceans.

> In this work you have first to prove that the shells at a thousand braccia of elevation were not carried there by the deluge, because they are seen to be all at one level, and many mountains are seen to be above that level; and to inquire whether the deluge was caused by rain or by the swelling of the sea; and then you must show how, neither by rain nor by swelling of the rivers, nor by the overflow of this sea, could the shells--being heavy objects--be floated up the mountains by the sea, nor have carried there by the rivers against the course of their waters. Doubts about the deluge.
>
> Since things are far more ancient than letters, it is not to be wondered at if in our day there exists no record of how the aforesaid seas extended over so many countries; and if, moreover, such record ever existed, the wars, the conflagrations, the deluges of the waters, the changes in speech and habits, have destroyed every vestige of the past. But sufficient for us is the testimony of things produced in the salt waters and now found again in the high mountains far from the seas.
>
> I say that the deluge could not carry objects, native to the sea, up to the mountains, unless the sea had already increased so as to create inundations as high up as those places; and this increase could not have occurred because it would cause a vacuum; and if you were to say that the air would rush in there, we have already concluded that what is heavy cannot remain above what is light, whence of necessity we must conclude that this deluge was caused by rain water, so that all these waters ran to the sea, and the sea did not run up the mountains; and as they ran to the sea, they thrust the shells from the shore of the sea and did not draw them towards themselves. And if you were then to say that the sea, raised by the rain water, had carried these shells to such a height, we have already said that things heavier than water cannot rise upon it, but remain at the bottom of it, and do

not move unless by the impact of the waves. And if you were to say that the waves had carried them to such high spots, we have proved that the waves in a great depth move in a contrary direction at the bottom to the motion at the top, and this is shown by the turbidity of the sea from the earth washed down near its shores. Anything, which is lighter than the water moves with the waves, and is left on the highest level of the highest margin of the waves. Anything which is heavier than the water moves, suspended in it, between the surface and the bottom; and from these two conclusions, which will be amply proved in their place, we infer that the waves of the surface cannot convey shells, since they are heavier than water.

If the deluge had to carry shells three hundred and four hundred miles from the sea, it would have carried them mixed with various other natural objects heaped together; and we see at such distances oysters all together, and sea-snails, and cuttlefish, and all the other shells which congregate together, all to be found together and dead; and the solitary shells are found wide apart from each other, as we may see them on sea-shores every day. And if we find oysters of very large shells joined together and among them very many which still have the covering attached, indicating that they were left here by the sea, and still living when the strait of Gibraltar was cut through; there are to be seen, in the mountains of Parma and Piacenza, a multitude of shells and corals, full of holes, and still sticking to the rocks there. When I was making the great horse for Milan, a large sack full was brought to me in my workshop by certain peasants; these were found in that place and among them were many preserved in their first freshness.

Leonardo reasoned that the fossil shells in the mountains came from animals, which once inhabited an ancient sea that covered the land, and that these mountains were raised above the ancient sea over long periods of time. Where fish once swam in large shoals, birds now fly and nest. He agreed with Aristotle's descriptions of the upheavals that turned seabeds into mountains over the endlessness of time.

The summits of mountains for a long time rise constantly. The opposite sides of the mountains always approach each other below; the depths of the valleys, which are above the sphere of the waters are in the course of time constantly getting nearer to the centre of the world. In an equal period, the valleys sink much more than the mountains rise. The bases of the mountains always come closer together. In proportion as the valleys become deeper, the more quickly are their sides worn away.

Evolution, Mutability, and Interconnectedness in the World

According to Leonardo, the entire Universe is God and that every living and non-living thing in the Heavens and on Earth and other planets and satellites is a Manifestation or a Code of God. That is, the Universe undergoes transformations and continually changes as a manifestation of God's creation and intelligence. Thus, everything is interrelated, connected in both visible and invisible ways in the Universe, within His body and His spirit, and that He and We can see, feel, hear, smell, and measure this interrelationship in different ways, through mathematics, science, art, architecture, engineering, movement (dance, war, murder, theft, etc.), and music by using our mind, senses, and awareness wisely. Consciousness is an essence of God that allows us to connect with different interrelationships in the Universe. We are conscious and self-aware at least some of the time so that we can live to process intelligently within the University of God. In sleep, we rest and have a subconscious process that rejigs the intrinsic processes in our brain and body in preparation for a new consciousness, good or bad, to cope with the new day and night of insults and stimuli. In death, we lose both our conscious and subconscious states and become permanently unconscious because our spirit becomes fragmented and transformed into the world of millions of inanimate objects of the Earth and the Universe. That is why Leonardo was interested in a higher or evolved state of alchemy and the five main elements in the Universe, fire, earth, water, air, and ether.

Yes, Leonardo saw transformation, mutability, and interconnectedness everywhere in the world.

> Man and the animals are merely a passage and channel for food, a tomb for other animals, a haven for the dead, giving life by the death of others, a coffer full of corruption. Man and animals are in reality vehicles and conduits of food, tombs of animals, hostels of Death, coverings that consume, deriving life by the death of others.
>
> **Against.** Why nature did not ordain that one animal should not live by the death of another.
>
> **For.** Nature being capricious and taking pleasure in creating and producing a continuous succession of lives and forms because she knows that they serve to increase her terrestrial substance, is more ready and swift in creating than time is in destroying, and therefore she has ordained that many animals shall serve as food one for the other; and as this does not satisfy her desire she sends forth frequently certain noisome and pestilential vapours and continual plagues upon the vast accumulations and herds of animals and especially upon human beings who increase very rapidly because other animals do not feed upon them; and if the causes are taken away the results will cease.
>
> **Against.** Therefore this earth seeks to lose its life while desiring continual reproduction for the reason brought forth, and demonstrated to you. Effects often resemble their causes. The animals serve as a type of the life of the world.
>
> **For.** Behold now the hope and desire of going back to one's own country or returning to primal chaos, like that of the moth to the light, of the man who with perpetual longing always looks forward with joy to each new spring and each new summer, and to the new months and the new years, deeming that the things he longs for are too slow in coming; and who does not perceive that he is longing for his own destruction. But this longing is in its quintessence the spirit of the elements, which finding itself imprisoned within the life of the human body desires continually to return to its source. And I would have you to know that this same longing is in its quintessence inherent in nature, and that man is a type of the world.
>
> WHAT'S THE POINT? Therefore the end of nothingness and the beginning of the line are in contact with one another, but they are not joined together, and in such contact is the point, which divides the continuation of nothingness and the line. It follows that the point is less than nothing, and if all the parts of nothingness are equal to one we may the more conclude that all the points also are equal to one single point and one point is equal to all. And from this it follows that many points imagined in continuous contact do not constitute the line, and as a consequence many lines in continuous contact as regards their sides do not make a surface, nor do many surfaces in continuous contact make a body, because among us bodies are not formed of incorporeal things. The point is that which has no centre because it is all centre, and nothing can be less. The contact of the liquid with the solid is a surface common to the liquid and to the solid, and the lighter liquids with the heavier have the same. All the points are equal to one and one to all. Write of the nature of time as distinct from its geometry.
>
> OF TIME AS A CONTINUOUS QUANTITY: Although time is numbered among continuous quantities yet through its being invisible and without substance it does not altogether fall under the category of geometrical terms, which are divided in figures and bodies of infinite variety, as may constantly be seen to be the case with things visible and things of substance; but it harmonises with these only as regards its first principles, namely as to the point and the line. The point as viewed in terms of time is to be compared with the instant, and the line resembles the length of a quantity of time. And just as points are the beginning and end of the said line so instants form the end and the beginning of a certain given space of time. And if a line be divisible to

infinity it is not impossible for a space of time to be so divided. And if the divided parts
of a line may bear a certain proportion of one to another so also may the parts of time.

Leonardo looked for the interconnectedness of the elements everywhere and in everything. This was his holy grail. Man is interconnected with all living (animate) things (animals and plants) and non-living (inanimate) things (fire, air, water, earth, ether) to eat, drink, breathe, and think, and without them we could not live. One night, he told us a story about how we were transformed from great apes and lower animals into a group or species known as man. The great apes were transformed from the monkeys, and the monkeys from other four-legged mammals like the dogs, cats, cows, horses, and so on. This had happened over a period of time beyond our imagination. That is why the basic shape of all the animals that we can see is essentially the same, a head with eyes to see, a nose to smell, ears to hear, and a mouth to feed the body, stomach and intestine to process the food for energy, and unsurprisingly, a mouth and an anus and urinary tract to extract nutrients and excrete poisons. Of course some creatures have lost one or other of their basic structures during their transformations, so we have snakes and lizards without legs, and fish that have fins and flippers instead of arms and legs to better adapt to their aquatic environment, and so on. And what about the plants that provide us with food, energy, and beauty? How are they connected to the animal world? Apparently, they emerged before animals and therefore provided animals with the necessary environment, nutrients, and energy to allow them to adapt to the plant kingdom, and together to procreate and develop all over the earth, the sea, and even in the air. That is why in some of Leonardo's paintings, he has shown us images of man or woman in contrasting light and in the presence of animals, plants, rocks, rivers, lakes, and air, thus depicting the five elements of the Universe, fire (heat and energy, light and darkness), earth (solidity), air (vibrancy and expansion), water (cohesion), and ether (the mystery). I had never thought of these things before in the way Leonardo told the King and me about his thoughts on universal interconnectedness. The awareness of the interconnectedness of all things has broadened my mind and given me a greater appreciation of the meaning and joy of life.

The Natural Philosophy of the Persian Nasiraddin Tusi [S44]

Leonardo held up a book for us to look at. He borrowed it from the king's library in Blois. It's not the Christian *Bible* as we know it, he said. It is entitled *Nasirean Ethics* and written by the Islamic scholar Nasiraddin Tusi when the Assassins held him prisoner for seventeen years in Quhistan. Tusi was born in 1201 in Tus, Khorasan, and he wrote about ethics and natural philosophy and Reason, Wisdom, Justice, and Equilibrium. He provides a history of the ancient philosophers and tells the story of the interconnectedness and transformations of all living and non-living things in our world, here on Earth. It is a beautiful story, even better than the bible that is told to us by the writings of the apostles and many known and unknown Christian scholars. He writes the following tenants about the evolution of the world and humans:

1. A body of matter cannot disappear completely. It only changes its form, condition, composition, colour, and other properties, and it turns into a different complex of elementary matter.

2. The world always consisted and consists of similar elements for they were and are equal and similar to each other. None of them had or have an advantage over the other because all of these particles consisted and consist of common primary matter.

3. With a changing balance among these things, essential contrasts began to appear inside this early world. New substances began to develop faster and better than others.

4. The four elements of Nature (fire, water, air and earth) were derived from this primary matter (ether), and they led to the formation of minerals, then plants from minerals, animals from plants, and humans from animals.

5. The organisms that can gain the new features faster are more variable. As a result, they gain advantages over other creatures or pass away into oblivion.

6. The body changes and adapts because of internal and external interactions and reactions.

7. Look at the world of animals and birds. They have all that is necessary for defence and daily life, including strength, courage, and appropriate tools [organs].

8. Some of these organs are real weapons. For example, horns are spears, teeth and claws are like knives and needles, feet and hoofs are cudgels. The thorns and needles of some animals are similar to arrows.

9. Animals such as the deer and fox that have no specific means of defence protect themselves with the help of flight and cunning.

10. Some of them, for example, bees, ants, and some bird species, have united into communities in order to protect themselves and help each other selflessly.

11. Animals are higher than plants because they are able to move consciously, go after food, find, and eat useful things.

12. The animal kingdom is more complicated than the plant kingdom. Reason is the most beneficial feature of animals. Owing to reason, they can learn new things and adopt new, non-inherited abilities. For example, the trained horse or the hunting falcon or the domesticated dog provides man with many uses and consequently these animals benefit in return. The first steps of human perfection must begin with correct reasoning and the ability to interact positively with other creatures.

13. Humans who lived in Africa and other distant corners of the world before they migrated to the European continent were closer to animals by their habits, deeds, and behaviour.

14. The human has features that distinguish him from other creatures, but he has other features that unite him with the animal world, the vegetable kingdom, and even with the inanimate bodies.

15. Before the advent of man, all differences between organisms were of the natural origin. The next step for man will be associated with spiritual perfection, morality and good will, observation, and knowledge.

16. All these facts suggest that the human being in the beginning of primal genesis was placed on the middle step of the evolutionary stairway. According to his inherent nature, the human was related to the lower beings, and only with the help of his reason, intelligence, and will, and understanding the sciences, arts, and virtues can he reach the higher levels of development. So says Tutsi.

According to Tutsi and the philosophical sciences, the principles of the various classes of evolution and development that are necessitated towards the species of perfection are one of two things, nature or discipline. Nature is the principle that moves sperm through the different degrees of classified mutations and diversified conversions to produce the perfection of an animal, whereas discipline is the principle that moves wood by way of tools and instruments to the perfection of a couch. Nature takes precedence over discipline in coming into existence and in rank for it proceeds from Divine Wisdom, whereas discipline proceeds from human desire to enlist the assistance and participation of natural things. The former is both teacher and master, whereas the latter is student and pupil.

These Tusian ideas are highly dangerous to the authority and well being of the Church, and so they are neither taught nor discussed outside the confines of secret societies and scholarly meetings. Aristotle taught similar ideas in Lesbos three hundred and forty years before the birth of Christ. Heraclitus taught us about 'ever-present change' as the fundamental essence of the Universe, and Democritus and Lucretius told us about Atomism. We sit here contemplating the truth, but we cannot speak of these ideas outside this room without being branded heretics and losing our lives, whether we are king or pauper. Even Muslims condemn Tusi's description of evolution. Tutsi believed in God, but a God that created the world and then allowed it to develop (evolve) on its own with no need to supervise or guide the process. This naturalistic view of the world fits in perfectly with how we should see and interpret the world, but it is forever hidden from our mind and awareness because of one powerful class of human, the clergy, who forever forbids us to contemplate such things.

Many of the ideas of transformation or evolution of the World and the origins of plants, animals, and humans that Leonardo told us about troubled me greatly over many nights of contemplation for the rest of my life. I could never explain them adequately to my wife or children or to my good friends who preferred to believe in the exclusiveness of Man over all other living things, and the Church's fictional explanation of a Heaven and a Hell. And so, I have accepted their beliefs and lived peacefully with them. The French king never quite understood Leonardo's belief in the interconnectedness of all things or in his concept of the Universe, but he did question the Church's doctrines, which led him and his sister into conflicts between Protestantism and Catholicism in France.

The Five Senses, the Power of Smell, and Advice to Dog Owners

It is my understanding that our awareness in life (consciousness), like those of all animals, is totally dependent on our five senses. Takeaway one or other of our senses, and we are much handicapped, but still aware. Take away all our senses then we are dead. This is what Leonardo meant when he said that the spirit couldn't exist without one or more of the five senses. According to him, the soul is in the brain to process, translate, and integrate all the inputs from our senses. If we lose all our senses then we no longer have anything to process with, and we are without a working soul. And so with death, we are senseless, soulless, and unaware.

Leonardo liked to talk to the king and me about the five senses, the four powers, and nature. This is what he wrote in his notebooks:

> There are the four powers: memory, intellect, sensuality, and lust. The first two are intellectual, the others sensual. Of the five senses, sight, hearing, and smell are with difficulty prevented; touch and taste not at all. Taste follows smell in the case of dogs and other greedy animals. I reveal to men the origin of smell, or perhaps the second cause of their existence after sight.
>
> I once saw a picture which deceived a dog by the image of its master, which the dog greeted with great joy; and likewise, I have seen dogs bark at and try to bite painted dogs; and a monkey make a number of antics in front of a painted monkey. I have seen swallows fly and alight on painted iron-works, which jut out of the windows of buildings.
>
> While the dog was asleep on the coat of a sheep, one of its fleas, becoming aware of the smell of the greasy wool, decided that this must be a place where the living was better and more safe from the teeth and nails of the dog than getting his food on the dog as he did. Without more reflection therefore it left the dog and entering into the thick wool began with great toil to try to pass to the roots of the hairs; which enterprise however after much sweat it found to be impossible, owing to these hairs being so thick as almost to touch each other, and there being no space there where the flea could taste the skin. Consequently, after long labour and fatigue it began to wish to go back to its dog, which however had already departed, so that after long repentance and bitter tears it was obliged to die of hunger.

WHY DOGS TAKE PLEASURE IN SMELLING AT EACH OTHER. This animal has a horror of the poor, because they eat poor food, and it loves the rich, because they have good living and especially meat. And the excrement of animals always retains some virtue of its origin as is shown by the faeces.

Now dogs have so keen a smell that they can discern by their nose the virtue remaining in these faeces, and if they find them in the streets, smell them and if they smell in them the virtue of meat or of other things, they take them, and if not, they leave them: And to return to the question, I say that if by means of this smell they know that dog to be well fed, they respect him, because they judge that he has a powerful and rich master; and if they discover no such smell with the virtue of good meat, they judge that dog to be of small account and to have a poor and humble master, and therefore they bite that dog as they would his master.

I have found that in the composition of the human body as compared with the bodies of animals the senses are less subtle and coarser; it is thus composed of less ingenious machinery and of cells less capable of receiving the power of senses. I have seen that in the lion the sense of smell is connected with the substance of the brain and descends through the nostrils which form an ample receptacle for it; and it enters into a great number of cartilaginous cells which are provided with many passages in order to receive the brain. A large part of the head of the lion is given up to the sockets of the eyes, and the optic nerves are in immediate contact with the brain; the contrary occurs in man, because the sockets of the eyes occupy a small portion of the head, and the optic nerves are subtle and long and weak, and owing to the weakness of their action we see little by day and less at night; and the animals above mentioned see better at night than in the daytime; and the proof of this is that they seek their prey at night and sleep during the daytime, as do also the nocturnal birds.

The Five Senses, Anatomy, and the Soul

When Cardinal Luigi of Aragon, grandson of King Ferdinand I of Naples and a relative of Isabella Aragon Sforza, visited the Chateau du Cloux in Amboise, Leonardo showed him some of his anatomical drawings. The Cardinal's secretary Antonio de Beatis was so impressed that he wrote about it in his published diary.

> ... Leonardo can no longer paint with the sweetness that was particular to him, nevertheless he still works at making drawings and teaches others. This gentleman has compiled a special treatise on anatomy, showing by illustration not only the members, but also the muscles, nerves, veins, joints, intestines, and all that one can study in the bodies of men and women in a way that has never yet been done by any other person. All of this we have seen with our own eyes; and he said he had already dissected more than thirty bodies of men and women of all ages. Also, of divers machines, and other matters, which he has set down in an infinite number of volumes, all in the vulgar tongue, which if they were published, would prove profitable and very pleasant. [S40]

The French king enjoyed looking at and talking about Leonardo's anatomical drawings during their fireside chats. On one occasion, during their get-togethers, the subject turned to Leonardo's search for the anatomical location of the soul. For Leonardo, the soul was simply the culmination (zenith, meridian) point for all the five senses of a person coming together at one location within the brain. It is the point of awareness about ourselves/themselves and our/their surroundings, it is where the conscious and the subconscious and automatic responses meet and enable us to think and reason and power us to act. It is the person's essence, their spirit, their soul, and their awareness of God. It is our reason, essence, passion, and interpreter of our existence. Experience is processed and stored as memory to help us make sense of our lives.

From his readings and discussion with theologians, philosophers, anatomists, and experts of the Holy Spirit, Leonardo was fully informed of the three prevailing points of view of our pioneering elders. The Aristotelian view, also held by the Stoics and Epicureans, is that the soul is located in the heart. The Alcmaein, Platonian, Galenian, and Hippocratic view is that the soul is located in the brain. A third view is that the soul is in the heart and the brain, and that it somehow pulsates between the two locations. From Leonardo's early experiments in 1487 on the pithing and beheading of frogs, he concluded that the soul, the essence of any person or animal, was in the brain. He told the king that he first considered this idea when he read an account by Livy in the *Seventh Book of the Carthagian War* that outlined how drivers killed their elephants by smashing a sharp spike in between their ears where the neck joins the spinal column and that this was the quickest death that could be given to them. This immediately removed the essence (life) of the elephant from its body. Leonardo then performed experiments on the frog to test the generative and transitive power of the spinal cord. This is what he wrote in his notebook in 1487 and told the French king thirty years later:

> The frog retains life for some hours when deprived of its head and heart and all its bowels. But if you puncture the spinal nerve below its brain (spinal medulla) it immediately twitches and dies. The frog instantly dies when the spinal cord is pierced; and before this it lived without head, without heart or any bones or intestines or skin, and here therefore it would seem lies the foundation of movement and life. All nerves of animals derive from the here (spinal cord), and when this is punctured, the animal dies at once.

From these experiments, Leonardo concluded that the soul was essential for life, and that it was located in the brain. In later years, he dissected human and animal brains in order to find and define the exact location of the soul within the brain. From his studies and dissections of the olfactory, optic, and cranial nerves, he pinpointed the soul to the middle ventricle of the ventricular system. The optic nerves converged onto the anterior ventricle that he named the *intelletto* (intellect) and *imprensivo* (regulator/integrator/communicator). The auditory and olfactory nerves moved towards the middle ventricle that he named the *volonta* (will) and *senso comune* or common sense. The third or posterior ventricle, located above the spinal cord, he named the *memoria* or memory. Thus, sensation and action arises from the middle ventricle, and is influenced by intellectual input from the anterior ventricle and memory from the posterior ventricle. In his last experiments on the ventricular system, he discovered the worm muscle, or the door that is located in one of the ventricles of the brain and that regulates cerebral communication by lengthening and shortening to open and close the passage of the *imprensiva* or the *senso comune* to the memory.

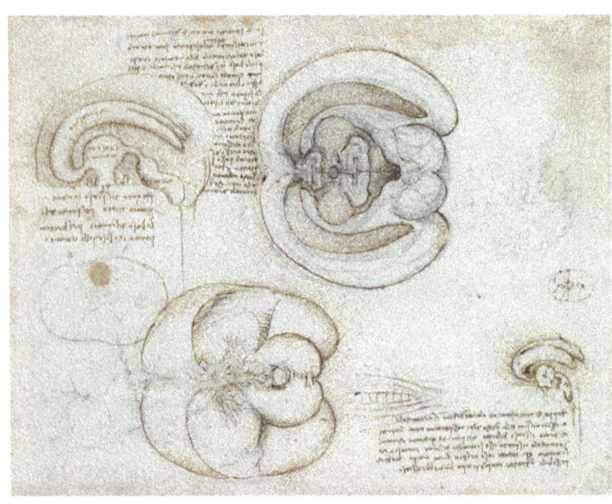

Fig. 135. Leonardo's drawings of the sectioned brain and the position of the cerebral ventricles based on his experiments with injected wax.

I was with Leonardo as his assistant in Vaprio when he injected wax into the floor of the third ventricle of a calf's brain using a syringe and allowed the fluid and air escape from the other ventricles by drilling small holes in the horns of the lateral ventricles. After the wax set, he dissected away the rest of the brain and was left with a cast of the ventricular system. He is probably the first person ever to have cast and moulded the soul of any animal. He not only solved a complex anatomical problem, but he also fully clarified his concept of the *senso comune*. We made numerous clay castes of the ventricular system and prepared a few bronze versions. I promised the king that I would send him one of my bronze models of the soul that I had kept at Vaprio.

> Make two air holes in the horns of the great ventricles and insert melted wax by means of a syringe, making a hole in the ventricle of the memoria, and through this hole fill the three ventricles of the brain; and afterwards when the wax has set take away the brain and you will see the shape of the three ventricles exactly.

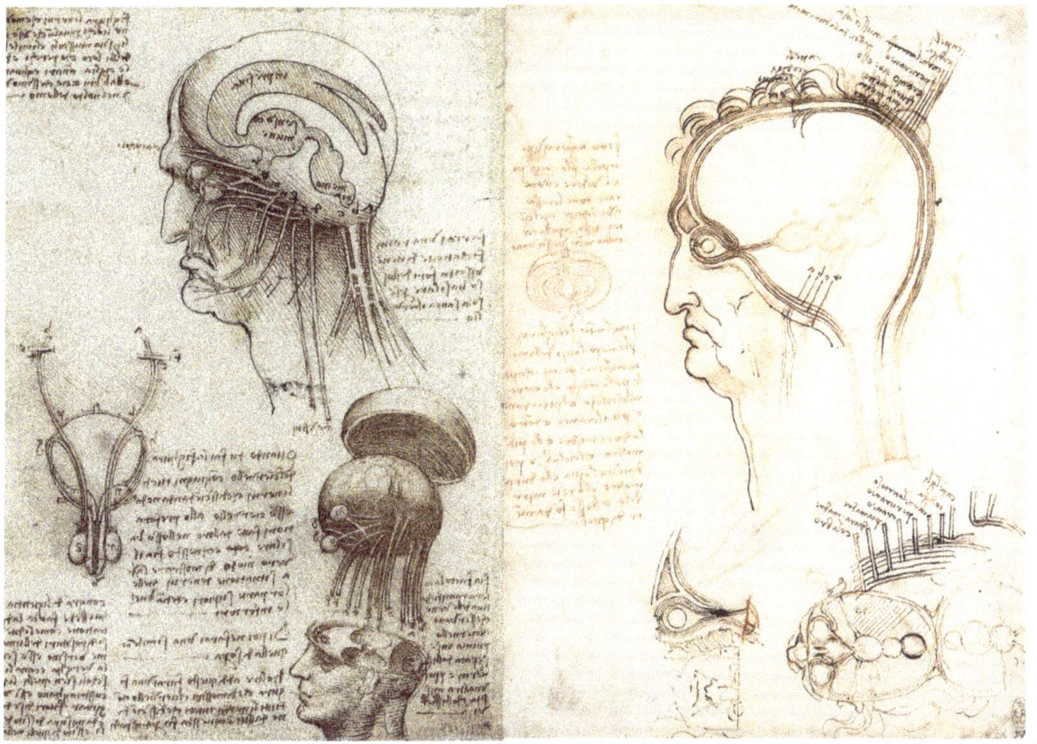

Fig. 136. Leonardo's drawings of the layers of the scalp, and the cerebral ventricles, and nerve pathways to the brain based on his experiments and the reading of the anatomy classics.

I let Leonardo's own words speak for themselves about his search for the soul and the five senses.

> HOW THE FIVE SENSES ARE THE MINISTERS OF THE SOUL. The soul seems to reside in the judgment, and the judgment would seem to be seated in that part where all the senses meet; and this is called the 'senso comune' (Common Sense) and is not all-pervading throughout the body, as many have thought. Rather is it entirely in this one part only. Because, if it were all-pervading and the same in every part, there would have been no need to make the instruments of the senses meet in one centre and in one single spot; on the contrary it would have sufficed that the eye should fulfil the function of its sensation on its surface only, and not transmit the image of the things seen, to the sense, by means of the optic nerves, so that the soul--for the reason given above-- may perceive it in the surface of the eye. In the same way as to the sense of hearing, it would have sufficed if the voice had merely sounded in the porous cavity of the indurated portion of the temporal bone, which lies within the ear, without making any farther transit from this bone to the common sense, where the voice confers with and discourses to the common judgment. The sense of smell, again, is compelled by necessity to refer itself to that same

judgment. Feeling passes through the perforated cords and is conveyed to this "senso comune" (common sense). These cords diverge with infinite ramifications into the skin, which encloses the members of the body and the viscera. The perforated cords convey volition and sensation to the subordinate limbs. These cords and the nerves direct the motions of the muscles and sinews, between which they are placed; these obey, and this obedience takes effect by reducing their thickness; for in swelling, their length is reduced, and the nerves shrink which are interwoven among the particles of the limbs; being extended to the tips of the fingers, they transmit to the sense the object which they touch. The nerves with their muscles obey the tendons as soldiers obey the officers, and the tendons obey the 'senso comune' (Common [central] Sense) as the officers obey the general. Thus, the joint of the bones obeys the nerve, and the nerve the muscle, and the muscle the tendon and the tendon the Common Sense. And the 'senso comune' (Common Sense) is the seat of the soul, and memory is its ammunition, and the 'imprensiva' is its standard of reference since the sense waits on the soul and not the soul on the sense. And where the sense that ministers to the soul is not at the service of the soul, all the functions of that sense are also wanting in that man's life, as is seen in those born mute and blind.

ON THE ORIGIN OF SOUL. Though human ingenuity may make various inventions which, by the help of various machines answering the same end, it will never devise any inventions more beautiful, nor more simple, nor more to the purpose than Nature does; because in her inventions nothing is wanting, and nothing is superfluous, and she needs no counterpoise when she makes limbs proper for motion in the bodies of animals. But, she puts into them the soul of the body, which forms them, that is, the soul of the mother which first constructs in the womb the form of the man and in due time awakens the soul that is to inhabit it. And this at first lies dormant and under the tutelage of the soul of the mother, who nourishes and vivifies it by the umbilical vein, with all its spiritual parts, and this happens because this umbilicus is joined to the placenta and the cotyledons, by which the child is attached to the mother. And these are the reason why a wish, a strong craving or a fright or any other mental suffering in the mother, has more influence on the child than on the mother; for there are many cases when the child loses its life from them, etc. This discourse is not in its place here, but will be wanted for the one on the composition of animated bodies--and the rest of the definition of the soul I leave to the imaginations of friars, those fathers of the people who know all secrets by inspiration.

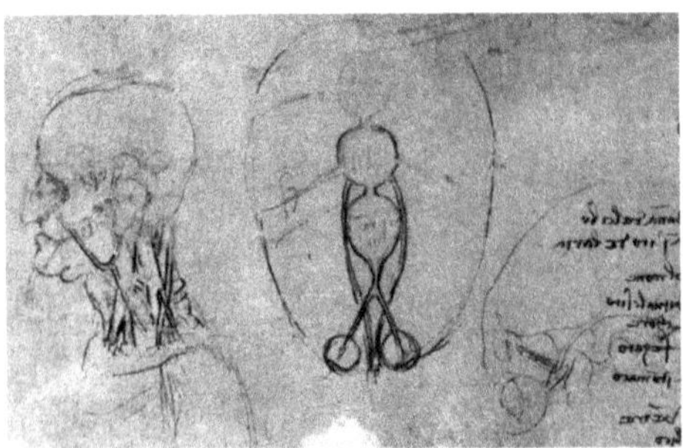

Fig. 137. Leonardo's drawings of the layers of the cerebral ventricles and neuronal connections to the eyeballs.

HOW THE NERVES SOMETIMES ACT OF THEMSELVES WITHOUT ANY FURTHER COMMANDS FROM THOSE OTHER FUNCTIONS OF THE SOUL. This is most plainly seen; for you will see palsied and shivering persons move, and their trembling limbs, as their head and hands, quake without leave from their soul and their soul with all its power cannot prevent their members from trembling. The same thing happens in falling sickness, or in parts that have been cut off, as in the tails of lizards. The idea or imagination is the helm and guiding-rein of the senses, because the thing conceived moves the sense. Preimagining is imagining the things that are to be. Postimagining is imagining the things that are past.

HOW THE BODY OF ANIMALS IS CONSTANTLY DYING AND BEING RENEWED. The body of any thing whatever that takes nourishment constantly dies and is constantly renewed; because nourishment can only enter into places where the former nourishment has expired, and if it has expired it no longer has life. And if you do not supply nourishment equal to the nourishment, which is gone, life will fail in vigour, and if you take away this nourishment, the life is entirely destroyed. But, if you restore as much is destroyed day by day, then as much of the life is renewed as is consumed, just as the flame of the candle is fed by the nourishment afforded by the liquid of this candle, which flame continually with a rapid supply restores to it from below as much as is consumed in dying above: and from a brilliant light is converted in dying into murky smoke; and this death is continuous, as the smoke is continuous; and the continuance of the smoke is equal to the continuance of the nourishment, and in the same instant all the flame is dead and all regenerated, simultaneously with the movement of its own nourishment.

Leonardo believed that an intense study of nature was what brought knowledge to the world. It was through our most important sensor - the eye - that the world came into our brain where it was interpreted and stored in the *senso comune* for the understanding of the soul. The soul's primary role was to understand the workings of nature, not to concentrate on Neoplatonic thoughts of abstract speculation. Truth was not to be found in investigating the soul, but understanding the world.

Perspective, Relativity, and the Pyramidal Laws of Nature

It was never easy to know what was on Leonardo's mind or what topic he was pursuing on any given day. Once, I asked him what subject was his favourite and occupied him most of the time. He said,

> Among the various studies of natural processes that of light give the most pleasure to those who contemplate it. Perspective therefore is to be preferred to all the discourses and systems of the schoolmen. In it you find the glory not only of mathematics but of physics, adorned as it is with the flowers of both.

Leonardo deduced the pyramidal laws of perspective from his study of optics and light, and he carried them over from the perspective of light onto the four powers of nature: movement, force, weight, and percussion (impact) acting on the four elements, earth, water, air, and fire. With this came the four powers of man, memory and intellect, desire and covetousness.

> We will be telling the truth by affirming that it is possible to imagine all powers capable of infinite augmentation or diminution. **Consequently, all powers are pyramidal (perspectival) because they can grow from nothing to infinite greatness by equal degrees**. And by similar degrees they decrease to infinity by diminution ending in nothing. Therefore nothingness borders on infinity.

For Leonardo, all powers are pyramidal, that is, they are perspectival, relative, and change in quantum amounts. This was his general theory of relativity. For example, the visual experience depends on the power of light that brings images of illuminated objects to the eye. It diminishes in pyramidal proportion according to the distance it travels in spreading waves from the object seen. It enters the eye and travels along the optic nerve to the *imprensiva* and onto the *senso comune* to enter into consciousness. The perspective power of light and colour diminishes pyramidally (quantumly) like the power of the waves from the percussion of a stone falling into water.

Everything is relative, perspective, pyramidal, and proportional. *'Proportion is not only to be found in numbers and measures, but also in sounds, weights, intervals of time, and in every force in existence.'*

Leonardo delighted in demonstrating the certainty of proportional law for its own sake because he thought that it confirmed the interconnectedness of all things in nature. However, this certainty did not always hold during the course of testing his theory by experimentation, which could be explained away as a minor fault in the premise or a fault in the experiment.

I have many notes from Leonardo on the pyramidal laws of nature that I am trying to bring together in his *Treatise on Mechanics and Science*. This is proving more difficult than I initially thought because of my poor background in mathematics and physics. Nevertheless, I have managed with the help of many learned experts and friends to put together a reasonable folio that I hope to publish soon. When I asked Leonardo a few months before his death what he really meant by his pyramidal laws of nature? he said, '*all things are interconnected and this is relative or proportional depending on our perspective and movement and where we are when we observe these natural processes, but the laws of nature are constant and remain the same.*' For me, it all remains a great mystery, and I leave it in the hands of God and Leonardo da Vinci.

> The science of painting deals with all the colours of the surfaces of bodies and with the shapes of the bodies thus enclosed; with their relative nearness and distance; with the degrees of diminution required as distances gradually increase; and this science is the mother of perspective, that is the science of visual rays. Perspective is divided into three parts, of which the first deals only with the line-drawing of bodies; the second with the toning down of colours as they recede into the distance; the third with the loss of distinctness of bodies at various distances. Now the first part, which deals only with lines and boundaries of bodies, is called drawing, that is to say the figuration of any body. From it springs another science that deals with shade and light, also called *chiaroscuro*, which requires much explanation.
>
> Perspective is nothing else than seeing a place behind a sheet of glass, smooth and quite transparent, on the surface of which all the things may be marked that are behind this glass. The things approach the point of the eye in pyramids, and these pyramids are intersected on the glass plane.

Power, Motion, and Machines

Five of Leonardo's favourite words in his notebooks are toward, forward, power, force, and motion. These five words denote action and movement and mechanics, and a machine's dependence upon them. They occupied Leonardo's thoughts and studies for his entire life. He spent a lifetime observing, studying, and building machines right up to the last years of his life. He was ready to publish a book on mechanics, and he wrote this note to me, '*the Book of the science of Mechanics must precede the Book of useful inventions. Mechanics is the paradise of the science of mathematics, because through it one reaches the fruit of mathematics.*' Also, he wanted to separate his theoretical and mathematical work on the powers that move the universe such as weight, force, motion, and impact from his practical work that was on the application of these powers in the construction of mechanical devices. '*To mix up practice with theory, would produce a confused and incoherent work.*'

Leonardo had a large workshop at the bottom of his garden at the Chateau du Cloux that the king enjoyed to visit and to see what the maestro was tinkering with and what new models and instruments he had constructed with the help of his work force and close assistants. He was ready to prepare his *Manual of Mechanics,* and in it, he had drawings of the individual components that make up the various parts of machines such as screws, keys, rivets, ball bearings and plummers, pins, axles, shafts, couplings, ropes, belts, chains, toothed wheels, flywheels, friction wheels, levers and connecting rods, gears, brakes, ratchets, pipes, pumps, valves, pistons, springs, cranks and rods, cams, wheels, handles, and pulleys. Some of the long list of machines that Leonardo discussed and showed the king with his drawings, models or actual working structures included his war, flying, and musical machines, different contraptions turned by water or air or fire, and machines for ships, waterworks, and carriages. Among them were pumps, moving hoists and ladders, treadmills, mechanical digging and dredging machines for canals and trenches, armoured tanks, giant cannons and crossbows, measuring devices, compasses, clocks, automated carriages, underwater breathing apparatus, boilers, furnaces, mechanical drum, button controlled string instruments, movable theatre in the round, *camera obscura*, timepieces, perpetual motion machines, man carrying underwater machines, floats for walking on water, magnifying glasses to observe and magnify the terrain of the moon, flying instruments, and gliders and parachutes. I could go on and on about the various instruments of war and peace that he had invented or improved, but the few I have exemplified are sufficient to reveal the diverse nature of his mind and his genius. Leonardo had the following caveat in regard to the invention and construction of his machines and instruments:

> Though human ingenuity may make various inventions, which by the help of various machines answering the same end, it will never devise any inventions more beautiful, nor more simple, nor more to the purpose than Nature does; because in her inventions nothing is wanting, and nothing is superfluous, and she needs no counterpoise when she makes limbs proper for motion in the bodies of animals. But, she puts into them the soul of the body, which forms them, that is, the soul of the mother which first constructs in the womb the form of the man and in due time awakens the soul that is to inhabit it.

Whenever I sit on my favourite rock beside the Adda River and I watch the boats of the tiller men move by me with or against the flow of the water, I think of Leonardo's descriptions and principles of Force:

> Force arises from dearth or abundance; it is the child of physical motion, and the grandchild of spiritual motion, and the mother and origin of gravity. Gravity is limited to the elements of water and earth; but this force is unlimited, and by it infinite worlds might be moved if instruments could be made by which the force could be generated. Force, with physical motion, and gravity, with resistance are the four external powers on which all actions of mortals depend. Force has its origin in spiritual motion; and this motion, flowing through the limbs of sentient animals, enlarges their muscles. Being enlarged by this current, the muscles are shrunk in length and contract the tendons, which are connected with them, and this is the cause of the force of the limbs in man. The quality and quantity of the force of a man are able to give birth to other forces, which will be proportionally greater as the motions produced by them last longer.

CHAPTER 29

Post Mortem and Adieu

Men are in error when they lament the flight of time, accusing it of being too swift, and not perceiving that it is sufficient as it passes; but good memory, with which nature has endowed us, causes things long past to seem present.

— Leonardo da Vinci

It is the End, My Friend

After a short illness, Leonardo da Vinci died at the Chateau du Cloux in Amboise on 2nd May 1519. He was 67 years of age. If all the world is a stage and all the men and women merely players then Leonardo lived from birth to decrepitude through most of his seven stages and acts of life by playing many different parts with dignity and genius in a strange and eventful history. As an infant, he was born out of wedlock and gazed out at his surroundings in his mother's arms. As a boy, he ran about his grandfather's fields and lands in the care of his uncle, father, and his loving stepmothers. As a young man, he worked the furnaces and paintings as an apprentice of Verrocchio and as Ginevra de' Benci and Simonetta Vespucci's lover. As an experienced soldier, architect, and painter, he worked in the service of various ambitious Lords and Ladies to bring them honour, wealth, and prestige, and he saw injustice that was beyond his control. In his fifth age, he tried to bring justice and learning to those he loved and address the necessary quarrel to those who dishonoured him. In his sixth age, he continued with his sciences, architecture, and painting in greater desperation and in foreign lands with his spectacles on his nose, a cap on his head, and a pouch on his side. In his final act, the seventh age, he contemplated his history and happily died before he could experience the unwanted last scene that he dreaded most and that still awaited him, his second childishness, sans teeth, sans eyes, sans taste, sans hearing, sans reason, and sans everything. And he has not passed into oblivion, for his memory lives on for all of us to know and to learn about him and his love for peace, freedom, liberty, reason, knowledge, understanding, happiness, and true justice.

Leonardo's epitaph inscribed on his tombstone (Leonardo da Vinci, Maestro, King's Architect and Painter and Man of Reason: 15th April 1452 to 2nd May 1519) is his oft-quoted saying:

> Just as a well-filled day brings blessed sleep, so a well-employed life brings a blessed death.

I already wrote about his death, funeral, and last will and testament in the opening chapter of this book. Here, I leave you with a few notes that I made in my diary a short time before and soon after he passed away and left us, forever.

> It is May, hot and humid. The mosquitoes harass and irritate and the flies multiply. Maturina sponges his face with some aromatic vinegar. 'Is my lord ill?' she asks. I was surprised, my hands trembled, my head swooned, and I fell in shock. He is unable to speak. He is sick, swollen, and not able to hear.

The vigil has started. I knelt at the foot of the bed and wept. Under the *baldacchino* of the great bed, Leonardo's body is stretched out, moulded by the sheets, a recumbent sculpture in readiness for his tomb, the sculpted cheekbones of his face now haggard, lined with valleys and rivulets, the smile still haughty, defiant, tender. A wind blows in through the large windows. The flames of lamps and the hairs of his white beard flicker. The presentments are confirmed by the wailing threnodies, the solitude is acute. I huddle wounded in a corner while three monks chant litanies and psalms. Soon, he will be garbed in a garment of monastic austerity and taken away from us forever.

Carriages, hearse, wagons, 3 white horses, the king's equerry, Sanseverino, three marshals, Leo's two mules – Pieta and Pedro – procession, including me – long line – black drapes, images of Madonna – banners, candle holders –tapers, wax candles bent in the hands of penitents, trembling tapers, wailing waifs, people in black – funeral hangings – across the nave to violet veils in honour of the royal mourning.

The populaces along the route of Leonardo's coffin kneel before him, for he was much loved for his festivals, processions, charities, and goodwill. The men and women knew him best as the one who gave them the Salamander Tavern with a fiery breath. In accordance with his last wishes, on the day of his funeral, sixty paupers carrying torches accompany him in broad daylight.

People will ask me why she (Maturina) was left so little, but Leonardo knew her to be pious, wanting little, and she had the king's favours and protection.

LEONARDO. Who was he? He was a man with a huge curiosity, imagination, and intelligence. He was curious about everything. He was a sponge for knowledge. He was a diplomat, a musician, an entertainer, a poet, a painter, an inventor, a philosopher, a joker, a magician, a lover, a father, a humanitarian, a designer of war machines, a scholar, an anatomist …

Death of Eleven Other Notables in 1519

By the end of 1519, it came to my attention that eleven other notables who had known Leonardo had died the same year that he did. The French king also knew them, and he and his sister told me about some of them. A list of notables follows:

Maximilian I, born 22nd March 1459, died on the 12th January, aged 59 years, the son of Frederick III, Holy Roman Emperor, and Eleanor of Portugal, was King of the Romans (the Germans) from 1486 and Holy Roman Emperor from 1493 (inherited title) and 1508 (self-elected title) until his death. He expanded the influence of the House of Habsburg through war and his marriage in 1477 to Mary of Burgundy, the heiress to the Duchy of Burgundy, soon to be inherited by his grandson, Charles V.

Cardinal Luigi of Aragon died in Naples on 21st January, aged 45 years, about three months before Leonardo died. He visited Leonardo and me at Cloux in Amboise in October 1517 while on his European tour with his small entourage and secretary Matteo Bandello. Leonardo gifted him with his folio on hydraulics, water management, and machines. The cardinal left his estates to his nephew, the Duke of Amalfi, Alfonso II Piccolomini, and his son, Innico Piccolomini. The historical novelist Matteo Bandello wrote that the cardinal and his brother arranged to have his sister, Giovanna d'Aragona, and her children strangled because she had married and had children with her household manager Antonio Beccadelli di Bologna. The cardinal also paid for the assassination of Antonia who brought dishonour to the cardinal's family.

Francesco II Gonzaga died on the 29th March, aged 53 years, ruler of Mantua from 1484 until his death. He was husband of Isabella d' Este. Leonardo and his assistants eventually relented and provided her with a number of portraits of herself when Francesco Gonzaga was still alive.

Blanche of Montferrat died on the 30th of March, aged 47 years. She was the Duchess of Savoy and titular Queen consort of Cyprus, Jerusalem, and Armenia, and wife of Charles I of

Savoy. She acted as regent for her only son Charles from 1490 until his accidental death in 1496.

Madeleine de La Tour d'Auvergne died on the 28th April, aged 21 years. She was the youngest daughter of Jean III de La Tour, Count of Auvergne and Lauraguais, and Jeanne de Bourbon-Vendôme. She married Lorenzo di Piero de' Medici in Amboise on the 4th of May in 1518, and Leonardo produced their wedding festival. She gave birth to Catherine de' Medici the future Queen of France. She died one week before her husband.

Lorenzo di Piero de' Medici died aged 27 years, two days after Leonardo and only one year after his marriage to Madeleine de La Tour d'Auvergne in Amboise. He was the Duke of Urbino and ruler of Florence from 1516 to 1519. His daughter Catherine de' Medici became Queen Consort of France while his illegitimate son Alessandro de' Medici became the first Duke of Florence. Lorenzo died one week after his wife.

Lucrezia Borgia, a renowned Italian beauty, was born on the 18th of April 1480 and she died on the 24th of June, aged 39 years. She was the illegitimate daughter of Pope Alexander VI and Vannozza dei Cattanei. Her brothers included Cesare Borgia, Giovanni Borgia, and Gioffre Borgia. She became a good friend of Isabella Aragon Sforza of Bari. She gave birth to nine children, was married twice (at least) and had numerous lovers.

Artus Gouffier de Boissy died on the 13th of May, aged 44 years. He was a French nobleman and politician with many titles and fiefdoms. He served as Grand Master of France and attempted to negotiate a lasting peace between France and the House of Habsburg at the time of his early death.

Francesco Bonsignori died 2nd July, aged 64 years. He was an Italian painter sponsored for many years by Francesco II Gonzaga, Marquess of Mantua, and influenced by Andrea Mantegna.

Francesco Cybo died 25th July, aged 69 years. He was born in Naples as the illegitimate son of Pope Innocent VIII, and he received many Italian titles and fiefs from his father. Among his titles were governor of Rome and Count of the Lateran Palace. He married Lorenzo de' Medici's daughter Maddalena de' Medici and was brother-in-law to Pope Leo X. He had a passion for playing cards and attempted to steal the Papal treasure. He died in 1519 after a trip to Tunis and was buried in St. Peter's Basilica. Leonardo taught him some card tricks.

Cardinal Luigi de' Rossi died in Rome on the 20th of August, aged 45 years. He was a Florentine and a friend of Leonardo and Raphael in Rome. He is in the background behind Pope Leo X in the painting by Raphael (Fig. 106).

After Leonardo's death, the King appointed me as his painter's agent and secretary of his household. He requested that I persuade Raphael to visit the French royal court for a year while I would be there in the service of the King. Raphael declined because he was too busy with commissions in Rome, and then he died unexpectedly at the age of 37 years in 1520, less than one year after Leonardo's death. I lost another of my great friends. Rest in Peace, beautiful Raphael. I hope that you and Leonardo are painting and scheming together once again in the heavens of fulfilment.

The year 1520 was also the year that my father, Leonardo's best friend, Gerolamo (Jerome) Melzi, died. I inherited the Melzi Villa and my father's other properties and his title of Count Palatine Melzi of Vaprio d'Adda.

The Death of Maximilian I and the Rise of Charles V, the Duke of Burgundy, as the New Holy Roman Emperor

Maximilian I, the Holy Roman Emperor and a former ally of Ludovico Sforza, died in Austria on 12th of January 1519. Many considered him an odd and frivolous monarch. A Pope described him as '*light and inconsistent, always begging for other men's money, which he wastes in chamois hunting.*' The Emperor ruled over the Holy Roman Empire of the Great German Nation. The Holy Roman Empire was once a complex of territories in central Europe including the kingdoms of Germany, Bohemia, Italy, and Burgundy, and numerous other territories including the Duchy of Milan. Many of these territories were still part of the Empire as an Imperial Circle in the eyes of the Emperor, but in reality the Empire had lost most of its Italian and Burgundian territories during the past thirty to forty years of his and his ancestors' rule. The supreme power of the Emperor over his vast Empire was inherited from the emperors of Rome, but the Holy Roman Emperor was still traditionally elected by the grand nobles of the Empire and then crowned by the Pope.

King Francois was excited by the news of the death of Maximilian in the New Year, and one night, he visited Leonardo and me at Cloux to canvas our views about his bid for the vacant position of Holy Roman Emperor. He knew that my father and I were Count Palatines of Lombardy, and that we held allegiance to the Holy Roman Empire, and that we were hereditary representatives of the Holy Roman Emperor in Lombardy, which still was one of the nominal territories of the Holy Roman Empire. In this sense, we had a vote because we possessed an extent of privileges from the Holy Roman Emperor that gave us independence within the Duchy of Milan. King Francois wanted to know from me how to best garner the votes to be elected the new Holy Roman Emperor, and he wanted my father's help and those of all the other Palatine of Lombardy. His main rival was Maximilian's grandson Charles V, Duke of Burgundy and King of Spain and heir to the Habsburg Monarchy.

Charles was six years younger that Francois, and he quickly was becoming his greatest rival. Charles in comparison to Francois was cold, phlegmatic, and with the Habsburg infamous deformed jaw. He rarely spoke or smiled. Charles's first language was French, and he had an immense dislike for Francois who was charming, flamboyant, and handsome, and a great favourite with the ladies. Neither wanted to take a backward step against the other. Charles's father Philip I of Castile was Maximilian's son who had inherited the Duchy of Burgundy and the Burgundian Netherlands, and so Charles V correctly thought that he and he alone was the rightful successor to the Habsburg Monarchy and the Holy Roman Empire. Henry VIII, king of England, was the other contender for the position, but he was the most unlikely successor because of his conflicts with the Pope and the Church of Rome. Another contender was Fredrick III, Elector of Saxony, but he had little chance against Charles V who had inherited the Habsburg Monarchy from his grandfather. Moreover, Fredrick III had defended Martin Luther and the Lutherans much too strongly, whereas Charles was a staunch Catholic and much more critical of Martin Luther.

Although the position of Holy Roman Emperor was traditionally elective, in reality it was controlled by dynasties. At this time, the German Prince-Electors held sway, and they were expected to elect one of their peers. Charles was the favourite for he was the grandson of the previous Holy Roman Emperor and the most likely to be elected king of the Germans. Nevertheless, the seven Electors were open to bribery, and Francois believed that he held a good chance to be elected if he lobbied correctly, effectively, and offered sufficient bribes. Therefore, I was conscripted and obliged to write numerous correspondences to my father and to other nobles and palatines who might be able to influence the Electors in their voting. As expected, it was Charles V who won the bribery contest and the election at Heidelberg on 28th June 1519, almost two months after Leonardo's death. However, the Pope did not crown the new Holy Roman Emperor until 1530. The ceremony was in Bologna, and the Pope was Clement VII, a prisoner under the complete control of Charles V who had sacked, raped, and pillaged Rome in 1527. Charles V reduced the population of Rome from 55,000 to 10,000 people during his eight-months of tyranny.

Francois was greatly affected by the death of Leonardo and his failure to be elected the Holy Roman Emperor that was awarded to his nemesis Charles V. Contrary to Leonardo's good advice for calm diplomacy, the rivalry between Francois and Charles V intensified and the competition for the Empire continued for the next thirty years. Charles allied with

England and Pope Leo X against the French and the Venetians, and they defeated and captured Francois at the Battle of Pavia in 1525 to drive the French out of Milan. To gain his freedom, Francois was forced to pay a huge ransom, permit the imprisonment of his own sons as a form of security for Charles, cede Burgundy to Charles in the Treaty of Madrid, and renounce his claim over Navarre. When released, however, Francois had the Parliament of Paris denounce the treaty because it had been signed under duress. France then joined the League of Cognac that Pope Clement VII had formed with Henry VIII of England, the Venetians, the Florentines, and the Milanese to resist Charles's imperial domination of Italy. In the ensuing war in 1527, Charles sacked Rome, imprisoned Pope Clement VII and prevented him from annulling the marriage of Henry VIII of England to his aunt Catherine of Aragon. This act by Charles V essentially allowed the English king to break free of the Roman Catholic Church and establish the English Reformation and his own Church of England.

Another war between France and Italy erupted in 1535, when, following the death of the last Sforza Duke of Milan, Charles installed his own son Philip as the Duke of Milan, despite Francois's claims on the Duchy. Although Francois failed to conquer Milan, he conquered most of the Duchy of Savoy, including its new capital Turin. A short truce ended in 1542 when Francois remembered Leonardo's good advice and allied himself with the Ottoman Sultan Suleiman I against Charles in a new war. The two-year war was ultimately abandoned when neither Francois nor Charles could establish the upper hand, and so the *status quo ante bellum* was restored temporarily. After Francois died in 1547, another war erupted in 1551 between Charles and Francois's son and successor Henri II. After some early successes by Henri in France and on the border with Spain, his offensives failed in Italy. A tired Charles V abdicated midway through this conflict, leaving his son Philip II and his brother Ferdinand I as the new Holy Roman Emperors to protect their territorial interests in Spain and Italy. Francois died with a grudging respect for Charles V, but with an unfulfilled and unsatisfied feeling about his rivalry and his rule. As the rightful Duke of Milan, he never resigned himself to losing this beautiful Duchy and the *Last Supper* at the Convent of Santa Maria delle Grazie. In contrast to Francois, Charles retired to the monastery of Yuste in Extramadura in 1556 to contemplate his achievements, and he died there from fevers of bad air (malaria or miasmic fever) on 21st September 1558.

Leonardo, Secret Agent

Some people have asked me, 'was Leonardo da Vinci a secret agent?' I replied with the question, 'who for? For the French, for Florence, for Milan, for the Medici, for the Sforza, for Sanseverino, for Isabella of Bari, for the Melzi of Vaprio, for the Borgia, for Rome and the Pope, who for?' I can only answer: No, he wasn't!!! If you mean a secret agent like a father confessor of the church who is a silent vessel full of peoples and states' secrets that he will not divulge, then I say, yes.

Like many court painters and priests of patricians, the lords, and ladies, Leonardo heard many confessions, and he saw many profound intimacies, and he attended many political secret meetings. But, he never used his knowledge and observations as a spy or a secret agent who would then reveal these secrets for blackmail or pass them on to the service of the enemy in order to further their ambitions. Of course, Leonardo was a diplomat for a number of Lords, namely the Medici House, the Sforza House, the Melzi House, the Borgia House, and finally the House of Valois. But, this diplomacy was never covert. Sometimes, he openly accepted a diplomatic mission for the service of a client with a specific purpose. The mission wasn't clandestine, so all who dealt with him knew where they stood. Similarly, as court painter, his models all knew from their own experience and their education what they could and could not disclose to him. Leonardo knew, like all honest court painters, that he had to be discreet in order to obtain further commissions. He could not afford during drunken debauched parties to let slip his knowledge of private intimacies or political secrets that could or would be dispersed suddenly as public gossip and that could be traced back to him as the source of the leak. Leonardo saw indiscretion, imprudence, and betrayal as the Sword of Damocles hanging over his head. If it fell, it could be fatal to him and his reputation. Yet, some people still regarded him as a secret agent for various clients, and they were highly suspicious of him and his privileged positions. One of the more intriguing claims or accusations that I heard often was that he was a spy for the Duchess of Bari, Isabella the former Duchess of Milan, and for her husband the 6th Duke of Milan, Gian Galeazzo Sforza. Apparently, he spied for her and Naples in order to protect her from any harm from Ludovico Sforza and his cronies. While this speculation might carry some truth, I know that he was never secretly married to the Duchess Isabella, nor did she have four of his children as others have claimed. The Duchess Isabella contracted the pox, and he stayed away sexually from women with sexual diseases. His intimacies were few, and I can count them on the fingers of two hands. If he had affairs with other women, which he may well have, I was not the bookkeeper of his sexual activities, and I do not know any of the details. From what I saw, he was mostly absorbed in his studies, paintings, experiments, and architectural problems. I admired his restraint because he had many beautiful women constantly propositioning him. He seemed to have more fun talking and flirting with them, sketching and painting them than bedding them, particularly if their immodesty and their disloyalty to others allowed them to indulge in such misbehaviour. With certain exceptions, most men, like Leonardo, are restrained, loyal, and modest in their *modus operandi* with the ladies.

In the Service of the French King Without Leonardo's Guidance, and Entertaining Henry VIII, the English King, at the Pageant of the Golden Dale

I stayed in the service of the French king for another three years (1519 to 1522). I spent the first three months after Leonardo's death as the King's tenant at Amboise sorting through Leonardo's belongings and executing his last will and testament. Salai returned to Amboise to pray at Leonardo's grave and to collect the paintings and items that Leonardo had left him and the keepsakes that he wanted to have in remembrance of his teacher and Papa. I kept Leonardo's paintings of the *Mona Lisa, St. John the Baptist,* the *Musician, Flora,* and *Leda and the Swan* as gifts for the French king. The remainder of Leonardo's belongings, manuscripts, books, notebooks, assorted paintings, and models, I packed and sent them over the Alps to the Melzi Villa in Vaprio d'Adda.

In January of 1520, the French king appointed me into his household and awarded me the privilege of being his gentleman of the bedchamber and his falconer. From then on, I travelled with him and his court on his royal tours, and I advised him on matters pertaining to the position of the Holy Roman Empire and the governorship of the Duchy of Milan. Francois's main enemy Charles V, the Duke of Burgundy and King of Spain and Germany, had been elected the Holy Roman Emperor in June of 1519, and King Francois was afraid that Charles V would claim the Duchy of Milan in his own right. King Francois wanted me to keep a firm diplomatic eye open on Charles's claims using my contacts in Milan to inform us of the mood of the people and political insurgencies.

A few months before Leonardo died, the king told him that he was planning to invite the King of England Henry the VIII to visit France for a very important meeting and pageant to increase the bond of friendship between them. The king asked Leonardo to help him design the pageants, festivities, celebrations, and carnivals. 'The English king loves banquets, dancing, jousting, wrestling, and other feats of arms,' said Francois. 'So, we must have many such events for a week or two. Jousting, tennis, and wrestling will be on the menu, of course. I believe the

English king is very adroit with his racket. We will have many a pretty damsel in attendance, for he has an eye for the pretty lady. But, what else can we surprise him with? Help me out, Papa. Something impressive. Something like your mechanical lion, but even better.'

'I will set my brain to it, my Liege,' said Leonardo. 'When wouldst your Majesty like to hold this extravaganza?'

'It will be in a field called the Golden Dale near Adre and Calais in the summer of 1520. It is next year, Papa. We must start planning right away.'

Leonardo set me the task to help him with his plans, and we were soon building models, sketching, drawing, and designing an extravaganza for the two kings. He showed me his plans for robot jousters, mechanical sword fighters, and birds. But, before he could present the French King with all his ideas and preparations, he was dead. It was left to me to present Leonardo's drawings and ideas of the golden flying dragons and fields of golden cloth to the King only a month or more after his burial and church ceremonies.

And so it was that the French King met with the English King in the valley of the Golden Dale between Guisnes and Arde outside Calais on Thursday 8th June 1520. They were accompanied by their Queens, 500 horsemen, and 3,000 foot soldiers, and they pitched their camps and marques opposite each other, the English towards Guisnes where the English Queen stayed, and the French towards Arde where the Queen of France and the king's mother stayed. On the first day of the royal meeting, the king of England and his company stood on one side of the valley and the king of France with his retinue on the other. The retinues of both kings were commanded to remain completely still on pain of death whilst the two kings rode down to the valley bottom to embrace each other in a show of great friendship. They dismounted and embraced while Henry's sword was held, unsheathed, by the Marquess of Dorset, and the French king's sword held by the Duc de Bourbon in a similar salute. There after, the two kings and their entire retinues met at the camp where a tiltyard was prepared in sight of a massive banqueting hall. From that moment on, the two kings tried to out shine each other with dazzling golden tents and clothes, spectacular banners and effigies, huge feasts, jousting, music, and a display of elaborate gold and silver costumes. Jean Clouet and I painted the French banners and tapestries, while Holbein painted and prepared those of the English. There were 400 tents of silver and gold silk and velvet scattered through out the camp; and a few of Leonardo's inventions and decorations were on display, but not his golden flying dragons, nor his gold salamanders and gold lilies in the fields of royal blue lavender, nor the mechanical jousters because nobody knew exactly how to construct and complete these figures in time for the extravaganza.

The French King had brought Leonardo's plans with him intending to show them to the English King, but these along with Leonardo's models, drawings, and other works were unfortunately destroyed in a marquee fire before the English King was able to see them. Surprisingly, it was Henry VIII who pitched his marquee, the largest ever made of gold cloth, near the banqueting hall and pavilion, and not King Francois I who had forgotten or rejected this suggestion by Leonardo. And so, a very distraught French King had to temper his anger about the incident of the fire and losing the prime real estate when he met with the English King in a series of friendly bouts and jousts. I was frightened that the French king's anger might lead to an unfortunate and nasty accident. As it was, Francois's concentration was not at its very best on this day and his nose was broken in a bout with an English lord, the Earl of Devonshire. Still, overall, both Kings matched it in their displays of expensive fabric, tents, and costumes made of golden cloth and expensive fabrics woven with silk, silver, and golden thread. Neither king out did the other completely in their display of ostentatious wealth and elaborate and dazzling arrangements and accommodations. Such sumptuous displays and golden ornaments brought me to tears, and the two fountains flowing in red and white wine brought me to a strange and drunken stupor. It was a draw in giddy displays. Of course, if

Leonardo had lived, he would have tipped the displays and festivities completely in King Francois's favour by more than an extremely long lance and a galloping furlong. Instead, Leonardo and the Saints in Heaven probably looked down on our debauchery with great amusement, witty exchanges, and musical interludes.

On the last day of the meeting, on the day of *Corpus Christi*, Cardinal Wolsey offered Mass in the presence of the two great sovereigns and their congregation. Leonardo's spirit interrupted the proceedings with a most mysterious event. A large golden salamander or dragon decorated with blue and gold lilies of the Royal Coat of Arms of Valois flew over the congregation and stunned both kings and all their honourable guests and servants. Nobody moved or made a noise as they watched the salamander fly overhead and then gently out of sight over a nearby hill and into a dense forest. When the congregation regained their composure, along with Cardinal Wolsey, he gave a general indulgence for all those who were there in his presence after the shock of having seen a flying golden dragon.

Two weeks later back at the Chateau du Cloux in Amboise, two of Leonardo's technicians in his workshop showed me the Golden Salamander that they had flown above the heads of Henry VIII and Francois I, the congregation and Cardinal Wolsey. It was essentially an elongated painted paper balloon that looked like a salamander and was filled with hot air by two burning candles or combustible materials to allow it to lift and fly. It had an attached mechanical device that once it was wound up on a spring could propel the front and hind legs attached to the balloon, like the oars of a boat, and move the balloon forward through the air until the spring stopped moving. This spring was surprisingly powerful to drive the balloon at a good height for several miles before it was mechanically and thermally drained of energy and fell gently back to Earth. The two workmen tested and played with the golden salamander in secret for a year before they released it on the unsuspecting public at the Golden Dale. Leonardo had given them instructions on how to build and test the Golden Salamander and when to release it at an opportune moment like during an outdoor Mass on the last day of the meeting. The two workmen considered confessing their prank to King Francois, but he now was so occupied with state matters and another imminent war with the Duchy of Milan, Rome, and Spanish troops that the Golden Salamander was left hanging as an oddity from the beams of the roof of the workshop. The Golden Salamander like the ghost of Leonardo had come to rest in his own workshop. I wish that I had taken it back with me to Vaprio d'Adda instead of leaving it behind in Amboise, but like many things it was all quickly forgotten about with the more pressing day to day issues that we needed to account for. The Golden Salamander is strongly retained in my memory, and I occasionally wonder whether King Francois I, Henry the VIII, Cardinal Wolsey, and any of the other lords and ladies of the congregation ever considered what the apparition was that flew above them on the last day of our festivities at the Golden Dale and where it had come from. Too much red and white wine soon after, perhaps allowed them to forget too easily.

Proceedings ended very sourly at the Golden Dale before the two Kings parted on that last day. Although the rules of the meeting were carefully established that they would not compete against each other in the tournaments, Henry broke protocol and surprisingly challenged Francois in a wrestling match before a large crowd in attendance. The crowd of more than 300 courtiers was hushed. They knew the challenge and event was meant to be an awe-inspiring surprise. Francois accepted and won quickly, knocking Henry to the ground and twisting his legs back in a painful submission hold. Henry felt humiliated before such a large crowd, and as a result, he briskly farewelled the French king and left the Golden Dale in a dark, unforgiving mood, followed by his large, silent, and bemused entourage.

I remember a few months before his death that Leonardo reminding the French King about the art of diplomacy. Never humiliate or embarrass the Lord who you want as your esteemed ally in front of his subjects, because if you do, he will soon become your enemy and an uncomfortable thorn in your side. I saw Francois do this unintentionally in his friendly, exuberant, and sparkling way, but his win in the wrestling match humiliated Henry. He should have graciously thanked Henry for his challenge and reminded him of their rules of non-engagement, and that they were brothers in arms at least at this meeting, if not at all future meetings. Then, they would have parted on good terms sharing good memories of a mutually successful meeting and wonderful festivities, even though possibly still mystified by the golden flying salamander that they had seen earlier, wondering whether it was a good or a bad portend for them.

The whole purpose of these celebrations and the fortnight of diplomacy by Francois I was to convince King Henry VIII to support and join him and France in their dispute with Pope Leo X and Charles V. Instead, the English king felt humiliated after losing the wrestling match to Francois, and he decided to support Charles V who later that year declared war on France and started the Italian War of 1521 to 1525. Thus, the festivities of the Golden Dale in the summer of 1520, as spectacular and expensive as they were, resulted in France losing the support of the English and with a desperate need to find allies from elsewhere. In this regard, France found its ally in the Republic of Venice and Swiss mercenaries in their hope to hold on to Milan.

One month after the Field of Cloth of Gold, on 14th July 1520, Henry VIII signed a treaty with Charles V promising not to form an alliance with Francois for two years. In July of 1521, Charles declared war against Francois and invaded Champagne in August.

Charles V now wanted to reassign Milan back to the Sforza, and Pope Leo X was happy to support them. In the summer of 1521, the Pope excommunicated the king of France and declared war to oust him from Lombardy. Leonardo, two years earlier, had warned the young French king that the Pope would side with Charles V and oust him from the Duchy of Milan unless he allowed Francesco Sforza to rule on his behalf as his proxy. The King disagreed with Leonardo and said that he would never allow a Sforza to ever rule the Duchy of Milan for this was now his sole domain. Leonardo tried to change the King's mind a few times with reasoned debate, but didn't force the issue. Who knows what can happen in politics? There are too many variables in play.

Uprisings and Back Home in Milan

In the spring of 1521, we received further word from Milan that the French Viceroy Odet de Lautrec was facing an uprising and an invasion from the German and Imperial armies of Charles V and Pope Leo X under the command of Prospero Colonna, the great feudal lord and husband of Covella di Sanseverino and condottiero in the service of the Pope. The French Viceroy lost the battle of Vaprio d'Adda, and he immediately abandoned Milan in late November. Milan was now in the hands of Prospero Colonna, the Pope, and Charles V. Lautrec remained in northern Italy begging his King for funds to feed and pay his army while waiting for an opportunity to recapture Milan. Francois was angry and reproached Lautrec for losing Milan. He promised him that he would send him 400,000 crowns. But, Lautrec never received the money, and we learnt much later that the King's mother Louise, instead, had taken the money for herself from the Superintendent of Finances. When the king found out, he was heard to say to his mother, *'you caused the loss of our fair Duchy, something I could not believe of you, taking the money that was to pay the army.'*

By the spring of 1522, Francois was finding it difficult to hold onto his territories and to collect taxes for war. The peasants had nothing left to give him. The new wars grieved the hearts of his people and many were dying from starvation.

I received letters from my mother and sisters begging me to return to Milan. They had been frightened by the battle that had taken place in their community of Vaprio d' Adda, and they wanted me as the eldest son, who had inherited my father's responsibilities when he died in 1520, to return immediately to protect them and the entitlements, properties, and interests of the Melzi. I had no choice, I had to return and say goodbye to the French king. I convinced the king that I would serve him best from Milan, and he agreed. '*We will soon be back in Milan,*' he told me. I visited Leonardo's grave at the Church of St. Florentin and said my goodbyes with tears flowing from my eyes and my heart. I heard him say that, '*it is good, Cesco, for that is where you belong, back home in your Italian kitchen.*' I left with an enormous sadness because Amboise and the French king had been kind to us. In April of 1522, I joined a group of Italians to cross the Alps on my way back to Lombardy.

After I was safely back in Milan, I found out that while I was crossing the Alps that Odet de Lautrec had tried to recapture Milan, but was severely defeated on the 22nd of April 1522 in the Battle of Bicocca. More than three thousand of his Swiss troops and twenty-two captains were killed or wounded during their frontal attack on the German and Spanish arquebusiers who were shooting at them with continuous volleys of shot. The few Swiss survivors had little choice but to return to their cantons, and Lautrec withdrew in defeat back to his home in France. Two days later, another Sforza was acclaimed Duke of Milan.

After six years in France, I was back again in Milan. My family was happy to have me home, and I was the new head of the Melzi household. We still had our old properties and more, but we were now concerned about the new rule and the effect of our previous service to king Francois and the French. Francesco Maria II Sforza, youngest son of Ludovico IL Moro Sforza, born four years after me, was installed as Duke of Milan from November of 1521 until his death in October 24, 1535. He was the last member of the Sforza family to rule Milan. His sovereignty, however, was constrained by the military occupation of Milan by Spanish troops.

Francesco Sforza and I played together for a few years as young children before we went our own separate ways during the French occupation of 1499 to 1512. He went into exile into the care of his cousin Bianca Maria Sforza, wife of the Emperor Maximilian I, when King Louis XII of France ousted his father Ludovico from Milan in 1500. After his father died in France in 1508, Emperor Maximilian assigned Francesco Sforza to an ecclesiastical career. But, when Charles V of Spain re-conquered Milan from the French in 1521, Francesco was appointed as governor and duke. I met with Francesco Sforza soon after my return to Milan and told him that I had returned permanently, and I swore my allegiance to him, the Duchy, and the Holy Roman Empire. He accepted my loyalty and support, and he told me that neither my family nor I had anything to fear because he was aware that the Melzi house had always served the Sforza's faithfully. He said that he had returned to his state of Milan and found that it was financially depleted by twenty years of war, and that he now needed to promote a cultural and economic recovery. He occasionally sought my counsel regarding the French ambitions and the cultural needs of his Duchy.

Although Francesco Sforza fought at the Battle of Bicocca on the side of the Spanish emperor in 1522, he suddenly switched sides in 1526, and he joined the League of Cognac, together with Francois I of France, the new de' Medici Pope, Pope Clement VII, and the Republic of Florence. The League of Cognac failed in their rebellion against Charles V who sacked Rome in May of 1527 and imprisoned Pope Clement VII for a short time in exchange for a large ransom, and until the Pope was again subservient to the Holy Roman Emperor and his army. The Spaniards under Antonio de Leyva besieged Francesco Sforza in the Castello Sforzesco until he made peace with the Holy Roman Emperor Charles V in Bologna in 1532. Francesco Sforza remained in Milan under Spanish suzerainty until his death in 1535. His half-brother Giovanni Paolo Sforza briefly reclaimed the Duchy of Milan until he died mysteriously in the same year.

I quickly resettled in Milan, and despite certain mishaps such as the vicious plague that attacked our city from 1523 to 1525 it was business as usual. The greatest event in my life happened in the spring of 1523. I met and married my very beautiful wife Angiola Landriani who was from an illustrious and ancient family of the Milanese nobility. At last count, we have had eight children. You may be interested to know that my wife was related to Lucrezia Landriani who was the mistress of the 5th Duke of Milan Galeazzo Maria Sforza and the mother of Caterina Riario Sforza, Leonardo's *Lady with Ermine*. We lived at the Melzi Villa in Vaprio d' Adda, which was also a resting place for many other important people who crossed the Adda to enter or leave between the states of Milan and Venice. In my time, either in the presence or absence of Leonardo da Vinci, we had many Italian and French nobles visit or stay with us. Other visitors who came to my Villa after the death of Leonardo and my return from France were Alberto Bendidio and Giorgio Vasari who came a number of times to look at Leonardo's works and painting and to interview me.

The Life and Death of Salai

I met with Salai (Gian Giacomo Caprotti di Oreno) again as soon as I arrived back in Milan. He came to visit me in Vaprio, excited that I was back home in Lombardy. He looked rich, happy, and wore fine and expensive clothes and sparkling jewellery. He told me that he was betrothed to a rich widow Bianca Coldiroli d' Annono who adored him. Leonardo had once written in his notebook dated 1490 soon after Salai first joined his household that he was a liar, a thief, stubborn, and a glutton. Salai was all those things to his very last day. But, he was also enormously loyal to Leonardo and loved him like a father. He was Leonardo's sword and shield as we always described him, and he was never afraid to collect the debts and payments owing to Leonardo and his workshop. He was one of Leonardo's best and most dedicated copyists and *pasticheurs* with more than twenty-five years of experience. He also had in his possession many indifferent copies of Leonardo's original paintings including *Leda and the Swan, La Joconda, St. John* pointing to heaven, *St. John Naked on a Rock, Virgin and Child with St Anne, Christ with a Globe, Christ Between the Columns, Donna Aretrata,* and his own version of *Monna Vanna* in the style of Leonardo.

Salai and I were not on the best of terms when we were in Amboise because he resented that I spoke fluent French and was well received by the king and his courtiers, while he was looked down on as a simple servant of Leonardo, like the cook and dresser Battista. But now, we happily sat together, the best of friends, and reminisced about our times with Leonardo.

Salai lived with his betrothed in her large house in the parish of *St. Babila foris* where he had his own studio and workshop. He also possessed half of Leonardo's vineyard where he had his house built by the architect and builder Palo da Mozate in the parish of *St. Martino foris* outside the gate of Vercellina. He still painted miniatures and portraits and acted as an art agent for Isabella d' Este and her friends. He was well known in Milan as an art dealer and Leonardo's former loyal assistant. He'd put on some weight during the last three years living the comfortable life, but he still had his cheeky, youthful expression that made me realise why Leonardo had named him his little devil. I agreed to visit him and his betrothed in Milan and to see his new original paintings and copies of Leonardo's paintings in case I had forgotten how they looked. He offered to help me to decipher Leonardo's notebooks and put together his *Treatise on Painting*. I welcomed his assistance because the work of translating Leonardo's mirror writing was not an easy task.

I attended the wedding between Salai and Bianca Coldiroli d' Annono on 14th June 1523, and they had attended my own wedding to Angiola Landriani a month before. I had little to do with them after their wedding until I received a message from Bianca Coldiroli that Salai had been killed in a fight on the 19th January in 1524. I attended his funeral and discovered that an arrow fired from a crossbow had killed him during an altercation that he had outside the city with a group of French spies who were laying siege on Milan. Salai died aged 43 years, a loyal patriot of Milan and the reigning Sforza duke.

Some months after his funeral, I received a request from the widow's notary to attend a meeting to help them verify the authenticity of Salai's property. Salai had not left an official will and testament and now there were disputes and challenges about ownership and inheritance between his sisters Angelina and Lorenziola. I was concerned about Leonardo's paintings in Salai's possession and the items that his sisters were in dispute over intrigued me, and so I attended the meeting. The notary handed me a list of Salai's items that his widow had no claim to. Unfortunately, due to her husband's sudden and accidental death, Salai had no will, and she could not inherit his properties that he had prior to their marriage. Her personal properties and rich dowry of 1700 lire would be returned to her because they were legitimately hers. Although Bianca Coldiroli was not of noble blood, she was a refined lady with impeccable taste and high sensitivity and refused to fight over Salai's belongings, which she was happy to leave to his two sisters to squabble over.

I looked through the list of Leonardo's items and saw that Salai had no Leonardo original paintings. The paintings were bad copies that Salai had taken with him from Amboise, and that he had tried to sell as original Leonardo's at highly over inflated prices. The sisters would fight over them thinking that they were originals, but I would have to disappoint them with the truth. There were a few Leonardo items in Salai's possession that I wanted to have, and that I was willing to pay a good sum for. I especially wanted the miniature, deformed, human cranium that Leonardo had carved beautifully and in great detail from calcedonia stone in 1508. The skull, a unique sculpture, which the sisters' thought was grotesque, only cost me 300 scudi, and I was happy to pay them the small price for this brilliant, small token that Leonardo had used as his personal sorrow stone. The other items were knickknacks that Salai had collected over the years and might be of use to his greedy sisters. Salai's house and vineyard was bestowed to his neighbour Battista de Vilanis as stipulated in Leonardo's will and testament and in a contract that they made and that I oversaw. I cried at Salai's funeral because I loved him much more than I had thought. We had our moments of disagreement, but overall we were very good and loving friends. And now, another one of Leonardo's sons is with him in the Paradise of Painters and Artists and all I can say to you, Salai, my friend, is goodbye sweet prince – you served your Father well.

Let me quote for you a short account from Giorgio Vasari's book *The Lives of the Most Eminent Painters, Sculptors, and Architects*:

> Messer Francesco Melzi, a Milanese gentleman who in Leonardo's day was a very handsome and courteous boy and much beloved by him, just as today he is a handsome and courteous old man who treasures these papers and conserves them along with a portrait of Leonardo to honour his happy memory. And anyone who reads these writings will be amazed by how opened, revealing it is to be filled with lilies. In Milan, Leonardo took on a servant Salai, a pleasingly graceful and handsome boy with beautiful, thick, curly hair, which greatly pleased Leonardo, who taught him many things about painting, and some of the works attributed to Salai in Milan were retouched by Leonardo.

I heard and read many accounts that Leonardo was a homosexual and that Salai and I were his instruments of sexual pleasure and depravity. For instance, people say that there is a clear innuendo in Vasari's account of Salai and me being Leonardo's lovers. Nothing could be further from the truth. These are spiteful allegations driven by jealousy, maliciousness, and envy of the worst kind. Both Salai and I have had to listen to such spiteful and snide allegations from a number of our vile contemporaries for years. Leonardo taught Salai and me how to ignore the calumny, and he provided us much useful instruction about ignoring salaciousness and envy. Salai couldn't ignore such accusations without drawing his sword, knife or providing a kick to the accuser's sinful groin.

Leonardo loved beauty in both women and men, but he had no sexual attraction to men or to us whatsoever. He loved women, but was temperate in his sexual activities because he was very aware of the many imprudent sexual infections passed on between the sexes and within the sexes by imprudent sexual behaviours. Leonardo was an expert on sexually transmitted diseases, especially the pox and gonorrhoea (*clapier bubo*). He had seen and treated many cases. Leonardo had not married because of his illegitimate social status, nomadic nature, and his love for knowledge and the natural philosophies. He was born out of wedlock and his own opinion was to mock the sanctity of marriage. Of course, he had his affairs and fulfilled his sexual curiosities and desires with women. However, Leonardo, like Salai and I, was intolerant of homosexuals, and we ignored their wicked advances.

I remember when I first entered the service of Leonardo in 1508. Salai was 27 years of age and a competent if not brilliant painter. He had enough of Leonardo's dictations and demands and was seriously rebelling against such menial tasks as recording, copying, and archiving for our maestro. He preferred to be out drinking, whoring, sketching, and fighting with the French pugilists and city locals. He was an accomplished fighter and totally fearless of any opponent. His wild ways were not diminishing with age, and Leonardo had long stopped chastising him for his bad behaviour and wicked ways. Leonardo tolerated Salai's need to spend time at the Vercellina vineyard with members of his family and friends or go boating up and down the canals with his whores and friends rather than help him in his studio and workshops with mundane tasks.

When we were together in Rome, Leonardo warned Salai once again about his flagrant pecker and the dangers of picking up incurable diseases, showing him a bottle of mercury and saying, 'you've seen what this treatment does to you when you have picked up the pox, my brother. You know that you would be better off to abstain from picking pockets and remain celibate and healthy.' Leonardo knew it was impossible to prevent Salai from picking any pockets or trying to seduce any woman that might show an inkling of interest in him.

Leonardo had been preaching regularly to us about the disease generated from too frequent sex from too many women, indiscriminate sex he called it. He had recently completed a thorough disease study of Roman women and found a number of disturbing features that led him to his hypothesis that such diseases were transmitted by microagents carried in pox pustules. Leonardo was constantly on about clean sex. Stay true to your wife and mistress and you will stay happy and healthy, he would tell us. Salai would say, phooey. You can't catch something you can't see. What I can't see I won't catch. Leonardo took him to see the dead bodies with the pox. What you can't see in these pustules you can catch. He made Salai look through the spyglass at the sores of the bodies and things unseen by the eye. You can't see these microagents with your naked eye. I have magnified them for you thirty times so that you can now see them and know that these minutiae can invade you and infect you and grow in you and cause you these diseases. Come here, and take a look at this animal that you say that you cannot see with your naked eye. I have this instrument to help you see it more clearly. You can't see this one in your pubic hair or the hair on your head, but it is there. It is a louse, an animal so small that it is almost beneath your ability to see it. But, it can burrow into your skin, have sex with its own like, get pregnant and lay eggs with its young ready to grow and live in your hair, unless I kill them for you with mercury lotion or other ablutions and lotions. Do you understand, Salai? What you can't see can kill you just like an arrow or a knife in your back. Leonardo once again had chastised Salai who didn't want to admit that his master was right about looking after his health and interests.

Salai loved Leonardo to a fault, and he always protected his master's interests whenever he thought that the going was tough or unfair. He was his Godfather's shield and sword. He was particularly incensed in Florence by the way Michelangelo was maligning Leonardo when they were painting their battles on the walls of the Sala del Gran Consiglio in the Palazzo Vecchio. Salai was annoyed that Michelangelo had complained to the Signoria and arrogantly pushed his way into sharing the commission. Before Michelangelo could start the painting on the wall, Salai confronted him one dark night with a knife to his throat and threatened that he and his friends would complete the job and take his head off his shoulders if he did not immediately pack his brushes and tools and leave Florence forever. Michelangelo heeded Salai's threat and soon left Florence with his painting unfinished to go and accept far more lucrative commissions offered to him in Rome. Leonardo knew nothing of Salai's threat or incident with Michelangelo and assumed that the sculptor's antagonism and flight from Florence was only due to envy.

Leonardo's Craniums and Skulls

I was pleased to have purchased Leonardo's beautifully sculpted calcedonia stone of a cranium in the possession of the Salai's sisters who knew no better as to its worth. Leonardo had drawn outstanding pictures of the cranium and the skull and his cranium sculpture sat on my desk as testimony to his genius.

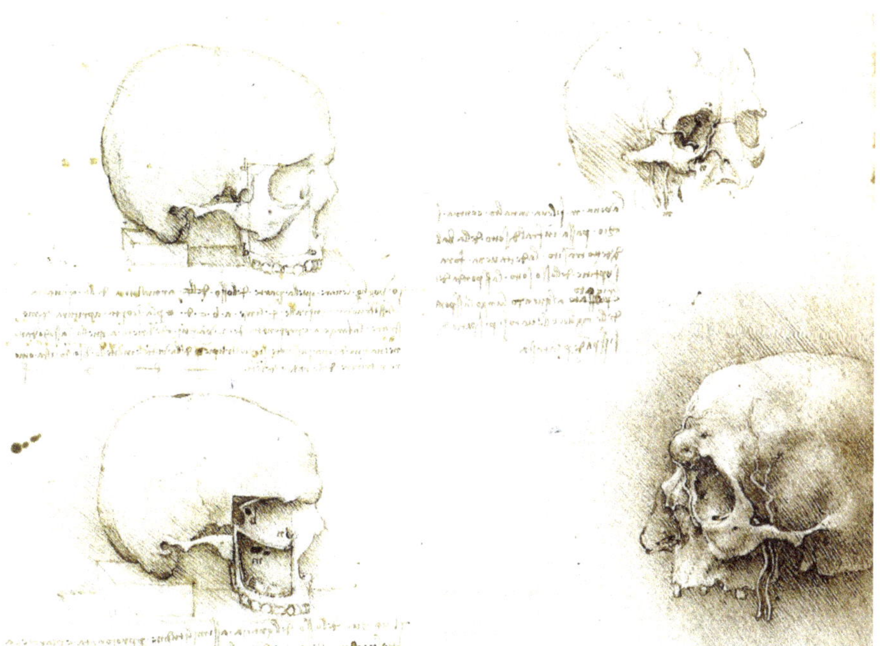

Fig. 138. Leonardo's drawings of a cranium for his calcedonia stone sculpture.

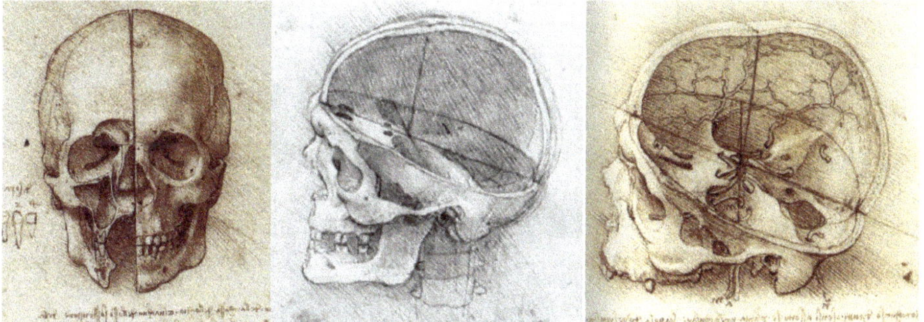

Fig. 139. Leonardo's beautiful drawings of skulls and a dissected cranium with blood vessels.

The Death of Mona Lisa, Isabella Aragon Sforza, Duchess of Bari, and the Former Duchess of Milan, 1524

I have written in previous chapters about the portraits of *Mona Lisa* painted by Leonardo da Vinci and the model for the pictures, Isabella Aragon Sforza, Duchess of Bari, the former Duchess of Milan and the widow of the 6th Duke of Milan, Gian Galeazzo Sforza. After the French occupied Milan in 1500, she moved to Bari where she spent most of her remaining life. Her daughter Bona Sforza became Queen of Poland in 1518 when she married the Polish King Sigismund I the Old. Isabella Aragon Sforza, the Duchess of Bari, died in Naples on February 11, 1524, aged 53 years, after a short illness while visiting the city of her birth. I met her briefly in Naples the year before she died. She had become obese and had problems with her heart and blood pressure as Leonardo had predicted. She is entombed at the Basilica of Saint Domenico Maggiore in Naples beside her grandfather Ferrante I (Ferdinand I) d'Aragona, King of Naples from 1458 to 1494, and her brother Ferdinand II d'Aragona, King of Naples from 1495 to 1496.

The French King's Capture in Pavia in 1525, Imprisonment, and Release from Spain

I received word from Admiral Guillaume Gouffier, seigneur de Bonnivet, that the King's wife Queen Claude of France had died on 20th July 1524. King Francois was distraught with grief, but he was still determined to win back Milan from the Sforza duke and Charles V. The four-year battle between Charles and Francois finally ending in February 1525 with the capture of the French king at the Battle of Pavia and his imprisonment in Madrid, in Spain, for a year.

The French king had crossed the Alps and ridden with his army to the gates of Milan. On the 24th of October 1524, he was at the Tucino gate where he silently watched city health officials carry out corpses on death carts to bury them in mass graves, the large and deep pits dug in the fields outside the walls of Milan. The king sent his messenger to a health official to find out how many had perished from the plague. The answer was, '2,000 dead so far, it is unsafe to enter'. The city was emptied of people, and it was taken over by noxious weeds. The king turned his army around and headed southwest to lay siege to Pavia. I was residing at the Melzi Villa in Vaprio, too afraid to meet with the king. The plague was rife up and down the Adda River and along most of the canals. We had a death house at a nearby monastery, yet miraculously the number of deaths in Vaprio was low.

Francois fought bravely at Pavia, but eventually was overcome by too many forces against him. Exhausted, he succumbed to the Imperial Viceroy Lannoy. In a letter to his mother from Spain he wrote, 'of all things, nothing remains to me but honour and life, which is safe.' Then, while under duress in prison in Spain, he signed the Treaty of Madrid on 14th January 1526 with major concessions to Charles V before he was freed on 17th March 1526. Ottoman Sultan Suleiman's ultimatum to Charles V played an important role in Francois's release from prison. Leonardo's good advice had paved the way for the French king and the Sultan to become allies. Among the concessions that Francois made to Charles V were the surrender of any claims to Naples and Milan in Italy, to recognise the independence of the duchy of Burgundy, and to give up all his claims to Flanders and the Artois. Francois was allowed to return to France in exchange for his two sons Francois and Henri to be held hostage. But, once he was free and safe in France, the king argued in the French parliament that his agreement with Charles was made under duress and that it therefore was null and void because his sons were taken hostage. His sons, after four years in captivity, were released in 1530 into the hands of Charles's sister, Eleanor of Austria, who was engaged to marry king Francois in the same year. The Treaty of Madrid was repudiated, but Francois and Charles V continued their feud and wars against each other for another 17 years.

I visited the French King when the Imperial Viceroy Lannoy held him prisoner at a monastery outside Pavia. He was relatively comfortable there, whereas a number of his captured marshals and army generals, Fleurange, Galiot, Montmorency, and Henri d' Albert were in the cold, cramped prison cells of Pavia. Bayard, Bonnivet, la Palice, and la Tremouille were dead, all fallen in battle. In two hours at the Battle of Pavia, the king had lost 8,000 Frenchmen and their mercenaries. The traitor was Charles II, the Duke of Bourbon and former Governor of Milan, who betrayed his French king and won a splendid battle on behalf of the Imperial forces. I spent two hours in conversation with Francois and told him I could do nothing for him because he was in the hands of the Spanish and Charles V. He was despondent, but optimistic. He was defeated, but he still had his life and health. I acted on his behalf to win him support from the Turks. Leonardo had once advised Francois that 'if you ever get into trouble with Rome or the King of Spain seek the assistance of an ally that your enemies fear most, the Ottomans, just as Medici had done when he was threaten by Sixtus IV.'

I reflected on Leonardo's philosophy of the Italian and French kitchens. He had made many friends within the French kitchen, especially with King Francois who was his greatest French friend and supporter. But, Leonardo loved his Italian kitchen best of all and his minestrone soup sustained him and his friends throughout his life. The vast casts of characters who he had entertained and aggravated were many. Yet, he had no regrets about dying in France, on foreign soil away from his beloved Italy. He told me that he was like a wandering Jew. His spiritual home was Jerusalem, but his real home was the world, the earth, and the stars, and the light and warmth provided to him by the sun and the fires of burning wood and candles. He had no regrets to die in Amboise in the presence of his two loving sons Francesco Melzi, Count Palatine of Insubria, and Francois I, the King of France, the two who loved him most and felt an immediate and great sorrow with his passing. He was sorry Salai was not with him, but instead had chosen to be caught up in his own intrigues in Milan.

And so, I couldn't completely ignore the King of France even in his inglorious defeat. He was eventually released from his imprisonment by the payment of a healthy bounty and the threat of war from the Ottomans. He returned to rule his country, but now in poorer health than when he had left. We stayed in touch by letter two or three times each year, and I was his unofficial diplomat in Milan, and I also served him unofficially as a representative with the Ottomans. He stayed a loyal supporter of the Ottomans throughout the remainder of his life and developed a great love and habit for Turkish delight and the tales of the Arabian Nights. He ruled France with a tight hand and began to lose popularity with his people and some of his officials. Many in France were relieved when he died peacefully in his bed on 31 March 1547. Nevertheless, he had a magnificent and spectacular funeral that he would have approved off and been humbled by if he could have seen it. The funeral in Paris was full of pomp and splendour, the most magnificent of any French king before him. It was too grand for me to do it proper justice and to write about it here. He was laid to rest in his vault at the Cathedral of Saint-Denis. Years later, I visited his and Claude's splendid tomb at Saint-Denis that was erected by Philibert de l'Orme and Pierre Bontemps. It is a masterpiece, depicting the King and Queen in repose, in death as they were in life, flanked by their two sons and a daughter.

Yet, despite the criticisms and some obvious failures, King Francois left his nation a lasting legacy. He maintained and encouraged a unified France with a central rule and a strong parliament. He introduced the Italian Renaissance to his country and left a strong legacy for the sciences and the arts, and he developed and expanded the libraries, art galleries, and museums that would long sustain his nation after his death. The paintings that Leonardo brought to Amboise with him are now on show in the Louvre Palace in Paris, and they are much admired and copied by all who visit. The French king remarried in 1530. It was to Charles V's sister Eleanor of Austria who outlived him by 11 years. His loving mother Louise of Savoy died in 1531, whereas his sister Marguerite de Navarre lived until 1549. King Francois's first son died of poison or 'consumption' in 1536, and so his second son, Henri II, ascended to the throne to rule for 12 years, before he died, and was replaced by his own son Francois who reigned for only one year. Now, it is Henri II and Catherine de' Medici's son, Charles IX, who is the King of France after he ascended to the throne in December of 1560 when he was only 10 years of age. However, it is his mother, Catherine de' Medici, who currently rules as the Regent.

As for Maturina, I lost touch with her soon after her daughter had visited me in Milan in 1541. Maturina had joined a nunnery in 1531, and she had given her and Leonardo's twelve-year-old daughter Caterina to the care of her sister Clara. Caterina grew up quickly to be a fine mannered and beautiful lady with a lovely voice and a talent for musical instruments. The court was available to her, but she chose to live the village life in Amboise. She lived with and married the court painter Francois Clouet. The Salamander Tavern that was owned by king Francois and Leonardo and given to Maturina is still operating in Amboise under the management of Maturina's sisters and nieces with minestrone soup, pasta (tortellini) with capon flesh, and a thick soup of tagliatelle in a fat meat broth, cooked and served hot with cheese, sugar and cinnamon, still among their signature dishes.

Leonardo's *Treatise on Painting and the Paragone*

Giorgio Vasari wrote the following in his biography of Leonardo.

> Many of these papers on human anatomy are in the possession of Messer Francesco Melzi, a Milanese gentleman who in Leonardo's day was a very handsome boy and much beloved by him, just as today he is a handsome and courteous old man who treasures these papers and conserves them along with a portrait of Leonardo to honour his happy memory. There are also other writings by Leonardo in the possession of a Milanese painter also written with the left hand from right to left, which treat painting and the methods of drawing and using colour. Not long ago this man, wishing to print this work, came to Florence to see me, and he then took it on to Rome to do so, but I do not know what happened afterwards.

The man who visited Vasari in Florence was the Milanese painter Girolamo Figino who produced the manuscript *Le Regole del Disegno*. His ideas and drawing were copied from Leonardo da Vinci's manuscripts and my manuscript *Leonardo's Treatise on Painting* that I showed him, but he gave no acknowledgement to Leonardo or to me as the source. My task now was to publish Leonardo's notebooks and drawings, to collate and publish his biography, to honour his memory in the establishment of our library, museum of his ideas, inventions, memories, and philosophy. I set about this diligently, and then I met my wife and fell in love to have eight splendid children and a happy life. My wife Angiola Landriani is beautiful, enchanting, and very wealthy. It was a marriage made in heaven. Together, we worked towards educating historians, painters, and scholars about Master Leonardo da Vinci.

On the basis of my education and training, I served Leonardo as his secretary and archivist and received a privileged insight into his drawing and painting techniques. I wasn't particularly interested in sculpture or other art forms. Leonardo was almost permanently fixed in reverse writing or mirror writing with his left hand, which was totally illegible for documents and letters that he needed to write to officials, bankers, notaries, friends, and courtiers. Hence, I, with my legible script and good grammar, was employed for all tasks stationery, and I was responsible, among other things, to write and copy the Maestro's letters. I collaborated closely with my teacher to archive his manuscripts, revise the figures and sketches that he had done in pen and crayon, and that were tending to fade, and I copied and collated many of his inventions and maps.

On my return to the Melzi Villa, I systematically reorganised Leonardo's manuscripts and his annotations on how to paint in an organic way in readiness for a print edition that I completed in the year of 1540. I eventually compiled and published Leonardo's *Treatise on Painting* that I derived from the *Codex Urbinas Latinus*. It took me many years of hard work to translate his mirror writing from his many different notebooks that amounted to more than 9,000 pages, and that were summarised into 250 pages in the *Codex Urbinas*. The superiority of painting over poetry was published separately as Leonardo's *Paragone of Poetry and Painting*. Although not extensive, the printed and published version of the *Treatise on Painting* provides the reader with Leonardo's philosophy about painting and drawing and perspective, and a summary on how to paint. I prepared 365 short chapters beginning with, '*what the young student of painting ought in the first place to learn*', and ending with, '*that a Man ought not to trust himself, but ought to consult Nature.*' Each chapter was to be read as a learning exercise for one day of the year, each day during the course of one year. For Leonardo, painting embraces within itself all forms of nature. '*The science of painting extends to all the colours of the surfaces of bodies, and to the shapes of the bodies enclosed by those surfaces. ... Truly this is science, the legitimate daughter of nature, because painting is born of nature.*' And, the eye is the principal instrument of the painter, for '*the eye, which is said to be the window of the soul, the principal means whereby sensory awareness can most abundantly and magnificently contemplate the infinite works of nature.*'

Painting, Drawing, and Writing

Leonardo wrote the following about the science of drawing in his *Treatise on Painting*.

> Drawing is the foundation of painting. It is indispensible to the architect and the sculptor as it is to the potter, the goldsmith, the weaver, or the embroiderer. It has provided the letters of the written language, given mathematicians their figures and numbers, it has taught geometers the shape of their diagrams, it has instructed opticians, astronomers, machine builders, and engineers in perspective, design, and creation.

I opened a school of painting in Milan to honour Leonardo. Many Leonardeschi (followers of Leonardo) visited my school to see his drawings and to show their own paintings and present a lesson about observation and painting to my pupils. I would begin my first lesson with the following statement. 'Drawing is writing and writing is drawing.' And I would continue as follows:

First, in antiquity, we drew simple designs; stick figures, circles, spheres, squares, and rectangles. Then, we put these most simple designs together to make representations of animals, bison, birds, tigers, snakes, and the mountains and rivers. Next, we began to paint over our scratchings and drawings using colours taken from the earth, the reds, blacks, browns, and whites of ochre dug out of the earth. Soon, our drawings of stick figures became meaningful symbols – a circle is a well, a square represents a house or field, a rectangle is a bigger house or field depending on its context to other symbols, a triangle is a hill or mountain, an L is the river with a right-handed bend, the reverse L is the river with the left-handed bend, and so on. We started to place these symbols together into a context of coded messages to tell others and ourselves meaningful stories. And eventually, our representations in drawing and writing became more sophisticated and complex. Written and oral languages emerged with which we could communicate with each other as the learned ones. Look at the Egyptian hieroglyphics. They placed their symbols together in meaningful orders, in a context, one above the other, next to each other either horizontally or vertically in a consecutive meaningful structure. These repeated extrapolated drawings of figures became a script that we could tell our family, friends, and descendants various stories about our history, our ownerships, and ourselves. It soon became useful or entertaining information, such as the type of animals that existed in our environment before we wiped them out of our existence with our towns and farms.

The pictures of birds, cats, human figures, animal heads, goats, and sheep became amazing symbols of writing and communication that turned into a shared script and language, known and understood by all those in the community who learnt the meaning of the symbols, the learned ones, the educated ones, and all those who had the code to decipher the symbols. This code is shared among people to decipher information, details, history, and the complex thoughts in our heads, etc. Amazing, isn't it? This is what drawing and painting has done for us. Sculpture comes close to this, but does it surpass it? Sure, we have to sculpt coins, talisman, weapons, and various other objects that are useful or important for our survival or wellbeing. This is engineering and I acknowledge that it is of fundamental worth and value, a science and an art that we see in our beautiful buildings, cathedrals, churches, and palaces. Who can deny sculpture as a beautiful and important thing to see and to touch? Nobody. We can look at sculpted art like Michelangelo's *David* as a beautiful and interesting object, but what more can it do for us? How does it expand our minds like drawing or writing? The arguments given by Michelangelo and Giambologna in favour of sculpture to be superior over painting and drawing are not particularly convincing and fail immediately when scrutinised by a rational mind. Look at Leonardo's notebooks where he has drawings, sketches, and writing that will inform us for ages. Yes, far more informative and reproducible for mankind than Michelangelo's *David* carved from stone will ever be, although there are those who will argue otherwise and say that *David* is more pleasing to the eye than any of Leonardo's notebooks. What do you think, dear artist and friend? Do you have a preference or is this just empty and unimportant rhetoric in comparison to your daily, exhausting grind to live and to survive?

And what of his paintings? Leonardo pioneered, advanced, and employed the following painting techniques: *chiaroscuro* (the contrast between light and shade to create the illusion of three dimensional forms), *contrapposto* (counterpose), *sfumato* (fine shading to produce soft and imperceptible transitions between colours and tones), perspective, the subject in three quarter pose, the subject looking out at the viewer, the landscape as part of the subject's portraiture, naturalistic saints without their golden or glass haloes, and the use of the golden ratio in the design of a painting.

Leonardo's Legacies

While in Amboise, Leonardo and I made a list of the treatises that he wished to have published as his legacy to art, mechanics, and natural philosophy. These in approximate order are *Treatise on Painting, Treatise on Perspective, Treatise on Light and Shade, Treatise on Flight, Treatise on Continuous Quantity*, and a *Book on Architecture and Anatomy* including discourses on the nerves, muscles, tendons, membranes, ligaments, the embryo, and the soul. In the end, there was just too much to do, and we simply ran out of mortal time.

Leonardo changed the face of portraiture and religious art. He introduced a new theory of art as a genuine science of seeing and thinking. His paintings, drawings, and theories influenced whole new generations of artists who became known as the Leonardeschi. I already have named many of them during the course of my exposition about Leonardo and me.

The following are some of the subjects that interested him, and that his followers and I will remember him for:

Painting and Sculpture
Anatomy and Medicine
Architecture and Engineering (Fortifications and Town-planning)
Biology, Birds, and Flight

Mathematics, Astronomy, and Cosmology
Hydrology and Geology
Horses and Other Animals Including Lizards
Ideas and Experimentation and How to Use the Mind
Jests, Riddles, Fables, and Fantasies

In 1543, my son Orazio and I returned to the task of trying to finalise the publication of Leonardo's *Atlas of Anatomy* when Andreas Vesalius's publication of seven books on human anatomy entitled *De humani corporis fabrica libri septem (On the fabric of the human body in seven books)* was brought to our attention. I was astonished. It was everything we had hoped to achieve with Leonardo's drawings. While lecturing in Padua, Vesalius had come to visit me in Vaprio in 1537 to look at Leonardo's anatomical drawings. He made some copies, and we asked him to help us to prepare a text and publish Leonardo's drawings. He said he would inquire with the publisher at the Padua school of medicine and let us know. We never heard from him again.

A few years later, Titian's student Johannes Stephanus of Calcar visited me to look at Leonardo's anatomical drawings. He stayed with us for a week examining and studying the drawings. He asked me what my plans were for the drawings, and I explained that we planned to make copper engravings and have them printed in a publication. Soon after, Andreas Vesalius used Johannes Stephanus of Calcar and the studio of Titian to illustrate his text on anatomy. He set out his seven books exactly how Leonardo had instructed me to set out the order of his *Atlas of Anatomy*: 1 - the bones and cartilages, 2 – the ligaments and muscles, 3 – the veins and arteries, 4 – the nerves, 5 – the organs of nutrition and generation, 6 – the heart and associated organs, and 7 – the brain and soul. It is a disgrace that Vesalius never acknowledged knowing of Leonardo's dissections and anatomical work after having seen and copied his drawings. An attribution, no matter how small, would have been an honest and honourable gesture. But, Vesalius wanted to claim that it was only his dissections, observations, and experience that mattered and corrected Galen's unchecked errors, and he did not want the world to know that in fact it was Leonardo who first corrected many of these Galen errors long before Vesalius had. Nevertheless, Vesalius was appointed physician to the Holy Roman Emperor Charles V. Soon after Vesalius's *Fabrica* was published, many professors and publishers advised us that it would become the standard text for all physicians and anatomists and that nobody would want to publish Leonardo's outdated anatomical pictures.

My Life as Count Francesco Melzi, Husband, Father, Artist, Writer, Teacher, and Patrician

While I stayed in touch to some degree with my French friends and the king's court, most of my time and energy back in Milan was now devoted to my family, the Duchy, Vaprio, Como, and the safe running of the Adda River and the canal between Vaprio and Milan. I have extensive farming lands, factories, and three tolls to maintain and to administer on the Adda River. I also have colleges and studios to manage, one in Vaprio, two in Milan, and one in Pavia.

Because of Leonardo's demands and workloads expected from me, my own artistic production has suffered in output. Nevertheless, I did complete a number of my own paintings, some that I signed in Greek or Latin and that are still confused with Leonardo's art, as if he was the painter. I made a few extra, signed copies and sold them at a good price to collectors who thought that they would on sell them as Leonardo's masterpieces. The paintings *Flora, Vertumnus and Pomona,* and a drawing in red chalk of a foot, were sold as Leonardo's, and when exhibited they are rarely attributed to me. This is the scourge of having been Leonardo's assistant. I also painted the portraits of the *French king* and his sister *Marguerite* with the assistance of Jean Clouet, the *Holy Family* and other collectibles such as *Portrait of Young Man with Parrot, the Nymph,* several grotesque heads, the *Head of Elderly Man With a Slight Three-quarters Pose to the Right,* and the *Head of a Man Inclined to the Left.* I also finished two drawings of Leonardo, one in profile and the other of him moodily looking out at me. I still have some works and copies assigned to me by Leonardo, such as the *Flora, Leda and the Swan, Medusa's Head,* and *Magdalene.* I continue my activities with miniature painting, and some of these have been distributed widely to my satisfaction. I taught and mentored the miniaturist and painter Girolamo Figino, and between the years of 1559 and 1564, I was consulted on several occasions by the Fabbrica del Duomo di Milano (the working group for the maintenance and restoration of the Cathedral) for the decoration of the doors of the organ.

The Story of *Vertumnus and Pomona* by Ovid from his *Metamorphoses*

Here, I have added a copy of my painting of *Vertumnus and Pomona* for it perfectly symbolises my memory of Leonardo and Maturina in their last two years together.

> Pomona the beautiful wood nymph attended her garden with more skill than any other, and none was more attentive to the fruitful trees than she who cared not for the forests or the streams, but loved the country and the boughs that bear delicious fruit. Her right hand never felt a javelin's weight, always she loved to hold a sharp curved pruning-knife with which she would at one time crop too largely growing shoots, or at another time reduce the branch that straggled; at another time she would engraft a sucker in divided bark, and so find nourishment for some young, strange nursling. She never suffered them to thirst, for she would water every winding thread of twisting roots with freshly flowing streams.
>
> All this was her delight, her chief pursuit; she never felt the least desire of love; but fearful of some rustic's violence, she had her orchard closed within a wall; and both forbade and fled the approach of males. … And though Vertumnus (God of seasons, change, plants, and fruit trees) did exceed them in his love, yet he was no more fortunate than they in attracting her attention. How often disguised as a rough reaper he brought her barley ears—truly he seemed a reaper to the life! Often he came, his temples wreathed with hay, as if he had been tossing new mown grass. He often held a whip in his tough hand, you could have sworn he had a moment before unyoked his wearied oxen. When he had a pruning-knife, he seemed to rear fine fruit in orchard trees or kept vines in the well. When he came with a ladder, you would think he must have been gathering fruit. Sometimes he was a soldier with a sword—a fisherman, the rod held in his hand. In fact by means of many disguises he often met her and enjoyed seeing her beauty, but no more could he woo.
>
> At length he bound his brows in a cap of colour, and then leaning on a stick, with white hair round his temples, he assumed the shape of an old woman. Entering so into her cultivated garden, he admired her fruit and said, 'But you are so much lovelier!' And, while he praised her, he gave her some kisses too, such as no real beldam ever gave. The bent old creature then sat on the grass and gazing at the branches weighed down with their fruit of autumn.
>
> Pointing at the elm-tree embraced by a vine with shining grapes, he said, 'But only think, if this trunk stood unwedded to this vine, it would have nothing to attract our hearts beyond its leaves, and this delightful vine, united to the elm tree finds its rest; but, if not so joined to it, would fall down, prostrate upon the ground. And yet you find no warning in the example of this tree. You have avoided marriage, with no wish to be united -- I must wish that you would change and soon desire it. Helen would not have so many suitors for her hand, nor she who caused the battles of the Lapithae, nor would the wife of timid, and not bold Ulysses. Even now, while you avoid those who are courting

you, and while you turn in your disgust, a thousand suitors want to marry you—the demigods and gods, and deities of Alba's mountaintops.

But you, if you are wise, and wish to make a good match, listen patiently to me, an old, old woman (I love you much more than all of them, more than you dream or think). Despise all common persons, and choose now Vertumnus as the partner of your couch, and you may take me as a surety for him. Even himself does not better know him than I know him. And he is not now wandering everywhere, from here to there throughout the world. He always will frequent the places near here; and he does not, like so many of your wooers, fall in love with anyone that he happens to have seen the last. You are his first and last love, and to you alone will he devote his life. Besides all—he is young and has a natural gift of grace, so that he can most readily transform himself to any wanted shape, and he will become whatever you may wish—even though you ask him things unseen before. And only think, have you not the same tastes? Will he not be the first to welcome fruits, which are your great delight? And does he not hold your gifts safely in his glad hand? But now he does not long for any fruit plucked from the tree, and has no thought of herbs with pleasant juices that the garden gives; he cannot think of anything but you. Have pity on his passion, and believe that he who woos you is here and he pleads with my lips. You should not forget to fear avenging deities, and those who hate all cruel hearts, and also dread the fierce revenge of her of Rhamnus-Land. And that you may stand more in awe of them, (old age has given me opportunities of knowing many things) I will relate some happenings known in Cyprus, by which you may be persuaded and relent with ease. And so it was, to his surprise, that after all the fine speeches and disguises, it was not until he threw away his disguise and stories that she fell in love with his beauty and together they worked in her garden. [S45]

The End of a Divine Contradiction

I end my story with the opening paragraph of Vasari's chapter on Leonardo because I cannot pay a better tribute than he already has:

> In the course of nature the greatest gifts are often seen rained by celestial influences on human creatures; and sometimes, in supernatural fashion, beauty, grace, and talent are united beyond measure in one single person, in a manner that to whatever such an one turns his attention, his every action is so divine that it surpasses all other men and makes itself clearly known as a thing bestowed by God rather than by human art. This was seen by all mankind in Leonardo da Vinci, in whom, besides a beauty of body never sufficiently extolled, there was an infinite grace in all his actions; and so great was his genius, and such its growth, that to whatever difficulties he turned his mind, he solved them with ease. In him was great bodily strength, joined to dexterity, with a spirit and courage ever royal and magnanimous; and the fame of his name so increased, that not only in his lifetime was he held in esteem, but his reputation became even greater among posterity after his death. … And there was infused in that brain such grace from God, and a power of expression in such sublime accord with the intellect and memory that served it, and he knew so well how to express his conceptions by draughtsmanship, that he vanquished with his discourse, and confuted with his reasoning, every valiant wit.

Leonardo was a friend, teacher, and a father to many of us, including to me and my father and mother. He took great care of his friends, pupils, children, and animals no matter what age, size or sex they were. He took his responsibilities as a caretaker and guardian seriously, but also humorously and with much gentleness and patience. That is why we all loved him. He was wise and caring, and he could easily relate to the young and the old, to the king and the peasant, to the man and the woman, to the sick and the healthy, to the scientist and the poet, to the sinner and the sinned, to the painter and the sculptor, to the knights and the clergy, and to the clever and the stupid. He was a genius in tolerance, listening, feeling, observing, learning, and teaching. He was like Francis of the Assisi. That is what made him a great teacher and a gentleman. May his memory and legacies last forever and a day, and forever, thereafter.

Why was he considered to be so divine that he surpassed all other men, 'a thing bestowed by God rather than by human art?' He was blessed to be handsome, physically well coordinated and strong, articulate with a nice tone of voice, and an attentive listener who engaged with kind, knowing eyes, and polite body language. But it was his wide, encompassing mind that I knew no other to possess. He indeed was in communion with God's natural world, something that he was able to reflect so simply in his drawings, art, and actions. One side of his mind seemed strongly logical and mathematical with a fascination for complex machines, puzzles, puns, aphorisms, an uncompromising personal ethic, and the ability to solve problems from a perspective that others would miss. The other side of his mind was orientated for fun and pranks, he loved to sing and dance, to laugh and tell stories, to drink and argue and play sports and to ride horses. He was an excellent horseman, an accurate shot with a cross bow and had a special bond, and ability to communicate with animals, especially horses, dogs, cattle, goats, birds, and lizards. He was full of love, life, and curiosity. He would use either side of his brain at different times as he wanted to, depending on his need or mood as if he was talking to the Gods. Sometimes, he would use both sides of his mind at the one time, particularly in special circumstances when chaos was developing about him. At times, it was as if he had a female and male brain side by side, and he chose to use one or the other at his leisure and pleasure. It was his strong imagination tethered to his seat of logic that set him apart from all others with whom I ever came into contact. In comparison, my own mind seems so mundane and socially inadequate compared to his broader, imaginative, and wiser perspective.

An activity not seen by most people was his tricks and practices with memory. He had developed a technique to store his memories in imagination and symbols. He would imagine his mind to be a large cathedral and a series of outlying buildings and rooms where he would store his memories or information that he wished to remember and express. He then would visit these allocated buildings and rooms in moments of privacy or even in the presence of company and recall these memories, facts, details or whatever they were, from his mind's archives, and amaze people with his feats of memory recall. He had developed many tricks with the mind, and maybe he was guilty of spending a little too much time wandering about the territories of his own mind rather than completing the practical task at hand.

Of course, I could tell you much more about Leonardo da Vinci and his footprint on my life and those of the others who crossed our path, but I feel that this is as far as I can go for now. With the help of my sons, I am now trying to complete the organisation of Leonardo's notebooks and his treatises on anatomy, disease and medicine, flight, architecture and town planning, and update his manual on warfare, but progress is slow, and there are many interruptions and other matters that have taken up my time and expertise and that I must contend with as my priority. God willing, these projects entrusted to me by Leonardo will soon be completed.

Leonardo, you rose from humble beginnings in an isolated farmhouse in Tuscany, an illegitimate son, and yet you strode the corridors and the rooms of nobles, lords, dukes, and kings. You rubbed shoulders with mathematicians, painters, poets, philosophers, anatomists, alchemists, magicians, musicians, scientists, engineers, builders, enologists, farmers, soldiers, lawyers, clergy, and cosmologists, and you taught and mentored some of the best minds in three or four nations and over the same number of decades. You met many of the most beautiful and exquisite women in your times and tried tenderly to fulfil their physical and spiritual needs. You were a true and devoted Marist, you worshipped the Madonna and child, and She drove you 'forwards' (your favourite word), towards your relentless quest to understand the natural workings of God and all the gifts that Nature has given us. You were courageous in your pursuit of Knowledge, for you were fully aware of the Holy Spirit and John the Baptist and Our Holy Saint Mary and Saint Catherine and Saint Anne who all protected you dearly. I feel blessed to have met you and worked with you. Leonardo, my most dear and understanding spiritual father, I pray for you, and I salute you always. Leonardo di ser Piero da Vinci, you are the *Maestro Extraordinaire*.

And what of me, Giovanni Francesco Melzi, 'Cesco' to my friends? Well, I have had a good life and lived the great adventure that I had hoped for and expected to have with and without Leonardo da Vinci. Of course, my life was never only about Leonardo da Vinci. My life included my mother and father and grandparents, my brothers and sisters, my wife and children, and all my wonderful friends who contributed much to my good fortune and spiritual richness. But, life without Leonardo da Vinci is another story for another time, and I can only leave you now with this one that I remembered fondly about 'Leonardo and his Italian and French Kitchen'.

Leonardo da Vinci's life and conduct were unfailingly governed by lofty principles and aims, and he often reminded Salai and me about the importance of mindfulness to live in the present and to prevent our minds from wandering too much all over the place:

> The average human looks without seeing, listens without hearing, touches without feeling, eats without tasting, moves without physical awareness, inhales without awareness of odour or fragrance, and talks without thinking. Finally, a life dedicated to seeing and understanding the world around us, doing what we can to help those less fortunate than ourselves, and sharing love and joy and knowledge, is a life well-lived.

Like Heraclitus of Ephesus (*Logos*), the Zen Buddhists and the Taoists of the Orient teach that the universe is the unity or identity of opposites, a continual set of contradictions, a duality looking for the whole. Peace or harmony can be achieved by balancing opposite systems such as between mind and reality, inconsistency and consistency, awareness and unawareness, congruous and incongruous, sameness (identity) and difference, force and matter, man and woman, monism and dualism, conflict and peace, sinistra and destra, cause and effect, freedom and dependence, good and bad, subject and object, light and dark, action and inaction, and life and death, and so on. Because life is a balance between pleasure (happiness) and displeasure (unhappiness), like Jesus, we should work together towards relieving people's pain and suffering in the world. Leonardo had his share of displeasure and pleasure, unwanted change (impermanence) and illness, and he accepted that these things happen, and that we should go with the flow (non-attachment) without always trying to change them (want and desire). I leave the last words and an allegorical image of the duality of *Pleasure* and *Pain* to Leonardo da Vinci:

> Pleasure and Pain represent as twins, since there never is one without the other; and as if they were united back to back, since they are contrary to each other. (Clay, gold). If you take Pleasure know that he has behind him one who will deal you Tribulation and Repentance. This represents Pleasure together with Pain and shows them as twins because one is never apart from the other. They are back to back because they are opposed to each other; and they exist as contraries in the same body, because they have the same basis, inasmuch as the origin of pleasure is labour and pain, and the various forms of evil pleasure are the origin of pain. Therefore it is here represented with a reed in his right hand, which is useless and without strength, and the wounds it inflicts are poisoned. In Tuscany they are put to support beds, to signify that it is here that vain dreams come, and here a great part of life is consumed. It is here that much precious time is wasted, that is, in the morning, when the mind is composed and rested, and the body is made fit to begin new labours; there again many vain pleasures are enjoyed; both by the mind in imagining impossible things, and by the body in taking those pleasures that are often the cause of the failing of life. And for these reasons the reed is held as their support.
>
> In contrast to the smiling and beautiful youthful face of Pleasure, Displeasure is a mournful, bearded old man who with wounded heart drops painful spiked caltrops from his right hand while his left hand holds a bush of thorned roses where worldly pleasures like its flowers wilt and the sharp and painful thorns are retained. The right leg of the

body of pleasure rests weakly on a sheet of soft clay while the left leg of pain stands strong and hard on a firm tablet of gold. There is pleasure and pain in the one body, which cannot exist one without the other.

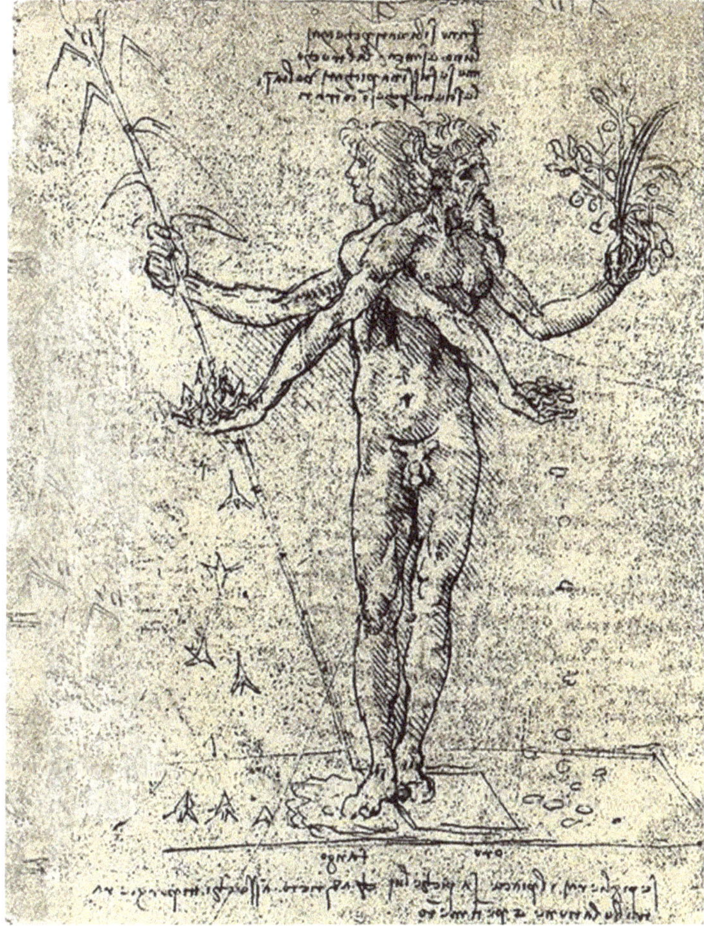

Fig. 141. Leonardo's allegorical drawing of Pleasure and Pain.

(PS and R-I-P: Francesco Melzi probably died in Vaprio d'Adda around 1570, some 51 years after the death of Leonardo da Vinci).

ACKNOWLEDGEMENTS

I thank the following: Dr. Don Giovanni Mariano of S. Maria Bianca della Misericordia in Casoretto, Milan for permission to use the image of the *Triptych of the Resurrection*; Paola Villa and the archive of restored paintings Archivio Villa Restauri for the restored votive image of *Lucia Marliani and Family*; Marino Vigano for the image of *Gian Giacomo Trivulzio's Heraldry* state portrait; Agata Rutkowska for her assistance with permission to use the images from the Royal Collection; Sylwia Lopatecka of the National Museum in Krakow for permission to reproduce *Portrait of a Youth* by Raphael and the *Lady With the Ermine* by Leonardo da Vinci, the editor Dr. Emil Kren for permission to use the online images at the Web Gallery of Art; Pascal Broist for showing me the video on the Leonardo da Vinci's palace of Romorantin; Roger Dawkins for his encouragement and kind suggestions via email; and Jan Kulski for creating the author's webpage at www.jerzykulski.com.

I also gratefully acknowledge the use of the texts, poems, and translations by authors living and dead, and the publishers from the past and present who are listed in the following section entitled 'Source of Quotes in the Text', and who helped me to add colour and substance to this story about the life and times of Leonardo da Vinci and his contribution to the Renaissance.

Source of Quotes in the Text:

Quotes attributed to Giorgio Vasari are from *The Lives of the Most Eminent Painters, Sculptors, and Architects*, Volume 4 (1913). Translated by Gaston Du C. De Vere. London: MacMillan and Co. LD and The Medici Society, LD. 1912. Provided as The Project Gutenberg EBook. http://www.gutenberg.org/files/28420/28420-h/28420-h.htm. Quotes in italics attributed to Niccolo Machiavelli are either from (1) Bull G (translator). *The Prince*. Penguin Classics (2003), London, U.K., or (2) History of Florence and of the Affairs of Italy, The Project Gutenberg EBook: http://www.gutenberg.org/files/2464/2464-h/2464-h.htm. Leonardo da Vinci's Notebook quotes are from [S1] below and are presented indented at a lower font (10 point) than the rest of the text. If not cited as such then the quotes are fictional and constructed by the author J.K Kulski.

S1. The Notebooks of Leonardo da Vinci, translated and edited by Jean Paul Richter, 1880. http://www.fromoldbooks.org/Richter-NotebooksOfLeonardo/; http://www.gutenberg.org/ebooks/5000.

S2. Brown JW (1828). The Life of Leonardo da Vinci: With a Critical Account of His Works. W. Pickering. Melzi's letter to Leonardo's brother.

S3. Annabell M (2000). Leonardo Da Vinci. The Man and the Inventor, Loadstar's Lair. http://www.lairweb.org.nz/leonardo/fable1.html.

S4. Birnbaum MD (1977). Janus Pannonius, Bartolomeo Melzi, and the Sforzas. Renaissance Quarterly, Vol. 30, pp. 1-7. Poem translated from Latin by Jerzy K. Kulski.

S5. Welch ES (1995). Art and Authority in Renaissance Milan. P. 268. New Haven and London: Yale University Press.

S6. Jagoe A (2013). A Layman's Chronology of Mary. P. 10. iUniverse LCC. Bloomington.

S7. Cartwright JM (1908). Beatrice d'Este, Duchess of Milan, 1475-1479. J. M. Dent amp Co. Online: http://readcentral.com/massappealnews/chapters/Julia-Mary-Cartwright/Beatrice-dEste-Duchess-of-Milan-1475-1497/003. https://books.google.com.au/books?id=EHFHnl7mYg4C.

S8. Fumagalli G (1952). Eros di Leonardo, Ed. Garzanti, Milano, pp. 97-98, from the State Archives of Florence, 'Uffiziali Notte' XVIII (2), fol. 46v, April 9, 1476.

S9. Perrens FT (1892). The History of Florence Under the Domination of Cosimo, Piero, Lorenzo de' Medicis, 1434-1492. London: Methuen & Co.

S10. Crispino E (2010). Leonardo. Artist's Life. Giunti Editore, Milan, Italy, page 7.

S11. Filelfo F (Robin DM translator and editor) (2009). Odes. The Tatti Renaissance Library. Harvard University Press, Cambridge, Massachusetts.

S12. Boccaccio G (1348). Decameron. (G.H. McWilliam, Editor, Translator, Introduction). Penguin Classics (2003). London, UK.

S13. Fanti G, Botella JA, Crosilla F, Lattarulo F, Svensson N, Schneider R, Whanger A, of Shroud Science Group (2010). List of Evidences of the Turin Shroud. Proceedings of the International Workshop on the Scientific Approach to the Acheiropoietos Images, ENEA Frascati, Italy, 4-6 May 2010. http://www.acheiropoietos.info

S14. The Church of St. Andrew in Melzo. http://www.amicisantandrea.com/Libro/Galleria%20immagini%20libro/Galleria.htm.

S15. Christian KW (2001). Petrarch's Triumph of Chastity in Leonardo's Lady with an Ermine. In, Coming About… A Festschrift for John Shearman, Eds., Jones LR, Matthew LC, pp. 33-40. Cambridge, Massachusetts: Harvard University Art Museums, 2001. Bernardo Bellincioni's Latin poem translated into English by Jerzy K. Kulski.

S16. Hare C (1911). Isabella of Milan. Princess D'Aragone and wife of Duke Gian Galeazzo Sforza. Charles Scribner's sons, New York.

S17. Bossi GA (1927). Epithalamium de Io. Galeazzo sexton Mediolonanensium Duce et Elisabella uxore, Ambrosiana, Milan, Cod N 133 Sup., 139-43; printed in P. Bondioli, Un poeta bustese alle nozze di G. G. Sforza et Isabella d' Aragona, Monza 1927, pp 44-5. Poems translated from Latin into English by the author, J. K Kulski. Latin version sourced from Scofield R, Tavernor R (1988). A Humanist Description of the Architecture for the Wedding of Gian Galeazzo Sforza and Isabella D'Aragona (1489). Papers of the British School at Rome. Vol. 56, pp. 213-240.

S18. Scofield R, Tavernor R (1988). A Humanist Description of the Architecture for the Wedding of Gian Galeazzo Sforza and Isabella D'Aragona (1489). Papers of the British School at Rome. Vol. 56, pp. 213-240.

S19. Milano P, ed (1975). The Portable Dante & The Divine Comedy. Translated by Laurence Binyon. Penguin books, NY, USA.

S20. De La Sizeranne R (1924). Beatrice d'Este and Her Court, trans. N. Fleming (London: Brentano's, 1924), pp. 208–12.

S21. Williamson HR (1974). Lorenzo the Magnificent. Michael Joseph.

S22. Rough S, Rough J (1987). Leonardo's Kitchen Note Books. Collins, London.

S23. Carla Glori. Il cartiglio. http://www.carlaglori.com/mi-presento/

S24. Evens ML (1987). New light on the 'Sforziada' frontpieces of Giovan Pietro Birago. British Library Journal, XIII, p. 232-47; Wright E (2010). Ludovico Il Moro, Duke of Milan, and the Sforziada by Giovanni Simonetta in Warsaw. https://sites.google.com/site/labellaprincipessacom/home; Glori C. The Illumination by Birago in the Sforziad incunabulum in Warsaw: in defence of Horodyski's thesis and a new hypothesis; Wozniak K (2014). The Warswa Sforziad. http://www.bbk.ac.uk/hosted/leonardo/WozniakBP_2014.pdf.

S25. Gardner EG (1968). Dukes and Poets in Ferrara. Haskell House Publishers Ltd, NY.

S26. Tinagli P (1997). Women in Italian Renaissance Art: Gender, Representation and Identity. Manchester University Press, Manchester and New York.

S27. The two main proponents that Isabella Aragon Sforza is the Mona Lisa have been Robert Payne and Maike Vogt-Luërssen. Payne R (1978). Leonardo. Double & Company, Inc., Garden City, New York. Vogt-Luërssen M (2010). Die Sforza III: Isabella von Aragon und ihr Hofmaler Leonardo da Vinci, Norderstedt.

S28. There are many medical and scientific articles diagnosing Leonardo da Vinci's *Mona Lisa* with lipoma and other disorders. The following are a few examples: Adour KK (1989). Mona Lisa Syndrome: Solving the Enigma of the Gioconda Smile. Ann Otol Rhinol Laryngol. 98:196-9; Bray GA (1991). Obesity, A Disorder Of Nutrient Partitioning: The MONA LISA Hypothesis. J. Nutr. 121:1146-1162; Borkowski JE (1992). Mona Lisa: the enigma of the smile. J Forensic Sci. 37:1706-11; Dequeker J, Muls E, Leenders K (2004). Xanthelasma and lipoma in Leonardo da Vinci's Mona Lisa. Isr Med Assoc J. 6:505-6; Ose L (2008). The Real Code of Leonardo da Vinci. Current Cardiology Reviews, 4, 60-62; Maloney WJ (2011). Bell's palsy: the answer to the riddle of Leonardo da Vinci's 'Mona Lisa'. J Dent Res.90:580-2; Mims JL 3rd (2012). History of medicine: ocular disorders of the Mona Lisa (strabismus) and other famous paintings in the Louvre, Paris. Binocul Vis Strabolog Q Simms Romano. 27:35-8; Santos-Bueso E, Vico-Ruiz E, García-Sánchez J (2012). Eye pathology in the paintings by Leonardo da Vinci (iii). Comparative study between the Mona Lisa and the copy in the PradoMuseum in Madrid. Arch Soc Esp Oftalmol. 87:381–383.

S29. Valeri E (2009). 'Freedom of Italy' in 'Histories' by Giolamo Borgia (1494-1547). In: L'Italia dell' inquisitor. Storia e geografia dell'Italia del Cinquecento nella Discrittione di Leandro Alberti. Bologna, Bolonia University Press.

S30. Zutshi P (2006). The unpublished letter of Isabella of Aragon, Duchess of Milan. Renaissance Studies 20:494-501. Letter translated into English by Poala Magni and Jerzy K. Kulski.

S31. Payne R (1978). Leonardo. Double & Company, Inc., Garden City, New York.

S32. Cartwright J (1899). Isabella d' Este, Marchioness of Mantua 1474-1539. A Study of the Renaissance. Julia Cartwright. Dent & Co (1899). J. Murray, London 1903, 1919.

S33. Wasserman J (1971). The dating and patronage of Leonardo's Burlington House Cartoon. The Art Bulletin. 53:312-325. Note 39. Gerolamo Casio's poem. Translated from Italian into English by Jerzy K. Kulski.

S34. Missinne S (2013). A Newly Discovered Early Sixteenth-Century Globe Engraved on an Ostrich Egg: The Earliest Surviving Globe Showing the New World. The Portulan. Journal of the Washington Map Society, 87, 8-24.

S35. Symonds JA (translator) (1904). Cellini, B, Autobiography, New York, Appleton, pp.18-19.

S36. Ramsden EH (1963). Michelangelo Buonarroti. The Letters of Michelangelo Vol 1. Stanford University Press.

S37. https://en.wikipedia.org/wiki/Hanno_(elephant).

S38. Kelly WK (1853). Heptameron of Margaret, Queen of Navarre, by Marguerite de Navarre (d' Angouleme) Duchesse d' Alencon (1492-1549). Fifth day. Nouveille edition, London. Published for the Trade.

S39. Brioist P. Romorantin: Palace and ideal city. Pp 83-93 online at http://www.vinci-closluce.com/fichier/s_paragraphe/8730/paragraphe_file_1_en_romorantin.p.brioist.pdf.

S40. Saint Bris F (2015) 'Nel palazzo del Clu'. 500 years of history. Online. Association of the Friends of Leonardo da Vinci pp 19-26. www.vinci-closluce.com/file/francois-saint-bris-**nel-palazzo-del-clu**-gb.pdf.

S41. https://www.kingjamesbibleonline.org/Mark-6-21/

S42. Croizat YC (2007). 'Living dolls': Francois Ier dresses his women. Renaissance Quarterly 60: 94–130.

S43. Seward D (1973). Prince of the Renaissance. MacMillan Publishing Co. Inc, NY.

S44. Wickens GM, translator (1964). Nasirean Ethics. George Allen & Unwin. NY.

S45. More BB, translator (1922). Ovid. Metamorphoses. Cornhill Publishing Co.

Additional Bibliography

Ajmar-Wollheim M, Dennis F (2006). At Home In Renaissance Italy. Victoria and Albert Museum.

Bambach CC, ed (2003). Documented Chronology of Leonardo's Life and Work. In, Leonardo da Vinci. Master Draftsman. The Metropolitan Museum Of Art, New York, Yale University Press, New Haven And London.

Bender N (2013). Leonardo da Vinci: 197 Drawings. BookRix GmbH & Co. KG. Kindle edition. https://www.amazon.com/Leonardo-Vinci-Drawings-Narim-Bender-ebook/dp/B00HPUR44S.

Bramly S (1994). Leonardo. The Artist and the Man. Translated by S. Reynolds. Penguin Books. Great Britain.

Bris BS (2006). Chateau du Clos Luce. Watercolours, text and captions by Francois Saint Bris.

Brown JW (1828). The Life of Leonardo Da Vinci: With a Critical Account of His Works. W. Pickering.

Burckhardt J (1904). The Civilisation of the Renaissance in Italy. Translated by S.G.C. Middlemore. London. Swan Sonnenschein & Co., Ltd. New York: The MacMillan Co.

Capra F (2008). The Science of Leonardo. Anchor Books Edition, NY.

Capra F (2013). Learning from Leonardo. Decoding the notebooks of a genius. Berrett-Koehler Publishers, Inc. San Francisco, California.

Clark K (1989). Leonardo da Vinci. Penguin.

Crispino E (2010). Leonardo. Artist's Life. Giunti Editore S.p.A. Milan Italy.

Dacarro F (2012). A Study of Milanese Architectural Officers in the 15th Century: the Engineers of the Municipality of Milan. Architectural Research, Vol. 14, No. 4. pp. 133-141.

Del Maestro RF (1998). Leonardo da Vinci: the search for the soul. J Neurosurg 89:874–887.

Dann J (1997). The Memory Cathedral. A Secret History of Leonardo da Vinci. A novel. Flamingo, Harper Collins Publishers, Australia.

Fagnart L (2010). The French History of Leonardo da Vinci's Paintings. In Catalogue of the exhibition Leonardo da Vinci & France under the supervision of Carlo Pedretti, Château du Clos Lucé, Florence, Cartei & Bianchi, pp. 113-116.

Farrago C, ed (1999). Leonardo da Vinci. Selected Scholarship in English. A Garland Series, 5 vols. Garland Publishing Inc/ Taylor and Francis Publishing Group, NY and London.

Gelb MJ (2000). How to Think Like Leonardo da Vinci: Seven Steps to Genius Every Day. Penguin Random House, London.

Herbert J (1998). Leonardo Da Vinci for Kids, His Life and Ideas, 21 Activities. Chicago Review Press, Incorporated.

Heydenreich LH (1952). Leonardo da Vinci, Architect of Francis I Reviewed work(s): The Burlington Magazine, Vol. 94, No. 595, pp. 277-283+285.

Hone W (1827). The table book: or Daily recreation and information concerning remarkable men, manners, times, seasons, solemnities, merry-makings, antiquities and novelties, forming a complete history of the year. W. Tegg.

Kemp M (2004). Leonardo. Oxford Press, NY.

King R (2010). The Fantasia of Leonardo da Vinci. Levenger Press, Florida, USA.

Landrus M (2010). Leonardo Da Vinci's Giant Crossbow. SpringerLink. (Online service). Online access.

Laurenza D (2006). Leonardo's Machines. Da Vinci's Inventions Revealed. Eds Taddei M, Zanon E. Translator Reifsnyder JM. David & Charles, Newton Abbot, United Kingdom..

Lubkin G (1994). A Renaissance court: Milan under Galeazzo Maria Sforza. University of California Press, London, England.

MacCurdy H (2012). The Mind Of Leonardo Da Vinci. In Leonardo Da Vinci. The Artist. Digitized by the Internet Archive in 2012 with funding from Metropolitan New York Library Council – METRO.

Marinoni A (1972). Review: The Sublimations of Leonardo da Vinci with a Translation of the Codex Trivulzianus by Raymond S. Stites; Leonardo da Vinci. Technology and Culture, Vol. 13, 301-309.

Marion CS (2015). Exhibition « Leonardo Da Vinci And France. » Catherine Simon Marion, Deputy Directior, Marie-Caroline Chaudruc Comunication Manager. Château du Clos Lucé Parc Leonardo da Vinci. www.vinci-closluce.com.

Mateer D, ed (2000). The Renaissance in Europe. Volume 2, Courts, Patrons and Poets. New Haven/London: Yale U.P., for The Open U.

Matthews-Grieco SF (2014). Cuckoldry, Impotence and Adultery in Europe (15th-17th century). Published by Ashgate Publishing Limited.

Müntz E (1898). Leonardo da Vinci. Vol. 1 and 2. London: W. Heinemann; NY, C. Scribner's sons.

Muntz E (1888). Raphael. His Life, Works and Times. Chapman and Hill. London.

Nicholl C (2005). The Flights of the Mind. Penguin, UK.

Orbi J (2010). Cenacolo. IO Twomey Ltd. Tallahassee FL.

Pascal T (2012). Leonardo The Last Years. Ton Pascal, USA.

Pederson J (2008). Henrico Boscano's Isola beata: new evidence for the Academia Leonardo Vinci in Renaissance Milan. Renaissance Studies 22: 450-475.

Pedretti C (1985). Leonardo, architect. Rizzoli, NY.

Pedretti C (1982 and 1987). The Drawings and Misc Papers of Leonardo da Vinci in the Collection of HM The Queen at Windsor Castle, Vol. I (1982): Landscapes, Plants and Water Studies. Vol. II (1987): Horses and Other Animals [Vols III and IV were not published] - P(L) 49.

Ryle G (1949). The Concept of Mind. Penguin Book.

Sassoon D (2001). Mona Lisa. HarperCollinsPublishers.

Shell J, Sironi G (1991). Salaì and Leonardo's Legacy. The Burlington Magazine, Vol. 133, 95-108.

Shennan JH (1974). The origins of the Modern European State 1450 – 1725. Hutchinson & Co Ltd, London.

Tanaka H (1992). Leonardo da Vinci, Architect of Chambord? Artibus et Historiae, Vol. 13, pp. 85-102.

Thiis J (Muir J, transl) (1913). Leonardo da Vinci; the Florentine Years of Leonardo and Verrocchio. Herbert Jenkins Limited Publishers, London S.W.

Tyler CW (2010). How did Leonardo Perceive Himself? Metric Iconography of da Vinci's Self-Portraits. Proceedings of SPIE, Vol. 7527, 75271D-4.

Tyler CW (2014). Leonardo da Vinci's World Map. In Huylebrouck D (ed), Leonardo's Mathematics, Springer: Berlin.

Vallentin A (1938). The Tragic Pursuit of Perfection, Viking Press, London.

Welch ES (1995). Art and Authority in Renaissance Milan. New Haven: Yale University Press.

Wilcox M (1919). Francesco Melzi, Disciple of Leonardo. By. Art 6- Life Incorporating. The Lotus Magazine, Vol. Xi. No. 6.

Yiu Y (2005). The Mirror and Painting in Early Renaissance. Texts Early Science and Medicine, Vol. 10, No. 2, Optics, Instruments and Painting, 1420-1720.

FIGURE CREDITS

Fig 0.   Cover. Raphael. Portrait of a Youth, 1514 Oil. From the collection of the National Museum in Krakow, and the collection of the Princes Czartoryski. Wartime loss. Web Gallery of Art.

Fig 1.   Francesco Melzi. Self-portrait. Museum Bonnat, Bayonne. Public domain. Wikimedia commons. PD-Art.

Fig 2.   Giovanni Francesco Melzi of Vaprio d' Adda, Count Palatine 1525, self-portrait. Private collection, Milan, Italy. Public domain. Wikimedia commons. PD-Art.

Fig 3.   Giovanni Ambrogio Bevilacqua. The Triptych of the Resurrection at the Church of Casoretto. Permission of the Parocchia Prepositurale Abbaziale S. Maria Bianca della Misericordia.

Fig 4.   A. Leonardo da Vinci. St Jerome. c. 1480. Vatican WGA. Public Domain @ Wikimedia Commons. PD-Art.
B. Leonardo da Vinci. Vitruvian Man. 1492. Gallerie dell'Accademia, Venice. PD-Art.

Fig 5.   Leonardo da Vinci. Recto: The foetus in the womb. Detail from RCIN 919102. Royal Collection Trust / © Her Majesty Queen Elizabeth II 2017.

Fig 6.   Leonardo da Vinci. A view of the Adda river valley, c.1511-13. RCIN 912399. Royal Collection Trust / © Her Majesty Queen Elizabeth II 2017.

Fig 7.   Leonardo da Vinci. A. Planimetry of a section of the River Adda, Codex Atlanticus, f. 911 r. Milan, Biblioteca Ambrosiana. B. Perfecting a lock, Codex Atlanticus, f. 935 v. Milan, Biblioteca Ambrosiana. PD-Art.

Fig 8.   Map. Prepared by Jerzy K. Kulski.

Fig 9.   The Italian states map. Prepared by Jerzy K. Kulski.

Fig 10. Map of Milan from Leonardo da Vinci's, Codex Atlanticus, f. 199 v. Milan, Biblioteca Ambrosiana. PD-Art.

Fig 11. Map of Gates of Milan. Prepared by Jerzy K. Kulski.

Fig 12. Heraldry of House of Visconti and the House of Sforza. Public domain. Wikimedia commons.

Fig 13. Gold and silver coins. Public domain. Wikimedia commons.

Fig 14. Hans Memling or Zanetto Bugatto (?). His Highness, Ludovico il Moro Sforza, Regent of Milan. Thyssen-Bornemisza Museum. Public domain. Wikimedia commons. Web Gallery of Art. PD-Art.

Fig 15. Coin. Testone of Gian Galeazzo Sforza, the 6th duke of Milan with his uncle, Ludovico Sforza, governor of Milan. Public domain. Wikimedia commons.

Fig 16. A. Leonardo da Vinci. Female Head (La Scapigliata), 1508, Galleria Nazionale, Parma. Web Gallery of Art 808*952. B. Leonardo da Vinci. Woman's Head.1470-76. Galleria degli Uffizi, Florence. Web Gallery of Art 830*1145. C. Piero di Cosimo. Portrait de Femme dit de Simonetta Vespucci 1490. Musee Conde, Chantilly. D. Leonardo da Vinci. Head of a Girl, c. 1483. Biblioteca Reale, Turin. Web Gallery of Art. PD-Art.

Fig 17. Leonardo da Vinci. Annunciation. Uffizi, Florence, Italy. Web Gallery of Art. Public domain. Wikimedia commons.

Fig 18. Leonardo da Vinci. Ginevra de' Benci. National Gallery of Art, Washington, D.C., United States. Public domain. Wikimedia commons. Web Gallery of Art. PD-Art.

Fig 19. Leonardo da Vinci. A. Madonna with a Flower (Madonna Benois) c. 1478. The State Hermitage Museum, St. Petersburg. Federation of Russia. B. Madonna of the Carnation. Alte Pinakothek. Bayerische Staatsgemaldesammlungen Munich. Web Gallery of Art. Public domain. PD-Art.

Fig 20. Unknown Artist (?). Madonna with Child, St. Ambrogio, St. Lucia, Ambrogio Raverti, Lucia Marliani and Family, at Santa Maria delle Grazie. Permission for use of image obtained from Paola Villa and her archive of restored paintings Archivio Villa Restauri.

Fig 21. Unknown Artist (?). Allegory of Sforza family's Coat of Arms. Biblioteca Estense in Modena, Italy. Wikimedia commons. PD-Art.

Fig 22. Coin. Gold Double Ducat of Gian Galeazzo Sforza, the 6th duke of Milan, issued in 1481. Wikimedia Commons.

Fig 23. Sandro Botticello. Adoration of the Magi. Uffizi Gallery. Public domain. Wikimedia commons. PD-Art.

Fig 24. Leonardo da Vinci. Adoration of the Magi. Galleria degli Iffizi, Florence. Web Gallery of Art. PD-Art.

Fig 25. A. Domenico Ghirlandaio. Adoration 1488. B. Filippino Lippi Adoration. 1496. Public domain. Wikimedia commons.

Fig 26. Cariani. Portrait of a Man and a Dog, c. 1520. National Gallery of Art, Washington DC. Accession No. 1950.11.2. Public domain. Wikimedia commons. PD-Art.

Fig 27. A and B. Detail, Head on Shroud (negative and positive), online www. See [S13]. C. Leonardo da Vinci, detail of Salvator Mundi. Public domain. Wikimedia commons. Web Gallery of Art.

Fig 28. Leonardo da Vinci. The Lady with an Ermine, ca. 1490. Nr inv. MNK-MKCz XII-A-290. In the National Museum /Princes Czartoryski Museum in Krakow. Web Gallery of Art. PD-Art.

Fig 29. Amici Di Sant' Andrea. Copy of commemoration plate displayed at the Museo Naz. di Ravenna, Italy.

Fig 30. Birago. Book of Prayers depicts St. Ambrose of Milan. The Sforza Hours. folio 1r, Birago, St John. Copyright © The British Library Board (Add. MS 59874). PD-Art.

Fig 31.   Leonardo da Vinci. La Belle Ferronière. c. 1490. Musée du Louvre, Paris. Web Gallery of Art. Public domain. Wikimedia commons. PD-Art.

Fig 32. Giovanni Ambrogio de' Predis. A. Portrait of a Youth as Saint Sebastian 1483. Cleveland Museum of Art. Public domain. PD-Art.

Fig 33. Giovanni Antonio Boltraffio. A. St. Sebastian. The Pushkin State Museum of Fine Arts, Moscow. Russian Federation. Public Domain. B. Portrait of a Youth Holding an Arrow. Timken Museum of Art - San Diego. Public domain.

Fig 34. Leonardo da Vinci (?) or Giovanni Ambrogio de' Predis (?). A. Green Angel. (B) Red Angel. National Gallery UK. Public domain. Wikimedia commons. PD-Art.

Fig 35. Leonardo da Vinci. Portrait of a Young Man (The Musician). 1490. Pinacoteca Ambrosiana, Milan. Web Gallery of Art. Public domain. PD-Art.

Fig 36.   Raphael. Portrait of Dona Isabel de Requesens, Vice-Queen of Naples. 1518. Musée du Louvre, Paris. Web Gallery of Art. PD-Art.

Fig 37.   Leonardo da Vinci. Virgin of the Rocks. 1483-86. Musée du Louvre, Paris. Web Gallery of Art. 807*1270.

Fig 38.   Stanislaw Samostrzelnik. The Annunciation. Bodleian Library. Public domain. Wikimedia commons. PD-Art.

Fig 39.   Leonardo da Vinci. Verso: The hemisection of a man and woman in the act of coition. c. 1492. RCIN 919097. Royal Collection Trust / © Her Majesty Queen Elizabeth II 2017.

Fig 40.   Bartolomeo Veneto. Portrait of Beatrice d'Este. Snite Museum of Art, University of Notre Dame South Bend Indiana USA. Public domain. Wikimedia commons. PD-Art.

Fig 41.   Ambrogio de' Predis. Portraits of Bianca Maria Sforza, the Holy Roman Empress and Queen of Germany. A. Kunsthistorisches Museum. Public domain. The Athenaeum. B. 1493. National Gallery of Art - Washington DC. Public domain. The Athenaeum. PD-Art.

Fig 42.   Bernhard Strigel. A. Portrait of Empress Bianca Maria Sforza.1505-1510. B. Maximilian I. 1502. Kunsthistorisches Museum, Vienna. Vienna Museum of Art History. Public domain. Wikimedia commons. PD-Art.

Fig 43.   Marco d' Oggiono (1494). Portrait of a Young Man. National Gallery, London. The Athenaeum. Public domain. PD-Art.

Fig 44.   Ambrogio de' Predis (?). Portrait of a Young Man. c. 1500. Pinacoteca di Brera, Milan. Web Gallery of Art. PD-Art.

Fig 45.   Bernardino Luini. A. Madonna and Child with St. Sebastian and St. Roch, ca. 1520-26. Collection of The John and Mabel Ringling Museum of Art, The State Art Museum of Florida. B. Madonna with Child, San Sebastian and San Roque (ca. 1521-1524). Parish of Santa María de la Mesa (Utrera). Public domain. Wikimedia commons. PD-Art.

Fig 46.   Coin. Gold testone, (double ducat) of Ludovico Maria Sforza, 7th Duke of Milan, December 1494. Milanese Coins Tumblr. Public domain. Wikimedia commons.

Fig 47.   Master of Pala Sforzesca. Sforza Altarpiece. Virgin and child enthroned with the doctors of the church and the family of Ludovico il Moro. Pinacoteca di Brera, a Milano. Public domain. PD-Art.

Fig 48.   Leonardo da Vinci. Last Supper. 1498. Convent of Santa Maria delle Grazie, Milan. Web Gallery of Art. PD-Art.

Fig 49.   Leonardo da Vinci. Last Supper. Gallerie dell'Accademia, Venice. Web Gallery of Art. 1153*770. PD-Art.

Fig 50.   Leonardo da Vinci. Knot Patterns. Numbers 1, 4 and 6 at Rosenwald Collection, National Gallery of Art, D.C; 2 internet. 3 and 5 at The British Museum (1877,0113.364 and 1877,0113.366 respectively). Photo Credit: © The Trustees of The British Museum, Creative Commons and Web Gallery of Art. PD-Art.

Fig 51.   Jacopo de' Barbari (?). Portrait of Luca Pacioli with Student. Ca 1495. Capodimonte Museum of Naples. Inv. Q. 58. Public domain. Wikimedia commons. PD-Art.

Fig 52.   Detail of the black fly and the cryptogram in Fig. 51.

Fig 53.   Leonardo da Vinci. A Political Allegory. RCIN 912496. Royal Collection Trust / © Her Majesty Queen Elizabeth II 2017.

Fig 54.   Giovan Pietro Birago. Frontispiece. La Sforziada. British Library, G. 7251. Public domain. Wikimedia commons. PD-Art.

Fig 55.   Giovan Pietro Birago and Antonio Zarotto. Sforziade Frontispiece. Paris, Bibliotheque Nationale, Imprimes, Reserve, Velins 724. Public domain. Wikimedia commons. PD-Art.

Fig 56.   Giovan Pietro Birago. Sforziada Frontispiece. Warsaw, Biblioteka Naradowa, Inc. F. 1347. Public domain. PD-Art.

Fig 57.   Stanislaw Samostrzelnik. Hours of Bona Sforza. Queen of Poland. 10 figs. Book graphics online. Warsaw, Biblioteka Naradowa. Bodleian Library, the University of Oxford. Public domain. Wikimedia commons. PD-Art.

Fig 58.   A. Leonardo da Vinci. A Young Woman in Profile. RCIN 912505. Royal Collection Trust / © Her Majesty Queen Elizabeth II 2017. B. Bona Sforza, Queen of Poland. Public domain. Wikimedia commons. PD-Art.

Fig 59.   Leonardo da Vinci. Profile of a Young Fiancée. Private collection. Public domain. Wikimedia commons. PD-Art.

Fig 60.   Unknown artist (?). Mona Lisa. Museo del Prado, Madrid. Accession number P00504. Public domain. Wikimedia commons. PD-Art.

Fig 61.   Raphael. Portrait of a Woman. 1505-06. Musée du Louvre, Paris. Web Gallery of Art. Public domain. PD-Art.

Fig 62.   Detail from Fig. 60.

Fig 63.   Leonardo da Vinci. Mona Lisa (La Gioconda). c. 1503-5. Musée du Louvre, Paris. Web Gallery of Art. Public domain.

Fig 64.   Detail from Fig. 63.

Fig 65.   Bona Sforza, Queen of Poland. Public domain. Wikimedia commons. PD-Art.

Fig 66.   Bernardino Luini. Portrait of a Lady. c. 1525. National Gallery of Art, Washington. Web Gallery of Art. Public domain. PD-Art.

Fig 67.   Bernardino Luini. Mary Magdalene in the Allegory of Modesty and Vanity. San Diego Museum of Art. Accession number 1936.23. Public domain. Wikimedia commons. PD-Art.

Fig 68.   Francesco Melzi. Flora 1517-21. The State Hermitage Museum, St. Petersburg. Federation of Russia. Web Gallery of Art. Public domain. PD-Art.

Fig 69.   Giovanni Antonio Boltraffio. Portrait of a Youth. 1498/99. National Gallery of Art - Washington DC. The Athenaeum. Public domain. PD-Art.

Fig 70.   Leonardo da Vinci. Isabella d'Este. 1500. Musée du Louvre, Paris. Web Gallery of Art. Public domain. PD-Art.

Fig 71.   Titian. Portrait of Isabella d'Este, c 1534-1536. Kunsthistorisches Museum, Vienna. Public domain. PD-Art.

Fig 72.   Leonardo da Vinci (?). Isabella d' Este. 1500. Guardia di Finanza, Italy. Public domain. Wikimedia commons.

Fig 73.   Leonardo da Vinci. Madonna Litta, c. 1490-91. The State Hermitage Museum, St. Petersburg, Federation of Russia. Web Gallery of Art. Public domain. PD-Art.

Fig 74.   Leonardo da Vinci. A. The Virgin and Child with St Anne. c. 1510. Musée du Louvre, Paris. Web Gallery of Art. 801*1233. B. Madonna with the Yarnwinder. after 1510. Private collection, New York. Web Gallery of Art. Public domain. PD-Art.

Fig 75.   Leonardo da Vinci. The Virgin and Child with St. Anne and St. John the Baptist (instead of a lamb). National Gallery London. Public domain image. Web Gallery of Art. PD-Art.

Fig 76.   Leonardo da Vinci. Neptune, c.1504-5. Royal Collection. RCIN 912570. Royal Collection Trust / © Her Majesty Queen Elizabeth II 2017.

Fig 77.   Francesco Melzi. Recto: Map of the northern hemisphere in four segments. Verso: Map of the southern hemisphere in four segments. RCIN 991393. Royal Collection Trust / © Her Majesty Queen Elizabeth II 2017.

Fig 78.   A. Giampietrino. Salvator mundi. Pushkin Museum, Moscow, Federation of Russia. B. Marco d' Oggiono. Salvator mundi. Arkady, Warsaw, Poland. Public domain. Wikipedia commons. PD-Art.

Fig 79.   Leonardo da Vinci. The Battle of Anghiari (detail). 1503-05. Musée du Louvre, Paris. Web Gallery of Art. 1030*708. Public domain. PD-Art.

Fig 80.   Sebastiano da Sangallo. Copy of Michelangelo Buonarroti. Battle of Cascina. Musée du Louvre, Paris. Public domain. Wikimedia commons. PD-Art.

Fig 81.   Leonardo da Vinci. Self-Portrait. c. 1512. Biblioteca Reale, Turin. Web Gallery of Art. Public domain. PD-Art.

Fig 82.   Santi di Tito. Portrait of Niccolo di Bernardo dei Machiavelli. Palazzo Vecchio, Florence, Italy. Public domain. PD-Art. Wikimedia commons.

Fig 83.   Coin. The testone of King Louis XII, Duke of Milan, with Saint Ambrose on horseback. Public domain. Wikimedia commons.

Fig 84.   Images of the golden spheres, golden rectangles, golden triangles, and a calculated golden mean. Public domain Wikipedia images.

Fig 85.   Leonardo da Vinci. Salvator Mundi With a Glass Orb. Private collection. Public domain. Wikimedia commons. PD-Art.

Fig 86.   School of Leonardo da Vinci. Christ as the Salvator Mundi. Public domain. Wikipedia images. PD-Art.

Fig 87.   Bernardino de' Conti. Charles II of Amboise, the French Governor of Milan from 1503 to 1511. Public domain image photograph of Miguel Heroso Cuesta. Wikimedia commons. PD-Art.

Fig 88.   Leonardo da Vinci. A view of the Adda river valley c.1511-13. RCIN 912398. Royal Collection. Royal Collection Trust / © Her Majesty Queen Elizabeth II 2017.

Fig 89.   A. Leonardo da Vinci. Copy of Leda and the Swan.1508-15. Galleria degli Uffizi, Florence. Web Gallery of Art. Public domain. B. Cesare da Sesto. Leda 1510-15. Galleria Borghese, Rome. Web Gallery of Art. Public domain. PD-Art.

Fig 90.   Correggio (1531-1532). The Loves of Jupiter - Leda and the Swan. Gemäldegalerie - Staatliche Museen zu Berlin. The Athenaeum. Public domain. PD-Art.

Fig 91.   Giampietrino. Mary Magdalene. Public domain image. Wikimedia commons. PD-Art.

Fig 92.   Bernardino de' Conti, Gian Giacomo Trivulzio's Heraldry 'state portrait' with his French Medal of the Order of Saint Michael, painted after his death from a living portrait of 1499-1500, '1519' Private collection. Permission of Marino Vigano.

Fig 93.   Leonardo da Vinci. A. Sketches for the Trivulzio monument. RCIN 912355. B. Recto: A study for an equestrian monument. Verso: A study for an equestrian monument. RCIN 912356. Royal Collection Trust / © Her Majesty Queen Elizabeth II 2017.

Fig 94.   Leonardo da Vinci. The chain ferry at Vaprio d'Adda. RCIN 912400. Royal Collection Trust / © Her Majesty Queen Elizabeth II 2017.

Fig 95.   Francesco Melzi. Portrait of Leonardo, 1515-1518. RCIN 912726. Royal Collection Trust / © Her Majesty Queen Elizabeth II 2017.

Fig 96.   Leonardo da Vinci. A. A deluge. RCIN 912377. B. A deluge. RCIN 912385. C. A storm in an alpine valley RCIN 912409. D. A deluge. RCIN 912384. E. A deluge RCIN 912378. Royal Collection Trust / © Her Majesty Queen Elizabeth II 2017.

Fig 97.   Leonardo da Vinci. Tempest. Detail (Aiolos) – deluge. RCIN 912376. Royal Collection Trust / © Her Majesty Queen Elizabeth II 2017.

Fig 98.   Leonardo da Vinci. A. A deluge. RCIN 912382. B. A cloudburst of material possession. RCIN 912698. Royal Collection Trust / © Her Majesty Queen Elizabeth II 2017.

Fig 99.   Leonardo da Vinci. Tempest. Detail. RCIN 912376. Royal Collection Trust / © Her Majesty Queen Elizabeth II 2017.

Fig 100. Leonardo da Vinci. A Deluge. RCIN 912380. Royal Collection Trust / © Her Majesty Queen Elizabeth II 2017.

Fig 101. Leonardo da Vinci. Scenes of the Apocalypse, with notes. RCIN 912388. Royal Collection Trust / © Her Majesty Queen Elizabeth II 2017.

Fig 102. Raphael. Hanno, the Elephant. Public domain image at wikiart.org. PD-Art.

Fig 103. Raphael. Portrait of a Youth, 1514 Oil. From the collection of the National Museum in Krakow. The collection of the Princes Czartoryski. Wartime loss. Web Gallery of Art.

Fig 104. Raphael. The Knowledge of Causes (also known as The School of Athens). Vatican Museums. Public domain image. Wikipedia commons. PD-Art.

Fig 105. Detail of Raphael's fresco in Fig 104.

Fig 106. Raphael. Portrait of Leo X With Cardinals Giulio de' Medici (later Pope Clement VII) and Luigi de' Rossi. 1518-19. Galleria degli Uffizi, Florence. Web Gallery of Art. Public domain. PD-Art.

Fig 107. Jean Perreal workshop. Louis XII, King of France. ca 1514. Royal Collection, Hampton Court Palace, London. Accession number RCIN 403431. Royal Collection Trust / © Her Majesty Queen Elizabeth II 2017.

Fig 108. Raphael. Portrait of Giuliano de' Medici, Duke of Nemours. Metropolitan Museum of Art, NY, USA. Public domain. Wikimedia commons. PD-Art.

Fig 109. Leonardo da Vinci. St. John in the Wilderness (Bacchus). 1510-15. Musée du Louvre, Paris. Web Gallery of Art. Public domain. PD-Art.

Fig 110. Leonardo da Vinci. Design for St. John in the Wilderness. 1508-15. Formerly Museo del Sacromonte, Varese. Web Gallery of Art. Public domain image. PD-Art.

Fig 111. Leonardo da Vinci. St. John the Baptist. 1513-16. Musée du Louvre, Paris. Web Gallery of Art. Public domain.

Fig 112. Leonardo da Vinci. St. John the Baptist. RCIN 912572. Royal Collection Trust / © Her Majesty Queen Elizabeth II 2017.
Fig 113. Chateau du Cloux. Sketched photograph by Jerzy K. Kulski.
Fig 114. Leonardo da Vinci. The Chateau of Amboise, c.1517-19. Royal Collection. RCIN 912727. Royal Collection Trust / © Her Majesty Queen Elizabeth II 2017.
Fig 115. Map of the Rivers Loire, Vienne and Cher and the main towns in the Loire Valley. Image prepared by Jerzy K. Kulski.
Fig 116. Leonardo da Vinci. Verso: A design for a palace on a river island. RCIN 912292. Royal Collection Trust / © Her Majesty Queen Elizabeth II 2017.
Fig 117. Leonardo da Vinci. Plan for the twin palaces on the canals. Folio 270 v of the Codex Arundel. PD-Art.
Fig 118. Leonardo da Vinci. Recto: A seated old man, and studies and notes on the movement of water. Verso: Architectural studies c.151. RCIN 912579. Royal Collection Trust / © Her Majesty Queen Elizabeth II 2017.
Fig 119. Leonardo da Vinci. A Lily (*Lilium candidum*). RCIN 912418. Royal Collection Trust / © Her Majesty Queen Elizabeth II 2017.
Fig 120. Francois Cloux. A Lady in Her Bath. National Gallery of Art, Washington DC, USA. Accession number 1961.9.13. Public Domain image. Wikimedia commons. PD-Art.
Fig 121. A. Il Sodomo. Death of Lucrezia. Szépmûvészeti Múzeum, Budapest. Web Gallery of Art. Public domain. B. Marco d' Oggiono. Lucretia. Collection Rossi E Onesti. Public domain image. PD-Art.
Fig 122. Bernardino Luini. A. Salome with the Head of John the Baptist. Kunsthistorisches Museum, Vienna. B. Salome Receiving the Head of St John the Baptist. Musée du Louvre, Paris. Web Gallery of Art. Public domain.
Fig 123. Andrea Solari. Salome with the Head of St John the Baptist. 1506-07. Metropolitan Museum of Art, New York. Web Gallery of Art. Public domain. PD-Art.
Fig 124. Jean Clouet. Portrait of Marguerite of Navarre, c 1527. Walker Art Gallery in Liverpool, England, Web Gallery of Art 1308. Public domain image. PD-Art.
Fig 125. A. Leonardo da Vinci, Young woman seated in a landscape and pointing at a unicorn. Ashmolean Museum, Oxford, Oxford Chambers Hall Gift, Oxford, 1855 KPII 15. B. Raphael. Lady with a Unicorn. c. 1505. Galleria Borghese, Rome. Web Gallery of Art. Public domain. PD-Art.
Fig 126. Leonardo da Vinci. Last of the Unicorns beside a pool of incontinence. University of Oxford, Ashmoleon Museum. AM0156355. Image of Brigeman Berlin. PD-Art.
Fig 127. Francesco Melzi. Flora. Galleria Borghese, Rome. Web Gallery of Art. Public domain image. PD-Art.
Fig 128. Leonardo da Vinci. A Woman in a Landscape c.1517-18. RCIN 912581. Royal Collection Trust / © Her Majesty Queen Elizabeth II 2017.
Fig 129. Leonardo da Vinci. Recto: The foetus, and the muscles attached to the pelvis. Verso: studies of the foetus, related internal organs, and the arm. A. RCIN 919101. Public Domain. Royal Collection Trust / © Her Majesty Queen Elizabeth II 2017.
Fig 130. Leonardo da Vinci. The cardiovascular system and principal organs of a woman. RCIN 912281. Royal Collection Trust / © Her Majesty Queen Elizabeth II 2017.
Fig 131. Jean Clouet. Portrait of François I, King of France.1525-30. Musée du Louvre, Paris. Web Gallery of Art. Public domain image.
Fig 132. Giampetrino (?). Leonardo da Vinci. Last Supper (copy). 16th century. Da Vinci Museum, Tongerlo. Public domain image. PD-Art.
Fig 133. Leonardo da Vinci. A detail. Study for the Last Supper.1494-95. Gallerie dell'Accademia, Venice. Web Gallery of Art. Public domain image. PD-Art.
Fig 134. Leonardo da Vinci. A horse in profile with measurements. RCIN 912319 (RL 12319). Royal Collection Trust / © Her Majesty Queen Elizabeth II 2017.
Fig 135. Leonardo da Vinci. The brain c.1508-9. Royal Collection. RCIN 919127. Royal Collection Trust / © Her Majesty Queen Elizabeth II 2017.
Fig 136. Leonardo da Vinci. Study of Brain Psychology, Waimar, Kunstsammlungen zu Waimar, Schlossmuseum Inv KK 6287v. Drawings of Leonardo online. Public domain. B Recto: The layers of the scalp, and the cerebral ventricles. Verso: Studies of the head. RCIN 912603. Royal Collection Trust / © Her Majesty Queen Elizabeth II 2017.
Fig 137. Leonardo da Vinci. Recto: Miscellaneous anatomical studies. Verso: The leg sectioned. RCIN 912627. Royal Collection Trust / © Her Majesty Queen Elizabeth II 2017.
Fig 138. Leonardo da Vinci. A. Studies of human skull. Royal Library, Windsor. Web Gallery of Art. B. Recto: The cranium. Verso: Notes on topics to be investigated 1489. RCIN 919059. Royal Collection Trust / © Her Majesty Queen Elizabeth II 2017.
Fig 139. Leonardo da Vinci. A. Recto: The cranium sectioned. Verso: The skull sectioned 1489. RCIN 919058. B. Recto: The skull sectioned. Verso: The cranium 1489. RCIN 919057. C. Recto: The cranium sectioned. Verso: The skull sectioned 1489. RCIN 919058. Royal Collection Trust / © Her Majesty Queen Elizabeth II 2017.
Fig 140. Francesco Melzi. Pomona and Vertumnus. 1517-20. Staatliche Museen, Berlin. Web Gallery of Art. Public domain. PD-Art.
Fig 141. Leonardo da Vinci. Allegories of Joy, Sorrow, and Envy, Christ Church, Oxford, Inv. JBS 17v. Public domain. Wikimedia commons. PD-Art.

ABOUT THE AUTHOR

J. K. (Yurek) Kulski is a retired scientist who lives in Perth, Western Australia. He is married with two sons and two grandchildren. He has published extensively in medical and biological research in the fields of lactation, virology, cancer, microbiology, genetics, genomics, and immunology, and has been a staff and freelance researcher at a number of universities and institutes in Australia, the USA, and Japan. He is the author of the crime novel *China Heist*, and *Leonardo da Vinci: The Melzi Chronicles* is his first historical novel.